Purebred
Soul of the Mixed Blood

JAMES TODD LEWIS
AUTHOR OF *THE THURIAN SAGA*

Artistic Credit:
Flourish, & Breaks: Kat Miller
(www.furaffinity.net/user/foxenawolf)

Cover: Ilya Royz (furaffinity.net/user/royz)

Editing and Review Assistance: James W. Lewis, Jr. & Deborah
Williford

"Honor to all. Honor from all. Honor … above all."

Revision 4.3.0

Contact e-mail: author @ jamestoddlewis.com
ISBN 978-1-940929-07-1

Table of Contents

Author's Note

Thank you for reading this book, and as always, I hope you enjoy it!

This is the fifth book in the Thurian saga, and a prequel to the events described in *The Rescue: The First Visitation of Thuria*. This story is about a world far away from our own. If a human were to visit there, they would find things both foreign and familiar. While our way of marking out time – days, weeks, years – would not be, a system for tracking the moments certainly would exist, and does. On Thuria there are mountains, rivers, beaches, and forests, but the continents would not be recognizable to us, and the mountain ranges and courses of rivers would be unfamiliar. Governments, families, and businesses still exist and serve much the same functions for Thurians as they do for humans, but not exactly as our own. This world is a different world.

Finally, this book contains some material not intended for children. Parents and other responsible adults are asked to do their part in ensuring that any story with mature subjects and themes does not end up in front of eyes too young and for which it was not intended. There are some episodes of violence, occurrences of suggestive material, and moments of coarse language; however, these are not prevalent.

Again, my sincere thanks. See you in the future.

James Todd Lewis

Introduction

They killed her! They killed ... my mommy! They killed her! Please ... oh, please, no!" the young mixed blood's heart screamed inside of her. Horrified, Vannie watched as the elder Faelnar dame crouched beside the still body of her beaten and blooded parent, reached out with a yellowish brown paw, and closed her mother's open eyes. The dame, with her back to the eight season old kit hidden in the bushes, sat very still, her green dame's robes blown about by the wind – a wind which hid the sounds of young Vanarra Anasto's terrified crying. The skies above echoing the kit's torment, the now young orphan dared not make a sound as her heart was ripped apart in grief.

After so many seasons of suffering and pain, her mother had reached out to her former family, house de Gonari, in complete desperation. They had no money, no food, and they were about to be thrown out of the pathetic lair they had called home ever since her mother, Shenaria, had been outcast for a crime against the honor of her family. That crime now wept, eyes closed, shivering as cold drops of rain started splattering through the leaves and wetting her reddish brown fur. "I'm sorry, Mommy! I'm so sorry!" she cried in her heart. "I should have run away! I should be dead, not you! Not you! Oh, Mommy!"

A slight scuffling sound altered the young mixed blood's activity, and through nearly tear-blinded eyes, she saw the house guards roll her mother's body onto a stretcher and carry it away. "Goodbye ... Mommy," she breathed as the rain started pelting down, driving even the remaining guards from the brick steps where her mother had died. She watched as her own parent's blood spilled over the steps, barely diluted by the torrent of rain. Vannie clawed the dirt in front of her in agony, and more than anything, in that moment, she wanted to be dead – to be with her mother.

"Vanarra, no matter what, you stay hidden and stay safe. Let all of my love and that of your father, wherever he is, protect you. Promise me, you will not come out of hiding!" The voice of her mother only a few intervals earlier penetrated her mind, overwhelmed as it was with pain and a longing to simply no longer live. "Promise me, you will not come out of hiding!" the memory repeated.

Rolling onto her side, Vannie wept, trying to ignore those words, but somewhere deep inside of her, she knew that she had to do what they asked. She had to obey the last wishes of her mother. She had to obey the one who died trying to save them both. "I ... I promise, Mommy. I promise. I love you, Mom," she breathed as mud splattered her fur. The lightening in the storm above her seemed to mark her words, thundering just after with the sharp tenor of a close strike.

As the thunder rolled away in odd echoes caused by the buildings and mounds and walls, she seemed to hear the voice of her mother echo back to her. "I love you, Vannie. Remember, I don't care what the world says about you. I will always believe in you."

Pushing herself slowly up on all fours, she looked around and realized that when the storm let up, she could be easily spotted beneath the leaves of the bushes sagging under the weight of so much water. As best she could, Vannie looked around the garden, trying to see if anyone else was there, and at a lightening flash, she could not only see that she was alone but the direction of the gate through which they had come. Looking up at the window on the second level, the window through which some old female had looked down in scorn upon her mother, she saw it was now covered by curtains. Fairly certain that no one was observing her, Vanarra backed out of the bushes and quickly darted to the gate.

With little trouble, she was through it, although her rain-soaked paws did slip on the latch the first time. Looking down the long, high-walled path, she could only see a few hundred tracks ahead in the downpour, but what she saw was clear. Vanarra started running as soon as she closed the gate – not a crazed run, but one she had used before to escape purebreds who wanted to beat her up. Dashing from bush to tree, looking ahead, looking behind, planning her next run, and then sprinting for all she was worth, Vanarra made swift progress away from the garden where her mother had died. She wasn't thinking about what she would eat or where she would go, she was simply doing. Thinking meant getting lost in grief once again, and to fulfill the promise to her mother, Van knew she could not afford such a luxury.

Nearly exhausted, she reached the gate at the other end of the path, and the heavy rain had slackened to a modest drizzle. As she peered out of the metal fretwork, she saw what she feared, de Gonari guards, but what they were doing was curious. They were gathered in front of a large delivery hover that imbedded itself in the ground, its thrusters seeming to have failed before the driver could properly land the vehicle. Now, the guards were helping the driver, one of their own kind, place the four jacks that would get the hover far enough above the ground to allow it to restart. As they went to the far side of the vehicle, Vanarra had a reaction – instinctual, the kind her mother used to chastise her for. Like so many other times, Van didn't think, she acted.

Carefully opening the gate, she looked in both directions and saw nothing other than the guards, the hover, and its driver. Noticing the sign on the side said "De Gonari Foods and Services," she darted across the thick grassy ground and tried the back hatch of the vehicle. It opened, and after only a quick peek, Vannie slipped inside. She banged her knees, albeit silently on the edge of the hole where all of the jacks had been extracted from. Realizing that if the hover got going again, the jacks would be put back in, she worked her way further back into the vehicle.

Fortunately, a couple of rows of boxes provided more than adequate hiding opportunities, so she slipped back behind them and waited. Her nose, after a few passes, started to speak directly to her stomach about the possibility of fresh food within easy reach. Almost before she knew what she was doing, she was raking a claw carefully down the seam of a nearby box and pulling out its contents. Raw creele, juice boxes, and crackers were in three of the boxes near her, and soon, she was quietly eating and drinking.

She almost gagged in surprise when she heard the driver climbing in and restarting the hover. It sputtered a little, but then it lifted gently off the jacks and righted itself. Working quickly, Vannie made sure that nothing she had pulled out to eat could be seen from the back hatch. Just as she slipped her paw out of sight, light poured into the space, and she listened as the guards and the driver chatted, replacing the jacks and talking about how the harshness of the rain and the old style of thruster the hover was using were probably responsible for the failure. The driver closed the hatch with a final thank you, seemingly unaware of her presence. As the driver entered and closed the door, Van started eating again, and quickly, realizing that this might be the only easy meal she might have for awhile, and that she would have to leave this hover quickly, lest she be trapped and found out. Her mother's admonitions about what happened to mixed bloods caught stealing was more than enough motivation to act judiciously.

The hover bounced along in traffic for almost an interval before Vannie felt it turn off the congested fast trail and back onto regular streets. It took her a moment to shake off the pleasant lethargy that had settled upon her – a comfortable, dark place with her stomach full was enticing her to sleep, but she knew she couldn't. Stuffing as much as she could into her pockets, the young mixed blood made her way to the back of the vehicle and, while it was still moving, carefully pulled on the release and peeked out the door. They were driving through a neighborhood, a poorer one by the looks of it, but several vacant and undeveloped lots sat next to one another, trees and brambles being their only feature. No hovers were behind them, at the moment, and as the vehicle slowed, she knew she had to move.

Without really thinking about what she was doing, Vanarra opened the door just enough to slip out, and she closed it behind her. She was going to carefully leap off the back of the hover, but her hind paws lost their grip, and she tumbled to the ground, rolling a couple of times before coming to a stop. Her knees and elbows stinging, she pushed herself up and darted for the safety of the trees. Without anyone seeing, she was gone.

With evening coming on quickly because of the overcast skies, Vanarra frantically searched the area around her for any place to rest. The edge of the wooded area was far too visible, and she had to duck behind a tree as a passing enforcement hover screamed by. Walking carefully into the forest, she found a small clearing lined with trees. She was surprised to find a wooden platform that had been nailed between two trees with a rope ladder dangling down – obviously a play fort for some local kids. It didn't look like it had been used in a long time. "It's something," she sighed and started to climb up. She was heartened when she made it to the platform that there was at least a tattered tarp covering it as a roof. Pushing the fallen leaves and seed pods out of the way, the eight season old kit tried to make her new lair as comfortable as possible in the waning light of the setting sun.

Intervals later, the chill of the night air forcing her into a tight little ball, Vanarra Anasto lay crying. It was her fault her mother had died; she knew that in her soul beyond question. She didn't know why her mother had done all those things – cleaned herself up, put on a fabulous dress, and taken her on that long journey into the heart of the de Gonari estate. The two of them had walked for what seemed like intervals with Vannie secreted beneath her dress, walking at almost a crouch to keep from being detected. It had all been a horrible mistake. "We should have just … run away! We should have stolen what we needed and found some place! Why did you have to do it, Mommy?! Why?!" she screamed in her mind.

A soft wind filtered through the trees all around her, almost making a shushing sound, and for a moment, a stunned Vannie looked up, thinking she heard her mother. Then there was the terror that it might be someone else – someone else who wanted to hurt or kill mixed bloods like her. As the wind died away, however, there was no one there.

Sitting up, she crossed her legs and put her head in her paws. "Will … will my life be like this from now on? Is this all I have?" she cried softly, and again, the wind blew.

"Now, Dame," Triana demanded officiously of her younger sister Sahnassa, "you need to take my message to the matron and have her tell all those ugly Anati to go away! They aren't allowed to come around here! They're stinky and mis-honorable!"

Sahnassa de Orturu, the pureblood Nephti daughter of Gonastir and Holana de Orturu, sighed, and her shoulders sank. "I'm tired of this game!" she complained.

"Well, I'm the matriarch, and you have to do what I say!" Triana stated as if it were a universally accepted matter of fact.

"Triana, Hylea doesn't listen to me!" Sahnassa complained bitterly. "She just wants to play with her stuffed prowler!" As if proving the point, the youngest of the three sat cooing to her toy animal and petted it, completely ignoring the rest of the conversation.

The elder sister looked into the frustrated indigo eyes of her younger sibling and sternly lectured, "The dame is always supposed to do what the matriarch says, and I'm the matriarch!"

"Oh, why do there have to be dames and matriarchs anyway?! I don't want there to be dames and matriarchs!"

"Now, now, Sahnassa," the deep baritone voice of her father admonished from a nearby chair, his data-pad momentarily lowered. "Families are made from all of us, as well as our matrons, our dames, and our matriarch. Each of us have our role in the family, and we are required to do our part to keep our family house strong and highly honored. We must respect and honor our matron, our dame, and our matriarch because they help us and watch over us. If they were gone, we wouldn't be any better off than the cast offs or the Anati – running around blindly trying to fend for themselves like wild animals."

"But ... but..." Sahnassa stuttered, "I don't want to play dame anymore!"

Her mother chuckled from the couch. "Oh alright, sweetie, you don't have to play dame."

"But I'm the matriarch!" Triana complained.

"Not yet," her father replied with an amused smile. "Perhaps one sol you will be, but not yet."

Unceremoniously, Sahnassa shirked off the nightgown she had been using as her "dame's robes" and stood there in her dark purple and silver white striped nakedness with only her under-things on.

"Young one!" her father almost barked. "We do not strip our clothes off in the middle of the living room!"

"We'll have no Primalists in this family!" her mother agreed tartly. "Up to your bedroom straight away and put on some decent clothes!"

"You're disavowed, Sahnassa!" Triana shouted at her sister, which set the nearly unclothed Nephti's lip at a quiver.

"Am not!" Sahnassa shot back, but clearly about to cry.

"Triana, that's not a nice thing to say. Apologize to your sister," Holana told her child.

"Oh ... alright. Fine. I'm ... sorry." Without saying a word, the angry and embarrassed middle child stalked out of the room and started up the stairs. "She's just going to play computer games, Mom! That's all she ever does now!" Triana started complaining, but Sahnassa started running up the stairs so she didn't have to hear the rest of her sister's protestations.

A few passes later, Sahnassa was dressed in her bed clothes staring out her window at the night sky watching the hovers slip back and forth on the paths of the de Orturu estate, when her mother quietly opened the door to her room. "You didn't come back down," Holana softly prodded her daughter.

"I ... didn't feel like it. Triana..."

Holana sat on the bed, watching as Sahnassa struggled to articulate her feelings, but then her kit simply sighed and laid her head back on the base of the window. "She hurt your feelings. I could tell. You're not really disavowed, you know?"

"Mom, would you treat me like I was dead, forget all about me, if I was disavowed?" Sahnassa asked.

"You're not disavowed, so that isn't worth worrying about. Only those who do something very wrong and dishonorable are disavowed, kit. You're not going to do those things, right?"

Sahnassa's eyes filled with tears as the evasiveness of her mother's reply gave her all the answer she needed. "I ... hope not."

"Well, that settles that, then. I ... brought your nightgown back up."

"Give it to Hylea, Mom. I ... I don't want it anymore."

"Don't be silly now," her mother gently chided, somewhat disregarding the way Sahnassa's voice broke at the end of her sentence. "You don't have to play dame anymore tonight, and I've told Triana she's not to nag you about it. Dinner is in half an interval; you'll make sure you come down, right?"

"Yes, Mom. I will."

"Alright then," Holana replied and then stood, walked out, and gently closed the door behind her.

"Honor, matrons, dames, matriarchs – is that all there is?" she asked herself, and Triana's shouting voice calling her "disavowed" echoed in her thoughts. Looking past the walls of the estate into the darkness beyond, she wondered fearfully what it would be like if that were true. If she was, indeed, abandoned, forgotten, and all alone.

Chapter 1: Progeny

Gonastir called softly back to his three little kits waiting in their best dresses in the living room. "Now everyone, be on your finest behavior! It's not every sol that our new matron comes by for her first dinner with us."

"Yes, Daddy," all three of them said – albeit with differing levels of enthusiasm and interest.

Holana looked at her well-dressed mate and smiled as they walked to the door. "You'll do fine," she offered quietly as she absently adjusted her own dress. "I've heard good things about this new matron. Minsanna had nothing but praise for her."

"We'll know soon enough, and here's hoping our terrible trio back there doesn't ruin the evening."

"I think they'll do fine," she assured him as they reached the door. Nodding to the Perratti butler, the pair stood, waiting to greet their new matron.

As the door swung open, both Holana and Gonastir fought to keep their expressions pleasing and welcoming. The matron before them was hardly what the two had expected. A slightly pudgy elder Nephti stood before them in robes which, while fitting the dress regulation, hardly portrayed the wealth or power or honor they had seen in their last matron – a matron now proudly serving as a dame of the family. Instead of robes which would have paired well with those commonly worn by the matriarch herself, this matron wore robes that – although clean – seemed more suited to gardening than matters of family honor. Deep purple eyes stared knowingly at them out of a face of graying black fur, with purple stripes. It was as if the matron could see the disappointment in the couple's faces despite their best efforts to hide it.

"Greetings and honor to you!" the male Nephti managed. "I'm Gonastir de Orturu, and this is my mate, Holana de Orturu. Welcome to our lair."

A slight smirk tugging up the side of her mouth, the elder matron stepped inside and said, "Thank you, very much. I've heard a lot of good things about you from your former matron. I'm Matron Shalarra. No need to be quite so formal – we all know what our last names are here, don't we?"

"Uh, yes, well, sorry," Holana apologized as they followed the matron who seemed to be making straight for the living room.

"Please, I understand. Your prior matron was big on … formality; well, I'm not. Oh, and who are these three beautiful kits?!" The matron's features, which had been a mask of patient tolerance largely unseen by her hosts, blossomed into an expression of absolute friendliness and affection at the sight of the well turned out children waiting in front of her. Instantly, she lowered herself to one knee so she could be on eye level with them.

Triana, with almost the same look of dismay her parents had tried so unsuccessfully to hide, marched forward two steps and announced, "I am Triana de Orturu, pleased to make your acquaintance, Matron." After a short, snappy bow, Triana took exactly four short steps backward, returning to within fur-strands of her starting point.

"Well, pleased to make your acquaintance," the matron replied, smirking just a little bit. "Looks like someone might have a future in the military." Triana grimaced slightly, bespeaking volumes to the matron about this family.

"Hiyah Maystron!" Hylea blurted and almost tackled the matron, her arms outstretched for a hug.

"Hylea!" Holana gasped in horror, but by then, the matron already had the kit in her arms and was offering her a gentle and reassuring hug.

"Oh, hello there, precious!" Matron Shalarra chuckled. Hearing the approaching clicks of Holana's paw shoes behind her on the polished stone floor, she glanced back over her shoulder. "It's alright, dear. I kind of prefer this greeting, actually." Turning back to the child, she asked, "And how old are you, sweet kit?"

"I'm two hundredths and fwenty tree!" the child replied looking up into the matron's eyes as if this was the real and honest truth.

"Well, you're actually older than I am; imagine that!" the matron chuckled, delighted. "And what a sweet dear you are. Oh, if they would only stay this way forever." Her musing was not all wistfulness, although she did not glance over her shoulder to emphasize she was actually making a point. With a devious sparkle in her eye, she suggested, "Hey, why don't you go give your sister Triana a great big hug! I think she really needs it."

"O day!" Hylea replied and turned on her sister with the maniacal fierceness that only the very young can truly manage. Shalarra suppressed a laugh as the oldest sister took on an expression of outright revulsion at the oncoming assault of her youngest sibling.

When the matron's eyes turned towards the middle child, she was surprised. As she, this one found the discomfiture of her older sister amusing, and the posture of her body – the set of the ears and tail – indicated that she wasn't anywhere near as stiff and formal as her older sister pretended to be. It was also clear that this one seemed to instinctively like her new matron – Shalarra's appearance had caused her to go a bit wide eyed, but the elder matron hadn't missed the child's grimace at Triana's over-formal greeting or the amusement at Shalarra's response to it.

Extending her paw towards the only child still standing was all that was required to draw this attractive little kit with indigo eyes forward. "Hello there. I'm … Shalarra."

"Sahnassa," the child offered with a nervous smile as she took the matron's paw and lightly grasped it.

"Oh, and indeed you are, rare flower," Matron Shalarra replied earnestly.

"Quit it! Hylea! I mean it!" came Triana's frustrated complaint from the floor. "You're messing up my dress!"

"Sissy hug! Sissy hug!" Hylea chortled with glee.

The matron and the middle child looked back at one another with almost the exact same smile of mischievous amusement – something which made a connection between the two instantly. "I … I'm really nothing special," Sahnassa almost whispered, looking away.

The matron took a paw finger and put it under the young kit's muzzle, bringing her eyes back to stare at those of the elder Nephti.

"You most certainly are very, very special," the matron asserted quietly, "and I can't wait to get to know you better."

The young Nephti nodded appreciatively and answered, "You, too." The matron couldn't help herself; she drew Sahnassa into an embrace, an embrace fully welcomed by the shy middle kit.

After a moment, the matron let go of her and stood, although not releasing Sahnassa's paw from her gentle grasp. Looking back for the parents, Shalarra found only the mother, and a quick turning of her head brought the answer of where Gonastir had disappeared to. He was quietly trying to pry Triana free from Hylea's tight embrace, without much success. The matron waited until Gonastir was just about to lose his temper before saying, "Hylea, dear. I think your sister's had enough hugging. Would you like to walk to the table with me?" The matron hadn't missed the smells of food wafting in from the dining room.

With the speed of a trained gymnast, the youngest was off her sister and grasping the matron's free paw with earnest glee – a disheveled Triana and a disconcerted Gonastir looking back at her. "Won't you come this way?" Holana offered nervously.

"Very kind," the matron replied as she led the two kits towards the table.

After a half interval of polite conversation and general questions about what each adult thought of their workplaces and what each child thought of their schools, the meal was concluded and Holana dismissed the children to their rooms, Sahnassa taking care of a very clingy Hylea who insisted on hugging the matron before departing. As the trio disappeared up the stairs, Shalarra affirmed, "Real treasures, every one."

"Perhaps not precisely on their best behavior," Gonastir uttered in apology, for the exuberant chaos of the youngest and the all too candid honesty of the middle child had forced the parents to call both of them down a couple of times. Triana, sensing that she was not favored for some reason, had sullenly eaten her meal while maintaining the pretense of decorum, but it was hardly an impressive performance in either parent's mind.

"Don't worry about it, now," Shalarra reassured him. "I've seen many, many families, being as old as I am, so by comparison, I'll tell you that this went pretty well against some of the others I've seen. At least no change of clothes was required for anyone, so on that, top marks. Now, I wondered if I might have a moment to go over with you some of what I've learned – perhaps some things that will help you."

"We would be very appreciative," Holana offered.

"Very well. I've spoken to the director in your office at the archive, and I've asked for some very direct feedback. Now, he's an old friend of mine, so he was kind enough to tell me that he thinks you're doing a very good job, Holana. However, there are two courses in antique preservation that he would like you to have prior to promoting you. Has he spoken to you about this before?"

Holana blinked in surprise. "Well, no, Matron, he hasn't. I … I had no idea he wanted me to move in that direction."

"I don't think he wants to change where you are or what you're doing, as far as an area of discipline, but I believe he feels that if you are to attain the next level, he wants to have the flexibility to move you between positions, if required. Would you be interested in looking at taking those courses?"

"If they're the ones I'm thinking of, most certainly," Holana replied, smiling nervously. "I've always had an interest, but … I've just been so heads down on the trail at work I never thought I had time to."

"Well, they're worth some effort, especially given the potential you've demonstrated."

"Thank you, Matron, very much," she replied earnestly. "It's quite kind of you to look into that for me."

"My pleasure. Now, Gonastir, I've done some poking around in your casework over the last few seasons, and I don't think you're being well utilized in your present position. You have a phenomenal ability to hold onto details and to state things with a degree of clarity that, well, isn't very often seen. Perhaps you might consider a lateral into the family enforcement law branch? A position there has opened up recently, and qualified applicants are hard to find. You have the basic qualifications; were you not aware of that posting?"

Gonastir swallowed. "I … I have to confess that I have seen it, but … it seemed they wanted someone more qualified."

"Yes, I've spoken to the head of that office before about their miserable postings. They ask for the qualifications of a senior director in just a junior manager. Suffice it to say, that I know what's going on in that office, and they are hurting for someone who demonstrates the skills you already have. The rest they are looking for I believe you can easily train up to. Would you like for me to put your name forward?"

"I ... well, I would be honored if you would," Gonastir replied gratefully, impressed and a little humbled about having misjudged his new matron. In the space of a few passes, Shalarra had given him and his mate more career advice than their prior matron had ever bestowed upon them.

Seemingly attuned to his thoughts, Shalarra leaned over the table and said nearly at a whisper, "The truth is that some matrons are matrons because, one sol, they will make a good dame. They are good at managing things – projects, situations, and staff. There are those, and I count myself among them, who wouldn't allow themselves to ever be promoted to dame; this is the job we love, and we love helping families grow. That's why I'm here. Now, can I dress up? Surely. If there's a formal occasion, I promise you won't have any cause to be embarrassed because of me."

She could tell the pair were about to disclaim any feelings of such, so she raised her paw. "I just thought I would say. However, if it's just us, then as wonderful as this dinner was, the formality isn't really necessary. I want to talk to you and help you, not attend a banquet. Now, have both of you been to the doctor in the last three moons?" They both nodded. "Good. Following the doctor's advice?"

"Well," Gonastir admitted, "except for tonight. I think I've been on-edge ... nervous about the transition."

"Then just relax. If chances are in my favor, we'll be at this for a very long time. Now, about the children, if I may?"

"Please," Holana offered.

"Triana is an excellent student and very ... diligent, according to her record and what I've seen tonight, but I wonder if she could be a little bit more well rounded. Her intelligence is high, without doubt, but she might benefit by pursuing some creative ... group activities – perhaps drama or dance?"

"We can look into that, surely," Gonastir replied, far too impressed by her prior advice to feel defensive, although Holana was clearly working to keep her expression pleasantly neutral.

"Hylea ... well, it's just best to let Hylea be Hylea for now, I suppose. Her care director says she thinks the child is doing very well in all areas. 'Coming along nicely,' I believe was the comment."

That report Holana warmed up to. "That's so good to hear! I was afraid she was creating a frightful mess for them every sol!"

"Hardly. I've got two that are biters in another family. Dear Hylea is as sweet as she can be," Shalarra assured them. "Now

Sahnassa – I honestly have to tell you, I was a little conflicted about what advice, if any, to give. She seems to interact well with her peers, does well in introductory music class, and her other academics are solid enough. If, perhaps, I could trouble you to let me talk with her a little, just the two of us. If I could do that, then I might be able to give you more helpful advice than just keep doing what you're doing."

"Absolutely," Gonastir answered. "I ... would welcome it, honestly. Sometimes we aren't sure quite where she fits. Triana's the eldest, and Hylea's the youngest – what's the middle child to do?"

"We are both 'only children'," Holana explained. "We're ... we're having to learn as we go."

"There were ten in my family," Shalarra admitted, smiling. "I was one of eight middle children, so I have an idea of perhaps how she might see the world. Could I just go up and talk to her for a little while? Would that be okay?"

"Certainly. Please, let me show you to her room," Holana offered.

Upstairs, Sahnassa sat at her large circular bedroom window, looking at the night sky and feeling the breeze as it circled around their lair. The new matron had been interesting, more interesting than she expected. Although some of the admissions she had made would probably draw the ire of her father or mother, the matron seemed interested in them. "Shalarra," she said to herself. She liked the name, she decided, and so far as she had seen, the individual who claimed it.

There was a soft knock at her door, and she swallowed in dread. "Yes?" she called back. The door opened, and instead of her mother or father looking stern, there was the gentle face of the matron. Surprised, the kit jumped to her hind paws.

"Please, please, Sahnassa! Don't get up. You looked quite comfortable there. Might I join you?"

"Yes, Matron," the Nephti child answered politely as she carefully took her seat.

"What are you doing at the window?" Shalarra asked as she gently sat beside the kit, opposite from her so she could look out the window as Sahnassa had done. "See anything in particular?"

"The ... clouds and the stars look so ... magical tonight," the kit replied, honestly. "With the breeze, it's just perfect."

"I would agree, just like this evening has been for me." When the kit looked up at her, uncertain, Shalarra explained, "It's been a great pleasure for me to meet your family. I think all of you are wonderful. You have good reason to be proud of your parents, you know? They are bringing great honor to our family, and they'll continue to."

"I am … proud of them," Sahnassa agreed.

The matron, however, heard a catch in the kit's voice that made her prompt, "But?"

"Matron, do I have to do what they do when I grow up? What they do seems a little … well, I don't think I'm interested."

"What are you interested in, kit? What gets you excited?" the matron asked.

"I like music and reading. My grandfa got me a recording of an orlure concert. I listen to it all the time."

"Perhaps you could play the orlure," Shalarra suggested. "Do you think you would like to learn how to make music like that?"

"I … I guess so. I didn't think I would be able to, though. Triana told me that I would have to go to math camp and language camp soon. I–"

The matron chuckled. "Dear Triana is quite the … intelligent kit, but hardly in control of your destiny, dear Sahnassa. That, after all, is your job."

"Matron?" the kit asked, clearly confused by the concept.

"Your parents will do all they can to help you, mould you into a successful adult, but in the end, when you leave this place to live on your own, when you're older, you'll make the decisions about who and what you become."

Sahnassa looked very afraid. "I … I promise to only do honorable things, Matron! I promise to bring honor to the family."

"You can't do that, child, if you're not being who you were meant to be. We are all given gifts, Sahnassa, special abilities that we are better at than most others. Even middle children like you and me have those gifts, but sometimes we have to work past what others want for us to find them. Have you told your mother and father how much you like the orlure concert your grandfa brought you?"

"Uh, well, no," the Nephti kit admitted. "I … I checked with a music teacher at my school, and he said an orlure can be very … expensive."

"I believe that we, as your family, Sahnassa, can help you with that. Your parents are also quite capable of buying you a trainer version and some lessons. The question I have for you is are you willing to practice – put the work in so that what you've been taught takes hold, and you can use it to make music as beautiful as what you've heard – a music all your own."

For the first time, Sahnassa thought about making a music that was hers, making choices that were all her own, and actually choosing who she would be. "If … if I could make music that was mine, I would. I would practice. It's either that or play dame all the time for Triana!"

Shalarra laughed. "I didn't much care to play that game either, whether I was growing up or even right now, for that matter. I am who I am, and I am who I've chosen to be. My family has encouraged certain things – to act honorably and kindly towards others are ideas I've listened to. Some of what the family has suggested I've all but ignored. Be a dame? Bah! What's the fun of spending all your time running back and forth between the matriarch and all those matrons?"

"Exactly!" Sahnassa wholeheartedly agreed. "But you make a much better matron than Hylea."

"I'm glad to hear you say so, kit. So, I'll tell you what – why don't I try to get you a practice orlure and help your parents find you some lessons. Then, we'll see what kind of music you can make, alright? I'm sure it will be absolutely wonderful."

Looking up into the kind, elder face, Sahnassa felt warm affection and gratitude for this gentle soul who seemed to truly understand her and believed that she could be something special. "Oh, thank you!" she breathed. "Thank you ever so much, Matron!" Sahnassa reached around and hugged the elder Nephti who gently and warmly embraced her.

"Kept by and keeper of, dear kit. Kept by and keeper of," Shalarra whispered as they held one another, their friendship sealed in that moment.

Vanarra was running, running terrified from the angry male voices behind her. She had woken up underneath one of them, pain searing her between her legs like she had never felt before, and a sense of horrible pressure, like something was being shoved into her. Terrified and violated, her claws had instantly expressed and literally carved the nose of her assailant in two, forcing him to fall back in intense agony. The shock her assault had caused was all of the distraction she needed to flip backwards off the hard table and scurry away from them.

She had returned to the tree fort the prior evening, where she had first taken refuge four seasons ago. There, she had grown a little too confident of her surroundings, and a group of teens had found her. She didn't remember much other than screaming in shock and going to sleep, but there wasn't time to dwell on why – she had to survive right now.

As she ran naked out of the small forest, a luxury hover almost ran her over and had to use its emergency thrusters to avoid her. The sound of her attackers still behind her, Vanarra didn't stop and look back; she only thought about how to get away. Up and over a fence-berm, she sprinted at a diagonal through a well-tended yard with manicured gardens. Jumping onto a low branch and quickly climbing, she was up and over the top of a shed and into the next darkened yard before the pet prowler could react. However, given the sounds coming from behind her, the pet prowler was all too aware of the males pelting after her, and its barks and snarls made it apparent it didn't like the intruders. Shouts and challenges diminished in the distance as she left another private yard and darted across another hover trail.

For nearly an interval, she put more and more distance between herself and her attackers. Finally, reaching a darkened lair with a paddling pool, she stopped behind a row of bushes and the berm fence and simply listened. There were no sounds other than those normal for nighttime in a residential neighborhood, and she sat still – her heart pounding, her crotch aching, and her legs stinging from nearly a solid interval of panicked flight. Trying to quiet herself, she kept listening, hardly realizing that she had also started to cry. She reached between her legs and held herself for a moment, then brought her paw up to her nose and sniffed. It was blood. Terrified of what they had done to her, she simply sat and wept.

Waking up with a start sometime later, Vanarra realized that it was well into morning. She panicked, knowing that being naked and a mixed blood hiding in someone's nice yard was a very, very dangerous place to be, and now she couldn't leave. Remembering what had happened to her, she reached down and felt between her legs, and happily the bloody wetness and the aching pain were largely gone. The Vulpi-Faelnar kit almost broke down again at the relief that whatever they had done to her seemed to be healing.

She then realized why she had woken up, someone was entering the back yard. Crouching into as small a shape as she could manage, she silently tried to "not be there" in any discernable way. Two Vulpi opened the back doors of the lair and started hauling equipment to the side of the luxurious paddling pond.

"So this is the Trialle de Caterra residence – very nice. Where are the owners?" one of them asked.

"Away on vacation, somewhere in Tapricia, I think," the other answered. "It will be half a moon before they're back, so don't worry about all the details. We'll polish it all up next time."

Vanarra watched them as they worked, cleaning the clear pond and adding chemicals, checking pumps, and then writing up details. As they left, she noticed that they didn't close the rear doors all the way. "Maybe they're coming back," she thought. Then, she heard their hover lift off and zoom away down the street. "They're going to remember and come back and lock it."

However, as the intervals passed, it became clearer and clearer that Vannie's initial thought wasn't true. As the shadows grew long, Vanarra began to feel some excitement about the treasure that lay in front of her. Only three other times had she come upon lairs that were unattended. Those instances had given her badly needed shelter, money, clothing, and food she wouldn't have otherwise had. Roaming the trails behind restaurants trying to pull food out of the garbage was a disgusting affair, but it kept her from starving to death.

As she continued to wait with growing expectation, she thought back over what had happened, tried to figure out what had gone wrong. "How did they find me?" she asked herself. She had been back to that spot several times in the last few seasons, secure in the knowledge that during the warm turn of the season, no one ventured there. That, she decided, was where she had made her mistake.

Her winter lair beneath the trails in the access tunnels of one of the corporate pack campuses was reasonably secure, and the steam lines running along its length made them fairly warm. Her other resting places were just as isolated – empty shipping crates at the back of a self-storage center, a nice long gap between a bridge and the ground beneath it, and an abandoned utility building in the center of an industrial facility. "I was too exposed. The forest is too small. They saw me going in," she thought to herself. With a sigh, she gave up on the thought of ever returning there – the first home she had known after her mother died.

Finally, with the shadows overstretching the entire yard, Vanarra quietly began to creep from her hiding place. Carefully looking in all directions to ensure she wasn't seen, the mixed blood kit demonstrated the hard won experience of the last few seasons. Several times, she had been ambushed and barely escaped because of her lack of patience, especially when intruding into somewhere she wasn't supposed to be. Breaking into lairs wasn't something she wanted to do, it wasn't something that her mother would have approved of, but she had to eat, and tonight, she was injured and needed a safe place to rest. Slinking around the edge of the yard in the shadows, she carefully made her way to the door and slipped inside quickly. Once in, she closed and locked the door, and drank in the relative safety of having some degree of protection available to her, even that of someone else's lair.

Looking around the lair, she realized that the owners had closed all of the window coverings and shades, which was a relief. The first lair she had slipped into had no such protection, and the first time she turned on a light gave her away. Enforcement had almost caught her that time. Now, she was wiser. Creeping below window level, she made a circuit through the entire lair, learning every room, looking for resources, food, possible escapes should she need them. The lair was nicer than anything she had ever seen, and it had several features she was instantly fond of. There was both an office and an interior bathroom that didn't have windows. These would serve her nicely. Everywhere else, she would have to go about in the dark, but in these two places she could enjoy the luxuries of light and comfort.

Vanarra then set about her primary tasks. In whatever light was left, she searched out a cloth bag in the ample laundry, went to the well-stocked kitchen, and started pulling out food. Eating and drinking some as she went, she had learned from prior misadventures that having a mindless feast was a bad idea. Unfortunately, the cooler had largely been emptied due to the extended absence of the lair's occupants, but she found the pantry nicely stocked with dry goods, and although her knowledge was a little dated, she made generally good decisions about what to take and what to leave. Once assembled, the modestly heavy bag would go with her everywhere she went in that lair, and she would sleep with it, if needed. She also took great care to not make a mess. Nothing told the owners they had been broken into like a big mess on the floor that they didn't make. Putting someone wise to the presence of an intruder made it harder for the intruder to get away, and it cut escape time.

With the edge off her hunger and the light quickly fading, she took the bag and made for the bedrooms, hoping for something to clothe her nakedness. The first child's room was that of a young cub, which wasn't all that helpful. The next room was the master bedroom, and a quick search through the closets didn't reveal anything practical or that would have fit her well. However, the next bedroom was what she had been hoping for. A young teen kit was the other child of this Faelnar family, and her wardrobe – although hopelessly impractical for the most part – did have the basics she needed. Soon after adding several pairs of under-things to her bag along with shirts, shorts, and paw-shoes slung over her shoulder, Vanarra made for the bathroom.

Closing the door, she flicked on the light and nearly screamed at the foreign image looking back at her. The reddish brown female was standing in front of her with her fur matted and dirty, caked with some kind of goo in places, and ribs were easily discernable on the painfully thin figure's body. For a few moments, she just looked at herself, barely able to recognize the kit she had been just four short seasons ago. She looked older than twelve, much older – her eyes, especially.

Not wanting to linger, she put down her things, and turned on the water in the generously sized tub. The roaring of the water frightened her, and as a precaution, she turned off the light and left the bathroom for a few passes while the tub was filling. "I have to be able to hear if someone's coming," she told herself. Finally, she returned and shut off the water. With the light still on, she placed items where she could easily reach them in the dark and then turned off the light and opened the bathroom door. Only then did she bathe.

The potent floral scents of the soap and lotions were almost overwhelming to her, as was the stinging that reasserted itself once she had lowered her backside into the warm water. Thankfully, both sensations dissipated, and Vannie was finally able to relax and clean herself. Ignoring the fur dryer in the corner which would have deafened her for far too many passes, she simply toweled off as best she could and then made for the interior office.

The lair was in full dark now, and it was a little tricky for her to navigate, but she managed, going to the teen kit's bed and pulling covers and pillows for her use. She had no problem leaving this part of the lair a bit of a mess, and after all, she knew the primary rule of what she was doing – enjoy it while you're there, leave, get as far away as you can, and then never return. Working herself between a couch and an inner wall, Vanarra finally laid down and drifted off into an uneasy sleep.

The next sol, she had awoken early, but seeing and hearing no signs of a threat, she used the facilities and went to the kitchen for a quick meal of sweet sticks and meat bars. Newly energized by this sudden rush of caloric intake, she set about her next task, useful thievery. Throughout the entire sol, every drawer was carefully searched, every closet, the pocket of every hanging garment, and every desk and cabinet. Items such as money and medicine, at least that she recognized, were added to her bag. Even that was replaced with a hiker's single-sol backpack. It was small enough to allow her to run if she needed to, but large enough to carry supplies worth mattering. In going through the lair so meticulously, she discovered quite a bit of loose currency, a number of specialty knives and stun prods, as well as jeweled bracelets and gold ornaments, things she knew she could probably trade for a meal or some other favor later. By the end of her first full sol in her borrowed lair, Vanarra had managed to fully obtain every advantage the place had to offer, or so she thought.

Awakening early the following morning, she was tempted to "break camp" and slip away, but a quick check of the office clock and calendar showed that the Faelnar family would not return from their vacation for at least ten sols. To make matters easier, the adults had even marked when the gardeners and pool service would return, so she had at least seven more sols that the lair should be completely available for her use.

For the better part of that sol, she had simply poked around the family's possessions, her interest not so focused on the items she could use as to simply understand what everything was. For the first time in a long while, Vanarra had the luxury of curiosity. She looked at everything, in detail, especially the kit's possessions. A portable music player eluded her understanding until she found a manual, and, although many of the words she didn't recognize, the pictures were easy enough to understand, and she was soon enjoying the teen kit's musical library (albeit through only one ear, just as a precaution). Also, the kit had a large selection of books, and for the first time in seasons, Vanarra found herself reading for intervals on end.

After exhausting the books in the daughter's room, she found her way back into the office and realized that the parents also had extensive libraries. Scanning through the titles on the spines of the books, she was able to make out the words, "Medical Reference." For the rest of that sol, those volumes had come down off the shelf and been perused with great care, one by one. A single volume caught her attention and held her fixated – "Reproductive Health." As she read through its pages, skipping over words she didn't understand, the realization slowly began to come to her about what had happened at the tree fort.

"I … I was rape-mated," she breathed after reading the term in the section about reproductive crimes and assaults. Instantly, she was beset by numerous worries. "Am I carrying a disease? Am I really hurt, or worse, am I carrying a child?" The section on reproductive maturity offered her a little reassurance, indicating that mixed bloods had a very difficult time conceiving a child, and some never did. Fighting with her memory, she struggled to recall exactly what had happened to her, and, as far as she could remember, Vannie had clawed that bastard's nose in two before he had a chance to finish what he started. Still, it was a very sobering and frightening thing to be faced with the possibilities such a incident could lead to. For the rest of the sol, she scoured the library for anything that would give her more information about what happened to her, and finally, she fell asleep in the office on her makeshift bed, a book on infertility in her paws.

The next sol, she found she was able to put aside many of her fears and worries and simply take in the rest of the family's library. Every pass she sat there, every interval she read, was like the opening of whole new worlds for her. While she couldn't read everything, every book was taken down, looked at thoroughly and replaced in its appropriate spot. A small pocket dictionary became a permanent addition to her possessions, and it received almost constant use as she struggled to catch up on so many seasons of missed schooling and mindless existence.

"If … if I could only stay here, and they would never come back, I would be happy," Vanarra thought mournfully to herself. Although still perpetually wary of sounds outside the lair that may indicate the need for a swift exit, she realized that she actually was starting to feel happy, content in her surroundings. "Maybe sometime, in the future, I'll have a place like this," she dreamed and even pretended as she took books back to the enclosed office and read them like they were "her" books.

Shuffling near the lair's entrance in the low level of light seeping through the closed curtains, Van accidentally bumped into a folio that had been left against one wall, and a whole pile of papers spilled out. "Mange!" she thought. She knew she would have to clean it up, but in the dark, it was too difficult to arrange and stuff the items back where they were supposed to go. Resigned, she picked up the mass and took it to the office where she could lay it out and put it back how it had been with the aid of an overhead light.

Upon reaching the office and laying out the documents, she just stared at them. They were odd, unlike anything she had ever seen before. They weren't words telling a story or explaining something; these were groups of drawings, and not child's drawings, either – very, very careful and precise drawings, she surmised, after looking at them for nearly an interval. A word in the corner of each document forced her back to the pocket dictionary. "Pinnacle," she said quietly aloud. "The top or apex of a structure or object. Archive? Ah, here it is. It's a place where documents and records are stored and preserved."

Dumping the rest of the papers in the folio to the floor in front of her, a shiny brochure fell out. She picked it up and marveled at the grandiose structure portrayed on the cover. With a single beautiful spire rising out of an enormous building mound, the structure defined the very essence of power and security. Although it took numerous checks of her dictionary to find what all the words meant, the brochure explained the purpose of the masterfully rendered building on the cover. "The Pinnacle Center Archive is the first multi-family, multi-species library and archive on Thuratan." Flipping through the rest of the document, she saw pictures of luxurious study areas, massive stacks of books, a restricted archives section, and a beautiful children's area.

"Oh, if I could only go there and see that," she breathed. Vanarra hung her head and started to cry knowing that such would probably never happen. Growing angry, she kicked the folio and another document flung out, one that had been fastened together with several others. It had bright red marks on it, and the word "Denied" caught her attention. Curious, she looked at it. The part that was paw-written seemed very angry. Again, going to her pocket dictionary, she was able to make sense of what it said:

To whom it may concern:

I have been a part of the Pinnacle Center Archive design team ever since its grand opening ten seasons ago, and I have petitioned for a redress of this building fault, time and time again. The lower level of the archive contains nearly six hundred square tracks of space that is utterly unusable, not to mention completely inaccessible through any means other than by crawling through the air vents! I have expressed my disagreement with the air ventilation architects numerous times, and every time, they have baselessly rejected my most reasonable assertion that this waste of potentially useful space is a folly and ought to be corrected. Every time they cite regulations about flow routing and variant pressures, but I have done my own research, crawled in the space multiple times, and I fully believe their judgments to be in gross error.

As the diagram in attachment A shows, nothing can be done with that space in its present configuration; the map clearly demonstrates the only access points through a vent shaft in the children's section leading to an access panel some sixty tracks later. My proposal to move the air handler channel back and widen it slightly is altogether reasonable, giving another five hundred and three square tracks back to the offices and store rooms on that level. Although many hundreds of square tracks in the archive admittedly are still unoccupied, it is rapidly filling up. If this isn't fixed now, then it will be too costly in the future to put this situation to rights. I ask that you please consider my proposal for remediation of this defect and that we begin demolition activities as soon as possible.

Vanarra then looked down to the hastily scribbled note in red ink. "DENIED! We don't have the money or the time, and the walls we would have to go through are in full use by the archive as document storage and computer rooms. Let it go! This is one imperfection that will just have to be lived with!"

The mixed blood kit rocked back on her heels from the crouching position she had been keeping, with the letter in one paw and the map – the so called *attachment A* – in the other. "In this … archive place, there's a room that you can only get into through the air vents. A safe place that no one else cares about except this designer, and they told him no, it can't be fixed!" She read over the letter again and looked at the map. The map showed, in bright blue, the way into the hidden space via something marked an "air return" in the children's section. Flipping through the rest of the documents, she realized that the pages she held were only the cover of a much larger document. Examining the rest carefully, she realized that everything she needed was here – the location of the Pinnacle Center, maps of the levels, operating times, private areas where hovers delivered their goods, and instructions for how to remove the grates and hatches that led to the six hundred square tracks of "unusable" space.

"Heh, I could sure use that space," Vanarra thought. "At least there, no one else would try to rapemate me. There, I could sleep like I'm sleeping here, not really worry about anyone finding me." The more she looked over the papers and thought about it, the more she got interested, even a little excited. In her gut, she knew that she had only survived as long as she had through blind chance and the infrequent kindness of others. She had nearly frozen to death several times, enduring nights of sleepless agony, shivering. If the elements didn't get her, then others like the ones who had tried to rape-mate her certainly would.

Stepping away from the pile of papers on the floor and looking down, she realized one other critical truth, as well. From time to time, she had seen mixed bloods like her working in jobs; they weren't great jobs, but they seemed to keep food in their stomachs and clothes on their backs. In order to get a job like that, she had to know something. Her mother was always the one who had taught her, whenever they had a free moment, and that education had obviously ended when Vannie was eight seasons of age.

All of this work she had done understanding what had happened to her and all about the Pinnacle Center Archive made her aware of a hunger she hadn't been able to sense in the last four seasons – a desperate hunger to learn. She knew she had to leave soon, and she knew she didn't want to give up the joy she had looking at all those books. In the Pinnacle Center, she knew that there would be more books than she could read in a lifetime. She found pen and paper to make her own notes about how to get into the building, and for the first time, she felt like she had a focus for her life, a prey for her hunt.

Sols later, just before the return of the pool cleaners, Vanarra slipped out the back of the lair she had entered seven sols prior a completely changed being. No longer starving, she had eaten. No longer ignorant, she had feasted on knowledge, consuming everything from maps and diagrams to an entire volume on air handlers. No longer hopeless, Vanarra finally had a frail dream she could hold onto, that with good chance and the resources of her prospective home, one sol Vanarra Anasto would emerge and find a way to survive on her own terms, with a job and respect and some small measure of happiness.

Looking back at the lair that had sheltered her over the last few sols, she breathed a silent "Thank you" to it as she turned and started to make her way in the midnight darkness towards her destination, what she hoped would be her new home.

The next morning, the same cleaners arrived that had visited eight sols prior. Seeing no sign of anything amiss, they began their maintenance as usual but were forced to stop when one of them received a PawLink call. "Hey, Arnassal. Have you made it to that lair of that de Caterra family?"

"Yeah, we're there now. What is it?"

"Well, leave and go to the next one. I just received word from that family's matron; the whole family died in a hover accident, sailed off the edge of a cliff and tumbled down a hillside. Their house is coming over this evening to take possession of the lair and all their belongings."

"Wow, I … I can't believe it! They've been our customer for seasons! Okay, damn sad, but we'll head out." With a sigh, the Vulpi closed his PawLink, shaking his head in despair.

Chapter 2: Identity

Triana complained bitterly as Sahnassa worked through her fingering drills on the orlure trainer, "Mom! She's screeching and howling again!"

"She's in her room, dear. That's really all we can do," her mother replied back calmly, trying to soothe her eldest kit's frazzled nerves.

The conversation was happening right outside Sahnassa's door, and she stopped playing momentarily to listen. "Nothing new," she sighed and went back to her fingering routines. In the past moon or so since she had the trainer, she had actually listened to Triana's complaints with emotions ranging from anger, to humor, to irritation, and finally, the indigo-eyed Nephti kit had reached the point of resignation. After a few passes, the conversations in the hallway would run their course, and she would be allowed to practice in peace.

Granted, Sahnassa knew that her playing was nothing worthy of a concert recital after a mere moon, but it felt good to almost change the air around her with the sounds she made, and although she still missed fingerings frequently, there were those magical moments when almost perfect music emanated from the instrument. Those were the times that made her feel like the intervals of drill were all worth it. "Well, that and getting the fur up on Triana's back!" she giggled to herself.

As if in response to that irreverent thought, there was a solid knock on her door. "Yes, Father?" she asked as she stopped playing.

Smiling, her father walked into the room. "How did you guess?" he chuckled, although he most certainly knew. "Sahnassa, you have a visitor," he announced and stepped out of the way. In robes far finer than when she had first met them, Matron Shalarra stepped into her room.

Seeing the Nephti kit's struggle to untangle herself from the instrument, the elder matron raised her paws to forestall the movement. "Stay where you are, dear one. Don't bother to get up. After all, the phrases, 'playing the orlure' and 'bounding to your hind paws' really aren't ever found together."

"If it's alright, Matron," her father stated with his blush furs in flight, "I'll go back downstairs and see about ... Triana."

"Thank you, Gonastir. I'm sure we two kits will be just fine," Shalarra offered as she sat on the bed. Her father then nodded and left, closing the door behind him.

"See about Triana, Matron?" Sahnassa asked.

The matron chuckled, "She was in a full out rant, complaining to your mother about your playing when I came up the stairs. Your father, well, he was not happy about it. He sent her downstairs directly, and I can imagine she probably will not dare complain about your practicing ever again. However, it was useful for me to hear her loud complaining because it led me to believe that you actually practice quite often, is that true?"

Sahnassa smiled broadly. "Oh, yes! Every night, if I can. I'm really starting to enjoy it."

"Really? I'm told this is the dullest part, just going over the basics time and time again. Why would you enjoy it so much?" the matron asked, truly dubious.

"Just listen to this, Matron," the kit suggested, and then pulled her bow across the strings. The tone was a little rough, and Sahnassa apologized. "Well, not exactly that but, let me try a few times. I can get it to come out every so often." Without any further prompting, Sahnassa pulled the bow back and forth across the strings working through some easy fingerings. After her third attempt, the nearly bone jarring sound harmonized into a sweet resonance, one that Sahnassa was able to keep going. Then, the young Nephti leaned into the voice box and tried to get her own voice to match the three notes she was repeating. It took a few more repetitions, but eventually, voice and bow, strings and singing all matched, circling slowly around the three notes played again and again.

Drawing the repetitions to a close with a rough stop, Sahnassa winced. "Oops, bad finish – sorry – but did you hear? For a moment there; it was right!"

The wide-eyed matron replied back to her, "Sahnassa, you've only had that thing for a moon, child! You're … you're harmonizing with it already!" the elder matron noted in astonishment.

"Only three notes," she replied, embarrassed.

"But dear, you've got good, solid tone and harmony in those three notes. You can keep it going, too; you don't fall apart! Dear one, I think you are doing exceedingly well! I'm very happy about this. I'm going to report your progress to our dame, you understand."

"Our … dame?!" the kit gasped.

"Surely!"

"But … but … it's only three notes!" Sahnassa contested.

"It's not that you can play three notes, child," the matron gently admonished. "It's that we found something you care about, that you have a passion for. What a victory that is for us and for you! It means that as your matron and as your family, we've help you find something … extraordinary in yourself! Moments like this are why I would be a matron and absolutely nothing else!"

"Thank you," Sahnassa replied, and then looking at the matron – her matron – smiling at her, she felt compelled to untangle herself from the instrument, walk over, and give her matron a grateful hug. "Thank you very much, Matron Shalarra. I am really enjoying it!"

"Very, very welcome, kit; you are so very, very welcome," the matron replied happily. "Now," she began as she broke the embrace, "I wonder if we couldn't find even more things like your orlure, eh? I heard from your parents that you like to play video games, is that right?"

"Well, I suppose so. It's just a waste of time; that's what Triana says."

"I would have to disagree, again, with your elder sister. I got a list of the games you've been playing from your mother, and I had some friends of mine check them out. You don't like easy games, do you? You're playing games that are … very advanced, if what I'm given to understand is true. Why do you like them so much?"

Sahnassa shrugged and admitted, "I don't know really; I kind of like learning them, figuring out what the tricks are, and then beating them. It's like I'm in a contest with someone, and if I can solve the game, I win."

"Yes, I thought as much. Sahnassa, I'm going to talk to your parents about getting you your own computer, up here in your room. Now, it won't be TransNet connected just yet, but it will be an excellent platform for you to learn how computers work. I have a friend of mine at the de Dothnar academy, and he's got some wonderful youth training programs – very entertaining, actually. Think you might be interested?"

Sahnassa wasn't sure, but given how well the orlure had worked out, she was starting to truly trust this new matron. "Okay. I'll try it. I mean, it's got to be better than math camp!"

Shalarra chuckled. "I don't think math camp is for you. Your grades are strong enough that you don't need any reinforcement."

"My grades are…" Sahnassa repeated. "I thought only the best students went to math camp."

"Well, perhaps it is best said the camp is for those who are striving to do … better," Shalarra replied with a bit of judicious tact. Watching Sahnassa work it out made the elder matron smile with pleasure. "Yes, that's right, kit. Not everything is as it appears, even with your elder sister. So don't be discouraged or think yourself second best just because you're the middle kit. You've got abilities in some areas that far surpass that of your sister. Now, she does have strengths in some places, but you are a talent in your own right, kit. Always remember that."

Buoyed up by the matron's candor and praise, Sahnassa looked at her smiling and softly offered, "Thank you. I will."

"Well, I must be off. I'm going to a formal dinner tonight with a bunch of dames set on babbling about the various achievements of their matrons. Bragging session, if you ask me. I hate going to dinners where I'm on display. I'll have to sneeze a lot or do something to make sure they don't try to promote me into their ranks. No, sneezing just gets tissues shoved in your face. I know, I'll fall asleep; they're bound to keep me matron-ified if I cut a good snore during the middle of the speeches. Perhaps, I'll pass gas – that always works at limiting one's upward mobility." Sahnassa, by this time, was starting to laugh.

"Matron! I can't believe you just said that!" Sahnassa cackled.

"Sometimes it takes great skill to keep oneself where you're happy; I'm an expert. The climb to the top of the hill can have a lot of loose rocks and sudden drop-offs. At some point, learning to be content no matter your situation is far better than any … position you could earn. Now, you take care, dear kit, and I'll check on you later, okay?"

Still chuckling despite her mind reeling over her matron's statements, she replied, "Okay. Thank you so much." Sahnassa embraced her matron and smiled, returning happily to her practice after the matron left.

Once leaving the de Caterra's lair, Vanarra had quickly put several courses behind her in the pre-dawn darkness, staying hidden as best she could, lest anyone see the clothes she was wearing and question her. The stunner hidden in her paw made her feel more confident, and she kept vigilant watch around her, specifically behind her. She found the trails and walks blissfully deserted until almost an interval before dawn. Reaching a major intersection just as the sun was coming up, she used the money she had appropriated to reach the center of Shanandrae via public hover transport. Sitting in the back and pulling her clothes around her made her largely indistinguishable from any other patron, and only those who saw her get on, knew she wasn't purebred.

Getting off at the central city transfer station, she purchased another pass which would take her to the archive stop. Again, sitting small in the back of the large hover transport kept others from really noticing her, and she even feigned being asleep, although her pack's straps never left her. At the archive stop, she slipped out of the back entrance of the vehicle and then walked away from signs pointing towards the archive so no one could gauge her intent. After checking her map and that no one was observing her, she slipped into the woods beside the path and made for the general direction of the archive – her goal, her prey.

After many tense moments in the forest, largely caused by small animals and the wind blowing through the trees, Vanarra emerged at the end of a large, well-manicured lawn which led up to the archive. Taking the borrowed distance viewers, she studied the archive building. In every way, it looked exactly as the maps and diagrams had portrayed, and the ring of forest around the building allowed her to make her way behind the facility slowly, carefully, and without much fear of being seen. Sitting in the dappled sunlight of the forest as the sol wore on, Vanarra patiently studied the building with her distance viewers and compared that to the documentation she had discovered.

Several possible methods of entrance had presented themselves, but by far, the most attractive was an exhaust vent just behind the rear of the central spire. That's where most of the heat exchange units were clustered, just behind the top of the hill so as to be invisible to the observer on the ground.

After sleeping uneasily in the secluded forest, she awoke to see a moon high in the night sky. The archive was nearly all dark, except for a few interior lights and the giant floodlights pointed up at the central spire. Once having taken care of her body's most immediate needs, she slipped onto the open ground behind the center and made it to the clusters of machinery with very little effort. What she saw there at the top of the mound, however, caused her no end of difficulty. Although there was adequate light bouncing off the shaft of the spire, it was hard for her to pick through the various machines trying to find which one provided the fresh air ventilation for the structure. Only when, at least half an interval later, a series of fans nearly startled her into a scream did she realize she had found what she was looking for.

Two banks of large, mechanical fans sat on either side of a doorway bearing a sign which read, "Warning: Heavy Machinery. Authorized Maintenance Staff Only." As the fans sucked in large volumes of cool night air into the building, Vanarra examined the doorway and its lock carefully. While not adept at picking locks by any stretch, she had learned some basics about how they worked, and the door's pull-lever had a built in lock she had seen before. While she waited for the fans to cycle off, she readied the tools she would need. About a quarter interval later, the fans spun down, and she started working on the slot between the door frame and the door where the catch kept the door closed. Yanking and pulling on the cheap and poorly installed catch for just a small amount of time produced the desired result – an open door. Carefully, she slipped in and quickly closed it behind her.

Taking a small UltraBright from her pocket, she was almost giddy as she looked for how she might use the access she had acquired to her advantage. It was a little disconcerting to realize that the only way she could make it into the steep shaft leading into the structure was to step right between the fans – a very tight squeeze, even for her. Realizing that the fans could come on at any moment, she quickly made her way over the motors and chains and worked herself into the gap. As she slipped between, she looked down at the long drop off in front of her. Shining her light down into the shaft, she tried to figure out how she could actually manage such a long descent.

Just as she was leaning over for a better view, the humming sound of electricity followed by the quickly increasing pitch of machinery signaled the activation of the fans. Knowing she couldn't escape in either direction and terrified, Van realized that she had no choice but to wedge her body tight between the fan casings. With wind whipping fast around her, she pulled her bag and her own tail between her legs and then sagged, effectively pinning both securely. Clamping her paws over her ears because of the intense noise, she just stayed as still as she could while the fans ran and tried not to move.

After what seemed like an eternity, the fans cycled off, and her ears ringing, Vanarra felt it was safe to move again. Shaking her head gently, she painfully brought herself up to a standing position. Leaning over, she sucked in a gasp of air as her UltraBright showed no less than a four level drop, almost fifty tracks down. "I'm never going to make that," she thought, wondering if she should abandon her entire plan and escape back to the forest while she still had the protection of night. Looking down again, this time leaning way out, she shone her light all around the shaft carefully. Beneath her hind paws, on the side of the shaft closest to her, were small paw-holds. "Ugh. That … that doesn't look easy," she thought. "One slip, and I'm a pile of Anati goo at the bottom, stinking up the archive." However, the thought of giving up or waiting through another run of the fans pushed her into action far quicker than she would have, otherwise.

Lying down on her stomach, her pack on her back, she slid backwards as carefully as she could, until her legs and tail were dangling out in space above the chasm. Her forepaws with claws bared grabbed the metal frames of the fans as best they could, but she felt like one good sneeze could send her to her death, and what was worse, her nose was itching. Literally banging her muzzle on the floor to fight the feeling made her eyes water, but it did give her a little relief. Stretching her arms and body as much as she could, Vanarra was able to get far enough out to bend at the waist and start searching for the small indentions she had seen earlier. Worry started to turn into panic as she realized that she would be unable to pull herself back up, even claws bared, using the smooth surface of the metal fan casings. "Oh, come on Vannie, for Mom! Do it for Mom!" she pleaded with herself.

A paw-shoe bumped something just as she was considering a desperate attempt to pull herself up. Quickly, nearly out of breath, she frantically searched for and found the indention. She tried to push her paw-shoe into it, but it was too big. "Oh, mange!" she breathed, her whole body seeming to tremble with exhaustion. In desperation, she used one hind paw to slip off the paw-shoe of the other, and the shoe dropped just as the fans started buzzing in their start-up sequence. Terrified, she reached back with her naked hind-paw and found the indention, hooking her hind claws into it.

It was enough to hold her, weakened as she was, but it wasn't a good position or one she could keep for very long. Straining to hold herself up one more moment, she lifted her hind-paw out and pulled off her other paw shoe, the fans now reaching their full roar. The screaming noise more than ample motivation for her to quickly retreat, Vannie found the claw-hold she had before, and searching down with her newly bared hind paw, found another just below it. Tired and scared to the point of nausea, she willed herself to keep on moving, even as the gale blew around her.

Using nothing more than the pressure of her paws on the flat surface of the ledge, she reached down with her other hind paw to find the next claw-hold. Using the spacing of the first two as a guide, she found it and started to slip her neck over the edge. Reaching in front of her, she frantically felt around for any sort of hold for her fore-paws. After a moment of desperate searching, she had it, and Vanarra finally started to feel like she was going to survive. Working her way down again, she was completely off the ledge, hugging it, all of her paws secure at last.

Resting just for a few moments, she started her descent. The fans still blowing away above her kept a steady force of wind against her, as if they were trying to drive her down. With what strength she had, she kept descending as carefully as she could. After several terrified passes, her dropping hind paw found not a claw-hold, but the flat surface at the bottom of the shaft. Testing the strength of the bottom to make sure it would bear her weight, she climbed down and lay on her back, gasping, trembling, all four of her paws aching painfully, strained as they never had been before. Before she even realized it, she was crying, sobbing in relief at not having fallen.

The spinning down of the fans was the only thing that quieted her, when she started to hear her own voice weeping. If she could hear it, others might, as well, so she rolled over, pulled herself into a ball, and tried to control her sobbing. "Okay, okay, we've done it, Mom. I'm in. I got in. I got in."

Retrieving her paw-shoes and donning them, she started trying to figure out where to go next. Pulling out the notes she'd made, she found that the air ducts she needed were not connected to these. If she followed these, she'd run into another set of blowers that sent the fresh air into the parking garage. Even if she could get past the blowers, the path would just lead her outside to locked doors and potentially, security cameras. Leafing through the pages while holding her UltraBright in her mouth, she eventually found the diagram she needed. Looking down the single horizontal vent leading away, she followed its line on the map with her claw. Almost right in front of the second set of blowers was an access panel that exited into an equipment room. Packing her notes and replacing her backpack, she started to make her way down the shaft.

She was caught up short by the noise she made, the metal vent flexing and groaning under her weight. Terrified by this, she was forced to wait for nearly an interval for the blowers in the system to turn on again. It wasn't time wasted, however. A quick drink of water and a meal bar gave her a badly needed resupply of energy. With nothing else to do, the tired kit laid down her head on her backpack and simply dozed.

Stirred awake by the sounds of the machinery and the air blowing across her fur, Van sat up feeling much better than she had when she laid down. Working her way along the vent was still noisy, but she felt like the sounds were manageable so long as she didn't keep a regular rhythm. Finally, just as the blowers were cycling off, she reached the panel. Worried that she would find a lock or something that couldn't be opened from the inside, Vanarra was pleasantly surprised. A simple latch was easily turned, and the panel swung open.

Depositing herself on the floor of the room, lit only by the light of the hallway spilling under the door, she closed the panel and eyed her surroundings, carefully.

"Well, the easy part is over," she thought to herself, darkly. From the drawings, she had determined that this maintenance room was fairly close to the back loading dock and parking garage. In order to reach the children's section, she would have to slip out of this room, down the employee's hallway, and into the main archive's library. After descending another two levels, she would need to find the children's section and work her way inside those vents to reach what she hoped would be her final destination.

She knew she had to move soon, however, because certain bodily urges were beginning to prod her with greater and greater intensity. There was a facility in the hallway she was on, but it was closer to the back dock than she would have liked, but with a sigh, Vannie realized she had no choice. A great puddle of Anati pee wouldn't be missed and could instantly lead to a search. So, stepping over to the metal door and quietly turning the knob, Vanarra peeked outside.

The hallway was dim and quiet, the lights obviously far lower than they would be normally. She waited and listened for nearly a pass before leaving the safety of the equipment room, but seeing and hearing no one, she was compelled to quickly slip out and down the hall to the restroom. Not daring to turn on the lights, she felt around and was able to find what she was looking for – the stall in the back with its own door and a small sink. With a little careful maneuvering, the sink served as the vessel of her relief, not the fixture normally provided for that purpose. In several other situations, the loud flush needed to remove any evidence of her presence had given her away, whilst the quiet running of water in the sink would easily dispose of anything remaining.

Her body no longer aggravating her mind for relief, Vanarra was able to think a little more clearly. "Not bad so far," she told herself, feeling a surge of pride at having been able to slip inside this daunting facility without apparently being detected. "Yet," she added mentally in self-warning and carefully cleaned around the sink with paper towels before edging back towards the door and listening for any activity.

As she pulled the door slowly open to peek outside into the hallway, her heart was starting to race. This was the most dangerous leg of her traverse. She had to make it into the archive's library through a door which could easily be monitored by cameras or alarmed. Nevertheless, there was no other alternative visible on the map without using an elevator. The stairs nearby the freight elevator had been clearly marked on her diagram as for "fire escape only" and "alarmed." So carefully and quickly, she darted down the hallway, crouching low until she reached the door which warned, "Quiet! Patrons Inside!" Scanning around the door, she didn't see any access control panels or wires or plastiform lumps which would have indicated an alarmed entrance. Pulling on the handle, she noiselessly swung the heavy door towards her, revealing a darkened space beyond.

Slipping through, she immediately moved off to one side, away from the meager safety light which illuminated the door. The smell of books and ink and paper and cleaning fluid assailed her nose as she huddled in the darkness, waiting for her eyes to adjust to this even darker area. With tentative steps, she felt along a shelf of books, letting it guide her forward. She passed across an aisle, and found herself drawn back and down that aisle to a cavernous space looming ahead.

In wonder and in awe, Vanarra beheld the grandeur of the great library, impressive even in the modest light filtering in through a paw-full of safety fixtures in the ceiling. The place had a mystery and a reverence that seemed to fix the mixed blood to the railing, compelling her not to move even though she was horribly exposed on this balcony, a balcony which overlooked another one beneath hers, both suspended above shelves whose number and height and orderly alignment seemed above the ability of normal Thurians to even conceive of. Its majesty overwhelmed her, and in that moment, the young mixed blood's life was forever changed.

The mere realization that so much information existed, more than she could ever consume, was exhilarating, and Vanarra actually giggled aloud, unable to control herself. Every possible dream she could have ever had for her life, from the ones she had while hiding in that de Caterra lair to ones she hadn't even conceived of yet, seemed to be laying in neat rows amassed beneath her. In many ways, it was the most hope and joy she had ever felt.

Her revelry was cut short by a change in the distance ahead of her. A light off to the left close to the front of the archive turned on, and a shadow fell across the polished stone floor – a silhouette of someone moving. Instantly backing into the dark safety of the stacks, she reached into her pocket and checked the time. "Damn!" she thought to herself. It had taken her nearly three intervals to make it this far, and morning was close enough that the library's staff had started showing up to prepare for the sol ahead. Sticking her head out and looking around, she easily found the steps leading down a level and availed herself of them, trying to strike a balance between swiftness and silence.

When she reached the lowest level, there was a measure of relief, but that was soon dissipated as several large lights started to illuminate the area of the library near where the first light had appeared. Remembering the layout of the building from her diagrams, she moved to where she thought the children's section should be, and she was grateful to find large signs along the walls directing her to where she needed to go. Thankfully, this put her farther away from the Thurian who now greeted a fellow worker who had also just arrived.

Quickly stepping around the low shelves and soft foam chairs and mini-tables, Vanarra found the air returns she was looking for. Although she hated to risk it, she knew she would never be able to find the catches without the aid of an UltraBright. She took it out of her pocket, placed her paw fingers over the light, and clicked it on. By parting her paw fingers ever so slightly, she was able to make a narrow slit of light that proved adequate for finding what she was looking for without giving her away.

After a moment, she found the latches exactly where the air-handler book said they would be, and slipping her claw-tips in and pressing, she was able to raise one of the grates and slip inside the duct. As she closed the grate behind her and carefully pulled it shut, light suddenly poured in through the slats. Smiling hugely, Vanarra realized that the library was now fully and completely lit, but she, by ingenuity and bravery, had managed to finally reach her goal.

Basking only for a moment in her achievement, Vannie realized she needed to get back away from the slats lest a cough or a sneeze give her away. She also knew she had to make that movement quickly lest the pinging and banging of her weight distorting the metal ductwork would also do the same. Carefully sliding back, she was surprised as no sound or complaint met her ears from the surface beneath her. A few more careful scoots, and she could still hear nothing. As it was her goal to work her way back into the vent to the access panel mentioned in the diagrams she carried, she simply kept sliding farther and farther back until the duct made an abrupt left, exactly as it had on her drawing.

Despite herself, she smiled and giggled mischievously. Not only did her potential lair have access to what seemed like the sum total of Thurian knowledge, it also had a silent entranceway, very useful and far more flexible than she had thought it might be after her trip through the other ducts. She had imagined that she would be a prisoner in her lair until the last employee left for the night. Now, she could leisurely make her way to the grate, perhaps sit and read not ten tracks away from other children, listening to their chatter, pretending she was one of them.

Just then, the air handlers switched on, and a stiff breeze blew in her face, pulled from the area near the children's section. That made her smile all the more. When the air handlers were running, she would always be downwind, able to smell everything in the children's area but completely masked as far as they were concerned.

Turning happily in the other direction and continuing to follow the map she had memorized to the access hatch, she felt an amazing energy running through her. Here, there was the promise of never being found. Here, no one would try to rape-mate her. Here, she could sleep and study and do whatever she wanted. She just had to reach this new paradise, and it just had to be real.

With her UltraBright now shining ahead of her, she looked for and soon found the hatch described in the de Caterra engineer's memo. Finding its operation no more difficult than the one she had used to exit the vents earlier in the night, she swung its door open and shone her light inside, smiling. "It's real! It's here!" she whispered, excited. After gauging the distance to the floor, she carefully maneuvered through the opening and put her hind-paws on the dusty cement. Shining the light around, she saw only a small space, but that agreed with what the diagrams said. She would have to slide between the vents and the wall to her side to reach the "main chamber."

Slipping off her backpack and holding it with one paw, she navigated the claustrophobic crevice deliberately, shining her light ahead, looking for anything that might snag her or hurt her – a skill that had been borne from getting raked and scraped by forest brambles or fence edges. Finally, she exited the gap and shone the light around the room.

"Yes!" she laughed. "Yes! Yes! Yes!" Although she gazed at a space whose floor was nearly covered with debris and abandoned building materials, Vanarra knew she had found the place she had sought so desperately. A place where she could be free from the perpetual fears and anxieties that came from the threats the purebred world imposed on those called Anati.

Putting her bag down, she started stepping through the large room taking inventory of all of the wonders it contained. More than a modest sampling of construction scraps littered the floor – bricks and buckets, food wrappers and containers, bags and even some wood. The number of bricks was astounding, in actuality, as it looked like a whole pallet of them had been spilled onto the floor and left – the effort to right and extract them too difficult. Vanarra made her way to the far corner by the wall and stood, her hind-paws turned at odd angles avoiding the debris on the ground. "It's so wonderful, Mom! I ... I wish you could see it! If we had only known about this place, we could have come here and hid from the world, together."

She stood for a few passes, awash in the memories of her mother. "Vanarra, no matter what, you stay hidden and stay safe. Let all of my love and that of your father, wherever he is, protect you. Promise me, you will not come out of hiding!"

"I'll never forget you Mom, ever," she breathed, "and I'll stay hidden." Now that she had made it to her destination, Vanarra realized she had to begin dealing with its realities. Carefully, she reached down and picked up a brick. It was heavy, and it required her to use two paws to shift it, but brick after brick, she slowly opened up an area for her to sit and rest, sleep beginning to demand its due.

Chapter 3: Probability

Vanarra slipped back in through the narrow crevice between the ductwork and the wall to reach her lair after a very productive night of scrounging. She had spent nearly a full season in the archive, and sol after sol since her arrival, she had learned more, adapted more, and made that forgotten corner of the archive's basement into her haven. Entering the room without the aid of an UltraBright, she walked confidently to its center where she had her table and clicked on her camping light. The light had been abandoned without power packs in the detritus left by the construction crew, but thanks to a frequently unlocked supply cabinet in the archive's book hold room, power packs weren't all that hard to come by. She only took exactly what she needed, no more, lest someone begin to suspect. That cabinet also supplied her with paper, writing utensils, folders, and tape. Those items were also pulled out and placed on the table she had made for herself with the bricks and wood left behind.

Next, she started removing food items. In the offices close to the loading dock, a number of Anati worked loading and unloading, sorting and recording, and doing all the supporting jobs the archive required, such as janitorial. In what amounted to their break room, there was a large cooler that had a sign affixed to its front. "All items in this cooler must be removed by the end of the sol, or they will be discarded," the sign warned. Vanarra was only too happy to assist the archive management in ensuring the cooler didn't become overcrowded. Some sols, there was very little, and those things she didn't want she did indeed discard in the trash. Some sols she feasted on the remains of someone's meal. Nevertheless, this location was not her only stock of food.

Up on the second level of the archive were the offices of the junior archivists and their aides. This group of purebreds kept a common "larder" of quick meals, drinks, and snacks in a cabinet near the center of their work area just in case they were staying late. As dedicated as they were, however, they weren't allowed to stay beyond high night, so for more than a few intervals each night, Vanarra was free to pick items from their pantry without much chance of arousing suspicion. This group was also provided with a cooler, and it, too, had a strict clean-out policy, happily enforced by Vanarra. As an added bonus, occasionally, this group ordered catered meals, and the remains of such an office event were a true feast for the mixed blood. Given the comparative wealth of available food over the last season, Vanarra had become more and more pleased with the image staring back at her in the bathroom mirrors. No longer did her ribs stick out into her fur. To her great astonishment, she was also developing into an older teen with a couple of notable attributes adorning her chest.

Regular patrols through each office area were productive and useful in another arena – equipment. Occasional office upgrades, staff departures, and employee clean-outs had rendered her a wealth of additional throw pillows (from the executive offices), power-pack TransComs, and even a few pretty nick-knacks. There was also a reasonable amount of funds that could be secured on her nightly hunts. Various office staff kept a spare change cup on their desks or in their drawers, and a few missing coins here and there rewarded her with trips to the vending machines for a special treat or a quick meal. She had even learned how to use the quick warmer to give herself the rare treat of a hot supper. Abandoned bottles and containers went with her every night and were filled, and at least once every night, the bucket that acted as her toilet during the sol was carried to a rest room, dumped, and flushed. She no longer worried about the sound since she was fairly confident that the archive was empty, except for her, during the night.

There was also a donation container near the front of the archive which Vanarra didn't go near except on very special occasions. If a particularly violent storm caused the power to go out, she would go, open the container, and remove several of the larger denominations of money from it. With that, she'd been able to sneak back out of the archive and take a public transport to a store that would actually allow her kind to purchase – usually the charitable discards of purebreds or the things they wouldn't buy. Occasionally, she would also buy medicine or other packable foodstuffs during those infrequent trips outside the archive.

She didn't like to leave the archive since she feared that one sol, she wouldn't be able to get back in, but the archive's most abundant treasure had also given her some confidence in that area, as well. Waiting outside of the archive in the trees she had watched the delivery hovers and garbage transports come in and out of the facility. As best she could, she made notes about what they looked like and how they operated. Once back inside the archive, she had been able to find volumes that detailed secret places in the garbage hovers that could easily hide someone of her size. She just had to be careful to get out before the hover landed, or she could be crushed. A little late night investigation of the garbage chute found that it was completely unprotected, with more than adequate places to hide while the container was being dumped. It wasn't something she had been forced to do yet, but knowing that she could, if she had to, gave her a measure of security.

Having eaten and read for several intervals, the exertions of the prior night started to wear on her, and she yowled out a long, satisfying yawn. Getting up from her padded sitting platform near her brick table, she stretched, closed the books on language and math she had been reading through, and then wandered towards her bed. The archive's shreds stuffed inside several abandoned coats made her pillow, and abandoned seat cushions wired together made her bed. Large jackets from what had to be overweight Pantera had been laced or fastened together to provide her with a reasonable facsimile of a comforter. Happily relaxing into the warm embrace of her self-made bed, Vanarra shucked out of all but her underthings and slipped under the covers for a good sol's sleep.

Unlike so many other peaceful sleeps, this one was interrupted by a vague sound that shouldn't be there – male voices. For awhile, she thought it might be a dream, but then, the voices got closer. Vanarra's eyes popped open, and she was horrified. Someone else was in the vents or near them, perhaps within moments of discovering her. Without turning on the light, she slipped out of her bed and carefully made her way in the pitch black of the room to the crevice entrance. Slipping through, she squatted in the small space outside of the open hatch and listened. With the air blowing, it was hard for her to tell how close they were, but it seemed that they were still some distance away. As quietly as she could, she swung the panel shut and closed it – comfortable with doing so since she took pains to lube it with oils taken from the repairs office.

A few passes later, she could hear a couple of males talking right outside. "So, hold it, where does this go?"

"Oh, that was just construction access. It isn't used now. The blowers are ahead; that's where the problem is."

"Are you sure they are turned off?"

"Yes. I locked and tagged the primary unit, myself. It's been over ten seasons. Those belts have to be changed out. We get one this sol, one the next sol, then they'll be in pretty good shape."

"Alright, let's get this done. I don't want to be home late tonight; my matron is coming over."

"Matron, huh? She like you?"

"Not very much, I really don't..." The shuffling outside and the voices growing quieter indicated that the two repair technicians had continued on their way. Vanarra breathed a sigh of relief, but just for good measure, she took out a broom handle she had purloined and fashioned for just such a purpose and slipped it under the lever on the door so it couldn't be turned, and therefore, couldn't be opened. Nearly shaking, she retreated from the entrance and made her way back to her bed, lying down but knowing that she wouldn't be able to sleep.

Sometime later, she heard them working their way back up the shaft after clanking and banging around for several intervals on end. Carefully, she slipped out of her bed, crept back to the entrance, and listened. "So Charlo disappears from work, no reason, leaves everything with me, and then shows up two sols later, complaining of a neck ache."

"Well, he's the one who's the pain in the neck," one of the Vulpi chuckled. Vanarra heard him slide close to the hatch and try the lever. "Damn thing won't move." Her heart pounding in fear, Vannie gently grasped the broom handle, ensuring that it wouldn't slip out of place.

"They welded it, most likely, on the other side when they were putting it in," the other commented. "Come on. We're going to be late. We've got that job at the de Caterra estate to take care of."

"Oh, alright. Still curious as to what's back there, though."

"Cement and dust. What's there to be curious about?" he replied, calling back as he had obviously continued along his way.

"Okay. Wait up," the other Vulpi called, and then he, too, started to move away. Trying not to gasp, Vanarra finally started breathing again, her whole body trembling in fear and nervous anxiety.

"It's that damned lever," she thought to herself. "Everyone who comes in here is going to try it. I've ... I've got to do something about it." Her mind instantly started calculating the best path to the reference books on air handlers, and she ran through the tally of supplies and discards she had saved that she might make use of. As she thought through the list, a glimmer of an idea started to form, but she'd have to check the toolbox near the back dock to see if she could carry it off. For now, she eased the panel back open as the blowers turned on, a flow of air circulating out of her lair and into the returns.

A light knock pulled Sahnassa's attention away from the viewer she had been staring at for the last two intervals. Looking at the clock, she was stunned that so much time had slipped by. "Yes? Please, come in," she called.

"Sahnassa," Hylea said sadly as she opened the door. "Triana won't play with me." While the older sibling tried to look back at the viewer, she just couldn't. Hylea's pleading purple eyes looked out of a depressed light purple face, and a silver striped paw gently reached up and touched her side.

"I'm sorry, sissy. Did she make you feel bad?" The kit firmly nodded in response, as if reporting the offense to the enforcement authorities. "Yeah. She does that. Come on. Let's go to your room and play. Perhaps we can make a tent out of your blanket and read stories under it."

"Yay!" Hylea giggled. "Thank you! I'll go get ready!"

"I'll be there in a moment. I just have to shut this down," Sahnassa replied, saved her lesson, and keyed the commands to power off her computer.

An interval later, Triana opened the door to Hylea's darkened room. She had rid herself of her pestering little sister, but after awhile, her schoolwork and chores done, the eldest had no one to talk to; her mother and father were both studying or finishing up other work. So, after peeking into Sahnassa's room and finding her missing from her computer, she decided to search out the youngest. She was even willing to play "run and hunt" another ten more times.

In the dim light of the window, she realized that all the pillows and blankets had been pulled off the bed, along with the majority of the stuffed animals. Instead of a chaotic jumble, the artifacts from off the mattress had been arrayed in the corner of the room, a corner lit by a softly glowing pink nightlight. Half tempted to walk back and turn on the overhead light, Triana faltered and stepped forward. There, on the floor, lay Hylea with Sahnassa snuggling behind her, the two of them completely asleep, several story books about stars and space stacked nearby. The feelings Triana hadn't been able to name earlier coalesced into something she definitely could bring to mind – loneliness.

Dejected, she was about to turn away, but as she did, a slight whisper sailed above the ambient noise of the lair's air handler. "Triana, come – if you want."

Looking back, she saw Sahnassa, indicating the space behind her. A pillow had been left for Triana, and her younger sister was pulling the covers back in invitation. Tears forming in her eyes, Triana slipped out of her paw-shoes and belt before stepping carefully over the "wall" of stuffed prowlers and slipping in behind Sahnassa. Carefully working the dark purple, ink-dipped tail between her legs, Triana soon found she was quite comfortable, and put her arm around both of her sisters, the youngest barely stirring at the touch.

"Thank you."

"You're welcome," Sahnassa replied before relaxing against her. Triana smiled at the warmth that passed into her, and she nuzzled the back of her sister's head, happily.

After simply enjoying how wonderful the closeness to her sister felt, Triana started to think and realized how truly grateful she was that Sahnassa had invited her to lie down. There were a lot of things she thought were wrong about her sister, but nevertheless, the love there was truly undeniable. "Sahnassa?"

"Yeah?"

"I ... love you, you know?"

"I know. I love you, too. Do you love me even if I play with computers and won't play dame?" she asked.

"I do."

"Mommy said hush," a sleepy kit voice whispered in front of Sahnassa interrupting their conversation. Instantly, the two behind Hylea smiled and quieted, and Triana pulled them all gently closer.

It had taken several sols for Vanarra to fully realize her plan, but now she looked at the blank panel that had been the doorway to her secret lair with a mixture of pride, accomplishment, and terror. The hint of terror was an echo back to when she had found the access hatch right where it was meant to be, and now, by any objective eye, the panel was simply gone. In its place was a trim piece, a flat panel, and another trim piece. According to the books she had referenced, this was the standard way of covering up such an access that was no longer needed. From the inside, it could even be locked into place so that no curious maintenance workers could pry their way into her lair, even if they wanted to.

Now, that had left her with another problem she had to solve, and that one had actually been a little easier to fix than the first. To ensure her lair didn't run out of air, she had actually crawled through the very narrow gap between the ductwork in the direction of the blowers and forced open a dead-end duct that had been closed up and abandoned. Using spare pieces to make it turn back and forth, no worker, sitting in the main ductwork, would be able to determine where the vent came from.

"It's perfect!" she said to herself. "Oh, Mom, if you could only see this…"

It was at that moment that a very profound, sad feeling settled across her soul. Her mother had been dead for five seasons, nearly six. For most of that time, Vanarra had been alone. She didn't have anyone to talk to. It was just her and the archive. The archive spoke to her through its books, and she talked to it, whispered to it, pleaded with it, and thanked it when she returned to its comfort and security away from the outside world. Still, it wasn't a someone, and now that she had some measure of safety, a part of her desperately wanted companionship. Slowly, Vanarra removed the panel and slipped back into her lair, closing it up behind her wondering how, if ever, she could just have someone to talk to.

She awoke at an odd interval, just after mid sol by her watch, an item abandoned in the lost and found for more than ten sols. The maintenance of the air handlers had thrown off her schedule, and she couldn't get back to sleep. Staring into the darkness above her, Vanarra felt the oppressive emptiness of her life eating away at her again. Without really thinking about what she was doing, she rolled out of the bed and slipped on some soft clothes after smelling them to make sure they didn't reek too badly. Fortunately, she had done laundry a couple of sols ago using the liquid soap in the bathrooms and then hanging the clothes up in her lair to air dry. Grabbing a couple of books, she slipped out of her lair and into the air vent.

"What are you doing, Vannie?" she asked herself. "I just want to hear what's going on in the archive, that's all," she answered. "You want that bad enough to get caught? No." Vanarra hesitated, but then kept quietly shuffling forward. "I'm not going to get caught unless you can't shut up," she hissed at herself. "Oh, right." With that conversation ended, she stealthily slipped closer and closer to the vent and the sounds of activity ahead.

"Gather around, children!" an elder Perratti archivist instructed the group of kits and cubs milling about in the children's section of the archive. "We have a very special guest this sol! Honored Dame Rahnahi de Dothnar is going to read to you a story! It's a story she has written called *The Tale of The Ugly Seed.*"

Obediently, Triana and Sahnassa, with Hylea in tow, tried to get close, but because they were returning from the facilities – thanks to Hylea – they ended up in the very back near the vents. Sahnassa ended up standing to one side of the vent, as the youngest sat upon the only seat left.

"Everyone settled?" the archivist asked, and the quiet group nodded politely until Hylea blurted, "Yes!" The tittering of the other children caused Triana to whisper harsh warnings into her sister's ear, and Sahnassa couldn't keep her blush furs down as every eye seemed to turn towards them.

"Sorry," she mouthed.

"Well, then!" the archivist replied, looking a little sternly in Sahnassa's direction. "Would you all please welcome Honored Dame Rahnahi de Dothnar!"

The group applauded politely as the somewhat stocky dame walked to the side of the archivist. Sahnassa noted how different she was from her own dame – so much friendlier looking, and she seemed genuinely pleased to be there. Her dame never looked happy to be anywhere. Dame Rahnahi's black and purple fur set off silver stripes that looked beautiful, elegant in their own way, like the dame had been painted as a piece of artwork. Kind purple eyes gazed out at them, and a wide smile graced her muzzle. "Well, now! What a good-looking group you are!" she exclaimed, her voice as friendly and kind as the rest of her appeared to be. "Would it be okay if I sat with you for a few moments and read you a story?" she asked.

In unison, the group answered in rehearsed monotone, "Yes, Honored Dame."

"Alright then," the dame replied, but Sahnassa caught in her expression that the response of the group of children didn't please the dame very much. "With all that enthusiasm, how could I say no?" she asked. Sitting on a stool upon the raised platform, Rahnahi de Dothnar opened her book, turned its beautifully illustrated pages towards the children, and began to read:

> There once was a seed, lonely and true; it fell all the way from the top of the moon. The plants of the garden looked down in disgust, at this poor wrinkled seed that was the color of rust. "You look very strange!" "Your markings aren't right!" "Your shape is all wrong!" "Oh my, you're a sight!"
>
> "But I'm from a moon," the seed tried to say, but all the big plants just looked away.
>
> From far up on high, the moon saw the plight, of her sad little seed, all alone in the night. A tear she then shed, and it fell to the ground and watered the seed and the soil all around. Then a small creature who also looked odd, took its small paws and covered with sod, that sad little seed amongst all those fine plants, fully assured of their own elegance.
>
> They paid no attention when its first sprout poked through, the top of the ground all covered in dew. And still they ignored as its branches stretched tall, until one fine night it was taller than all. They awoke and looked up in surprise the next sol, at gorgeous gold blossoms – a sight to behold. With awe, they confessed that the sad little seed was worthy and special and honored, indeed.
>
> So be kind when you see someone different or new, for that sad little seed, after all, could be you.

The group applauded politely, and with as much tolerance as she could manage, the dame replied, "Thank you."

From right beside Sahnassa, a small voice shouted, "That was great! Read it again!"

"Oh, Hylea!" Triana groaned quietly.

"Now, that's what I like to hear!" the dame replied, chuckling happily. "Thank you, dear kit! What's your name?"

Sahnassa tried to sit small as every eye around them turned in their direction once again. "Hylea de Orturu!" she replied proudly.

"Well, Hylea, I'm Dame Rahnahi de Dothnar. I'm so glad you came! Thank you!"

Nervous, the archivist wanted to end this before any other children chimed in. "Thank you very much, Honored Dame. Again, everyone please thank our special guest for reading to us!" The polite applause of the group of children was punctuated by Hylea's much louder cheers. "Alright everyone, you're dismissed back to your reading groups."

"Except dear Hylea!" Rahnahi interjected. "If I may?"

Anxiously, the archivist nodded and ushered away the other children. "I'll take her," Triana told Sahnassa as she started to lead an excited Hylea forward into the crowd. "You wait here and watch for Dad."

As much as Sahnassa would have liked to have met the Honored Dame, she realized her older sister was right; the last thing they needed was for her father walking up without any knowledge of the Honored Dame's presence. So, she leaned against the return vents, enjoying the feeling of the air being sucked past her fur. Next to her, however, two young Faelnar were having a conversation which she couldn't help but overhear.

"I don't like that story. It almost makes you wonder if she isn't talking about Anati. How dishonorable!"

"Ugh! I know what you mean – nasty, foul-smelling beasts. And I don't care how her story goes, an ugly Anati kit will grow up into an ugly, stupid Anati."

"Better than being two ignorant, stuck-up thin-tails," Sahnassa murmured, not quite under her breath.

"Excuse me!" one of the Faelnar looked at her, green eyes snapping.

"Oh, I'm sorry," Sahnassa replied, not quite apologetically. "I thought I heard you two calling an Honored Dame 'dishonorable.' She's talking to my sisters right now; would you like for me to pass your observation along?"

The second Faelnar suddenly had a terrified look on her face, but green eyes was walking right in front of her, threatening. "You wouldn't."

"I might, if you don't back off and get your bad breath out of my face, and ugh, how dare you talk about anyone else's scent – I mean, really!"

"Is there a problem here?" a deep baritone voice sounded from behind Sahnassa, and the two Faelnar kits backed away, surprised.

Looking up into her father's eyes, smiling, she replied, "No, Daddy. No problem at all. Did you see? Hylea is getting to meet with Honored Dame Rahnahi de Dothnar. She read us a story."

"My goodness! What an honor! Uh, do you know what they're talking about?" Gonastir asked with barely concealed anxiety.

"I'm not actually sure." It seemed that the Honored Dame was deep in discussion with Triana as she held a very happy Hylea on her lap.

"Let's go over, dear. I think it would be … prudent."

"Yes, father. I don't like the smell by the vent, anyway," Sahnassa replied, joining paws with her dad.

As they walked away, her father was curious. "That's a return vent, dear. How did you smell anything coming from it? I didn't smell anything."

"The smell wasn't coming out of the vent, actually," she said, turning and scowling at the two Faelnar as they retreated down the hall.

Vanarra was literally shaking with the emotions coursing through her. The honored dame's booming voice had easily carried into the vent, and the story had left her breathless and stunned. That an honored dame would even consider telling such a story nearly electrified every fur-strand on her body. She silently repeated the dame's name so she wouldn't forget it. Then, the conversation afterwards had caused her claws to express and her blush furs to rise. A part of her wanted to claw through the metal grates and show the two purebloods just how bad an Anati could be. Then, that other kit, the one whose scent was covered with a soft perfume of flowers, seemed to come to her defense – she seemed as repulsed as Vanarra had been at the ugly attitude of the two "thin-tailed" Faelnar.

Taking a great risk, Vannie wedged her claw-tips between the slats of the grate and tried to get a look at the dame or the kit who came back at the two Faelnar. Of the dame, she could see nothing, as an adult Nephti male and his daughter stood beside him. She gazed at this Nephti kit, sure she was the one who had talked back to the other two arrogant purebreds. All she could see was that the kit had dark purple fur and silver-white stripes with a tail that was ink-dipped, the last track or so a purple so dark it might as well have been black. "Thank you, kit," Vanarra told the stranger at a whisper before removing her claws.

To her surprise and dismay, the slats popped back into place making an audible noise. Terrified, Vanarra didn't know what to do for a moment. Carefully and silently, she started slipping back into the ductwork just in case someone wanted to investigate that sound. To her great relief, as she pulled her head around the corner, no one had seemed to notice.

With her vibrating alarm, Vanarra had been awakened at her normal excursion time, just after high night. It took her longer than normal to wake up thanks to her activities during the previous sol, but as she emerged into the dark of the children's section, Vanarra had a very definite target – she wanted to find the book the dame had read. She guessed she could spend about an interval looking for it before she needed to get started on her normal chores of food-gathering, laundry, and waste disposal. Chanting the name to herself quietly, she was soon able to use her partially shielded UltraBright to find where the book should have been. In disappointment, she sighed, "It's not here. It got checked out."

Looking just above on the shelf, she saw a number of flyers that had been left. Taking one and sitting down in the comfortable seats – a luxury she rarely afforded herself – she looked at the page carefully. There, printed on it, was an image of the book. Again, she was disappointed, because the artwork of the book looked beautiful, perhaps the most beautiful she had ever seen. There was one nice feature of the flyer, the image of the author. "She looks kind of nice," Vanarra considered. After reading over the accolades, and turning it over, she saw something that made her stand up. "Additional titles by this author include the following…" Instantly, Vannie was back, looking through the stacks for any other book written by the dame. She found two more in the children's section and slipped them into the vent to go back to her lair in the morning. Four more, however, including one that was highly acclaimed, were located in the adult section of the archive.

She blinked and tried to remember where that was. "Philosophy?" It was a section she had never been to before. "It's not on the lower level." Carefully, she stepped out of the children's section and started to stalk towards the information desk, far in the front, near the entrance to the archive. Looking at the weather, she groaned inwardly. It was a perfectly clear night, no rain to obscure her movements should someone just happen by. Still, she was so intensely curious about this dame and her writing that it pulled her forward, almost irrationally. Approaching the front of the library with its great glass windows, she was nearly shaking in fear as – step by careful step – she crept forward.

When she was just starting to emerge from the cover of the stacks, her paw-shoe crinkled paper left on the floor, making a sound which seemed to echo throughout the entire archive. "Damn!" she thought and fell forward on her forepaws. Unable to tell if the sounds she heard around her were echoes of her noise or the sound of someone starting to search for her, she lay still. Waiting for a moment, she tried to back up, but found that her rear left hind-paw had the piece of paper stuck to it, and it wouldn't come loose. As silently as she could, she rolled onto her back and extended her claw-tips to remove it.

Finding in the soft light radiating from the entrance that she actually had stumbled across a library brochure, she smiled. Staying hidden where she was for a few moments more, just to make sure no one else was around, her sensitive eyes perused the map on the page she held and easily found the section she wanted. After waiting a few moments more, Vannie rolled back onto her hind paws and quietly slipped away back into the rows of books, headed for the staircase hidden amidst the stacks.

For the first time she could ever remember, Vanarra climbed to the highest balcony three levels above the children's section. She had never been up so high, and while the staircase was well concealed by the shelves of books on the lowest level, that protection became less and less the higher she went. Here, at the apex, she felt nearly naked, terrified, and thrilled being so high above the entire archive. "Oh …

my … gosh…" she breathed, smiling hugely, nearly panting. A part of her marveled at how she could have lived here more than one season and never availed herself of this magnificent sight. "Mom! I … I wish you could see this … maybe you did, but I … I never…"

Again, despite the joy she felt, a wave of sad loneliness washed over her. To see such a wonderful sight and to have no one to share it with seemed such a shame and such a waste. "If only I … had someone." For the first time, she started to consider what it would mean to bring another Anati to the archive. The secret that had kept her safe could get out, and someone stronger than her could kick her out of her own lair or cause her to be discovered. Vannie thought about the other Anati children she had seen on her various trips outside of the archive – many of them in worse condition than she, living in the open, living on scraps from garbage bins. "You can't trust them, Vannie," she told herself and sighed. "You just can't."

Turning away from the railing, she made her way back into the stacks and started trying to locate the books by the honored dame. The books were actually easy to find, to her surprise, and several of them had multiple copies. One volume, *Light, Warmth, and Hope*, had been loudly proclaimed on the flyer, so she took a copy of that. Some of the other titles looked interesting, but holding the first book in her paws, she felt it was pretty substantial. "This … this will do for now," she whispered.

Sometime later, as she brought her wet laundry back downstairs in a bucket, she startled. More lights were on than normal, and she realized that someone had come in early. Looking at her watch, she realized that she had also been running late, thanks to her expeditions and research earlier. Normally, she could afford for the bucket to jostle a bit on the stairs, but now she realized she had to be both quick and deathly quiet. She heard voices talking – several, not just two, and her heart started beating hard inside of her chest. It beat so loud that she swore the sound it made was going to give her away. "Down the stairs in the center of the stacks," she thought. "That's the safest way."

She was about to put her hind paw on the lowest level when a voice that was far too close to her said, "Look, would you simply tell me where the controls for the lights are? I'm not a fan of guessing games."

The male voice froze her in her tracks as she tried to ascertain where it had come from, and listening to the paw-steps only a few tracks away, she realized he was leaving the stacks headed back up towards the front.

Someone called out to the male as Vanarra slipped quietly to the ground and started to quickly step towards the back entrance of the children's section. "Where? I can't hear you!" the male called back, and as Vanarra got close to the corner where she could see the vents, she heard someone answer, but couldn't tell what was said. "Oh, the children's section, by the vents? Okay!"

Vanarra was nearly there, but now she was terrified. Setting down the bucket too quickly it tipped over, and her wet underthings landed on the smooth carpet. Righting it and realizing that she had just given away her presence, she struggled to slip her claw-tips where they needed to be and get herself and the bucket safely inside before the library employee made it to the children's section. Finding the panels, he started switching on the lights.

"Oh, so you finally found them?" a sly male voice asked, coming up.

Vannie was frozen in fear mere tracks from them, trying as hard as she could not to breathe.

"Yeah, alright, alright. Pick on the new guy. Hey, what's this?"

"I don't know. How'd the carpet get wet?" By the shadows falling across the slats, Vanarra could tell one of them was bending down.

"They're going to find me! They're going to find me!" she screamed in her head, wanting with all that was within her to flee but still too afraid to even move a single strand of her fur.

There was a sniffing sound. "Smells like the soap from the bathrooms."

"One of those damned Anati cleaners, I'll bet. Must have dropped the thing here and been too damn lazy to clean it up. I'll report it. Maybe they can fire them and find another one."

"It's not that bad, Sharris. It's barely even damp." At that moment, mercifully, the air handlers turned on and all of her scent and that of the bucket she carried was pulled away from the opening of the vents. "Just let it be."

"Oh, come on. Why not?"

"You don't play with someone for sport like that, no matter what you think of them."

"It, you mean," the other said.

"Whatever. Just get this section organized and presentable. The Honored Dame is coming by again at mid sol to read to a couple of school groups that are being brought in."

"Ah, you going to help?"

"No."

"Why?"

"Because you're the new guy!" the second one said, chuckling, and then walked away.

As the muttering, angry male stomped off, Vanarra reached for the bucket and slowly, carefully, made her way back to her lair, grateful that this time, she had avoided discovery, and she was thoroughly determined to never get caught like that again. However, as she slipped into her lair, she made another decision – at mid sol, she would be back, listening to the dame read her story once again.

Chapter 4: Insecurity

Vanarra read aloud in her lair, "Isolation is the creator of madness, and a life without trust is empty." The words of the dame struck her to her soul, and she put down the book slowly. "I've been … in here for … nearly three seasons." She had read all the way through *Light, Warmth, and Hope* several times. That book simply didn't get returned anymore. In Vanarra's mind, it was hers. She had even started making notes in it. Now, she was reading *Finding the Way*, and its tone frequently touched her heart – sometimes in warm and caring ways, sometimes in very painful ones. This one made her ache inside. "Fifteen seasons," she said to herself. "I'm fifteen seasons old this sol, and I don't know … anyone."

Strictly speaking, that wasn't entirely true. The archive's books and stories had been her companions for that time. They had taught her math and reading and writing all the way to the tertiary school level. Every sol, she had school, just like her mother had taught her. She graded her own tests against the answers in the back, working ever so hard on the one dream she had – to walk out of the archive ready and able to begin a life that was independent, on her own terms. Other interests had started to intrude on that dream, somewhat.

The weird aching and strange emotions of heat were difficult for her to process until she found books explaining male and female relationships. In many ways, that was her entertainment. Romantic novels, including those by her favorite author, were the prize she held back from herself until all of her other work was done. While it would have been easy to simply give herself over to her teen desires, the dire necessities of life – the careful scrounging, the need to hold to an exact schedule, the discipline to remain quiet and clean as to be undetectable by the maintenance staff which seemed to be in the ductwork twice every moon – were all potent reminders that she couldn't simply give in and satisfy her new-found passions to the exclusion of all else. If she did, Vanarra knew she wouldn't eat or worse, she would get thrown out.

Trying to shove a little balance back into her life – a strong suggestion from her dearest friend Rahnahi, the author-dame – she had just finished taking a sample academy entrance exam. After scoring it and smiling to herself for having done reasonably well, Van slid into bed with her newest Rahnahi acquisition. However, unlike the wonderfully supportive things that had helped soothe the horrible emotional wounds she had endured, tonight the Nephti dame seemed to be almost scolding her. She had found this place of safety, and it had sustained her and kept her alive. However, Vanarra had mentally written off every other Anati; she was completely unwilling to offer any of the desperate souls she saw roaming the outside world any sort of shelter or help. *Finding the Way* had convicted her in a manner she was finding difficult to dismiss.

"Alright, Rahnahi. It may cost me everything, but … I'll … try."

She awoke with enough time before high night to start gathering her things together for a little self-cleaning and fast scrounging before starting her trek to the garage venting system. With only an interval until the first staff started to arrive, Vanarra, dressed with a small pack and a decent stash of "donated" funds in her possession, worked her way into the equipment room and into the garage ductwork. As she reached the top of the vertical assent, however, she was faced with an unhappy discovery. The fans which had been there since her arrival had been replaced, and the new casings created a full seal between the two larger fans. As she leaned to one side and shone her light through the grating surrounding the fans to the door, she saw another problem. New, heavy locks had been placed on the door. These were locks that Vanarra knew she couldn't bypass or trip. "Oh, great," she groaned.

Starting to feel her muscles tire of holding her weight, Vanarra retreated back down the shaft. Leaving tonight was out of the question, and she knew it. Quickly and quietly, she made her way back to her lair, fuming, angrily wondering what had happened to cause the archive to install the new fans, and why those new locks had been necessary. She had always been careful not to be seen or leave any trace, but there had been a few times, now that she thought about it, that Vanarra had found evidence of someone else seeking shelter by the fans. That had to have been a horrible place to try and stay, but the rain this season had been very bad, and she supposed she could understand how someone desperate enough might have tried to lay just behind the door and hope for the best.

Slipping into the stacks for a moment, she retrieved a book on the garbage hovers' design before heading back to her lair. Frustrated, she pulled out her archive diagrams and started looking at them, planning out her new means of entering and exiting the archive. Exiting wasn't a real problem. All she had to do was sneak out one of the side exits soon after the archive was closed to the public. Watching the janitorial staff, she knew that they commonly propped open a side door so they could do garbage clean-up along the building mound. So long as she didn't try to carry any archive material through the doorway, the theft detectors wouldn't go off.

Getting back into the archive was the problem and a very risky proposition. Truly, she only had to get herself into the garage and then into the garbage conveyor access-way, which was commonly left unlocked. Granted, it wouldn't be the cleanest way to make an entrance, but at least it would serve reasonably well. So long as she could make it across the hallway to the equipment room, she could wait until night granted her the freedom of movement she needed to get back to the vents in the children's section. Making it into the garage, however, relied on two possible solutions: secreting herself aboard a delivery hover bound for the archive (which was very difficult) or jumping aboard the extended thruster spar of a garbage hover. Being that these vehicles were so top-heavy, they tended to need additional support as they travelled about, so the thruster spars extended a good ways out during normal travel. When the hover started to work its way into an area where trash bins were, the spars were almost always retracted as the vehicle was about to land. Having watched the hovers come and go numerous times, carefully studying them through her distance viewers, she knew exactly the moment to approach them and hop aboard, and exactly the right moment to hop off. The only problem is that she had never actually tried it.

A part of her wanted to just give up and not worry about leaving the archive anymore, but she knew she couldn't actually do that. A number of storms had enabled her, on several recent occasions, to raid the archive donations and gather enough money for a few pieces of clothing – clothing she desperately needed. The copy of

Finding the Way also stared back at her accusingly. It reminded her that, while this wasn't going to be easy, Rahnahi believed that she had to find someone, had to trust someone or else Vanarra's existence didn't matter. If she didn't build some relationships, then she wasn't whole, and her sanity was at risk. "Okay, Rahnahi, I will. I will … tomorrow night." The garbage hovers came every other sol, so at least that way, they could bring her back the very next evening.

Resigned to her course of action, Vanarra kicked off her paw-shoes and sat down on the bed. Right at her bedside was a small box – a box that contained her most special possession in the entire world, her most prized. After being rape-mated, she hadn't returned to the tree-fort for nearly a full season. It was quite some distance away from the archive, but having public transport fare had enabled her to visit it one last time and retrieve the lone item she had held onto ever since she fled from the de Gonari estate – the paw-woven sweater blouse her mother had made for her. She had hidden it in a plastiform bucket with a lid and tucked it into the hollow of a rotted tree. When she returned, stunner ready in her paw, she had retrieved the item and immediately returned to the archive. Whenever she was worried or felt especially lonely and sad, she would do what she was doing tonight, opening the box and pulling out that item, laying it reverently on the table, and staring at it, letting her paws gently touch it.

"I remember you, Mom. I love you, Mom," she breathed softly, "but, I have to come out of hiding, sometime. I'll … do my best to stay safe, and always, always, I'll remember you, but I have to do this. I can't be alone anymore." Without truly understanding how, she seemed to sense that her mother would agree, and with that small bit of imaginary assurance, she placed the item back in its container, and slipped beneath the covers.

It was evening, and an odd, smoky smell made Holana's nose twitch as she walked through the hallway upstairs by her daughters' bedrooms. Instantly, the proud delivery of Triana's commendation letter became her secondary concern, and she started urgently sniffing around trying to find where the smell was coming from. "Ow!" Sahnassa's voice came from beneath her door, and Holana – with no preamble – flung that door open. The room was actually warmer than the rest of the house, due to the open window, and the pungent smell of smoke was even more in evidence here. Sahnassa looked up at her in surprise, one paw holding the other as if in pain.

"Sahnassa de Orturu!" Holana shouted. "What in the two moons are you doing?"

"Uh, soldering an expansion socket onto a main board," her daughter explained, apologetically. Indeed, as Holana glanced around the room, her training computer was disassembled, and a smoking soldering gun was sitting on the top of her desk along with several other computer parts. As she walked forward, Holana's nose wrinkled all the more.

"Really? Smells more like you're singeing the fur off your hide; let me see," Holana demanded. A little unwillingly, her daughter offered her paw finger, and it was easy to see the painfully swollen line of skin beneath a clear channel of missing fur. "Oh, just fantastic, Sahnassa! The very night before you're to have your orlure recital! How are you going to perform now?! Answer me that!"

Sahnassa was clearly surprised by that reminder, and realized that she had indeed given herself an injury that would make the following sol's recital difficult, if not impossible. "I … I don't know, Mom; I'm sorry! I … I just wanted to be able to add more memory to it so I could run some of the more advanced training programs."

"Well, turn that thing off right now before it burns us out of our lair!" her mother demanded sternly. As Sahnassa complied, Holana continued her disparagements. "And look! Your closet door is wide open! Everything in there will probably smell like singed fur for a moon, not to mention your bed coverings and carpet! You didn't exactly think about that, did you? Oh, and just wonderful, just wonderful! Look at your desk! What are these … globs of –"

"Solder," Sahnassa meekly supplied.

"Yes! They've burned right through the finish of your desk! Wait until your father hears! What were you thinking, child?!"

"I'm sorry, Mother," Sahnassa apologized humbly, her head falling to her chest, and her blush furs rising in shame as she again cradled her hurt paw.

As angry and frustrated as she was, Holana could see that her kit's paw was indeed hurting. "Just wait here," she demanded, "and don't do anything else!" With that, she quit the room and headed for the hallway where the emergency aid supplies were.

"What's going on?" Triana asked, sticking her head out of her room.

"Sahnassa's … oh, just never mind it; it's the usual. Here is your commendation letter, signed by our new dame, Rothnerra. I wanted to bring it to you as soon as I received it. Let me try to take care of your sister, again, and then I'll be in to see you about it. Your father will be so proud. You always make us proud!"

"Wow! This is cool! Signed by our dame! Thanks, Mom!" Triana bubbled and took the piece of paper carefully into her room.

Smiling at her eldest daughter's reaction, Holana reluctantly pulled herself away and started retrieving what was needed to tend to Sahnassa's minor injury. Returning to her daughter's room almost broke Holana's heart. Her daughter had laid her head upon her desk and was sobbing, hard, her tail tucked beneath her chair. The edge off her anger at such a sight, Holana sat by the long alcove seat at the window and bade her child to come over. In absolute defeat, Sahnassa slowly exited the chair and sat down beside her mother, crying silently.

"Give me your paw," Holana said softly. Sahnassa complied, and her mother started to look at the injury more deliberately. "I'm going to have to shave you a little." Her daughter didn't react, and carefully, Holana used the mini-clippers to remove enough fur so there was room to treat the burn with ointment. She also made sure to catch the singed clippings on the top of a book she laid on her lap. In a few moments, Holana had the injury treated and covered with a protective bandage.

"Thank you," Sahnassa whimpered as her paw was released.

Holana took the book and carefully tipped it towards the trash bin, brushing away the fur. Putting the book down, she looked at her middle daughter, still sullen and depressed. Without any reservations, she loved Sahnassa, but in many ways, Holana just couldn't understand what drove her kit to do such strange things. From the time the child had shaved off all of her fur as an "experiment," her mother had realized that the compulsions that drove Sahnassa were ones she would never understand. Even in her own youth, Holana had never heard of such a thing, and now this kit – not even out of primary and sitting in her room soldering computer boards – was completely out of her realm of experience. The matron of their family seemed uncommonly attached to Sahnassa, perhaps trying to help her make up for her deficiencies, but now Holana wondered if that influence had been completely helpful.

Holana's statement to her daughter, while truthful and a bit more candid than perhaps it should have been, was the first confession she had ever made to the kit. "Sahnassa, I don't understand you.

Really, I don't. I want to, and ... I want to help you. I love you, but
... I don't know why you do these things. You take no interest in
family projects or honors; your first visit to the hall of honor was a
disaster – you were bored the whole time. The matron leading the tour
thought you were sick. Are any of your other friends spending their
nights soldering computer parts together, or are they calling one
another and playing, talking about cute cubs, anything? Sahnassa, do
you even have any friends at school? I never hear you talk about any."

Sahnassa's body slid off the seat and onto the floor, and she sat
with her knees pulled up to her chest, tail wrapped around her body,
her head down, and facing away from her mother. "I hate to see you
like this, kit. I don't take pleasure in it, whatsoever. Perhaps you need
to think about the things you want and the way you are – the choices
you are making, kit. Honors can come to you, but you have to work
for them. Friends can be yours too, but you won't find them if you're
always up in your room playing computers. I'll ... I'll talk to your
father, and see if he can help you finish what you've started, and then
... we can make a decision about the recital. Okay?"

"Okay," Sahnassa whispered, and added, "sorry."

"I'll ... I'll be back in to check on you later," Holana replied
standing, and quietly, she left the room and closed the door.

Later that evening, after Triana had listened to their father
come home and give Sahnassa another stern lecture about
responsibility and priorities, the eldest sister stepped from her room
and quietly tapped on Sahnassa's door before entering. She truly
ached inside at what she saw. Sahnassa was seated on the sill of the
window, her legs draped off, and her tail flat on the alcove seat.
Thanks, in part, to the sloping nature of their lair's exterior, her
younger sister was in no danger of falling, but Triana sensed another
danger, as if she could read her sister's thoughts. "Don't ever think
about leaving us, Sahnassa, please," she whispered.

"Why should I stay? I'm as good as disavowed; they don't
love me, and ... I'm nothing but a disappointment to them. Maybe it
would be better if I asked Matron Shalarra to take me, put me in the
family orphanage. She, at least, isn't always upset by what I do."

"But then you wouldn't live here, with us, and ... I'd miss
you," Triana contested gently as she walked up and sat beside her
sister. "I love you, sis. You've helped me so much, even on math. I
... I actually got a commendation from our dame for it. I couldn't
have done that without you." Sahnassa leaned into her sister a little,

and Triana put her paw around Sahnassa's shoulders. "So, I heard what happened. I'm going to talk to Mom and Dad, and ask them to give you a place in the garage to work. They need to give you some safety gloves, and a couple of other things, too."

"How would you know about that?" Sahnassa asked, looking up at her sister, curious.

"Simple, my friend Tralla's father has a Vulpi who does repairs on their executive conferencing systems. He actually told us all about the safety equipment he has to use. You're trying to do the same thing he does without the right equipment. Where did you even find a soldering gun?"

"It was in the bottom of a box in the garage. I think I saw one of the kitchen staff using it once. That's how I knew where it was. Would you really talk to Mom and Dad about this?"

"I would," Triana asserted.

"Thank you. You're … a great sister. I was feeling pretty … alone."

"You're not alone," Triana added, hugging Sahnassa. "And you're not going to be alone tonight. Come on. It's kind of smoky in here. Let's go see if Hylea would be willing to sleep with us."

Snuggling into her sister's neck, Sahnassa agreed. "Yes. Thank you, Triana."

Vanarra swallowed, listening carefully for just the right time to pop open the vents and slip out. Doing so before high night felt so strange, so dangerous. Thankfully, the returns were not visible from a long distance away, so there was a pretty good chance that if she couldn't hear anyone, it was safe. Preparing for this moment, she had actually lubricated the latches and hinges with oil-gel the night before, making it relatively easy for her to slip the vents open with little to no noise of her exit. She had even practiced this maneuver many times before finally going to sleep.

After taking a deep breath, she opened the latches and pushed the right side of the vent open far enough for her to slip a mirror out. Using the mirror to scan around, she saw no one, and then she checked her go-to hiding place in a corner nook. With the strength and finesse created from moons and moons of complex physical exercises (another

Rahnahi suggestion), Vannie was out the vent and into her spot with the speed that an ill-timed eye-blink could have missed.

Ready to move along the route she had mapped out and trained on the night before, Vanarra took a deep breath. Just as she was about to move, a nearby noise made her freeze. It was a grunt, but a grunt like someone young waking up and rolling over. Peering over the low bookcase, she saw a Faelnar cub, sleeping with a book in his paws. Sighing in relief, she started quickly dashing from one place of concealment to the next along her route.

"Vannie! Vannie? Are you there?" a very worried female voice called through the archive. Vanarra startled – someone calling her name, and it sounded a lot like her own mother! Pulled forward by this voice, she quickly crept to find where it was coming from. Looking over the last set of shelves, she saw the mother, a Faelnar like her own mom, but she sighed. Standing beside one of the Lupar security guards was indeed a Faelnar, but the coloring of her fur was different, and dark glasses also betrayed that she was unable to see. This Faelnar was clearly not her mother, so she shrank down, and started to dash away towards her exit.

The more steps she took, however, the worse she felt. The mother was clearly panic-stricken, and Vanarra knew the fear her own mother had when she had disappeared from sight, even for a moment. Groaning softly, Vanarra turned around and dashed back towards the children's section. Creeping right next to the sleeping cub, she gently shook him. "Hey, are you Vannie, cub? What's your name?"

The cub stirred, and Vanarra slipped back from him and turned her eyes away, holding her tail in front of her. "Wha?" the cub asked.

"I asked you if your name was … Vannie?"

"My name isn't Vannie," the cub replied, now waking and sounding embarrassed. "It's Vannashar!"

"Well, Vannashar, your mother is terrified she's lost you. She's in the front of the archive calling for you; can't you hear?"

"I don't hear real good," the cub confessed, standing up. "I … I don't see real good either. Where are you?"

Curious, she turned to look at the cub. He was staring blankly in her direction, but it was clear he couldn't really see her. Walking closer, she asked, "You can't see what I look like?"

"Not … really. Can … can you please take me to my mommy?" he asked.

"I can't, but I can take you most of the way. Take my paw and go very quietly, okay?"

"Alright," the cub answered, and fully trusting, put his paw in hers. Gently, she led him forward, past the air handlers. After a few more steps, he said, "Uh, oh. I think I can hear her now."

"She's scared she's lost you, cub. Keep coming. Now, I need a favor, okay? You can't tell anyone I was here and helped you. It has to be our secret."

"Okay," the cub agreed. A few steps later, they were at the edge of the stacks.

"Now, count to ten slowly and then call out for your mommy as loud as you can. That will give me time to get away."

"Thank you," the cub replied, but then pulled her down to his level. Now, it was as if he could fully see her, and his eyes widened but not in shock. "You know what?"

"What?"

"You're the prettiest Faelnar I've ever seen," he replied, honestly.

The comment warmed her heart in a way she had never felt before. "Thanks, and you're the bravest. Don't ever let anyone tell you you're second best, okay?"

"Alright."

"Good, now start counting," she replied, nuzzling him, and then sped away.

"... nine ... ten. Mommy! Here I am! Here I am!" he called, and one of the archive security guards immediately exited the stacks and walked towards him.

"Here he is! We found him!" the guard called. At that moment, the Lupar saw a shadow move out of the corner of his eye and heard a door close. Looking over, he didn't see any alarms going off or anyone who wasn't supposed to be there. Taking the cub's paw and starting to walk him back, he simply dismissed it and reunited the cub with his mother.

For Vanarra, walking away from the archive this time was difficult, especially since she knew getting back in could be very risky, but a few factors were starting to convince her leaving was worth the trouble. First, the evening sky was marvelously beautiful, and a light, comfortable breeze sailed around her. Second, Vanarra knew she had a purpose, and this time, it was more than just clothing or medicine, although those things were certainly on her list. She was looking for ... someone. She thought it might just be someone like that cub who needed her help – just a little bit. It may be someone who needed to share the marvelous gift she had managed to find – someone to share her lair with her.

"It wouldn't be bad to have some help," she thought. There had been a few times in the last three seasons when she had been fairly sick, and there was no one to take care of her. Regardless of how bad she felt, the bucket had to be dumped and cleaned, the food had to be gathered, and her own hygiene had to be attended to. From Rahnahi's writings, Vannie was also coming to realize that it would build her up inside to actually care for someone – try to help them. "But it has to be the right Thurian; I can't take a kid or someone elderly. I have to find someone who can live like I have, without being caught."

As she entered the tree-line of the forest surrounding the archive, Vanarra moved far enough in so it would be difficult for anyone to see her from the archive's windows, and if she kept a good pace, she could catch one of the public transports into the city. From there, it would be a long night. She wouldn't dare fall asleep, but would find a decent place to hide while she awaited morning, and the opening of the stores she needed.

She was pleased as the wind blew through the trees above her; it covered the sounds of her movements as she worked her way forward. However, it also started to bring something interesting to her nose – wood smoke. It was not a smell she was used to, so it made her instantly wary. As she approached the area where the forest broadened, the air grew still, and the smell intensified. Slipping a paw down to her belt, the stunner was unsheathed and held at the ready. Clearly, someone was camped ahead, and her experience at the tree fort was one she was adamant would not be repeated.

As she worked her way into a place where the trees thinned out near a stream, she could finally see the cause of the smell. A Thurian, an Anati by what she could tell from the firelight, was tending a small fire by the stream, a rickety lean-to his only shelter. She watched him for a long time as night truly started to fall. He seemed to be fairly young, like she, and it was clear that he had food in a bag he was eating from occasionally. It was a little difficult to gauge his true colors in the firelight, but if she had to guess, she would have called his main color brown, with silver or white stripes. She also noticed how nervous he seemed, terrified even. For at any crack of a branch or sound, he startled, picked up a big stick he placed beside his campsite, and stood, looking around. While he was doing this, Vanarra turned her head away, preventing any reflection from her eyes to find his. He also seemed to be getting sleepy, and this appeared to terrify him all the more. When he woke up, he startled awake, perhaps at a sound or even at nothing at all.

"You're certainly not in your element out here," she thought to herself, looking around to double check how well she was hidden. "I guess I should be moving on." Vanarra was about to leave, but a quick check of her watch made her blink and check the time again. "I've been sitting here watching him for what ... two intervals?! No!" She could scarcely believe what her timepiece displayed. She leaned back against a tree in surprise, accidently braking off a dry branch.

Instantly, the terrified male was startled awake and looked around in all directions, unsure where the sound had come from. "I ... I heard you! I know you're there! Come out ... show ... show yourself! I'm not afraid of you!" the male called out in warning.

Rahnahi's words played into her mind, "Have pity upon those whose lives are unschooled and terrified, and care for them as you would for the sick, for ignorance and fear are as crippling as any disease." She had watched him long enough to trust that he was alone, and that his appearance in the forest wasn't intended as a trap. So, nervously, with her paw on the stunner, she unwound from her crouch and stood up.

She stood for almost a full pass before he saw her, which surprised her. "Who ... who ... are you?" he demanded, his voice quavering.

"Just another Anati, like you," she answered, slowly stepping closer, "and no one to be afraid of." Still nervously holding his stick as protection, his eyes followed Vanarra's every movement as she approached. With some amount of amusement, she watched as his expression turned from terror, to curiosity, to outright fascination as she drew to within a few tracks of him. "Hello," she offered. "My name's Vanarra Anasto."

"I'm ... Ashalam, Ash is the short version," he replied, still obviously afraid of her.

"Hmm ... Ash," Vanarra mused, as she drifted closer. "I like the short version. I ... I used to go by Vannie, until ... well. But I heard a little cub called that earlier so I don't know if I'm really okay with it anymore. So, what are you a mix of?"

"Some Perratti and Lupar, I think. I ... I didn't really know my parents."

"Oh," Vanarra replied, realizing that as difficult as her life had been, there were others who hadn't even been blessed with eight seasons of either parent taking care of them. "How did you survive?"

Finally, he started to lower his stick as she stared at him steadily. "Orphanage, until ... until this morning. They threw me out."

"Really? What for?" Vanarra asked, looking into the forest beyond.

"Stealing food," he replied with a nervous smile. "Not really much of a choice, actually. They never feed us enough, and some have even starved to death."

"So that's what you're doing here?" she asked. "This is your first night with no lair, isn't it?"

"Yeah, but ... but I can manage," he replied with insubstantial confidence. "No one knows I'm out here, and I have ... well, I have a few things, and it should be safe enough?"

Vanarra's shoulders sagged a little at his ignorance. "Thurians have noses, you know? I could smell your fire a hundred courses away. There are some very bad ... ones out here sometimes. Best find a place where you've got a good solid door to protect you, and you don't need a fire for heat."

"Oh, then ... then what are you doing here?" he asked, a little challenge in his voice.

"Passing through to the hover stop. I've got to hurry if I'm going to make the last one headed for the Brook Office Park. That's where I'm bunking tonight. Ash, you're welcome to stay out here if you want, but if it were me, I wouldn't," she said softly, something in the air telling her that they were beginning to draw attention.

"Can ... can I come with you?" he pleaded. "I ... I'm not sure about anything. I've never been out like this."

"Sure," she whispered, as she started scooping loose dirt onto his campfire, snuffing it out. "Grab your things and stay quiet. I heard something."

All Ash grabbed for was his bag, and then he stood ready. An audible crunch and groan in the forest behind them made Vanarra reach out for his paw and lead him away down towards the stream. Carefully, the two of them followed a path, barely visible in the moonlight. In just a few passes, they were emerging onto a paved walkway along a lighted hover trail. "We need to be careful and hide who and what we are until the hover stops. Once the door is open, I'll pay our way, and the driver should let us ride in the back."

"Okay, Van," Ash replied absently, sounding a little drowsy.

"Van?" she asked as she led him forward. Chuckling, she replied, "Well, it can't get much shorter than that, I suppose. I mean, what's left? Va? Vee?"

"I guess not," he chuckled, as well. "I'm sorry. I hope you don't mind; I'm just really tired. They kept me up all night yelling at me, trying to get me to tell them where I find food."

"Oh?" Vanarra asked as she took her seat on the empty bench by the hover stop. "Did you tell them?"

"No. It's why they threw me out. It's not like they didn't keep all the food I found, either," he huffed quietly as he sat beside her. Vanarra's attention was fixed on a couple of large Lupar making their way down the path on the other side of the hover trail, and Ash asked her, "Trouble?"

"Not if we don't attract attention. Lean against me and rest, Ash. Best if we're quiet right now."

"I … I can barely keep my eyes open," he admitted softly. "How are you staying awake?"

"Now is normally when I am awake. Hush now, Ash, and sleep. Van is watching out for you," she assured him, and to her surprise, he was already breathing slowly, his eyes fully closed.

Vanarra was getting quite used to the feeling of Ash's body against her, and it reminded her of when her mother used to snuggle against her in bed. It also made her keenly aware of how long it had been since anyone else was physically this close to her. She wondered if she shouldn't feel uncomfortable, but still, she simply didn't.

"Van," she thought to herself. "That's not bad. Sounds a bit more grown up than Vannie, I suppose." Carefully, she put her right arm around Ash and gently held him, tears starting to well in her eyes. "Oh, mange, Rahnahi was right! I've … I've not really been living." She didn't know if she could trust Ashalam or if she would after she got to know him, but more poignant than it had ever been was the need for her to have someone to care for, who would also care for her.

"Ash, wake up," Vanarra whispered in his ear as she shook him gently. "The transport is here." Ash startled and backed away from Vanarra quickly, not realizing where he was. "Calm down; I'm not going to hurt you. Remember me? Van?"

"Oh, uh, right, well," he replied, voice shaking.

"Great, now shut up and keep your head down, and follow me," Van ordered and then stood just outside the focus of the lamp above their heads, it's odd color masking her unusual Vulpi-like coloration. Keeping her tail almost between her legs meant that, for the most part, the driver couldn't see it. The transport slowed, the door opened, and it pulled to a stop. With money in her paw, Vanarra walked up the steps of the transport and paid for their fare before looking at the driver – a Pantera who looked back at them with disgust and pointed his big, chunky paw-finger towards the back of the vehicle.

Vanarra coquettishly dipped and very nearly bowed to the driver before sauntering back past the few purebloods and casually taking a seat in the rear. Ash followed, a short distance behind, but as she turned and looked up at him, she saw a very nervous, but very earnest, appreciation of her in his eyes. "Half-breeds," a Faelnar grunted in disgust as Ash stepped past.

"Ugh, the smell," another from across the row complained.

"Sorry," Ash apologized, turning back, but the two just ignored that he had said anything. As he sat down next to Vanarra, he complained at a whisper, "You would think they'd at least acknowledge I apologized."

"You expect too much from them, obviously," Van replied coolly as she leveled her gaze at the haughty Faelnar. "Sometimes, I wonder if it's really 'purebred' or 'in-bred' that's a better description." Ash looked at her in shock for such a statement. "They consider themselves so much more perfect than us," she added. "If they didn't slight us and keep us down, there would be nothing to stop us from doing as much or more than they. Now, it's a long ride, Ash; just close your eyes and relax. I'll keep watch over you."

Ashalam looked at the two Faelnar who were now glaring at them both. It was clear that while the two hadn't been able to hear what Vanarra had said, some of the tone of what was said had made it to their ears. One even looked like he was going to stand up and approach them, but Vanarra opened her jacket, and the Faelnar's eyes went wide before he sat down very carefully. "You heard me, Ash. Get some rest."

"Oh … okay," he replied nervously, and then tried to relax, but he wasn't able to close his eyes until the two Faelnar got off at the very next stop.

Almost an interval later, Van's voice sounded in his ear, and this time, he didn't react with as much terror. "Wake up, Ash,"

"Uh, thanks," he offered, rubbing his muzzle. "Are we there yet?"

"Next stop. We're going to leave out the back door. No use getting any closer to the purebred than we have to. After that, just follow me, and don't say anything."

"Okay." Ash had to do what he agreed to immediately, because the transport stopped, and Vanarra was getting up, moving fast towards the rear exit which had just opened. Once that was done, he followed her as she walked alongside the hover trail. They continued for some time, one behind the other, not speaking.

After a moment, Vanarra coughed – the only warning that she gave him of a change in direction. She was diverting down a walking trail which was supposed to be closed at dusk, according to the sign posted alongside. As it was only a few passes to high night, he followed her rapid steps getting out of sight of the main road as quickly as possible. "Very good," she told him quietly.

"Thanks, but … where are we?"

"Like I said earlier, the Brook Office Park. A number of small and medium companies rent or buy-out space here. The buildings here have a few nooks I can slide us into, and we can wait there until morning – get some rest. Come along. There's a nice one ahead, if we can get into it."

As they approached the building's side entrance, Vanarra started walking up the building mound, leaving the path. Surprised, Ash followed her as her change of direction took her basically straight up the four level structure. Walking around to the left, away from the front entrance, they were soon at the top, behind the crest of the hill where a small utility building sat amongst several air-handlers.

Nervous and tired, Ash watched with amazement as Vanarra took out a small set of tools and started working on the lock to the utility building's door. "How … how do you know about all of this?"

"I read," she answered. "Quite a bit, actually."

"How did you keep those two Faelnar from jumping us on that transport?"

"One thing at a time, Ash.   One thing at a time.   Let's get inside, and then, we'll chat.   There, got it!"   Carefully, she opened the door, shining her UltraBright inside.   When she was satisfied, she stepped in, pulling him along by his paw.

With the door closed behind them, Vanarra reached to the side and pulled out a pole to wedge between the floor and the door pull, effectively barricading the door.   "What's that for?" he asked quietly.

"Don't want anyone else coming in this way.   I don't think anyone else knows about this place, but I don't take chances," she answered, turning towards a panel ahead of them.

"How … how did you know about this place?   Who told you about it?"

"No one.   I looked it up on my own.   I have access to all of the building plans in the city," she answered, smiling.   "And this one has a central route.   The upstairs and downstairs of this lovely building have all of their facilities, washrooms, and kitchens along a series of central walls.   It makes changing out fixtures or checking pipes and electrics easier.   It's narrow, but," Van paused as she opened the access panel and shone her light into the two level tall chasm, cluttered with pipes and conduits and ductwork.   "It works."

To Ash, it was amazing, truly something he had never seen before.   "I … that's incredible.   So, that's where we're staying?   Down in there?"

Vanarra smirked at him and shook her head.   "No way.   That's just how we're getting to where we're spending the night.   Come on, climb down after me," she bade.

"Alright," he replied a little nervously as he watched her slide down the service ladder.   He was content to climb down, but as he turned round, he found her already a good distance ahead.   His eyes widening and shaking his head to ward off sleep, Ash struggled to step through the maze of multi-colored pipes.   After a moment, he saw Vanarra squatting and fiddling with something on the wall.   "What are you doing?"

"Opening the door to our suite," Van replied, nearly giddy with pride at being able to show off her knowledge in front of such an easily impressed audience.   Slowly, she opened the secured access hatch and peered into the darkened room.   "Perfect.   No one here.   Slip in behind me, but keep your voice low. Someone may be working late."

Ash nodded and then followed Vanarra. What they emerged into appeared to be a rather nice, albeit vacant, series of offices. "What is this place?" he asked, looking around.

Vanarra was already at the windows, lowering the covers and closing the curtains. "It's rental office space, but the management's never been able to rent it out. They use it as a storeroom, mostly."

"Why haven't they been able to rent it out?"

"Too close to the females' restroom. I guess some lawyer or accountant doesn't want their clients to hear 'flush, flush' every time they come visit or call," she chuckled. "I'm just going to check the door to make sure it's nice and blocked off, and then we can take to the couches and sleep out the rest of the night."

"How ... early do we have to leave?" he asked, yawning.

"We can actually stay around until mid morning. We're not leaving the way we came in. It would be too obvious when it's light out." Now, pick a couch and get some sleep. I'll make sure we're safe." He nodded, but then looked at her, staring silently. She noticed and walked over to him. "What's wrong?"

"I'm ... just really glad I met you," he confessed. "I wouldn't have known about any of this. This ... is far better than the orphanage where I was. Thank you, Van, very much."

She patted him on the shoulder with her paw and replied, "You're welcome. Now, get some rest."

After Vanarra had quickly stepped to the front door and wedged a tall chair under the door pull, she walked back into the room where Ash was and found him already laid out on the sofa, sleeping soundly. Looking at him, she wondered how much she could trust him, and although she thought it was unlikely that she would awaken to find him trying to do what those at the tree fort had done, Van didn't feel like taking any chances. Slipping away to another office, she closed and locked the door. Then she, too, settled on a nice thick couch and closed her eyes for a rest.

At morning's light, a soft, but urgent, series of taps on her door brought Vanarra to consciousness. "Yes, what is it?"

"Oh, good! Uh, Van, I ... I have to like go pee, really, really bad."

Rolling her eyes and chuckling a little, she got up and stretched for a moment before walking to the door. Opening it, she said, "Did you miss the fact they had a small kitchen in this suite?"

"Uh, well, no. I got some water out of the tap last night but…" Vanarra looked at him a little askance and smiled suggestively. "What? You mean go in … there?!"

"Unless you want to crawl through the service hatch and find your way to the females' restroom," she chuckled. "Which from the way you're dancing, makes me think you won't make it."

"Right," he agreed and immediately turned from her, moving towards the front of the suite. Smiling, she mostly closed the door to give him some privacy. However, as she rearranged the area where she had slept back to the way it was, she couldn't help but overhear him. "What? How am I supposed to make this work?" She grew more interested in his struggles and stepped quietly over to the door and listened to him trying to arrange himself, grunting occasionally in discomfort. Despite herself, Vanarra started to laugh. She kept it silent, but she actually heard him fall onto the floor once, and that sent her over the edge. "Van, this isn't working! I … I can't reach it! I'm … built … differently than you!" he whispered harshly in her direction.

Swallowing hard, she managed to say in a half controlled laugh. "Well, yeah, but … just lay across the counter – face down."

There was a silence, and finally, she heard Ash say, "Oh! Well, yeah, I suppose that would work. Just … just don't come in until I'm done, okay?"

Vanarra wanted to reply, but she was laughing too hard, something that started to make her want to pee, as well. After a moment or two more of shuffling, she heard him groan – a groan that could only mean one thing. This had her nearly pounding the floor in hysteria. When she heard him finally dismount and turn on the faucet, Van was able to control herself, although just. Crawling off the floor, she was able to open the door and met him coming out of the kitchen, looking much more at peace. "Well?" she asked, unable to keep from smiling.

"It … worked," he replied looking far more calm, but his blush furs were at full rise.

"Good, because it's my turn. Start putting your room back the way you found it. We'll be going soon."

"Oh, okay, sure," he answered, and rapidly retreated to his room. After Vanarra had ensured that both she and he had left the kitchen as they had found it, she went back and packed her gear, slung it onto her back, and then went to go find Ash. She found him sitting on the couch, staring into space. She cleared her throat to get his attention, and he turned to look at her. "Oh, sorry. I was just trying to figure out what I should do next. I mean, you've been kind and all – amazing, really, but ... I suppose I can't ask you to keep taking care of me, can I?"

His forlorn look evoked a slight smile from her, and she stated softly, "I suppose not, but perhaps, we just might agree to ... take care of each other for awhile? I've been on my own for ... a very long time." Unable to keep her eyes on his, she admitted, "I've read ... it's not healthy for me to not have anyone to talk to. I've got a place we can stay, a safe place. I don't really ever have to leave it anymore, only if there's a piece of clothing I need or medicine I can't find inside of it." She looked back at him, and Van could see from his expression what he was thinking. "It can only be you, Ash. There's not enough available there for me to take any more with us. So, it's just you and me, or I send you on your way."

He looked up at her, his eyes haunted. "There's ... just so many at the orphanage who are ... worse off than I am."

"Perhaps with you gone, they'll have a little more. I'm sorry, Ash. I wish I could take care of all of them, but you or I starving to death or getting caught won't help anyone. Our goal is just ... to stay alive right now."

"Until?" he asked, standing and looking at her, questioningly.

She considered for a moment before answering. "Until something changes, and we can, perhaps, one sol, take care of ... well, a few more."

Defeated, he replied, "Okay. You're right. We'll never be able to change anything if we starve. So, how do we get out of here?"

"Back through the panel, and then I'll go up top to where we came in last night and remove the bar."

"We're not leaving from there, I get it," he stated, confused, "but where are we leaving?"

"Females' restroom, then out the side door," she replied with a smirk.

"But I'm not supposed to be in the—"

"I'll look out for you, Ash. Don't worry," Vanarra replied. Nervously, he nodded and agreed.

Chapter 5: Associativity

Dasahar de Mistral nearly purred into Sahnassa's ear as she carefully finished seating the last memory wafer into place, "You see? Not so hard, is it?" A light puff of breath from his nostrils sailed into her ear in that moment, and she yelped in surprise.

"Dasahar! You ... you are so ... so ... impossible, sometimes! I – every strand of my fur is now standing on end!" she exclaimed.

"But you still managed to get the wafer installed perfectly," he rumbled smugly in a low voice as he leaned back, chuckling and smiling.

"So this is like what – computer assembly and construction while being tortured?!" she asked him, smiling back in good humor. The two had been lab partners in computer hardware design for nearly two moons and had gotten to know each other pretty well. Sahnassa was fond of his rich accent and his mischievous sense of humor. He had drawn her out of the shy little ball she had kept herself in since being transferred to the Academy for Interdisciplinary Studies. Although she really would have rather kept going to school on the de Orturu estate, such wasn't possible because of the courses she wanted.

"Some forms of torture are not torture at all, yes?" he purred out seductively, making her blush furs stand on end. "Got you!" he exclaimed, finally breaking character and laughing so hard his eyes were closed. This she was grateful for, as she felt the tip of her tail brush her own shoulder, and she had to fight to pull it back down. She felt heat under her fur and little prickles of excitement in some very tender places, and her pulse was starting to accelerate.

Forcing herself to reply angrily, she said, "Oh, alright, pick on the Nephti! She's an easy target! She's just a naïve mothered kit—"

"Oh, so mothered it's sad, but … kind of cute in a way," he replied, recovering and looking at her with affection. "I'm honestly glad that they put us together. I've never known a Nephti before, at least, not as well as I know you."

"Well, same here," she replied, kindly. "I mean, seeing it was either you or Byetsea…"

Byetsea was a Nephti from de Dothnar who was overweight, difficult to get along with, and always had something wrong with her fur that smelled bad – whether it was the disease or the cure that had such a pungent odor, neither Dasahar or Sahnassa wanted to know. Byetsea was paired with a Pantera male who unfortunately lived up to the many stereotypes of Pantera as being a little clumsy and unable to perform delicate work. The professor had to supply that pair with replacement memory wafers three times, and now only Byetsea was allowed to install them.

"Ugh, don't make me think about that, please," Dasahar groaned. "We're almost done, and it's dinner for me after this. My appetite would be truly ruined if you started to go through that list of things you think make her fur stink."

"Okay, then, so what's next, and no more ear-tickles, Dasahar, I'm serious! If we have to request a new circuit board because you made me snap it in two—" she warned.

"Alright, fine, fine, just be a boring little Nephti kit, then," he countered, sourly. "It's the power supply that I think should go on next."

The two sat close together, finishing the build of their computer project until finally, they slipped the case on the unit. "Come on, power it up!"

"We've already powered it up without the case," Sahnassa replied giggling. "What's the difference?"

"You can never tell until the case is closed," Dasahar insisted extravagantly. "We could have jostled a board, dislodged a connector, and then where would we be with our presentation?"

"Alright, alright!" Sahnassa replied, smiling at his over-officiousness and theatrics. "Turning it on right … now!"

Both of them, their heads nearly touching, watched anxiously as the system began to start up.   "Very good," Dasahar said breathlessly. "Very good, very nice."

"I think it's going to work," Sahnassa whispered back. The pair was sitting so close together that as their tails began to swish with excitement, they occasionally knocked together. "Oh, sorry. Excuse me," she offered.

"It's alright, Sahnassa. I'll keep mine lower," Dasahar offered.

"Oh, okay, alright," she agreed, allowing a little more loft into her tail.

As the system completed its startup sequence and displayed the initial control screen, they both knew that the many long intervals of difficult work were over, and that they had succeeded. In celebration, Dasahar reached out for Sahnassa and put his arm around her shoulder, pulling her into an embrace of sorts as they laughed and cheered. In turn, she also reached out for him around his back.

Just then, a very hard and intentional cough from behind made them turn around, and Sahnassa looked to see the department proctor staring at them, clearly disgusted and angry. For a moment, neither of them could tell what they had done wrong, but the Faelnar proctor pointed sternly behind their seats, and Sahnassa looked back to see that her tail and Dasahar's were wrapped around each other. Worse still, the loft of their tails were just on the edge of suggestiveness.

Quickly, an embarrassed Sahnassa untangled herself and stepped off her stool, folding her paws in front of her. "Sahnassa … de Orturu," the proctor ordered, "please remove yourself to my office and stay there. Dasahar and I need to have a discussion."

The pair looked uneasily at one another, and at the same time, realizing what they had done, mouthed "Sorry" to the other, and then Sahnassa quietly left the room, wincing as she heard the door shut hard behind her.

For nearly an interval, Sahnassa sat in one of the hard chairs of the proctor's office waiting. She tried to think about everything that she and Dasahar had done. It was all innocent enough. They had become close, good friends, and Sahnassa did like him, but they hadn't done anything really intimate, not until the moment they were caught, that is, and that had just sort of happened. The longer she waited, the more she dreaded what was to come. It wasn't a quick clarification with Dasahar that nothing was going on as she had hoped. She realized that if she was waiting this long, someone had been called.

She hoped, beyond hope, that it would be Matron Shalarra. She felt for sure she could explain it to her, and that the elder matron would understand, give some good advice, and then things would be back to how they were. Now that she had been caught and realized what she was doing, Sahnassa felt sure she could keep an incident from happening again.

It wasn't more than a half pass after that thought when the door to the proctor's office opened, and Sahnassa's hopes for a gentle reproach sank. Dame Rothnerra de Orturu was stern, almost uniformly gray, with a mottled nose, and violet eyes that were now snapping with indignation. Sahnassa had caught scent of the dame's sour disposition by way of hints from her matron. In one moment, she knew all of those warnings barely clawed the surface.

The dame closed the door to the proctor's office and then took a seat in his chair with absolute assurance as if this was her own domain. Sahnassa bowed her head and tried to sit small.

"So, you're Sahnassa de Orturu," the dame stated evenly, coolly. "I don't believe I've actually met you before. If all the ways to meet your dame were numbered and cataloged, this method would rank pretty near the bottom of the list. Don't you think?"

"Yes, Dame. Sorry," Sahnassa replied.

"Well, let's get to it, then. Have you actually mated with Dasahar?"

Sahnassa's head raised up in shock. "No! Uh, uh, no, Honored One! We ... we're just friends! Really!"

With a smirk, Rothnerra pulled a picture out of her robes and placed it on the desk facing Sahnassa. "Your tail's a bit high to be ... 'just friends,' don't you think?" Sahnassa was instantly aghast. During the one moment she had lost control of her tail, the proctor had been watching and silently snapped a picture with his PawLink. What was worse, Dasahar's tail was nearly as high as her own. "Now, would you care to revise your last answer?"

"No ... Honored One. I'm certain. I didn't ... we haven't ... really," Sahnassa pleaded.

"To just the casual passerby, the proctor in this case, it was far from certain. Not only were you violating this academy's rules for physical contact between students, you were dishonoring your house. From what the proctor can tell from that picture and this one," Rothnerra added as she placed a second picture next to the first, "you two might as well be a mated couple."

The second picture showed the two of them celebrating and embracing, their tails wrapped around one another. Sahnassa shook her head, desperate to try and explain. "I know what the pictures look like, Honored One, but Dasahar and I are just friends—"

"As of this moment, you're most certainly not, little kit!" Dame Rothnerra growled out the directive. "As of this moment, he is not your friend, he is simply a classmate, and you are forbidden to speak with him or come near him or even look at him. I have spoken to your instructor and made him fully aware of the situation. He has reassigned your lab partner to one of our own kind and a female. That should remove any … temptation from occurring during class or lab time. As far as removing any temptation from the time you spend outside of class, both of these images will be provided to your parents. I trust they will have a few things to say about where and with whom you spend your spare time."

Sahnassa started to cry and pleaded, "We didn't do anything, Dame, really! Why … why does it have to be this bad?!"

"Because the honor of our family is far more important than some random hormones and a senseless teen's lack of good judgment. You will mate who you hunt, kit, and your over familiarity with another species is a warning sign I cannot permit to go unaddressed. You must fully and completely understand that this will NOT be tolerated in the future, and if you rebel against these punishments, you will find yourself subject to the most severe censure house de Orturu has to offer. Do you understand?"

Completely terrified that the dame was ready to disavow her, Sahnassa gave up trying to plead her case. "Yes, Honored One."

"Very well. You are to remain here until your father comes … and claims you," she stated, rising. "You are not attracting the sort of attention young kits should be seeking, like that of your sister. Triana's honors in familial studies and legal preparatory are top rate. So you need to ask yourself what's wrong with your focus in life. We will be keeping a very strict eye on you now, make no mistake. I would say farewell, but in your case, let's just hope you fare far better than you did this sol."

With that, the dame left the room, and a shattered and heartbroken Sahnassa sat alone, horrified, embarrassed, and weeping.

Pulled out of an important meeting to go and retrieve his errant daughter, Gonastir was nearly beside himself with anger until he called Holana. "Please, be gentle with her. From what the matron told me, she believes nothing actually happened, but that it just looked bad and our dame … perhaps, was seeking to make a … very firm point with Sahnassa. I would imagine that she's … pretty badly shaken, utterly devastated, even."

"And where was Matron Shalarra during all of this?" he asked, crossly.

"At her lair, recovering from a fainting episode. She said she feels fine, but the doctors still want to check her out. She saw Dame Rothnerra's note and … the pictures."

"There are pictures?!" Gonastir almost shouted into the PawLink.

"The proctor took them. I'm not happy about that!" Holana nearly growled. "Those could get into other paws and be taken out of context. I intend to have a word or two in the director's ear."

"If she was doing what she should, Sahnassa wouldn't have to worry about someone taking pictures!" he growled.

"Listen to me, please!" his wife pleaded. "There's no reason to believe anything else happened other than these two kids were caught at a moment when they weren't paying attention to what they were doing. Young kits make mistakes, and I'm sure young cubs do, too; am I right?"

"Yes," he replied, cooling a little.

"Then please, be careful. Yes, I was upset when I heard, but Triana told me a few things just now – things I … never knew about Sahnassa. We've hurt her, really hurt her on more than a few occasions. There were times when Triana really thought she was going to just … leave. If that's not what you want, and as her father I would hope it's not, then please, Gonastir, just be a father for her right now."

"There have to be consequences, love," he replied in warning.

"There will be, and there already have been. We obviously have to be more careful about where she spends her time and with whom, but in all honesty, one has to ask why two teens were left together for so long. In my mind, the picture is as much of an indictment of the proctor and the school as it is of our little one. I know you have to be firm, but … don't forget to be loving, okay? Sahnassa has told Triana she doesn't believe that we really do, love her, I mean. Please, don't prove her right."

Gonastir was silent for a moment. "Alright, Holana. Alright. I'm here now. I'll … see you when I get home."

When he entered the academy, he went to the office. "May I help you?" a Faelnar asked him.

"I'm here to pick up my daughter, Sahnassa," he replied.

"Oh, so you're the father," the Faelnar replied with disgust.

"And you're the proctor?" Gonastir asked, his eyes tightening.

"Yes, I was the one who found them–"

"You can stop right there," he warned. "You know, I've got a legal brief up in front of me right now. I wonder if you would find it interesting. It involved an individual taking a picture of someone else in a … compromising position. When it was discovered that the picture simply was snapped at an inopportune moment and that no true family crime had been committed, the attention turned back upon the one who snapped the picture. The individual had been so … foolish as to circulate that image to others, and in the end, he was sentenced to a fine of one hundred thousand and six moons in jail for a libelous attack on another house. He might even be disavowed for the offense. If you're interested, I can send you an update on the final disposition of that case – although I can tell you the outlook isn't promising … at all. Do you and I understand one another? Perhaps you should just delete those images now, while I'm standing here, to avoid any … accidents."

The Faelnar scowled and looked as if he was going to refuse, but then the Nephti director stepped up behind him at that moment. "I believe that would be a very prudent idea. I also believe that a review of policy and practices for proctors is in order. It seems that we both have some issues to address."

"Well said," Gonastir replied, watching as the director took the PawLink out of the paws of his subordinate and started keying commands. When the director turned the display to Gonastir so he could see that every image had been deleted, Sahnassa's father quietly said, "Thank you. Can you please take me to her?"

"Certainly," the director replied, putting the device back in his humiliated subordinate's paws. "Come with me." After they had made it a few steps away, the director stated, "I want you to understand that Sahnassa is an excellent student – by far the best we have in that program, and … to be perfectly forthcoming with you, her lab partner has been disciplined before for being too familiar with those of other species, and even within his own species—"

This brought Gonastir up short. "Then, why was he paired with Sahnassa?"

"We have been trying to work with him, coach him, and we thought he fully understood, but … it appears not. The conversation I'll be having with his parents tonight will be very different. He won't be coming back, and we don't have any other problem students remaining in the program."

"Except one, perhaps," Gonastir admitted grimly.

"I don't think so. I'm not from your house, so I can get away with saying this – your dame was way out of line. She crushed the poor kit, scared her to death. Sitting behind that door down the hall is one of the smartest and sweetest kits I've ever seen grace these halls. You should be proud, not ashamed."

"Thank you," Gonastir replied.

"You will tell me how that case turns out, won't you?" the director asked as he stepped away. Seeing Gonastir's confusion, he clarified, "The one with the individual who circulated the compromising picture."

"Well, now that you … mention it, it isn't an actual … brief. Sorry about that."

"Hey, I'm a dad, too. I would have done the same thing. Now, go take good care of her, okay?"

Gonastir smiled and nodded at the kindness of the director, who winked and then walked away.

When he tapped on the door to the proctor's office and opened it, he saw Sahnassa sitting, her head leaning against the wall. When he sat down beside her, he could see the deep furrows in her cheek fur, and when she glanced over and saw him, she put her paws over her face and turned away from him, crying aloud now, "I'm sorry… I'm sorry…"

Never had he been so grateful to his loving wife than at that moment. He could see that his daughter's spirit had been utterly crushed, and if he had stamped into that office and ripped the fur off her hide in shreds, Sahnassa might never recover from the blow. Gently taking her paw in his, he softly replied, "I know, kit. I know. I … I still love you. I … will always love you. It's going to be okay."

He wrapped his paw about his daughter's shoulder and drew her close. Seeming a little stunned, she went along with it. "But … but I … dishonored … I … the picture, I…"

"That picture has been deleted off of the proctor's PawLink, by the director." Then, Gonastir looked on the desk and saw the two images. He saw where it was possible to interpret the pictures in a certain way, but still, there was significant cause for doubt, specifically when he saw how Dasahar's tail was entwined tightly around Sahnassa's, but her own was fairly limp, and the embrace was companionable – not intimate. He collected the two pictures off the desk and slowly placed them in his coat.

Sahnassa looked up at him in fear. He reached out and kissed her on the cheek and replied to her obvious question, "We'll talk about it, and … there will be consequences, but only to protect you and perhaps, do a better job of equipping you to avoid such … accidents in the future. You're my daughter, Sahnassa, and I love you. Please, kit, never doubt that."

"Thank you," she replied, looking up at him, still horrified by what had happened, but the relief and gratitude in her eyes brought tears to his own.

"Come now. Let's go home," he bade her, and the two, father and daughter, stood and left the office together.

"Thank you, Van," Ash replied, embarrassed as he looked at his new shirt and pants. "I … I can't thank you enough for this. I've never had new clothes – I mean like ever. How did you get the money?"

"There's a place inside where I live that has a container for donations," Van explained quietly as they walked down a path beside a hover-trail. "It's intended to help the less fortunate, and … it does, although perhaps not as the owners of that place would intend."

"Haven't they noticed you, I mean, taking from it?" he nervously asked.

"I take very infrequently, and then only a couple of large notes that are … exceptional. The secret to getting by where I live is that you have to graze and hunt very carefully. You can't make things disappear too quickly; it has to look like normal use."

Ash furrowed his brows as he thought about it. "So, there is food there, but you can't take all of it at once; you can take a little at the time, here and there."

"Enough to get by, but not enough to be noticed, plain and simple," she replied. "If I were to bring anyone back with me, they would have to follow those rules and do what I said; after all, I've managed to stay undetected for three seasons."

"I … I know I didn't do a good job at the orphanage living up to the rules, but … we were starving. You've already put more food into me this sol than we see in ten sols. I can't thank you enough, but why are you helping me, Van? I … I don't want to seem ungrateful, but I am curious."

Vanarra's shoulders sagged and some of the confidence that she was putting on display faded a bit. "Perhaps, although I've been really good at living in the special place I've found, I … I haven't shared it with anyone – I've been pretty rotten about that, actually. I haven't had anyone to talk to, either. You say that I've given you more food than you've ever had before. Ash, I'll be honest with you, I haven't talked to anyone this much since … well, since before I lost my mom."

"It is nice to have someone to talk to," he agreed. "That's … that's what I was afraid of, when you found me in the forest. It wasn't running out of food—"

"I think not! You've broken the code on how to get and find good food out here!"

"Who knew restaurants and groceries were so eager to have someone dispose of pre-packaged food that was still good, but they weren't allowed to sell?"

Van chuckled, "And all the while as you provide this 'service,' Ash gets to pick through what he wants and keep it. Nice! It's a real pity that you could only escape the orphanage every couple of moons to go scrounge. If they'd just freely let you go, everyone there could have eaten like matriarchs!"

"Well, there are a few good-hearted Thurians out there. Just never ask a de Caterra for anything like that, or a de Gonari, for that matter." Van scowled angrily at the mention of her mother's former family, but she turned her head away so Ash couldn't see. "I make you a promise, Van, the best I can possibly make," he continued, "that I'll … I'll do anything you ask me to if you would be willing to share your lair with me."

"You'll do anything I ask?" she queried, surprised, looking at him. "That's a lot of trust, Ash. Are you sure? You don't really know me that well."

"I know enough," he replied, warmly looking at her. "No one has ever treated me so kindly or made me feel more welcome. You know, everywhere I go I'm a freak; the purebred Lupar and Perratti just look at me as if I'm so … revolting, and yet I'm half of both of them! How can I be this disgusting and unwelcome when I am what they are?"

"I know," Van sighed. "On my little trips away from the lair, I haven't looked forward to the transport drivers, the shop clerks, and even enforcement looking me up and down as if I was some kind of … I don't know. It's like some of them look at me as if I would be a great hunt for them, and some of them look at me like I'm walking crap! How … how can I both be … attractive and – like you said – revolting all at the same time?"

"Well, you're not revolting," Ash countered quietly. "Not … not at all."

"You're being nice," Van replied.

"Well, no actually," he offered. "You're … well, I shouldn't say. Just that you're not, in any way, unattractive."

Vanarra felt her tail lift a little bit at his shy compliment. "Thanks. You're not a bad looking cub yourself, Ash. So, are you ready to see what it's like inside of a … *secret lair*?"

"Very much so. The thought of trying to find somewhere to live, especially trying to go to the bathroom in a disused office is kind of … terrifying."

"And you'll do exactly what I tell you to? Trust me completely?" she asked, serious.

"You've been so kind to me, why wouldn't I?" he replied, but he could tell that didn't satisfy her. "Yes. I will do what you say and trust you."

Looking hard into his eyes for a moment, Vanarra's expression softened, and she smiled. "Okay, then. First thing you have to trust me about is getting into my lair. It was pretty simple in the past, but some additional security measures and other upgrades make it a bit more difficult than it used to be. We're going to have to ride on the thruster spar of a garbage hover."

"Do what?!"

"You said you would trust me, Ash. Do whatever I said?" she countered in warning.

"Alright," he replied, swallowing. "You ... you just have to tell me what to do."

Half an interval later, Van and Ash were waiting in the bushes behind a large warehouse, staring at the large garbage bins arrayed side-by-side just off the back loading dock. "So, why are we here? Why is this the place to pick up a ride to ... wherever it is we're going?"

"Well, I suppose I should tell you, so long as you're not going to stick your tail between your legs and run away. We're going to the Pinnacle Center Archive. Ever heard of it?"

"I haven't," Ash confessed. "What is it?"

"A giant library and archive storage that services multiple families and houses. That's why it's not on any of their well-guarded estates. I used to get in through a service entrance at the top of the mound, but they redid the venting system, and now there's no way through. So, that's why it has to be a garbage hover. Once we get past their cameras by hiding on the spars, we can duck out when it lands and slip behind several recycling bins. I've checked the space in the past. We can stay hidden there fairly easily. When things settle down, we go up the garbage conveyor and out into a service hallway. Then, we're in!"

Ash shook his head. "Sounds ... complex and ... fairly smelly. So, right now, how do we do this part?"

"The smell isn't bad at all. This garbage hover only handles recyclables like clean plasti-forms and paper. When it drives up, the spars will be extended. As it gets ready to land, however, they start to pull back in. While the driver has his load up in the air, we scoot around in back of the hover. When he puts the container back down, he'll gently lift off and slip over to the other bin. When he's done with that load, he'll have to extend the spars again in order to retract the landing skids. That's when we slide under the vehicle and crawl up onto the spars. I'll take the right; you take the left."

"Okay, you take right; I take left. Then what?"

"The next step on his route is the archive. We just hang on and ride until he gets to where he's going. Ash, listen closely to this. The moment you hear the skids pop open, you've got to get off that spar, beneath the hover, and in the middle. Stay on the spar, and you'll be crushed. Drop down on the outside, you'll get cooked. We both jump off at the same time – there'll be enough room. Then, just take my paw and let me lead you. I know where the cameras are and where workers are likely to be. If we play this right, no one will have any chance of seeing us. Got it?"

"Scared out of my mind, but … yeah."

"Me, too. I really wish they hadn't closed off that access door, but I'm not giving up my lair that easy. So, all we have to do is wait."

It was another half interval before the garbage hover showed up, and Van tapped Ash on the shoulder and motioned for him to get ready. "Now, what side am I going to crawl up on again?" he asked.

"The left," Vanarra replied, slightly annoyed.

"Sorry, I just need a way to remember that," he sighed in self disappointment.

Van smirked at him. "It's easy. I'm always right!" He smiled back at her in a way that made her feel that he not only got the joke, but in a way, he also got "her." A sound from the garbage hover attracted her attention, and she looked back to see the skids lowering and the thruster spars retracting. "Alright, Ash. We go!"

She shot through the brush line and was pleased to hear Ash quietly padding after her. Coming up behind the big crimson-colored vehicle she knew they would be visible for a moment, but everything looked perfect. Ducking under the camera but still a good ways from the hover, she grabbed Ash's paw and held him down in a crouch behind her.

Both shielded their eyes as the thrusters fired and reoriented the vehicle towards the second and final bin. As it set down and the thrusters shut off, Vanarra waited until the vehicle had lifted the bin about half way up before she squeezed Ash's paw and pulled them both under.

Obviously terrified, he moved to the left side under the thruster spar and looked at her nervously. "It'll be okay, Ash. I'll look after you," she reassured him quietly.

Just then, the spars began moving, opening a large gap on either side right above them. "That's … amazing!" Ash gasped, realizing the space would easily accommodate him.

"Move, Ash!" Vanarra demanded, and he looked over to see she had already disappeared off the ground. Quickly, he leapt up onto the spar, and found he had no problems finding a secure position. "Ash, are you in there okay?" Vanarra queried, sticking her head down.

"I'm good. You were right! This is incredible. How many times have you done this?" he asked as the thrusters warmed up.

"Including this time," Van called back from her compartment, "one!"

"Oh, mange!" Ash groaned as the thrusters came to full power and drowned out all possibility of further communication. However, he still thought he could hear laughing coming from not too far away.

Sahnassa sat, small and ashamed, in a chair in her parents' bedroom. Her mother had told her to wait there while she had a conversation with her father, and the silence clawed into her heart. She knew, without a doubt, that the two of them were deciding how to get rid of her, disown her from the family. If they decided to keep her, they would probably pull her out of her school and force her into the same kind of training that Triana seemed to love, but that Sahnassa simply couldn't enjoy. About to cry, she heard the door of her parent's bedroom open and close, and after a moment, the sound of her mother sitting quietly on the bed, facing her daughter.

"Sahnassa, kit?"

"I'm … I'm so sorry, Mom," she replied, looking up into her mother's worried expression.

"I know, I know. Please, kit, understand that if anyone is at fault here, it's me," Holana stated quietly, making Sahnassa blink in surprise, and in return her mother just nodded and confessed, "I … I didn't prepare you for what you might run into, and a situation which I believe was truly innocent – on your part – was intentionally misunderstood by a proctor who seems to have had his own agenda. Let me ask you kit, did you have … feelings for Dasahar? It's okay to be honest with me; I'm not going to be mad at you."

Sahnassa looked away and stared intently as if she was trying to put into words something that was very difficult and complex for her to understand. Finally, she breathed out, "I … I suppose I did, but … but I thought they were because he was my friend. I enjoyed being around him. He was funny and nice to me. I've … never had a friend like that."

"But it was more than just friendship, wasn't it? What you were feeling?"

"I ... I had some feelings, but I kept just trying to shove them down. My tail—" and she pointed to it like it was the third individual in the room. "My tail would not stay down! I'm sitting there talking and having fun, and then it's brushing me on the back of the neck! I'm ... getting these weird, prickly tingles in ... like places, but I got through that. I finally managed it, and then we got everything working – we finished our project. We were celebrating when we were caught."

Holana nodded and sighed. "I really should have talked to you sooner, kit. You're old enough that your mating urges are going to start affecting you." Sahnassa's curious and doubtful expression was exactly what her mother expected, and she smiled as if recognizing the same surprise she had once experienced as a kit hearing this from her own mother. "Your body was having a reaction to Dasahar. It appears that he was ... quite skillful in ... making you feel appreciated, safe, and cared about. You knew that he was concerned about you, right?"

"Well, yes ... I suppose," Sahnassa replied, unsure.

"Sweet kit, you need to hear that the academy has had problems with Dasahar before. He's been caught a couple of other times trying to start up a hunt with someone he shouldn't have been. They had talked to him on two other occasions, and the academy director thought Dasahar had understood, but apparently not. They've dismissed him for this offense. You won't be seeing him again."

Sahnassa's face was a picture of dismay. "He ... he didn't touch me anywhere he wasn't supposed to! He didn't ask me out! He didn't even try to lick me on the side of the muzzle!"

"I know, I know," Holana replied, motioning down with her paws to calm her daughter. "But, he didn't exactly keep his distance respectful and ... professional, did he? Did he do things you wouldn't expect ... say, Triana, I suppose, to do?"

"He ... well, he kind of blew in my ear a little, but that was just trying to get me to drop what I was working on, I thought," Sahnassa admitted, now starting to feel doubtful, herself.

"Oh, no," her mother chuckled. "Not to be too, well, forward, kit ... but, that's ... well, let's just say that's a well established way to get certain Nephti females interested in hunting." Seeing her daughter's surprised and now embarrassed face, Holana added, "Some Nephti ... really like that, and Dasahar may have known about that little trick, too." Her mother's expression turned sad. "He may have intentionally used it to try to get ... intimate with you." Holana watched with some regret as Sahnassa's expressions changed, the pieces starting to come together in her daughter's mind.

"So he was just using that to ... like, mate with me?" she asked, doubtful.

"Or something short of that, but as females, we have to face an unfortunate reality. The males of our species and others are drawn to us, and we to them. Eventually, for all the right reasons, this is okay. However, there are some males who look at females as just ... well, toys for a moment's pleasure. They only want the pleasure of a successful hunt; they aren't interested in all of the heartache and consequences that can come from it. Consequences like ... children, or even ... Anati children."

Sahnassa's eyes went to the floor, and her eyes welled up with tears thinking that Dasahar could have just been using her and had tried to use two others. "He ... he didn't really care about me, did he?" she asked, her voice breaking.

"Maybe he did, at some level. You're certainly beautiful enough, inside and out," her mother answered lovingly. "Perhaps he just wasn't mature enough to understand the consequences of his actions. I would be willing to grant you that, with his dismissal from the academy, his matron and yes, probably his dame will make those consequences painfully clear to him. My guess is that right now, Dasahar is having to grow up quite a bit in a short time, just like you, kit."

"Anati children, though," Sahnassa countered, thinking about it. "I ... not that I want to have one, Mom, but why is that such a problem? Wouldn't any unwanted child scream as loud, need as much food, and well, poop just as much? Why are those children so ... bad?"

"Sahnassa," her mother breathed and looked away, surprised at her daughter's question. "For whatever reason, our society and our family have decided that creating children from two different species of parents is ... dishonorable. Now, I don't honestly know what makes those children worse than any other, except this – because everyone else thinks they have dishonor woven into their being, it might as well be true. There can be an Anati who is just a wonderful soul, but no one will ever stand by them. If no one ever stands by them, the Anati would likely become bitter and angry. They would turn dishonorable because no one ever expects anything more from them. It's sad, in a way, I suppose. Purebreds are afraid of the shock and scandal of such a mating or the result of one, and just because of that, Anati are dishonorable."

"But isn't that wrong, Mom?" Sahnassa asked.

"We may not always agree with the dictates of our family, Sahnassa, but remember, it's to our family we owe our first allegiance. If our family believes that such a pairing would harm its honor, we are obligated, for the love of our family, to keep such a thing from happening."

"Did you ever have ... feelings for someone of another species?"

"I did," Holana confessed. "I was in a situation a lot like yours when I was about your age, and my mother told me something that helped. It's a little something you can say in your head over and over to help you get control of yourself again and remind you of your family's requirements. It went like this, 'We can be friends, loyal and true, but for my love, only a Nephti will do.' Say it with me, Sahnassa."

"We can be friends, loyal and true, but for my love, only a Nephti will do," Sahnassa repeated with her mother.

"Very good. If I was having a really difficult time, I kept it short. Basically, I would say over and over again, 'Only a Nephti, Only a Nephti, Only a Nephti.' Remember that, and you probably won't have to worry about any other ... difficult conversations with Dame Rothnerra."

"It's like she hates me, Mother!" Sahnassa replied, afraid. "How will I ever achieve anything now that she hates me so?!"

"Matron Shalarra said that she and Dame Rothnerra had some very ... active discussions about what happened. I think Matron Shalarra is a very apt and able champion for you, Sahnassa, and that's what your father and I want to be, too. Okay?"

"Okay; thank you, Mom."

"No, kit. Thank you. Again, I'm sorry I didn't tell you any of this sooner. I just thought you weren't there yet, but ... then again, you've always been beautiful to me."

Sahnassa reached out for and embraced her mother, fully grateful to still merit her mother's love and for how kind her mother had just been to her. "Love you, Mom, and thanks."

"It's okay, Ash. You can breathe now," Van chuckled quietly as they both sat in the darkness of the garage ductwork.

"That's easy for you to say! That was terrifying!" the Lupar-Perratti complained quietly. "Those thrusters retract really quick – I mean, you can feel the heat in your fur!"

"Well, if it makes you feel any better, it's a lot easier to leave than it is to get in."

"How did you used to get in?" he asked.

"Come back here, I'll show you," Van offered, "but go slow. We don't want a lot of noise. Walk with your forepaws and knees on the outside, like I showed you, in the places I showed you."

"I can't see anything."

"You can feel, can't you? Besides, once we get to the air shaft, we'll be able to stand up."

"Okay, now you're talking," Ash replied, obviously brightening at the suggestion. "Spending another four intervals cramped in here doesn't sound all that attractive, actually."

"It may not be that long," she noted. "They might close up early. Come on."

After several passes of carefully shuffling along as Vanarra had instructed him, Ash emerged into a small room of the main shaft and accepted Vanarra's paw as he uneasily stood. Light was seeping in from somewhere high above, and as he looked up, he marveled. "Oh … wow! That's … that's horrifying!" he breathed.

"It's a lot easier than the garbage hover," Van commented, surprised.

"Uh, not for me. I'm kind of … scared of heights. You climbed all the way up there?" he asked, looking at her, amazed.

"Sure," she replied, matter-of-factly. "Climbed down the first time; I had to dangle myself over the edge and try to hook in with my paw-shoes. In the end, that didn't work; I had to kick them off and just use bare hind-paws." Even in the dim light of the ventilator shaft, Vanarra could see all of the color drain out of Ash's nose and lips. Barely under control, Ashalam backed-up against the side of the shaft and slid down to the floor, sitting and panting. "Ash? What's wrong, cub?"

"I'm … sorry, Van. Even the thought of that … terrifies me!" he admitted, closing his eyes. "I … I can like see you doing it, in my head, and falling."

Vanarra slid down beside him, and put her paw around his shoulders. "Hey now; I'm here, I'm okay. I take it you wouldn't want to climb up to have a look at the fans, right?"

Ash opened his eyes and looked up. "Oh no, please, and ... please don't climb up there, yourself, Van, okay? I ... I would be terrified for you," he confessed.

His earnest statement and pleading look into her eyes touched her in a way that made her smile. "I ... I won't, Ash. So, you're going to be pretty happy that we don't have to do any climbing like this to get to your new lair, huh?"

"Really, really happy about that," Ash replied uneasily. "If this was the way in, the only way in, I wouldn't have been able to do it. Sorry about that."

"It's alright, Ash," she reassured him, leaning against him companionably. "You don't have to worry. That's one of the real blessings of this place. I just hope you're okay with small spaces."

"Reasonably okay," he admitted, "just so long as I've got a way out."

"You'll be fine. Here, put your paw in mine." A little uneasily, he lifted his right paw and put it in hers. She put her other paw upon his and gently held him. "I will look out for you, Ash. Don't worry."

With a gentle smile, he reached under her paw and grasped hers in his, as well. "Thank you, Van. You're ... you're a miracle."

"Thanks," Van replied. "You, too, Ash. You, too."

Chapter 6: Generosity

Vanarra felt almost a giddy excitement as she led Ash around the archive that night. He was perpetually amazed and intrigued by her observations about not only the techniques she had used to survive and feed herself, but about the specific individuals who worked at the archive. Vanarra hadn't realized just how much she knew about most of the library staff. She was able to tell Ashalam an enormous amount of detail about the various Anati and purebreds who worked there. With morning nearly upon them, Van brought him back to the children's section, their bags full of the night's scrounging. "Quite the bonus coming back from being away," she whispered as they closed the vents behind them. "Obviously, no one else is keeping the coolers clean!"

"I'll say! This … this is an amazing amount of food, Van, and no one misses it?" he asked, incredulous.

"The policy posted on the cooler doors says it all. They have no reason to be suspicious if the policy says that's what will happen. Although I have to admit, it's not the food that's got me excited," she explained as she turned and started making her way down the shaft.

"Oh, really? Is it … me?" he asked.

"Well, Ash, of course," Van chuckled, "but my favorite author has a new book, and I found a copy on the shelf! I can't wait to read it!"

"Hey, be careful with that tail, please," Ash chuckled, stopping for a moment. "I'm getting swished to death back here."

"Oh sorry, Ash, really," Van apologized looking back at him. "I just … *love* her writing. There's this book I want to show you. It's called *The Tale of the Ugly Seed*. It's one of my favorites."

"This … this is just amazing, everything you've found, everything you've learned, everything you've done! It's … it's just amazing!"

"I'm glad you like it," Vanarra replied, feeling very warmed by his earnest appreciation. "Now, let's get these things back. We have to start work on building out a bed for you."

"Oh, right," he replied. "I'm completely losing track of time. I may fall asleep on you. Wait, that didn't sound exactly–"

"Don't worry about it. I'm not offended. Since we're going to be living here together, we're probably going to get very familiar with one another. I've already spotted a few knits in your fur I want to work on."

"I … don't know about that," he replied, following her into the lair. "I might be a little … embarrassed."

"Alright. Don't worry, and trust me, Ash. I won't hurt you."

"Thanks," he replied and then worked his way through the tight gap into her lair.

Almost an interval later, the two had finished eating, and Ash was working on sewing together the various cushions Vanarra had found over the seasons into his new bed. He had also been fairly quiet, which made her wonder what he was thinking, but she had steadily picked up on the fact that, while he was appreciative for what she was doing for him, he was perhaps overwhelmed or still unable to trust her. Thinking back, she realized that she had been a complete show-off, and if she truly admitted it, she had mothered him more than a few times. She tried to combat her embarrassment at going so overboard with Ash by telling herself that he needed reassurance, and in some places, like the garbage hover, her careful instruction had kept him alive. Still, as she read through Rahnahi's first chapter of *The Open Soul*, she couldn't help but wonder.

"Van, would you mind if I asked you a question?"

"Go ahead. What's wrong?" She could tell that something was clearly disturbing him.

"Here I am, making a bed out of items that have been … well … stolen from others, with a stomach full of food that was also stolen from others, in a lair that well, is also kind of stolen from other Thurians. Does that ever bother you?"

Vanarra raised her eyebrow fur. "I'm surprised it bothers you. Weren't you thrown out of the orphanage for stealing food?" she asked, a little accusation in her voice.

"Yes, I was, but … we were starving. I didn't have any other choice. You … you're smart enough that you could find a job. Someone would pay you for what you could do. You can … read and plan and organize such amazing things in your head. You don't have to live here; you could probably live away from here if you wanted to. How long do you intend to stay down here, living this way?"

"If it really bothers you, Ash, you could leave at dusk," she replied, a little coolly.

"I don't mean it that way," he carefully offered and then just sat there, waiting for her to answer.

With a sigh, she put her book down and looked at him. "Purebred Thurians kept me and my mother on the edge of starvation most every sol I was growing up. Because they don't approve of Anati mix-ups, they kept my mother from getting a job, and when – because she loved me so much – she tried to go back to that damned family of hers to get help, they beat her to death, Ash. I watched my own mother die right in front of my eyes. So if you're asking me if I have any guilt living off the purebreds in this place, taking their food, their money, their books, or their medicine, the answer is no, I don't! Do I always want to live this way? I … I don't know, honestly," she stated, her temper evening out. "I … guess that would depend on if I was … happy or not."

"Van, I'm sorry those things happened to you, and you have every right to want the purebreds to make up for what they did. I'm just saying that you're … special. I can't imagine you living out your entire life here and no one ever knowing about you."

"Maybe, it's best for everyone," she replied, looking at him gently smiling. "It makes me wish that there were no purebreds – that it was just mix-ups like us. We'd treat everyone the same, like you and me talking here – no insults, no back of the transport, just … living in that light, warmth, and hope Rahnahi talks about."

"Who?" Ash asked, although he had been smiling wistfully at Van's imaginings of an Anati paradise.

"My favorite author – the one I was mentioning earlier."

"Oh, right, when I was getting whacked in the face with your tail – a very lovely tail, actually," he chuckled.

"Okay, now," she warned, but in good humor. "Rahnahi says that would be her perfect society, too. In her books, I can almost feel like she's calling out to me, teaching me. Some of it, I really get; some of it, I don't, but she just seems so nice."

"Is she an Anati like us?"

"Actually no," Van admitted. "A Nephti dame of house de Dothnar, believe it or not."

"Would you feel as comfortable taking things from her?" Ash quietly asked.

"I don't get the sense I would even have to steal anything from her," Van mused, staring at the wall. "She would offer it, willingly – not that someone like me could ever get that close to one of the de Dothnar dames."

"That was like the first family I had that took care of me. They were Nephti, an older couple. They said they found me in the bushes behind their house. They did their best to take care of me, but … they were really old – a lot of health problems. When one of them fell, both of them were sent to a medical assistance facility, and … one of the matrons put me into the orphanage. I … really miss them." Vanarra put her book aside and stared at him, intently. After a moment, he sighed and continued, "They were like my mother and father. One of the disavowed de Caterra who helped run the orphanage told me a few moons ago that they had died … alone and without any family around them. I was their family. I would have wanted to be there."

Something about the sadness of his expression reached into her soul, and almost without understanding why, Vanarra started confessing, her voice breaking, "My mom … was … just so wonderful to me. She … gave me life … then gave her life for me! She could have just … abandoned me! I … I wish she would have! If it weren't for me, she … she'd still be alive!" Ash watched as the strong and confident Vanarra emotionally collapsed and started crying like a little child. Unsure of what to do, he put down what he was working on and stepped close beside her. Carefully sitting down, he put his arm about her shoulder, and she leaned into him – so many seasons without that comfort causing a flood of grief and release to pour out of her soul.

After several passes, Vanarra was literally trembling, unable to stop herself from crying although she desperately wanted to. With

Ash's arms around her, she couldn't rally her inner strength; it simply wouldn't come. She was weak, broken in his embrace. "I'm … sorry … Ash," she cried.

"Who … who have you had to talk to, Van, since your mother died?" he asked.

"No one."

"Van," he responded, now beginning to cry himself. "I'm sorry. Just cry, Van. Just cry until you can't. You're due, kit. You're due."

Vanarra couldn't understand what he meant, and a part of her wanted to struggle, get away from him, but all of the things Rahnahi had spoken to her through her books were working upon her very soul, and the tears and his touch were causing something inside of her, something that hadn't been alive in seasons, to live again. Memories came back to her, memories she had buried – not only of the moments when her mother was beaten, not only of her rapemating in the tree fort, but other horrible memories she had buried. She had been tied down, drugged, and molested by a group of teen Faelnar who only fled when enforcement came up. The purebred officers had let her go, but ordered her to leave, offering her no help. She had begged from lair to lair, only to have purebreds slam doors in her face or spit on her. At one lair, they tried to pull her in, and something had snapped inside of her. She didn't remember anything other than wiping blood from her claws in the grass outside.

"Oh mange, Ash. I … I remember what … what they did to me … I'd … forgotten."

"I'll stay with you, Van, as long as you need. I will watch over you, Van."

His reassurance brought cries anew, cries of a broken soul that had never been able to start healing, one that had gotten by on just hiding horrible memories, shoving them down and away. Finally, helpless and crippled in the arms of Ashalam, she finally understood what Rahnahi had meant. "Isolation is the creator of madness, and a life without trust is empty." Until that moment, Vanarra realized she hadn't been fully sane.

Completely unnerved, Sahnassa stood just outside her lair, waiting for Matron Shalarra to arrive. Her mother had been quite happy about the call she had received several passes ago, but she hadn't been willing to tell Sahnassa what was going on. Holana had just helped her daughter change from sleep ruffled fur wearing soft shirts and shorts to fully groomed and dressed in her finest in less than half an interval. It had only been three sols since the incident with Dasahar, and she had sadly presented their mutual project, pleased that at least the two of them had been given a perfect score. He hadn't tried to contact her, and she certainly wouldn't have dared try to reach out to him, but she had to admit to herself, and to her mother, that she was mourning his loss. Her mother had been very kind about it, but again reminded her, "Only a Nephti. Only a Nephti. Only a Nephti."

As a large limo-hover pulled into their driveway, Sahnassa was surprised. She stood at as close to attention as she could manage. She just knew that the dame was going to be inside of that vehicle, and dreaded spending any time in the presence of the "gray one." As the hover landed and its door opened, Sahnassa bowed her head and looked at the ground. After a moment, a voice she recognized called to her. "Come on in, Sahnassa. It's only me, after all." She looked up to see Matron Shalarra's paw waving to her from the door, so, quickly, Sahnassa stepped inside.

The inside of the hover was nearly filled to capacity with not only the matron, but with many other females and males of her own age, some she recognized from her primary school. They greeted her happily and invited her to come inside. "What's … what's going on, Matron Shalarra?" she asked as she took a seat next to one of her old classmates.

"Well, you're all about to enjoy a very special honor. You see, our Grand Matriarch likes to reach out to young Nephti like you and interact with you, get to know you, know what you're feeling. She also wants to tell you the stories of our family, so you'll be able to know and understand why our family is the way it is. Finally, our Grand Matriarch will take all of you on a tour through the Legends Archive, where the important and honorable achievements of our family are recorded. It will be only you ten who get to spend time with her. It's an important opportunity – one to be treasured."

Sahnassa's mouth dropped wide open, and she shook her head in disbelief. Less than three sols ago, she thought for sure she was about to be banished from the family, disavowed. Now, she was being permitted to spend time with the most powerful and influential member of her family. "Thank … thank you, Matron!" she nearly screamed. "I … I can't believe it!"

The other children laughed in agreement, and Matron Shalarra smiled as she chuckled, "Every single one I've told has had the same reaction as you, Sahnassa. What you don't know, children, is that Sahnassa has been engaged in a special program of study, one that is very difficult and technical and one that she has demonstrated great aptitude for. I certainly believe that you will make a great contribution to our family, one that is most unique."

"Oh my, Sahnassa," her once friend in primary, Allilae, breathed in surprise. "I ... I had no idea! What are you doing?"

"Please, Sahnassa, may I?" Matron Shalarra asked, and willingly, she nodded. "Sahnassa is studying information systems, logic, advanced hardware design, and is just about to begin programming class. This is in addition to the normal courses she is taking."

"You must spend all of your time studying, Sahnassa," Allilae offered.

"It's a lot, but ... I kind of like it – the technical pieces are just ... very interesting to me."

"She is also getting to interact with those who are not Nephti, and that has been challenging, hasn't it, kit?"

"Yes, Matron," Sahnassa replied, embarrassed. "That's ... been difficult, at times."

"Be aware of this, my young ones," the matron gently admonished. "Those of you who have ambition for house leadership or business would find it to your benefit to seek out the kind of opportunities Sahnassa is struggling through. It is easier when we deal with our own, but Thuria is filled with those who are *not* our own. We must learn to accept the diversity of the world around us, and we must learn to not only adapt to it, but make it work for us."

"Does that mean having Vulpi do jobs like gardening and repair?" one of the young males asked.

"Perhaps," Matron Shalarra replied, shrugging. "Although they do seem to do and prefer many of those jobs, we must always be careful never to judge a new individual of a species we meet by others we have met or especially by what others say about them. We cannot judge any individual by a group society has placed them in, can we Sahnassa?"

"No. We have to be careful, too, or the things we do might be ... accidently misinterpreted," Sahnassa carefully admitted.

The matron nodded thoughtfully, and it was clear that several of the other students were considering what had been said. "If you will forgive me in the present company, Sahnassa, I do have your marks for the last semester. It may encourage you to know that you achieved a perfect score in the system design class. Very impressive."

"My family deserves the honor, Matron. Thank you," Sahnassa replied, giving her head a polite bow, and trying as hard as she could to keep her blush fur under control.

"I always knew you'd do well," Allilae whispered in her ear, and a pleased smile crossed the matron's expression at that exact moment. Sahnassa was stunned and nodded thanks to the kit seated beside her. She had never conceived that anyone other than perhaps her parents, sisters, and matron had ever taken notice of her or her schoolwork. Looking into Allilae's smiling silver eyes, she knew she had misjudged, and part of her was instantly saddened by the fact that her own choices and interests had taken her away from kits like Allilae who might have otherwise been her friend.

"That means a lot," Sahnassa told her quietly. "Thank you."

"Now, everyone," the matron spoke up. "We are arriving at the matriarch's keep. Needless to say, but I will just in case, that one's behavior here should be the most respectful, most attentive, and most well spoken possible. When we exit the hover, we will do so in a line, and you will follow the matron who meets us. I will follow behind you. This meeting you are about to have is an extreme privilege. The Grand Matriarch of house de Orturu does not spend more than two intervals per moon meeting with students as she is about to with you. You know how many there are in our house, so do the math and relish this opportunity. Doubtless, you will remember it for the rest of your lives."

By the time Matron Shalarra finished her speech, Sahnassa's heart was racing, and she just knew she was going to do something horrible. Taking a quick glance at Allilae, she found that kit nearly frozen with terror. "Hey, hey," Sahnassa reached out with a shaking paw. "It … will be alright. We'll … we'll be fine, okay?"

Allilae's paw gripped hers desperately. "I hope so."

A quick look around the other faces in the hover showed that all were as terrified as she. However, when she locked eyes with her matron, Shalarra winked conspiratorially, bringing Sahnassa out in a slight smile.

The hover landed, and the door opened. A subtle gesture directed at her by the matron kept Sahnassa in her seat as the others filed shyly out of the vehicle. Finally, as Allilae left ahead of them, she obeyed another gesture and preceded the matron out of the vehicle. They were entering a magnificently decorated and furnished entrance that had no less than four ceremonial guards, adorned in purple raiment. They passed by the guards nervously, and then the line was brought to a halt in front of an ornate and majestic doorway.

As they waited, Matron Shalarra leaned forward and whispered. "A bit surprised, kit?"

"Stunned, especially after … but are you okay? They … they said you fainted," Sahnassa whispered.

"Nothing all that serious. I'm old; we do that sometimes. Just an adjustment to my medication. Now listen, here's a secret about our Grand Matriarch. Don't be afraid to answer when she asks a question, and if she questions you again, just do your best to answer honestly. Don't tell her what she wants to hear; tell her the truth, as politely as you can."

"Oh my gosh, okay," Sahnassa replied, but turning around, she noticed Allilae step forward. "Thank you," she added as she began to follow the group. A soft pat on her back both moved and reassured her all at the same time. Walking through the beautiful doorway was an experience in itself, but the room beyond was greater still – warm and rich, refined and approachable, and infused with the very essence of power and authority. Antique pictures and artwork adorned walls that were recessed with alcoves containing life-sized statues of great and noble Thurians. Looking to where the others were moving, she realized that in front of an expensive-looking ottoman were a series of smaller ones arrayed in two semi-circular rows. The other students had availed themselves of the ones in the back, leaving the dead center front row the only choice for Allilae and Sahnassa.

Sahnassa glanced behind and saw that her matron now stood by the door, nodding for her to take her seat. Trying to remember everything her mother had ever said about sitting with poise and modesty and grace, Sahnassa was about to sit, but then Allilae stumbled in front of her and fell to the floor, face first. Completely forgetting everything about where she was, Sahnassa exclaimed, "Oh, my gosh!" and dashed to her friend's side as the others gasped and murmured. Allilae was already struggling to get up, her blush furs at full, her eyes full of tears – humiliated by what she had just done.

"Are you alright? Are you hurt? Please, let me," Sahnassa offered as she helped Allilae come to a sitting position.

"I'm … okay," the kit admitted, as Sahnassa gripped her paw. "I'm not used to this dress," she added quietly. "It's … so heavy."

"Now, that is something I can truly sympathize with," an elder female voice sounded kindly from in front of them. Hearing the gasps all around them, both looked up into the face of a graying black-furred female with gentle silver eyes, but it wasn't the face alone that grabbed their attention – it was the ornate, jeweled and gilded neck and shoulder-piece of the Grand Matriarch that nearly pulled the air out of their very lungs. "Are you injured, child?"

"No … no, Honored One," Allilae managed to say.

"Come on," Sahnassa whispered into the light purple ear beside her, and she guided Allilae carefully back to a standing position. "Okay?" she queried again, her paws still around the kit's back. Almost imperceptibly, Allilae nodded.

"What is your name, child?" the Grand Matriarch asked, her eyes tightening a little as she stared in Sahnassa's direction.

"I … I am Sahnassa, Honored One," she managed and bowed her head slightly, but she did not let go of Allilae's trembling frame.

"Well, Sahnassa, will you help your friend to her seat?"

"Yes, Honored One," she replied and did as she was asked, making sure that her friend was safely seated before she let her go.

As she turned back around, the Matriarch had moved towards her seat, but had not yet taken it. "Most Thurians entering into these chambers, Sahnassa, would be very concerned about the necessities of protocol and decorum. Yet I enter not only to find one youth spilled upon the floor, but another diving to the ground after her. I also find that when I enter the room and address you two … misplaced youth, you keep your focus upon your fallen friend and do not do me the appropriate honor and respect – and I really couldn't be prouder of you for that, kit! Well done. Well done."

Sahnassa felt light-headed as she smiled back at the matriarch and replied, "Thank you, Honored One. Thank you."

"Please, Sahnassa, take your seat." After she did, the matriarch looked upon the assembled group. "What you've just seen, in a microcosm, is the entire nature of family. Why are we here? To have ceremonies? To wear pretty robes? To scare the tails off of everyone we pass by because of all this jewelry? Certainly not! Anyone who lives that way or believes that is … misguided, and that's being kind. Sahnassa took care of her family, just now. When you are a member of this family, regardless of the position you are in, you are 'kept by and a keeper of' everyone else in this family. Sahnassa aided her fellow family member. What's more, her friend didn't let pride stand in the way of accepting help she needed. She *accepted* help. Sahnassa was the keeper of, and her friend was kept by. Both performed rightly. I would bet this sol, if they are not already dear friends, they might most certainly become so."

Sahnassa reached her paw over and grasped that of Allilae, who grasped back in gratitude.

The matriarch sat down and continued. "I could tell you story after story, describe familial law and honor, and every one of you sitting here will never have a better object lesson in being a part of this family than what just happened here. You will find members of our family, during your life, who have fallen on difficult circumstances, become sick, or need someone to help them out of a deep and dark depression. Do not pass them by. Do what you saw her do. This is why we have families. Now, I already know your name, Sahnassa. Why don't we get introductions from everyone else?"

For the next half interval, Sahnassa sat spellbound listening to the Grand Matriarch of her family open up whole new worlds for her, describing the negotiations between houses and the ways she had to manage the interests of the family both at home and across Thuria. Then, the matriarch had led them into the Legends Archive and invited them to explore whatever might interest them. While most of the students went down the line of statues and displays in order, Sahnassa was drawn to a large stone statue of her matriarch holding the paw of another, a Vulpi matriarch. Stepping around the statue, Sahnassa was shocked to see that a good portion of the Vulpi matriarch's beautiful tail was missing.

Sahnassa continued to slowly walk around that single statue, studying every detail. Something about it spoke to her deeply, more deeply than she could put into words. As she stopped and looked up at the two of them, she felt a presence behind her. Thinking it was Allilae, Sahnassa quietly asked, "Who is that? Do you know?"

"I should, since I am up there, as well," the matriarch replied in good humor.

"Oh sorry, Honored One!" Sahnassa apologized. "I … I thought you were one of the … well, you're not, but—"

"Her name is Saekia. Actually, by full title, she's Grand Matriarch Saekia de Khaetria. Her house has its primary estate on Ricia – lovely, lovely continent. They've had some desperate troubles there – pirates, raiders and all kinds of nasty sorts. It's … a poorer continent in some ways than Thuratan. Saekia's house isn't as strong as ours is in terms of numbers or wealth or influence, but still, she is a valuable friend."

"Forgive me, Honored One, but she looks like a dear friend of yours," Sahnassa noted with the honesty Matron Shalarra had suggested to her. "May I ask how she lost some of her tail?"

"Defending her family, Sahnassa. Think about this, if you will. She had this statue commissioned for me, as an act of thanks for our support of their house during the worst of their wars with the criminals who used to scourge them. She could have easily had the artists gloss over her missing bit of tail; she … she could have worn an extension and ordered them to blend it in, but no. What you see before you is my friend, Saekia, just as she is, and I wouldn't have her any other way."

Sahnassa looked into the matriarch's eyes as she continued. "Saekia and I met when we were young, and neither of us knew what to make of the other one, at first. She thought that I wouldn't see her as socially equal, and I admit, I was a little put off by some of their ways. I've put this statue here for one reason, and for one reason only. While it may remind us of how we came to another house's aid, it serves better as a reminder of how to be an authentic friend. Be authentically who you are and allow your friend to be who they are, missing bit of tail and all. Some of the most … wonderful and meaningful souls you will meet in your life will be found in the unlikeliest of packages. While we must hold to our family's honor, there is nothing that says we should not take risks in friendship. Sometimes, it's worth risking a little dishonor. What you might find you gain could well become worth more to you than you might ever guess. Saekia is that to me, and I to her – or so she tells me."

"I think this is now my favorite, Honored One," Sahnassa replied, looking back at the statue, smiling broadly. I … it's … just, thank you, Honored One."

"You are most welcome, kit. Most welcome," Matriarch Selena offered, and then reached around and gently embraced the surprised Sahnassa.

"What is the meaning of this, Shalarra!?" Dame Rothnerra nearly growled into the ear of the matron standing at the door of the Legends Archive watching Sahnassa and the matriarch speak almost companionably with one another.

Unperturbed, the elder matron replied calmly, "I understand, Dame, that you are newly promoted – more or less, but this activity has been common for quite some time. What about it unsettles you so?"

"You know very well, Shalarra," Rothnerra replied icily. "You've brought that disreputable kit of Gonastir and Holana to this event – an event which should be reserved for students who are displaying appropriate behaviors in their studies, not ones who appear … on the cusp of committing acts worthy of disavowal!"

"I think, perhaps, Honored Dame, that you lack a certain amount of … experience in dealing with Sahnassa. When I heard of the incident and saw the pictures, I saw our little kit in a position she'd never been in before, and yes, she was having reactions she shouldn't have had. I also know that her mother has been slow to warn her children about such things, and prepare them – a fact I reminded Holana of when I spoke to her."

"A young kit should know, Shalarra, not to—"

"If you don't mind, Dame Rothnerra," Shalarra replied, annoyed, turning towards the dame. "I would prefer you use my name more sparingly. I am not a little kit that you can terrify with your bluster and bullying. At my age, there's little left to fear, and certainly not from a dame that can't seem to understand that the young make mistakes. That is when we teach them, and they are most apt to listen. You ripped apart her heart, Rothnerra. You injured one of our family unnccccssarily, one of mine, and it's not the first time you've overreacted. The other matrons who report to you are also growing tired of this … attitude of yours. It will not be tolerated forever … Honored … Dame."

"You forget your place," the dame replied quietly, stewing at having been spoken to in such a way by a subordinate.

"Look there, at the two of them." Rothnerra did, and her jaw dropped. The Grand Matriarch and the disreputable Sahnassa were hugging. "Tell me now that your judgment isn't flawed. I will not be alive to see it, I'm sure, but something tells me that one sol you will look back upon this moment realizing that you saw two matriarchs embracing one another."

"I would expect the color of my very fur to suddenly change before that happened!" Rothnerra nearly spat and left the room.

"Oh, we can only hope," Matron Shalarra retorted dryly.

"Are you okay?" Ash asked the quietly shivering Vanarra, still in his arms. It had been intervals; some of that time, she had been able to talk, confess how far down the pain went, and sometimes she nearly wailed – inconsolable. She had looked into his eyes after she bared her soul's pain and expected him to push her away, dismiss what she had said, but every time she looked up into his eyes, she saw only understanding and shared pain.

"Not ... really," she admitted. "I ... guess I haven't been okay my entire life. You ... you don't have to do this. You don't have to stay."

"I'd be completely heartless if I didn't stay with you right now," he stated firmly. "Have you ever talked to anyone about these things before?"

"Never," she whispered, looking away. "I ... couldn't stop myself, Ash. It all just ... came out." She rolled out of his grasp and looked at him, not truly understanding why he was still there. "And you ... listened to it all. Why?"

"You needed me to," he replied at a whisper. "I have known others, at the orphanage, who hurt, and they came to me and talked, but I've never met anyone who had so much hidden deep inside of them."

"I ... never meant to tell you all that. You ... you have to be so tired," she reached up and stroked the side of his muzzle.

"I can't tell you why, Van, but for some reason, I feel like doing that for you – just listening – was the most important thing I've ever done or ... ever will."

"Oh, Ash..." she breathed. "I ... I feel so ... broken inside. I'm ... not even the same Vanarra I was when I crawled into here with you. I'm ... not sure of a lot."

Despite himself, the Lupar-Perratti yawned, and then apologized, "I'm sorry."

"S'okay," she replied, smiling at him. "You need to rest. You've had a … difficult sol."

"Not so bad," he offered, taking her paw and holding it in his. "I … I haven't finished my bed yet."

"There's room on mine, and … I need someone close to me, Ash. I … I've been alone for … so long." Without any hesitation, Ashalam laid down beside her, lying on his back next to her – his paw in hers. "You are the best thing I've ever found."

"You are the best thing ever to find me," he replied, and with his free paw, reached over and turned off the light.

The next evening, Vanarra woke up, Ash still lying beside her, quietly sleeping. It had been difficult trying to sleep – her mind was so raw from what had just happened, this immense catharsis that had left her soul utterly naked in front of this comparative stranger. He knew everything about her, details vomited out of a sick spirit that had been unable to purge itself, just trying to stay alive. Ashalam had every reason to abandon her, belittle her, or shun her for what Vanarra had confessed. He didn't; he was just there, lying beside her. Ash needed her – that was easy to parse from his actions and what he said, but he looked at her in a way that wasn't tolerant or threatening or anything negative. It was a little like how her mother looked at her.

Not fully knowing what she was doing, Vanarra rolled onto her side and faced him, he lying on his back. Glancing over his body at the clock beyond, she realized that in a few intervals, they would need to begin preparing for the night's activities. In the soft amber light from the clock, she could see his body outlined in the darkness, his chest rising and falling in regular, slow waves. From her romance novels, she understood how much males loved physical intimacy and the affections of a female willingly given. Something inside was driving her to reach out for him, for her to place her paw gently on his chest, stroke him and touch him.

She could tell from the change in his breathing that he was waking, but slowly, not at a startle. Finally, his breathing stopped for a moment, and his body tensed in fear. "Don't worry, Ash. It's just me."

"Van … Vanarra? What … what are you doing?"

"Waking you up, hopefully in a way that's not too … disturbing for you," she breathed quietly.

"It's … really … amazing … actually," Ash replied softly, and he made no move to stop her. After a few moments, he ventured, "Van, do you … like me?"

She made an affirmative sound in her throat and shuffled up closer alongside of him. "Why shouldn't I, for how kind you were to me? I know I'm not the most … attractive Thurian, being a mix-up and all—"

"Van, you're gorgeous!" he exclaimed, and sat up to look at her in the pale amber light. "You're so beautiful! I'm the one who should apologize! I'm a real mess – my fur's matted, I haven't washed in—"

She put her paw alongside his muzzle and cheek, gently cradling Ash; it was a gesture of affection that instantly silenced him. "Not after tonight," she asserted. "I'll take care of you, make sure you have enough food and help you stay clean. All that … stuff isn't important when you are already wonderfully keen in the most important way."

"What's that?"

She leaned in close, put her head right alongside his and breathed, "Rahnahi says you have a beautiful soul, Ashalam. The most … beautiful soul I've ever met." Very gently, remembering the advice from the romance novels, she tentatively licked him on the side of his muzzle. Ash's reaction was instinctive, like he had been shocked, and he sucked in a fierce breath of air. "Come on, now. Let's get our sol started. We have a lot to take care of tonight, including you."

Vanarra started to get up, but he put his paw right where hers had been, and she found herself equally transfixed. "Vanarra, you're a miracle, and … I'll do whatever I can to help you work through everything. I will." She felt the warm-moist feeling of his tongue lap the side of her muzzle, grazing across her lips, and the same, stunned gasp came from her. The stirring of her emotions again touched deep and painful memories, and although his touch had been kind, she realized that this level of intimacy was just about as far as she could go. She gently reached around and hugged him, and he hugged her back.

"Come on, Ash. One lesson you learn here is that no matter how … nice a distraction may be, the clock doesn't stop and wait for you. We've got to get ready."

"Okay, Van," he replied and reached over and turned on the light.

"Ash," she told him, "don't ever think you aren't keen. Those Perratti and Lupar who look at you in disgust. It's not disgust – it's envy. You got the best bits of them both."

His smile was all the thanks she could have hoped for.

Chapter 7: Tragedy

Gonastir shook his head as he entered his daughter's room, "It's only two intervals to high night, Sahnassa,"

"Sorry. I'm … just trying to work out how to merge these two files so I can complete my assignment."

"When is it due?" he asked walking over to her and looking at the display. "By the moons, I can't make ears or tails out of that! It looks so … random."

"It is a mess," she chuckled, "but it does have a pattern – it's just a very long pattern. I wanted to get it out of the way tonight, but it's not due for two more sols."

"Is that because we're going to the coast for our vacation?" he asked, kindly.

"Yes. I don't want to have to cram this in when we get back."

"I understand. Kit, would you mind if I asked you a question?"

"It's fine," Sahnassa breathed. "I need to take a break anyway."

Gonastir sat on the bed and looked at his middle daughter. It was a subject he had been wanting to broach with her for some time, and now seemed as good a time as any. "Kit, you're really putting your heart into these … computer classes, and I appreciate that you really enjoy them, but … you're in tertiary school now. You need to start thinking very hard about lining yourself up on the track of a good academy and a career that could bring you honor and respect."

Instantly, Sahnassa knew where this conversation was going; it wasn't unlike the one she had with her mother a moon ago. In some way, she was surprised that the two of them hadn't talked and cornered her together. "Dad, it's perfectly possible to gain honor and respect as a technologist."

"Fixing other Thurian's issues," he replied dismissively, "just so they can do real work – the work that gets noticed, the work that gets appreciated and honored. What's the difference between a technologist and say … a plumber or maybe even an electrician? No one sets the destiny of a house as a technologist, Sahnassa. You've got a better mind than that! You've started to develop the right connections and at the highest levels! You're the only one from our family to be directly requested to attend the Grand Matriarch on two occasions. Can't you understand the kind of influence you could wield and at such a young age?"

"In the end, Father, isn't it my decision? Why can't I just choose the career that suits me? I've made plenty of my classmates happy by what I've done for them – my teachers, too! I've … won awards; even the matriarch is interested in what I'm doing. She asks me about it—"

"Now, *that* I understand," Gonastir replied sternly, "because there are hardly any technologists in all of de Orturu! Kit, have you wondered why that is?"

Sahnassa was now angry at her father, and she snapped back, "Is that because all of the fathers and mothers in de Orturu won't allow their kits and cubs to do what makes them happy?!"

The fur on Gonastir's back went up. "Now you listen to me, you impudent little kit! Mothers and fathers in de Orturu give a damn about their children's futures, more than you can say for any … Vulpi house!" The comment stung Sahnassa, since her current instructor was a Vulpi who had been very kind to her. "We understand the way this world works, far better than a kit who can't even count twenty seasons of her own life! I've seen how technologists work, stuffed in cramped little pens – even at the most senior levels! Their destinies are controlled by individuals with not even half their education or intelligence, and what grand accomplishment comes from their labors, eh? A new financial accounting system – oh, well that is sure to stir the world, yes!" he mocked.

"You're not being fair!"

"I'm not being fair, right," he agreed fiercely. "I'm being accurate! Technologists are seen as … odd, socially dysfunctional is the kind word for it. They don't attract the best mates, and they certainly don't bring honor to the family. If you're so desperate to underachieve, you should just give up studying and be a fur dresser—"

"Dad! That's so not the case!" Sahnassa interjected. "My counselors at school are telling me that if I continue my studies at academy—"

"You are most certainly not going to study video games at an academy I'm paying for! And who are these vaunted counselors, anyway? How much stock am I to put in someone working at an academy who isn't even teaching?!" he shouted angrily.

Sahnassa, at that point, just backed away from her father and sat on the bed. "You've already decided. Why ask me to make a choice when you've already chosen for me?" Her voice wasn't raised, and much to her credit, she had calmed down. Looking up at her father, her face was a mask of disappointment – not in his decision, but in him. That, more than anything, stopped him from escalating the argument any further. "Dad, I have no desire to do what you or Mom do. It's not that I don't respect you for it. This–" she said, pointing to the computer with her open paw. "It's who I am. It's where my heart is. It's where I can make a good living. It may not be … as honorable, but Triana and Hylea both want to follow you and Mom – isn't that enough?"

"You have the ear of the Grand Matriarch of our family, child! Doesn't that mean anything to you?" her father asked, frustrated.

"The ear of the matriarch is good, but … I couldn't live under the eyes of our dame. I … just couldn't," Sahnassa admitted, looking away from her father. "I'd have to intern with the dame, our dame, to – she hates me, Dad! My matron likes me, and even the matriarch, but our dame clearly doesn't, and even if she did – I'm … sorry, my heart isn't in those things."

"It's such a waste, Sahnassa," Gonastir said in resignation. "When I think of what you could do, kit; it's just such a waste. I'll leave you to your … choice." With that, he quietly walked out of the room and closed the door, leaving Sahnassa to sigh and try to get herself back into the frame of mind she needed to finish her work.

Ashalam woke early, by Vanarra's estimation, given the "night" the two of them had together, and Vanarra reached out and interlaced her paw fingers with his. It had been nearly two seasons since she had first invited the scruffy looking mix of Perratti and Lupar to join her in her secret lair within the archive, and although she had been somewhat worried about taking someone into her confidence, she found Ash to be every bit as trustworthy as she could have hoped for. Throughout her entire period of knowing him, she had never had cause to doubt his motives. That trust, after a certain amount of time, began to weave itself into something else.

While Vanarra was content to live within the confines of the archive, Ash pulled Vanarra out into Shanandrae – extending their stays outside of the isolation of the Pinnacle Center basement. While she had taught him so much about how to survive undetected within their shared home, he had done as much for her on the outside. Although he was as much an outcast as she, he had lived more in the world, been sent on errands, met other Thurians, and even come to know a few purebred who seemed to actually accept and like him. While they weren't willing or able to give him a job that paid anything, he hadn't had any shyness about promoting Vanarra to his contacts. The pair had helped move boxes onto a hover when a warehouse was running low on staff, and they had even helped a somewhat crass old caterer get his storage area cleaned up. This, they had done exceptionally well on, largely because of Ash's newly developed ability to read – a gift from the patient Vanarra who happily took his education on as her own assignment.

In every way, their lives had started weaving together. Ash's shyness about matters of intimacy helped keep their progress very slow, slow enough for Vanarra not to feel threatened by the ghosts of her nightmare rape-matings. He loved her, just loved being close to her, taking care of her, and she enjoyed taking care of him. It had only been very recently that their contact had become lovingly and sensually intimate. Ever since she had first taken him in, in every way, he had been healing her; the first painful flood of confession had been followed each new sol by some other admission. Now that they had consummated their love for one another, Van had been granted another gift from him – the ability to appreciate sexual intimacy without fear. As she held his paw, Vanarra felt complete and content for the very first time, and her dreams of walking out of the archive one sol into a life of independence were gone now – she always wanted to be dependent on him, wherever she was.

"You alright?" she asked as she felt him tense up.

"A little out of sorts, that's all," he grunted, wincing a bit.

"I wasn't that much of a paw-ful, was I?"

He chuckled, "Oh, you were a paw-ful, alright – two very full and firm ones, actually. No, this has been bothering me for a few sols, just a bit, ever since I was punched."

Vanarra scowled at that reminder. One of the teen purebred who also worked the back-dock – she was disavowed, Vanarra thought – had come up to Ash and punched him hard in his lower gut for no good reason at all. A fierce claw-raking had been the Vulpi's reward, courtesy of Vanarra, and she ran away in need of many stitches. Ash had been doubled over for nearly a quarter interval, and it had been difficult for him to move again, but finally, with some kindness offered by the store owner, they were able to give him some drugs and make him able to walk.

"I'm still not sorry for what I did to that damned bitch," Vanarra spat. Then, her mood turned lighter as she rolled over on her side. "It certainly didn't seem to slow you down at all, you rabid prowler. You ... dear Ash ... were amazing!"

Turning on the light and looking at her, he smiled and said, "No, kit, you are amazing." Vanarra reached out and stroked the side of his muzzle, but something about his appearance made her concerned. The color of his nose and lips seemed to be a bit off, just a bit paler than they should be. "What's wrong?"

"You look a little ... tired. Say, why don't you leave the scrounge to me tonight. Just rest here. Who knows, that damned purebred Vulpi may have actually hurt you in some way. I'll break out a couple of quick meals for us so you can relax, and it will give us a good, hot meal tonight."

"Sounds nice. I am ... pretty tired. I thought it was the male who was supposed to do most of the work during mating, though," he leaned over towards her and winced a little, but he still made her smile.

"You are so good to me. I ... wasn't afraid that way. Thank you," she stated softly.

"My pleasure, surely," he replied tenderly and kissed her.

Instantly, she backed away. "Ugh, Ash! Your breath! Okay, I'm hitting the vending machine up for those mouth freshening things, too."

"Alright, just be careful, okay?" She leaned over and kissed him on top of the head, and then she got up, ready to begin her nightly chores.

Two intervals later, Vanarra had made good progress on those chores in the archive, emptying the buckets, gathering the food from the coolers, as well as some spare change from the donations. She was worried about Ash but tried to reassure herself that he had performed so very well earlier, that he couldn't be that bad off. She was just about to take the steps up to the second level to grab another language book for Ash, when she heard his pleading voice calling to her through the vents in the children's section.

"Ash?!" she replied, suddenly afraid at how he sounded. Darting back down to the vents, and pulling them open, she actually yelled back to him, something she never would dare before. "Ash! Are you okay?!"

"No! I … I'm really … I'm really sick, Van! I … I … something's wrong!"

Vanarra's pulse, which had already been quickening at his tone, now started racing, and so did she. Scurrying through the vents and finding the entrance to their lair, she found him hanging in the opening, his nose and lips much paler than they were before. "I've … I've been throwing up, and … my insides are just – they hurt Van, they really hurt! It's … it's getting worse." His eyes, sad and afraid, were all the confirmation she needed.

"Take my paw, love," she told him, and carefully they both hauled him into the vent so he could lay on his back. "Now, stay here. I'm going to get the stashes and get you some clothes, and then I'm taking you to a hospital. I've got to get you to the transport stop in the next … oh, mange, it's like half an interval before the last one. It goes by Shanandrae Commons Hospital, though. We'll take you there. Okay?"

"Okay, Van. I'm … sorry; I'm so sorry," he told her, wincing again in pain and clutching his abdomen.

"Hey, you're worth everything to me, Ash, please! Don't apologize. I'll be back in a tick." She nuzzled him for a moment and then nearly jumped through the opening and almost ran through her lair grabbing things on instinct. Taking one last look around, she closed the lid of the bucket Ash had been using, turned off the light, and went as quickly as she could to rejoin him.

After resealing the entrance to their lair, she helped him dress in soft clothes, and they slowly made their way out of the vent. As they were working their way out of the children's section, Ashalam fell to his knees and started retching, streams of rancid vomit coming from his muzzle. Vanarra tried her best to help him, knowing that he was doing something that would be discovered. Finally, he recovered enough to move again, apologizing all the while.

Looking at him, Vanarra realized how desperate his situation was, and a circuitous trip out the side entrance and through the forest wasn't going to do. Taking him forward towards the main entrance, she stopped to let him rest at the donations box. Looking at it, and realizing that they might need what it held, she pulled off the cover and shoved the entire contents into her bag.

"Why … why are you doing that?" he asked, confused.

"Because we might need money to get you taken care of, and right now I don't care about anything more than you – not even this place," she asserted as she almost threw the box's cover back on.

"You are wonderful, Vanarra. More than anyone could ever deserve," he told her earnestly, but then grunted in pain and clutched his lower abdomen.

She rushed to his side and supported him. "Come on, love. You're too wonderful to be in this kind of pain. Let's get you taken care of." With that, she helped him to the front entrance, and the two left the Pinnacle Center Archive together.

"I … didn't hear an alarm," he grunted as they made it down the walk to the hover trail.

"You won't. It's an exit door. However, I'm sure they probably recorded it or something."

"They'll be … ugh … looking for who was in the archive, Van," he said as they made slow progress.

"They won't find the lair. I made sure of that before I left. We may have to wait for them to let down their guard again, but we can just hide out somewhere else until then. Don't talk. Let's just focus on making it to the transport stop, okay?"

"Okay. Thank you, Van," he offered, hugging her around the shoulder.

The wait at the transport stop wasn't more than a few passes, but Vanarra was steadily growing more worried. Ash's pains were growing more intense, and he seemed to be getting weaker, curling up into a ball on the bench.

When the transport arrived, she saw the driver and didn't recognize her, but saw the instant look of worry on the Nephti's face. Vanarra reached into her pocket and drew out some of the money she had appropriated, with her paws open, offered it up. The driver stopped and cracked open the door. "What do you want?"

"Please, my friend is very sick, and … I need to get him to the hospital. I'm begging you! I'll pay anything; just help us!"

The Nephti looked at Van and then at the form of Ash lying on the bench, holding his guts. "Bring him to the door, first."

Vanarra nodded and darted back, helping Ash up onto his hind paws. When the pretty gray Nephti saw him in the lights of the transport, she immediately opened the door, her dark blue eyes wide and her expression nearly horrified. "Oh mange, there's no way he's shamming that! Come on! Get in! I don't have anyone else on the route right now, so I'll take you straight to Shanandrae Commons, okay?"

"Bless you!" Ash groaned, looking up into her eyes, and instantly, the transport driver was out of her seat and helping Vanarra get him aboard.

As she belted back into her seat, the driver noticed that her new passengers were trying to shuffle to the rear of the transport. "Hey, you don't have to go back there! Have him lie down on one of these! It will be more comfortable, okay?" Stunned, Vanarra looked at the purebred and nodded. "I'm taking my bus off duty so I can get you there quicker." The Nephti then turned around, picked up her TransCom, and called into her dispatch station indicating she had a sick patron aboard who needed immediate transport. Although her station manager tried to convince her to wait for emergency services, the Nephti wasn't having any of it, and from the reply, the station manager trusted her judgment. "Okay, we're clear! I'm taking you to the hospital."

Van found it difficult to speak, and she looked at Ash who was likewise surprised they were being treated so well. "Thank … thank you. Who are you, if I may ask, please?"

"My name's Sorla de Dothnar. What's yours, kit?" the driver replied, obviously used to having conversations over her shoulder.

"Vanarra Anasto," she answered before she knew what she was doing. Belatedly, she realized that if someone from the archive reported a break in, the driver might well be in a position to identify her and the fact she held a large sum of money up to convince the driver to stop.

"And your friend?"

"His name ... is Ash," Van replied.

"Just relax, you two. I'll get you there in five passes," Sorla called back to them, and with the hover trails clear ahead, the Nephti pushed the transport faster and faster.

As she held Ash's paw, Vanarra felt him grasp hard as a wave of pain overcame him. "I'm here, Ash. I'm here. Hold on."

When the pain subsided, he looked up at her and said, "You're ... you're always watching over me. I ... I love you for that, you know?"

"I love you, too," Van whispered in his ear. "I'd do anything for you. Even risk jail ... risk my life." He nodded slowly, looking into her eyes with a longing that made tears fall from hers and onto her cheek fur. Paw-in-paw, the two rode as the Nephti took them towards their only hope, Shanandrae Commons Hospital.

"I'm sorry I can't get you closer," Sorla called out to them, worried. "My transport won't fit in there."

"It's close enough," Van replied. "Come on, Ash. Let's go." With a groan, he was able to come to his hind-paws and stumble forward with her help. Sorla came to his other side and helped them down to the ground.

"I ... I hope he'll be alright," the Nephti said sincerely, sounding worried, herself. Although it was difficult for her to let go of Ash, Vanarra left him holding onto a signpost and walked back to the driver. Reaching around, she quickly embraced the Nephti, who readily accepted the action.

"Thank you. You've ... been far kinder to us than any purebred I've ever known."

"The best compliment I've heard. Please, Vanarra. Go get your friend taken care of." The two released, and even Ash waved at the Nephti before again accepting Van's assistance to begin the walk to the hospital's emergency entrance.

Several intervals later, Vanarra watched helplessly as Ash languished in an Anati waiting room, filled with others wounded or in pain. They had been ushered into the foul-smelling space almost immediately upon entering. The Vulpi desk clerk who saw them took nothing more than the barest details of Ash's problem before dismissing them. There was no mistaking the double-standard – a crowded Anati waiting room full of the suffering and a purebred lounge that seemed more like a luxurious hotel lobby than an emergency ward. As Vanarra had held Ash's paw and shoulder as he groaned in pain, she had watched the single doorway to see if anyone came in. Twenty five passes went by, and then twenty five more, and still no one – either Anati or purebred – crossed that threshold.

"Oh, Van ... Van I'm going to be sick again," Ash whispered, and quickly Vanarra ran for the waste bin. She made it back to him with no time to spare, and again he was spewing the vile smelling contents of his digestive system until nothing was left but crying and dry heaving all at the same time. She cried, too, feeling as helpless as the time she was rapemated. The other Anati simply turned away, unwilling or afraid to help.

When he finally recovered enough to sit up, she cleaned his muzzle the best she could with the rags she had brought. Looking at him, panting for breath and his muzzle streaked with tears broke her heart. "Oh, Ash, I'd ... I'd do anything if it could be me and not you going through this."

"It's ... not that fun, actually. I ... I'm glad you're not, love," he whimpered, trying to smile.

"This place," Vanarra cried, shaking her head. "It's supposed to be a hospital, but there isn't one grain of mercy here at all! Being ... Anati shouldn't make you disposable."

"We know that. I wish they did," he replied, sobbing. She wrapped her arms around him and held him. Finally, the door opened, and a young male Lupar doctor looked in as if he had been sent there as punishment. Quickly, he pointed at an Anati mother and a kit with a bandaged head and ordered them out.

Vanarra was starting to get angry and loose her inhibitions against confronting the hospital staff. "Can I leave you for just a moment? I ... I want to go dump this and get you some water, okay?"

"Yes. Thank you, love," he said, but she looked, and he was already clutching his stomach again.

"I'll be quick. I'll ... find someone. Hold on."

He nodded, and she was away carrying the wastebasket. Not two steps out of the room, she was met by an orderly. "Where are you going?"

Angry, she shoved the rancid container in his face, forcing him to step back. "I'm going to dump this and get some water for my friend, okay?"

Coughing, his eyes watering, he didn't answer her but did step back out of the way. Vanarra stalked through the refined and comfortable purebred waiting area to their restrooms before anyone could stop her. With the door locked, she ignored the insistent knocking of the nurse demanding she leave the restroom immediately. Dumping and rinsing the basket, using the toilet, and filling a water bottle she had in her bag, she finally exited when the security guard started banging on the door.

"What were you doing in there?" the Pantera officer demanded.

"Dumping out vomit, using the bathroom, and getting water; that's all!" she pleaded as he grabbed her and pulled her away towards the exit of the building. "Please, no! My friend's dying in there! He … he needs me!"

She pulled back so hard that he actually stumbled and lost his balance. Losing his grip for a moment, Vanarra slipped away from him and darted back towards the waiting room, but another guard grabbed her roughly at the shoulder and stopped her. "Please … don't you have a heart?" she begged, looking up into a stern Lupar's expression. "I love him, and he's so very sick. Please!"

"Wait here and don't move. If you move, I will throw you out myself." While the two guards conferred about her fate, Vanarra had the opportunity to see into the emergency area. Save for one room where the curtain was pulled, nothing was happening. Purebred nurses were gathered around one another in a group, talking and laughing softly while one told a story about having to shave the tip of her tail on a dare. In the corner, a Vulpi doctor was asleep on a chair, scratching his nose. The purebred waiting room was completely empty. Inside of her, she hated every one of these purebloods for ignoring the suffering happening not twenty tracks away.

The Lupar was in her face again. "Go back into the waiting room, and wait until someone calls you."

"You mean *if* someone calls us," she muttered, but started walking. The Lupar followed right behind her until she was completely back in the waiting room. After that, she didn't care where he was; she couldn't find Ash. Stepping around, she found him laying on the floor at the hind paws of several other Anati, curled up into a ball, clutching his stomach, moaning. "Ash! Tell me what's happening."

She knelt beside him, and he answered, "I'm … like ripping inside … apart. Hurts … so much! Oh mange, Vanarra! If … I don't make it, please promise me, promise me! Ugh, ow! Ugh. Promise me that you won't stay and hide in the archive," he whispered intently, straining hard to say the words as the pain racked his body. "Promise me you'll leave, live in the outside world, bloom like … oh … oh … the flower you are! Promise me, Van! Please!"

"Ash, anything, but … please don't leave me, please don't!"

"I … would stay if I could, love–" he started, but then his mouth went wide open in a horrified scream, and then his eyes rolled back into his head. He collapsed in her arms, just as an angry Faelnar doctor burst into the waiting room.

"What is the cause of all this damned noise!?"

Vanarra shouted back at him with even more fury. "My friend's dying because you won't help him! He says his insides are ripping apart! We've been here for intervals and intervals and no one has helped! All of you are just willing to let him die here, while you've got an empty waiting room out there, nurses gossiping, and doctor's sleeping in corners! Haven't you any pity at all?! Even for lowly Anati?"

The doctor just stared at her for a moment and the still form of Ash she was holding in her arms who seemed to be barely breathing. Slowly, he stepped forward, knelt, and looked at Ash's mouth and nose. "How … how long has he—"

"Ten intervals since he called out to me in … our lair," she told him, sobbing.

"I'll … I'll go get someone," he replied, his own nose and lips looking a little pale in shock.

"Hold on, Ash, love, please," Vanarra pleaded, leaning over him. "Hold on. Help's coming, love. Please stay."

In a few moments, two orderlies worked their way through the two sets of doors and gently came for Ash. They lifted him off of Vanarra's lap, and slowly, Ash's paw unclasped from her own, limp and lifeless. A Vulpi nurse came in behind them, just as they were turning to leave, and as Vanarra tried to follow the pair carrying Ash, the nurse held up her paw. "No. You stay, Anati. You stay here. We'll tell you when there is something you need to know."

Vanarra stepped forward and stared at her, her back fur up and her claws expressing of their own accord. "You listen to me, you arrogant, heartless purebred – you had better do everything you can to save him, because if he dies, nothing will save you!"

Shocked and afraid, the Vulpi backed out of the room and left. All of the other Anati looked at her, some with shock, some with fear, and some with approval.

Vanarra then sat, sick with worry, for more than six intervals. At six and a half, the two big orderlies came back into the room, followed by the Faelnar doctor who had come in earlier. When they turned towards her, something in her knew. "No! No! He's ... dead? Oh, please! Please no!" she cried, standing up, and the orderlies instantly moved to restrain her, grabbing her by the arms.

As she struggled in their grip, crying, the doctor explained with only a trace of sympathy. "The damage was too severe. There was nothing we could do." Vanarra collapsed, howling and crying with soul-rending grief; the only thing keeping her on her hind paws were the strong arms of the orderlies holding her fast. "I ... it ... if you had only–" When he said that, Vanarra stopped crying and looked up at him with a look that seemed to shatter his purebred pretense of superiority. In that moment, the doctor's heart was touched with just enough of the searing pain she was experiencing, that he did something that was almost never done for an Anati – he apologized. "I'm ... so very sorry. It ... wasn't your fault."

"Can I see him?" she whispered intensely.

Again, the doctor knew what was coming and turned away, unwilling to have his heart lanced a second time. "They've already disposed of the body. Again, I'm ... sorry."

Against the horrified and soul-torn cries issuing from behind him, he turned away, unwilling to look back. As she watched him leave, Vanarra could only weep. After the door closed, one of the two Pantera holding her said, "Because you threatened a nurse, you are being evicted from the hospital grounds. We'll have enforcement outside. Don't make this worse by trying to come back in here and do something stupid, Anati."

Harshly with little mercy or concern, the orderlies hauled her up and crammed her into the space between the two doors where three Lupar security guards reached in and again, roughly and painfully, took hold of her and nearly dragged her out of the hospital's emergency ward. Not content to simply shove her out the door, they escorted her for nearly five passes until they were well past the hospital's main vehicle entrance. There, they shoved her to the ground and stepped away.

As Vanarra, broken and hurting, looked back up into their eyes, all three of them drew their stun prods and held them at the ready. In the pre-morning darkness, the mixed blood was forced to pick herself up, take hold of her bag, and slowly walk away, crying and calling out to her lost love, begging that what had just happened wasn't so.

It had been a stupid decision, diving in front of one of the other whisk players, trying to prevent a goal. Sahnassa had been goaded into it by one of the others in the dame's social sol – a large outdoor gathering which supposedly was to create cohesion and foster connections within the families affiliated to Dame Rothnerra. It was very clear to the young would-be technologist exactly what the sol was for, namely putting the young on display for the dame to consider. It was a pointless exercise, but still smarting from her father's comments, Sahnassa had decided to try her best.

Technologists, however, did not appear to make the best whisk players, and the daughter of Gonastir was no exception. She was almost comically left behind as others bobbed and moved across the field, pounding away after the lumpy spheroid which was the object of the game. After a few sets and being called down by the official for making an improper move, she had been sidelined in the penalty area – the only one of the team who had. Other than giving her blush furs a good airing, her time there had been useful in that she was finally able to objectively view the game and pick up on the underlying processes and systems required to score a goal, and when the official waved her clear, Sahnassa was far better educated and started to contribute more effectively.

That was when she had taken things just a little too far and found herself doubled up, the breath knocked out of her, and her ribs aching from being kicked in the chest by an opponent's hind paws. She had given her team the goal, putting them ahead, but Sahnassa had to be removed from the field via stretcher and was now resting in Shanandrae Commons Hospital, Gonastir having a friend and contact who worked in the emergency services. As Sahnassa listened to his lecture after she had been released to her hospital room for the night, she realized that her father hadn't taken her to the family hospital because he was embarrassed by her. More than the aches in her chest, that hurt. "There's no way I can make him happy anymore," she said to herself after he left her.

All alone in the room, she was sad and bored. The doctor told her she would likely be released in the morning, but interval by painful interval, she'd just have to ache her way through the night. The hospital VidStar was about what she expected – poor, and she had been told that the hospital gift shop and library were already closed. So, with some inane show about family procedural law softly gibbering away on the screen, the Nephti slowly pulled her way out of bed and made it to the window. Opening it, she looked out onto the peaceful grounds of the facility. A clear night, lit by only the trail lamps along the hover path, spread out before her almost completely devoid of any movement. Glancing over at the clock, she knew why – it was only a few intervals until morning.

Every now and again, she'd hear the alert siren of an evacuation hover, but they would silence themselves at the edge of the property and come in quiet, without so much as their lights blinking or flashing. She couldn't see directly into the emergency entrance area from her vantage point on the third level, but still, it was something to watch.

Eventually, her eye caught a Thurian, a female by the look of her, wandering slowly away from the hospital. The light was too poor to see anything more than a silhouette, but good enough to see that this individual was either in great grief or horribly ill. What's more, others passing by her on the path ignored her, walked the other way as she fell to her forepaws and knees, crying – the heaving of her back and body and the set of her tail easily making that all too discernable.

"Why doesn't anybody stop and help her?!" Sahnassa thought to herself, angrily. If her whole upper body weren't aching with every movement and she had more than a skimpy and embarrassing medical gown to wear, she knew she would quit her room and go to the side of this poor individual. "It's just … decency!" Shaking her head and feeling a tear slip from her eye, she watched as the tortured soul slowly made her way down the path, disappearing behind a hedgerow after more than twenty passes, dawn still more than an interval away. "The coldest, darkest part of the night," she thought. "Whoever you are, I … I hope it gets better for you. I truly hope it does."

Saddened and disappointed in Thurians as a whole at that moment, Sahnassa turned away from the window and slowly made her way back to the bed.

Vanarra ached in every possible way, and she barely felt alive. Ash's loss felt like it had ripped away half of her own soul, even her desire to keep on living. "What's the point?" she had cried into the dawn, seated on a bench by the hover trail. Now, she knew it only took one sickness, and then she would be dead. She had been sick before, very sick, but Ash had taken care of her. Together, the two of them had discovered she had Altian-B, and she had been miserable but had made it through. What happened to Ash, however, was horrifying. Not more than a sol ago, they had been making love, and now his body had been "disposed of." She had to get away from that horrible building. A part of her feared seeing Ash's lifeless corpse atop a pile of trash as the garbage hover removed the detritus of the night.

As she crouched in their usual spot, waiting for the garbage hover, a part of her wanted to mount the hover and then purposely not get off when the spar retracted – simply end it. Ash's last request of her begged she didn't, begged she keep on going. "Dammit Ash, I'd give anything to be where you are right now, to be with you," she said mournfully, but she was brought up short as two enforcement hovers arrived, parking to either side of the hover lot. "Oh, great," she groaned and slipped further back into the bushes.

A few passes later, the garbage carrier arrived, and the Lupar enforcement officers exited their hovers. They motioned the driver to land, and he did, stepping out of the vehicle presenting all of the proper identifications. Vanarra watched with a growing sense of dread as the driver walked the pair around his vehicle. Finally, the driver stepped back into the cab and extended the thruster spars. Then, he rejoined the officers at the rear of the vehicle and started pointing to places Vanarra knew all too well. "Oh, no. Please, Ash, not this, too!" Vanarra begged silently.

One of the officers slid under the vehicle and then, after a moment, reemerged nodding, motioning for the other officer to try it. Soon, both officers had walked some distance away from the truck and had a private conversation – nearly on top of Vanarra. "It's possible," one said. "I wouldn't have believed it, but it's possible."

"Well, security cameras don't lie. You can clearly see two figures dart out from behind the garbage hover when it lands in the archive's parking deck. I wonder if this was the first time."

"Don't know," the first replied, "but whoever they were, they made a right mess of the archive. One of them yacked in the floor, and another seems to have knocked over the donations container."

"Do you think the driver is at fault?"

"No, I don't think so. He says he's reported the problem before, thought he spotted some mixed bloods dropping back behind him and then disappearing. No; they can't blame him for sloppy procedure. They weren't even checking their own camera recordings, and they're supposed to be archivists!"

They both chuckled before the other asked, "So, what's the fix?"

"Well, they'll install some more security cameras here and tap them right into the enforcement net. Also, after this sol, they're bringing in an upgraded trash hauler. That one has fixed spars and no place to catch a ride. This is going to be a one-time deal, one way or the other."

"Yeah, I'll bet the archive is going to put some new cameras in, too."

"The director said as much to the investigators before they left. That place will have tighter security than de Caterra's home estate. Shall we give the driver the good news?"

"Yeah, sure. Poor guy looks like he's about to have a fit."

As the two walked away, another huge rip ran down Vanarra's soul. Her love was dead, and now, her lair was unreachable. In her desperation to save her love, she'd lost everything. Save for the small amount of currency she still held, and her second pair of clothes, Vanarra Anasto had nothing left. Unable to do anything more than hurt and weep, the poor mixed blood stayed in the bushes, wishing that something or someone would come and finally end her misery.

Hoping that the officers were wrong, Vanarra eventually made her way to the forest surrounding the archive, feeling like her very soul was bleeding onto the ground as she approached. Sure enough, the outside of the archive was literally crawling with Vulpi contractors, installing external cameras, putting up a pass system to the parking garage, and pulling up any shrubbery that could have offered concealment. As she worked her way behind the archive, she even saw a pair of lock specialists working on the door she had originally used to enter the vents, seasons ago. It was done; she knew she had lost her home.

As night was falling, she wandered along the far edge of the forest, not truly knowing where she was or having any direction. Without really meaning to, the exhausted and distraught Vulpi-Faelnar returned to the exact transport stop she and Ash had been at less than a full sol ago. Sitting upon the bench, she folded herself into a ball and wept as so many regrets and sorrows came along side of her. "I ... I should have protected him better, kept that damned walking piece of crap from hitting him! Oh, Ash ... I ... I should have taken care of you."

There were no words adequate to describe how alone Vanarra felt at that moment; none that she could grasp. To sit upon a bench where, moons ago, she and Ash had tickled one another, and where less than a full sol ago, she had waited with him as she tried to get him help, was heartbreaking. Now, he was dead. "Why can't I be dead, too?" She closed her eyes and tried to will her own heart to stop, hoped her breathing would end, and that the corpse of just another Anati would be found and discarded by some passerby the next morning.

She had no idea how much time went by, but then light burst in all around her. The hum of a hover and the opening of a door slowly brought her senses back to the world. A voice started to penetrate the six track thick rock that had covered her mind, and her head tilted up to look into the light.

"Kit! Can ... can you help me, please! I was attacked!"

Vanarra snapped out of the trance she was in and looked up into the desperate eyes of a Nephti, her arm cut and running with blood. Slower than she would have liked, Vanarra uncurled herself and moved to help the only pureblood she had ever known to show her any kindness. "What ... what happened?" she asked stepping aboard and trying to focus herself.

"This damned Lupar comes in here and slammed me up against the door because I told him he wasn't allowed to ride! Raked me with his claws! I ... I stunned him and drove away!" Sorla was almost hysterical.

Van reached into her bag and pulled out her last clean shirt. Sighing, she cradled the Nephti's arm and looked at it. There were claw marks there, but the injury wasn't bad – certainly not as bad as some Vanarra had delivered to others in her past. "We ... we need to wrap it until we can get it shaved and bandaged." Looking up into the frightened blue eyes, she added, "It's not too bad. I'll … I'll make a bandage for you."

"Oh, thank you, thank you! I've never had anything like that ever happen before!" With her other arm, the Nephti landed the transport and secured the doors. "I would have called on the TransCom, but it's not working, and my PawLink's dead and…"

"Listen to me – what was your name again?"

"Sorla … Sorla de Dothnar," the Nephti replied nervously, almost frantically.

"You've got to settle yourself down, or you'll go into shock. A cut up arm I can fix," Vanarra offered as she ripped apart her spare shirt. "Shock's a lot worse. Don't let that damned mange-ridden bastard who attacked you do you any more harm, okay?"

Van's tone of voice was firm and fierce enough that Sorla stopped talking and allowed Vanarra to do whatever she wanted. As the bandage took shape, Vanarra listened to Sorla's breathing, becoming calmer and more regular. Quick glances up into her face showed good color making its way back into her nose and lips. "You've done this before?"

"Yes. I … had to learn."

"Your friend, is he still at the hospital?" Vanarra froze in what she was doing, unable to reply to Sorla's question. "Oh … no, kit! Please … please tell me it isn't so!" the Nephti whispered, starting to cry.

"He's … he's dead," Van barely managed as she tried to keep wrapping the bandage. "Didn't make it."

"I … oh, no. I'm so sorry! I should have driven you there faster! I should have driven the transport up to the door; I –"

Vanarra looked up, and through her own tear streaming eyes stared in amazement at the Nephti. "It … wasn't you. You … were kind. You helped us. They wouldn't see him until … until it was too late."

"Be … because you're Anati?" Sorla replied, horrified. "Oh, I … I should have gone in with you! I … I was worried about that, and I … I just drove away … oh, kit! Oh, kit, I'm so sorry!"

"Sorla, you … you look at me. It wasn't you. It wasn't your fault! It was mine! I…" Vanarra faltered, staring blankly ahead at all of the things she could have done that might have kept Ash alive.

"It wasn't yours either, kit. If those heartless bastards refused to see someone in that much pain. They – how can they even have souls?!" Sorla looked away and couldn't meet the golden eyes staring up at her. Vanarra, at some level, knew that she wasn't to blame, at least not fully. She could also see how much Sorla grieved the loss and the injustice of what had happened to her and Ash.

Vanarra quietly finished the bandage, making it as perfect as she could under the circumstances. "It's done," she stated quietly. "It will hold until you can get back to your lair." Numbly, Van started to turn and walk towards the closed door.

"Wait. Are … you going back home? Do you … have a home?"

Van sighed and leaned against the railing. "I – no, I don't have a home, not anymore."

With a touch of anger in her voice, Sorla growled out, "That's not true! That's not going to be true, anyway! Sit in the seat behind me, kit! I'm – you've taken care of me. I'm … I'm going to take care of you now."

She looked back into the Nephti's hard set expression, the determination and outrage all too plain to see. "What is it with you?" Van asked. "No one treats us like we're anything. Why do you?"

"I grew up as an outcast, without a family. I was recently adopted back into de Dothnar. I … I know what it is like, and you and I are not so different that I can't care about you. Please, kit. You helped me."

Vanarra's eyes ran freely as she whimpered, "I … I don't have anything, Sorla! I can't pay you anything!"

"You're not going to pay me, kit. You've taken care of me. That's the only payment I need. Please, sit. I'll take us back to the depot."

Van tried to make it back up the short stairs but found herself kneeling, looking back up at Sorla, muttering "Thank you." The Nephti left her seat and knelt down and embraced her, and for several passes, the two new friends cried.

"Where have you been? What the heck happened to you?" a big Pantera asked Sorla as she stepped off the transport. "Dispatch says they got two calls about no one showing up at the stop when they – is that a bandage on your arm?"

"Yes, Bashall, I was attacked!" Sorla replied angrily. "That damned TransCom didn't work, and since the power port on the console isn't fixed, I couldn't charge my PawLink to call for help!"

"Uh, well, sorry. Are … you okay? I'm sorry, Sorla. I'll talk to dispatch and get a guard put on your route. I'll make sure the transport gets fixed up, too," the Pantera – although standing a full head taller than the Nephti female, was intimidated and clearly aware of his fault. He then noticed the Vulpi-Faelnar descending the transport steps. "Is she the one who did it to you?"

"No! She's the one who patched me up," the Nephti stated firmly.

"Anati?"

"*Vanarra,*" Sorla replied back at him, making a point. "She has a name, and it's not that one! I'm taking her back to my lair tonight."

"Are you sure, Sorla?" he asked her quietly, but not quietly enough that Vanarra didn't hear it. "She looks a little rough."

"You can't tell me that she intimidates a big, strong Pantera like you, Bashall. She's fine. She … she did a marvelous job on my arm."

"You'll have to report the injury to the office, you know. It's work related."

"I'll do it," she sighed. "That will take some time, though. Come on, Vanarra. Let's see if we can't find a place for you while I deal with the paperwork."

Quietly, Van followed the Nephti. After nearly an interval of Sorla calmly reporting what had happened, then shouting about it, and finally filling out a statement, she finally exited the office and retrieved Vanarra from the driver's break room. While she had waited, Van had tried to stay inconspicuous, and although a few asked her pointedly why she was there, the mention of Sorla's name brought an eye-roll or a knowing head nod as the questioners returned to their tasks. The Nephti had even pulled out some food for Vanarra before she left, and surprised by her appetite, the Vulpi-Faelnar had eaten hungrily and drank quite a bit, too.

"Come on. My hover is out back," Sorla nearly growled as they left the building.

"What … did they say?"

"I have to get it checked out in the morning by their physician. They did give me the next two sols off and said they would file an enforcement report; so that's something, I suppose."

"You don't sound … happy with how they reacted," Van carefully observed.

"It happens all the time, or so I was told. You … you can bet I'm going to be more prepared next time, and I'm darn sure not taking out a transport that isn't in good shape." The Nephti seemed to let go of her anger and turned towards Van as they walked. "Thank goodness you were there, kit! I … I was terrified!"

"Being scared … isn't fun," Vanarra replied, looking away. "I … was glad I could help."

Sorla clicked her entry controller, and a modest blue hover opened its doors and started warming up. "I really needed you. Thank you. Now, go ahead, and get in."

For awhile, neither spoke – Sorla angrily muttering beneath her breath, and Vanarra overwhelmed by what was happening. After awhile, the Nephti finally recovered enough to speak civilly once again. "Hey, are you still hungry, Vanarra?"

"Yes. I am. I … I have a little money. I can pay," she offered.

"Vanarra, what would have happened to me if I had gone into shock?" the Nephti asked without looking at her.

"You could have actually died. It's not … certain or anything, but if you have a medical condition already and something bad happens to you, an injury or something else…" Van let that trail off.

"You may have saved my life tonight, then," Sorla stated firmly. "I'm buying, Vanarra. Any preferences?"

"I'm … okay with anything, really, Sorla. Thank you." Still entangled in her inner turmoil, the Nephti didn't answer but simply nodded and kept driving. The comfortable seat and the sounds of the hover were having an effect on the exhausted mixed-blood, and without her realizing it, Van had fallen asleep.

"Vanarra, kit? Can you wake up?" Instantly Vanarra was awake and terrified, her claws expressing of their own accord, and her teeth baring to the Nephti quickly stepping back from the hover's door. "It's … it's alright, please! Don't be frightened. You're okay. I'm Sorla. Remember? The one you helped."

Her adrenaline abating slightly, Van tried to reign herself in. "Yeah, right. Uh, Sorla. Sorry … I've … woken up in – I'm not good about waking up somewhere new."

A little afraid, but understanding and sympathy clearly coloring her tone, the Nephti responded, "I can see that. Are … are you going to be okay?"

"Sure, sure," Vanarra replied, grasping her own paws and trying to relax enough for her claws to go back in. "I'm sorry, Sorla."

"It's alright, kit. Come on; we're here, at my lair. Can you get out? I got us some food."

Hunger and thirst had started to take hold of her again, and the promise of anything to abate those sensations was enough to bring her fully back under control. "I can do that. I'm so sorry, Sorla. I frightened you."

As the mixed blood stepped out of the hover in front of a small lair, the Nephti observed, "You've been seriously frightened in the past; that much is clear. Come on. I want you to come in and eat, and then we can get to bed, okay?"

"This … this is beautiful, Sorla," Vanarra observed, feeling tears prick at her eyes.

"It's not much," her host chuckled, embarrassed as she opened the door. Just a place to lay my head. It's got more than its share of squared-off corners."

As Vanarra entered, she saw that, indeed, it was a compact living space, but it had its own kitchen and bathroom as well as a den and bedroom. What's more, the Nephti had attractively decorated it in soft natural tones which set Vanarra completely at ease. "It's beautiful. It's the nicest place I have ever stayed."

"Your lair before wasn't all that nice?"

Vanarra knew that she had to be careful with answers about her past, since Sorla may well have known about the security issues at the archive. "Not as nice as this. It … was just a room. The furniture was nowhere near as good as what you have."

"Much of it was gifts from my matron. She was a friend of mine for a few seasons before they adopted me back in. Some of the families she watched over were getting rid of some things, so she was able to send a few pieces my way. Why don't you go into the bathroom and clean up a little, and we'll sit down and eat."

"Okay," Van replied, and did as Sorla suggested. Soon, the pair were eating together at the small table, but Vanarra's appetite got the better of her. "This is amazing! I've never tasted food like this!"

"What have you been eating? This isn't much better than your average QuickMeal," the Nephti replied, surprised.

"QuickMeals are the best food we ... I had access to. This ... this is so fresh and tastes so good!" Van replied.

"I'm glad you think so, Vanarra," Sorla stated, clearly somewhat sad at the realization of how little Vanarra had. "I was worried you might be really hungry, so I ordered enough for three meals."

Van just shook her head, again on the edge of tears at the Nephti's kindness. "I don't know how to say thank you, Sorla. You're ... you're the best purebred I've ever met."

"You're welcome, and ... I'm sorry for that. You should have met better," the Nephti replied softly. Van considered that while she ate, the food infusing her with a desire to keep on living nearly as much as the Nephti's behavior towards her.

The two remained quiet for the rest of the meal, but as Vanarra started to finish her last bite, Sorla ventured, "It's very late. You've got to be tired."

"I ... I am," Van chuckled ruefully, "but normally, I'm awake in the overnight intervals. It is – was the best way to avoid ... problems."

The Faelnar-Vulpi's vagueness wasn't lost on the pureblood. "I see. Vanarra, I know things have been very tough for you, and I'm sorry about that, but..." Vanarra stopped in mid chew, worried that she was about to be thrown out for some reason. "I ... I want to trust you, kit. I do. I don't doubt that you've had to do things that were ... not exactly legal in order to survive. I know because ... I did."

Vanarra stopped and just looked at her, curious. "Why ... would a pureblood have to?"

"Disavowed, at least my parents were," Sorla explained, pointing at herself. "They had a hard time finding work, and ... I got jealous of the other Nephti children. So, I took things. I don't have any of that stuff anymore, and I actually don't own much that's valuable. I just had to make a choice, at some point, to stop. So, after ... a good scare, I stopped stealing. Vanarra, I don't know what's happened in your life so far, and you don't have to tell me, but I have friends, friends that might be able to help you get a new start. You've got to be trustworthy, though, reliable. If you can't be those things, then…"

Vanarra considered Sorla for a long moment but finally confessed. "You're right. I do steal – food, supplies, money. I … I don't want to, but I have no other way to live. If no one gives me a chance, ever, should I just let myself die of hunger?"

"I don't suppose so. Do you have any education at all? Can you read?"

"Sure," Vanarra replied, shrugging. "I'm pretty good at math, too." Sorla just stared at her for a moment, appearing as if she was trying to decide if the statement was sarcastic or honest. "No, really. I can. Test me if you want," Van replied, her food now gone.

"Alright," the Nephti replied with a slight smile. Standing, she went over to a bookshelf and removed a single volume. "Pick anything from this."

Vanarra took the book and then recognized what it was. "Oh, Sorla. No fair! You'll have to pick something I haven't memorized! This is *Light, Warmth, and Hope* by Dame Rahnahi de Dothnar—"

"Matriarch, now," Sorla corrected with a twinkle of pride in her eye.

"Really? She so deserves it, but I'm kind of surprised she accepted," Van replied thoughtfully and found the passages she was looking for. "Here, in the forth chapter – all power tempts deceit of the self and nearly demands erosion of perfect ideals. The greater the power, the greater the temptation." Vanarra looked up at Sorla and shrugged. "If she still believed this, it's hard to see why she would accept."

The Nephti was shaking her head. "You act as if you know her, directly – like you're her friend or confidant!"

"I've read everything she's written, even the children's books," Van replied with a shrug. "She's … just so good at helping you sort your life out."

"I agree. It's very clear you can read; I'm sorry. I didn't mean to offend you."

"I'm surprised you asked. I did patch up your arm, after all."

Sorla sighed in self disappointment. "I know. You're … an Anati, and I judged you because of that. I'm sorry."

"It's been that way my whole life, Sorla. Why should you be any different?" Van asked, the question stated in a harder tone than she intended.

"Because I had hoped myself better than that," the Nephti replied, not meeting her gaze. "If I do it again, don't just accept it. Correct me – in private – but still, please, set me straight. Don't allow me to assume you can't do something."

"You're willing to help, Sorla. I'll do whatever you ask," Van replied reaching across the table. "Thank you for trying to help us. If we had found anyone in that hospital with even … a small portion of your kindness, Ash … would still be alive." The Nephti reached across the table and grasped the mixed-blood's paws, matching her tears to Vanarra's.

Vanarra awoke the next morning in a strange mix of fear and comfort. A nightmare had put Ash within her grasp, but then his stomach had burst into flames, consuming him in the very same screams she had heard him making in the hospital. Even with so harsh and ugly a wake-up, there was no denying a sense of physical well-being. The soft cushions of the couch were beneath her; blankets were around her, and her stomach was still pleasantly full from the night before. Beside her on a nearby table was a bowl filled with fruit and snacks and a large glass of water.

She leaned up and put her hind-paws on the floor, rubbing the sides of her muzzle and drawing in a breath. Instantly, she knew she was being watched. "Good morning," Vanarra croaked out in a rough voice. "And … thank you for keeping your distance. I'm sorry about last night in the hover."

"No problem," Sorla replied, surprised. "I … I heard you call out. You okay?"

"Nightmare," Van explained. "Thank you for the food, though. That was very nice to wake up to."

"I … I hope it's alright. I … just don't have – I don't keep…"

"Sorla, forgive me," Vanarra replied, turning around and looking at the tentative Nephti. "I think you're doing it again. Be honest. What are you worried about?"

The Nephti sighed and looked away. Quietly, she admitted, "Fermentum."

"Not available where I was staying. I have nipped at the stuff, but I honestly don't do too well with it. Too much makes my whole muzzle itch, and I hate that."

"It makes your muzzle itch?" Sorla replied, a bit of humor in her voice.

"Ash told me once that when I'd had a little more than usual, I was really annoying and wouldn't stop talking. I've seen some Anati make real tails of themselves by drinking too much of it. I don't need that trouble; I already have enough."

"I ... thank you for telling me. I ... keep worrying about you – all of the things I've heard over the seasons. They're just ... wrong." She stepped around and sat across from Vanarra who was now taking a few bites of fruit. "Anati are vicious, drunken, smelly, violent, and deceitful. I'm sorry; you're just not living up to your reputation."

"I think that's a good thing," Van replied at Sorla's almost joke. "However, the violent thing actually has a little bit of truth to it. I ... well, I've had some other Thurians try to do things to me ... take advantage like ... they shouldn't have. They ... paid for it."

"You killed them?" Sorla asked carefully.

"I don't think so, but I did put some nice, long claw marks in a few muzzles and in ... other places," Van admitted. "When some guys get ready to hunt, they forget where my claws are."

"I've had a couple of guys try to do that to me."

"Oh really?" Van asked, curious as she munched another piece of river fruit. "What did you do?"

"Stunner. Knocked them both out cold; me, too, since we were all sort of ... well, touching, but I woke up first," Sorla replied and then smiled deviously before adding, "and I did it to them again!"

Vanarra laughed, seeing Sorla's expression. "I would have liked to have seen that! So, what happened then?"

"They were disavowed, the two of them, and that allowed me to meet a matron of the de Dothnar family. That ... kind of started getting me into their good graces. Oh, but ... I suppose it's kind of rude for me to talk about that."

"Talk all you want," Van chuckled. "You're feeding me and giving me a place to stay when I really, really need it."

"Vanarra, I have to confess that you're absolutely shocking to talk to," Sorla said, obviously frustrated.

Van was worried. "I'm ... sorry. Did I say something wrong?"

"No! You ... you're saying everything right! When I told the shift supervisor why I'd taken you back with me, he gave me this whole long list of things Anati do and can't do! But ... but you can practically quote a Grand Matriarch! The way you speak is perfect, like you've been studying at an academy, and ... you're so mature and ... well, grateful! I've known you just a short time, kit, but ... you're pretty amazing. It's hard to accept that something I've been told my whole life, now that I have a real, live Anati in front of me, doesn't seem at all true!"

"For some of us, it is true," Vanarra sadly confessed. "Sometimes, we live down to what everyone thinks of us. I mean, if you keep doing right and no one gives you credit, why try?" Understanding flashed in Sorla's features, and she nodded. Van smiled weakly and continued, "It's nice to hear someone finally tell me I've done something right. It's just – Ash was so much better than I. He ... he worked out ways to live, at least get food, without really stealing. He's the better example." Van stared blankly ahead, her expression bleak and aching. "The best."

"Would you like to tell me about him?" Sorla offered cautiously, but compassionately. "Rahnahi says that those we've lost still live in our memories, especially those we've cared about. It's like a candle we burn in honor of them, but in our souls. Telling their story is like sharing that flame, and instead of one light, there are two. If you wish, Vanarra, I would happily listen and make him live in my memory."

Vanarra looked at the Nephti, and the offer touched her so deeply she started trembling and tears rolled out of her eyes. "To ... have ... another ... cherish his name ... like I do..."

Sorla came and sat beside Vanarra and held her close around the shoulder, and the two clasped paws. "Teach me, Vanarra, and I will listen."

"First," she replied, snuffling back tears and grabbing a tissue. After she blew her nose, Vanarra continued, "First, you have to know that he didn't call me Vanarra. I know that's all ... proper and everything, but he called me Van. His name wasn't Ash, either. It was ... Ashalam."

"May I please call you Van?" Vanarra nodded, smiling. Slowly, and with many tears, the mixed blood started to share all she felt she could about the dear one she had lost.

Chapter 8: Horizontality

Sahnassa tapped lightly at the door of her matron's quarters. Because of her recent bouts of illness, Matron Shalarra had been confined largely to the precincts of the keep and her own lair. That was no barrier to Sahnassa who, more and more, cherished the elderly female who had become her mentor, friend, and advocate over the past few seasons.   Deflecting the concerns of her father regarding Sahnassa's choice to be a technologist and keeping the dame at bay were more than enough to endear the matron to Sahnassa. Still, her matron did so much more for her. Sahnassa had been before the Grand Matriarch at least once per season, sometimes twice, and each time Matriarch Selena remembered the kit, asked her questions, and seemed appreciative of the answers. Hylea and Triana tried not to seethe with jealousy when these occasions happened; they hadn't been to see the matriarch a single time.

"Come in," Shalarra's voice called, and the young Nephti was happy to hear that voice sounding strong and certain. Entering, she carried with her a bunch of pink and red sahnassa flowers, and the sight of those made the elder Nephti sit straight up in her "favorite chair." "Sahnassa, you wonderful dear! Look at those! They are positively beautiful! How did you ever afford them? I know your father didn't give you the money." There was a distinct air of complaint in that last statement.

"No, he didn't," she agreed. "I've got a pretty good part time job now helping out the other students in my tertiary school. It's not bad work, and the pay from the parents is surprisingly good."

"I've heard about your tutoring, and how badly Tagathar needs it," Shalarra commented as she touched and smelled the flowers. "So wonderful! Could you please get a vase from the top shelf of the kitchen and set them up for me? I'd do it myself, but I'm having a little difficulty getting around right now."

"I'm sorry to hear that, Matron. Is ... is there anything I can do?" Sahnassa asked as she obeyed the instruction and moved into the kitchen.

"No, no. I have medicine. I just have good sols sometimes and bad sols other times. This one is kind of in the middle. I'm okay sitting, but moving isn't much fun. Just be glad that the universe has decided to put being old at the end of your life. If it hit you when you were young, you wouldn't have built up the stamina."

"Speaking of fun," Sahnassa chuckled and then commented, "Tagathar is truly a paw-ful, two in fact. I get the distinct sense that there is a very good reason why his schoolwork is suffering."

"Spending too much time practicing his music and not enough on his math and composition, I'd wager," the matron replied a little grimly. "What's the group he's formed called again?"

"Rebel Monsters," Sahnassa replied as she carefully arranged the flowers into a nice presentation.

"Well, the honorable rebel monster had best terrorize his grades into running up a steeper slope to a higher place. They've been languishing in the valley for some time now. Do you think he'll improve?"

Sahnassa sighed as she brought the arrangement in and set it beside Shalarra on a nearby table. "Only if I or someone else tutors him, keeps him on task. He's okay if he does his homework; it's just getting him to do it that's the challenge." Shalarra chuckled and motioned for Sahnassa to sit. Then, she just stared at the young Nephti for a moment, smiling. "What is it, Matron?"

"I was just remembering the little kit I met so long ago. She's grown up now, in many ways. You are quite accomplished for your age. It makes me sometimes wonder if the concerns of your father aren't worth a thought or two. You have such a way with Matriarch Selena, and she earnestly does seem to like you. Your tutoring, in a way, is like the counseling we do as matrons. I've had other reports from the headmaster about your involvement in substance abuse peer counseling, and I've heard you've had some measure of success. You also … just treat others with respect and honor, something your dear elder sister could learn from you."

"Oh, no," Sahnassa replied, shaking her head. "What has she done now?"

"I think I probably shouldn't tell you exactly how she offended her professor in advanced legal preparatory, but … just make it a matter of practice, kit, never to tell your professors they're too sheltered to understand what's really going on in the legal profession." Sahnassa groaned and put her head in her paws. "Yes, yes. She also did it in class in front of others, so an apology had to be made in front of the class."

"Triana, please, just keep … your … muzzle … shut," Sahnassa uttered in frustration. "She always has to be out there sticking her tail in places and faces."

"She does, but see, kit, that's my point. I would never have to worry about you doing something like that. I … I could see you accompanying a major diplomatic mission to another house and doing quite well, as an assistant to a matron or dame. You might even provide discrete good advice—" Shalarra stopped, because she could almost see Sahnassa withering in front of her. "But your heart's not in that, is it?"

"I've … tried. I've so tried to fake my way through it and pretend—"

"To make your father happy," Shalarra interjected.

"And my mother," Sahnassa agreed. "I've had to endure Triana and my father talking over new and exciting case law over dinner. Hylea's playing the game, too, asking them questions, but I … am just left out."

Shalarra nodded, as if she had come to a decision and then asked, "When are you the most happy, Sahnassa? What makes you content?"

"When I solve a problem in a programming class – one that's hard, one that's driving me feral. To finally get it solved is like finishing a hard video game, but unlike a game, it means something."

"You've been helping the Nobel Society Pack with their computers, I hear," Shalarra commented.

"They're a great bunch – helping kids read. It's sad, though, the kids who are disavowed … are just so lost."

"I know. It's hard that sometimes we make the children pay for the misdeeds and poor choices of their parents, but in time, perhaps they can be adopted back in, should they prove themselves with honor. My point in these questions, kit, is that it's time to decide your academy goals – what you want to be when you grow up."

"A litigator, I suppose," Sahnassa replied bleakly.

"I don't think that's true, kit, and we both know it."

"An archivist, then?"

"No, I don't think so, either," Matron Shalarra countered. "Just because your parents chose those professions and seem to be pressuring you doesn't mean that they have the right to decide for you. They have their callings, their professions, and what makes them happy. Picking what makes someone else happy – but not you – isn't choosing a profession; it's enduring a prison sentence. You've committed no crime, dear kit, in having a differing focus in life than your parents. So long as you respect them and what they do, you are not dishonoring the family by choosing your own path."

"With all respect, Matron," Sahnassa replied apologetically, "my father has had Dame Rothnerra over for dinner time and again, and when she's there, he … they…"

"Lean on you? Try to push you in their direction? Doesn't surprise me," Shalarra harrumphed. "That's all they can do, you see. Your matron helps you decide what your options will be, and then the dame helps choose from among those options. If we don't list litigator or archivist on the form, then there truly isn't much choice either of them have."

"He's not going to pay for it, you know?" Sahnassa asked, shaking her head.

"Oh, Gonastir may come around, and that thought hadn't escaped my notice, either. You'll be happy to know that I've put you in for the matriarchal scholarship. It won't cover a top school like Harnard, but it would easily fund your full tuition at Dothnaria or one of the other institutions who have good technologist programs. Add a part time job, which you're already doing, and then you'll be set, regardless of how … fixed your father wishes to remain in his thinking."

"But … but what about Dame Rothnerra?" Sahnassa sputtered. "There's no way she'd go along with this!"

"Oh, now, don't discount your wily matron just yet, little kit! You see, the duty of career approvals and assignments rotates to prevent those with *hardened attitudes* from having undue influence over someone such as yourself. I chose to contact you now because that duty rests in the paws of one Shaelia de Orturu, dame extraordinaire. I have never met such a ... progressive and an artful soul as Shaelia. I have to say, she's given me hope for the future of this house that I never had before. We've ... become good friends, actually. I've been explaining your situation to her for some time, and she's very sympathetic."

"She sounds like someone I would really like to meet," Sahnassa replied, surprised.

"A regretfully difficult prospect, now that she's been posted off continent, but she's back for a short time for dame studies and so forth, covering Rothnerra while our dame tends to ... disciplinary issues on Ricia. Those do seem to attract her attention more often than not."

"I'll say," Sahnassa replied, wincing at the memories. Not only had there been that somewhat flirtatious incident with a different species when she was younger, the dame had set about lecturing her on a number of occasions for all sorts of infractions, including her "discounting" of the professional achievements of her parents and failing to have a desire to emulate them. Each session, no less than once per moon for the last season, was accompanied by both berating and interrogation. After each one, Sahnassa had gone to Shalarra for encouragement. Suddenly, a smile started to turn up the corners of the young Nephti's expression – a smile that bordered on the devious.

"Be careful, now," Shalarra warned, holding up a paw finger. "We dare not gloat about end-running Dame Rothnerra. She's likely to be furious. If you're not careful, she can create trouble for you in a hundred different ways – seems to be her specialty, remember?"

Sobered, Sahnassa nodded. "But to actually be able to do what I want. That ... that would be amazing."

"It will be hard work," the matron countered, "perhaps harder than going for an archivist degree or some such to placate your parents. You'll need to do well in it, both in school and afterwards. Then, if you achieve results as a technologist, not even your parents or Dame Rothnerra can argue with it. Pay your family dues and win the occasional commendation for some of that volunteer work you do, as well, and stay as close to the Grand Matriarch as you dare, especially when she's speaking in public. Any kind of relationship you can maintain, however thin it may be, will work in your favor and help protect you until our dear Rothnerra moves on, hopefully."

Seeing that Sahnassa was clearly absorbing the advice she was giving, Shalarra admitted, "You know, you and I might not be doing the future you any favors by the choice we make this sol, but if I've learned anything about you, kit, it is that you are willing to risk pain and difficult situations to get your heart's desire. In my mind, that makes you brave so long as the desires of your heart are noble. For the entire time I've known you, kit, they have been." Sahnassa reached out and grasped the matron's paw in her own. Smiling, Shalarra asked, "So, do we go ahead with it?"

Sharing that same smile, Sahnassa de Orturu gripped the matron's paw just a little tighter and nodded yes, her tail swishing with excitement.

Vanarra woke up, still feeling weak, but finally not feeling worse than she had in the last five sols. Perhaps as a consequence of her visit to the hospital ward or her wanderings elsewhere, she had gotten sick, very sick. It was the worst she had felt in her life, and had it not been for Sorla, she knew she would have probably died.

Looking over, she saw Sorla asleep in a nearby chair, hind paws propped up on a small table. Van smiled at her sleeping form and whispered, "Thank you." Vanarra had been telling her everything about Ash when a wave of nausea and dizziness hit her, and she barely made it to the bathroom in time. At first, the pair thought that the food they had bought was tainted, making Sorla worried for her own safety, but as Vanarra's body added diarrhea to her list of unfortunate symptoms, the Nephti had no ill effects whatsoever.

After several intervals of Vanarra's continued deterioration, Sorla called her matron and all but demanded any available nurse with a spare moment. When the Nephti nurse had arrived, a male one, he had been a bit surprised to see that his patient was an Anati, but noting Vanarra's mix of heritage had actually made her problem easier to diagnose. Altian-B was not a new word to Van, and she was very firmly convinced she didn't like meeting it a second time. What was worse is that this unwelcome disease affected only Vulpi and Faelnar, and Vanarra, being a combination of the two, had managed to get both the Faelnar's digestion problems and the Vulpi's dizziness. Both were worse now than when she suffered through Altian-B at the archive with Ash.

Providing Sorla with numerous samples of appropriate medications, the nurse had informed them that the disease would take several sols to clear itself from Van's system. He also said that although the local hospitals weren't in the habit of admitting anyone – disavowed or Anati – who couldn't pay, Sorla's lair would do as well as a hospital room so long as he checked in with them every sol and Sorla played nurse. Sick as she was, Vanarra was stunned how readily her new friend accepted that responsibility. They had been fortunate in one regard, at least. The nurse was actually qualified to look at and treat Sorla's injuries from being attacked on the transport, and, as an added measure of kindness, he had written an excusal from work for ten sols because of "emotional distress."

It was then that Vanarra truly started to admire and appreciate the Nephti who had taken her in. Sorla gently turned away requests from her matron and supervisors for a visit, even accepting counseling for the attack over the LineCom, all while she cared for Vanarra. When Van wasn't feeling miserable, she eventually realized that Sorla could have probably gone back to work the very next sol, but she was using the attack as an excuse for taking care of her.

Smiling at the memory of that realization, Vanarra slowly tried to push herself up. The sound instantly brought Sorla out of her slumber at a start. "What? What is it, Van?"

"I'm okay ... kind of, I think," came the raspy reply. "I ... still feel awful, but better than I did. I might be getting—" Vanarra coughed a few times and couldn't continue.

"I'll get you some tea, dear kit," Sorla stated and then was gone before Vanarra could stop her. Resigned to accepting the Nephti's help, she simply sat and tried to take inventory of how she felt. "Here you go."

"Thank ... you," Van managed and then consumed the tea, cautiously at first, but then all of her bodily impulses demanded that she drink as fast as possible. "Wow, uh, thanks. I ... I guess that means I really am feeling better."

"I'll get you another."

Before Sorla could take the glass, Vanarra grasped her paws. "I'm so sorry about this, and ... I can't thank you enough."

"Don't feel bad. Everyone gets sick, although I have to say I'm glad that I'm a Nephti and not a Vulpi or a Faelnar."

"Worse if you're both," Van chuckled. "That ... that was awful. The dizziness was bad enough, but ... ugh. You ... you are just the sweetest kit ever for taking care of me. Don't think I haven't noticed you talking to work and everyone else on LineCom, keeping yourself here and keeping them away. You … you did that for me. Thank you."

Smiling, Sorla nodded. "I'll get you some more now, and … you're welcome." As she walked towards the kitchen, she commented, "I've never seen someone so sick before. You … poor thing – you were miserable!"

"To think, Ash died in that hospital, and I … I certainly could have from this. I would have if it wasn't for you, Sorla. Thank you."

"My pleasure," the Nephti said, reaching out and putting her paw on Vanarra's knee.

Van covered that paw with her own and patted it. "You know, you're very kind to say that, but at some point, caring for me is going to lose its shine. Even if you're willing to, Sorla, I … I don't want to be a burden to you. You've got a life."

"What are you saying, Van?"

"I wish – I'd give anything to be able to take care of myself and make my own way! I don't want much more than to have a job, do work, get paid, and go home to some lair that is half as nice as this one! That would be *so* good."

The Nephti folded her paws in her lap. "Well, you don't have a family house, but you do have a friend, and a friend who has other friends can be almost as good."

"Really?" Van asked, smiling and now starting to feel even better.

"There's a caterer I know – Gorta. She's … got her problems, but she's good at heart, and she could use someone to help her get ready for events, manage inventory, things like that. She's not avowed, but she has a lot of friends in Nephti and Perratti family houses. What's nice is that she can usually make a pretty good amount of money, but only if she can carry off an event almost perfectly. Since she's by herself, she's limited in what she can do. I could talk to her if you wish."

Vanarra shrugged. "It's a place to start, I suppose."

"It would be a lot of hard work, and she does events at all points of the clock, middle of the sol or late at night."

"As long as I was making a little money and could feed and clothe myself, have a lair I could shelter in, I'd be happy. I … I would appreciate anything you wanted to try, Sorla. We've ... well, that's kind of how Ash may have gotten hurt. We tried the short time laborer thing. It was ... we were in too much danger, since we were disposable."

"I understand. Hopefully, catering wouldn't be as hazardous. Who knows, you might even like it."

"I am certainly willing to try. Ugh, I think ... I think I'm going to lie down for a moment though. I'm really tired."

"The nurse said you'd be pretty weak for awhile. Don't worry. I'll take care of you and help you get better."

"Sorla, thank you. I don't know what I'd be able to do for you to repay you, but ... whatever I can, I will." The Nephti stroked the side of Van's muzzle and nodded, and then gently guided her friend back down to the soft cushions of the couch.

"Gonastir," Dame Rothnerra de Orturu said gravely as she met the litigator in his private office. "I ... have troubling news, I'm afraid. It appears that Sahnassa has made her choice regarding an academy placement."

Taking the piece of paper presented him, he read it and was almost instantly shaking with rage. "How, how could this happen, Dame Rothnerra! I thought you and I had discussed this."

"You and I had discussed it," she replied, slightly on the defensive. "We've exercised every opportunity for reinforcement and tried to persuade your daughter, but as I was ... reminded, we are not allowed to make Sahnassa's choice for her. She has chosen in consultation with her matron, and a dame of our house has approved it. It's done."

Defeated, he sank back into his chair, no longer seeming to care about paying the dame the proper respects. "Now what?" he asked, sighing. "Let her attend Dothnaria, like she wants? Let her settle for a ... mediocre profession, like she wants?"

"In accepting this unfortunate reality, I was able to do some research that might grant a measure of solace to you. She has listed Dothnaria, but I believe I can arrange matters so that her application would be denied. In point of fact, I believe I can ensure that Harnard will be the only school that accepts her, and only in their top program. If she wants to be a technologist, and such is her dream – so be it.

However, as her family, we will demand that she becomes the most educated, certified, and respected technologist ever to graduate from Harnard. The program is ... incredibly challenging and expensive."

"I'm not paying for that, Dame," Gonastir said, fixing her with an almost stern look. "I refuse, and that is my choice."

"Exactly!" the gray dame replied as if she expected him to realize the marvelous trick she was playing. "Conserve the funds you had intended for Sahnassa and don't supply them to her. If Sahnassa has the unquenchable thirst to achieve greatness as a technologist, then she will literally have to work the fur off her tail to do so. To pay for such a noble school without familial support will mean that she will have to work nearly full time. Her degree will take her a long time, Gonastir – plenty of time for her to bravely try, struggle, fail, and then come back to you with her tail dragging behind her, accepting the grave mistake she's made. Then, once she has realized her error, she can ... reconsider her options, as well as our advice."

"Make it impossible for her to succeed?" he asked, curious.

"Oh, it's not impossible. It's just so difficult that she likely won't finish. As a favor to your family and because of all of the grand work you've done for us, we'll happily absorb the costs of any loans she has accrued in her failed attempt. In life, some are able to see reason without the need for a hard lesson, and regretfully, some must receive that in order to put themselves to rights and move forward."

"I don't know. I don't ... understand her choice, nor do I approve of it, but ... to sabotage her deliberately – that's going to be difficult to sell to Holana."

"I have to confess that I've already had this conversation with your mate, as well, since my route here took me by the family archive, first. It seems that she is as angry as you are, and she seems quite insistent that Sahnassa needs to learn to listen to the wishes of her family. It may have had something to do with the fact that everyone in her department was keeping track of what their children were signing up for. I get the sense that Holana ... was embarrassed by Sahnassa's choice."

Gonastir nodded. He knew his own mate well enough to know that was the absolute truth. She had been worried for moons about how the others in her office and directorate would perceive their daughter's choice. "And you can make Dothnaria Academy appear to have rejected her application ... on what grounds?"

"Full classes, a key professor on an extended leave of absence, improper scheduling – there are a host of good reasons," Rothnerra replied, shrugging.

"So, all we have to do is sit back, wait for her to fail, and then help her start over again?"

"All the while looking amazingly beneficent when she comes crawling back, and she'll finally appreciate the honored legacy in which she can partake. What you do now doesn't even have to be acrimonious. Simply state your decision, firmly and resolutely. Don't even bother to lecture her or try to persuade her right now. I'm sure that she's thoroughly convinced in the rightness of her choice. Disagree agreeably and move on."

"One sol, she's going to find out about this conversation."

"And by then," Rothnerra quickly added, "she'll be mature enough to appreciate and thank you for it."

"Very well," Gonastir replied, although doubts clearly bothered him.

"I will be available if you need me. Matron Shalarra continues to be … ill, so don't hesitate to reach out to me."

"Thank you, Dame. Much appreciated," Gonastir offered, standing and nodding a short bow before Dame Rothnerra quit the room.

"Now, don't worry, Van. You look fine, and I've already told Gorta all about you."

"Sorla, are you sure that was a good idea?" Vanarra asked, nervously, forcing her tail to stay largely hidden behind her and keeping her eyes lowered as they approached the entrance to the small business. Of all of Van's traits, minus her overall coloration, several purebred schoolchildren had teased her on these attributes especially. From a distance, she might be able to pass as Faelnar if the flash of her golden eyes and the full width of her tail wasn't visible.

The Nephti turned back to look at her and then stopped as they stood under the short overhang of the roof. Putting her paw on Van's shoulder and lifting her chin, she stated, "A very good idea, and don't lower your eyes or try to hide what you are. Remember, Gorta's disavowed, too, so on the social scale, you are both equal."

"At the lowest level," Van replied, looking away.

"Perhaps even that can change in time, but first we need to get you into an honest and honorable living, and Gorta needs your help, kit. She really does. Come on now," Sorla bade, and after a quick knock on the door, Vanarra followed her friend into the building.

"Oh, yes," a scratchy Faelnar voice called back to them, one which could be defined as female, but only just. "Sorla, kit. So nice to see you!" Trying to heed the Nephti's advice, Van lifted her eyes as she saw an overweight female push herself out of the chair and step around to hug the first of the new arrivals. "How's your arm, kit?"

"Almost all healed, and thanks in no small part to the kit I want to introduce you to. This is Vanarra, and she's become a very good friend. If it hadn't been for her, I might have died that night."

Vanarra's blush furs raised as she nodded and tried to smile at the yellow-eyed female with graying brown fur and a yellowish brown nose. "I see. That's quite … impressive, considering," Gorta stated evenly. It was immediately clear that although Sorla saw the Faelnar and Van on the same level, the proprietor of this business certainly did not. However, to her credit, she added, "Thank you for keeping Sorla safe. She's … she's been a heroine to me and more often than I would care to admit."

"You're welcome, and I owe her my thanks. She's taken care of me when I was sick and … helped me through a hard time."

The Faelnar cracked an ironic smile and glanced at the Nephti. "Seems to be a habit of hers. She's done the same for me, so we have that in common, at least. Name's Gorta – I haven't bothered to pick up a suffix since de Mistral dismissed me from the pleasure of their company." The Faelnar reached out for Van, and tentatively, the two briefly clasped paws. "Now, Sorla here says you need and want honest work. She also says that I make horrible messes and have a psychotic talent for not throwing things away."

"I didn't exactly say it that way!" the Nephti replied, embarrassment and accusation in her voice.

"Hah!" Gorta chuckled, pointing. "Got you! Oh, she said it alright, just real nice and proper. You know, even without the last name, she was always polite … and kind. Sadly, she's also kind of right about me, and a health inspector is coming tomorrow. If I don't get this place straightened up, they'll likely revoke my business charter, or at least threaten to. Problem is, I have a function I have to get to tonight, and I won't be available until morning—"

"Gorta!" Sorla interrupted. "You … you should have told me! I would have brought her by sooner."

"Well, you said she's a hard worker—"

"She is. You should see what she's done for me just in my little hole of a lair," the Nephti countered.

"And you said I could trust her," Gorta replied, looking at Vanarra. "So, kit, think of this as your … job application. Prove to me that I can leave you here and that you can make the storeroom back there clean and well-organized as, well, the de Mistral family archive, and then you'll have a place here. If something gets thrown away that shouldn't or I find something stolen or out of place, you're done. Fair enough?"

Although Sorla's tail was lashing a bit in indignation, she kept her peace as Vanarra answered, "I will."

"You will pay her, either way, right?" the Nephti pointedly asked.

"Sure, sure. Basic wage, though. We're not a business that caters to the moneyed house elites."

Before Sorla could intervene, Vanarra answered, "I'll take it. At the very least, I'll be doing something useful."

"It's done then," Gorta replied nodding, evidently relieved to put the agreement beyond Sorla's ability to question it. "Come on now. Let me show you what you're up against." The pair followed the fat Faelnar as she got up and made her way to a door on the far side of the room and down a short hall.

Sorla and Van followed her through a door at the end and into a darkened room where they stopped short once Gorta turned on the light. "Mange!" Sorla nearly shouted. "And you have an inspector coming tomorrow!" Van couldn't help herself; her mouth was agape. There were shelves in the room, but they were surrounded on all sides with a mass of paper and boxes and equipment and all sorts of other detritus nearly as high as Van's chest. A narrow path through the mass slithered towards a back door which certainly would be a challenge for Vanarra to navigate – for Gorta, she reasoned it had to be near impossible.

"I've been running behind, a little," the Faelnar replied without much embarrassment.

"A lot!" Sorla replied and then looked at Van. "Are you sure you want to take this on, kit?"

"I said I would, and that's what I will do," she replied, although she swallowed afterwards.

"Very well," Gorta said. "There's a facility back in the hallway, and I have some leftovers from last night's event on the table over there that you could help yourself to if you get hungry. I'll lock the doors after I leave, and there's trash bins out back. I think they were just emptied. I'll leave you to it, then."

After Gorta had left the room, Sorla took Vanarra by the shoulder and said, "Look kit, I had no idea it was going to be anything this bad when I suggested it. She's … she's gone pretty far downhill – I mean, this could take you all night! More even!"

"It's okay, Sorla," Vanarra replied as her eyes started to roam across the mass. "I think I can do something to help her."

"Alright, but you have my PawLink number. If I need to jump off my route to come get you or if you need help, I'm willing."

Vanarra reached around the Nephti and hugged her. "I want to do this on my own – to prove it to myself, if nothing else, and it's my first test. If I can help her with this, maybe she'll keep me on."

"Alright, then, if you're sure?" Sorla asked, releasing the mixed blood to look her in the eyes.

"You said the way forward for me was honest work. This … certainly looks like honest work."

Sorla sighed. "Alright, then. Call me when you want me to come pick you up, okay?"

"I will," Vanarra replied smiling, "and thank you."

"I don't know what for," Sorla chuckled, gesturing at the piles in the room.

"For caring enough to try," Van offered, and then leaned over and nuzzled the Nephti along her muzzle.

"Anytime, kit. Anytime. I'll talk to you soon, okay?"

Vanarra nodded, and reluctantly, the Nephti left the room. As she turned back to face her task, Van had to chuckle, remembering the way her lair in the archive looked when she first discovered it. "Time to make a new home," she said to herself and started working her way down the narrow path towards the back door.

Pulling into the depot, Sorla was relieved. "I'll finally be able to call Van and check in on her." Although it had been comforting to have an off-duty enforcement officer riding along with her for safety, he did little more than call or type on his PawLink the entire time. Unfortunately, she didn't feel any freedom to do the same. He was a passenger, but she was the driver. Anything she did outside of the realm of normal policy would have a chance of getting back to the station manager – a Thurian she had been on poor terms with ever since she was attacked. With Vanarra, her jobless lodger, finances were starting to get clawed pretty thin – so thin that her family dues were almost late, something her matron did make mention of.

The opportunity with Gorta was truly the one with the greatest capacity for income, but it was also a job fraught with problems. Gorta had a real issue with drinking too much fermentum, and her inattention and distraction meant that she failed to come through for her clients, from time to time. As the Nephti said goodbye to the guard and walked over to tell the maintenance manager about a steering problem she'd noticed, Sorla shook her head. The sight of that horrid storeroom almost had made her physically ill. It wasn't only the smell – a stale and nearly rotting odor – it was the very idea of keeping that much garbage around. Gorta had been on her own for a long time after her mate was struck by lightning and killed. Disavowed and with no one checking in on the details of her life, the Faelnar had obviously gone into decline.

As she was keying the wall screen with a few quick presses to indicate she was leaving, her PawLink was already open and dialing. She could only call Gorta's office number, since Vanarra didn't have her own PawLink, and as she expected, the call rang and rang. After almost half a pass, the line picked up, Vanarra sounding like she was out of breath. "Gorta's Gatherings, Vanarra speaking, can I help you?"

Sorla was forced to chuckle. "Now where did you learn to do that?"

"Oh hi, Sorla! Yeah, sounds pretty silly coming out of my muzzle, but I heard her answer the LineCom that way, so I thought it made sense. I've actually taken a few calls from prospective clients since she's been gone."

"Good for you!" Sorla replied, heartened. "Have you made any headway on that awful mess?"

"Quite a lot, actually. In some parts of the room, you can actually see the floor. Thrown away a ton of things, though. I've been able to yank out business records and receipts, and I've tried to keep a sample of any flyers or programs she's created, but ... I mean when there's a whole stack at the bottom of a pile for an event dated two seasons ago—"

"Oh no, you're joking! Oh Van, you have to be!"

"I'm afraid not. There were also a few ... well, biology experiments that I was more than happy to take out of here."

"Oh my goodness," Sorla replied, groaning. "I just got off my shift. Do you want me to come by and help?"

There was a deep breath as Van considered. "I don't think so, but it's very kind of you to offer. You can't lose a night of sleep and still drive safely tomorrow night. I'm actually doing okay. I've made a little tea, and Gorta left some really tasty leftovers in her office before she locked up. She said I could finish them off if I wanted to. Say what you will about how clean she keeps her place, but that Faelnar can positively cook!"

"It's the only thing that's saved her, I think," Sorla observed as she stepped out of the building and headed towards her vehicle. "So, should I just wait for your call? Are you really going to work through the night, kit?"

"I am, but that's the time of the sol I'm used to working, really. I'll be tired and need to sleep, but if this means getting a job and earning a little money, it's worth it. I know what you've been doing for me, Sorla, and I know things have been difficult. I don't want to be a burden to you."

"It's not been without its challenges to be sure, on that front, but I've never met anyone so amazing as you. I mean like – how did you know to keep the receipts and all of that other stuff?"

Van paused for a moment, and Sorla knew what that meant. In talking to Van, anytime she asked about the mixed blood's past, there was always that pause. The Anati wanted to answer her, but there wasn't enough trust between them to allow for the full truth. In a way, that hurt Sorla's feelings a bit, but the raised blush furs on Vanarra's muzzle and the drooping tail and ears spoke truth to Sorla in a way that Van, by her mouth, was unable to. In time, Sorla had come to realize that Vanarra was ashamed of her past, however beneficial it had been to her education. "Let's just say," Van answered, "that there were a lot of … loose facts floating around where I was living. I guess … I guess I kind of picked up on that through just being there."

"It's okay, Van. I understand," Sorla answered. "I'm sorry. I try to stop asking about your past, but you just keep surprising me!"

"Let's hope Gorta's surprised, and pleasantly," Vanarra replied.

"Can I ask you something?"

"Sure, but I really should get back to it."

"Oh, you!" Sorla chuckled at Vanarra's almost sarcastic tone. "What will you buy with your first paycheck?"

"Buy?! You've got to be joking! I'm paying you back!"

"Okay, yes, that's true, I would appreciate a little to ease the pinch right now, but … maybe something small. What would you want?"

Van considered for only a moment. "I … well, heard that Matriarch Rahnahi has come out with a new book. That's what I would want."

"Sounds like a good goal to keep you going. Now, call me if you need me, kit. Okay?"

"Sure enough. Get some rest, Sorla, and for once you won't have to worry about my coughing or my nightmares. Just relax and rest. I'll be alright," Vanarra replied confidently.

"Okay then. Take care, and I'll be by just a few passes after you call me, okay?"

"Alright. Thank you, Sorla."

"And thank you, kit. Bye."

As the Faelnar owner of Gorta's Gatherings pulled up to her place of business and landed her hover, she growled out softly, "Well, at least the building is still here." Slowly, and with some difficulty, she slipped out of her vehicle as quickly as her aching head and painful joints would allow. She winced a bit as she closed her vehicle's door, its cool exterior touching a nearly exposed patch of skin on her arm sending a chill through her, a sensation she intensely disliked. Her bare spots were becoming more than just a nuisance – they were becoming noticeable. Pulling the long sleeves of her blouse down to cover the embarrassing patch, she picked up her bags and started trudging to the door.

Opening the door brought an unfamiliar and somewhat pungent smell to her nose, one she wasn't used to – the strong smell of cleaning fluids. "Hello," she said after a sneeze. "Is … is that you, Anati?"

"Yes, Gorta! I'm in the back."

The Faelnar's nose twitched again, and a chuffing sneeze almost made her drop her burdens. "What … what's that smell?"

Vanarra was coming forward as she answered, "It's the cleaner you keep under the sink. I'm sorry, but there were a couple of places I couldn't get clean without it."

"Did you—" and again, the Faelnar sneezed. "Did you use the whole bottle in one spot?!"

"No, Gorta. I used it exactly according to the instructions on the label. It said one part cleaner for every four parts water."

The Faelnar's eyebrow fur raised. Although it was a distant memory, she did recall that being the exact instruction. "Oh, okay. I'll … I'll have to—" Gorta was interrupted by a sneezing fit at that point, and Vanarra stepped forward to take her bags and offer her a tissue. As the Faelnar tried to right herself, Vanarra propped open the front door and then went to the back. After a moment, the strong flow of air pouring in from the front door eased the Faelnar's symptoms and helped her regain control. The buzzing of a large fan, one she thought was stolen some time ago, met her ears and started to draw her back into the storeroom.

When she walked into the room, she screamed, "It's empty!"

"Well, not … completely," Vanarra quietly disagreed.

"What?! What did you throw away!?" In answer to that accusation, Vanarra produced a list where, in very precise and readable paw-writing, a description of everything that had been discarded had been logged. "Seventeen boxed lunches, contents out of date and packaging damaged. Six stacks of programs that were for previous events – five samples kept of each. Two – Anati, this can't be right!"

"I'm afraid so. They were kind of scattered throughout."

"Oh by the moons," Gorta replied in a mixture of embarrassment and self-frustration. "Sixteen unopened boxes of food, all the contents expired, some leaking. Well, I … I guess then that would tend to empty the place out a little. Were there any … forms or invoices that you kept?"

"Kept and filed."

"Filed!? All of the filing drawers in the front office were locked!" the Faelnar replied, stunned.

"In ... this filing cabinet. I kind of had to come up with a replacement for folders. I ... I can do better if I could get some real ones."

Without so much as another word, the Faelnar walked to the small piece of furniture and stared at it with amazement as if it had suddenly appeared from another planet. "Was ... was there anything in it? When you found it?" Gorta asked after she went through the files of both drawers with an exposed claw-tip.

"Yes. There was a stock of well-aged fermentum. I've placed that up on the shelf, over there, according to what it said on the label." Gorta then walked over to the shelf and started looking around. Everything that had been salvageable, it appeared, had been neatly ordered and organized with a diligence and precision that made the Faelnar shake her head.

"How does an Anati learn to do all of this?!" Gorta asked, finally returning back to Van.

"I ... I've helped, and I'm familiar with a few other places that have to sort things and put them on shelves. I hope it's okay."

Again, the Faelnar looked at the list she was carrying, and with her blush furs barely under control, discovered that her new employee hadn't thrown away anything without noting it, including why the item was discarded. "Well, kit, that's ... that's pretty impressive. You may have just worked yourself out of a job, though. I mean, what else is left?"

"Well, you had a number of calls last night, and your LineCom answerer didn't seem to be working, so I took down the client information for you. Really, Gorta, I'll do anything to help you, and ... what you left – the meat rolls – were really very good. I'd love to learn from you. That's the one thing I couldn't do where I was. I couldn't exactly ... cook."

Gorta stood back and looked at the Anati in front of her. "Well, granted you are a scrambled rulla egg, but you're pretty in a way. I ... I could probably take you along to my events, at least some of the time."

"The others – I would love to help you get ready for them. Really, Gorta, please. I'll do anything to help you I can!"

Quite beyond her control, the Faelnar started to smile. "Oh, alright. You've sold me, kit. Here, let me pay you for the time you've worked and then some. That ... well, more than anything proves that I need another set of paws around here."

"Thank you, Gorta! Thank you! You won't be disappointed!" Vanarra replied, sounding giddy.

"Well, make sure I won't, but ... otherwise, I think this may just work out."

"Triana, where are they?" Sahnassa asked nervously as she looked out into the audience gathered for the tertiary school graduation. "I know they're mad, but they're not actually going to bail on me, are they?"

Triana sighed at her younger sister, dressed in graduate's robes. "They're here. They're ... well, in the back – the very back."

Sahnassa's lips nearly curled up into a snarl. "As close to not being here as they can get without actually not showing up. I suppose they have an ... important engagement to go to right after this that prevents them from spending any time with me."

Triana closed her eyes and again admitted, "Yeah. Something like that."

"I have a perfect average, will probably be rated top in my class, and I may even get a scholarship to something nice like Dothnaria, and ... dammit." She looked away from her older sister and wouldn't say anymore.

"I'm sorry, you know that, right?"

"You didn't do anything, at least not to make them mad at you," Sahnassa said bitterly.

"There's been plenty of things for them to be mad at me about ... just not this one. You should know that Dame Rothnerra is here, too."

That made Sahnassa even angrier and stirred her resentment. "Oh, she would be! Sitting with them, right?"

"Stalking around just a bit, but yeah, she's camping out in our row," Triana admitted. "Not surprised by this very much, are you?"

"No. Matron ... Shalarra," she started, but a lump formed in her throat. It had only been a few sols since her matron's memorial service, and the loss still grieved Sahnassa badly. Collecting herself, she looked into her sister's sad eyes and explained, "Matron Shalarra called every bit of this. So, no, it doesn't surprise me. It just makes me wish that the one adult who cared about me and was happy for me was actually here."

"Hey, I'm here," Triana offered, putting her paw on her sister's shoulder, "and I'm an adult."

That made Sahnassa smirk a little. "More or less," she shot back. Looking towards the podium at the instructors assembling, Sahnassa warned, "You'd best get back, Triana. They're about to start."

"I care about you, kit. I really do, okay?" Sahnassa accepted the hug and returned it briefly before Triana sped away, and Sahnassa was left to gather with the other graduates of her class.

As Triana slipped into her seat, beside her mother and Dame Rothnerra, she almost visibly bristled at her mother's question. "How … is she?"

Knowing the answer would undoubtedly be eavesdropped upon by the dame, Triana replied as smoothly and respectfully as she could, "She's looking forward toward receiving the honors of her studies. She only hopes what she's done will bring some honor to our house."

"Very doubtful," Rothnerra put in at a low volume.

Sitting on the other side, Gonastir quietly asked the dame, "So, tonight will be when she finds out that she's only been accepted by Harnard?"

"Yes. And that should put the matter to rest very quickly, since you've already informed her that studying there will not be supported by either you or your mate."

"And we can reapply for entrance in the de Orturu Legal or Archivist programs?"

"Certainly," Rothnerra assured. "She'll start a moon or so behind, but with diligent work, it should not be a problem."

Although Triana couldn't hear their words, the tone nearly made her claws come out. Her father and the dame were up to something, and her poor, hapless sister was the target. She could just imagine the intervals of consoling that would be required later, and then seeing her sister walk around the lair like a shell of a Thurian, all of her dreams crushed. Although Triana's dreams had the fortunate aspect of being aligned to those of her father, it didn't take much imagination for the elder sister to empathize with what the younger was going through. She envied Hylea, who had volunteered to pass out programs and open and close doors – she wouldn't be stuck sitting with her parents and the dame.

The ceremony began with much the same cadence as hers had a few seasons before – the call to order, the welcome, the speech by someone of honor or merit, and then came the presentation of each graduate and the listing of their honors. Sahnassa was in the middle, due to her name, so Triana had to simply suffer through listening to this kit or that cub who had done this or that and was going somewhere or other.

As it came Sahnassa's turn, however, she felt her mother tense, and that brought Triana back to the moment and the proctor's words.

"It is seldom that we are able to recognize someone who has achieved not only an academic record of perfection, but has also found high esteem and honor in the eyes of all of her professors and many of her peers. Sahnassa de Orturu is graduating with full honors in the hopes of becoming a technologist. Her application to and acceptance at the leading and most prestigious academy for the study of that field, Harnard Academy, speaks greatly to the capabilities of this young Nephti. Dothnaria and Counterlan academies have both surrendered their claim, so Harnard it will be."

Triana swallowed as she saw Sahnassa's tail dip. Being appointed to Harnard was a top honor, but unless her mother and father recanted their promise not to fund her technology studies, she knew her poor sister had no way of attending. A glance at the dame indicated a smug satisfaction at seeing Sahnassa's discomfiture, which made Triana's stomach churn with anger. However, the proctor had more to say. "Not only Harnard is recognizing Sahnassa tonight. Her own house is supporting her with the full weight of the Matriarch's Scholarship, paying for all of Sahnassa's tuition and books and study material for the duration of her time there."

As applause and cheers burst forth and Sahnassa's paws went up to her muzzle in astonished surprise, a second glance at the dame's features didn't demonstrate the same smugness that had been there a moment before. For once, the gray dame was utterly and completely stunned. Looking a little longer, she noted her father grinding his teeth – something he only did when he was either really embarrassed or really, really mad. Her mother looked as if someone had told her she'd never be able to drink Aster tree tea again.

With the cheers still roiling through the crowd, Triana listened as the proctor tried to call the assembly back to order. "Now, now, yes … that is certainly something to celebrate. Sahnassa, I know this comes as an immense surprise to you, but I can't think of a kit more deserving and, in truth, the Matriarch's Scholarship is not all of the support you'll be enjoying. Added to this are the Finder's Scholarship, the Technologists Pack, and the Brissaine scholarships which, with the support of her family will mean that Sahnassa will be able to devote most of her time to her studies – something she will truly need at Harnard. Sahnassa, would you like to say a few words?"

"Oh … oh my! That's … that's just amazing!" Sahnassa bubbled as she stepped forward to the microphone at the proctor's urging. "I … I just want to give my thanks to all of the instructors and to the proctor and my classmates and to my wonderful Matriarch and … well, to someone very special who would have given anything to see this tonight. My matron, my … best friend, passed away at the turning of the last moon. This night my thanks go out to her wherever she is – oh, and to my sisters and to my mother and father and dame. I hope to bring honor to my house. Thank you!"

"Dame, a word," Triana heard her father say as Sahnassa retired from the platform to join the rest of the students on the stage. It was surprising, since it was nearly an order – the kind she and her sisters had received so many times. The two exited the row and made for the lobby without saying anything else.

As her mother looked at them go, Triana asked softly, "Mom, aren't you proud of Sahnassa?"

"What? Oh? Well now, I…" Triana's expression must have had an impact on her mother, because she stopped trying to prevaricate.

"Mom! She's received honors much higher than what I have, or even what you did, or Dad! You're not proud of her?"

"I … can't call it pride, Triana," her mother replied, looking away and sounding hurt.

Leaning over and whispering into her mother's ear, Triana pleaded, "Mother! You and Father are going to push Sahnassa away until she leaves and never speaks to us again! She'll be a part of de Orturu, and she'll be earning honors, but she'll have nothing to do with us because of how you are treating her right now! Don't you love your own child, mother? Would you treat me like this if I wanted to become a technologist?! You are forsaking your own daughter!"

That stung her mother, and she swung around to look at her daughter angrily. "Fine," Triana replied into her mother's fierce expression. "You tell me how you aren't shoving her away, and I'll take it all back. Who matters more to you, Mom? Sahnassa or your dame?"

A shock of fear went through her mother's eyes, and then she hung her head, refusing to face her daughter. "Mother, I will be out tonight," Triana said firmly, "celebrating with Sahnassa and her friends – Hylea, too. Now, if you'll excuse me, I'm really feeling sick."

The sneer in her daughter's voice and the near head-swipe with her tail left Holana sitting disconsolately alone, and conspicuously so.

Chapter 9: Compactly

Utterly resigned, and unhappily so, Sahnassa finished packing her travel cases with the belongings she thought she'd need, and given her parents' icy silence since graduation, she had given the list some very deep thought. One of her prized possessions, her orlure, would have to stay behind. There wasn't a student's lair anywhere near the academy that would be able to accommodate such a large and bulky musical instrument with all of its tubes and bows and oils and so forth. The sad little practice version, although capable of most of the same sounds via technological trickery, would be the only thing beyond basic necessities she could bring with her. "Fine, it will remind them of me," she growled quietly.

"It's … it's not like we're going to forget you, kit," her mother said softly from the doorway.

Not startled and still angry at them, Sahnassa didn't flinch. "Really? I would have thought you would start cutting me out of all the pictures in the lair once I'm gone, changing my room into a … another law study or your own little archive."

Her mother clearly took offense, and her tail lashed indignantly. "There's no cause to be disrespectful."

"I have every reason to have lost respect for you!" Sahnassa shouted, turning to face her mother. "You and Dad! I have *friends* at Dothnaria academy, Mother! They found out what Dame Rothnerra did and told me! She made them think that I was simply applying there to fill out the three spaces on the form! I wanted to go to

Dothnaria! There's no way you and Father couldn't have known what she was up to; Dad probably came up with it!"

Shocked by this revelation, her mother was now on the defensive, and yelled back, "We're just trying to look out for you, do what's best for you!"

"By kicking my hind legs out from under me, Mother?! Really?!" Holana was stopped cold by that image, and Sahnassa closed in on her. "You and father have disavowed me!"

"We have done no such thing!"

"Yes! You have," Sahnassa replied, her voice quavering. "You ... you refuse to help put a roof over my head or food in my muzzle, but I bet your pack memberships and trips to the coast and elegant dress shopping won't even miss a paw step! Will they?" As Holana stammered, Sahnassa turned away from her. "How ... disappointed all of you must be that your clever little trick didn't work out! I ... I figured it out, and yes, when I heard that it was only Harnard that had accepted me, I felt it like bared claws across my stomach. Now, I have enough scholarships to pay my way and at least take care of one season in the academy students' lair. I promise you; I'm going to get a job, and I'm going to make my way ... somehow."

Sahnassa turned and saw that her father was at the door, as well, having heard the commotion. "You're not going to change your mind, are you?"

"No, Father, and neither are you. So ... thank you for giving me a home – until now. Thank you for feeding me and helping me get an education – until now. Thank you for ... for loving me – until now. I ... I was honored to be your daughter – until now."

Staring into her father's face, she knew there were things he wanted to say, but he simply frowned and walked away, his wife following him. Through almost tear-blinded eyes, Sahnassa continued packing.

As Gonastir retreated into his bedroom, Holana followed closing the door behind her. "Damn arrogant kit!" he growled. "Would that I could disavow her, myself!"

"You heard her, Gonastir. We ... we only have two daughters now. I ... I hope this is what you wanted."

"Hardly," he grumped. "The dame's schemes have turned to absolute rot at every turn while Matron Shalarra's seemed to have worked out perfectly. Even from beyond the grave, she claws at us."

"I thought I *was* ashamed," Holana whimpered as she sat upon their bed, "when everyone found out that Sahnassa was going to be a technologist. Now, when they ask how she's doing, what do I tell them, Gonastir? When they ask me how proud I am that our ... daughter won the Matriarch's scholarship, what do I tell them? If she graduates, do we not go? What do we tell everyone, then? For seasons and seasons to come, when kits or cubs she used to know come up to us and ask us what she's doing or how she is, what will we tell them? When she—"

Gonastir interrupted angrily. "Is there an actual point to this ... self-indulgent supposition?"

"Yes. We're losing our daughter," Holana replied, standing up and walking away from him.

"She will come back, when things get hard enough," he affirmed, although by the tone of his voice, it was clear he wasn't certain either.

"She might not! We've crawled so far out on this branch, we're trapped! If we decide to support Sahnassa, we risk alienating our dame! If we decide not to help her, as we have, then ... then we could lose her. She'd be like silly old Villiana's cub who left and made millions upon millions! He never calls! From the things you and ... I have said to Sahnassa, she ... she won't call us either. She won't have anything to do with us."

"What do you want me to do!? You've done a masterful job explaining our situation, but what do I do?! What do we do?!"

"We love our daughter!" Holana shot back. "We ... try to work something out, Gonastir!"

For a long time, Gonastir stewed and paced. Finally, he looked at Holana and said, "Alright. I'm ... willing to talk to her, but I'm not going to be treated with disrespect."

"Fine. Let's go see if we can give her some reason to treat us with respect. I don't think we've given her much reason to, lately."

Slowly, the pair exited their room and made their way back to Sahnassa's. As her father came to the door, he said, "Sahnassa, your mother and I –"

"It's no use, Dad," the voice of their youngest said from Sahnassa's bedroom. "She's gone." The two parents looked into Hylea's paws and saw the kit holding a stack of letters and cards, tears rolling down her cheek fur.

"What … are those?" Holana asked.

"Every note you ever wrote her, every card you sent to her, and every message she got from you while she was away. She … she told me that … the parents who wrote those things to her are gone now, and that I should … pretend they were written to me and forget … forget she ever lived here." Holana just turned away and walked down the hallway, and her father shed a tear. "I don't want to forget her, Dad! She's my sister."

"What have I—" he started, but then he clenched his eyes shut and walked away.

Quietly, realizing that her father wouldn't change his mind, Hylea pulled the batch of paper to her chest and hugged it. "You did live here, sis, and … I'll miss you."

"Hey, Anati!"

The voice called Vanarra from the back storeroom where she was just shelving a new shipment of napkins that had arrived. "Coming, Gorta!" Van called, and then walked up to the front, once she had secured the back door. In the last three moons of working for the Faelnar, Vanarra had actually gotten used to not being called by her name. As far as she could determine, the purebred didn't actually say it to hurt her feelings, intentionally.

Stepping into the front office, Van asked, "What can I do for you?"

"Look at the numbers we're piling up in receipts!" Gorta chuckled happily. "We're … we're really starting to see more and more events come our way, and good events, too! This is starting to make me think it wasn't a mistake bringing you on."

"Gorta," Van groaned. At every turn, the Faelnar teased her about giving her a job, but at some level, Vanarra was now aware that the disavowed female was truly relying on her, more and more every sol.

"I know, not a fair swipe at you, anymore. You've done really well for me, kit, and I mean that. I'm giving you a raise – two steps above base wage."

Vanarra's eyes widened. "Well, thank you! That will make Sorla happy, as well!"

"Still paying her back?" Gorta asked, curious.

"Yes. I ... I owe her a lot."

"Hmm... kit, I think I should tell you a secret." Vanarra stepped close as the Faelnar motioned her over and spoke quietly. "Sorla will never let you pay her back, not completely. It's maddening, and I've tried. She always gives you more."

Vanarra smiled as she thought of her only purebred friend. "I can see that. She's ... special and wonderful."

"A true rare spirit," Gorta mused. "She's also been tunneling into my ear about a disservice I've been doing you. I haven't taken you with me to any events. The truth is ... I'm getting to where I need a little help. These new events are ... big, and they're a lot for me. Now, you'll have to behave yourself, and don't expect to get treated like a matriarch or dame, either. These are avowed, purebred events, and having an Anati there probably won't make them all that happy, but if you can help me set up and take down and then maybe just find somewhere out of the way during the event, help in the back or what not, it ... it could work. It would mean bonus time, too, just in case I forgot to mention it."

Vanarra's eyes went wider still. Not only was she getting a nice raise, but Gorta was kicking in additional overtime on top of it. "Wow, Gorta! I can't say thank you enough! That's the best news ever! I ... I only wish –"

"What?" Gorta asked, crossing her arms and twitching her tail, expecting the Anati to want more. Instead, Vanarra sat down on the chair, not looking at her and seemed to be suddenly very sad. "What is it, kit?"

Tears in her eyes, Van turned towards Gorta and confessed, "There's someone ... dear to me I lost. I only wish he could have been here to hear you give me the news. He – it would have made him happy."

Gorta leaned back in her chair and let her paw drift towards a picture she always kept close to her when she worked. "I know, kit. I know. It hurts. I miss my special someone every single sol, every interval. I go to these events where ... someone was just joined or celebrated a hundred seasons of being joined, and ... then there's me. Alone."

"Is it hard to be there, when that's going on?"

"Not so much," the Faelnar confessed. "You've got a job to do, and you do it. It's ... after that it hurts, when the room's ... empty." Vanarra watched as Gorta took a glass from behind her, poured something from a decanter into it, and drank it down. "Well, that's enough of that. You going to celebrate?"

"Just by telling Sorla. I need to finish putting things away first."

"For once, kit, just leave it. Go. You're done. Here," the Faelnar ordered as she pulled out a draft and scribbled in the amount of Vanarra's pay. "Go have a good time. Tell Sorla I said to, as well, okay?"

"Alright. Thank you, Gorta! Very much!" Vanarra took the draft and was about to leave the office when she heard the Faelnar reach for the decanter again. "Are you going to be alright?"

"Sure. Go on now. Don't make me wish I hadn't done anything nice for an Anati."

Feeling the Faelnar's defenses prick up and seeing the slight bristling on the back of her employer's neck, Vanarra nodded, offered her thanks again, and left.

Sahnassa had been crying the entire time since her friend dropped her off at the transport station outside of the de Orturu estate. In some ways, it felt like she should just call herself Sahnassa. Looking back at the gates to the family estate, she could easily empathize with anyone who had been ejected from the family. "I … I have to make my own way now, alone," she thought bitterly. In a sense, she knew that wasn't true. Her new matron would be expecting her to call in once she was settled in the students' lairs, and the same matron would be checking in with her once a moon – probably more – inquiring on her progress. After all, it was only through her matron that she would actually be able to collect the scholarships.

However, maintaining her connection to the institutional de Orturu family wouldn't be any replacement for what she felt she'd lost over the last few seasons – namely the love and support of her parents. In rebellious indignation, she thought through all of the ways she could give the matron as little information as possible. "I'm happy. I'm well. Everything's okay. I have lots of friends. I really like it here." She could spend all five seasons telling her matron that, and her parents and the dame would just have to accept it. Again, however, reality intruded on that pleasant fantasy as she boarded the transport for the long ride to the Harnard campus. The matron would be talking to her instructors, perhaps making suggestions – if what she had heard from others was right.

That thought made her very soul ache. "Great, Dame Rothnerra and my parents could still kick my hind legs out from under me by souring my instructors on me or convincing them to give me impossible assignments!" Angrily staring at the floor, Sahnassa grimaced.

"You okay, kit?" the Nephti driver asked her.

Looking up in surprise, Sahnassa suddenly realized that her claws had expressed themselves and her tail had cleared the seats on either side of her quite effectively. "Sorry," she said to the other patrons who, although nodding, still kept their distance. Looking up at the driver glancing back at her through a mirror, she repeated the apology.

"Come up here, kit," the female driver suggested, and somewhat shamefacedly, Sahnassa obeyed, pulling her travel cases along with her clumsily. "I wanted to ask you quietly, kit. Did you just get … some very bad news?"

Instantly, Sahnassa knew what the driver was thinking – an obviously upset Nephti with travel cases at a transport stop outside of the house de Orturu gates very definitely suggested someone just disavowed. "Oh, no. I'm … I still have my last name, thankfully. It's just an argument with my parents. I'm going to academy, settling in – just without their support. They … don't agree about the field I'm studying in."

"What's that?" the driver asked, curious.

"Technologist," Sahnassa admitted.

"What!? Do they have any idea how much a technologist can pull down in salary a season!?" the driver nearly shouted with indignation. "I wish I was a technologist! If I was, you sure wouldn't see me driving a transport, let me tell you!"

Sahnassa was forced to smile at the driver's indignation that so clearly mirrored her own. "Oh, but see I'm not going to be a litigator or an archivist. Those are the only 'chosen' fields."

"Chosen, right!" the driver countered, quietly. "Like we don't have enough of those already! Sometimes, I downright admire Vulpi houses because they aren't afraid to send their members after careers where your paws can get dirty."

"I know."

"I suppose you've tried convincing them."

"So many times until I was just told to keep my muzzle shut on the subject," Sahnassa offered. "I don't disagree with what they do; I … I just know I wouldn't enjoy it." The driver shook her head. "What?"

"I know a kit who is happy to take any job, the worst job if necessary, to make it. You have a future, the potential for a great career—"

"It just isn't enough for them," Sahnassa interjected sadly.

"So, if your parents aren't supporting your choice of going to school – if you don't mind me asking – how are you able to still go?"

"Scholarships," Sahnassa answered as the transport came to a stop.

The driver looked back at her, dark blue eyes snapping with offense. "And you're a good student, too! Top rank, I'd bet!" Sahnassa's embarrassed shrug was all the confirmation that was needed. "Oh, I'm sorry, kit! I really am. There are parents who would give anything to have a daughter like you. There are kits I know who would give anything to be you, and still, that's not enough? I'm sorry; that's just wrong!" the driver said firmly before looking forward. "I hope you ace everything, kit! I hope you prove them wrong, and that one sol, they have to come crawling back to you."

"I'm sure they think it will be the other way around – that I'll come crawling back to them, tail between my legs, begging their forgiveness. Thanks, though. That's the kindest thing anyone's said to me in a long while."

"You're welcome. Now, don't let them fuss you, kit. There are good Thurians on the path ahead of you – be sure of that."

"Thank you very much. It's nice to know someone else can see things my way."

The driver wasn't quite done with her. "Hey, you're going to be on this transport for awhile, so I want you to do something for me."

"What?" Sahnassa asked, bemused.

"I want you to concentrate on how good it feels … to be free and heading towards a future of your own making. Enjoy it, kit. I'm sure there are things you're worried about, but still, why waste the time, right?"

Sahnassa was forced to chuckle a little. "You're right. Thank you."

"Glad to help," the driver replied, and sitting back in a nearby seat, Sahnassa tried to take the driver's advice and simply enjoy the trip towards her new future.

"Thank you!" Sahnassa called back to the transport driver as the door closed and its skids retracted. With a wave back at her, the transport was away. "What a nice kit," she said to herself, and Sahnassa had to admit that she actually did feel better. Only a few other students were around, and having been to Harnard only once before, the beauty and regal grace of the buildings and gardens all around her filled her with awe. All of the buildings were old, but far more than simple mounds with doors and windows scattered along them; these stately shapes sported spires and ornamental walls and shaded gardens with seats all around. In many ways, it reminded her of the Pinnacle Center Archive, which was a newer structure standing all on its own. This was like a forest of small Pinnacle Centers, each one bestowed with its own uniqueness and grace. Beyond her ability to control it, she just stood there admiring everything before her.

In time, however, a part of her became afraid that her father and mother and dame would come driving up any moment to stop her or interfere with what she was doing. As quickly as she could, she started following the signs that led her towards the student center.

After nearly an interval filling out forms and having to answer, time and again, where her matron was and why she wasn't being escorted, Sahnassa found herself burdened additionally with a satchel full of academy documents and a key card for the tiny lair she'd be sharing with another student. Thankfully, she had been made aware that the hall wardens had a storage area for her travel cases once she had unpacked. The heavily laden and panting Sahnassa continued down the stone path until she reached the females' lairs. Hauling her possessions up the three levels nearly caused her to pass out, and once at the top of the stairs, she had to rest. Thankfully, there was no one around since she had arrived at the very beginning of the registration period and on the very first sol.

Huffing and grunting her way down the narrow hall, Sahnassa finally found lair 314 and knocked quietly on the door, not truly expecting anyone to answer.

"Yes? Who is it?" a sing-song voice called back to her.

"I … I'm Sahnassa de Orturu. I think this is supposed to be my new lair."

"Hmm…" The Nephti waiting outside in the hallway shook her head a little in surprise. Normally, she would have expected someone to just open the door or at least call back to her to come in. The sound she heard was very much like the Thurian within had just decided to consider the matter, like someone who would get back to her in a few sols.

"Uh, would … would it be okay if I came in?"

"I suppose…" Sahnassa's head cocked this time. Again, the tone was nothing short of someone considering an abstract theory or an idea. With a grunt, she put her travel cases in the hallway along the wall and searched for her key card. "But I'm not really sure yet."

"What would it take to make you sure?" Sahnassa asked, confused.

"Well you see, we're really not going to know how okay it's going to be until after you've already come in."

Sahnassa chuckled despite her frustration. "You have a point there. May I please?"

"Do you mean would it be pleasing if you came in or that you would be willing to please me by coming in?"

"Uh, I … think I'm asking for your permission to come in, as a courtesy," Sahnassa replied, realizing this was the longest conversation she'd ever had with a door before, still trying to keep any sign of testiness out of her voice.

"If you are sharing this lair, then you do not require my permission to enter, you only need to prove the truth of your assertion."

"How?" Sahnassa asked, but there was no response. Then, she looked down at the keycard in her paw. "Well, you have a point there, too. Okay."

With no other preamble, Sahnassa slipped the keycard into its slot and opened the door. The small room that greeted her was nothing like the austere little lair she had seen on her one and only tour. Because of its unique situation in the building, it was somewhat deeper than the rest, and the current occupant had obviously brought in copious amounts of wall-hangings, curtains, and other décor that turned the still smallish room into a sort of meditative haven. The room, however, wasn't anywhere as singular as its occupant, who sat calmly on a bed along the far wall, looking at the new arrival appraisingly. Dressed only in her underthings with her legs crossed, the Nephti looking back at Sahnassa had light purple fur that was a very attractive color, accented with exquisite striping that made her look nearly like a painted piece of artwork. Calm purple eyes stared at her, not unkindly, and a pink nose took a brief, subtle sniff, as if trying to sample a trace of Sahnassa's scent.

"I ... uh ... hi," she greeted the sitting Nephti. "I suppose that's pretty good proof."

"Sufficient, yes," her new companion mused.

Trying to be the kind and polite Thurian, Sahnassa stepped forward and stated, "I'm Sahnassa de Orturu, and I'm pleased to meet you."

"Really? Why?" What was shocking to Sahnassa about that question was that she now had a facial expression, ears, and tail to gauge the intent of the one speaking. There was a little anxiety and self doubt in the question, and this Nephti actually seemed to be a season or two younger than she was.

"Well, I'm beginning to think that you're really interesting, and I kind of like interesting. You've made me think more in the last few passes than I did on the way over here. Also, this ... what you've done with the hangings and the decorations – it's ... beautiful! My old room was nothing like this, and I've never seen anything like it, but it's so ... peaceful and warm. If all of this," she said motioning all around, "is any sign of who you are, I think I am pleased. I just wish I knew your name."

"Merialla de Fantar. I have an exceptionally high intelligence rating, but no social filter whatsoever – or at least that's what I'm told."

"Social filter?" Sahnassa asked, curious.

"I say what I think without taking into account the feelings of others," Merialla answered, looking away. "At least that's what the doctors have told my parents and matron and dame; my diagnosis is fairly complex. I have a copy of it if you'd like to read it."

"It's okay. You just ... think differently than others around you do," Sahnassa stated as she sat down on the empty bed closer to the door, a touch of sadness in her voice. She wondered, absently, if that was an idea her own parents had considered – taking her to a psychoanalyst to discover why Sahnassa didn't want to be an archivist or a litigator.

"You think differently, too?"

Sahnassa nodded, still not looking at Merialla. "Yeah, but I don't have a diagnosis. My parents think I'm just doing everything because I don't respect them or don't want to follow in their paw-steps."

"They injured your soul, and you *have* lost respect for them." Sahnassa's head snapped back to Merialla who was gently considering her. There was no malice or accusation in what she was saying, and Sahnassa nodded in agreement, the emotional pain welling back up inside of her. "Oh my, and deeply! Even I can see it. That was very dishonorable for them to hurt the soul of their own child."

"Yeah," Sahnassa replied, sniffing a little, her eyes welling as she looked at the floor.

"When you came into the room and saw me, you said it pleased you. Now, you're crying. I guess you're not pleased, anymore."

"But I am," Sahnassa replied, chuckling a little. "I … I finally found someone who understands. It sounds like your soul has been injured, too."

"My parents love me, but they don't understand me," Merialla answered in acknowledgment. "I don't even understand me, all of the time. Every doctor they took me to made me wonder why I was this way, and they tried so many things to fix me, like I was broken. I don't … feel broken. I feel alright and kind of happy, except when they try to fix me or push me away. My parents aren't very happy, at least with me. I've been here for two sols, and the campus wasn't even open until this morning."

"You think they did it on purpose?" Sahnassa asked, wondering if Merialla's parents had moved her in early just to be rid of her.

Merialla looked at her, just a hint of admonition in her tone. "Everyone does what they do on purpose. If there were no purpose, there could be no exercise of free will. Some may not think through their purpose or control its results very well, but – aside from those who are mentally damaged or not formed properly – everything that is done is done on purpose."

Again, Sahnassa couldn't argue with her logic. "Yeah. That doesn't make it hurt any less. It hurts more. I … I came to the unhappy discovery that my parents care more about what my dame thinks than they do about loving me. And yes, you're right. They did it on purpose. I'm even afraid that they'll try to trip me up or kick my hind legs out from under me while I'm here."

"Physical violence is illegal in this case, especially for those of the matriarchy," Merialla replied in something akin to surprise, but the reaction was more analytical than it was emotional.

"No ... not physically, but they might ... talk to my professors and counselors and have them make things harder for me, try to get me to quit and go back to them, tell my parents I'll be whatever they want me to be."

"Hmm... That's illegal, as well, especially if you reference section three seventeen, assertion twelve of the Crearnum Triad Compact."

Sahnassa shook her head. "I'm sorry. I don't follow." That statement clearly confused Merialla, so she clarified, "I mean I don't understand how the Crearnum Triad Compact can actually keep my dame and parents from ruining my time here."

"Oh, so you haven't read the full compact, just the parts they teach you in school. That's completely intentional, especially when you review that section."

"What does it say?"

Closing her eyes, Merialla replied as if she was quoting directly, "Such as have authority over those beyond the age of childhood shall in no way make a hindrance to them where they, now recognized mature, are engaged in the pursuit of lawful, good, and honorable goals. Those raising opposition to such are guilty of great dishonor and shame, and if such as have authority over those beyond the age of childhood cannot involve themselves for the good and in truth, they should reserve their judgments and make no effort to either hinder or help, lest they be guilty of dishonor, purposeful or not." Opening her eyes, Merialla added, "So states the Compact."

"Wow!" Sahnassa replied, surprised. "I ... I've never heard that one before! Does it still apply?"

"It's why I'm here and not in a psychological ward or being given drugs to adjust my condition."

"Again, wow. I heard those words at the end – purposeful or not?"

Merialla tilted her head, considering the problem and said evenly, "I can only reason that the author of that statement knew there were parents, matrons, and dames who were mentally malformed."

Before she knew what she was doing, Sahnassa was rolling on the bed in laughter. In a round-about way, Merialla had suggested that Dame Rothnerra was crazy. The light purple Nephti looked at her with a mixture of curiosity and amusement. "It seems that you are quite pleased, now."

Righting herself, albeit with difficulty, Sahnassa answered, "Oh yes! Oh, yes! If ... if you can tell me how to ... keep my dame and parents from ruining my life, oh yes! I am ... I am so wonderfully pleased, and ... by you!"

"I think I am now pleased, too, Sahnassa," Merialla replied, smiling, the two becoming friends in that instant.

Sahnassa soon finished putting her travel cases in storage and organizing her possessions. During the process, Merialla had actually commented on much of what had come out of those cases. Some of her observations were very candid and a little shocking, such as "I don't like soldering irons. They are only meant to burn." Some of the words coming from her muzzle were almost poetry. "Oh, orlure music opens the soul and pours in sweetness and understanding." Based on that comment, Sahnassa had asked, carefully, if she could play something for Merialla, and the Nephti agreed, more or less. Sahnassa was just putting on her paw-gloves when a knock came at the door.

"Yes, who is it?" Sahnassa asked, her new friend still sitting, captured and fascinated by the practice orlure in front of her.

"Matron Drualla de Orturu. I would like to speak with Sahnassa."

Swallowing, she pulled her gloves off and rose to open the door. Bowing slightly to the graying matron with the stern expression and hard silver eyes, Sahnassa greeted her and invited her into the room. Looking at both the room and Merialla as if they were an unwashed plate that had been accidently overlooked in the cleaning process, she said, "I would like to hold this conversation in private, if you don't mind."

"If you wanted to hold a conversation in private," Merialla retorted in an even tone of observation, "you should have gone to someplace where no one else was."

This fussed the matron considerably, and she shot back, "I'm telling you to leave, you impudent little kit!"

"Yes, I suppose you are," Merialla agreed, much to Sahnassa's amusement, albeit concealed.

"Well?!" Matron Drualla queried.

"A hole dug into the ground until the porous layer of rock can be reached, and water can be extracted."

"I am telling you to leave and give Sahnassa and I some privacy, now!"

"Yes, you are," came the soft, analytical response.

Dumbfounded by the Nephti not instantly complying with her order, the matron looked at Sahnassa accusingly. "Have you already engendered such … disrespect in someone else in the short time you've been here?!"

"Matrons are supposed to be respectful, not disrespectful as you are being to both my new friend and to me right now. A matron as old as you should know that," came the detached observation from the light purple Nephti still not moving from where she sat.

"Well, I never have been so disrespected in my life!"

"Truly? Given the length of time you've been alive, surely some opportunity for that has arisen. Interesting…"

The matron looked back at Sahnassa in something akin to helplessness, and Sahnassa explained, embarrassed, "She … does have a point about staying. This is her lair, as well. She's also de Fantar, with no allegiance to our family. And," Sahnassa added carefully, "she has the entire Compact memorized. Perhaps it would be better if we were just okay with her staying here."

Seeing that she had precious few choices and apparently unwilling to remove herself to somewhere else for this discussion, the matron's tail lashed angrily. "Very well. Sahnassa, I am here to discuss with you what classes you will take and the course load you will carry."

"With all respect, Matron," Sahnassa replied, emboldened by Merialla's earlier revelation, "I believe those are my choices to make, and I already know what courses I'm going to choose."

"Since we are your family, you have an obligation to heed our advice and wisdom," the matron replied, angrily. "As I am now your matron, that counsel is given through me."

"Again, meaning no disrespect, Matron, I believe those are my choices to make, especially now that I am out of my parents' lair and living on my own. The scholarships have funded my way, and the Matriarch's scholarship nor any of the others require I take any specific courses. I asked the matriarch about that when she presented me the award in the keep."

"But do you honestly think that as a kit of not even twenty seasons, you should refuse the wisdom and guidance of your family, the sage advice of those who have lived nearly ten times as long as you have?!"

Sahnassa rose from where she sat, standing between the door her matron. "Yes, when I have cause to believe that advice to be … intended for harm to the 'lawful, good, and honorable goals' I wish to pursue as an adult. Matron, I have had friends at two other academies tell me that Dame Rothnerra intentionally misled their administrators to think I didn't want to attend. They showed me the forms, and I have copies." At this revelation, much of the matron's huff and bluster drained away. "I wanted to go to those academies, and this one was too expensive for me, especially since my parents refuse to support me."

"Your … your parents aren't … supporting you here?" the matron asked, confused. "But this is Harnard! This … is a prestigious academy, the *most* honorable."

"But I'm not becoming a litigator or an archivist. They don't agree with my career choice, so they've cut me off from their help … and even their love. Before the death of my previous matron, who I truly loved as a dear friend, they – my parents and my dame – were doing everything they could to push me onto a path they approved. There is nothing about being a technologist that is not 'lawful, good, and honorable,' Matron, is there?"

"Not in and of itself," Matron Drualla replied quietly. "I take it by the fact you've used the words of the Compact, that you know your rights in this matter."

"I do, and I am terrified, Matron, that someone from my family will work against me here, pick classes for me that are too difficult or too many in number. I'm afraid they'll talk to my professors and make them … not like me or give me more work or … I don't know – grade me more harshly? Although I've truly enjoyed the favor of the Matriarch in any and all ways, and I love her for that, and I love my family, I just know that my parents and my dame do not … even like me, and they've tried to make my path more difficult. So, yes, Matron. I want the protection of the Compact."

Looking into the face of the matron, Sahnassa knew that Drualla had clearly been given false information about her. However, it was as evident that Sahnassa's candor and honesty, something she always exercised with Matron Shalarra, was resonating very strongly with this elder matron. Pulling a piece of paper from her robes, Matron Drualla opened it and invited Sahnassa to look along with her. "Oh, no! You've got to be kidding me! Those ... those are third season courses! I don't even meet the prerequisites!"

"I can see that, now. I'm ... going to go back and check your tertiary school record, myself. I had been given to believe that you had taken advanced placement courses that would prepare you for these, and there ... was some worry that you might go back and retake easier courses ... well, I'll look into that. Can you get me copies of the documents you mentioned from the other academies?"

"I can, Matron."

Folding the paper and putting it back into her robes, the matron replied, "You are well within your rights to do this, and if what you say is true, then ... you will receive the protection of the Compact. You can also imagine that ... well, Matriarch Selena will be hearing some of this. There's only a certain amount I can take to her, but it will be enough to clearly signal to our dame and your parents that it's time they let you make your own decisions." The matron just looked at her for a moment and added, with a measure of respect, "You know, it took a lot of courage to do what you just did. If what you say is true, then ... I'm rather sorry you had to. You realize that by seeking the protection of the Compact, it's going to cut you off from the good we could do for you, as well as anything that might be interpreted as a hindrance?"

"I know," Sahnassa replied hopelessly, looking aside. "I am so sorry about that; I wish there was another way."

"As do I," the matron replied. "Oh, Sahnassa, you've given me a very difficult task – but it's not like I haven't had those in the past." Turning around and looking at Merialla, she added, "And you're right. I have most certainly been spoken to more disrespectfully than you did."

"Ah, now that fits better."

Looking concerned, Drualla leaned over and asked Sahnassa, "Is she ... alright?"

"She just thinks differently, sees the world in a different way. She doesn't mean to offend anyone, and neither do I. We both just want to seek out what is honorable and makes us happy."

Looking back at the seated Nephti, the matron replied, "And so you shall. Very well, Sahnassa. As your matron, I will take this course for you. You'll hear from me within the moon, possibly quite soon. I wish you well."

"Thank you, Matron." Sahnassa stepped out of the way, and allowed the matron to pass out of the room.

As the door closed, Merialla stated, "She needs to hear your music, I think."

"Perhaps, but you gave me such a wonderful gift, Merialla, I will play for you whenever you like."

"The orlure touches me, every time I hear it."

Sahnassa looked at the beautiful and strange Nephti sitting opposite her, eyes closed. Everything she said was just different, and it made her think. Putting on her paw-gloves, Sahnassa quickly thought through the pieces of music she knew the best and decided on one that fit her new friend. Gentle, mystic, and charming sounds started to issue from the instrument as she played, and as she was playing, Sahnassa glanced up and looked at her friend – her eyes still closed, muzzle raised towards the ceiling, her mouth slightly agape, and tears shedding from her eyes.

After the song came to an end, Merialla seemed to come back to her senses. "My … fur is wet," she observed softly, feeling the sides of her cheeks and muzzle.

"The song … touched you, Merialla. I think that's why."

"Not the song. You touched my soul, and now I know you. You are part of me."

Sahnassa nodded and smiled. "And you are a part of me. Thank you."

In the matriarch's study within the keep, Matron Drualla sat with Dame Rothnerra and Matriarch Selena performing her tri-moon status review. Both knew her well, and there were truly no surprises in how easily she had assumed stewardship of the families once under Matron Shalarra's care. With the status nearly done, the matriarch asked if there was anything else that needed to be covered before the meeting was concluded.

"Regretfully, yes, Honored One. It is very … infrequent, in my experience, for anyone we watch over to feel the need to invoke the familial protection clause of the Compact, but … someone I now watch over has done just that."

The revelation stung the dame who had no idea this was going to be discussed.

"My goodness," Matriarch Selena replied, concerned. "Who would feel a need for such a drastic measure?"

"It is Sahnassa de Orturu, daughter of Gonastir and Holana, Honored One."

The matriarch's black nose twitched and her brow furrowed over her silvery-grey eyes as she concentrated, recalling the name. "That's ... that's the kit we awarded the Matriarchal Scholarship to! Matron, you must explain to me why this has happened."

Not looking at her dame, the matron answered, "Yes, Honored One. It appears that her parents and ... others have been trying very hard to steer the kit into a specific career – one that is more to their liking."

"But wasn't Sahnassa studying to be a technologist? Are you saying she doesn't want to do that?"

"No, Honored One. She wants that very much. However, it appears that some in our family have a passionate desire for her to become say ... an archivist or a litigator, for example. It's been more than a simple suggestion. There has been some level of pressure and interference and, perhaps, purposeful harm done."

"You don't say! Who has done such a thing?" the matriarch asked.

"I believe specifics would not be fruitful to mention – Matron Shalarra has passed after all, Honored One. Let us just say that with the evidence I've gathered over the past few sols, it was clear that either someone was working against her or doing a completely incompetent job of trying to help her. To be specific, someone ensured that her application to Dothnaria would be turned down without a true examination of her qualifications or desires to attend that school. Further, the courses that were suggested to her for academy were completely in disharmony with her tertiary school record; they were so far off that had she signed up for them, they would have made it impossible for her to succeed. I have validated all of the available facts and consulted with three other matrons. All agree – Sahnassa has a right to invoke the Compact."

The matriarch turned towards Dame Rothnerra who was sitting very still, her eyes boring into the face of the matron. "This report disturbs me greatly. We've placed the full confidence of our house and many resources into the paws of young Sahnassa, and now I find that she is being pressured so severely that the resources we have provided are in danger of being wasted. I know the transition from child to adult can be difficult for parents and others in the family, but ... this is alienating! In many ways, the use of this provision of the Compact is akin to disavowing some members of your own family. Dame Rothnerra, I charge you to resolve this issue with her parents and any of those who might wish to hold sway over her to follow the demands of the Compact and giving this young adult the freedom she is due. Please make it very clear."

"I will, Honored One," Dame Rothnerra replied evenly. "I will make sure that Gonastir and Holana are made aware of ... Sahnassa's wishes."

"Very good. Matron, is there anything we can do to get her into Dothnaria?"

"Sadly, no, Honored One. The registration slots are all full in both of her other choices, and since her parents are refusing to support her financially, the scholarships will be insufficient to cover the costs of Harnard academy."

"I will speak to the scholarship committee and see if there can be some adjustments there since her choice appears to have been ... tampered with. I believe that they have some extra in the budget they can shift around. So, her parents are refusing to support her, at Harnard? This does not please me in the slightest, especially since Gonastir and Holana have more than adequate resources provided by this house. Matron, in your conversations with these two, I would highly suggest to them they reconsider their lack of support, especially since the rest of our house is generously providing for their daughter."

"I will speak to them on that matter, Honored One. However, we should all be ... diligent," the matron warned, "to uphold the requirements of the Compact. Sahnassa's request to invoke those protections was witnessed, Honored One." A glance between the dame and the matron at that point warned the dame that the matron knew all too well who the true source of opposition was, and that the dame was getting off easy – this time.

"I see. Very well. Inform anyone who may be tempted to interfere, the pair of you. We need to prevent situations like this from occurring in the first place. How can we say we are kept by and keepers of our own when those we try to watch over feel threatened by us?" The matriarch's PawLink beeped, and she picked it up for a quick glance. "Our time is up, and I must move on to another meeting. Anything else?"

"No, Honored One."

"No, Honored One," the dame added to her matron's statement.

"Very well. I'll leave you two. Good sol to you." With that, the matriarch left the room.

When the door was closed, Rothnerra nearly exploded. "What was the meaning of that?!"

"The meaning is that I, Dame, was utterly humiliated and ashamed of what I found out. You know better than to try and interfere at this level, this aggressively! We have a checks and balances process for a reason, and you are now being checked. You are intentionally trying to ruin this kit! Why?"

"Not ruin – redirect. You are ruining this kit's future by helping her—"

"What I want to do with her future is completely immaterial. You've provided more than enough justification for invoking the Compact. Anyone who interferes now is subject to a hearing in front of the matriarch. Regardless of what you have wanted for this kit, Dame; it is now her choice, as it should be."

"You are no more agreeable or helpful than Matron Shalarra was—"

"Then," the matron replied sternly, "I will consider that a compliment. We all looked up to Matron Shalarra, especially since we suspected that you made life continually difficult for her. The other matrons are watching you carefully, Dame Rothnerra. I will not do anything to prove out their suspicions about you. Just make sure that you do not."

"You order me … as if I was the matron and you were the dame?!"

"Shall I open my files and lay before the matriarch all I've found? Shall I bring Sahnassa here to tell exactly what she discovered – face to face with the matriarch? Shall I question her parents to determine where this idea for cowing and bullying a daughter of this house truly came from? Even worse, shall I take the contents of Matron Shalarra's private files and bring that to the other matrons who serve under you. Votes of no confidence are not for matriarchs, alone, *Dame* Rothnerra. In the time that I've lived, a considerably long trail actually, I have never come upon a dame such as yourself. Keep your attentions upon your duties, and let us attend to ours. You have harmed Sahnassa and disgraced her parents, either maliciously or through incompetence. Leave off, or I will do what I need to in order to protect this family – even from you! Is understanding now resonating between us, *Dame*?"

The dame's tail was lashing, her back fur was up, and she held her arms crossed, hiding the disposition of her claws as she attempted to cool her burning temper. "I hear your council, Matron, and … I will strongly consider it."

"Very well. Now, if you will forgive me, I plan to have some discussions with the scholarship committee and see what can be done to give our house's daughter adequate support." With that, the matron turned and left, Dame Rothnerra almost unable to move because of the embarrassment and rage coursing through her.

"Matron Drualla," Holana greeted her warmly as she opened the door to her lair, "so nice to see you this evening."

"Very kind of you," the matron replied, but then made no further attempts at pleasantries. "I need for you and Gonastir to meet with me in a private room, where we are likely not to be overheard."

"The … his study should do well. I'll go and get him. It's right in here."

"Thank you very much."

When Gonastir and Holana returned, the matron was examining some of the books on the shelf but turned immediately and nodded, acknowledging their presence. "If you would please close and lock the door."

His eyebrow fur raising, Gonastir complied and then joined Holana on the couch in front of the desk. The matron took the chair facing them, and the couple could see that the news was not going to be good. "What's happened, Matron?"

"In plain terms, Gonastir, your daughter, Sahnassa, has invoked the protection of the Compact, specifically the clauses relating to the familial protection of adults." A look of shock passed across both of their faces, causing the matron to nod and add, "So you do know the implications of such an action."

Gonastir was still finding his hind legs, figuratively speaking, but Holana nodded. "As you might imagine, this has been brought to the matriarch's attention, and I think the pair of you should consider the implications to be quite serious. Matriarch Selena is ... most discouraged by the lack of support that has been offered a student deserving of the Matriarchal Scholarship. I ... have had words with Dame Rothnerra on this issue, and she is now quite clear about what I'm going to remind you of. No one from this family is to interfere, in any way, with Sahnassa's academy training or the decisions she makes from now on as a fully recognized adult. I and several other matrons have reviewed the application process, and we have found flaws – no, that's too polite a word – we have found deceitful statements made by certain individuals to discourage them from accepting Sahnassa into their academy."

"Matron, we never talked to anyone about—"

"Please, Holana, let me finish. You did know, the pair of you. You may not have been the ones going to the various offices and saying these things, but you knew they were being said. You knew things were being said to undermine the future of your own daughter, and you not only allowed it to happen, you were in favor of it. Dishonorable ... is a polite description of what has happened. Now, let me be clear about the consequences of this. First, Dame Rothnerra is not going to have any contact with you that doesn't go through me. Houses have a structure, and when that is violated, problems arise. Second, this house, your family, is supporting the education of your daughter, but because of the ... fraud that was perpetrated, the funds she has to live on are insufficient. She barely has enough to cover room, board, tuition, and books. There's nothing for medical care; there's nothing for clothing; there's nothing for transportation. Your daughter went to one of the most prestigious academies on the planet riding ... a public transport. It's a disgrace."

Gonastir and Holana both hung their heads at that point, their blush furs up at full. "Imagine if you will, a brilliant student, walking into class in threadbare clothes, coughing like a disavowed Anati cast-off, and begging rides off of anyone she can. When she finally claws her way to graduation, there she'll be, nearly furless with mange, wearing nothing but what she can get from charity organizations."

That stung Gonastir's pride, and he looked up in anger, but the matron's expression was nothing short of menacing. "This ... is ... your ... daughter! You will either adequately support her in these areas of basic necessities, or I will have liens placed against both of your wages to ensure Sahnassa gets what she deserves in terms of your support." In frustration, the matron looked away from the pair, now staring back at her, horrified. "To think of it, that I would have to say these things to one of the most prized litigators and one of the most cherished archivists in our family. It would be different if she had dishonored herself, then you would have cause to be ashamed but no requirement to support her. It would be different if she had just decided to take things easy and go for a job that required no real schooling. It would be different if the resources of this house were not already committed, by right, by merit, and by honor to assist her."

"But ... that's not the case," Gonastir said quietly.

"Certainly not, and the matriarch knows it. Correct this quickly – that's all the advice I can give you. You don't have to talk to her, you don't have to agree with her decisions, but you must support her adequately. The sooner you make this right, the sooner your reputation with this house's senior leadership can begin to recover." Looking back at them, she asked pointedly, "Is anything I have said not understood?"

"We ... we understand," Holana replied, holding back tears.

"Very well. I will leave you two to discuss this," the matron told them as she stood. "I will want an itemized list and first payment sent to me via PawLink no later than mid-sol tomorrow. If I were you, I would make sure I sent it early, just to be safe. The matriarch is likely to query me on this point the next time she sees me. Please make every effort to ensure I have something *very* positive to tell her. Good evening to you both."

The matron then quietly left the study, closing the door behind her.

"I will never trust our dame again," Holana wept. "She ... she led us astray ... ruined us!"

"It's not ... that bad," Gonastir said grimly, "but it is ... bad. Very ... bad. Come; we'd best get started figuring this out."

"So, are you going to talk to Sahnassa?" Holana asked.

"Could you? What ... what would you say? I don't have any idea where to start. I ... I don't think I can without ... courting dishonor, and I've had more than enough of that. Let's just do what we have to, and hope ... hope things turn out in time."

Shaking her head, Holana leaned into her mate and held onto him. The pair then just wept together, their hearts broken by how far they had gone astray in dealing with their daughter.

Chapter 10: Opportunity

Vanarra keyed back into the lair she shared with Sorla at the end of a long sol, feeling tired, but relatively happy. Gorta had intentionally left the evening clear, since she had some friends she wanted to gather with, and after the nominal stocking and reporting had been done, Van was free to go with her blessing. When she opened the door, however, she saw something that made her concerned. "Sorla? What's wrong?" The Nephti was sitting on the couch, just staring into space – obviously distressed. Thinking she knew the cause, Vanarra offered, "I just got paid by Gorta. I can give you all of it. She's letting me nibble off the leftovers and–"

"It's not that, Van. I'm sorry," Sorla replied, trying to shake off whatever spell had been entrancing her.

"I … I know I'm early. If you had plans, I could find somewhere to be." At that moment, Sorla started crying, and Vanarra was completely beside herself on what to do. Putting down her things, closing the door, and locking it behind her, Van walked over and sat beside the weeping Nephti and tried to comfort her. "Please, Sorla, please. Let me help." Sorla looked at her with a heartbroken expression and reached around the mixed blood, continuing to cry. "Oh my gosh, Sorla! Please! Oh, I'm sorry. What happened? Let me help."

Sorla shook her off and walked across the room, putting her paw up in warning when Vanarra tried to follow. Sitting down, Van waited anxiously as the Nephti tried to control her emotions. After a few passes, Sorla was forcing herself to calm down, taking deep breaths and swallowing – occasionally groaning in frustration at how difficult it was to pull herself together.

"Please, Sorla, what is it?"

"In … in less than five sols, I'm … moving … overseas," Sorla replied, putting her head against the wall, still unable to face Vanarra. "De Dothnar, my family, has … assigned me as the driver of a dame on the Rician continent."

"Assigned you? Don't you have a choice?" Vanarra asked, her heart pounding in her chest, realizing that in less than five sols she would be without the help and protection of her friend and their lair.

"Not … really. The transport service is reducing staff, and I'm … I'm a junior driver – so, they informed my matron that they would be eliminating my position. My matron … found me something, but … it's … I can't stay here, Van. That's … what has me so…"

"Should … should I just pack my things right now?" Vanarra replied, her anxiety and fear turning to anger. "Oh, purebreds! I should have known it!"

Standing up and striding to the door, Van was about to walk out, when Sorla turned and begged her, "No, Van, please! Don't … I … I feel so horrible about this! I want to find somewhere for you. I asked for the extra time just so I could do that!"

Putting her paws on the door and leaning her head against it, Vanarra asked quietly, "Who's going to want to share their place with an Anati?"

"I did," Sorla insisted, "and I've never known a closer friend."

"Until now," Vanarra said in return, feeling betrayed and hurt. "Purebreds always see us as disposable."

"You are my friend, Vanarra Anasto, and I don't think of you as disposable. You've paid me back so much, I have a good little bit saved up. It's all for you! On Ricia, my lair will be provided for me; my food will be provided for me. Everything will be taken care of for me, and that is going to rip my heart apart bit by bit unless I know that you are somewhere safe!"

Vanarra turned and sagged against the door, looking into the sorrowful eyes of her friend. Sliding down to the floor in defeat, she put her head in her paws and answered, "For Anati, that just doesn't exist, Sorla. You know what I make, and I won't be able to afford a small rental lair, even if someone would rent it to me."

"I'm going to make calls all tomorrow, Van. I'm going to search everywhere I can for you." Despite herself, Van started crying – the thoughts of having to find a place like the Pinnacle Center or the office buildings to hide out in made her once again feel like she was losing everything. Now, it was Sorla who knelt down and sat in front of Vanarra. "You are the most wonderful kit. I have friends. I will try everything I can!"

"Thank you, Sorla, but ... but there won't ... be..."

"No, Van, I promise. Somehow, somewhere," Sorla insisted as she took Van's paws in her own, "there will be a place for you."

The next sol, Vanarra made it to work, and numbly went about her duties in the back. Gorta noticed the change in the disposition of her Anati employee, but didn't give it much thought, that is, until Sorla called her.

"Gorta?"

"Oh, hello dear! What can I do for you?" the Faelnar asked, her head still buzzing a bit from her pleasant time with her friends the night before.

"First, please make sure your office door is closed and your LineCom is not on speaker. I have to tell you some news," Sorla's voice warned her.

"Alright, kit. Just a moment." Grunting a bit and wincing at how her head felt, the Faelnar made the trip to the door and back to her desk. "Alright, I'm back on. What's going on, kit? You need something?"

"It's Vanarra. I need a favor, and it's a big one."

"Alright, what?" Gorta asked.

"I'm being relocated to Ricia, and when that happens in a few sols, Vanarra's not going to have anyone or anywhere to stay. I was hoping you might be able to take her in."

That thought didn't appeal to the Faelnar in the slightest. There were so many things about her lifestyle that she just didn't want others to know about or bother with. Rearranging and cleaning out a storeroom was one thing, but the last thing she wanted was for her Anati worker to become her lair mate. "I don't think so. My lair really isn't set up for two."

Disappointed, Sorla sighed. "I'd hoped since she's done such a good job for you that you'd be able to think of something. If I can't find her anything, I'm not even sure she'll be able to stay in this area!"

As distasteful as bunking with an Anati might have seemed, losing the employee who had helped turn her business around was far more concerning, and Gorta's mind cleared rapidly. "Wait a tick, wait a tick. Let me think!" Gorta flipped through the piles of notes on her desk and came upon a notice from the building manager offering her the adjoining fur-dresser's office, since they had gone out of business. "Now, that's … something.   Hold on, Sorla. I'm looking at an idea here."

Sorla quietly waited as Gorta flipped through a few more papers, pulling up bank statements and some of the new income charts Vanarra had managed to create. "Kit, do you think that between the two of us, we could get her set up in the rental office space next to mine? I've got an offer from the building manager right here, and for once, the inventory space we have is so full that we need more room. I was thinking about annexing that. It's got running water, a shower, and a door could be cut that would allow her to come and go between there and here. I mean, it wouldn't be a big place—"

"It doesn't have to be, Gorta. She's lived this entire time on my couch! She doesn't make big demands, and you have learned you can trust her, right?"

"She's done a good job for me, kit. Without a doubt. It's kind of made things possible for me – to keep going, that is. I owe you, too," the Faelnar softly said. "She'll have to work some more events, and … she's got to keep her area clean."

"You're keeping her from becoming homeless, Gorta; believe me, she'll do whatever is needed."

"What will she sleep in over there? It's pretty cleaned out."

"I'm dumping most of my furniture, since I won't need it in Ricia. She can have whatever I have that will fit. It's the least I could do for her."

"Okay.   Let me make some calls, kit, and make sure I can swing this, but if I can, I'll do it. I'll tell her this sol if it's going to be something we can do. If it's not going to work out, I just won't mention it to her."

"Thank you, Gorta. So much! I'll keep trying to find other places for her, just in case your idea doesn't work out, but please try! I haven't had any good leads all morning."

"You're welcome, kit. You're welcome. Talk to you soon, with good news I hope."

"To good news, by Gorta." The Faelnar hung up the LineCom and instantly started to dial the local building manager.

Vanarra had started to unpack and shelve the same items three times, and each time, she became distracted by her anger at the purebreds for causing this to happen or her fear of again being abandoned or her guilt at having spoken so harshly to Sorla. "Anati?" Gorta called, and then Van realized that she'd actually been holding a box in her paws, a track away from the shelf, just standing there for more than a pass. "Why don't you put that on the shelf and come up front. We need to talk about some things."

Gorta's statement, given Van's experience the prior night, seemed foreboding, and that was just enough motivation to make her move. Soon, she was walking out to the front. "Ah, there you are," Gorta began. "You know, kit, you've done a really great job for me, and, well, Sorla called and told me what's going on with her. I'm … real sorry about that. She called me this morning and asked if I could help in some way. Now, I'm not exactly able to put someone up in my lair, but … she and I, well, we did come up with something. Are you interested?"

"I'm … really interested, Gorta. I … I don't have anywhere else to go!"

"Well, you've done such a great job for me, I didn't want to lose you, either. Come with me. I just got a key from the building manager for the place next door. The fur dressers have moved out, and he's anxious to start getting rent from it again. It took a little dealing, but we can get it for a pretty good price. Let's go over and have a look, shall we?"

"Alright, sure," Vanarra replied, surprised.

As Gorta managed to get to her hind paws, she explained, "I don't know if you've ever been to a fur dresser before, but they need at least one shower to rinse out all of that crazy stuff they put in your fur. I'm hoping if I can get the water turned back on, you could use that. They should have a small facility, I think. The whole front part I want to either convert into office space for me or use as more storeroom."

"Well, we need that, for sure," Van confessed.

As they walked outside the door and stepped along the walk to the next office, Gorta snorted, "It's funny, but when you came, the storeroom was just as full as it is right now, but only with garbage, not with stuff we actually use. I'm going to have the building manager check to see if we can punch a hole between our current office and this new place. That way, you could just carry the stock through. Have to get some shelves, though," Gorta mused as she keyed into the abandoned storefront. Opening the door, she walked in, Vanarra following behind her. "Great," the Faelnar grunted in disappointment. The room was cluttered with equipment, dusty, and there were a few holes in the walls and ceiling.

"I can take care of it," Vanarra replied stepping in and looking at the items scattered all around. "There are some things in here we might just get a little money for. That salvage place we've used for some of the old cooking things – I saw stuff like this in the back of their hover when they came to pick up. Then if we can get the room clear, it's a good size for adding to our storage."

"Well, let's see what the back of this place looks like. That's what is going to matter, for you at least."

The pair walked around the clutter and carefully made their way to a darkened space in the back – the light from the open door all that was available to them. As they reached a small hallway, Vanarra found a light switch, and a bare fixture lit up pitifully above them. Opening a door, they found the small shower and facility – both badly in need of cleaning. Walking back further there was a small storeroom with bare walls, square corners, and industrial building block as the only wall covering. "Well, this … is cheerful. Maybe … this isn't such a good idea, kit."

"If you'd be willing, Gorta," Vanarra replied as she walked over and felt the wall. "It would be perfectly fine. Believe it or not, this … kind of reminds me of one of the lairs I've had. I could make this work, and I would be able to work extra intervals every sol to make up for you letting me stay here – time I wouldn't put on the books."

The Faelnar shifted her head back and forth, thinking it over, and finally replied, "Well, I'll get it for us, if you're sure. It's going to take a lot to put it in order, though – funds, too."

"If I can get a little bit for everything that's up front, I may be able to patch the walls and ceiling and make this place pretty nice, actually." Vanarra then looked at Gorta and offered, "I can't thank you enough for doing this!"

"Well, I'm sure as mange going back to that building manager and telling him he's got to discount this for all the expense it's going to cost me. I'm not going to just take this at his price!"

Worried that Gorta might make the deal untenable and ruin it, Van offered, "I'll do whatever it takes to earn back anything you have to spend above what you think you should. This ... this would be a real find for me, please!"

"Alright, then. Alright. I will make this happen, regardless of what that miserable crook wants to charge. So, you think you might be able to concentrate a little better, now?" Gorta asked, a tease in her voice.

"I ... have a place to lay my head in five sols. Yes! Thank you!" and the Vulpi-Faelnar was reaching around Gorta and embracing her gently, but earnestly.

The Faelnar chuckled and replied, "There, there, kit! Come on. So much to do, and I think I should call Sorla and ease her worry, as well. You know, she really cares about you."

"I know," Van sniffed as they parted. "You, too, you know?"

"You've got my business back in the hunt, kit; there's just no denying it – stupid purebred pride or not. Come on now, let's get back to work."

As Gorta started making her way out of the room, Vanarra looked back and smiled. "My ... own place. My own place, like it was before. Thanks, Ash," she whispered and then stepped out of the room, following her boss.

Sahnassa was hunched over the desk in her student lair studying while Merialla was in class. Spending time talking to her new friend and confidant had actually started taking too much of both their time, and now she was falling behind. She knew she'd have to find a way to spend less time with her new friend and more time with her books, but she dreaded trying to explain that to Merialla. Still, not a moon into the academy's starter courses, she knew she'd have to try. The course load, even having chosen a mix of classes she thought would balance the easier with the more difficult, was teaching her one essential truth – at Harnard, all of the courses were hard. Every one of the new students was feeling exactly the same as she, completely overwhelmed and in horrible need of catching up for perhaps not always taking the hardest classes at their tertiary schools.

She could only barely imagine what her life would be like right now if her parents and dame had gotten their way. "I would have given up," she sighed aloud, but then she put her head in her paws.

"Oh, I still might have to – I will if I can't find free time to work a job!" One of her outfits had torn on a sharp corner of the closet door, and instantly Sahnassa had realized her plight – clothes were something her parents had just provided, and now she had to provide her own. "The money's going so fast," she breathed, depressed.

Glancing at the clock, she was then angry – angry at herself for wasting time being distracted, angry at her parents and dame for putting her here, and angry that her situation seemed completely hopeless. As she tried to force herself back into the books on composition and persuasive writing, an unhappy thought crossed her mind. "I won't be able to attend here more than a season or … less."

Just when she tried to apply herself to her studies once again, a knock tapped upon the door. Frustrated, she sat up, sighed, and answered, "Yes?"

"I'm sorry. Is Sahnassa there? It's Matron Drualla."

Curiosity almost shoving her frustrations aside, she stood and opened the door. "Matron? It's … good to see you."

"Might I come in? I need to talk with you for a moment." As Sahnassa stepped back and allowed the matron to enter, Drualla noted, "It looks a trifle more … lived in than when I saw it last." Turning around, she saw the matron was smiling slightly. "Still much neater than my own in academy. I'm sorry your friend isn't here to comment on what I've got to tell you. It would have been priceless, I'm sure!"

Despite her anxious state, Sahnassa giggled, "That's certainly true! The things she says – I'm sorry. She was kind of rude to you last time."

"Well, the way I stamped into your lair before, I probably deserved it. I can tell from the books that you are horribly busy, but this is important enough to deserve an interruption, and it may make what you're doing easier."

Sahnassa blinked in surprise and asked, "Would … would you like to sit down?" The matron nodded, and the two of them sat beside one another on the edge of Sahnassa's bed.

"I'm very sorry it's taken me so long to get back to you; I had hoped to get here much sooner, but other family situations just wouldn't allow it. There's quite a bit of shuffling going on right now in the matrons under your dame – some much-needed changes are taking place. However, family politics are not what I came here to speak with you about. Sahnassa, your house is placing significant resources into your paws for you to use to better yourself, but the actions of your parents and your dame have caused you harm. The matriarch has seen fit to grant your request for protection under the Compact, although it truly grieved her to do so."

"I ... I know. I wish there was another way, and ... in the end..."

Sahnassa trailed off, unwilling to meet the matron's gaze. "What, child?"

"In the end, it may not matter. I'm ... buried, even with the courses I chose. Even with the scholarships, I can tell, I'm not going to have enough to make this work! I ... probably can't afford to stay more than a season, if that!"

The matron reached out and put her paw on Sahnassa's back. "Oh, no. That's what I'm here to speak with you about. There are many things we learn from our parents and those in family leadership, but I'm afraid the way your parents and dame have behaved are lessons in what not to do. Matriarch Selena was nothing short of ... furious at your parents for failing to support you while you're here, at this *prestigious* institution and studying for an *honorable* field. I was angry, as well. However, when you invoked the Compact, that created a problem of sorts and some logistical issues in providing you extra support. Last sol, with your parents and the familial account office, we worked out a solution."

"They're actually going to ... like ... what?" Sahnassa asked, confused.

"The Compact requires that your family do absolutely nothing that could be interpreted in any way as doing you harm or trying to thwart your efforts here. Giving you advice on what courses to take, trying to steer you towards certain professors and mentors – all of those things have potential issues in light of the Compact. However, the giving of gifts and the provision of funds, free of any impediments cannot be considered an issue."

"They're going to give me money? Really? How ... did you ever convince them to do that?"

"Threaten to take it out of their pay if they didn't. Now, please understand that this is a fixed amount, and it will remain a fixed amount throughout your time here. In our best judgment, it is minimal but sufficient to supply your basic needs of medicine, transportation, clothing, and food. This will not be enough to live ... luxuriously, by any standard, or allow you to buy as much as your peers. Still," the matron said as she pulled a piece of paper out of her robes, "this is what they've agreed to."

Sahnassa took the paper, paw shaking, and looked at it. "You don't mean it! I'll actually … need this much?! I … was kidding myself! I … if I need this, I … I wouldn't make it one term!"

"It's still going to be very close, even with this much support," Drualla warned as she withdrew her paw. "You should also know that it came with a higher cost to your parents then just the funding amounts you see there.   In the eyes of your matron and your matriarch, your parents have dishonored themselves in how they've treated you. They will have a long climb to make it back into the esteem of our family leadership. Both have been … relieved of some familial duties and honors, and a commendation that our matriarch was due to present to them will now be withheld – indefinitely."

Sahnassa dropped the paper and shook her head. "No…" she breathed, sadly, imagining how her mother and father would have taken such news.

"Your parents, probably with some urging, acted dishonorably towards you, and as those kept by and keepers of this family, the matriarchy cannot support that. I can imagine they regret what they've done very much, but – and it pains me to say it – I don't believe they are anywhere close to being able to reconcile with you, in any way. What they've done has wounded you, and what you've done, by invoking the Compact, as was your right, has wounded them. While I'm not trying to direct your course, please hear from me that they need time. It may be seasons, kit. At some point, when these unhappy events are a distant memory, it may be possible."

"I love my parents, Matron. I … I'm sorry for what I've done. Invoking the Compact was a mistake," Sahnassa stated, tears welling in her eyes.

"So has said nearly everyone who has ever done so, but that doesn't mean it actually was a mistake. In your case, Sahnassa, it was needed.   The evidence is painfully clear.   Your parents made a grievous error, and what you've done, in time, will help them correct it. Take some comfort in that, and take comfort in the fact that what's now being provided to you was done with their input, even if it was not given voluntarily. You should also know that your little red hover is also parked in the hover lot behind the library archive." The matron pulled out the activator and presented it to Sahnassa, laying it softly into her paw. "Your family believes in you, Sahnassa, and we trust you. We're offering you comfort and consolation by way of an apology and by way of support. We hope that even if the bonds with your parents are not as strong as they once were, the bonds with your family still hold firm."

"They do … because of Matron Shalarra, and … because of you and the matriarch," Sahnassa replied, tears rolling down her cheek fur. "Thank you! Oh, thank you!"

The matron reached around Sahnassa and hugged her, causing the young Nephti to cry all the more. After a few moments, they parted. "She'll want to see you, you know? At the end of the term, I'll contact you and set up a time and date. It's a part of the scholarship, but … Matriarch Selena just wants to, as well."

"Okay. Please, tell her … I look forward to it."

Standing and smiling, the matron replied, "I will. Now, turn to your studies with a good heart, Sahnassa. Things are getting better, and in time, maybe even more so. Good evening, dear kit."

"Thank you again," Sahnassa replied as the matron quietly left the room. "Things are getting better," she said to herself, looking down at the paper, and then, following the matron's advice, left the bed and returned to her work, finally able to concentrate.

⟨⟨⟨ ❀ ⟩⟩⟩

"Hi there." Sorla's voice startled Vanarra a little as she was reorganizing her things in her small lair.

"Oh, hi there," Van replied, and recovering, had a chance to look into the Nephti's sad blue eyes. "This … this is goodbye, isn't it?"

Sorla nodded, sniffling a little, clearly torn. "Yeah. It's … all packed up or put out–" Van's sad nod instantly made the Nephti regret what she'd said. "Oh, no! That didn't … that didn't come out right."

"True, though. I am going to miss you, Sorla. You've … really given me a lot."

"Not enough," Sorla replied bitterly. "Not as much as I should have! My family–"

"I know. With purebreds," Vanarra stated sympathetically, "family must come first. It's … the way things are."

"And why is it that an Anati can make me see so clearly it's not always the right thing? Why … why did it have to be someone so nice and so clever and kind ... that my family forces me to leave? I'm sorry, Vanarra. I've–"

Van's heart was touched by how much Sorla was struggling in this moment, and although she was still angry and hurt, the Nephti suffering through this conversation in front of her was someone she loved. Vanarra stood and walked over to her, and gently drew her into an embrace. "I don't blame you, Sorla. I don't have that right. You've done more for me than any purebred ever has, except my mom. I'm alive; I have a job; I have a lair. It may not be the best life. It may not be the best job. It may be a tiny lair, but it's more than I had sitting on that bench at the transport station after Ash died. Thank you."

Crying hard, Sorla surprised Van by reaching around and hugging her tightly and burying her muzzle in the neck of the mixed-blood. Returning the embrace, Vanarra began to cry, as well.

After several passes, the two let go of one another. "Please, Van, be careful! Stay as safe as you can."

"You, too. Remember what I've taught you about taking care of yourself and keeping an eye on what's around you – the emergency aid skills, too. Those are skills that even your dame might appreciate."

"I can imagine so," Sorla laughed, wiping tears from her eyes. "I ... I left a contact card with Gorta. It's the family information number. It will help you locate me. If you need anything, and I can, I will, okay?"

"I know, and ... you know where I'll be, right?" Van asked, leaning against the frame of the door, smiling.

"Yeah. I do. Take care, Vanarra."

"You, too, Sorla, and ... thank you." The Nephti reached around Van one more time for a quick hug, and then without looking back, quietly walked away.

With the noise and merriment of a joining celebration coming from a banquet room nearby, Vanarra leaned against the wall of the darkened hallway thinking about Sorla. Almost the moment she had left, Vanarra's life got ten times busier, or so it seemed. There was the obvious work of getting the new expansion cleared and ready for use, a task Van had excelled at, getting more than enough funds from selling off the junk from the fur dressers to pay for the repairs and more than a few modest shelves. Gorta was so impressed that she added more shelves and wall-units from the business budget, all of which her live-in assistant had gladly put together. There had also been a notable uptick in business to contend with; her employer's name was starting to make the rounds among matrons, or so it was said, and those purebreds looking for a caterer charging well below the standard demanded by avowed family businesses started lining up for the services of Gorta's Gatherings.

Other than being tired, Vanarra had only one additional complaint – she was lonely. She had grown so used to talking to Sorla that losing that opportunity seemed almost like solitary confinement, or at least, work release. It had been this loneliness that had, perhaps, contributed to what she noticed more keenly as she set up and then brought out trays of food. Several of the well moneyed Lupar were taking notice of her, and one or two were eyeing not only the creele rolls but Vanarra with a certain degree of hunger. As more of their purebred peers came in, the males who had been watching her carefully wandered off to talk to those attending the gala, and Vanarra was left to simply do what she always did at times like this – wait for intervals until it was time to clean up or something else was needed.

"You were working hard tonight," a deep male voice said from nearby, causing her to startle. "Sorry. I can tell you were deep in thought."

Van looked up into the eyes of a very keen looking young Lupar. In the soft light coming from the banquet hall, his brown fur, soft hazel eyes, and black striping reminded her distantly of Ash, and despite herself, Vanarra's blush furs raised. "It's … it's okay. I'm sorry," Van replied, lowering her gaze submissively. "I was just waiting … until I'm needed for something."

He leaned up against the wall along side of her, and she could smell him – clean, masculine, and again with just a hint of Ash's scent. Glancing to her right, she got a good look at him – he was fit, his muscles were well toned, and his fur looked as soft as a newborn's. "Well, I need you for something. I'm finding it a little boring talking with all the same Thurians. They show up at these things all the time – the same ones with the same jokes and drinks and complaints. Not at all appealing. You're the first new thing I've seen in a moon, and I have to say, that you are surprisingly appealing."

Vanarra furrowed her brow at this, unsure. "I'm a mix-up, an Anati – what could you find appealing about me?"

"A few things. Let's just say that in a world where there is so much sameness, you are ... exotic. It's strange; you carry yourself as if you were one of us, fully avowed and self-assured. There are more than a few females circling that dance floor that could learn a thing or two from you. And you, working so hard to serve us. It should be the other way around."

"It will never happen," Van replied, but added somewhat shyly, "although it's nice of you to say."

"No, I mean it. Please, wait right here, just for a moment. I'll be back in a tick or two," he offered. She nervously watched him go, her tail starting to ride up a little higher on the wall as she saw his attractive back-side and his tail that was fairly generous when compared to most other Lupar. She had to control herself when he came back carrying two drinks in one paw. "There. A little something for the sweet and lovely kit who did so much for us tonight," he offered as he held a drink out to her.

"I'm really not supposed to ... while I'm working."

"Like you said, though, you're just waiting. I promise not to tell," he replied, conspiratorially. Shyly, she took the drink and sniffed it; a sweet berry aroma drifted into her nose, and something of a light touch of fermentum was in it too, making it intriguing to her.

"Thank you," she told him.

"Oh, it is my pleasure, surely. Now, here's a toast to you, the dear kit who made this party so much more than usual."

"Thank you, again," she replied, and as he drank, so did she. "So, what are you ... I mean, what do you do?" The luscious tastes in her mouth demanded she drink again.

"Let's just say I'm in the chemicals business," he answered with a toothy smile that was growing by the moment. "I've learned more than a paw-ful of interesting tips and tricks. They can make for ... some really interesting times."

"You ... don't ... you..." Vanarra tried to reply, but it felt like all of the strength was draining out of her, and she started to slip down the wall – an odd euphoria making her lift her head up and causing her muzzle to gape open. Strong paws took hold of her and guided her down to the floor and into complete unconsciousness no more than a tick later.

The next coherent thought Vanarra could muster came amongst a swirl of weird noises and pain in between her legs and up into her guts. That pain was matched by nausea and a headache that nearly made her want to return to unconsciousness, but a familiar voice was calling to her, demanding she answer.

"Anati! Dammit, where are you!?" Gorta's voice rang inside of her skull, and she could just make out that the Faelnar was slurring her words appreciably.

"I'm … I'm here…" she called back feebly.

A door opened and struck the poor Anati with a shaft of harsh white light that seemed to cause her ears to ring and made it feel like her eyes were bleeding – they hurt so much. "Well, now. Look at you! Someone had a … nice time tonight! Come along, now. We've … we've got to clean up so drive you can me back. Well, that didn't … make sense. Come on. We've … gotta get outa here. They want to close up." Gorta turned her back and left, walking unsteadily away.

Struggling and reaching for the nakedness between her legs, Vanarra finally began to understand what had happened to her – she had been rape-mated, and by the feel of it, repeatedly and fiercely. Pungent male scents were oozing out of her, and she started crying in humiliation and pain. The truth struck her to her soul – she had been used as a plaything for purebreds. She felt truly horrible, and the more she tried to wake and get up, the more she realized just how bad off she was. Barely able to walk, she made her way out of the small office and stumbled, grasping the walls, to reach the bathroom.

After many painful moments of washing herself and trying to drink water from the faucet, the abused Vanarra was able to exit the bathroom and make her way painfully down the hall towards the now empty banquet hall. When she arrived, she saw Gorta, sitting in a corner, snoring.

"You have to be out of here in half an interval, or you won't get paid," a Faelnar told her who impatiently came into the room.

"Okay … okay," Van replied, nearly crying. Through a supreme act of will, the mixed blood managed to clean up and get her inebriated employer out of the hall.

Grudgingly, the Faelnar had presented her with a secured draft as they left, and then, with a smirk, added, "Oh, and here's a little more for … services rendered." As she took the crumpled currency from his paws, she caught a whiff of his scent, and she knew instantly that he had been one of the ones who had taken her. Angrily, she took his offering and picked up Gorta, who was again napping on a nearby sofa, and made it to their vehicle.

Grateful that the Faelnar had actually taught her to drive, albeit illegally since she had no license, Vanarra took them back to the office. After seeing Gorta onto the office couch, Vanarra placed the draft on the desk and then, aching and crying, made her way back to her bed.

"You really are cute, you know," Merialla observed with no preamble or warning. Sahnassa shook her head and looked up from her studies at the kit who was carefully considering her.

"I ... uh, well."

"You don't think you are, but you are."

A little unnerved, Sahnassa asked, "Merialla, why are you telling me this?"

"Because you need to hear it. I'm taking a psychological observations course. I thought it would be interesting. I've been watching you as you go across the commons between classes."

"You been ... watching me?!" Sahnassa asked, a little alarmed.

"Yes. Every sol now since the last moon. You are an interesting case study."

"But ... why tell me I'm pretty?"

"Your tail and ears and other body signals are transmitting that you're inferior to those around you, in particular the other females. You nearly carry yourself as if you were disavowed."

Sahnassa was shocked and a little offended. "I do not! I meet everyone I talk to eye to eye, with honor!"

"You do meet them with your eyes, but your head inclines down and your tail goes still, and you hunch your back; your ears droop just a bit." Sahnassa stopped and thought, trying to remember. "You won't be able to recall doing it. It's instinctive. You're naturally submissive."

"You should ask my parents and dame about that!" she shot back.

"You are *assertive* when you need to be," Merialla gently contested. "Your current relational archetype when dealing with others is still submissive. It's most likely because you don't think much of yourself in comparison to others, specifically when you compare yourself with other females."

Now, Sahnassa was somewhat struck by the veracity of that statement. One of the reasons she had gotten along with Merialla as well as she had was because she learned early on that the strange Nephti almost always had a point to what she was saying, and it was almost always important regardless of the shock or offense she inadvertently caused. A little sadly, she looked over at Merialla and replied, "Well, yeah, I suppose. Take yourself, kit. You're ... like this beautiful and fascinating piece of art, your striping is like none I've ever seen! I'm just kind of ordinary – especially when I'm next to my sisters."

"Your sisters are not here. No one can compare them to you." Sahnassa was quiet, thinking about that. "You should stand tall, like you do when we talk in the commons. The males I've seen looking at you turn away when you talk to someone else, or their interest goes to the female you're talking to."

"Males ... like, guys, have been looking at me?"

"Yes," Merialla smiled at Sahnassa as if someone finally understood her. It was the smiles like that one Sahnassa truly appreciated. "They look at me, too. So long as I say nothing, they are quite interested." With a little sadness, she watched as Merialla's tail and the expression on her muzzle both faded, as if forced to think about something difficult.

"So, I should try ... standing a little taller, swishing a bit? Casually, I mean?"

"Yes. That will probably work for you. Sahnassa, do you think I am mentally unstable?"

The abruptness of the statement again shocked her, but she tried to stop and think. "You ... can surprise ... a bit. When we met, you told me that you are really intelligent. That's true, and that can be intimidating. My sisters told me that; it was one of the reasons they told me males weren't attracted to me. You are also ... very direct in what you say. Not everyone appreciates that."

"To get a male to like me, I should appear to be less intelligent than I am and not say very much."

Sahnassa chuckled. "Not really. I've just been reading some ... articles, here and there. They said that if you try to pretend to be something you're not, you'll eventually fail. The real you will show through. It doesn't mean that at first you're not ... more careful, but as you get to know someone, like I've gotten to know you, you ... open up and let them see who you are, little by little. If it works out, great. If it doesn't, then it was probably not meant to be."

"You like me. I can tell it, by the way the iris of your eyes opens up when you see me and the set of your tail. It's a little higher when I'm around."

"You ... you're the only real friend I have here."

"We are not friends, Sahnassa," Merialla corrected gently. "We share the same space – forced together by this school."

"It is ... true," came the soft reply, the darker furred Nephti stinging from the reproach. "I ... guess it takes more time ... to be a friend ... if ever."

"I don't think you can ever be my friend, Sahnassa." The harsh statement was delivered as if it were merely an observation of an unimportant fact.

"But why?"

"Friend is a word those around me use and never mean. They think they are close to my soul, and yet they speak about me when I'm not around like I'm not even real – to them; I am a curiosity. They smile and never visit; they answer but never call. They won't talk and walk away. Friend is a word that lies more than it tells the truth. Friend is a score that is kept but is a collection of emptiness."

In that instant, although she was hurt by what Merialla had said, Sahnassa understood. So many in the unique Nephti's past had likely been called her friends, perhaps at the behest of parents or matrons or school teachers or counselors. In some ways, Sahnassa had grown up without many friends, as well, only a few, and all of those had drifted away and abandoned her, much as Merialla's had probably done to her. "I understand."

"And that is why you cannot be my friend, Sahnassa. You are too close to my soul to be called a friend."

The statement made her put her paw over her chest, as if this elegant Nephti had suddenly reached inside of her and made the hurt she was feeling go away. "I'm ... honored, Merialla, to hear you say that! You ... you have become close to my soul, and ... I mean that!"

"I know you do." Sahnassa stood and walked over and sat beside Merialla on the bed, gently lifted the Nephti's paws, and put them into her own and held them. "I have spoken more with you than almost anyone else."

There was a bit of fear and regret in the normally placid Nephti's tone that made Sahnassa feel intensely sorry for her. Merialla wasn't bad, and she wasn't crazy – she just saw the world so very differently, and in many ways, she saw it more truthfully than anyone Sahnassa had ever met. "Merialla, have … you ever slept next to someone, for comfort – to feel someone else's presence, for reassurance when you were feeling bad?"

"No. I've always slept alone, as much as I can remember."

Sahnassa nodded, sadly. In their prior conversations, Merialla had confessed that certain memories of her childhood were missing, victims of the drugs her parents tried on her at the behest of doctors. In many ways, the light purple Nephti was like an adult with very little emotional past to draw upon, and Sahnassa wondered if that's why she didn't understand empathy or tact or social norms very well. "I don't know if you would be willing to try it, but … it's something my sisters did when they needed comforting or when I did. Even though my parents and I are not on good terms, I know … I know my sisters still love me."

"I will try. Is this how you show that you are close to my soul?"

"It is," Sahnassa answered, standing. "Let me finish up my work, and then we can get ready for bed, okay?"

"This will be interesting," Merialla observed, but a gentle smile tugged up the corners of her muzzle.

The next morning, Sahnassa awoke, feeling a little weary. The night, from her perspective, had not gone well. She had slept behind Merialla, as with Hylea, but into the small intervals of the night an increasingly excited series of questions had come forth from the Nephti in front of her, about what she was feeling and what she should feel. Some of the questions were a little concerning, but as patiently as she could, Sahnassa answered every one. However, at some point, she realized she must have fallen asleep in the middle of an answer. What also added to the difficulty of the experience was Merialla's refusal to accept any change in position, and it had taken some very subtle movements to relieve a cramped arm or leg. Generally, when she and her sisters went to sleep, they awoke separated, if only slightly. Sahnassa's body told her that she had been fixed in the exact same position all night.

"Sahnassa, are you awake now?" came an anxious question from in front of her.

"I … am. I … I have to get up. I've … I've got to … go."

With a voice that sounded truly bereft and laden with disappointment, Merialla acknowledged, "Oh, well … I … I understand."

Following through, Sahnassa got up, stretched her aching muscles and said, "Okay. I'll be back in a bit." When she arrived back from her trip to the facilities, she found Merialla, curled up on the bed, sitting with her legs close against her chest and wrapped with the heavy blanket all around her. Her eyes were intently staring into the space ahead, into nothing, and something about the way she was acting worried Sahnassa. "Kit, are … are you okay?"

"I … don't know, Sahnassa. I … all night felt like I was drinking in something … from you. I was afraid when I woke up this morning, you'd be dead behind me – all the life drained away."

"Well, I have to admit, it wasn't the most comfortable night's sleep I've ever had, but I'm certainly still alive. Did I like stop breathing or something?"

"I don't remember. I don't think so. I … feel different this morning. I feel different," Merialla insisted, still not really looking at Sahnassa. "The doctors required me to not eat for almost a full sol before some of my tests. When … when I was allowed to eat again, it felt … like … like I feel right now! I … I don't understand it. I wasn't hungry. I didn't eat."

Although still tired and fatigued, Sahnassa started to get a small inkling of what was causing the normally composed Nephti's distress. She walked over, opened Merialla's blanket, and slipped in beside her. As she closed the blanket around them both, Sahnassa ignored the stunned stare pointed back at her. "Perhaps, in a way, you were. You have no siblings. Your … parents aren't that close to you. Like me, you kind of have an issue with … fitting in. You've been alone for so long, when you're finally not alone … it can feel pretty strange, I'd imagine."

"It's like I've had something taken from me, and you've given it back, but it shouldn't have been *you* that gave it back! I … I hope I didn't hurt you by what I said just now."

That made Sahnassa turn and look at Merialla, amazed. Never before had she been asked directly about how she felt by the light purple Nephti. It was appalling to think that the aloofness, the detachment Merialla demonstrated was because no one had bothered to give the poor kit the closeness and connectedness every Thurian needed. "No, but I have a favor to ask. Don't tell anyone we did this. There's nothing wrong with it, but those of ... lesser intelligence may misunderstand."

"Certainly. Can we ... sleep like this again tonight?"

"Will you let me move around a little? Perhaps we could go to sleep a little earlier." Merialla nodded emphatically. "Okay." Sahnassa's agreement brought out the broadest smile she had ever seen on the Nephti's muzzle, like that of a child – full of joy and innocence. "You've never had this kind of closeness, have you? Not with your ... dad or even your mother?"

"No. We ... almost never touch."

Reaching around to comfort the light purple Nephti, Sahnassa realized that, in a way, although she was still sleepy and ached a bit, she felt much the same as Merialla. Finally, she was close to someone, a friend, even if this "friend" couldn't bring herself to use the word.

Vanarra listened as her small alarm clock sounded, and she simply reached over and turned it off, continuing what she had done for the entirety of the sleepless night she had endured. "What if I'm pregnant? How did this happen to me? Why?" Van's memory of the entire evening was essentially missing or hopelessly distorted until the point she had woken up in pain.

"Anati!" Gorta's voice, rougher than usual, called out to her. "Anati!"

Wincing in pain, Van slowly rose, grateful that she at least didn't stink of her assailants' scents anymore – almost a full interval in the small shower had given her at least that amount of peace. Walking with her legs ajar and a paw over her lower abdomen, she finally made it into the office to the sounds of Gorta retching into a trash bucket. Stepping back into the hall washroom, she grabbed some of the disposable cloths, wet them, and poured a cup of water. Hearing the coughing and heaving stop and the cursing begin, she made her way back to the office.

"I brought you some water and something to wipe your muzzle," Van quietly stated, and nodding, the Faelnar took both of them. "I'll take care of this for you," Vanarra offered, trembling as she picked up the bucket and held it away from her. In a few moments, she returned to the office to see Gorta sitting up, looking dazed and weak.

"Thank you, Anati. Must ... have been a fun evening. Did ... did we get paid?"

Feeling like she was about to fall down, Vanarra reached out for and held the desk. "Yes. Yes, we did," she answered, her voice full of bitterness.

The Faelnar looked up at her, her bleary eyes tightening a bit. "What's wrong with you?"

"I ... I was ... rape-mated last night. I don't remember it, though. I ... don't remember much of anything."

Gorta cocked her head and then, slowly, got off of the couch and made for her chair. Likewise gripping the desk, she sat, and her eyes fixed themselves to the draft left on the top. "That's not the full amount. That's barely more than half! Why didn't you tell me before we left?"

"I ... couldn't ... wake you up."

"You didn't try, you mean," the Faelnar grumbled. At that moment, Van's knees when out from under her, and she sank to the floor, still holding the desk. "Oh, dammit, and this, too! Go lie down on the couch. Are you bleeding?"

Vanarra didn't answer until she was lying down, and that effort left her panting. "I ... I don't think so. I ... don't remember ... anything about what happened to me!"

"So, you're weak this morning, aching all over, memory scrambled?" Van nodded. "Someone dosed you. I had someone try it on me when ... when I was younger. Stupid Anati – you should know better! I told you don't take anything from anybody. That's why. Now you see, right?"

Grimly, Van nodded. "I ... I'm sorry! Now, I could be ... pregnant." Despite herself, Vanarra was crying.

"Oh, mange!" the Faelnar nearly growled. "You know Anati can't get pregnant very easily, so you probably have nothing to worry about." Van's crying became more intense, and she put her paws over her eyes in shame. "Oh, please. That I have to put up with this! Alright. I'll ... there's something I can get you that will make sure what they did doesn't take, but it's expensive, and it's coming out of your pay since you were the one who messed up." Van calmed down and nodded. "Now, do you know who did this to you?"

"I ... I don't remember it happening, but from the scents, I'm almost certain that the one who gave me the draft last night was one of them."

"It's not enough.   Even if you had pictures and signed confessions, it would be difficult for an Anati to prove any case against anyone at that party last night.   You're just going to have to take this as a lesson and learn from it.   We can't have you hiding in corners or down hallways, I guess, either.   Oh, won't that be fun to explain!"

"I'm ... sorry, Gorta!"

"Well, you should be," the Faelnar groaned as she rose. Reaching for a walking stick that had become a recent addition to her office, Gorta grabbed her bag and slowly walked towards the exit.

"Thank you," Vanarra offered when the Faelnar opened the door and had to turn her head against the onslaught of the morning sunlight.

"You're welcome, Anati. I'm ... sorry this happened to you. Just ... rest. I'll be back in awhile."

Sahnassa awoke, as she had for every morning in the last moon, behind Merialla. She would have tried to resist the light purple Nephti's pleas to keep repeating the practice, but there was a tangible change in the one who had grown "close to her soul." Although it wasn't quite as present in the conversations she had with others, Merialla's discussions with her had taken on an air of connectedness and ease they didn't seem to have before. Slowly, her distant and analytical roommate started asking about the effect of a statement – questions like "Did my saying that hurt your feelings?" It had been a fascinating time of discovery for both of them, and although Sahnassa almost missed the airy detachment, this emerging spirit seemed as marvelously intricate and exquisite as the stripes on Merialla's fur.

"How are you, Sahnassa? Did you rest well?"

Smiling a bit, she answered, "I did. Do you always wake up before me?"

"Whenever you start to wake, I ... can tell. It's not bad that you wake me up, and it doesn't hurt my feelings. Are you still okay with this? I have to ask."

"It's fine, so long as we don't share it with anyone else. It's just for us."

"Just for us." Merialla slipped forward and made way so Sahnassa could rise. As Sahnassa stretched and got out of the bed, the light purple Nephti said, "I've watched you coming across the commons and talking to others. You're ... doing better, but still, you just need to focus on standing to your full height. I think Jazan has taken notice of you. If you can project a little more confidence, he might actually come over and talk to you."

"Jazan?! You're kidding, right? He doesn't even look at me."

"When you're looking, he doesn't; when you look away, he does. Can't ... can't you feel his stare? I can feel everyone's stares."

Sahnassa turned and looked at her roommate with a mixture of embarrassment and sympathy. "I ... I can't, I guess. I'm ... sorry that you feel like others are staring at you."

"They are. I'm starting not to mind it. I've caught ... Lashahar looking at me, and I like that, but when I look back at him, he looks away, like he shouldn't have been doing it."

"When you look back at him, are you smiling? Do you smile more when he holds your gaze or looks back at you?"

Merialla cocked her head. "I ... I don't know. I'll shall have to try that. I've heard him talk; he's interesting. He reads strange books – books about things that can never be. I like that."

"You know, there are some who think Lashahar is a little too caught up in his space fiction."

"But he smells nice," Merialla contended.

"How'd you get close enough to do that? To figure that out?"

"He kind of ran into me by accident. I ... actually didn't mind."

Sahnassa chuckled, her muzzle drawing up into a smile. "Oh, I think you two are definitely starting to think about a hunt!"

"Perhaps," Merialla replied in something of her old detached tone, but Sahnassa couldn't help but relish the spark of happy curiosity in her roommate's eyes or the noticeable loft in her tail.

Vanarra stood, leaning against an entrance wall at yet another banquet hall, finally feeling as if the pains in her groin had stopped. It had been nearly a full moon since she was rapemated, and now, as she stood watching this joining celebration, the first since she was attacked, a whole new sense of wariness and alert observation pervaded her.

There were two reasons – the attack being only the first. Second, she had learned that she had to watch out for Gorta as much as for herself. Thurians were always trying to give her drinks, which she too readily accepted and then, after awhile, she was incapacitated, and Van was left to carry on alone. So Vanarra had discovered that making up little emergencies and jumping in at the right moment kept the Faelnar out of trouble, and it also – to the obvious chagrin of some of her customers – ensured that they were paid fully for their services.

To some extent, the interruptions – polite as they were – made Gorta annoyed, angry even, but once they were back together in the transport in possession of a draft for the correct amount, the Faelnar seemed to bid her no ill will. After a successful night, she would leave Van in peace and go back to her own lair to celebrate. Generally, Gorta arrived late the next morning, still not completely over her celebrating or, in some cases, not finished with it. As she watched the Faelnar move around greeting guests, Van studied her. More and more she was moving like a wounded animal, and her endurance had seemed to be flagging as of late. Vanarra had even brought her drinks – fruit juices – to try to keep her going, but more and more of the responsibility of keeping the event on trail was resting upon Vanarra's back.

"Well, hello," a smooth voice from beside her said.

Turning around, she averted her eyes downwards and greeted the keen-looking male. "Good evening. How may I assist you?"

"A little talk, a little conversation, perhaps?"

Intentionally glancing in Gorta's direction, she realized that they were being double-teamed. A nice female was holding two drinks and seemed to be talking Gorta into taking one. "I'm sorry. We're out of creele rolls at the table. My boss requires me to keep them stocked, or I don't get paid."

"They look fine to me," he tried to say, but she already had her back towards him and was waving to get Gorta's attention.

Sighing, Gorta returned the drink to the female Lupar and asked, "What is it now, Anati?"

"A moment, please?" she asked.

Leaning over, she whispered into the Faelnar's ear. "They just tried to double team us! It's ... intentional! They're trying to get out of paying!"

Gorta looked at her, and then back at the Lupar who was standing only a short distance away, obviously wanting to come back and deliver Gorta that drink. She glanced behind Vanarra and saw a male Lupar carefully watching her employee. "Dammit, and I thought they were straight on the trail," Gorta whispered back. "What do we do?"

"Cross them up. I'll take her, and you take him, okay?"

"This should be interesting! Okay, kit. We'll try it your way."

After they separated, Gorta moved off towards the male, and as the female tried to follow her, Vanarra stepped in the way. "Good evening. I hope you're finding everything satisfactory?"

Now, slightly annoyed, the female replied, "Yes. Fine. Very nice."

"May I take that extra drink from you?"

"Well, Anati, I actually wanted to give it to someone."

"Yes. Gorta asked me to let you know that she'd been offered her limit of drinks for the night, and although your kindness is appreciated, we want to give full value to our clients. She hopes you'll understand."

The female Lupar's shoulders sank visibly, and a glance at the male Lupar trying, without success, to extricate himself from a conversation with Gorta, nearly dropped her tail to the floor. "I ... suppose I will have to. Here," she said, shoving both drinks into Vanarra's paws, and Van couldn't help but smile viciously as the Lupar retreated back into the throng of guests.

Intervals later, the two celebrated the full payment in the office, drinking fruit juices and recounting the event. "You know, I think he was up to something. He was holding something in his paw, and when I started to walk towards him," Gorta explained, "he almost dropped it trying to get it out of sight. That ... damned Lupar had been trying to put drinks in my paws all night. Great catch, kit. I ... I owe you."

"I owe you, Gorta. Thank you for letting me interrupt."

"From making a tail out of myself and costing us money, do that anytime. I'm finally realizing that I've been making some really stupid calls, and ... you're helping me not to do that. I want you to know that I've also added you as joint on the business's bank accounts. Now, I'll still see every statement, and they'll only approve small withdrawals for you, but … I've learned I can trust you, Anati. I really can."

"Thank you," Vanarra replied, surprised. "But … but what do I need access to the bank accounts for?"

"Ordering, of course! I'm just asking you what we need, anyway," Gorta chuckled. "There's no reason why I have to be your administrative assistant."

Van ducked her head and apologized. "I'm … sorry if you felt that way."

"I'm just joking with you. As of this morning, you have all you need to order and deposit and withdraw. Just run things by me first, okay? I'm still the owner here, but … I … I wouldn't be if you hadn't come. I would have … messed it all up."

"Sorla did us both a favor, then, didn't she?" Vanarra asked, thinking fondly of her friend. It had been awhile since either of them had heard from her; her last message stating that she had been very busy with the dame's schedule.

"She did," Gorta replied. Van just stared at her for a moment. There was something wrong with the Faelnar, that much she knew already, but there was something else, tonight. "What are you looking at, kit?"

"Are … are you okay?"

"More or less," the Faelnar replied. "Now, go on to bed. I … I know you're tired. I certainly am."

"Are you going back home?"

"I don't think so. Unless you have an objection, I'm … going to be here tonight. I just … am not feeling much like being alone right now."

Although there was something truly strange about Gorta's demeanor, Van simply nodded and replied, "Alright. Good night, Gorta."

Just as Van was about to leave the room, the Faelnar added, "Vanarra?"

"Yes?"

Looking down, embarrassment causing her blush furs to rise, Gorta said, "Thank you, kit. You've been very good to me, kept my business from failing. I am grateful you've helped me regain some small bit of honor. I ... never had a daughter, but if I did, I wish she could have been like you."

"You're welcome," Vanarra replied, surprised by the statement since Gorta had never really thanked her like that for anything she did, let alone talk to her as tenderly as she was doing now. "And thank you for that. You've ... helped me in so many ways."

"More than both of us probably realize. Rest well, Vanarra. Tomorrow's a big sol."

Not truly understanding the comment, since there were no functions booked for a few sols, Van simply shrugged it off and told her boss good-night a final time before going to her room.

Van awoke a couple of times during that night, listening to the sounds of her boss celebrating by downing fermentum, but as she carefully listened, Vanarra thought it was just a little bit. Finally, things got quiet, and Vanarra faded back into a sound sleep.

The next morning, the alarm woke Van, and she groggily got out of bed. Trying not to disturb Gorta, she quietly went through her morning routine, got dressed, and then went back into her room to wait for the Faelnar to awaken. After nearly two intervals of reading Matriarch Rahnahi de Dothnar's latest book, Van was growing hungry and a little impatient. Quietly, she slipped off her bed and slowly made her way to her boss's office door.

Leaning in, she saw that it was quiet, but she was surprised that Gorta wasn't sleeping on the couch as she had suggested; she was asleep in her chair. "Gorta? Are you awake?"

There was an odd smell in the room, like urine, and then Van noticed that Gorta didn't stir at all. She was perfectly still. Van's heart then started to beat in her chest a little stronger as she watched Gorta, sitting, her head back, her tail limp, and absolutely not moving whatsoever. "Gorta? You're not playing a trick on me now, are you?"

Van slipped into the room and walked forward. Clicking on the desk light, she gasped. "No! Gorta!" The Faelnar's mouth was open, and her lips and gums were almost completely without color, and her eyes were open, fixed at the ceiling. Rushing to her boss's side, Van put her paw on the Faelnar's chest and put another alongside her neck. The cold touch beneath the Faelnar's fur told her all she needed to know. "Oh, no! Gorta! Please, no," Vanarra groaned, heartbroken. Stepping around behind her, Vanarra looked down at the desk and saw that the Faelnar had written a note. Her paws shaking, she picked it up and read it:

Vanarra, I need to find peace, and I finally will tonight. My life has been unending misery for so many seasons, and the only joys in my life the last few seasons have been Sorla, and then you. You let me finish my last banquet, my last hurrah, and finish it well. Thank you for that. I've done more than add you to the bank accounts. I've lived a life without honor, but here, at the end, I choose to do something good for someone who truly deserves it. What I have is yours. The keys to my hover and my lair are on the desk. They're yours. You'll find a red envelope in the file folders; that should give you all the legal support you need to take over – it effectively makes you my partner. Kit, I've known for awhile now that the end was coming, but I've decided to end things now on my own terms. Forgive me for leaving you in this way. I wish you well.

Love, Gorta.

Reaching down for the LineCom, Van picked it up and dialed. "Emergency services. How may I assist?"

"I … hi, my name is Vanarra Anasto. I've … I've just found my … business partner dead in her office."

"Are there any signs of a crime?"

"No. I just think she accidentally took too much of her medication or something," Van commented, seeing the empty bottle of pills in the garbage.

"Very well. Please do not touch the body. We have your address, and we're dispatching enforcement and the coroner."

"Yes. I won't. Thank you."

"Very well. Good-bye." The callous attitude of the purebred on the LineCom didn't surprise her, and she placed it back on its rest, carefully. Gently, she took the keys and activators off the desk and placed them in her pocket. Going to the file cabinets, it didn't take her long to find the red envelope with the documents inside. Sitting on the couch, she slipped the documents out and read them. As far as her limited experience could tell, the documents did exactly as Gorta had promised, give her equal status as a partner. Her eyes running with tears, Van folded her boss's note and put it in the envelope with the rest of the legal papers – overwhelmed that she, an Anati cast-out, was now the owner of a business. Looking at Gorta's still form, Van mouthed over and over again, "Thank you. Thank you."

Chapter 11: Fanassaragatti

The next six intervals were a frantic and frightening blur for Vanarra, for when enforcement arrived, two big Vulpi pinned her against the wall and searched her thoroughly before questioning her on the death of Gorta. They had her sitting in binders on the sofa until an older Nephti doctor asked, "Why do you have her locked up?"

"We want to make sure she didn't have any part in the death," the Vulpi said officiously.

"Yeah, right. This Anati – single-pawed – made a Faelnar drink too much fermentum for nearly fifty seasons and then stuffed a pawful of pills down her gullet in the middle of the night while the victim was fully awake," the doctor nearly growled. "Let her go, you idiots. There's no way she's done anything other than what she said." The two guards hesitated, forcing the doctor to add, "Well, I can always play the part of expert witness at a wrongful arrest hearing with internal investigations. Your call." He started packing his gear after examining Gorta's corpse, still upright in the chair.

Looking a little humiliated, one of the guards walked over and unlocked the binders from Vanarra's wrists. "The body is ready to be taken out. Did she have any family?" the doctor asked her.

"Not that she ever said or talked about. A few friends, but … not much else."

"They can take care of the body for you, if you'd like."

Van thought for a moment, with the doctor watching her. "Just … promise me she'll be treated with respect. She treated me that way."

"I'll see that the coroner ensures her death has some meaning. There are a number of medical academies who have new doctors, doctors who could stand to see the damage to her organs that I just saw on the scope. If you agree, your friend will help others save lives."

A tear fell out of Van's eye as she looked up at the doctor. "She wanted to die with a little bit of honor."

"Saving lives is a lot of honor, in my book," the doctor commented.

"Alright," Van agreed. "Please, make it like you said." The doctor signaled the two officers, and they brought in a hover gurney, softly whooshing as it came into the room. In only a few passes, with no one speaking, Gorta's body was pulled back from the desk, gently laid down, and removed from the office to the waiting hover outside.

"What's your name?" the doctor asked, now that they were alone.

"Vanarra Anasto," she replied, looking down.

"Nadar de Orturu. I'm not actually a coroner; I'm just filling in for a friend. Would you mind if I had a look at you? This … had to be difficult for you. How long had you known her?" he asked as he shut and locked the front door.

"A few moons, not even a full season. She gave me a place to stay, and she gave me her business just before she…"

He was kneeling down in front of her, looking at her. "Now, I'm not going to hurt you. Just let me have a look." For the first time she could remember, Van was being examined by a doctor. "I'm going to prick your paw and draw a little blood. It will help me screen you for anything worrisome."

"Ow! Oh," she exclaimed, surprised. "I … I've never had that done before."

"Well, just put this on it and keep the pressure on." The doctor pulled out a specialized device that looked like a large PawLink and slipped in the little glass tube he had used to collect her blood. "Well, now. You're surprisingly healthy. A lot of your kind don't get what they need in terms of food. Have you had any problems, injuries, or anything like that?"

She didn't know why, but Vanarra understood that she could trust this Nephti, perhaps because Sorla had been one, and he was so gentle and kind to her. "I ... I was rapemated about a moon ago."

"Do you know who did it?"

"It ... was ... had to be several of them. They dosed me with something. I don't remember any specifics."

"Alright. Now, you have my attention. Vanarra, I want to examine you, and I mean down there, where they did this to you. I think it's in your best interest to make sure you didn't get anything in terms of a disease from them. I take it you're not pregnant?"

"No."

"Alright. I'll check only if you want me to, but ... if it were any of my regular patients, I would strongly encourage them."

Van's blush furs were in flight, but the fears that had nagged at her since that episode demanded she do something. "Alright."

Half an interval later, the doctor was packing his gear and giving her the result. "You're very lucky. I can tell they really treated you poorly, but there's no evidence of tearing or scarring. The disease filter is coming up with nothing, so that's good. If you're just ... more careful from now on—"

"Oh, I will be."

"See that you are," he insisted. "Someone who has their mind on using you for a good time doesn't have your best interests at heart, and they could as have easily overdosed you, and it would be two of you serving medical science, not just one."

"Thank you. Can ... I ask you a question?"

"Yes, but I do have to be going," he warned.

"Just a quick one. Are ... are all Nephti ... nice? I've ... known a few, and it's silly, but they just are."

"Well, I'd love to tell you that's so, but as a doctor I've seen far too much. Just let me say there are a couple of good houses here in Shanandrae – de Orturu and de Dothnar. Generally, they do pretty good."

She stood and approached him cautiously. "Thank you. You're the first doctor I've ever seen—"

"As old as you are?" he asked, stunned, and she nodded. "Generally, we see your kind during the free clinics and ... look, take this. It's a card that tells you when some of the charitable organizations offer free clinics. Come in once a season, at the very least. If you're sick, come as soon as you can. You may have to wait, but if you're bad off, you won't have to wait for long."

"Oh..." Van replied quietly, and her heartbroken expression saddened the doctor.

"They couldn't have helped your friend here. She'd been killing herself for a long, long time."

"It was someone else. This ... little card could have saved him."

"You didn't know, kit. You didn't know. Someone should have told you, and you should have been in a position where you could have found out. That's my belief. Now, though, you do know. So, use it. Tell others. I wish you well."

"Thank you, Doctor. I ... I can't thank you enough."

He chuckled, "Well, you're always welcome to try, but by no means is it required. Take care."

He had left her then, alone, sitting in the office. When she went to the door some time later and opened it, everyone was gone – the coroner's hover, the enforcement vehicles, everything. Walking back inside, she smelled the foul smell from underneath the desk and went about cleaning it. It took her a moment after she had done so to realize that she wasn't doing it for Gorta, anymore. She was taking care of the business for herself.

Carefully, she sat down in Gorta's chair, trying to decide what she should do. She started thinking through all of the parts of the business, and she found, to her surprise, that there wasn't really anything that she didn't know how to do. In the last moon, Gorta had been showing her more and more of her cooking secrets, and Van had taken over some of the simpler tasks. The finances, the ordering, the administration and organization, sales, running an event – she thought through everything, and there were a few parts that she wasn't exactly sure of, but her experience helped convince her that she could cover those areas she was weak in. "Okay, so ... my choices are sell everything and try to find another job working for someone ... or try to take over this business."

Still unsure of what to do, she knew that there was one other thing she should look at. Going through the files, she found the ownership papers for Gorta's lair. In her heart, she knew that the last thing she wanted was to take over the lair of the old kit, but depending on what it could be sold for, it might just help her do what she'd always wished Gorta had done – hire more help. With more help came security in numbers, and with more help came the ability to manage bigger events, with bigger profits. She'd always found it irksome when Gorta walked away from an event that was just a little too big for the pair of them to manage.

"I've … I've got to see that lair – see if there's anything there we can sell. See if we can sell it, too." Reaching for the building keys and hover activator, Vanarra strode out of the door, locking it behind her.

Flint Bonar had just been fired, and he was literally sitting out on the curb. The great, hulking Anati was a mix between Pantera and Lupar, two of the largest species of Thurian. Although the few other pairings he knew about between such had rendered children roughly equivalent in size to either of the two, Flint's parentage had emphasized the genetic tendency towards a larger size and put him a full head taller and wider at the shoulders than any Thurian he had ever met. On the positive side, there wasn't a purebred or Anati who wanted much to tangle with him. Flint liked working out, which made his size all the more impressive. The negative for this great gray Anati was what had got him fired – fear.

He had been working as a masseuse and an assistant manager at a small business in Shanandrae. The intervals were long and frequently weren't as rewarding as he would have liked, but it had been steady pay and sufficient enough for a small rental lair, food, and a gym membership. Now, because he had done a good thing, that was gone. Some purebred outcasts had barged into the business, wielding long knives and threatening the nearly full establishment in order to convince everyone to give over every valuable they owned. When the thieves had come in, Flint was bent down trying to rearrange the fur lotions on the bottom shelves – not his favorite task. When he stood up, however, growling at his adversaries, the effect was all anyone could have imagined. One assailant nearby dropped his weapon instantly, and his body made a perfect projectile for dealing with the other three. In short order, all four were unconscious and bleeding, held down beneath Flint's paws, his claws extended just to make sure they didn't awake and escape.

After enforcement arrived and dealt with the miscreants, Flint had dusted himself off and turned to walk back into the establishment to continue what he had been working on before. Much to his dismay, the short Perratti who ran the place was standing at the door, barring his entrance. He held a bag with all of Flint's things and a financial draft. "This is your final pay. You aren't working here anymore. Everyone in that building behind me is six times more terrified of you than they were of the thieves who came in. I ... I hired you because I thought you were a gentle giant, not a terror. Please, just go."

Looking into his stern little face, Flint knew there wasn't any hope of negotiation or compromise. Sadly, meekly, he had taken the items presented and walked away. What should have been, in his mind, appreciation if not a hero's welcome, was met with fear and disdain, and it was that bitter realization and regret that ached in his soul, along with everything that he might now lose.

"Uh, hey there. Muscles!" Flint looked up a little grimly; that wasn't the first time he had heard that particular name. However, what met his eye was surprisingly pleasant. She was an Anati, as well, a mix of Vulpi and Faelnar, but what a mix! Both of those somewhat lithe species had their own attributes of beauty and attractiveness, but the one before his eyes now surpassed them both by the particular combination woven into this keen looking female.

"Hello. What can I do for you?" It was much the same thing he asked several hundred times each sol, and it came out with a practiced ease that made the Vulpi-Faelnar mix cant her head a little thoughtfully.

"Well, I ... I am a small business owner. It's a catering business, and well, my business partner just sort of well – she died, actually."

"I'm sorry to hear that. A business ... owner?"

"Yes, I am," she answered, and although there was a little hesitation in the answer, that was soon explained when she added, "I was actually a partner with her until this morning, when she passed."

"I'm very sorry to hear about your loss. Seems to be a bad sol all the way around."

"Really? Why's that?"

"Just lost my job ... as a reward for protecting the clients and staff from a group of thieves. Seeing me fight them off ... scared them."

The eyebrows furrowed, and the tail lashed angrily to match the irritation in the response. "I see. Typical purebred behavior! I'm Vanarra Anasto, and I'm looking for some help. It may just be for a few intervals, but if things work out, it might be longer. Pay is at the standard basis, plus six – at least for a start."

"Flint Bonar," he introduced himself. "I guess I'm available. What's the job?"

"My partner, Gorta, had a lair, and I need to go over and clean it out – see what can be sold and what can be thrown away. My goal is to eventually sell the place to cover any outstanding debts she may have had and plow the rest of the funds back into the business for expansion."

"Sounds ... like a really good idea," he replied thoughtfully. Beyond her physical attractiveness, Flint picked up on the fact she seemed endowed with good judgment in addition to her more obvious assets. Slowly, he stood up, and as usual, Vanarra took the customary single step back. "Don't worry. I'm actually a nice guy unless you're trying to rob the business where I work."

"Yeah, and I would never fire you for that! In fact ... in my business, it may be good to have someone around to ... dissuade certain rowdy party-goers from trying to take advantage of our employees. Come on. You can ride in the back of the delivery hover." The offer was made with outstretched paw, paw-fingers splayed open, awaiting to be clasped. Surprised by this gesture, since most believed it to be physically impossible, Flint very carefully reciprocated, and although it was more like touching paw pads at first, she managed to stretch just enough to make it a real clasp – something he hadn't experienced in ages.

He nodded gratefully and then followed her down the trail the short distance to where she had parked. Now, his eyes couldn't help but confirm every bit of appreciation they had indicated at having seen this Vanarra from the front, for her going was as beautiful as her coming. Her all-business attitude, however, and relatively level tail were a bit of a warning and enough to council him to behave respectfully. After all, the most beautiful thing about her at the moment was her willingness to provide him with employment, and Flint had no intention of messing that up.

"Well, thank you very much for stopping and talking to me," Flint said from behind her. "It ... was kind of a bummer. You think you've helped someone and..."

"Purebreds," Vanarra growled in response, but then corrected herself. "Not all of them, just almost all of them. Also, don't expect

me to set any speed records getting where we're going. I actually …
kind of … don't have a license, yet. I'm going to."

"Well, I actually do. If you want for us to get there and not
worry about it, I'd be okay with driving."

"Fine by me," Van replied surrendering the spot. "I have to
look at the map to figure out where her place is."

"You've never been there before?" he asked as he adjusted the
driver's seat as far back as it would go, leaving his real question
unsaid, but Vanarra was quick enough to take him up on it.

"Gorta … had some issues – with drinking and not throwing
things away," she explained. "I'm a little worried about what we'll
find."

"Hopefully not her," Flint quietly stated.

"She passed away in the office last night – one drink too many
and too many pills, period. Okay, here's where we're going. 221
Hush Trail, Course Point 21."

Flint raised his eyebrow fur, as he lifted the skids. "I know
where that is. I've had clients over there before – nice area, actually."

"Well, let's get over there."

"You got it, boss." Vanarra couldn't keep herself from smiling
when he said it. For as long as it lasted, she was actually the boss.

Pulling up in front of the moderate-sized lair, Van breathed, "I
had no idea she could afford anything like this. Her business was
hanging on by only a few fur-strands."

"How long did you know her?"

"A few moons, why?"

"You said she had a problem with fermentum?" Van nodded
in answer as they both got ready to get out. "Usually, most can hold it
together for a really long time, until the end, that is. Perhaps she did
really well before."

"We'll see," Van replied. "Either the key will fit, or it won't."

They walked up carefully to the front, and Vanarra started
trying keys. "What's that smell?" Flint asked.

"Doesn't exactly smell like fresh-cut sahnassas, does it?"

"More like the space underneath someone's tail," Flint
groaned, but just then, the lock released, and Vanarra flung the door
open. "Oh, mange!" Flint cried at the sights and smells that assaulted
him.

"Oh my," Van sighed. "We … we've got it right. This is definitely Gorta. Her storeroom was like this when I got hired on, but wow, it … wasn't this bad! Looks like we've got a lot of work ahead of us."

With that, the two waded in and started trying to open windows and doors to let some of the smell out. When Van directed Flint to start collecting the piles of trash and hauling them away, she removed her outer shirt, revealing a sleeveless top that made Flint just stop and stare. "Ahem," Van stated, annoyed. "Flint, we're not going to get much work done if you can only look at two things."

Flint shook himself when he realized that Vanarra was pointing at her own chest with two expressed claw-tips. He apologized, "Sorry, but … you are kind of an attention-getter."

"Yeah, well I've had about all of that kind of attention I can stand. I'll go work in her bedroom … if it will help your concentration. Keep your eyes open for anything valuable, okay? Well, more than just what you were looking at."

"Alright, you got me, Vanarra," he chuckled. "Point taken."

"You know what, Flint? For you, it's just Van. Just call me that. It's okay."

"Alright, Van. Thanks."

After an interval, Flint and Vanarra had started to make the barest dents in the mounds of material that Gorta had left behind when he looked out the window at an enforcement hover pulling up, its alert lights flashing. "Van! Enforcement just showed up!" he bellowed.

"Oh, right!" she called back from the bedroom. "I should have known! I'll take care of it."

She strode back into the room, her top replaced, holding her satchel. She emerged from the front door, just as a Nephti and Faelnar officer were approaching it, their paws on their stunners.

"Good morning, officers!" she called to them, her eyes on their waists, trying not to offend. She lifted a piece of paper and held it in front of them.

"What's this?"

"Legal note. Gives me the right to access this property and all of its possessions. The owner, Gorta, of Gorta's Gatherings, passed away this morning. I'm her business partner."

The Nephti took the paper gently and started reading it. "I heard about that call this morning. Doctor said she died from an overdose or something."

Looking up into his eyes, she corrected him. "She was already dying. She just decided to choose when."

The Faelnar was looking at her with a measure of disgust, but the Nephti was poring over the document very carefully. "What are you doing here this morning? The neighbors called thinking it was a robbery."

"Yeah, right! The slowest robbery of all time, and when you take a look in there, you'll know why. It's full of just … stuff! Everywhere!"

"What's that smell?" the Faelnar asked. "Don't you ever bathe?"

"That's what the whole inside smells like, and I'll warn you – it's worse the closer you get."

"Just a moment, please," the Nephti told Vanarra before calling in the information on the paper. After a few moments, the dispatch center confirmed that the legal instruments were properly filed and in-force. "Well, okay then. Just be careful not to annoy the neighbors. We got like six calls."

"Well, we're harmless. The smell aside, do you want to have a look inside? We're basically just cleaning it out and selling off whatever we can."

"I think we have to be going," the Faelnar replied, disgusted, and started walking towards their vehicle.

"If we went in for a look, we can answer the calls we know are coming next," the Nephti officer countered. "If you wouldn't mind?"

"Sure. I have someone else with me helping. He's harmless, too."

"Okay."

"I'm going to work on paperwork," the Faelnar said, disgusted and walked away.

The Nephti officer followed her in, putting his paw in front of his muzzle. "Wow! You … you weren't kidding! Uh oh!" The Nephti's paw went to his sidearm the moment he saw Flint.

"Easy there. He's the one who's helping me. I needed someone with big muscles."

"For shoveling," Flint supplied, motioning to the mass, but the joke made the Nephti chuckle.

"Yeah, I can see that. How ... how did it get like this?"

"I don't know," Van replied. "It's the first time we've seen it. She never let me come over before. Now, I can see why."

"I'll bet I – hey, oh ... oh ... oh my! By ... by the moons! She ... she has one! She ... really, really has one!" the officer shouted, almost jumping up and down as he pointed to a hanging on the far wall.

"One ... what?" Flint asked.

The excited Nephti was nearly climbing over the piles trying to get to it. "Oh my gosh! She's really got one! Oh, this is ... you never see these anymore!"

Vanarra was chuckling. "What?!"

"Let me see if it's ... oh ... by ... the ... moons! It's original!" he breathed with absolute reverence. "It's a copy of the Familial Ordering Accord, written in Nephti, Faelnar and a few other of the old languages. This should be in a museum somewhere!"

"You want it?" Van asked. "We're selling!"

"Huh, I ... I don't think I could pay you what this is worth. It wouldn't be enough to set you up for life or anything, but ... it's more than I make in a season."

"Could you, perhaps, do something in trade? Give us some help from time to time? Anati usually get the reaction your friend gave me. It would be nice to have someone in enforcement to ask questions to."

He shook his head. "I can't do that. The ethics review board would never go for it, but I tell you what I *can* do. I have an older brother who owns a waste removal and damage recovery service. If you part with this hanging, I'll make sure he has a dumping bin brought out here and put out front so you can have a place to throw away all of this ... stuff. When you've got the floor clear, he can re-do the inside, make it look good – if selling is what you want to do."

"Sounds good, but I want it in writing, please. I've occasionally been treated poorly by purebreds who think they can just get away with anything because my parentage is a little mixed up. My eyes are an odd color, but my brain works just fine."

"Yeah, okay. Not a problem. Can we draw it up now? I'll ... I'll make the call to my brother, and you'll have the bin and a signed contract before I leave, but … if we don't do something with this, it's going to get stolen. It's just too damn valuable."

Vanarra walked over to him and put out her paw for him to clasp, and to his credit, he did so without hesitation. "What is it with Nephti?" she asked him, smiling. "It's like you're the only ones who don't treat us like we're disposable."

"My dame was Rahnahi de Dothnar. If I did, she'd have the fur off my back in strips."

Vanarra went wide-eyed, and now her excitement mirrored what the officer demonstrated only a few moments before. "Oh, you have got to be kidding! Oh, I love her stuff! Is she doing alright as matriarch? I was so worried about how she would do!"

He smiled at her, seeming pleased. "She's doing great. She's put some tough dames up underneath her to do a lot of the hard stuff – disavowals and the like, but yeah, everyone of us just loves her. She's … she's trying to change how Thurians think about mixed bloods, about a lot of things."

"I know that!" Van countered. "Ever since the *Tale of the Ugly Seed*!"

"We've got that book! I read it to my cubs!"

"Well, that's just wonderful! Okay, you get all that stuff put in motion, and I'll draw us up a contract."

Two intervals later, a very pleased Nephti and an exceedingly unhappy Faelnar were leaving, just having finished a conversation with Van, Flint, and six of the recovery firm's workers who were now helping Vanarra and Flint quickly unload the massive amount of debris from the lair and place it in two large bins that had been very quickly brought to the site.

"You should have told them about your business," Flint whispered to her.

"Oh, right! Darn! Well, I might hear from them again. I … you know the truth is I don't know what to call it. I can't keep calling it Gorta's Gatherings; she's dead!"

"Something with your name in it, then," Flint suggested. "You're a catering business. What kinds of things to you cater?"

"Gatherings, celebrations, joinings, and … hey, what about Celebrations?"

"Needs your name in it. Celebrations … by Vanarra?"

She tilted her head back and forth, sifting the name in her thoughts, and found it to her liking. "Yeah! Celebrations by Vanarra. That works! I'll need to get some cards drawn up."

"I know who can do that," Flint supplied. "We had to do that ourselves at the massage business."

"Flint," Van said, looking at him, pleased, "so long as you don't try to paw me or stare at my … 'attention-getters' too often, I think this is going to work out. Speaking of work, we still have a lot of it to do, even with the help. So, let's get going."

"You got it, boss!"

Again, Van couldn't help but smile when he said it, and she went back into the lair feeling like her life was finally moving in the right direction.

"You seem a lot more relaxed, Sahnassa, than you normally are," Lashahar commented as he and Merialla sat next to one another on the bed in their room. The pair had been slowly getting to know one another over the last season, and as Merialla's spirit had opened up and blossomed, the bookish male was the happy benefactor. In many ways, he was as odd and brilliant as she, just in a slightly different spectrum, and although Sahnassa's patient closeness with the light purple Nephti had helped Merialla develop empathy and caring towards others, it was Lashahar that had made her laugh, really laugh for the first time.

"I just finished my last exams for the season! I'm … thrilled and relieved, regardless of what grade I get. I don't think I care anymore!" Sahnassa sighed as she lay back in her bed.

"You do care, and I think you're going to do alright," Merialla offered. "Although I know that advanced theoretical mathematics course was a challenge to you."

"Yeah, probably only get 85% in that one, if that. Still, box checked!" Sahnassa stated.

"So, what are you going to do during the break?" Lashahar asked, reaching around Merialla and drawing her close.

"Well, I'm staying here. I … can't exactly go home—"

"Why?" he asked.

"Fight with her parents," Merialla said quietly in warning.

"Oh, sorry."

"Don't worry about it. It will probably work out better for me, anyway. I'm going to work in the student administration center setting up TransNet sites for them, maybe even the library archive. They're offering fairly decent pay – well, for a student. I'm going to try to save up my money, too. I've been running pretty even with what I'm getting, but that hover repair really set me back."

"I still say your parents should have paid for it," Merialla commented, sourly.

"I can't go back to them and ask. What little communication I've had with my matron over the last season has indicated pretty clearly that my parents are still licking their wounds from when I invoked the Compact—"

"You did what?!" Lashahar almost shouted. "Why would you ever do that?"

"It was her idea!" Sahnassa replied, chuckling, pointing at Merialla who was now turning her head to hide her blush furs.

"Well?" he asked.

"Her parents were working with her dame to ruin her time here, put her in classes she wasn't qualified for, sour her professors against her. It was either that, or she'd leave."

"Oh, Sahnassa, I'm sorry about that."

"My parents were, too," Sahnassa added, "after our matron got through with them. It also seems my sisters are, too." Sahnassa's tail drooped, and her ears fell. "I … I thought for sure they'd at least come visit me. They're busy, I guess. So, I guess I'll be here for about a couple of moons, working, and probably bored out of my mind."

"You could have a little fun? Go out? Check out some of the clubs?" Lashahar suggested.

"Not much in the way of funds. My parents are providing the bare minimum, as required by the house – but no fun money."

"Well," Lashahar offered suggestively. "You could always do what I do."

"Read space fiction?! Yeah right," Sahnassa replied, rolling her eyes.

"Oh, now don't be that way, Sahnassa," Merialla chided her. "I've actually been reading a little here and there, trying to … well, learn more about my dear one." He squeezed her a little tighter whenever she said that. "Now, I've been thinking about two or three titles that are part of a series. I think you might like them, and since I know you so well, I have a high likelihood of being right."

"Okay, I suppose," Sahnassa agreed. "Let me know what they are. I guess I might as well push the technologist stereotype to its maximum; it's not like anything else is happening for me right now."

"I … I thought you had an interest in someone," Lashahar said sadly.

"Oh, I have an interest, and so do they, up until they find I don't have much money and can't spend what I have. That doesn't make me all that … fun."

Merialla got up and sat beside her roommate. "It's not fair. You're wonderful and kind. I only wish we knew of someone who was worthy of you, kit."

Sahnassa hugged the light purple Nephti. "Thank you. Alright, I've held you two up long enough! Go have a good time."

"No, Sahnassa, not tonight," Lashahar stated firmly. "Merialla and I have been talking, and she … told me a lot of what you've been doing for her. I … can't thank you enough. I would never have gotten to know her if you hadn't been so kind. If it's okay with you, dear one, can we take her out to dinner? There's a new place on the other side of Shanandrae. It's a bit of a drive, but it's supposed to be very good. It's called de Kesto's. Let's make it an evening, for … all of us. I'm buying!"

"Are you sure?" she asked Merialla.

"Certainly, close to my soul," the light purple Nephti offered, pulling her into an embrace. "You've showed me what I was missing in my life, and you helped bring it to me. Please, join us."

"Alright," Sahnassa relented. "It's so very nice of both of you. It will be the closest I've been back to home since I came here."

"Sounds good. Now, let's get going. It's a long drive," Lashahar bade, and happily, Sahnassa rose from her bed and donned her paw-shoes.

Vanarra was walking along the trail in front of a number of upscale businesses, several of which were catering companies. Although the sale of Gorta's lair and possessions had netted a very tidy sum, there were only a few sparse opportunities presenting themselves to Vanarra and her three new workers. Flint had chided her for being overly concerned, but Van had run the numbers. They were making enough to break even, mostly, but she was still living in the back of the office, and she refused to not pay Flint or the other two enough to live on, even if she wasn't making anything close to that. Mostly breaking even also meant that they were sometimes not, and the money would bleed out of the business like a small wound that wouldn't close up. The losses were small, but they would still kill off Celebrations by Vanarra if something wasn't done to offset them. Worse still, problems with the delivery hover had caused her to seek out some small loans to pay off the mechanics. Sighing, she knew it wasn't going well.

She turned and walked towards the businesses, and started strolling along the mostly empty walk under their awnings. She was glancing in the windows, trying to get ideas when a door suddenly burst open in front of her, startling her and making her take a step back. From it, came a rather keen Faelnar, she noticed, but what was most noticeable about this particular individual was that he was angry, tail lashing, and the fur at the back of his neck was up – standing on end. "He's angry, coming from a catering house? Did he just get fired?"

When she saw the rather expensive looking hover he was walking towards, her hind paws started moving before her mind actually knew what she was doing. "Excuse me! Excuse me!"

"What!?" he turned on her, enraged, and when he saw what she was, he added a measure of disgust to his repetition of the question. "What do you want, Anati?"

Keeping her eyes down, she quietly stated, "I'm so sorry for disturbing you, but I noticed you came from that business very upset. I … I was wondering if you … if they didn't … just if you needed any help, that's all." Van groaned inwardly. That was about as convincing a sales pitch as a stack of rotten creele.

The Faelnar looked at her with a mixture of pity and contempt, but answered truthfully, "Not unless you have a catering business that doesn't charge the fur off your back!"

"As it happens, I do, actually. We … don't have the overhead that those large family businesses have, so we can offer our services at much reduced rates. Here … is my card."

She gave the card to him, and to her surprise, he actually took it and read. "Celebrations by Vanarra. Who is that, your boss?"

"Well, actually, as it happens, it's me," she replied, looking up into his eyes just for a moment. Something strange happened in that instant, and it made them both pause. His golden eyes were so very close to hers in their shade, and his deep brown fur, nearly black, accented with softer brown stripes, made him appear kind and thoughtful.

"You think I would hire an ... Anati business?" he asked, but she didn't interrupt or answer, for he looked away and started pacing back and forth a bit, a smirk beginning to curl up the edge of his lips. "Well now, wouldn't that be justice! Okay, Vanarra. Let's say I did hire your company, and I wanted heavy snacks, drinks, and some sort of celebratory dessert. For fifty individuals, what would it cost me?"

"There are a lot of factors," Van commented, running some quick numbers in her head, "but the range is from about 850 to 1,800 or so."

"You've ... you've got to be kidding! The ... rapemating bastards in that building wouldn't quote me anything below 2,500, and that was for nothing! How in the heck are you able to pull that off?! Feed guests stuff you pulled out of the garbage?"

"We provide a sampling in advance, and guarantee that your guests will get what you have sampled, or you pay nothing. We ... just have a lower overhead, that's all. No ... family dues, smaller operation, and we don't keep our business in a high-rent storefront. We have a modest facility, but it serves the needs of our clients very well. Would you be providing the room?"

"I would. I want to have it in our office. I'll tell you what, just because I'm so utterly ... frustrated with those rapemating bastards behind you, I'll give you 2,500, what they were going to charge me for what I could have bought at the local market and done myself. You show me what you can do, Anati, and I'll put the word out on you, a good word. Dammit, if there isn't a single project manager in every company we've partnered with who can't reward his employees with a good celebration because budgets are so tight."

"Okay, wow, we ... we can do really well for you on that," Vanarra replied, her eyes still tenuously fixed on his, and for some strange reason, he hadn't grown disgusted with her or looked away. She thought, actually, as his eyes quickly surveyed her now, that he might even be a little attracted. "Attention getters," she thought, bringing herself up to her full height, although still keeping her head tilted down. "Who do I have the honor of serving?"

"Fanassaragatti ... de Caterra," he replied, and fished out a card from his own pocket and gave it to her. "When can we do the tasting?"

"Whenever you'd like before the event, but at least a sol before. When's the event?"

"Three sols away," he stated dubiously. "Can you manage that?"

"We will, and we will try to impress you."

"I hope so. There's someone ... special to me coming, and I don't want to look the fool. If I do, you won't get anything, are we clear?"

"Absolutely, but we'll spell it out in a contract so we're both clear on exactly what's expected, okay?" she asked, tentatively.

"That's fine. Can you bring by samples tomorrow, say at mid sol?"

"I will. Just make sure that I don't have any issues coming to visit you. Sometimes, we've had problems."

"I'll bet," he replied, almost kindly, she thought. Most of his anger had bled away, and now he seemed genuinely hopeful.

"I can tell this means a lot to you. When I come by, I would like to spend some time talking with you to understand exactly what's being celebrated. We can adjust our theme appropriately."

His eyebrow fur raised. "Good point, I suppose. Damn, none of them asked me that!" He looked beyond her to the deserted store fronts. "And they haven't even tried to follow me or work out something. If you can make this work, Vanarra, I ... I would be grateful. My team worked so hard, and it so often goes with no thanks at all."

"You care about them. I'll see that my company does, as well."

"Good. I need to get to my next meeting. Thank you, Vanarra. I hope ... I hope this works out. If it does, both you and I will have a good laugh at *their* expense," he offered, pointing back to the other catering businesses.

"Until tomorrow, then," she replied, smiling and bowing – averting her eyes down and lowering her tail.

"Until tomorrow." She turned away from him and started to walk, just as he did, but after a moment, curiosity got the better of her, and she looked back. She waved, smiling, realizing that he had actually stopped at the door of his hover and had been watching her. He was surprised at having been caught, waved nervously, and then quickly ducked into his vehicle.

"A great event, and he's kind of cute, too," Van said to herself. "Bonus!"

Their meeting the next sol went far better than Vanarra expected, for his administrative assistant had been clearly given orders to spirit her into his office with no resistance whatsoever. When she walked in, he was on the LineCom, talking some technical gibberish with another individual, but he smiled and motioned her in. As she started unloading the cases from her rolling cart, the room filled with the smell of succulent swimmer fish and creele soup, along with perfectly seasoned roots, baked to perfection.

Instantly, she had his attention, and after she motioned to the desk in front of him, he quickly cleared it of all paper and other work-related debris. In a few short moments, Vanarra set before him an elegant place-setting with the hot food still steaming. "Uh, Challa, I ... I need to finish this later. Some ... lunch just arrived, and yeah, I ... kind of need to go, unless you want to hear me drooling. Yeah, guess not. Okay." He hung up the LineCom and exclaimed, "This?! This is what you're going to serve?! It's a full meal! This stuff smells like it came out of the ovens at Rangelands or Moonrise or something like that!"

"Please, try it. I've already eaten, so no shyness, now. You need to know what you'd be paying for."

No other invitation was required. Instantly, he was on the food, eating hungrily. "Damn ... caterers – the other ones, I mean, sorry! And you really can do this! For ... for everyone?!"

"I can. As soon as we finish here, with your approval, I'll get the purchasing started so we can begin preparations."

He took a couple of additional bites and then picked up the LineCom and dialed a number. "Hey, it's ... yes, it's me. Can you come to my office a moment? I want you to try something."

"I have a second plate, if you'd like for me to set it up?"

"Yes, my partner. If we can convince him, he might even throw some more funds into the gathering."

By the time Vanarra left her new client's office, she was in possession of a draft for 1,000 and several additional suggestions and requests that she knew she could easily satisfy, although she and the others would probably be working through the night to get them done.

"That doesn't matter. We have the job!" she giggled to herself as she left.

The evening was going as well as Vanarra could have hoped. The Anati twins she found were not only fantastic cooks, they were also very willing to help with serving – swelling her ranks to six. Flint's two other add-ins he had found were also excellent help. After the frantically exact preparations, Vanarra and her team had the whole group sat at their tables unable to do anything but continually comment how nice everything was and how much money their bosses had spent making sure the evening was delightful. There were, of course, comments about the Anati serving them, but most just presumed she was a member of the staff, not the business owner, and that suited her alright. If things went bad, she could always present the complaints to her "boss." Thankfully, once the food was set in front of the group, all anxieties seemed to have been allayed.

Now that the group had eaten heartily, Fanassaragatti had risen to speak and after that, his partner. They spoke about the project they had been working on, and happily pointed to the large banner Vanarra had printed for the occasion, stating "The accomplishments that bind us together are the greatest ones of all." It was one of Rahnahi's quotes that she liked, and one she used to good effect in her pep-talk to her own group, earlier – a suggestion from Flint.

She was quickly surveying to see if there was anything they had missed, but as Fanassaragatti's partner was a trifle overlong in his speech, Van had an opportunity to just look around and survey the group. They were an interesting bunch; many were slightly pudgy, but not a one of them had been rude to her. It was clear that they had felt overworked and underappreciated, and it was as evident that the banquet was thoroughly pleasing them and making them glad to have worked on the project. "That's a win for us, too," she thought.

Her eyes came to rest on Fanassaragatti, the de Caterra Faelnar she had run into outside of the catering businesses. He certainly wasn't hard on the eyes, and there was something about his manner, how he treated her, that made her wonder if he, like Sorla and to a lesser extent Gorta, was a purebred that she might actually like getting to know. Although it was clear he had chosen to use her out of spite, how he had dealt with her and complimented her made her feel almost like his equal. That was refreshing, and she thought she might like to get to know him better as a friend or maybe even more. However, something else was starting to come to her attention.

Sitting next to the Faelnar that hired her company was a very attractive Vulpi with flowing fur and feminine graces that were teaching Van a thing or two about how to make a male feel appreciated. She was trying to keep her actions respectful and polite, but it was clear that she adored Fanassaragatti. His eyes frequently returned to her, and whispers into her ear drew out giggles and snickers that were as well staged and alluring as any Vanarra had ever seen. "Wow, she certainly knows how to use the gifts nature gave her," Van thought with a bit of disgust.

She didn't get much more opportunity to think, because she realized the long-winded speech was finally over, and Fanassaragatti was rising to join his partner in giving out project rewards. Being close, she stepped quietly to the side of the table and gave each one to them in turn, ensuring they didn't have to walk over. Some of the rewards were quite humorous: "Most likely to code overnight," "most likely to find a missed requirement," and "most likely to fall asleep at their desk" were just a few of the choicer titles bestowed upon members of the group.

Once that portion was over, the attendees began a large scale video-game tournament; thankfully this was something she hadn't been required to organize, but her team dashed from station to station providing additional drinks and snacks. Sheffer, one of Flint's friends, tapped her on the shoulder and leaned in to talk into her ear, as the noise from the video games being played on the huge monitors made conversation very difficult. "That Fanassa-whatever, who hired us. He wants to see you. They're in his office."

"They?" she asked, and he mouthed "Vulpi" back at her.

Knocking on the door, and again, a little louder as was required by the din of noise in the office space, Van then waited until her client, his shirt loosened and his jacket off, opened the door. He was happy, which was a good sign. Stepping in at his invitation, she stood quietly with her eyes down until he closed the door. "Is there something you need me to take care of?"

"No, no!" he replied happily, but then corrected himself. "Well, maybe, but first, Vanarra, I have to say it – you're amazing! Before anymore of the night gets away from us, I wanted to settle up with you. Here ... here is the payment plus a nice bonus for your team. They were awesome!"

Smiling as she took the draft from his paw, she breathed, "Thank you so very much! It's been a pleasure serving your group. Everyone was so nice, and they really seemed to appreciate what was being done for them."

"I'll say," the female Vulpi sitting beside Fanassaragatti on the couch offered. "You've done more in one evening to improve office morale than we've been able to do in six moons. They ... we, all feel very well taken care of."

"It's our privilege. We would, of course, be grateful if you kept us in mind for any other celebrations you would like to have."

"Oh, there are a few in the group you served tonight that have already asked for your contact information. I gave it to them, unreservedly. Now, I ... I hesitate to ask, but ... could you do us a little favor?"

"If it's legal," Vanarra replied with a large grin and a smile at her client's obvious embarrassment.

"I suppose," the Vulpi stated. "Is there any way you can ... absolutely ensure that we won't be disturbed for awhile?"

Thinking about the arrangement of the building and where the office was, she could recall one rather large Thurian who could easily dissuade anyone from wandering down the hallway that led in that direction. "I think I can accommodate your request. How long should I have someone taking care of that? I'm scheduled to let my team go very soon."

"Well, until high night," her client requested, embarrassed, but hopeful.

Doing some rapid calculations in her head, she realized, "I'll have to leave some of my things here if I split my staff. Can I just pick them up from you later?"

"Sure. Come by tomorrow – the office is closed because of tonight, but I have to be here in the morning, say an interval before mid-sol?"

"Very good. I'll speak to Flint. He's ... rather imposing when it comes right down to it. I very much doubt anyone will try to walk past him."

"Oh, thank you, dear kit," the Vulpi nearly purred out. "Your consideration is so greatly *appreciated*."

"Then I must get to it. I will happily see you tomorrow, in the morning?" His nod was sufficient, and she performed a short bow to both of them and left the room, locking the door before she closed it.

Stepping outside, she found Flint. She had to walk right up and touch him to get his attention; the sounds of the games had grown far more intense, as had the cheering. "We've been paid!" she nearly shouted into his ear. "But our client has a special request. Can you move the drinks and snacks over there, in front of that hallway, and bar anyone from getting back there? I have a feeling that our Faelnar and Vulpi friend want to try a little interspecies relations!"

He looked back at her, curious. "For how long?" he asked, and he grimaced at the answer.

"I'll take the rest of them back so they can go home, and I have to deposit this. We can't take any risks, and we need him to recommend us to other clients!"

"Yeah, yeah, okay. I get it."

"You'll get overtime for it, I promise. He gave me enough."

"Plow it back in," Flint demanded. "Put it back into the business. Like you said, we need it."

Putting her paw gratefully on his enormous shoulder, she nodded gratitude to him and then said, "Leave the bigger pieces. Just take the small stuff in your hover. I've got permission to leave them here and pick them up tomorrow morning. Okay?"

"Okay. Have a good night, Vanarra."

"Too late! Already did!" she shouted back, smiling widely as cheers erupted from a nearby group. Flint smiled as well, and then went about his tasks. Van, looking back at the tumultuous affair, smiled to herself. "We're doing it – Ash, Gorta, Mom! We're really doing it!" Then, she turned and went to collect the rest of her group.

Vanarra strode up towards the door of Fanassaragatti's office the next morning feeling pretty good. With what she and her team had earned the night before, she was able to pay off the loans, pay her staff, and make the rent on their office space, with just enough available to keep her decently fed. It was a bright sol, and she was happy – happier than she'd been in a long time. She knew she'd have to really thank her client. A steady income of jobs like the one last night would allow her to expand and hire more staff, and perhaps, eventually allow Van to rent and furnish a lair of her very own.

When she walked up to the door of the office, she found it open, and stepping inside, she found it was quiet, a far cry from the noisy and happy din that she had left behind. Quietly padding past the empty receptionist desk, she found the large conference space that had been the location of their activities last night, and she was pleased to see that someone had actually washed out all of their serving-ware and placed it neatly in a corner. "Well, that was kind of them." She then bent over, picked up a couple of pieces, and started the first of her many trips back to the delivery hover.

A few passes later, when she was making her final search for anything that might have been left behind, she grew a little curious. "There has to be someone here, Fanassaragatti if no one else – they wouldn't just leave it open."

Quietly, she padded down the hallway to where his office was, and she didn't see any lights on. However, the door was cracked open just slightly, and she thought she heard something, like shuffling and gasping. "Oh, come on!" she thought. "I know Vulpi are supposed to be good, but really!"

Drawing closer, her ears picked up on sounds that didn't match her first guess at what was going on. As she drew near, it sounded a little like crying. Slowly, Van leaned on his office door, sliding it noiselessly open. What she saw there in the dim light from the hallway almost made her heart stop. Fanassaragatti was there, alone, sitting in his chair, with his head upon the desk – still and unmoving. "Oh, no. Not again!" she shouted in her head. "It can't be!"

Suddenly, a deep wailing sob came from the figure lying in front of her, and she realized that something awful had happened, something so awful, that if this Faelnar purebred could have died from sheer heartbreak alone, he would have indeed been a corpse. Carefully, she walked around the desk, not trying to be quiet specifically, but trying not to make any loud and jarring noises. As his crying continued, she slowly reached out her paw and placed it on his back. He didn't react in the slightest, but simply continued his weeping.

"Hey, there. Now, now. I'm here. It's … it's going to be okay, whatever it is. I'll help you … in any way I can."

"Dis … disavowed … dishonored," he whispered. "How … how could you help?"

"I've never been anything *but* that," Van offered. "It makes life harder, but not impossible. You … just have to learn how to try."

"I … I don't know how to live without…"

"Just breathe," she replied softly, rubbing the fur between his ears soothingly. "Take one breath, then another, and only think about that. Once you've got that down, you can start to live tick to tick, pass to pass, and then interval to interval. You let someone help you, and you don't give up on yourself. Last night, things may have been different, but you are still so very smart and accomplished. Your house dishonoring you doesn't change that."

He opened his eyes and slowly lifted his head. Her paws gently guided him up to a sitting position, and she started carefully massaging his temples, exactly how Ash used to like it when he felt unhappy or sad. "You … why would you want to help me?" he questioned her, although he still accepted the gentle touches coming from her paw-fingers.

"You helped me, gave me a chance. With what you paid me, I was able to take care of those who work for me. Your willingness to give us a try just means the world to me. We honor you for choosing us. That's why I'm here, and I'm not going to leave you until you're okay. You need to go home, and I can sit with you, watch over you."

"Are … are you sure?" he asked, compelled to consider what she was offering as her paws went to his shoulders and neck. "This … wasn't what you signed up for."

"Last night, you were my client. Right now, you're my friend. You need me. Come on. Let's get out of here and get you back home. You haven't been back since last night, have you?"

"No," he said, shaking off her touches. "I … haven't."

"Come on then. You need to rest, and you need to eat, and you need someone to talk to. Consider this a catering job that's free of charge." She offered him her paw, and slowly, he took it. "Come on. Lock up what you need to lock up, and we'll go."

"I … I have to go to the … facilities."

"Fine, but I'll be waiting for you. I'm not going anywhere," Van assured him. She was heartened that he was starting to show a few more signs of life and strength than he had moments ago.

While he was occupied, Van was quickly dialing her PawLink and leaving a message. "Flint, I'm leaving the delivery hover at the office where we had our event last night. Can you get someone else to come over with you and retrieve it, load the stuff back into the office? I hate to ask, but something's come up, and I need to help a friend. Thanks, Muscles. Bye."

A pass or two later, he appeared back in the hallway looking as if walking was a supreme effort of will. Again, she offered her paw, and he seemed to draw strength from her as he took it. Walking him towards the entrance, she gently guided him. "Come on. I'll ride with you or drive your hover. I've called someone to come get our company vehicle."

"Are … you sure about this?" he asked as he locked the door. "I'm not keeping you from a…"

"It's a quiet sol for us, resting from last night. You need to rest, too, and you need someone to take care of you, just for a bit. Don't worry about me."

"Thank you, Vanarra."

"Van … will do just fine," she replied as she took him by the paw and followed him to his vehicle.

About half an interval later, they were entering his somewhat luxurious apartment. As the door closed and he locked it, she said, "Now, I want you to go and change into something comfortable. Then, I want you to come talk to me, okay?"

"Okay. You … you know this trail best," he breathed out in a ragged sigh. Reaching around and hugging him first, she gently sent him on his way. While he was changing, she took off her paw-shoes and her outer jacket. She hadn't gone sleeveless, since it was cold, and having taken a hint from Flint's reaction to her, she wore underthings which didn't over-emphasize her "attention-getters." Quickly, she started making tea.

Before long, she became worried that he might have something in his bedroom that could do him harm, if he wanted to. So, she walked to the door and asked carefully, "I'm making tea for you. Do you like sweetener?"

"Yes, please. That's … very kind," he replied, opening the door. She smiled as she looked at him; as distressed as he was, he was still quite keen, and the soft shorts and shirt he was now wearing emphasized his strong arms and upper body.

"Come on, then. Sit on the couch and get comfortable. I think you should talk to someone about what happened, and I'm willing to listen and help, okay?"

"Okay," he replied and trudged over to the couch.

"He really is completely deflated, like the life's just gone out of him," she thought, watching him. "I … I wonder if this is what Mom felt when they disavowed her because of me. Oh, Mom, I'm so sorry!"

She brought him the tea and set it in front of him. He smiled and said, "Thank you. See you used the nice stuff."

"Caterer," she answered at his appreciation that she had used a finer cup for his drink. "Now, tell me what happened. I promise you, it will never leave this room. You have my word."

"Do the disavowed have honor?" he asked, depressed, shaking his head.

"Absolutely. We have *real* honor, the honest kind, the real kind. It's not defined by a particular house. At our best, we treat one another with respect. Not because we have to, but because it's the *right* thing to do. Come on, now. Let me carry a little of your burden. Talk to me."

"My … friend, you met last night. We spent time together. It … it was wonderful, and this morning, early, she left. It wasn't two intervals later, and I was napping in my office when a dame from my family barged in with three matrons alongside of her. "She held a letter of grievance, filed by Nissalani – a letter of grievance against me. It said I had rape-mated her, that she asked me, begged me not to. It wasn't that way. She … was after me. She … was so … beautiful and … seductive and just … special. They told me she never wanted to see me again, and that she had quit her job and wouldn't be returning. They also told me that her parents demanded the satisfaction of honor, and although they couldn't press charges against me that enforcement would recognize, that my family – de Caterra – did recognize the offense and had summarily decided against me. They disavowed me – cut me off from my family. To … to everyone I loved, Van … I'm now dead!"

He broke down and cried again, putting his head into his paws. She sat alongside of him and put her paws on his back, and gently guided him so that he lay with his head upon her lap. "You're not dead, and your family doesn't realize what a wonderful Faelnar they've lost. You don't have to be purebred to realize that something's wrong with what they did. How could she love you and in only a few intervals, all of this comes to be?"

"I ... I can't fight it. My family doesn't recognize me anymore," he answered.

"Yeah, and isn't that convenient, too? You know, my ... mom was Faelnar, and my dad was a Vulpi. Maybe your family was afraid something would happen; someone like me could have been born. Maybe that was the real reason."

"We ... we took precautions. She ... was spiked. It couldn't have happened. We ... were just enjoying being together. It was exciting. I thought we both liked it."

"Something happened; someone had it in for you."

"My dame ... has hated me ever since I helped start this business. We take in those who aren't avowed and let them work. Technologists sometimes run afoul of enforcement when they realize their skills can allow them access to information they shouldn't have. One tapped the security cameras and got images of his dame ... getting all primal - those kinds of things."

"And ... because you allowed those who were disavowed to work for you, she hated you for that?"

He nodded, and she could sense that he was starting to rationally think through what had happened. "I guess I should have suspected they'd do something. I guess Nissaliani just gave them an excuse."

"So they don't control your office, your business? They ... they must hate that. Most purebred families want to be in control. I've ... read a lot about that."

"What you've read is right, then. They decide for you ... everything, almost. You can make a request, but it's just that."

"Then, although I'm sorry for what's happened to you, they have given you a gift."

"What?" he asked, dubious, but still accepting her caresses on the fur of his head.

"I know you feel like you've lost a lot, but ... you're finally free. You ... aren't beholden to them anymore. They walked away from you, and now you can do the same." He rolled over and looked up at her, and found she was staring ahead, her expression angry. "You don't have their support, so you'll have to make it on your own, but when you make it, and you will, it will be because of you. They can't claim any part of your success. It may be harder, but what you win ... is yours."

"So that's what it's like for you?"

"Yeah. My mother's family ... just ... it's more than I can talk about, but we'd have been better off if they never existed. They were ... murderers and ... cowards and heartless." Seeing the pain in her eyes, he raised his paw and placed it alongside her muzzle. "Oh, listen to me. I'm supposed to be making you feel better."

"You are, Van. You are. I ... I want your help, if you wouldn't mind doing something?"

"What are we going to do?" she asked, looking down at him.

"I want ... I want to get any sign of that damned house out of my lair. I want you to take it out of here and just ... dump it somewhere. Burn it if you want. Destroy it for ... for the harm the houses have done to both of us. Would you like that?"

"Yes. Yes, I think I would."

The next morning, Vanarra awoke beside the Faelnar, and she turned over to look at him. Although they had shared a bed, that was all they had shared. Fanassaragatti was starting to find his hind-legs again, but he had so many worries about what would happen to him with his work. However, the more she heard him talk about his job, the more it sounded like he was completely essential to the place, and avowed or not, they had to keep him. They had talked about that late into the night, and finally both had drifted off to sleep.

Soon after she had awoken, his alarm went off, and he also awoke. After encouraging him once again, she sent him to the bathroom to get ready while she made his breakfast in the kitchen. Soon, she was helping him finish dressing, when he asked her, "Now that I'm disavowed, what am I supposed to call myself? I'm so lost I can't even think up a name."

"Buck up," she had told him gently. "You're stronger than you know – stronger than an old harlock, if you give yourself credit." The reference to the great hardwood trees renowned for their staying power in a storm had brought a smile to his muzzle. He kissed her on the cheek, and then they had said goodbye, Vanarra catching the transport station right in front of his apartment complex to ensure he wouldn't be late for work.

When she returned to the office, a flood of invoices and ordering consumed her so that she didn't even realize that it was well after mid-sol, and she hadn't eaten. Just as she was about to search through the stores for something to eat, a courier appeared at her front door. "Hi there. You Vanarra Anasto?"

"I am," she replied to the young Lupar.

"Package for you. Please sign here." She did so, and he presented the package to her and quickly went on his way. As she brought it in, she suddenly realized that there was hot food inside, food that smelled pretty good. Opening the package, she saw a small bowl of fruit and steamed creele, and a rather large grazer steak from a place called de Kestos. Also inside, she found a note:

> You were an amazing friend to me. I can't thank you enough. I found out this morning how right you were, and how foolish I was being. You were right. I am now free, and I made it to this sol only because of you. Thank you.

> Buck Harlock, formerly Fanassaragatti de Caterra.

"Aww," she nearly purred. "That's so nice of him! What a great guy, even if he is a purebred." Taking the card, she slipped it into a special place in her desk so she would always keep it, and then, without anything else to distract her, she started to happily attack the food he had sent.

Chapter 12: Primality

Van answered the LineCom early the next morning, "Good sol to you! Celebrations by Vanarra, can I help you?"

"Hi there, it's … well, it's Buck."

"No, it's Buck Harlock, if I recall!" she giggled. "I love the name you chose. That's awesome!"

"Well, I owe you a lot, and now, I'd like to pay it back."

"Really? How so?" she asked, curious.

"Well, I was passing your name around the office, and one of my senior analysts asked me a question, and I … I didn't know what to tell her."

"What's the question?" Vanarra asked, curious.

"She asked if you only did events that were fully avowed – sanctioned by the families, I mean."

"You could have answered that question," she replied quietly, almost angrily. "You know how I feel about them."

"Fair enough, but I guess what she was looking for was … permission to send someone to your office to ask you about catering an event. They're looking for confidentiality, and from what I can tell, she's quite serious about the confidential part."

"If you'll give me a time, I'll meet her when she wants and where she wants, Buck. Anything I can do to make her comfortable."

"Okay. How about … at your office, the address on your card, at … say, 22:00 intervals?"

"Fine. Ask her to park out front, we're the door on the right, and it's not fancy – just warn her. What's her name?"

"I'm not sure it will be her you'll see, but she said she'd pass your name along to the member of her … pack that has the purchasing authority."

"Vague, mysterious, but sending someone who can write a draft," Van chuckled. "I like her already! Okay, fine. It's a quiet night, tomorrow, so we should be good."

"Excellent. Thank you, Van. Take care."

"You, too … *Buck Harlock!*"

"Thanks."

As she hung up the LineCom, Flint came in. "New business?"

"Sounds like it. We really seemed to impress that group. Did we pay the twins?"

"Yes, we did. They were thrilled. It's a damn shame, being so gifted at cooking food and nearly starving. They'll eat well … for awhile. They were grateful."

Vanarra nodded, and offered, "And I was grateful to them, very much so. They had that Faelnar's mouth almost flooding the moment I stepped in with the samples. Thanks for finding them, Flint. You're really turning out to be my right paw around here."

"Well, your right paw has a lot of shelving to do while you hunt for business."

"I know," Van replied thoughtfully, "but I'll be interested to see where this latest lead goes. Some purebred in the office we were at wants a private meeting for her pack or club or something. Buck – that's Fanassaragatti's new name by the way – sounded completely confused about what she was asking, but … it's new business, so he called it in."

"Thank him for me," Flint replied and headed back towards the storeroom.

After nearly two full sols of searching for new jobs, absolutely nothing was showing up, and Vanarra was frustrated. The other catering firms had taken precautions against another grab of one of their clients; new cameras and security were featured in addition to signs promising to match any reasonable offer by a competitor.

Apparently, they were only going to allow her to easily hunt upon one of their prey. As she wondered how they had found out so fast, Buck's disavowal came to mind. "Oh, yes – purebred families, great!" As she drove the delivery hover back to her office, Van hoped that Buck's odd referral would end up being something good. They all needed that about now.

Pulling up in the small hover lot a half interval before the scheduled meeting time, Vanarra noticed a rather nice blue hover sitting in front of her business. Pulling up a space away, Van landed the hover and checked herself in the mirror. Leaving her vehicle, she waved to the occupant of the other hover – she wasn't even sure there *was* one through the heavily tinted window – and then keyed into her office. Flint and the twins were also out, trying to find some new business at her request, so the office was empty. Leaving the door unlocked, she went to her desk and sat down, glancing at the notes Flint had left her.

"Excuse me," a timid female voice from the doorway called. Van looked up to see an attractive middle aged Nephti poking her head into the room. "Is this … Celebrations by Vanarra?"

"It is, please, come in," she offered, standing and walking over to greet her guest. "I'm Vanarra Anasto, and you are?" Van intentionally dropped her gaze, as form required, and couldn't help but notice that the Nephti was rather ample up top, given her otherwise lithe appearance.

"Please, I … I don't follow that practice," the Nephti stated, ducking her head and lifting her eyes to meet Van's. "I'm Mavia de Fantar."

"Well, you're certainly are keeping my opinion of Nephti quite high," Van replied, raising to her full height, which put her in a position of looking down on Mavia, who seemed stunned by the statement.

"Oh … well, uh, thank you … I … you're … you're actually quite … nice," Mavia shyly uttered.

Van couldn't help but smile at the nervous compliment and decided to put her guest at ease. "Thank you. Now, why don't you sit down and let me get you something. What would you like? Una juice? A little wild berry fermentum?"

"Water would be just fine for me, thanks," she apologized. "Ambient temperature, if you don't mind."

"I'll see what I can do," Van replied, smiling, but her mind raced as she tried to remember what ambient meant. She'd run across it in some of the coursework books in the archives. To herself, she thought, "Oh, there's hot, there's cold, and there's ambient, okay!" She walked into the storeroom and pulled out some bottled water and got one of the better carved serving glasses and brought it out. Opening and pouring it in front of her guest, she noticed the somewhat unhappy expression. "Oh, I'm sorry. Did I not get what you want?"

"It's not the water; it's the glass. I'm … I'm used to more … primitive serving ware."

"For your event?"

"Yes, exactly!" Mavia brightened up. "Do you have some?"

"Why don't we walk to the back and take a look?" Van asked as she put her paw into her pocket, where it rested around her new stunner.

"Oh … okay," she said, standing.

"After you," Van offered. "Straight down the short hallway there."

"Oh, thank you. Is … is anyone else here?"

"No, it's just as you asked," Van replied. "In point of fact. Let's make sure we're not disturbed." Mavia watched with approval as Vanarra went back and locked the door. After a quick glance out the circular window, she turned around and confirmed. "Nobody but us."

"You're so kind about this," Mavia effused. "It's been so very hard to talk to anyone about our group or our event. Either they don't understand us or don't approve, or … they just won't go there."

"Well," Van countered, relaxing the grip on her stunner just a little, "we have low overhead, as you can see, and we don't have any … familial overseers watching us. We're … free to serve. Ah, now here is what you asked for."

"Hmm…" Mavia hummed as she picked up the fine fired cup. "Do you have anything that's a bit more … primitive, irregular?"

That question left Van searching her memory. "I do, but it's not in here. It's next door. This is where we keep all of the nice stuff since it's close to the office. Walk back through here."

Mavia followed Van through the rough-cut doorway into what had been the fur dressers' establishment. Van's rough patching of the wall and the mis-matched shelving seemed to make the Nephti take in an extra deep breath. "Bit of a mud-hole; I apologize," Van offered.

"No … it's fine. Just fine." Lifting a rough cloth dustcover off a set of items on the shelves made Mavia gasp. "Oh … oh, they're perfect!"

"They're perfect? And they're the worst ones we have?" Van thought to herself as she watched Mavia pick one up, nearly fondling it as she inspected. The edges were somewhat irregular, and the clay to make them hadn't been colored in any respect, and the glaze on them was very light. "I have to admit, Mavia. You have my curiosity on the hunt. Can you tell me about your group and their event?"

The Nephti almost dropped the cup at that question, but steadying herself, she carefully put it back on the shelf before she spoke. "Can … can we sit here and talk?"

Van looked around, and there were only two somewhat sad wooden stools sitting near what had been the front of the prior establishment. "So long as you don't mind the seating."

"Suits me fine," Mavia replied, and although still nervous, it was clear to Vanarra that these settings were far more comfortable to her prospective client than Van's office, which she tried to keep well tended and neat for guests.

As they sat, Van could tell that the Nephti was still very nervous, and she wouldn't look at Van. Reaching out, Vanarra put her paw on Mavia's, which was resting on her knee. "Hey, it's okay. Just talk to me. Nothing you say to me here will ever go outside of these walls unless you want it to."

"On … your honor?" Mavia asked, uneasily.

"I guess that's something our kind are not supposed to have. How about I promise you on my livelihood – the business here that keeps me fed and with a place to lay my head? If I don't keep your confidence, my reputation suffers, and as you can imagine, I truly don't need that."

That seemed to satisfy the Nephti, and she nodded, still not looking at Van. Her blush furs were up full, but Mavia began to speak, after a deep sigh. "I've … always been different in what I liked, different than many in my family. We live in nice lairs, but … they don't look anything like what our ancestors used. We're living in unnatural circumstances, working in unnatural occupations – yours is far closer to something our ancestors could have been capable of than mine."

"What do you do?"

"Head of accounting, TranStar Enterprises," Mavia replied, albeit ashamed. "It was possible for those kinds of cups to be used, for rough-hewn bowls to contain the food, for … no other adornments to be present when we eat. I … am a part of a group called Primalists. There are quite a few of us, and many of us are actually very well off, by everyone else's standards. We just feel this *need* to reach back to simpler things."

"I've lived that way, somewhat, in the past," Vanarra admitted, looking away. "I … still do, a bit."

"Don't feel that way. You are so much more self-reliant than almost anyone else who is grown up mothered in a family house. You've … lived by your instincts and what you were able to learn, haven't you?" Van nodded, a slightly proud smile gracing her muzzle. "See, it may have not been perfect, but you are more competent, capable, and resourceful because of it. So, yes. I'm here, sitting in front of you as a purebred, fully-avowed, telling an Anati that you are better than I am."

"Pretty … refreshing, actually," Van agreed.

"That's … what we need from you, for our gatherings. We hold gatherings once every two moons. They're large gatherings, very well attended and … funded, but we've not been able to get anyone to cater them."

"I don't understand why. It sounds like a great event to cater! I've got a bunch of ideas scrambling around in my head on things that might work for you!"

"Well, you might understand when I tell you that … at our events, we shed all of the pretenses of our modern existence. That includes … clothing." Van's eyebrow fur shot up. "I know, I know, but … in the context of our celebration and our ceremonies, it works. Everyone is still treated with respect, and perhaps, even more so, since we see who they are beneath all of the beautiful clothes and adornments, the technical trappings. We are who we honestly are. We hold these gatherings in various places, away from the public eye and the eyes of the matriarchy. The locations are strictly confidential, and any firm we hire must keep those secrets as vigilantly as we do."

"As I said, no problem with that. Would … our staff also need to be without … clothes?"

"If you could keep what you were wearing very simple, and with no technology whatsoever, that would probably suffice."

"And I take it that you want the food to be fairly simple, as well, right? Good, but simple?"

"Exactly!" Mavia exclaimed, seeing that Vanarra hadn't turned and ran hearing the one detail that kept every other catering firm from accepting the job. "Whole fruit, or cut if it's got a hard shell, but still rough cut or cracked, not sawed or cut with a modern knife. Use your imagination!"

"That I can do," Van chuckled. "That I can do. Okay, I think I'm in. I'll discuss it with my staff. Just how, Mavia, is your group getting by now?"

"Everyone just brings something. Sometimes it works out, but it's never … nice. It's always a burden, and the way we have to do it – coolers, boxes – it just … ruins the atmosphere. It would be perfect if those things were invisible. They can be in a rough sort of tent, not a purchased synthetic one, and they need to not be seen."

"Okay. So, what kind of a budget did you have in mind?" Vanarra asked.

"Well, we've figured in travel and a pretty large staff, and … frankly, we really, really want someone to help us. We're thinking about 45,000 to 50,000 for the event."

Van's eyes went wide, and her heart started pounding. "Well, how … how many heads … attending, that is?"

"The next event we have is booked for about 150. If we get a bump in attendance because of the catering at this event, for the next event, it would be more."

Van swallowed. "Okay. I've … I've done events that big, and a little bigger. You're … I mean I have to be honest here, Mavia! You're paying way above the market rate!"

"There is no market rate for caterers who do our events – they didn't exist, until now," she replied, smiling. "We would be so grateful to you if your company could help us."

"I think we can, Mavia. I think we can. For what you're paying, though, I really want to make sure I have every detail just perfect. I'll want to pull several of your group into a room, if we can, and hash out the details. Under no circumstances do I want you to feel like you're not getting your money's worth."

"The biggest value you can give us is privacy. Once others learn that you're helping us, I'm sure you'll get some matrons or other house agents snooping around asking your staff about the guest list."

"I will keep your secrets, I promise."

"You will, but what about your staff? Can you absolutely ensure they'll keep quiet?"

"My partner, yes. For the others, I'll need ... I'll need to think about appropriate ways to ... convince them, require them," she answered thoughtfully, looking towards the wall. Then, she turned back to Mavia. "It is a problem I will solve, I promise you."

"It would be hard for us to use someone a second time, if we suddenly started getting visits from matrons and dames that didn't happen in the past," Mavia confessed.

"I understand you, and you're making it valuable enough for me that it will be worth every effort I can make to take care of your group, in all respects."

"Great!" Mavia exclaimed in a sigh. "Oh, we've been hoping for something like this forever. If ... if you could make it work, that would be just amazing for us! Now, what do we do first?"

"Well, first I think we need to draw up a brief understanding, and I need to give you some documents about our rules and policies, and then I'd like to hold a meeting somewhere with you and several others from your group to get a real ... flavor for what they would like. I'd have things to sample, and I'd make sure that based on whatever you've already told me, I would tailor it as much as I could. From there, we just work out what needs to change. Can you give me an overview of the times and schedules you'd want catering for?"

"Oh, I ... I guess, yes! I'm ... sorry; I'll have to spend a moment and put my thoughts together. I've never gotten this far in the conversation before!" Mavia was almost giddy, and Van thought it gave her a rather cute aspect.

"Well, let me bring some things in here, and then we'll get started."

"Okay!" she replied, standing along with Vanarra. "I'm ... I'm sorry to ask, but would it be okay if I ... gave you a hug?"

"Not a problem, kit! You're being so very good to me," Van replied as she gently embraced the Nephti, having to stand a bit to the side because of their mutual "attention-getters." What completely impressed Vanarra was the level of trust and relief she was sensing from the Nephti. Instantly, that made her keenly aware that if she broke that trust, Mavia would never honor her like that again. When they parted, she held Mavia at the shoulders and looked her directly in the eye. "I will do everything that is within my power to keep your group's activities and participants a secret. I will fire anyone who says anything, and I will let them know that I will tell everyone in Shanandrae I work with that they can't be trusted. I mean it."

"I can see you do. Vanarra, you're ... you're someone special."

"And you are, too! Now, let's get to work," Van replied, slipping her arm about the shoulder of the Nephti and guiding her back to the office.

Sahnassa eagerly awaited the return of Merialla for the beginning of her second season at Harnard. She had actually taken an additional refresher course to prepare her for the rigors of a full course load, and thankfully, her parent's provisions included a surge in payments to cover the period where room and board would be at a higher rate over the break. She had also taken two part time positions on campus, and although the pay was minimal, it was something. It gave her some interactions with various professors and instructors, as well, which she realized she sorely needed. Normally, these introductions would have been accomplished by way of a matron, but since that wasn't allowed, the various odd occupations available to her as a student helped.

One of these positions was covering the front desk of the academy's archive library. Generally, there wasn't much to do, and after she had gone through the normal list of tasks, there could be as much as one or two intervals each sol where there was literally nothing to do. Into this time, she'd actually started using the free resources all around her, and after burning through a couple of steamy romance novels, she decided to pick a couple of selections from Merialla's list and give them a try. The first was so good that she had literally clocked out of her shift and went back to the long couches in the library and read it until closing. Then, she checked it out and completed it at three intervals after high night.

Although bleary-eyed the next morning, she had some cause to reflect on why she liked the book so much. It had just as much romance and intrigue as what she was used to reading, but the book was cast on this idyllic planet, one without the problems of houses and matriarchy, or even species prohibitions. The main characters weren't Thurian, but they had many of the same emotions and desires and struggles that made Sahnassa want to jump into the book and get involved, fight alongside the main characters. There was even one lone male who, in the end, was left disconsolate and emotionally wounded, and instantly, she felt herself fantasizing about being the one to comfort him.

"Oh, how well Merialla knows me," she sighed, as she looked at the collection of new books sitting on her shelf in the small student lair.

A knock sounded on the door, and a voice called, "Sahnassa? Are you there?"

"I am! I am!" she replied and swung open the door to see Merialla and two older Nephti – clearly her parents – standing alongside of her. All of them looked very pleased and delighted to see Sahnassa, and Merialla embraced her warmly and happily. "Oh, I missed you so much!"

"I missed you, too. So very deeply!"

At that moment, Sahnassa heard a sob from in front of her and stepped back. "What's wrong?" she asked the mother, who was clearly crying.

"She's changed so much, and … it's all because of you, you dear sweet kit! We … we have no idea how, but she's so much more connected, so much more alive, and she says it's you."

"Well, and Lashahar, too," Merialla clarified. "Just a little."

"I want you to know," her father said softly, "that we've spoken to our matron about you, and asked that the commendation of our house be given to you. You've … made our daughter … whole."

"But still unique," Merialla corrected in that detached and contemplative tone of voice Sahnassa had so missed over the break.

"Always unique," Sahnassa assured her, putting her paw on the light purple Nephti's shoulder. "Your daughter has been a joy as a roommate, and I … can't wait to catch up with her!"

"Well, we won't keep you," her mother replied, reaching out for and hugging Sahnassa, "but we wanted to meet you, ourselves, and tell you thank you. Merialla told us a little about what's going on with your parents. Please, I want you to come back with her and spend time with us over the next break, if you can."

"I can try. Finances are a little tight, so I have to keep working, but … you are so kind to offer, and I do want to see where she grew up!"

"Very good. I love you, daughter," her father stated, reaching out for and hugging his daughter. The same was done with her mother, and then the pair departed.

"They've changed, so much," Merialla observed as the hallway door closed behind them.

"You've changed so much."

"Not fully, although I guess we could rejoin our old arguments about objectivity and perception," the light purple Nephti teased.

"Let's not. Your cases are in the hallway?"

"Sure."

"Great, I'll help!"

"Oh, while we were coming in, we picked up your mail, well our mail," Merialla explained as the pair moved her heavy cases into the room.

"Thanks! I … I haven't been down there in forever. It just stopped coming."

"There wasn't much. Well, now. Look at that shelf!" Merialla exclaimed.

"Okay, you got me! I'm hooked on space fiction now. Thanks! Just one more thing for guys to avoid me for."

"Not unless they're unintelligent. You're a great Thurian, Sahnassa, and one sol there will be someone who sees that … beyond myself."

"Uh oh," Sahnassa groaned, looking at one of the pieces of mail. "Class fees. Let's see how bad the damage is." She slit the envelope open with a claw-tip and exclaimed, "You've got to be kidding me! How do they expect me to pay this!? I've saved up … enough, but this will wipe me out completely!" Frustrated, Sahnassa sat down hard on her bed, just staring at the piece of paper.

Merialla slipped down beside her and drew her close. "There, there, Sahnassa. My parents and I had a talk, like they said. You have done so much for me; they want to give you a gift. They asked me what it could be, and now," she stated slipping the paper out of Sahnassa's paws, "I know exactly what."

"You … you're not going to do this! You shouldn't feel obligated to do this."

"I have, and I am," Merialla said quietly, folding the paper. "On one condition; you continue to give me the … support you have in the past. I could feel myself slipping away these last few sols, letting go of those things I should care about. When I saw you, that changed. One sol, I know I'll rely on a mate for this kind of help, but ... even Lashahar isn't there, yet. Please, remain close to my soul."

"Regardless if you pay for this or not, you are close to my soul," Sahnassa replied, a little hurt.

"See then, it doesn't matter if I pay," Merialla stated smugly, smiling her delicately pleased smile. Sahnassa could only hug the one close to her soul and laugh with her.

Vanarra awoke in the small lair at the back of the old fur-dresser's business at the soft chiming of her alarm. Surprisingly, given the long sol of preparation prior and the very long sol now ahead of her, she had managed to sleep without worry. It wasn't that there weren't things to be worried about, given such an insanely large event, but Van knew that if she stayed up all night worrying about each detail, each fear, holding onto them in her mind and staring at them all night, she would be in horrible shape to do what she had to do this sol – run the event that would decide the future of her business. If she and those she had hired were able to make this work, the Primalists would keep coming back with enough money to completely change the way she was living and help her expand her business in ways she couldn't even dream of. If something bad happened and she failed, she would be just another Anati outcast, proving the purebreds right about her. "That's not going to happen," she said to the empty room as she lay there. "I'm more than just a mongrel Anati mix-up."

Sitting up and propping her back against a pillow, she thought about that. "Mixed blood. What does that really mean? Like my blood is purple where others are red or blue? Like Vulpi and Faelnar blood can't flow in each others' veins? Not true; they can get transfusions. Now, that's funny. If a Faelnar gets Vulpi blood for some reason, doesn't that make the Faelnar a mixed blood, too? Damn, it's not that – it's just the way we look. Nothing more. Mavia's right. I've had to live on my own, claw out a life – they ... have everything given to them by the soft paws of a family house. What ... if I was avowed? An avowed Anati?" She snickered aloud as she stood. "Yeah, like that's possible. In the end, do I care? If I can take care of myself and those around me, what does it matter? Gorta wasn't smarter than I was; she wasn't stronger or more ...

honorable. No, it's not just the way we look. It's not just about being pure in body; it's pure in reputation. But what about the event, tonight? The best of the purebred avowed running around all naked-tailed, hiding it from their families, but willing to show it to me? It ... it's a game, that's all it is. It doesn't make sense," she thought darkly before adding aloud, "it just makes them feel better by treading on us."

The concept made her angry and resentful for all of the pain she had been through. Yet, as she opened the door to her shower and stepped inside, she knew this was an anger she had to let go of, just as she had let go of her worries the night before. Both were equally dangerous now. For her mother's daughter and for those others she'd gathered around her, eating and having shelter was more important than being angry about things that couldn't change, would never change. There were also some strange benefits that were coming to her as a part of taking this job.

Van had found three disavowed purebreds, and although it was a little out of her comfort zone, she had hired them for the work tonight. The first was an artist – Saiphar, a Vulpi. Another Vulpi, Tresk, was very mechanically inclined, although somewhat rough around the edges and a little crass. Finally, there was Muriella, a disavowed gold-on-gold Faelnar from a family called de Mistral. Her accent was actually very pretty in its own way, but the way she moved, her pale yellow striping, the color of her nose – everything reminded Van of her own mother. Of course the facial features and the striping were different, but they were fairly close. "If ... if I can pull off this event tonight, if we can, I can help her, too," she thought. Perhaps, in time, she might even become friends with Muriella. It wouldn't bring her mother back, Van knew, but ... she was the only individual she had seen in so many seasons that even resembled her mother.

That was an aching chasm in her soul, having nothing to cling to that was from her mother or like her in any way, shape, or form. There were no pictures, no letters, and no gifts – the clothes her mother had made for her were lost in the archive, in the lair she could never return to. Van nearly always shed a tear when she thought about how her mother's body had probably been treated, and she believed her parent had probably been "disposed of" like her dear Ash had been.

Toweling off her fur, Vanarra shook off these thoughts. She had to get started, get going, and focus on what was to come – the most important event she'd ever catered. Now was the time for all of those worries and concerns and plans to draw into focus. Now, she had to be something above what purebreds considered when they looked upon Anati. When she had dressed, she stepped into the office at the front and unlocked the door for Flint and Saiphar, who would be coming in soon to start loading the rental hover they had secured.

Opening the door made her smile; the warm light of a bright and crisp morning shone upon her and caused her to breathe deeply, feel inspired – like the souls of those she lost were trying to speak to her, encourage her, and give her strength. "Oh, Mom, Ash – wherever you are, I will make you proud this sol; let all of this be for you!" Slowly taking in a deep breath of the magnificent cool air made her close her eyes and smile. This sol would be special, and every part of Vanarra's being was now ready to make it that way.

Two sols later, Vanarra unlocked the front door of her office early in the morning, and it was yet another glorious sol that greeted her. She yawned to a full yowl, nowhere near as chipper and focused as she had been before they catered the primal. That was because most of the last sol had been spent either picking up from the event, travelling back to Shanandrae or sleeping, since the event had nearly lasted all night. Still, there was that draft for 55,000 sitting in her business bank account that made her feel quite good about the whole experience.

The event had been eye-opening in quite a number of respects, and the most obvious one had been what she had expected. No one that was in their group could have ever claimed, to that point, having seen anywhere near that number of purebreds walking around without clothes. It started normally enough, with a big banquet, but then, there had been the games Mavia talked about and the whole "shedding" ceremony. Vanarra not only had to keep herself from looking at the Thurians dropping their clothes, she had to get her staff focused, as well. Flint, having tended the male's camp, reported much the same issue.

Vanarra was so intensely focused that when Mavia came up to her, Van simply greeted her as if she was just another one of the attendees. It had taken a moment and an amused look from Mavia to make her realize who she was talking to. Van smiled at the memory as she walked to her desk. Never had anyone been so appreciative and kind to her in what they'd said. Their group had been completely satisfied in all regards, and Van's team was going to get a bonus well above the 40,000 they had settled on. Mavia had also been very kind about Vanarra's shy compliments on her physical appearance; the Nephti had invited Van to look, and she even stated that she thought Vanarra would be a real beauty to behold. Having been given quite the sum of money, generous thanks, and a somewhat surprising compliment were good memories Vanarra knew she'd always treasure from her first "primal."

There were some unhappy memories, however, and those had to be dealt with. This was the time to do so, since each one of the staff would be coming in, one-by-one, to receive their pay for the event. First, there was Tresk. The Vulpi purebred had lived up to the reputation of his kind by making inappropriate comments, comments that made Flint wrap his paw-fingers around the Vulpi's muzzle to shut him up. Tresk had taken the hint and had behaved the rest of the night. Still, Vanarra felt that, as the owner, she had to comment on and reinforce the requirement to stay silent about what went on at the primal. Then, there was Saiphar. When things got set at the males' competition, Saiphar started talking to the guests and stopped serving. Flint wasn't sure what was going on, but the purebred Vulpi was very popular. He had even been escorted away by some of the participants, which had worried Van. When they had found him, he was in an area called the commons banging some water plants flat and drying them in the fire, all with an avid set of onlookers who were apparently learning from him how they might do the same. It was great he was well-liked, but she wasn't paying him for that.

Finally, and perhaps the most disappointing, was Muriella, the purebred Faelnar had given Van a lot of back-talk and sass that had been observed by a few of the guests, and that was embarrassing both to her and her business. Vanarra was berating herself now for hiring the Faelnar, although she really needed females to service their camp at the primal. Something had been warning Van about Muriella during the interview, some sense coming off of her, but the resemblance to her mother had kept her from paying it much attention. "Never again," she growled.

"Never what?" Flint asked, opening the door. "You can't be sour so early in the morning. It has to be a rule or something."

"Oh, you know what it is. I'm … I'm just disappointed in our purebred staff for the event. Every single one of them screwed up in some way! Sheffer managed to get through the whole event. Raska, too. She did fine! Why was it our purebreds who failed to stay on task and keep it together?!"

"I don't know," he groaned, sitting in the chair in front of her desk. However, since I know you're going to ask them about it, you may want to hold these discussions on the other side of the building. Everyone comes in here. It's not right to chastise someone in front of others. They might have been doing something innocently out of ignorance."

"Oh, I like this more and more!" Vanarra groaned. "The Anati mongrel mix-ups are less ignorant than the pretty little purebreds."

"We're ... naturally more cautious about offending, I think," he reasoned. "Still, I think Tresk and Saiphar are salvageable. Tresk helped me repair a table on the spot; had his tools with him, even with what he was wearing. Saiphar – I have no idea what he said that fascinated the group he was talking to, but he was enthralling them. We really didn't need him so much at the point he was taken away. I was just worried about him."

"Well, Muriella and I are going to have quite the talk. She's pushing the little purebred is better than Anati thing farther than I can stand it. I don't care what she says; she's collecting her pay from me, not the other way around!"

"I don't disagree, but again, please, Van. Hold the discussions with them in private, okay?"

"Alright. We'll have them wait here. You're getting quite a haul from this, you know? You deserve it. I would never have been able to do it without you."

"Thanks," he replied, smiling at her.

"Flint. I'll take off twenty percent if you don't get your eyes up," Vanarra stated, annoyed.

"Dammit!" he cursed. "I'm honestly trying not to do that, Van! I'm sorry."

"I'm going to have to dress like a matron to avoid this from you, aren't I?"

"No, no," he stated. "I'll ... pay attention to ... well, not paying attention. Again, I'm sorry."

The sound of someone approaching the door put an end to the conversation. "Well, here's your pay, Flint. Non-discounted – well, not yet."

"Thank you, boss," he said, and then they both warmly greeted Sheffer as he poked his head in the door.

Taking Flint's advice, Vanarra had moved her employee reviews to the fur-dresser's storage area, and seen Tresk, Sheffer, and everyone else excepting Muriella and Saiphar. "I'm sorry, Vanarra. I have a habit of my mouth getting me in trouble. If it wasn't for eating and breathing," Tresk confessed, "I'd get rid of it. I'll ... behave myself if you ever choose to have me back."

"You did help us, Tresk," Van offered in consolation as she walked the Vulpi back towards the front, his draft in his paws. "If you and your mouth can come to an understanding at events, I'll have no problem at all bringing you back, okay?"

"I'll do better next time, I promise. I—" They had nearly reached the entrance to the little hall that connected Van's office with the storeroom when Van interrupted him by putting a paw-finger to the end of her muzzle. From the way her back fur was up and her claws were expressed, Tresk had no problem obeying. As the two listened, they heard Muriella's voice from Van's office where she was having a conversation with someone over LineCom.

"Oh, and I have never seen anything like this. So many well-to-do, walking around as if they were in their full business attire, with only the fur they were born with. For instance there was–" Van's claw-strike severed the cord connecting the office LineCom to the earpiece, surprising both Muriella and Saiphar. Flint was nowhere in evidence, and Tresk was staying well back. It was clear that he at least had the experience to know when the fur was going to fly.

"What in the mange are you doing?!" Van screamed. "What in the mange do you think you are doing?!"

"Trying to talk on the LineCom!" Muriella shot back, clearly not connecting Vanarra's body language with the level of physical threat. "If you don't mind."

"Mind?! You ... you were told by me, directly, not to say a damned thing to anyone about what happened or where you were or who you were serving! And I come up here to find that you're not only doing exactly that, you're ... stupid enough to be doing that sitting at my desk using my own LineCom! You hopeless bitch! Whatever made you think you could get away with that and still have a job here?!"

"Hey now! At least I'm not some kind of Anati trying to pretend she's a business owner!" Muriella was standing now, finally realizing by the bared teeth and claws that Van was truly angry, so angry that the Faelnar might need to defend herself.

"Easy now, Van," Tresk quietly begged. Saiphar was too stunned to even move.

"Not a chance! You think you can drag your purebred little self in here and pretend that you're the one in charge? The one who makes the rules? You did nothing but back-talk me the whole time! Listen to me you hopeless purebred bitch, you're not getting one sliver of a payment from me! You're fired! The only pay you're getting from me is this."

Van reached into her desk and pulled out a black envelope and presented it to the Faelnar. "What ... is it?"

"It's a transport pass to Lassinon. You could stay in Shanandrae, but I'm going to contact every one of my suppliers and everyone I do business with and tell them that you can't trust Muriella. I'm going to look for you in any place where you work and make sure they know you can't be trusted! I will ruin you and your name everywhere I go because you were going to share secrets about what happened at the primal!"

"You ... you're not paying me?!" the Faelnar shrieked. "How ... you're a criminal, dammit! You're stealing from me! I deserve to be paid for slaving for you like that!"

Van was bearing down on her now, literally backing her up against the far wall. "Oh dammit, Van, please! Don't let this get out of control!" Tresk begged, and Saiphar was starting to stand up now, as well.

"It has gotten out of control, already! When anyone thinks they can, for their own ... enjoyment ... spout off and ruin the best opportunity any of us have ever seen in our lifetimes! Your cute little conversation could cost us this account, and if it does, every one of these who are out of a job are going to be looking for you! I don't know what they'll do, but I wouldn't trust them to have your best interests at heart – you surely didn't! Now, get the mange out of here, and if you tell anything about what happened at that primal, I will make it ten times worse for you than you can possibly imagine! Now, out!"

"Muriella, get out, please! Just go," Saiphar begged.

"You ... you can't agree with her!" the Faelnar shouted. "You're purebred! Like me!"

"I agree with her," Tresk stated firmly if not angrily. "I'm about broke. I really need this job, dammit!"

In shock, the Faelnar turned to Saiphar, but she found no sympathy in the artist's expression. "You signed a contract. You made a promise not to talk about what happened at the primal. You broke that promise. This is what happens. Don't hurt the rest of us, just ... take the transport and move on."

Seeing there was no one who had any sympathy for her, the Faelnar shook off Saiphar's paws and said, "Fine, but I wasn't even talking to anyone who was avowed," before turning around and nearly walking right into someone Van never realized was there – Mavia.

Muriella pushing past the Nephti forced Van to actually see the shocked countenance of her client. "Oh ... no," Van breathed and put her face in her paws.

"I ... I can't believe it! That was indescribable," the Nephti said, panting. "No one ... no one has ever stood up for us like that before! You actually fired her! I saw you fire her! You gave her a transport pass out of town!"

Looking up, Van nodded sadly. "She's the only one we had a problem with. I made such a mistake hiring her. I never will hire someone like that again. I'm very sorry, Mavia. I ... I would understand if ... you didn't want..."

"Wait until the rest of the group hears this!" Mavia nearly shouted. "Some of them had doubts! I mean, not to say that the food didn't do a lot to make them not doubt, but still. When I tell them this!"

Vanarra was nearly crying. "I'm so ... so sorry about this. I would have given anything for you to not know that had happened, for you to see me that angry."

"About protecting us!" Mavia replied, walking forward and embracing Van. "I can't believe it! I ... I mean I should have, but really! Oh, when you come back for the next one, they are going to be so much more comfortable about you."

"You want us back?" Van asked, pulling away and staring at the Nephti, confused. "Even after you've seen me ready to nearly claw the fur off someone?"

"Hey, I'm a Primalist," the Nephti cautioned. "I live for raw emotions. That was ... real! That, more than anything, tells me where your heart is."

"Well, thank you," Van replied, still embarrassed. "You ... you saw that even Saiphar and Tresk here were upset with her."

"I'm definitely going to watch what I say now," Tresk replied. "I thought I was good in a fight, but ... those damn claws of yours, Van!"

"I want to paint you that upset, but ... I won't," Saiphar stated, nervously.

"Oh my goodness!" Mavia breathed, her paws on the sides of her muzzle. "You're Saiphar?! Oh, I so wanted to meet you! Vanarra, may we please have Saiphar back? Did you say you paint, too?"

"I ... I do," he replied, and then looking at Van added, "I suspect I'm in trouble from what Flint said. I ... was trying to make your group happy, but I wasn't where I was supposed to be."

"Well, it appears you made our client very happy, and after Muriella, I'm very grateful someone did. Let's talk some more about what Saiphar would be doing, but let's do that on the other side away from the office so we can have some privacy. Tresk, can you bring enough stools and chairs for all of us?"

"Absolutely, boss. Anything you say; not going to make you mad!"

Van smirked, but Tresk was already moving, so the rest of them followed until, after a pass or two, all were sitting in the fur-dressers' storeroom. "So, Saiphar, what were you talking to the primal guests about? Flint saw you were popular, but he didn't know why."

"Vanarra, he has an amazing knowledge of how to make pigment from natural sources and paper from plants using only the most basic of tools," Mavia effused. "He had a group completely spellbound by his discussion of pottery clay and early firing techniques. He even knows things about weaving from natural materials!"

"I had no idea that I had hired someone so talented," Van stated, eying him carefully. Saiphar was still very nervous, clearly understanding that he hadn't been hired to be an artist, and that his pay might still be hanging in the balance.

"And ... and if he could paint with those natural pigments and that paper of his. That would make amazing decorations or ... some might even want him to paint things for them, as well!"

"Mavia, I have to confess that while there wasn't a terrible disruption to our activities, Saiphar's absence did leave us short. If I bring him back, I'll have to augment with additional staff. For what you're paying, I truly don't mind doing it, but ... I just don't want there to be a problem with us not being able to meet your needs."

"I think he would be worth more from us, Vanarra, certainly."

"Vanarra, if I was at an event where you hired me for painting or teaching," Saiphar quietly offered, "I would surrender the proceeds to you. You could pay me whatever you think is fair, and you most certainly would be within your rights to claim the largest piece. I ... I wouldn't have that venue if it wasn't for you."

Saiphar's gratitude and willingness to work with Vanarra made her reach out and gently grasp his shoulder. "I'm sure we can work something out. You did impress them, and that is what I was hoping for."

"He certainly did," Mavia affirmed. "There's been a little scheduling mix-up with the moon cycle, and we're going to need you for another primal sooner than we'd thought. Is that okay?"

"How long?" Van asked.

"We need you in fifteen sols."

"Mavia, I want some time to do some very careful hiring. I was in a bit of a rush this last time, but I think I can manage the timeframe you're talking about. I want to make sure I can have staff at these events I trust completely."

"I understand," Mavia replied. "You probably haven't had the hardest part yet. I'd expect the family jewels to start showing up here pretty soon."

"Family jewels?" Van asked, smiling.

"Our term for matrons, dames, and matriarchs. They wear so much jewelry to show their authority, just ... ugh," the Nephti said, obviously revolted by the practice.

"I think we can manage the 'family jewels.' Now, let's start talking about your next event. Tresk, would you mind taking notes?"

"Not at all. Back in a moment," Tresk replied and went to go get a pad.

Just then, Flint walked inside. "Oh, sorry. Van, why was Muriella getting on a transport out of town? I saw her when I was driving back."

"That's because if I ever see her working in this town, I'm going to tell her employer I fired her because she couldn't be trusted to keep her mouth shut."

"And I think we're really going to love doing business with you for just that reason," Mavia stated happily.

Chapter 13: Destiny

As Sahnassa stood at the very back of the line of Harnard graduates, she unhappily reviewed her last five seasons. Her first season was fairly good, and her grades were pretty decent. The second season had been tougher, with the expenses and class fees gnawing at her persistently, but she was able to manage. Her third season was where things had started to get difficult financially. Her roommate, who had been helping her here and there with expenses, simply wasn't able to do so any longer, and Sahnassa was forced to get a job off of the campus answering LineCom calls for a retailer. That job had cut into her study time, and her grades had shown it. By the time the fourth season had come around, she thought about trying to make some sort of plea to her matron, but for some strange reason, her matron was always off continent, leaving the only alternative her dame – Dame Rothnerra. She couldn't go back to her parents, so, in the fourth season, she nearly worked herself to complete exhaustion, and her grades were sub-par, at best.

The end of the fourth season brought another unhappy change. Merialla, who had been a support to her in so many ways, graduated with honors, pledged herself to Lashahar as a mate, and accepted an extremely lucrative position at a Nephti academic think-tank on the Anthurian continent. That had been a heartbreaking loss for Sahnassa. Only Merialla understood and sympathized with her, and Merialla owed much to Sahnassa and gave much. They had their own lives to live, she knew, and they had to leave. As much as her closeness to the light purple Nephti had been therapeutic in the first two seasons, Merialla had been consolation for Sahnassa the last two they were together. The departure of the dearest friend she'd ever had left a great open gash in her heart, and a new first season roommate did nothing to fill that. She never got to know the female Perratti who moved in, and her life was achingly lonely for the last full season of her schooling. It felt as if she was living life in a wilderness, solitary and disavowed from everyone else.

Then, there had been the silence from her parents and sisters. It was, in some part, mutual, but what little Sahnassa learned from news in the family TransNet mails, both her mother and father had recovered much of their former prestige – the situation with their errant daughter left far behind. Both had received multiple commendations from de Orturu and other houses, and Triana's name had even appeared on the rolls of those gaining honor. As she crossed the stage to receive her certificate, she didn't even look for them. She knew they weren't there; they weren't coming. She hadn't even asked or sent any word – their silence and lack of support hurt too much. She knew they would learn about her grades, and that would be enough to keep them away.

As the ceremony disbanded, Sahnassa walked to the upper tier of seats, took off her graduation robes, and shoved them into her tattered backpack. Sitting alone, she cried, and no one came to ask her what was wrong.

Finally gathering the strength to return to her lair, she boarded the transport for the long trip back to the campus. Arriving well after high night, she opened the door to find her roommate's belongings removed and three notices under the door. The first told her that her room, the room she had called home for five seasons, had to be vacated within the next five sols, now that she was a graduate. The second was a notice from the company that held her student loan – a necessity for her to survive her fifth season – congratulating her on her graduation and reminding her of when payments would begin. Third, there was a package from her house indicating the cessation of all benefits of the matriarchal scholarship now that her schooling was completed, and a reminder about how to pay her family dues – through her parents.

Letting the papers drop to the floor, she buried herself in her pillows and cried once again. She had never felt more alone and abandoned than in that moment.

Van carefully directed Flint and the others as they moved stock into their new office space. The past few seasons had been amazing for Celebrations by Vanarra, and her business had grown so fast that the biggest problem she had was screening potential staff. What she had come to learn was that Mavia's Primalist group was only one of four in the local area, and as several members intermingled between groups, word about her little firm had spread. In less than a season, Vanarra had moved out of the office and into a nearby rental lair. Within the second season, she managed to have that place relatively well furnished, and then during the third season she had purchased her very own lair, a nice one by most standards. This sol, she was celebrating the latest accomplishment of her company – moving out of the pathetic space that she had inherited from Gorta and into one that she purchased. It was three times the size of what she had before, with multiple offices and workspaces.

It wasn't, however, as if the seasons since her first primal had been without incident or problem. At least once every season, she had to fire someone for talking about what happened at a primal. The greatest number of those she had problems with were purebred, so except for the two disavowed Vulpi, Tresk and Saiphar, she generally shied away from taking any purebred applicants seriously. There had been times when that had cost her – she nearly had to cancel events at two primals because her staff was almost too thin to manage.

There had been, as Mavia promised, visits from several family elites – matrons and even dames, from time to time. What was interesting to Vanarra was that these purebred family jewels always assumed they had the power wherever they went. As nicely as she could, she reminded them that wasn't the case in her office and had developed an interesting technique which seemed to work against them very well. To simply suggest that someone of note and rank from one of their houses' matriarchy was present at a primal was more than enough to make their lips and nose go pale. What was interesting to her was this technique worked, time and again, as did the suggestion that someone would release the incriminating information publicly if anything happened to her. They never tried detaining her, not even once.

Then, there was the sordid turns of her own private relationships. Amongst the party-goers and Primalists, there were always some who were "into" this strange looking mix between Vulpi and Faelnar. At first, Van was afraid and defensive, based on her prior experiences, but now, she … dabbled, from time to time. Her sense for feeling out an interested male was growing very precise, and she'd managed to avoid anymore incidents like the mass rape-mating she had endured when working for Gorta. None of those relationships were for very long, nor did they in any way resemble the intimacy she had enjoyed with Ash. Van made the most of those short dalliances, and when they ended, she simply moved on.

Buck Harlock, however, was still very much a friend to her, and continued to use her company and recommend them. She was proud of how the disavowed Faelnar had recovered from the blow of being dumped by his family. Now, he didn't seem to worry about that at all, and other than the fact he was almost as busy as she, Buck seemed pretty happy with who he was. Flint continued to serve very well as her second in command, and he, too, had enjoyed the lifestyle benefits that came from their mutual success. The results of his newfound prosperity were surprisingly contemplative for a muscle-bound mixed blood. He had purchased his own computer and started writing novels. Some of what he had written was even enjoyable to her, but she eschewed reading it on an ongoing basis because of their work relationship. Saiphar and Tresk she had picked up full time, along with a somewhat surly administrative assistant named Mauft. All in all, it was a crew that worked together very well.

Still, there were some things about her business that concerned her, and sometimes kept her up at nights pacing the floor. The TransNet was a place that the other catering firms had her outclassed, and Vanarra couldn't see any way to bridge that gap. The technical expertise to set up a TransNet site with an appropriate amount of security was something she didn't have time to learn. Even sending Saiphar to the Pinnacle Center Archive to look for references did nothing but underscore how little she grasped in this domain. While the Primalists didn't have any interest in VidStar recordings of their events, there were more than a fair share of joinings and other celebrations which really seemed to be crying out for it. She had even lost a few contracts because, despite her low prices, some clients believed that these services were a must. Van's attempts to get anyone to partner with her on such events were also fruitless. It was a bitter truth that no one wanted to partner with an Anati caterer.

"Is that all of it?" Vanarra asked, looking at how little of the new space their gear seemed to fill.

"Believe it or not, yes," Flint commented. "It did look a lot bigger back at the old place."

"It did," Van replied, walking around, looking at everything. "Have you picked your office, yet?"

"I like the one up the hall, to the right. Fairly quiet, I would think, and within … shouting distance," he teased.

"Yeah, I know, that's like fifteen courses. Very funny."

"You know, this is kind of a big sol for you, one I thought you'd be a little happier about. What's wrong?"

"Oh, nothing much. We've just taken on a whole new debt, our company growth is flattening out, and we still don't have any way to make a break into TransNet. Damned what I wouldn't pay for a Thurian who would do that stuff for us. Any luck finding someone who might fit that job?"

"None yet," Flint admitted. "Most of my contacts have drifted away to other jobs or … simply disappeared. I've been doing some discrete asking around, but … we just don't know anyone. Tresk and Saiphar have been after it as well; Sheffer, too. Mauft doesn't know anyone like that. I guess … I guess we keep looking."

"Damned purebreds. Avowed and all plugged in with their own little inside network and inside game no one else can play! We've got to do something, Flint. We may be able to limp along, but after awhile, our competitors will catch up with us."

"Yeah," Flint replied, worried. "I keep thinking about what would happen if the primals got shut down."

"That would just kill us. We don't have enough outside of that to make a go of it. That would be devastating. Uh, to that point, Flint, go over with everyone again before they pull out tomorrow. I'm not going to be kind to anyone who, because of accident or stupidity, puts our competitors' teeth at our necks. They're going to find out about our move to this new office space, and things are going to get even uglier."

"Well, for now, let's just work what's in front of us and hope for the best. I'm sure we'll run into someone who can help us, eventually."

"Yes, I hope," Van replied. "It is a good sol, though. I can't believe we're here, moving into such a nice place. We … we could do amazing things here."

"You mean more amazing things, Van. You've been doing amazing things since I met you."

"Thanks, Muscles, and thanks for sticking by me."

"It's an honor, boss."

"I always like it when you say that," she said, turning to look at him and smiling.

"And that's why I think I'd be a good member of your team," Sahnassa replied, as convincingly as she could, to the review board of the last corporate pack she had on her list. The Star-Quest pack was a global shipping operation, and it had a fairly large stock of technologists to manage its high-speed information systems and complicated distribution centers. As with every other single interview she had gotten in the last two moons, it had been very difficult to schedule since any applicant with house representation invariably got first choice of the time slots. Here and now, she was struggling to maintain their attention as it was almost time for lunch, and they – by their own admission – had been interviewing since early morning.

The heavy-set Lupar sitting across the table from her looked at his three companions, and the looks passed between them made her heart sink. The words which next came from his mouth were words she now knew by heart, and she could have saved him the trouble. "We appreciate you taking time to come and talk with us, and although we agree you might make a good match for this organization, there have been several other more qualified and represented candidates in front of us this morning. While you will receive notification through your family house, I would suggest that you work through your matriarchy to search out other opportunities."

"Thank you," she replied, trying very hard not to cry. Without saying anything more, Sahnassa walked out of the room and closed the door behind her. Walking through the bustling office, her visitor's identification card in her pocket, she was on the verge of collapse. The little money she had was running out, and the squared-off little lair she had rented was bare of everything – food or furniture. In less than a moon, she would lose even that pathetic habitation. Then, she would have no choice. Crawling back to her mother and father and begging their forgiveness would be the only other option to being without a lair and without employment.

Turning down a hallway, she was starting to keep her paw on the wall to steady herself. "The last five seasons of my life, everything I went through, all the time I spent working and studying … is now … worth … nothing!" A sob burst from her chest, and she swallowed hard to hold it back. Desperation fought with grief as she realized that she was losing complete control of her emotions, and she was about to have a nervous breakdown in front of an office full of Thurians. Seeing a conference room door ajar, she pushed her way inside, finding it thankfully deserted. The closing sound of the wood hitting the metal frame triggered her immediate collapse onto the floor heaving out great sobs as horrible images of her future came to her mind.

One sol, she'd take her pathetic hover back to her lair to find everything she owned piled outside, perhaps even picked over by her neighbors. Ashamed, she'd have to try to put as much of it as she could into her hover and then go to find her matron. Her matron, however, would probably still not be around, so she would have to seek out Dame Rothnerra. In front of her dame, she'd have to apologize and surrender her rights under the Compact, admit that she had acted foolishly and had wasted the house's resources. The dame would probably disavow her on the spot, she thought. If she did take pity on the broken Nephti cowering before her, she would probably assign Sahnassa to menial duties as punishment, and she'd have to beg her parents to provide for her. After their long silence, she doubted whether or not Gonastir and Holana would even claim her as their daughter. A part of her wanted to simply die rather than be disowned, but some small part of her pleaded in her mind that there was hope. She just had to keep trying. That small hope, dashed and battered, struggled to keep Sahnassa from the abyss as she knelt on the floor of the small conference room.

"Dammit, dammit, dammit!" Van thought inwardly. "This is a really crappy time for both of my purebreds to get sick!" She had barely been able to land this deal with "Star-Quest" for their executive luncheon, and now she was down two sets of paws – Tresk and Saiphar – who had both fallen ill. The event was almost about to start, but even with her pitching in, there wasn't anyone to cover one of the serving stations. If she couldn't pull this one off, word would spread through the corporate packs and that business would dry up – business she had fought long and hard to gain entry to. "What the mange am I going to do, what the mange am I – I need a LineCom." Van's PawLink had been behaving badly for awhile, and she had been delaying a replacement, and now that was costing her, as well.

Looking around the hall where she was, she saw a conference room door. It was closed, but the sign beside it didn't show occupied nor did the schedule posted on the wall. There was no light coming from underneath the door that she could tell, so she decided to risk it. Flinging it open, she was surprised to see a cute female Nephti leaning against the table. Startled, as well, the Nephti turned and looked at her, embarrassment evident in her features. The dark purple Nephti with silver-white stripes, indigo eyes, and a pink nose looked at her in confusion. It was also evident to Vanarra that this individual was distraught, her ears were flat down against her head, and her tail was solidly on the floor.

"I'm ... I'm really sorry for disturbing you," Van apologized, looking down.

"I ... didn't know anyone else had this room. I'll go," the Nephti breathed out sadly. Something in her voice demanded Van's attention, a weird echo of a child's voice she had heard once.

"Say, kit. Are you alright?"

"I ... I just need a job," Sahnassa replied, shrugging fatalistically.

"Well, if you want one right now, I need you. I have an event I'm catering for the execs here, and I'm down a couple of paws. If you could help me out, I would very much make it worth your while. I need someone like ... right now!" Van exclaimed, looking in alarm at her watch. The event was starting within the next pass.

"Sure," the Nephti replied, resigned. "I'll do anything you want."

Vanarra blinked in surprise. There was no delay in her acceptance, no pretense of purebred superiority. The kit was desperate, Van could tell, and also heartbroken. "If you can do a good job for me, kit, I will make it pay for you. I'm really in need right now. Have we got a deal?"

"Sure. Yes," she replied.

"Great, follow me," Van ordered, and the Nephti complied immediately. As they walked quickly down the hallway, she added, "I'm Vanarra Anasto. I run Celebrations by Vanarra. I had everyone scheduled for this event, but then two of my staff called in sick, and no one else lives close."

"I'm Sahnassa de Orturu. I'll do whatever you need me to," came the reply, making Vanarra curious at what had happened to this poor Nephti to completely crush her spirit. Most times, even the hint of a purebred avowed working for an Anati would have created downright anger. This Sahnassa accepted it with something akin to gratitude.

"Well, right now, I just need you to do easy stuff. I need for you to serve the food from the chafing dishes and when you run out, go back and get a replacement from the hot box we've got set up in the room next door, can you do that?"

"Yes. Sure. I will," the Nephti replied.

"Oh, and I hate to ask," Van stated as they entered the company theater where the luncheon was being served, "but I need for you to put away what's got your tail on the floor for awhile. I need a few smiles and a little eye contact. Okay?"

The Nephti shook off her despair and replied, "Oh, yes. I'm ... sorry about that. I will ... try."

"Buck up, kit," Van offered, putting her paw on the Nephti's shoulder. "There are a lot of hard things you can live through if you can just realize your value. Now, here's where you'll stand, and here's what you're supposed to serve. Just one ladle of each of these, and three of the fish. No more, or we might run out, okay?"

"I understand. Thank ... you, Vanarra. I'll do my best for you."

Van again couldn't help herself; she put her paw around the back of the Nephti and gave her a brief pat. "That's the spirit, kit! Now, I'll be around in a bit to check on you, okay?" The Nephti nodded, and Van left her to finish the last few preparations.

As Sahnassa served the food to the line of Thurians queuing in front of her, she was struggling to understand what had just happened. She had just about worked out what she would say to her dame that would keep her from getting disavowed when an Anati had burst into the room. She was actually very attractive – shapely with golden eyes, reddish brown fur with gold highlights mingled all through. Of all Thurians, she had offered Sahnassa a job, and the promise of any pay at all bought Sahnassa what she most needed – time.

What was as curious was that Sahnassa was actually enjoying herself a little. Smiling and serving others, accepting their thanks, and chatting briefly with them was more social interaction than she had enjoyed in a very long time. It had actually made her a little proud when she had been able to find the back-stock of food to resupply her station without any help, whatsoever, and she only kept the line waiting a pass or so.

When the line was starting to thin out, Vanarra appeared beside her. "Well, look at you, kit! Nicely done! Now, when this finishes up, I need for you to start going around and collecting plates and taking them to the back. Can you manage that?"

"Yes. I will take care of it. Thank you for what you did, asking me to help. It's ... making me feel a lot better."

"And you haven't even been paid, yet!" Van shot back. "Trust me. If you keep this up, you're going to see my thanks in a very tangible way. Now, I'm back to what I have to do, and when the time comes for something else, I'll come get you, okay?"

"Okay. Thank you."

Again, Van patted the Nephti on the back and went about her work. Scanning around, she saw that things were actually going quite well. Sheffer was taking care of drinks, and Flint was directing the stragglers and late arrivals where they should go. Stepping back into the shadows a bit as the Lupar in charge got up to make his comments, Van took a long, careful look at the Nephti purebred. Working the serving line had actually made the kit's tail rise a little, and Van was somewhat fascinated to see an ink-dipped tail, the last track or so a noticeably darker shade of purple than the rest of her fur.

"I wonder if she could be a regular or maybe on-call," Van thought to herself, but instantly, she dismissed the idea. She had clearly heard the Nephti introduce herself as "de Orturu." An avowed kit would never stoop to work at an Anati-run business, she thought, but yet, here she was, working for Vanarra right here and now. The kit was just a few seasons younger than she, and there was something about her, something Van just couldn't grab hold of in her mind, that put this kit into a category all her own. She didn't seem proud, either. "She was certainly willing to take the offer, and ... she's not doing a half-bad job," Van observed as she watched the kit go and get another container of food from the back.

As she turned and walked around to where Flint was, she made a decision. Vanarra wanted to talk to this kit, not just put her pay in her paws and send her on her way. "If for no other reason than to just understand what makes her tick. The Nephti, what is it with them?"

Sahnassa continued serving the food even as she listened to the Lupar in charge talk about the "challenging business environment" and the "need for finding additional efficiencies." "All that, and you're still catering this bunch of Thurians like they're the matriarchy! What sense does that make?" she wondered.

"Excuse me?" a Lupar in front of her asked. Turning away from the presentation, she realized that a small group of late-comers had gathered, hoping there was some food left. When she realized who they were, her heart instantly sank. It was the very group who had interviewed her.

"How may I serve you?" she asked quietly.

"Is … is there any left?" one of them asked, shamefacedly holding a plate.

"Certainly," she whispered back and served him, her own blush furs riding high.

"Thank … you," he replied. "I'm … sorry about earlier. I … I hope you find something." Not knowing what else to say, he turned and left.

"I suppose I have," Sahnassa thought darkly to herself. In turn, each one of the interviewers accepted the food, looking ashamed and somewhat haunted to see the kit they had dismissed earlier here in front of them. She looked each of them in the eye, and each one of them turned away in shame and wouldn't hold her gaze. When the last one was through, Sahnassa closed down the station and started going to the large areas where the Thurians had set their used plates. Carefully and quietly, she took them, disposed of them, and came back for another load.

As she did so, she caught glimpses of the interviewers looking at her. It surprised her that they didn't ignore her or look on her with disdain. It was more like they looked at her afraid, afraid that they, too, might be there in her place one sol. As she listened, it became more and more clear to her that this company wasn't doing well. It was losing market share to its competitors and had several big lawsuits pending, including one from her own house, de Orturu. "I wonder if Dad or Triana will be going after them." In some perverse way, it actually felt good to think of her father coming after this company. They had hurt Sahnassa, humiliated her, and now – even if he didn't know it – her father might still be defending her, after a fashion. That thought gave her some small measure of solace as she removed the dirty plates from the room.

Vanarra peeked around from where she had been organizing the gifts that were to be given out as the attendees left. "Hey, the purebred little kit closed the station and cleaned up. Nice," she mused. "I wonder how much she'll ask for," her mind added darkly. As the speech continued, Van worked her way quietly along the edge of the room and into the area they had been given to stage what they had. Flint was helping the Nephti quietly clean what they had brought in terms of serving ware, and they looked up as she moved in and closed the door. "Hey, you two, how's it going?"

Flint answered, "Pretty well, actually. I have Sheffer making runs back to the hover, and Sahnassa's doing a good job of getting things ready. How's everything outside?"

"I think they're starting to wrap up. Sounded pretty depressing to me," Van commented. "I hate when that happens. It's hard to get good recommendations from events where everyone walks away all sour. Kit, you've done so much for us, might I impose again?"

The Nephti looked up at her and nearly smiled. "Sure. What do you need me to do?"

"Can you give out the gifts as they leave? I think some in this crowd may receive them a little easier from your paw than from any of ours."

The Nephti closed her eyes, and her ears dropped slightly along with her tail, but she replied, "Okay. Should I go now?"

"I think so. I'm not entirely sure when he's going to stop yapping." Without more than a nod, the Nephti walked out of the room. "Kind of an odd kit," Van commented.

"She hasn't said two words the whole time she's been helping me, and ... I wouldn't ask her. Something's wrong with her, bad wrong, Van."

"Like unstable or–"

"Depressed, very," Flint supplied. "The kind of depressed when Thurians sometimes think about doing something pretty bad to themselves."

"Oh, damn!" Van cursed. "I'd better go out there and keep an eye on her. I'd hate to have her flip out or something."

"I don't think she'll do a bad job for you, but ... Van..."

"What?"

"If there was ever a purebred you took pity on, let it be that one, okay?"

"No promises," Van replied in warning, but then took a breath which she let out in a sigh. "Okay, I'll pay her real nice."

"I don't mean it that way. Talk to her, Van. When this is all over; just ... talk to her."

Van tilted her head a little and then sighed. "Oh, wonderful. I get to be everyone's shoulder. It's going to get water-logged if I keep this up."

Flint's smile broadened at Van's self-pity routine, and she just shook her head at him and left.

A short time later, the last attendees were leaving, and Vanarra was being given her check. "I sincerely hope everything was to your liking," she stated as she took the envelope from the administrative assistant.

"Well, everything but the message. Uh, they could learn a lot from your group on how to run things," the Perratti groaned. "That Nephti on your staff was very good. She was very kind to the latecomers, and she did a marvelous job giving out the gifts. Everyone loved her. I had to chase a few away actually who were ... a little interested."

"From what I've been able to tell, it was probably good that you did. She's ... going through a rough time."

"Well, I hope things get better for her, and I should let you know - the director mentioned to me he wants your firm back in ten sols for the management conference. It's a smaller gathering, but the food is much more upscale. I'm sure they'd like to see your Nephti come back, if she's able."

Van furrowed her brow a little bit. "I wonder why she got such a positive response."

"Couldn't tell you other than the director spoke to her for several passes after his presentation. He started writing things down, and then asked me to make some calls into the de Orturu legal directorate to find their arbitration branch. The director is the one who asked me about her."

"You do understand that our staff can't ... socialize with our clients?" Van asked, dubious of the director's intentions.

"Oh, sure. You don't have to worry. He's joined and all that, but he certainly recognizes talent. I just wish everyone in our corporate pack did, too." Van nodded, her mind racing trying to categorize all the facts about this young purebred. "Well, we'll contact you with the location and details and contract and all of that, okay?"

"Yes. Thank you so very much! We can't wait to serve you again."

After she had said her goodbyes to the admin, Van walked around to where the Nephti was putting the unclaimed gifts back into boxes that had been slipped under the table. "Hey there, kit," Vanarra said quietly. "You … really do a good job."

Smiling a weak smile, Sahnassa replied, "Thank you. It's nice to hear someone say that."

"I really owe you for helping us out," Van offered as she leaned back against the table, facing out towards the meeting hall and not looking the Nephti in the eye. Her emotions were in such conflict. There was a part of her that wanted to pay this sad Nephti and send her away, but there was this feeling like she really did now have a debt to this Sahnassa. If Van's organization had failed here, it would have cost them all dearly.

Glancing down, she saw that the Nephti had returned to putting things away during the break in conversation. Looking at Sahnassa, there was something familiar about her, and Flint's statement earlier about taking pity on this purebred was nagging at her. "For helping us out, I was thinking about making it 150, but … I really should throw another fifty on, since you're not a part of the normal staff, and … you did pull me out of a serious hole."

"Oh, wow! I … uh … well, thank you, Vanarra. I'm very grateful," Sahnassa replied, stunned. That was enough money to keep her afloat for a few more sols.

"Yeah … sure, but I have to ask you, kit, and you don't have to tell me, are you alright?"

"I … really, really need a job, and I've had a hard time finding one."

"What do you do?" Van asked, looking at the Nephti eye-to-eye.

"I'm a technologist. I work with things like TransNet sites and programming systems for businesses and things like that."

Vanarra was thunderstruck, but she kept her composure. "Really? Well, that's … pretty interesting. I'm actually the owner of this catering business, and I've been wanting to get us some kind of presence there for awhile. Do you think we might be able to work out a little something? It would just be temporary, but … perhaps if you and I could help each other – I don't know – it could kind of … keep you going until something better turns up, right?"

"You mean it?!" Sahnassa excitedly asked the mixed blood. "I … I would love to! That's exactly the kind of work I trained for!"

Van felt a need to tamp down the purebred's unabashed enthusiasm. "Whoa, whoa, kit, just a tick! We haven't talked about pay yet, and whatever we come up with is going to be put down in a contract that we both sign. I don't want any of your purebred family lawyers coming back at me." She saw the Nephti's shoulders sag. "What is it?"

"You don't exactly have to worry about that, really. There's a situation with my family that's … well, kind of complex and … just know that you don't have to worry about it."

That made one of Vanarra's eyebrow furs raise. She knew purebreds came in two flavors - avowed and not - but didn't know about this third category. "Alright. Here, let me give you a card, and let's talk … tomorrow, just after mid-sol? We're working an event tonight - ugh! That's another one I'm short pawed for!" Vanarra realized that her situation this evening at the Core Pack's moon celebration was actually a much more dire circumstance than the one she had just managed to squeak through.

"I could help," Sahnassa offered shyly. "I'm really not doing anything, and I would appreciate the work."

Vanarra looked at the Nephti carefully. "She actually means it!" she thought. "How desperate is this kit?" "Are you kidding me?" Van asked. "You worked pretty hard, already."

"I've been working really hard for a long time, without anyone noticing, Vanarra. I … it is nice to find someone who actually is happy with what I do."

Van shrugged. "Okay, kit. It would be a help to me, and you'd likely walk away with another 150 for your trouble. We won't be done until a couple of intervals after high night. That suit your purebred sleeping schedule?"

To her surprise, the Nephti laughed. "I … I so don't have one, not for like … the last five seasons, anyway. I will be fine, Vanarra. I promise."

"Well, just be sure. Tonight is important to us; every engagement is important to us. We get by on doing a really good job and not by having some matron or dame toss our name around."

"I understand. If there's a particular way I should dress or something, please tell me."

"For you, I'd need you in a black dress, just below the knee and a white pair of paw-gloves, oddly enough. Think you could manage?"

The Nephti's brow furrowed, and she was clearly thinking hard. "I ... guess I could. What time is the event tonight? What time do I need to be there?"

"24:00, six intervals before high night, just so there's no possibility of a math error," Van stated, smiling.

"Okay, okay. I should have enough time ... to get ready. Where should I show up?"

"Be in the main ballroom of the Astillon Resort Hotel on the south side of Shanandrae right at 24:00. Understand, kit, that I'm relying on you. You disappoint me, and there's no chance I'll even think about using you for anything else."

"I understand, Vanarra. I'll do my best," the kit dutifully replied.

Vanarra cocked her head, amused at the prospect of having this winsome Nephti working for her. Unlike Muriella, there were no warning alarms in Van's mind that she was beating down. In fact, there was every indication that this purebred might be one of the best hires she'd ever made - it was always a good idea to have a purebred to post at certain places at certain events. "So ... we'll see. What's your full name again, kit?"

"Sahnassa de Orturu," the Nephti replied, and she ducked her eyes a little as if she was ashamed of that fact, which really surprised Vanarra.

"Having a purebred defer to me," Van thought inwardly, a smile pulling at her lips. "How rich!"

"Vanarra?"

Van blinked. She hadn't realized she'd been staring. "Oh, sorry, kit. Just one thing. That's a pretty name and all, but even I don't go by my whole name. You can call me Van. As for you, has anyone ever given you a 'short name', something quick and familiar?"

"I ... don't think so."

"Would you mind?"

The Nephti clearly had to think that one over for a tick, but then said, her blush furs up in embarrassment, "If it's standard practice around your office, I would need to be okay with it."

"Hmm, Sahnassa ... Sahna - no that's not good. Nassa? Hmm, don't like the sound of that one, either. Let me think about it. I need something quick. I'll have it by the time we're done tonight, and I promise I won't tell any of your purebred family about it."

"They won't ask. Not for me."

"And you are really avowed, kit?" Van couldn't help herself. "No, no, don't answer that! I'm serious. That was a bad slip on my part. I never ask about my employees' pasts ... because I don't want to deal with the same questions. Okay?"

"Yes, Van. Whatever you say."

"Alright, kit. You've done your bit. If everything works out, I'll see you in a few intervals. Remember, I'm relying on you."

"And that sounds very good to me, Van. Thank you ... for that trust."

Taking the draft now offered by Vanarra, Sahnassa nodded in what was almost a bow, and then turned and quietly left, leaving Van amused, confused, and curious.

"So, what did you think?" Flint asked quietly, coming up behind her a pass later.

"I ... I don't know, Flint. This one has me stumped a little. She shouldn't have wanted to help us at all, but she did, and she did an okay job. She wants to help tonight, too. She's a technologist; did you know that?"

"Yeah, found that out in the short conversation I had with her. I wondered if that might interest you."

"You didn't tell me," Van complained.

"Honestly, I didn't expect it'd be an issue, other than she might know someone. You think she might help us out directly?"

"Says she wants to; going to come by tomorrow after mid-sol to make a pitch - show me what she can do."

"What does your gut tell you about her?" Flint asked, for the question often brought entirely different answers than the one he had asked previously.

"On instinct? Damn, I'm baffled, too. I ... I have no idea, Flint. None. This is completely new ground for me. Is it normal for

Nephti to act like this towards us? Respect us, treat us as equals. Could she … would she really treat me as her boss?"

"Not all of the Nephti we've run into have been nice or even accepting of us," Flint countered.

"More often than not, though. We'll just have to see. Look, in case she comes to her senses and blows us off, call around and make sure we scare up another one or two more paws for our event tonight, okay?"

"I'll try. Our roster is pretty thin at this point, boss."

"Yeah. I know; let's not have the discussion again about booking two events tonight. Tell you what. I'll finish the clean up so you can start making calls." Flint nodded, and the two set off to get started on their tasks.

Shopping for a dress that matched Vanarra's requirements, Sahnassa felt very strange about what had happened. At some level, it was the most humiliating experience she had ever had - to be summarily dismissed from an interview and then end up serving food to them like some kind of hired help. Still, being at that gathering gave her a perspective she never would have had if she had simply slinked out of the building with her tail between her legs. Then, there was this Anati, Vanarra. She … was just different - different looking, different thinking, different acting, but unlike so many of her professors and instructors, who dealt out grades as if they were dealing out house commendations to the disavowed, Vanarra treated her with respect. It was also a little money in her pocket, something she desperately needed.

As she took several dresses in to try them on, she thought about what would be needed to put the Anati's business on a TransNet site. She had been required to create a fully functioning commerce site in one of her final classes, and she still had the code. It was a little rough around the edges, something she had been penalized for heavily by her perfectionist instructor, but Sahnassa knew how to make every one of the changes that were required. She had just run out of time. Now, hopefully equipped with a contract and a paycheck, she'd be able to make a site that would put everyone else in her former class to shame. "Now that would be very nice - theirs were only projects. Mine will be making money for a business."

She found a dress that fit, and it was a little more expensive than she had hoped for - its price taking a sizable bite out of what she had just been paid. Finally, trying on the white paw gloves to go with it, she knew it didn't matter. She needed work, and this was the only thing available. "Perhaps if I can show someone a fully functioning website that's making money for a business, they might want to hire me."

An interval or so later, she was pulling up to the hover lot of the Astillon Resort Hotel, and the gate guard motioned for her to set down. "Good evening, what can I do for you?"

"I'm ... working at a function here tonight. This is who's catering it," Sahnassa replied, offering the card.

"I'm sorry, we don't have a record of that," the guard replied. "You'll have to pay for parking if you want in."

Sahnassa bristled, inwardly, but she maintained her composure. "You sure? I could call her to verify."

The Perratti guard frowned and pressed some more keys on his large PawLink. "Oh, here it is. Are you on the list of staff?"

"I'm an add on, kind of last tick or so. If you like, we could call her?"

"Well, they had to pay parking, too."

Sahnassa could easily see where this was going, and again, giving up some of the pay she had managed to earn earlier, Sahnassa paid for parking. Pulling up to the entrance, she looked for a place to land, but "Valet parking only" signs were everywhere. Looking around again, she sighed and pulled up to the front. "There goes more of it," she sighed as she took her claim ticket, ignoring the somewhat disgusted expression on the face of the Faelnar who presented it to her. She guessed her sad little hover didn't impress anyone.

Walking into the lobby of the huge hotel resort, she knew she needed a map or some way to find the function. Looking down at her watch was also making her nervous. She was very nearly late.

Finding a map, she located the banquet spaces and rushed to reach them. Going down a large hall that seemed completely empty almost made her want to sob until a door burst open, and Vanarra emerged, a rather large Nephti Lupar mix following behind her. "Excuse me," Sahnassa called, and since Vanarra was headed the other way, she didn't hear, but the big, gray Anati did, and she turned on Sahnassa and stood in her way.

"The banquet area is not open to guests until five passes before the event."

"I'm sorry. I ... I'm Sahnassa de Orturu. I'm here to work for Vanarra tonight."

The gray Anati looked at her with a mixture of humor and disbelief. "Oh, really? And I'm a Grand Matriarch."

"No, really! I ... I worked for her earlier this sol. I bought the dress and the gloves."

"Mauft! What are you standing around for?" Van shouted, but she was rapidly advancing on them. Seeing Sahnassa, her eyebrow furs went up in surprise. "Oh, well now! Stunner! I would have thought you might come to your senses, kit. You sure you want to throw in with us tonight?"

"Very sure, if you'll have me." The statement made Mauft and Vanarra both nearly step back with surprise.

"Okay. Where did you park?"

Embarrassed, Sahnassa admitted, "I ... I had to valet and pay parking. They wouldn't let me in unless I did. I told them about you, but they wouldn't listen."

"Typical," the big gray Anati chuckled. "Put her right down the purebred path, they did."

Vanarra was smirking a little, shaking her head. "They cheated you, kit. They don't charge parking for caterers or their staff - it's part of the fee I pay. Give me your valet slip, and I'll get something worked out. Nice dress, as well. Oh, no," Van put her paws in front of her muzzle to stifle a laugh.

"What? What is it?" Sahnassa asked, embarrassed.

Very gently, the Faelnar-Vulpi reached around to the hem of Sahnassa's dress and lifted it up so they all could see the tag still attached to it. Flicking out a claw-tip, Van nicked out the tag's string and presented it back to Sahnassa who was nearly in tears with shame.

"Oh, don't feel bad, kit. Everyone's done that at some time or other. Did you like buy that dress this sol?"

"I did. Is it okay?"

"Surprised you didn't have one already," Van commented, but then caught herself and stated, "It will do very nicely for tonight. Do you have the paw-gloves? Oh, good, too! Okay, I'm going to pair you up with Mauft here, Sahni. Hey! That ... that just kind of rolled out there!"

"I'm sorry?" Sahnassa queried, confused.

"Short names. Sahnassa de Orturu is a lovely name, but if I have to get your attention quickly, I need something shorter. Can you manage being called 'Sahni'?"

"I suppose I can," the Nephti replied as she shrugged. "I … it kind of sounds nice."

"Good. Now, let's get to work. We've got a long night ahead."

"Thank you, Van. Very much," the Nephti offered as she turned to look up at Mauft. Mauft looked back down; she kind of grunted and chased down Vanarra who had already bounded a few steps away.

"What, Mauft?"

"What am I supposed to do with her? What do you expect her to do?"

"Anything anyone else is doing, period. She's one of the staff; I don't care about families or titles. Now, scoot, Mauft! I've got to get busy, too."

With a groan, the Anati who was almost as big as Flint returned to the Nephti who, although thoroughly embarrassed, was still waiting patiently. "We've got to arrange all of the chairs and tables. Do you think you could manage?"

"Just show me what to do," Sahnassa replied, and Mauft nodded, leading the way.

As Vanarra made her way to the main office of the resort, she realized that she had completely blocked the Nephti from earlier out of her thoughts. She had managed to get Mauft, her admin, to come in and help, so she wasn't in as desperate need as she had been. "Still, here comes this winsome little Nephti purebred, paying parking, buying a dress, and getting herself here on time for the pleasure of working for Van the Anati." Beyond her ability to control it, she started wondering about all of the possible circumstances that could have caused that to happen, and her policy about trying to turn a blind eye to her employees' past was in serious jeopardy. Forgetting an Anati's past was one thing, but purebreds supposedly lived by their honor if they were avowed. "What the heck has she done? She's ticked off someone important, for sure."

After a few tender words in the ear of the concierge who had booked her for the event, all of Sahnassa's fees were rescinded. The full guest list was also presented to her, and that made her happy the Nephti was there after all. Out of the normal ten or fifteen percent who sign up to attend and then don't, almost none had followed the pattern. "The lair's going to be full tonight," she breathed as she walked quickly towards the banquet hall.

Opening the door, she saw that Mauft and Sahni had made some excellent headway already on the chairs and tables, unfortunately. "Hey, you two! We just got word. The lair's full tonight! Mauft, you were building out for 150, right?"

"Yeah. What's the total?"

"We're damned near 180," Van replied walking close. "Sahni, I'm really glad you showed up, because I think we would have been really short pawed if you didn't. As it is, we're going to have to run. I'll tell Flint and the others in the back. Mauft will show you how to rearrange the room. I've got to have it ready in like less than half an interval."

"Oh, crap! Come on, Sahni de Orturu, this is where the job gets crazed," Mauft commented, and Sahnassa followed her to the nearest table, where the Anati was already pulling chairs out from underneath it.

The next interval was a complete blur for everyone Vanarra had brought to the event, and Sahnassa watched amazed as the Vulpi Faelnar did everything from cook to organize to prep to lead and direct. Sahni was grateful when Van put her beside the entrance door to guide the guests into the hall; the Nephti was just about panting at that point. There was also an air of excitement that filled her, watching the rather bland banquet hall transform itself in less than an interval into a space that could be defined as nothing short of magical. She felt more than a little pride when the somewhat jaded conference goers entered the space, and they were just as captivated.

An interval into the event, Vanarra was rapidly working her way through the various stations, making notes about what was running out and what wasn't. Everything, outside of the drinks, were running perfectly, and Vanarra knew she needed to slip out to get some from her back stock in her company hover. Just as she was walking up the hallway towards the open door, she heard two Faelnar talking to one another. "I just found out; this was all put on by some … Anati outfit."

"Really? I thought they were just 'the help'. You saying the place providing our food tonight is actually owned by … an Anati?"

Van held her place and bristled. She just knew this pair was going to make trouble for her or complain about something.

"Good evening, is there anything I can get for you?" Van's eyes went wide; it was her new purebred Nephti. A part of her wanted to jump through the doors and intervene, but stronger still was her desire to actually listen to the conversation.

"Sure, sure. I'd ... I'd like one of those, I guess," the Faelnar replied, a little disgusted. "Say, are ... are these things alright?"

"I'm sorry. Is something wrong?"

"Well, just ... this is like an Anati catering company, right? These things ... okay?"

To Van, it seemed like Sahnassa didn't know what was going on. "Do they not taste good?"

"They do, they do," the other Faelnar interjected. "It's just ... I mean who knows how they were prepared."

"I do," Sahnassa replied firmly. "I saw every phase of their creation. I've watched when my father - he's the head litigator for de Orturu - had events catered. The meat containers were kept strictly at temperature, cutting gloves were used, and all of the produce you're being served tonight came to this building in the sealed containers from the growers. If anything, I saw this group taking more care over a creele salad than I've ever seen before."

"She's got you there," one Faelnar said to the other. "It's not like the last event we went to catered by Glorious didn't make me sick. This stuff tastes better."

"I suppose. So, why are you here?"

"I work for them," Sahnassa replied, straightforward.

"You ... still carry a last name?" the Faelnar asked her, and Van leaned towards the door to hear her response.

"Yes, de Orturu - Sahnassa de Orturu to be exact. Recent graduate of Harnard and winner of the matriarchal scholarship," Sahnassa replied directly.

"Oh. Well, why work for this outfit?"

"I found someone who would treat me with respect and pay me. I'm hoping to work on the technology side for them, as well. It's a growing business. Now, are you sure I couldn't get you anything else?"

"No, no. I ... appreciate it. Everything is just fine," the Faelnar replied, and the pair walked away.

Sahnassa watched them go, trying hard not to smirk. "They were just fine with everything until they knew who was putting on the event, and then look at them." Just then, a warm paw gently grasped her shoulder. Turning around, she looked into the face of the mixed blood who hired her. Her golden eyes, nearly always snapping with focus and direction had gone somewhat soft, and she looked at Sahnassa kindly.

"Thank you, kit," Van told her softly. "But just be very careful how you respond to things like that. If there's any question, let me do it, but still ... this time..." Van squeezed her shoulder again, and Sahni nodded, a little embarrassed by the gratitude she was receiving. "Now, stay focused and keep yourself circulating. We're about halfway through."

"Yes, Van. I will."

"Good, Sahni. Good to have you with us tonight," Van replied before stepping away to deliver the extra fermentum bottles to Flint.

As the last few guests departed, Vanarra called the staff together. "Okay everyone, how did it go?"

Flint spoke up first. "They were way far into the fermentum more than I thought they'd be, but they still were pretty peaceful. We may want to bring more of it inside for the next one of these we do. I had to redirect a couple of guests to other drinks."

"I was really getting the Anati eye," Mauft exhaled. "They ... didn't want to take the food from me at first, but then, as they got a few more drinks down, they didn't seem to care as much."

"Always, be thinking of ways you can make it easier for them," Van cautioned. "Don't take it as an insult."

"But that's what it is!" Sheffer complained.

"Of course, but don't take it that way. Let the purebred avowed live in their own little world, and we'll live in ours." Van almost bit her tongue in two when she realized that her new employee was standing right there. "Sorry, Sahni - everyone, this is Sahnassa de Orturu." Instantly, the group turned to look at the Nephti who had been standing mostly outside of the circle of Van's team until that moment. Nervous, she ducked her head and kind of waved. "Sahni jumped in to help us out tonight, and ... as far as I can tell, she was very good."

"She's not disavowed?" Sheffer asked one of the others, but Van heard it.

"Nope. She's got a de Orturu tacked onto her name all nice and proper, but for as long as she's working with us, she's just one of the team. Treat her with respect, but not as a superior. That, after all, is my job!" Van belted out, proudly, which left the group groaning and took some of the focus off the Nephti.

"Any other comments about tonight?"

There were a few more about waste during food prep or problems with the facility, which the group discussed. Then, Van began making clean-up assignments. Sahnassa and Mauft were again paired for some of the easiest and dirtiest work.

Feeling exhausted, Sahnassa helped Mauft haul out the last bit of trash and stow the rest of the supplies back in the transport. When Sahni glanced at her watch, she realized why she was tired; it was two intervals after high night. "Is that all?" she asked.

"I think so," Mauft replied evenly. "I'll go back in and check with Van."

Sahnassa nodded and sat on a box at the back dock, breathing in the cool night air. It felt so strange for her to be there, but special in a way. A light breeze blew through the ornamental trees that screened the dock area from the places normal guests could see. Before she realized it, the delivery hover for the caterer was pulling away. She was alarmed that she might have been left without having been paid until a draft appeared over her left shoulder.

"Don't panic, kit. I haven't forgotten about you," Vanarra's voice came from behind her.

Taking the draft gently, Sahnassa replied, "Thank you. I'm sorry. I was just worried I had forgotten something."

"No, no, kit. You did fine. I'm … actually grateful to you. There haven't been that many purebreds who ever stood up for me, and … you did it after knowing me half a sol." Van's tone was appreciative, if not just a little suspicious. "You stand up for Anati, often? If so, you'd be the first purebred I know who makes a habit of it."

Sahnassa was a little too tired to be very careful what she said, and Vanarra was counting on that. Something about the Nephti just bothered her, but not in a normal way. It was a sense that nearly demanded Van trust her, but that was blind trust - and knowing very little about this Nephti kept her from paying any more than curiosity as tribute to that impulse. Watching carefully for any signs of a lie, Van studied her as she answered.

"The truth is I haven't had many opportunities to stand up for anyone. I'm usually stuck doing that for myself. I didn't like what they were saying, and it didn't match what I saw. No reason they should make a snap judgment like that."

"That happen to you a lot?"

"Yeah, kind of. Technologists get a bad reputation as being a little … socially insecure. It's probably deserved. We spend so much time studying or working, we don't get out."

"I don't socialize that much either. I don't have time for it. There's too much to do. So, I … was curious about what we discussed earlier. Do you think you'd still want to come over and help us with a TransNet site?"

"I would. There would be some equipment to buy," Sahnassa explained. "We'd need a room with good ventilation and power. I'd need to interview you and whoever else you think should contribute, pull together the site flow and graphics. Then, there's setting up the software and configuring it–"

"Whoa, whoa, whoa!" Van replied, chuckling. "That sounds like you'd need to be working in our office … for a good long while. You serious about that? You know, I have a couple of purebreds - a pair of Vulpi - but disavowed purebreds. You'd be the only family-blessed one of the bunch. You'd do that?" Van looked at her, curiously.

"Why not? Everyone I've worked with tonight was nice enough. I mean, Mauft wasn't all that friendly, but she wasn't ugly to me, either. It actually felt really good to help get this event done." Tired as she was, Sahnassa realized that Van had doubts about the arrangement. "You're worried about something. What is it, if I may ask?"

Vanarra sighed and sat down beside her on the box, and then looked at her. "You didn't move away."

"Oh, I'm sorry," Sahnassa replied and shifted herself to give Vanarra more room.

"No, that's just it, kit. You were perfectly okay with me sitting beside you just now. There are purebreds who won't even stand in the same room with me for fear someone in their house - a matron or dame - might find out. I don't understand you, kit. I tend not to trust what I don't fully understand."

Sahnassa was instantly worried, sensing her one possible job avenue was in danger, so she closed her eyes, sighed, and decided to confess. "You said I wasn't to tell you about my past, but you should be aware of something. I've … invoked the Compact."

Van shook her head. "I have no idea what that means, kit."

"I … have asked my family not to help me. They … they were interfering a lot with what I was doing, getting into school, so I used a fairly drastic method of getting them off my tail. In short, it means that you won't see my matron popping up on your door or my house questioning if I sit close to you or not. Besides, I … I don't feel like moving away from you, Vanarra. I'm too tired, and there'd be no good reason for me to."

"No good reason?" Van nearly scoffed, but managed to keep most of the derision out of her tone. "I've been treated like that my whole life, kit. It's a bit unusual when a purebred just up and treats me like I'm one, too. It's only happened once in my life before, and it was a Nephti, so that's a point in your favor. If you were to come and work in my office, you'd be doing the technologist bit, for sure, but in case we need help, like we did tonight, you'd be on-call. There'd be no special treatment for you, and if you mess up, I'll boot your tail out the door just like anyone else. Is that the kind of arrangement a purebred avowed really wants to live with?"

"If it's a good place to work and … if you treated me with respect, like you have this sol, yes. I need a job, Vanarra, I won't lie to you. I have school loans coming due and food to buy and rent to pay. I want to prove to my family and to myself that I can manage on my own. I've worked hard for five seasons learning. I want to put that to use."

"Even if it's for an Anati business?" Van questioned. "That doesn't make sense to me."

"I've seen catering firms my father hired do half as much for twice what you charge. That was one of the nicest banquets I've ever been to, and I'm not flattering here - that's the truth. I don't care about labels - I … want to live better than that, if you'll have me."

"On a trial basis," Van replied, looking forward. "That's how everyone starts. You'll have to impress me if you want to stay. I don't give a lost piece of tail fur for what your family says about you.

You've got to prove to me that you're worth keeping and that your ideas makes sense. I'm the one who makes the call; there's no argument; there's no debate. It's my business. I'll hire who I like and fire who I don't."

"That's how it should be," Sahnassa agreed.

That surprised Van a little, and she looked back at the Nephti, trying to gauge how honest that reply was. Seeing no signs of deception, she continued, "Okay then, second thing. We serve some events that are … interesting, from time to time. Perhaps some would even consider them a little … racy. The Thurians who hire us demand we keep quiet about what they do and who was in attendance. If you can't keep your muzzle shut, let's just forget this right now, because I'll kick your tail out the door and ruin your name with every business partner I know if you blurt out something. If someone asks, you were in the back and didn't see anything. Got it?"

"I do," came the earnest reply. "I will keep quiet, but if anything … illegal is going on, I won't be able to stay."

"Improper in the minds of some, but nothing that is illegal in the eyes of enforcement. Houses make a bunch of different rules, and frankly I don't care what they think. You're working for me, not for them," Van asserted firmly. "Oh, and another thing - absolutely no hunts in the office or with our clients. I won't have it, and it's bad for business."

"I … understand, oh - I'm so sorry," Sahnassa replied, but a stifled yawn in the middle of her sentence caused her blush furs to go up. That humiliated expression looking back at her from an avowed Nephti reminded Van a little of Sorla.

"It's okay, kit. It's late. Here," Van offered, reaching into her pocket and tossing a fruit stick to Sahnassa. "It has a little something in it to keep you going and alert. It's totally natural, and legal - thank you very much, but I won't have you driving your hover into someone's lair because you were too tired. Don't show up before mid-sol, tomorrow, either. Get some rest. We can talk other details then."

"Thank you, Van, very much."

"You too, kit. You, too. Here's your valet ticket. Don't even worry about tipping them. They were caught with their paws somewhere they shouldn't be, and the catering director was none too happy with them. At any future events, I'll see that you get clear instructions on where to park and what to do."

Sahnassa stood, turned around, and gently took the ticket from Van's paw. "I can't thank you enough for that."

"Good night, kit."

Sahnassa nodded in something like a bow and then walked back into the building, leaving Van looking up at the sky and thinking. "What do you think, Ash? Is this one going to punch *me* in the gut?" Something inside of her said no, but her confused instincts still wouldn't permit that answer to be accepted on faith.

Chapter 14: Initially

Nervous and nearly shaking, Sahnassa drove up to the building whose address was on the card Vanarra had given her the previous night. "Looks … pretty alright," she observed. Double-checking the address before she set down, Sahnassa was distracted and tried to shut off the engine before the skids were lowered. A loud beeping and a countdown made her scramble for the controls to land properly. "Oh, I hope nobody saw that," she said to herself, shaking her head. She was trying to get by on only a few intervals of sleep. Most of the morning, she had been working on the presentation and sample TransNet site for Vanarra's business, making a lot of guesses, but hoping that it would showcase her abilities to the mixed blood. "Oh, I've got to make this work," she told herself. On the way over, she had deposited her pay from the resort engagement, but it wouldn't be enough to even cover her initial student loan installment.

Trying to be careful, she opened the squeaky wing door of her hover and stepped out. With very deliberate intention, she extracted the portable computer she had used in academy, shut the hover door, and made for the building. Taking in every detail, she saw that the structure was relatively new. It was strictly functional, having little more than tapered corners that suggested the normal smooth lines and natural features that were almost universally preferred. "Still," she thought, "it *is* in good condition with a pretty sign."

Walking up to the door and opening it, she was instantly nearly face to face with the large admin, Mauft. "We're not open yet."

"Oh," Sahnassa apologized, "I'm … I guess I am a little early. Should … I come back?"

Mauft rolled her eyes and stepped back to allow the Nephti to enter the small waiting room. "Have a seat. Vanarra will see you when she's available." Then, the Nephti-Lupar mix walked back to her desk and started going through her paperwork.

"Okay," Sahnassa said as quietly as she could and put her things down. Sitting, she tried to look busy by taking out a pad and making notes about what she was going to say. In many ways, she was more nervous about this interview than any of the others. If this one failed, then she'd have no choice but to go back to her parents and plead for mercy. Time was simply running out.

The passes dragged on, and Sahnassa's lack of sleep started making itself known. She was halfway through a stifled yawn when Vanarra burst into the office. "Mauft, has there been any sign of that Nephti – oh, well now! You came after all!"

"I'm sorry. I guess I was a little early … and you were busy," Sahnassa explained, standing up.

Van looked down at Mauft curiously for a moment before replying, "Oh, okay. Well, I set some time aside for you. You've got something to show me?" Van asked, pointing to the computer on the floor.

"Yes. Just a sample TransNet site. I wanted to show you the kinds of things I could set up for you."

"You mean set up for my customers," Van corrected. "If I'm going to put something out on TransNet, I want it to outclass everything else the other catering firms have out there."

"Well, I … I guess then perhaps we should start by seeing what they have," Sahnassa replied, nervously, picking up her portable computer.

"Sounds good to me. Come back to my office. Mauft, please make sure we aren't disturbed, will you?"

"Yes, Van," the gray one replied.

Sahnassa was now terrified that she had completely failed in her preparations to meet with Van. Her one course on requirements gathering stressed that non-technical users wouldn't be impressed with technology or its abilities. They simply wanted their requirements fulfilled; much of what she had prepared showcased how scalable and flexible the site would be – technical points of merit, but not much that flashed or had wonderful graphics. "So, did you get some sleep? Kit?"

The Nephti scrambled to answer, realizing that she'd been lost in thought when her perspective employer was asking a question. "Yes, well, some … I guess. Sorry. I … I wanted to have something prepared for you."

"Good … initiative," Van offered, again bemused by how much this Nephti wanted to please her. "I will definitely want to see it. Do you want to start there, then?"

"No, Van. I … I think your way is best."

"Oh, the boss always likes to hear that," Van chuckled wickedly.

For the next half interval, Vanarra listed out her competitors, and Sahnassa searched the TransNet and found them. As they went through the sites, Sahnassa was really surprised at how technically simple they were. Many were just pattern sites, made from taking some cheap template and throwing material in. As Van looked at them, it was clear that she was disappointed, too. "I … I can't believe I'm losing market share … to this!" she finally said, looking at the Glorious Celebrations site. "What do you think?"

"I'm appalled, honestly. It's like they didn't even try. I mean, the graphics are nice, but you can't even order anything on-line. Everything just routes back to LineCom, TransNet mail, or … courier? Really? I … this is like first season … wow, really … lacking much structure and well now!" A big warning appeared on the screen of Sahnassa's computer indicating a suspicious response had been received and deflected.

"Maybe this TransNet site business is just a fad or something," Van mused.

"Actually, there are some really great sites out there. They're not catering, but, can I show you?" Van nodded, and Sahnassa took her on a quick tour of a videographer and a photographer and several corporate pack sites, and she pointed out features of the sites to Van.

"Wow," Vanarra breathed. "That looks really nice! Are you saying you could do that for me, kit?" she asked, dubiously.

"Let me show you my sample site. It's capable of all the basic functions I showed you, VidStar preview, music, on-line ordering, and even creating private sites for individual clients to go and see their pictures, make comments, whatever." Van leaned forward, in rapt attention, watching as Sahnassa clicked through her demo.

"And you could actually do this, kit? You could make this happen?"

"The graphics need some work—"

"Oh, I have an artist that works for me, don't worry about that. You want images, you'll have them," Van asserted. "Now, about those private sites – how private can they be? I have clients who are absolutely insistent on security."

"We can give them a pass phrase that's very difficult to guess, one that would even take house security some time to break."

"How long would it take them?" Van asked pointedly.

"If I use the strongest ciphers I was taught, it may take them ten moons or more, even with the very best equipment," Sahnassa stated, and that made Vanarra smile.

"I'm liking what I see, kit. Now, let's talk seriously for a moment. I've been doing my own research, and there are a few things I want to make clear. I'm not going to hire you, if we decide to move forward. I'm going to place you under contract. From what I've heard from a friend of mine, that's the best way to keep your house off your back and see my interests are protected. I'll also pay upon the delivery of features. So, for example, you get a prototype up and running locally, that will be one paycheck, and so on. Once the site is up and stable, we'll discuss maintenance."

"Would I still be able to work events, as well?" Sahnassa asked.

"Yes, but … not every event. There are some events I keep open for only certain staff. In time, maybe, but no promises," Van warned. "Now, the other part of what I was told. I don't want to buy the most expensive equipment to run this. I want to be absolutely sure that what I buy is helping my business and not going for any other purpose. I want to spend as little as I can to get as much as I can."

"I'll do everything I can to keep your costs down, and I already have a basic idea of what it would take. Here," Sahnassa offered as she changed to a different application, "is what I think you'd be looking at in terms of equipment. This is basic, reliable stuff with good ratings."

Van shook her head, looking at the bottom line. "I … would do everything I could to get discounts on that, find used equipment in good condition," Sahnassa put in.

"Well, it is higher than I want to go, but ... I could do it. It had better work, though, kit, or you and this equipment would both be out of here. Everyone else working here has no house family to fall back on if things don't work out. If we don't succeed, we don't eat. You've got to appreciate that and understand it fully if I'm going to contract with you."

"I'm, believe it or not, much in the same situation. If this doesn't work out for me, some very unpleasant things will happen that will pretty much ruin the rest of my life."

"Then it sounds like you're motivated, kit. Okay, let's work on a contract and talk through some of the details. After that, Sahni, you're going back to your lair with an advance to get you started and an order from me to get some sleep. You've held up well, but ... you're struggling. Okay?" Van's understanding smile made Sahnassa smile back, and relaxing, the Nephti felt a yawn coming on, and she turned her head to hide it. "Oh yeah, kit. I can tell."

A few passes later, Vanarra was saying her goodbyes to her new technologist and watching her leave. "You hired her?" Mauft asked, a little accusatorily. "You going to use her for events, too?"

"I put her on contract. She did alright last night, didn't she?"

"I suppose I can't say she was any less useful than anyone else on their first sol, but ... avowed, Van? That's going to make some in the office really nervous."

"I'm not sure I'm alright with it all the way, to tell you the truth," Van admitted. "With purebreds, the family comes first, if they have one, that is. We'll keep her in reserve for everything but primals and pre-joins; I'll have to know Sahnassa de Orturu a long while before I let her do one of those."

"She'd probably run right out and tell her matron all about it," Mauft grumbled.

"Yeah, about that. If any of her 'family jewels' show up, I want to know. She's working for me, not for them, and if she can't figure that out, she'll be gone so fast her tail will beat the rest of her out the door."

"Came dressed for work, I see," Vanarra commented upon seeing Sahnassa at her door the next morning. The Nephti was dressed in clothes that were nearly threadbare, with splotches of paint on them.

"I'm sorry," Sahni apologized. "You said something casual, and I kind of don't have much. The school had a uniform, but ... it wasn't made for doing anything physical."

"It's okay. Just stay out of the front lobby in case any clients show up," Van warned, as she stood. "Now, what's the first thing you need to do?"

"Well, we need to find a place for your servers – the computers that are going to run your TransNet site."

Van's eyebrow fur cocked over her right eye. "Do they need to be somewhere special?"

"Most companies I visited during school did have them in a place where ... no one who was visiting could just walk in. For many of these companies, those servers represented a lot of money and revenue, so they were pretty cautious with them."

"A lot of money and revenue," Van quoted back. "Can't say I can argue with that. Shall we take a look around?"

"Oh, yes, please."

As Van walked into the hallway, she saw a fairly nice satchel sitting on the floor. "What's that?"

"Oh, my tools. I had to buy a set when I was in school for my hardware courses. I ... just wanted to be prepared," the Nephti said tentatively.

"Okay," Van replied slowly, and nervously, Sahnassa stooped down and picked them up, sensing her boss had some displeasure at things being left in the hallway. "Let's start in the back and work our way forward, shall we?" Sahnassa nodded, and Van reached into her pockets for the keys. Inwardly, she was chiding herself for making the Nephti feel uncomfortable about her clothes and what she was doing. However, there was an aspect of fun that Van found difficult to resist. This Nephti ducked her eyes and head a bit whenever she spoke to Van, acknowledging her as a superior – not even Saiphar and Tresk did that.

Van toured the Nephti past an office that was filled with boxes. "That's probably too large and ... the power isn't right. It's a lot of space to spend on servers."

"How big a space does this need to be?" Vanarra asked as they entered the warehouse. Sheffer and Raska took instant notice of Sahnassa, and words were discretely exchanged.

Her blush furs raised, Sahnassa answered, "Only a few tracks long by a few tracks wide, but power and air handling need to be there."

Van cocked her head as if she was sifting her thoughts. "Back this way," she said and reversed directions. Coming to a closet, she keyed the lock and opened it. Turning on the light, she revealed a room chocked full of small boxes on little shelves. "This is where we keep a lot of the expensive fermentum – the stuff normally comes in small bottles but … a lot of clients and, well, some of our staff, find it pretty tasty. That's why we have to keep it in here."

Sahnassa stepped in as far as she could, her head turned as if she was trying to recognize something. Seeing it, she almost laughed but caught herself. Fixed a couple of tracks in front of a wall were "shelves" that had been extended with custom-made pieces to one side – allowing someone to stack boxes behind them. "Something funny?" Van asked.

Grimacing to herself that she'd been caught, Sahnassa turned – embarrassed – to face Van. "Uh, the shelf here, is … it's where the computers are supposed to go. This was the room the architect designed for it. It's got air, main power, and … this part of the shelf, what I'm guessing was originally here, was … is meant to hold computers and TransNet communication equipment. I'm sorry; it just … caught me by surprise."

Vanarra frowned as she looked at the Nephti. She had actually been quite impressed by Tresk's little bit of carpentry that had made the space useful. Now, all of that had to be undone, and she had the problem of where to securely store all of this expensive stock. A little mental shifting of her inventory reminded her that she'd recently acquired some storage cabinets, and they could be locked. "Are you sure this is what is needed?"

Sahnassa looked at the floor, sensing the displeasure from her boss, but answered truthfully, "This is very much like what I've seen, and because of the heat the computers generate, the space really shouldn't be any smaller. Any larger, and you'll probably feel like you're wasting space."

"I'm starting to feel like that already," Van grumped, and leaned out into the hallway. "Tresk! Come up front, please! Sheffer, you too!" Leaning back in, Van asked Sahnassa pointedly, "Are you damned sure this is the only place for your … servers?"

"Unless there's another room like this you haven't shown me yet..." and Sahnassa hesitated as Van held her fixed in a snapping appraisal. "Well, yes," she answered softly, "this is where it needs to be."

Van's scowl grew worse just as the pair walked up. "What'cha got, boss?"

"Our new technologist says this is where our computers should go. What do you think?"

Tresk's brow furrowed, and he crowded Van a little looking in. "Uh, yeah – maybe. How many computers?"

"Four, with a TransNet switch, emergency power units, and a few viewers."

"This room won't handle the heat load, well – as is," Tresk contested. "We'd need to cut ventilation into the door, maybe reroute a vent. Power might be a problem, too."

"It depends on what we buy," Sahni put forth shyly. "Some of the newer stuff is fairly reasonable and doesn't get quite so hot."

"Is there any place else we have, Tresk?" Van asked. "Couldn't we just lock them in a cabinet or something?"

"Yeah, if you want them to burn up, get spilled on, or if you want them to sprout hind legs and track it out of here. I worked contract at a place before yours, and they had a set-up like this one."

Van turned on Tresk, confused. "Then why did you build this up as storage?"

"You told me to, and you didn't have anything other than the one office computer," Tresk countered. "But Nephti de Orturu here is right. If you're going to set up computers in here, we need to clear it out."

"Well, can you and Raska and Sheffer help 'Nephti de Orturu' get all of this unloaded, secured someplace else, and then make it ready for the arrival of our new equipment?" Looking back at Sahnassa, she asked, "You don't have a problem with lending a paw, do you?"

"No, certainly not." Van's back-fur went up, her lips curled above her teeth, and her claws slightly expressed. "I'm sorry, I meant I don't have any problem with helping, really!" Sahnassa apologized, backing as far into the closet as she could.

Settling down again, Van was now more angry at herself than anyone else. "Flint!" she shouted. Shuffling in the room next door and the heavy steps down the hall signaled his approach.

"You bellowed?" he asked.

"Take charge of this project, Flint. It's … just pissing me off!" With that, Van turned on her heels and strode past Tresk, went to her office, and slammed the door.

All too cheerily, Tresk told Sahnassa, "And welcome to your first purebred avowed sol at Celebrations by Vanarra! I suppose we should get started. No use ticking her off even more."

With a knot in her stomach, Sahnassa followed the lead of the others by grabbing a few boxes and heading towards the warehouse.

On the other side of her door, Van sat down on her office couch and put her head in her paws. "Why the mange did I just do that?" she asked. "Why?"

"Purebred telling you what to do," her mind answered quickly. That made her angry all over again, and she stood up, intending to walk out, fire the Nephti, and be done with the whole project. As her paw touched the door, she stopped. At some level, Van knew she was being irrational and unfair. Hesitating, she turned back and started pacing. "I'm not going to let some little avowed purebred tell me how I can run my business!" she mumbled to herself.

"Uh, well, you did hire her," Flint replied from the doorway. "You … aren't okay about this, Van," he noted, stepping in and closing the door behind himself. "We had a computer room like this at the place where I used to work. I don't think she's making an unreasonable suggestion. You know, you … you were pretty harsh to the kit. She's pretty well cleaning the floor with her tail as she walks, right now."

"Just … take charge of the clean-out and … getting the closet ready. If everything gets stored and secured okay and doesn't cause too much of a problem," Van sighed as she went and sat in her desk chair. "I … suppose I can be alright with that."

"Okay," Flint said softly. Turning towards the door, he looked back at her and started to add, "Just—"

Leaning over the desk, she knew what he was going to say. "She has to learn who's the boss, Flint. She doesn't set the order of things around here."

"It's not a problem with her knowing who the boss is; it's now a question if her boss can be fair to a purebred avowed or if that's impossible. I was in the storeroom when she came in, walked past you two when you went in the closet. I'll talk to her about … being careful around you, and I'll have her work through me so you don't have to deal with her, if you want. Just understand, she'll have no chance of getting us up on a TransNet site if you can't have a little compassion for her."

All the fire went out of Van, and again, she put her head in her paws. "And we need that damned TransNet site, I know. Okay, Flint. Okay. Just … take care of this for me right now. I … I need to … take a pass or two – maybe intervals."

"Alright, but just think if you want her to leave the office this sol with what you said to her as your final word." Flint quietly left the office, leaving Vanarra alone, trying to work out her swirling emotions.

Flint looked at the work the trio had been doing over the last few intervals. All of the fermentum that had been stored in the would-be computer room was now safely stored in the various locking cabinets in the warehouse. They had moved those together on one wall after all of the other material within had been unloaded and placed in other areas. It had taken some effort to find all of the keys, since the cabinets had never been locked before. There was some fermentum that was out of date, which was good, since the cabinets were filled to capacity. They would need at least one more to carry the normal stock, which he knew would make Vanarra all the more irritable. Still, he put the best face on it he could.

"Good way to work together. I think this will work out."

"I guess I need to start taking down the shelving in the closet," Tresk sighed, looking accusingly at Sahnassa.

"I'll … help," she offered, meekly.

"Well, in a few passes. Sahni, I'd like to talk to you for a moment. Tresk, if you wouldn't mind getting started on taking down the shelves."

"It's work; you pay me if I mind or not!" he replied, shrugging and went towards the front of the building. Sheffer and Raska had already gone back to their tasks. While Tresk moved towards another part of the warehouse to get his tools, Sahnassa meekly followed the big mixed blood into his office.

"Close the door and have a seat, Sahni," he directed her. As he sat, he was pleased to see that she had done exactly as he asked without question. She, like nearly everyone else he interacted with, was intimidated by his size, but she was managing to keep herself under control and not get angry or flighty.

"Sahnassa, you impress me as someone who's had to live through some tough things, am I right?" She shrugged a little and nodded, but didn't look him in the eye. "You need to understand some things if you're going to avoid what happened with Van. Although what you went through was probably very hard, I can tell you that what Vanarra's dealt with in her life has been much, much tougher. Most of that pain came from purebreds. She hasn't told me many details of her past, but I can read Thurians pretty well, especially Anati. She's worked very, very hard to get this business to where it is, and without question, she's in charge."

"I ... understand. I ... didn't think I did anything to question that," Sahnassa quietly replied.

"You may have done so unintentionally. Did you tell her there was something she had to do? Did you phrase it like that?" he asked helpfully.

Sahnassa sat up and looked at him, and then furrowed her eyebrow fur. "I ... I was ... trying to be nice about it, but ... maybe? Yes?"

Flint nodded, knowingly. "That was it. You may not have meant it to sound that way, but Van reacted as if you told her what to do. In time, you might have that kind of rapport with her, but you don't right now. If anything, and I hate to say this, who you are and what you are will make that tougher."

Sahnassa nodded. "I'm ... beginning to appreciate that. I'm really getting a taste of what it's like to be ... different."

"Oh, and I'm sure some will do that intentionally. We've all suffered in some way because we were treated like we were less than fully Thurian. If you are going to succeed here, you are going to have to accept that fact and do your best to overcome it."

"How? I ... don't know what to do," Sahni confessed, sadly.

"Well, start by asking, not telling. Think about the different ways you could have let Vanarra choose the right alternative. It may have taken more time to go around the office, but if you could have given her options, she would have chosen the right answer."

"So when she asked me if the closet was the right place, I shouldn't have answered that it was, even though it was," Sahni asked, a little disturbed by the illogical nature of that approach.

"If she asks you if that is where it has to be, you answer, the decision is yours, Vanarra. You're the boss."

Sahni shook her head. "But she *is* the boss! She knows that; I know that!"

"Right, but she's not seeing that level of respect from you, and it's going to have to be more respect than the others show, fair or not. If she feels you don't respect her, you'll take a bite into her pride, and let me tell you that's a mistake that's hard to fix. I've done it in different ways, and I've had to change how I deal with her. She is ... very kind inside, but she is tough, and some in the past – purebreds – have tried to push her around, even when they were working for her. They were fired and given a transport ticket out of town – literally."

Sahnassa's eyes were wide as she nodded acknowledgement to what he was saying. "Oh, okay! I'm ... I had no idea."

"Well, be attentive to it, and never forget it, no matter how familiar she gets with you or how light-hearted she might seem to be. What you just saw is never far underneath the surface if you approach her the wrong way. The others, too. The outside world might consider you purebred and avowed, but in here, you – in many ways – are the Anati outcast."

"Wow," Sahni breathed, nearly slumping over with recognition.

"In time, you might be able to work up to being treated as an equal. That will be a long trail that will require you to sacrifice your pride, but ... I think you'd eventually be happy with being here if that was true."

"Happy or not, I ... really need for this to work," she admitted to Flint. "I'll try to do better."

"I know you will. Now, if I had to make a suggestion about your next move, I would offer to cart away from the closet anything that Tresk tells you to, and put it where he tells you, okay?"

"Yes, Flint. Thank you."

"Thank you for listening, Sahni. You're an exceptional kit for doing that much," he told her, offering his paw. Smiling, she took it, as best she could, returning his gentle clasp.

Vanarra had skipped lunch and kept herself busy with paperwork, at first, and then office cleaning, and then finally surrendered to Flint's suggestion and thought about what she was feeling. Over her history, even with Sorla and Gorta, there hadn't been anything like this little Nephti in her experience, she thought at first. Then, she remembered Muriella. The Faelnar who looked somewhat like her mother had drawn ire out of Vanarra she'd never really felt before. It came up from time to time when she had to fire someone for an indiscretion, but never like it had with Muriella.

She and Tresk had talked through that incident, and Tresk – a spectator of many watering hole fights – was amazed that she hadn't unleashed a claw-strike. Since that conversation, she'd tried to keep a cap on her anger. For the most part, she had been successful. "Stunk like crap, this sol, though," she admitted to herself. "Sahnassa … she didn't really do anything wrong. I could have still said no, couldn't I have? Was I … angry because I was afraid I'd go along with what she said? Damned silly, Van. Ash would have called me on that one."

Sadly, she remembered an argument with the one she had loved so long ago. They had almost gone their separate ways one evening because he had warned her off doing something he thought was risky. He was only protecting her, but it felt like he was suddenly calling her "stupid." Deferring to the knowledge of this new Nephti was much the same issue. "I can't put the damned thing in myself. She's shown me really great-looking stuff I'd love to have. I'm … yeah Ash, okay. I'm … intimidated. You got me again."

Van leaned back into her chair and looked at the clock. It was near the end of the nominal work intervals, and the banging and other various noises she had heard coming under her door had tapered off. "Oh, this should be just wonderful," Van sighed to herself as she stood, fully aware of what was required of her.

Opening her office door, she found the hallway quiet, and the door to the computer closet was open – a strong smell of paint wafting to her nose. "Hmm… I wonder where the Nephti went?" she thought to herself, presuming it was Tresk who was doing the painting.

"Hey, Tresk—" she called, but as she leaned in, a startled yelp came from the Nephti who almost spilled her paint. Some of it was streaked on the fur of her face and on her clothes. She recognized Tresk's wall patching work, which the Nephti was now painting over. "Well, now. Is this looking more like what you had in mind?"

The Nephti was quiet for a moment and answered carefully. "I … it matters more what you think of it."

Van leaned against the doorframe, a little bemused by her response. "I don't think I've seen that many server rooms, actually. It seems a little silly to have that one rack all by itself. Is that really necessary?"

Again, the Nephti was thinking furiously for a moment before she answered. "There … are options, I suppose. The computers need the airflow, but if we had several racks in here, I … I suppose we could use fans, perhaps cut a couple of holes in the door for airflow, cover them with metal grates."

"How did we do storing what was in here?" Van asked, still finding this conversation somewhat surprising.

"Would you like for me to show you what we did?" Sahnassa asked, for clarification.

"Sure," Van replied, and Sahni quickly put down her paint, rubbed it off her paws onto a rag, and stood up.

"Most of it went to the storeroom, in the back," Sahnassa explained, hesitating, waiting for Vanarra to go first.

"Oh, okay," Van replied walking ahead. Entering the storeroom, she instantly noticed what had moved. "Hey, what are all of those doing along the wall?"

"That's where Flint had us put all the expensive swill," Tresk said from nearby. "At least it's together."

"What happened to the stuff that was in these?" Van asked as she tried a cabinet door, finding it locked.

"It was all regular inventory, and we had room," Tresk supplied. "But Nephti de Orturu here's little adventure in the closet is going to force us to buy another cabinet. We don't have enough space. We had to throw some of the old stuff out."

"Was it out of date?"

"Yes, but Sheffer said we had some coming in tomorrow," Tresk warned. "We really should have a cabinet in here ready for it."

"Can you stay late?"

"Long enough to go get it, but not to put it together."

"I'll do it," Sahnassa supplied, "if you'd like," she corrected quickly.

Van nodded and said, "Tresk, you two go up and buy one and bring it back here. I ... have some work to do. I can stay late with her."

"Suits me. Come on, Nephti de Orturu. Head out back, and I'll join you in a bit," Tresk directed her. Looking to Van for permission, the Nephti waited.

"Go ahead. I'll see you when you get back."

As Sahnassa disappeared out the back door, Van slipped a little closer to Tresk. "So, what do you think of her?"

"Eh," Tresk scoffed. "Nothing all that special. Cute and all, but not as keen as a Vulpi is to my eye."

Van chuckled. "Tresk, I didn't mean if you wanted to hunt her or not, what do you think of her?"

"I think she's scared, can't figure out how she stepped on your tail, but Flint must have set her straight. She came out of his office a lot ... well, I don't know."

"Yeah, I picked up on that, too. In the store, do a little experiment for me. You go ask the price for a cabinet. Then, have her come back and ask the same thing."

"Take the cheaper?" Tresk asked, smirking.

"Yep. Now get on with it," she replied in good humor.

An interval later, Sahnassa's stomach was grumbling a complaint that it hadn't eaten in quite awhile. As she was nearly done assembling the new cabinet, she ignored it. The warehouse was very quiet now, except for what she was doing, and the feeling of loneliness was starting to gnaw on her as much as her hunger was. As she finished putting together the lock, she thought about the little exercise Tresk had told her to do. The Nephti at the supply store had quoted Tresk one hundred and sixty for the cabinet. Yet even as bedraggled, paint-smeared, and poorly dressed as she was, when she showed her family identity card, the price dropped to one hundred. That had made her angry, and it gave her some cause for thought.

"They really do have it so much harder, and ... for no real reason. This cabinet didn't have any less value to a Nephti than it did to an Anati. Why overcharge him so? It's wrong. It's just wrong," she said to herself.

"What's wrong?" Vanarra asked from the door to the warehouse.

"Oh! I'm sorry! I ... it's this," she said, pointing accusingly at the cabinet.

"Problems putting it together?" Van asked.

"Well, honestly ... it has more to do with what we paid for it."

Van shrugged. "Heard from Tresk we got a sweet deal on it, thanks to you."

"Yes, but it shouldn't have been thanks to me. They should have quoted Tresk the same price," Sahnassa complained.

"That's how life is for us, kit. Get paid less and get charged more," Van asserted, resigned. "Not everyone plays by those rules, but many do. So, is it done?"

"Yes. I have the keys," she said, offering those up to Van.

Van took the keys gently from Sahnassa's open paw and replied, "Thank you, kit. About ... earlier," Van started, realizing she had forgotten to apologize.

"I am so very sorry for that," Sahni interjected, bowing her head and turning to the side. "I ... approached that the wrong way. My fault."

"Yeah. Especially when, upon a little deeper reflection, I was kind of ... ugly about what you were like ... telling me. Sorry about that – some raw places there for me. Things I need to work on," Van replied, and she hadn't been looking at the Nephti at all while she said it. Looking back, she saw those big indigo eyes of the Nephti looking at her with an expression of surprise and appreciation, even a little admiration.

Just then, a weird gurgling noise echoed in the otherwise vacant warehouse. Sahnassa's blush furs flew straight up, and Van's eyes went wide. "That was ... you!?"

"Yes, sorry," Sahni apologized, embarrassed. "I ... kind of skipped lunch. I'll be alright. As soon as I finish painting, I'll ... what?" Sahni asked, seeing Van's smirk.

"Come and see," Van directed her. As she followed her boss down the hall, she was amazed to find that all of the patches had been painted, and very well. "I've been busy, too – by way of apology. Now, you're hungry, and I'm hungry. De Kesto's is pretty empty this late. Why don't we go get something? I'm buying."

Despite how she looked and how worried she might be about trying to carry on conversations with her new boss, her memory of eating there with Merialla and Lashahar was more than enough motivation for her to agree. "Oh, yes, thank you! That ... would be very nice."

"We could talk about next steps for the TransNet site, perhaps get to know one another a little better?" Van queried.

"Yes, thank you. That's sounds good." Given the bare state of her lair, Sahnassa was in no hurry to return to it.

"Good. If you want to hit the washroom in the back, I ... might have something around that you could throw on, just for dinner. Sound okay?"

"Oh, wow! Thank you, yes!"

As Sahnassa turned to go to the facilities, Van thought to herself, "Well, she's not ashamed of being seen with me, so we're on the right trail. Either that, or she's really, really hungry."

"Look at that hover!" Sahnassa breathed in awe as they stepped outside. The shiny gold hover looked like it was capable of actually flying.

"Just a little something I picked up," Van said proudly. "You want to follow?"

"Sure," Sahnassa replied, a bit embarrassed, walking towards her own bedraggled red vehicle.

"Well, perhaps you could ride along ... this time," Vanarra offered, seeing the sag in the kit's shoulders and tail.

"Okay!" Sahnassa replied happily. "Thank you again for the clothes!" The long black skirt and fitted white blouse were far better than anything she now owned.

"It's actually a serving uniform, so be careful and don't get anything on it, if you can help it."

"You actually serve at banquets wearing something this nice?"

"From time to time," Van stated as she keyed the button on her entry coder to cause the doors of the hover to raise and the engines to start.

"Oh, wow! It's … it's like a spaceship!"

Van chuckled, "Get in. You'll find it rides like one, too." Sahnassa worked herself inside, surprised by the tight-fitting seat. "It's a five point harness," Van explained as she got in.

"Five point what?" Sahni queried, confused.

"Like this, kit," Van explained, and then reached over and pulled the two halves from either side of her and the base strap from below. Sahni's eyebrow fur went up in surprise, and carefully, she tried to emulate what her boss had just done. "Oh sorry, kit," Vanarra apologized when the two halves wouldn't reach around the Nephti. "Would you mind?"

"No, please go ahead," Sahnassa explained. Popping out of her harness, Van quickly leaned over, adjusted Sahni's with a few deft motions, secured the Nephti, and then was back in her own harness in under ten ticks. "Wow! Uh, whoa!" Sahnassa shouted as the last motion in Van's series of fluid movements sent the hover zipping off the ground and speeding out of the lot with a force that shoved her firmly back into her seat.

"Has nice pick-up, doesn't it!"

"Like … being … launched!" Sahnassa exhaled, panting as the craft attained its cruising speed. That made Vanarra laugh, and for the moment, she forgot she was with a purebred avowed employee from her office.

"Sorry, kit. I can be a bit of a show-off sometimes, I suppose. So, is this your first time in a sports hover?" Van asked as she roll-cornered onto the next trail.

"Well, yes, wow!" Sahni replied nervously. "You're … a really great driver!"

"Was that little red hover yours?"

"I've had it since before I left home, five seasons ago. I … I didn't have a lot of money to keep it up like I should, and it's had its share of misadventures. Van!"

Sahni's shout made Vanarra giggle as she pressed the over-thrust control to push over an abandoned hover in front of them. Sahnassa screamed, terrified, until she realized what had happened. "You … you've got over-thrust!"

"Keeps me out of trouble, more or less. I take it you've never had a ride like this before?"

"Uh, no, and I'm thinking it was a good thing I rode with you. I'd … never be able to keep up!"

Vanarra laughed again and then continued to give her passenger the ride of her life until they pulled into the lot at de Kesto's.

When Sahnassa stepped onto the smooth ground in front of the restaurant, her legs were trembling. Vanarra had already unstrapped and was striding forward resolutely, and she looked back to see where Sahni was. "You coming?"

"I … I am," the Nephti replied, her voice quavering as she took only a couple of tentative steps away from the vehicle.

"Well now," Van commented, a little contemptuously. "There's something this Anati has over a purebred."

"Not quite a … fighter pilot, no," Sahnassa admitted, walking forward and stumbling. With a heavy sigh, Van walked back to her and took the Nephti's shoulder and fore paw. "Where did you learn to drive like that?"

"I've catered a number of times for various security companies in town, protection companies, too. They all teach some kind of driving course in their self-protection curriculum. They said I was an exceptionally good student."

"I can see that," Sahni replied, turning to her boss. "I … I think I can just about manage, now. Thank you."

"Well, I can see that unless I want to clean the inside of my hover, I better drive a little more conservatively taking you back to the office after dinner."

"Yeah, probably a good idea," Sahni giggled lightly. "I'm surprised enforcement isn't after us."

"We were only going a little over the limit!" Van replied defensively as they walked up the steps. "The difference is that in a sports hover you actually can feel something, as opposed to what most everyone else drives. Besides, I cater most of their events!"

Sahni shook her head in surprise as she followed Vanarra inside.

It wasn't long before they were seated at a table, and a nice one at that. Sahnassa had watched how Van received good, respectful service – something that surprised her, in a good way. "You seem a little shocked they were decent to me," Van replied, accusation in her voice again.

"I am, but I'm happy they were. They seemed to know you," Sahni replied, not looking at Van at first, but then eyed her questioningly. "Do you know everyone?"

A smile broke out on the mixed blood's muzzle. "Quite a few, kit. Quite a few. I'll bet you made your fair share of contacts ... at academy. At least, that's what I'm told happens."

"Yeah, I was told that, too," Sahnassa sighed. "Didn't seem to work out that way for me."

"So let me get this straight, you are avowed, but your matron doesn't continually run around and smooth everyone else's fur for you?"

"The Compact," Sahnassa gently reminded her boss. "Until I ... forsake it, what you said is true."

"So, you don't get any support from your family, kit? That seems like a bad deal. Do you still pay dues? Is that something I have to worry about?"

"No, not usually. They'll compare the government records you submit with what I've sent them. If I haven't paid what I'm supposed to, it's my tail in trouble. You'd be clear of it."

"So they haven't supported you at all?" Van asked, dumbfounded, and then realized she had asked about the Nephti's past.

Sahnassa was too quick with her answer for Van to retract the question. "They paid ... most of my school costs, but not all. That's why I have the loans. They also placed me in a school and program that was ... a little more difficult than what I would have liked. All the better for what I'm able to do for your business, I suppose."

"Hmm..." Van mused, and realized that because she'd forced the Nephti to disclose something about her past, she was now in debt.

"As long as we're sharing little bits, just know that my experiences with families growing up were ... very poor – horrible, in fact." Van's pause and haunted expression made Sahni cover her mouth.

"I'm so sorry," the Nephti breathed.

"It's in the past, and I don't talk about it, except for now so you'll know where not to tread. Now, enough about ancient history, what do you like to do? What do you do for fun?"

"Well, since I started school, the fun has been pretty limited. Mostly, I read books from the library."

"Oh really? Which library?" Vanarra asked, an odd tingle in the back of her brain.

"The academy library, until now. I guess if I want to get something, I'll have to borrow it from Pinnacle or somewhere else." That word shot a bolt of lightening up Van's spine, and Sahnassa saw the reaction. "I'm sorry! Did I say something wrong?"

"Uh, no, kit, no," Van hastily covered. "It's just that … I have wanted to get books from there for a long time, but they won't loan to me. You don't suppose it would be okay for you to get a book or two for me … perhaps on TransNet marketing or something?"

"Sure," Sahnassa replied earnestly. "I'd be happy to."

"I wonder what that place looks like, inside, too. Anati aren't exactly welcome, but … I've heard good things."

"If they have a brochure or something, I could bring that back. I could find a copy of their index and bring it to you so you'd know what they have."

"Sounds … good," Van replied, feeling an odd excitement about having any connection back to her old lair. "So, what sort of books do you read?"

"Well, I'm a little embarrassed to admit it, but I started with fairly … heated romance novels. While I was in academy, though, a friend of mine got me started on reading space fiction. That's mostly what I read now."

"Space fiction?" Van queried, trying to remember if she had ever read anything like that. She had vague memories of pulling a few titles off the shelves in her secret archive lair, but finding them odd and little frightening, she hadn't read anymore. "Hmm… not what I generally go after. Mostly, I'm a follower of the Grand Matriarch, Rahnahi de Dothnar."

"Really?" Sahni replied in surprise. "I've read several of her books in school – they're required to graduate."

"So, tell me what you've read…"

Having sprung upon a subject of Van's interest, Sahnassa and her boss discussed everything she could remember about the books she had read, and during the meal, Vanarra gave commentaries on the books Sahnassa hadn't yet read.

As they finished eating, Sahnassa asked good-naturedly, "Is there any book of hers you haven't read?"

"Only the ones she's still writing," Van replied proudly. "I try to use a quote or something of hers at every single event. The truth is, I learned a lot from her. There ... was a period of time when ... I read everything she had in print, several times. She ... gave me hope. If you want to get fired quick, just bad-mouth my favorite author; then you'd be leaving as shreds of fur."

"Oh, no! I respect her too much for that." Leaning in close, Sahni confessed, "De Dothnar is what I wish de Orturu could be." Leaning back and looking into Van's amazed expression, Sahnassa added, "Please don't tell anyone I said that. It ... could get me in trouble. It's not that ... I'm not loyal to them. It's been rough, but they are still my family. I just sometimes imagine what life would be like if ... Rahnahi was in charge. What if someone like her was in charge of every family?"

"It wouldn't be the same world, surely," Van mused solemnly. "She hints at giving my kind freedoms and equality, makes us sound like we're deserving of it."

"But you are," Sahnassa contested. "Look at what you've done!"

"I'm just an Anati caterer, when all's sifted and sorted, kit."

"You are who I work for, and I do what you say, not the other way around," Sahnassa protested quietly. "Greatness is where you find it."

"If you're going to use Rahnahi quotes against me, then you'd better be ready for trouble," Van replied back, just a touch of menace in her voice.

"I'm sorry. Thank you for dinner. It ... was very kind of you," Sahnassa replied as humbly as she could, looking away.

Vanarra took a deep breath and tried to relax. "Sure, kit. Sure. You do sometimes wander into those rough spots of mine, but if you learn to back off, you should survive pretty well when you do." Reaching across the table, she opened her paw to Sahni. "Thank you for trying."

Again looking at the mixed blood with admiration and gratitude, Sahnassa returned the gesture and clasped her paw. "You know, kit," Van admitted, "I don't do this very often, but ... I thought it would be good to get some understandings set between us." Letting go, she added, "I had a friend who started out as disavowed and got adopted into a family, de Dothnar, actually. She ... left because her family told her to. It was difficult, and I have to admit – I was mad at her. The truth is, I haven't spoken to her, largely because she's crazy busy off continent. I tell you this just so you know I understand where your first loyalty is. Now, you need to understand my first loyalty is to all of those who work for me who have no family house. Nobody hurts them or makes them feel less than they should. Be very careful about how you treat them. You're smart, you're pretty, you're purebred, you're avowed. They will be watching to see what you do, what assignments you get, and how willing you are to complete them. You're off to a pretty fair start, but just understand, okay?"

"Okay," Sahnassa agreed. "You know, I feel like I've learned more in this first sol working for you than I did in five seasons of school about some things. I ... hope you'll be patient with me. I wouldn't willingly hurt anyone. All I want is to do a good job for you."

"Fair enough. Let's get you back to your hover so you can head home. What time are you coming in tomorrow morning?"

"What time do you need me?" Sahni asked.

Van nodded and replied, "I have some time at ten to go over things, like the equipment you want to purchase or whatever you need to. I'm going to be tied up the rest of the sol. Oh, and we might need you for an event tomorrow night."

"Whatever you want, boss," Sahnassa stated, and Vanarra couldn't help but smile.

Chapter 15: Inequity

Sheffer whispered to Raska as the pair folded and rolled dining utensils in preparation for the event later in the evening, "There she is again." They sat and watched the Nephti hauling in a heavy box from the back dock. Both looked away and pretended not to notice.

"So, she bothers you that much?" Raska quietly purred back in a tease. The Nephti-Vulpi female was a striking mix of purple and reddish orange with sleek black striping that made her very attractive.

"The way she prances through here, flaunting her avowed name," Sheffer growled softly. The Perratti Faelnar's shades of blackish brown with somewhat irregular white striping and a mottled nose didn't make him particularly attractive, but understanding he had no chance with the female sitting beside him had allowed a kind of friendship to develop between the pair.

As Sahnassa nearly dropped the box and had to set it down quickly, Raska giggled. "Doesn't look much like prancing now, does it? You know, you're not a good observer of her stance, are you?"

"Stance? What's that?"

"How she holds herself. Around here, I've noticed, she's not prancing so much as slinking around, trying not to anger anyone or rub fur the wrong way. She's signaling non-dominance."

"Meaning?"

"Some … find that attractive," Raska mused. "But here, I think she's just putting us on."

As Flint walked in and started talking with the Nephti, Sheffer asked, "Putting us on?"

"Yes. I was close to her the other night when a couple of purebred tail-for-brains started making trouble about the event being catered by Anati. You should have seen the change in her. Little slinky straightened up and took them on, politely, but she came to her full height and looked them dead in the eye. She also pulled out the fact that her parents are head litigators in de Orturu."

"Powerful friends, just like all purebred avowed," Sheffer sighed.

"Well, not all, but this one? Yes. She's got a hard center for all that show she's putting on, ugh, like now. She's got Flint completely fooled," Raska scoffed as they watched Flint pick up the box easily and begin to take it down the hall, Sahni following behind. "Manipulative, clever, book-smart – Van may just lose her business if she's not careful."

"And we'd all be out of a job, Raska. If this place fell into avowed paws, we'd all certainly be gone; I promise you that."

"Oh now, don't fret. You can always run back to mommy or daddy, Sheffer dearest," Raska teased, since both of his purebred parents were still avowed, living separate and single, at least officially.

"Fine for me, and I'm sure one of them would help find me something but ... what about you?"

"Clever kits always find ways of keeping their options open," she offered cryptically. "There ... would be some reshuffling for me, but some of the others here, they would lose everything."

"We'll have to watch her," Sheffer stated crossly.

"You watch her. I don't find her that entertaining."

"You only watch out for cubs who are rich. If she did something to threaten the way things are, you wouldn't do anything?" Sheffer asked.

"If I actually thought something I'd say would matter, I might say something. Vanarra can be so painfully hard headed sometimes."

"Like forbidding us from socializing during an event or in the office?"

"Keeps your tail nicely in its place," Raska chuckled. "But yes, those kinds of things she doesn't want us to do – very restricting. Makes me grateful she's not hovering over the rest of my life. I do so love my hobby."

"What … is your hobby, Raska? You've never said."

"Let's just say I enjoy taking care of pets."

"Like pet prowlers?" Sheffer asked, confused.

"Yes, some of them certainly are prowlers, albeit easily tamed ones," Raska offered glibly as she stood. "As we're finished, I'll leave you to put away. I have to tick through the inventory of fermentum before I go. I have … a pet to tend to tonight."

"If it's the stuff in the little bottles, you'll have to get the keys from Flint. It's all in those cabinets now – thanks to our prancing, slinking little Nephti."

Raska gave a grunt of dissatisfaction but swished her tail a little as she stepped away, leaving Sheffer confused.

"Well now," Van mused as she looked into the small room cluttered by multiple empty boxes and partially unwrapped equipment mounted in the shelf rack. "This is really starting to look like something – what exactly, I'm not sure, but it's clear something … technical is happening, obviously. How's it going?"

"It's still got a long way to go, but so far, everything is checking out," Sahnassa explained, but then excitedly added, "I was able to find a couple of really nice deals for you! This TransNet gateway router was being offloaded by a corporate pack. It's last seasons' model, but we got it for a fraction of the list price, less than half. The server here we got twenty five percent off because we bought two. The runners were included, so we don't even have to buy that software."

"Not bad. How much do you think we've saved?"

"About a thousand or so. I have to work on how to get the power centers at a discount. Those things hardly ever go on sale."

"Sounds pretty good," Van admitted. Seeing the equipment in the rack gave her a little tingle of excitement she didn't quite understand. The Nephti actually seemed very competent like she could make good on her promises, but, as she had several times already, she'd be inviting Buck over in the evening to have a look. So far, her work had passed his review. What still confused Vanarra was Sahni's willingness to work for her. Muriella started politely enough, but then seemed to get comfortable and slip into a kind of disdain that made it easy for her to dismiss Van. "She's ... trying so hard," Van thought.

"But I can keep looking," Sahnassa said nervously, and Van realized that she'd been staring.

"Oh no, sorry, kit. I just got stuck for a moment. So, let me ask you," Van started as she stepped into the room and closed the door behind her. Having nowhere else to go, Sahni backed up against the boxes. "You've been here about ten sols or so, worked a few events – what do you think? Do you enjoy what you're doing?"

"Surprisingly, yes," came the admission, and Van frowned instantly. "Oh, no! That totally isn't what I meant! I ... just, school was really, really hard and not a lot of fun. When I started out doing this – the computer thing – as a hobby growing up and then at secondary school, it was neat and cool, and I enjoyed it. Every season I was at academy, though, yeah I was learning, but ... it wasn't fun anymore. It was just this unending series of tasks with not much reward and no real praise ... and no one else around who ... well, cared."

"Well, I'm paying you, so I certainly do care," Van stated dryly. "But if it doesn't do what you promised, that certainly isn't going to be fun."

"Yes, but I'm sure it will. I know it will," Sahnassa offered. "While this has it's challenges, putting the systems and site together for you isn't the hardest thing I did in academy, and it was something I enjoyed doing. I know I can do this for you, and like you said, you're paying me. I paid the academy for the privilege of doing it the last time. And, I'm not trying to stroke your fur here or anything, but ... you do care. It's important to your business and to you, and ... I can see that. It's not just an assignment. It matters."

Van, although it was a struggle for her to see Sahnassa's perspective, said questioningly, "And because it matters ... to me and my business, it's more fulfilling than, say, some school assignment?" Vanarra could tell by the Nephti's anxious smile and nod that she had spoken a truth that truly connected with Sahnassa. Van smiled a little, too; she could sense that somehow, the immense library of Rahnahi de Dothnar's works and philosophy rolling around in her thoughts had somehow allowed her to make the jump to understand the Nephti's point of view. Unbidden, a new concept from that same stream dropped into her perceptions, one that shocked her. "She cares about me."

Van didn't utter that thought, and its appearance embarrassed her, although she fought her blush furs down adequately. "Well, good. I'm … I'm glad it's work you enjoy. Makes it easier, I suppose," Vanarra stated, turning around to look at the equipment contained in the rack. "What about the events? Surely serving creele bake isn't a hobby you had growing up."

"But that's kind of neat, too," Sahnassa confessed. "It's this … odd mix between doing something that helps others and it's not … like … so mental," Van had turned her head back towards the Nephti and was looking at her critically. "Well not in the same way. I … it was all papers and programs and assignments before – never anyone real. I have to think about how someone else is feeling and what they want and try to give it to them. I can tell when they're disappointed or might be, and that makes me try a little harder. If I make them happy, it's like I've won something. It may only be their thanks, but still."

Van's frown at what started to sound like a disrespectful comment had now transformed into a wide smile. "She gets it," Van thought, but again tried not to react impulsively. Vanarra turned and leaned against the wall, casually. "You know, kit, I suppose that's a good way of thinking about it. I guess I do the same thing. There's all this … office work and figures and so forth, inventory and planning, but when I'm actually at an event, it's … like a race, a competition. And you can totally win or lose, really, but at least here, running this place, there's a *chance* I could win. It's … not always been like that for me. I like winning. It means I get a good place to live and food to eat and … a purpose that matters."

"I'm sure your employees appreciate that," Sahni stated happily. "I know I do."

"It's not just the employees you see who benefit. Kit, there are Anati like me who don't have any parents, and … they're wandering around with no lair and no family, victims of everyone and everything that wants to go after them. So, one of the things that keeps me going is that I get to do something about that – something that wasn't done for me. There's an orphanage that I donate to that takes in our kind. They are protected, fed, and … loved, even. So, it's not just about me, Sahni, or those who work for me. If this business fails, then those orphans – those defenseless little kits and cubs I care about – don't get taken care of. Just understand, in your heart, how much that means to me, and how much it matters that we do everything we can to protect them and provide for them."

Sahni's expression had been growing more serious as she listened, and then she promised solemnly, "I will get you the absolute best price I can on those power centers."

Despite herself, Vanarra laughed at how her heart-felt confession about supporting orphans got translated as looking for bargains on computer equipment. "You do that, kit! You do that! When your contract is up, I don't want to be stuck with a system that costs us our tails to run, okay?"

Van's merriment, she noticed, wasn't shared by the Nephti, whose ears dropped a little and tail sagged. "Of course. I will do my best."

"I'm sure you will," Van offered, patting her on the back. "I'm sure you will. Alright, I've got to get back to work and so do you. Check with Flint if you need anything."

"Yes, Van, I will," Sahnassa replied quietly, and watched, numbed, as Vanarra left the little room.

Sahnassa felt an impulse to cry, but fought it off. "When my contract is up," she thought, "then where will I go?" She liked Van and Flint, and even the others – although they were still pretty distant. She liked working events. Even though she clearly wasn't part of the group, she was at least around other Thurians.

At some level, she knew this was a limited contract; Van had stated as much when she signed it. That wasn't a surprise. "Why is this upsetting me so?" she wondered.

Reaching into her pocket, she found the reason why. Pulling out a card that had been sent to her from her parents caused her to reach over and push the door shut. It was a response to her first family dues payment, money she really needed to keep but surrendered willingly nonetheless. Reading it, she sat in the floor and truly started to cry.

Sahnassa, your father and I are relieved you were able to locate employment. We have sent your first dues payment, as honor requires. You should also understand that the requirements we were placed under during your schooling no longer apply. You wished to be on your own and do things your own way, and so you will.

The message's cold formality, detachment, and contempt ached inside of her as much as her anger at how they had abandoned her. It was a futile anger, she knew, for there was nothing she could do about it. "Just keep earning a living, feeding myself," she groaned as she stood, wiping her tears. "That's all I can do."

It had taken Sahnassa nearly three sols, and more than a few intervals of driving around, but now she stepped up and looked at the rack of equipment all nicely arrayed in front of her. "It looks like an altar of some kind," Saiphar – a purebred disavowed Vulpi – said as he looked in from the hallway.

Sahni chuckled. "I suppose it does a bit. Want to see something neat?"

"I guess."

"Come in; I'm going to close the door and turn off the light." A little hesitantly, the Vulpi complied, and Sahnassa did as she said. "What do you think?"

The artist carefully considered the ambience of the whirring, humming, and twinkling equipment in front of him. "It is … curiously compelling," he whispered. "It's almost kind of … alive, with its own presence."

Sahnassa flicked the light back on and shrugged. "A presence that's not doing a whole lot right now other than eating up power and looking cool."

The Vulpi looked at her quizzically. "Why do you think that's impressive, Sahni? Why show me that?"

"I … I don't know … I guess, perhaps," Sahnassa stuttered, "because of some of the stuff I read – space fiction, mostly. I … I guess I can almost imagine it being alive in a way."

"Ordered, regular, clean lines and even tones," Saiphar added, running a paw along the casing of one machine. "Nearly organic pulsing and here, a warm breath being blown out – I can see that. Something … inspiring to you?"

"It is," Sahni admitted, a little ashamed. She'd started reading some of the more adult space fiction she never could bring herself to read in academy for fear of being found out by a roommate. "A little … I don't know, compelling in a way, like what you said." Opening the door, she nervously shrugged. "Just thought you might find it kind of interesting, being the artist and all."

He put his paw on her shoulder and said, "You do find it inspiring, to your soul and your being. That, more than anything, impresses me. I'm glad you're here, Sahnassa de Orturu."

"Thanks," she replied smiling, and he nodded and then left her.

As she turned back to check one of the connections, another Vulpi voice piped in. "You know, if you're going to invite Vulpi in here with you in the dark, someone's going to talk."

"Oh, Tresk. Do you want to see, too?"

"See a computer closet with the light off? No. Techno doesn't get me going. I guess as a techno-tail, it does it for you."

"In a way," she replied. "Makes me feel like I've done something when I get it to work."

"Yeah about that," Tresk chuckled. "You do realize that ... there's no LineCom in here. Even if you are going to sub-band that into the master switch, you do have to have a piece of wire."

Sahni blinked and looked around. "You ... you're kidding me. I ... oh, I can't believe it! Where ... how?"

"The boxes are up above you, in the ceiling. You'll need to splice in a line down here, just thought I'd let you know," he teased. "Hate to have our only avowed purebred look like she didn't know what she was doing, Sahni de Orturu."

Her blush furs at full, Sahnassa replied quietly, "I ... I appreciate the observation, Tresk. Thank you."

"Oh, anytime!" he said easily as he strode out of the room, not giving her a backwards glance.

"14:30 on the claw-tip," Raska said to herself. As it was very near mid-sol, the others were sitting down to eat lunch at the tables near the kitchens portion of the warehouse. Slipping through the door, she made her way towards the back dock through the storage shelves via the wide center aisle. Listening carefully, she wanted to make sure no one was following her or in the storage area; she didn't want to be overheard.

Turning a corner, she pulled a scrap of paper out of a pocket. "Got to keep this short and to the point," she thought to herself as she reached for the LineCom on the back dock. As she put the set to her ear, she frowned. It was dead. Placing it back in the rest, she pulled out the paw-set and listened again. Still dead. "Damn! I can't afford to lose this one! He's just gotten dependant on me."

Striding quickly to the front, nearly panicked, she went past Vanarra's office to where Mauft was sitting. Smiling her best, she asked, "Mauft, the LineCom in the back is dead, and I … I need to make a private call. Are we completely unable to call out?"

Picking up her LineCom, Mauft dialed a quick number, and it rang through. "Not a problem here. However, I have a good guess as to why the one in the back is dead."

"Why's that?" Raska asked, and Mauft pointed to the ceiling. Just then, something up there shuffled, and a little grunt and sneeze punctuated the silence as they listened. "It's the little techno-Nephti, isn't it?"

"What's going on, you two?" Van asked, sensing some tension in her office.

Raska was quick witted and well prepared. "The de Orturu has cut the LineCom in the back, and I desperately need to make a private call! There's an Anati who was injured by a purebred, and he's gotten sick. Several of my friends are watching over him, but none of them are available. I'm trying to find someone. If I can't find someone, I'll have to go watch him – there won't be anyone else."

"Ow, and we have an event tonight! You can make the call from my office. I'm not having any problems; I just got off the LineCom."

"Thank you, Van, for understanding," Raska replied gratefully and made for Van's office.

"In the meantime," Vanarra sighed, "sounds like I need to have a little chatty chat with our Nephti kit."

"Just keep her from falling through the ceiling. It sounds like she'll be in my lap any tick," Mauft complained.

"Alright." Van started looking around for how the Nephti had made it up into the ceiling. When she opened the room where the new servers were, she found her answer. Perched precariously on a table was a ladder leading up into the ceiling, where a couple of rounded tiles had been removed. Stepping in, she closed the door, and noticed with some appreciation, that although there was a fair amount of insulation and dust on the floor from the goings-on above, the servers had been powered down and covered with a plastisheet. "Kit? Sahni? You up there?"

"Oh yes, Van! I'm up here."

"Might I have a word?" Van requested in a tone that bespoke the action was definitely not optional.

"Sure," Sahnassa replied, hearing the displeasure in her boss's tone. Carefully, she worked her way back to the entrance and peered down into the somewhat stern face of her employer. "Uh, hi there. Something … wrong?"

"Well yes, kit. Yes it is. What time is it?"

"Uh, about … mid-sol or so?" Sahnassa answered as a question. Her watch had been left on the table below.

"Uh huh," Van agreed. "And there are those in the back on their lunch break who had been hoping to make a private call or two. Now, they can't. These aren't purebred avowed who have a PawLink on their hip whenever they need it. For some of these, it's their only chance to call someone. Raska was trying to check on a sick friend, trying to arrange coverage so she could work tonight. I let her use the one in my office, but now I'm kicked out of my own office so she can make that call. That doesn't make me exactly happy, Sahni. Why is the LineCom not working back there?"

"Oh, I'm sorry, Van. I … I thought the opposite – that everyone would be eating and … not … I'm sorry."

"But why, kit?" Van pressed.

"I … had to run another line into the server room from the branch station up here so we could put the site … make it available, that is."

"Sahni," Van chided quietly, "you need to ask and not assume about doing anything to the systems of this business. We may have been about to receive a shipment and get into one of those damned arguments with the suppliers. That LineCom in the back is needed! If this was the work you had to do, you should have asked in advance and arranged a time, like this evening, when everyone would be gone to the event."

Sahnassa sighed and realized her mistake. She had wanted to leave the evening free for shopping, to perhaps buy a bed of some sort for her barren little lair. "I'm … sorry, Vanarra. I … I tried to rush through it. I'll … I'll fix it."

"How long?" Van insisted.

"Five passes, no more."

"I'm holding you to it, kit," Van replied seriously. "Now, when you're done, come to my office so we can discuss a more appropriate time to do this work, okay?"

"Yes, Van. Sorry."

There was a knock on the door, and Van opened it. "Raska, what's wrong?" she asked the distressed Anati.

"I'm … sorry, Van. I … the last one who might have stood in for me agreed to pull overtime at his job. He … he can't back out, and now there's no one."

Van's eyebrows furrowed, and her back-fur stood up. "Well, now. Sahni, Raska wasn't able to make a call in time, and now she can't cover my event. That leaves me a paw short. Who do you think should stand in for her?" she asked, crossly.

"I'll … I'll do it. Sorry, Raska," Sahnassa apologized from above.

"You've cost me a night's wages, de Orturu! Now my rent is coming due!" Van looked at Raska, and then looked back up at the Nephti with a sternly expectant expression.

Inwardly, Sahnassa groaned. "I'll … work it. You … you can take the pay, Raska. My debt to you."

"Sounds like a fair deal to me," Van stated, seemingly done with the matter, looking at Raska who nodded, albeit still clearly annoyed. The pair left the Nephti looking down at an empty room from the ceiling, wishing she could have just crawled into an actual hole and disappeared.

Several intervals later, Van asked Raska, "Are you sure there isn't anything I can do to help? Does he need money?"

"If we can just have someone with him, I think he'll be alright. Thank you, Van. I hope things turn out well tonight."

"Oh, they will. Sure there's nothing you need?" Van pressed.

Raska frowned and answered, "Just make sure the de Orturu doesn't take anything else away from us, make it easy on herself while making it hard for the Anati."

"Oh, don't you worry, kit!" Van replied brightly. "You should see what duty I have picked out for her tonight. Sheffer's going to have an easy one."

"Sounds good," Raska replied, knowing that Sheffer generally got stuck with most of the carrying duties when Flint wasn't around. She reached over and gave Van a brief hug and then stepped away.

About a quarter of an interval later, she left the transport in one of the nicer parts of Shanandrae – the banking quarter. By then, she had put on an exceptionally nice jacket – kept discretely in her bag, and changed into expensive paw-shoes. Striding confidently past the business workers and bankers and litigators, she worked her way into a parking garage where, waiting beneath a cover was her hover – a Strider special edition sports hover, a mix of purple and crimson to compliment her own colors.

After slipping the cover off and stowing it in the front, she stepped back to marvel at the sexy ship glistening in the overhead lights. "There's my little pet," she purred and pressed the control to activate the engines and open the doors. As if it was purring back at her, the vehicle came to life – it's perfectly polished and luxurious interior beckoning her in. Sitting in the comfortable, contoured seat, the mixed-blood giggled. Closing the doors, she lifted the skids and slipped from the reserved spot into the trail leading to the exit. Waving to the gate guard, she sped away towards the wealthy residential neighborhoods east of the town's center. As soon as she was in sunlight, and elegantly shaped claw tip pressed a control which darkened all of the windows, making it nearly impossible for anyone outside of the vehicle to see within.

As evening was giving over to night, she left her luxurious multi-bedroom condo clean, brushed, and dressed for the night's activities. In a few passes, she was turning into a large gated community where the guard passed her vehicle without even stopping it or querying the identity of the driver. With her point finder working perfectly, she was soon pulling up to a very large lair surrounded by pleasant gardens. "Very nice, as promised," she purred. Slipping her vehicle around the back, she found the open garage door just as she had instructed, and pulling into the empty spot and landing, she smiled as her own activator lowered the door, making it impossible for anyone outside to see who had just entered the lair.

Raska's heart was pounding now, pounding with predatory excitement. It wasn't only the money that kept her going; it was the thrill of it, the power she felt. Stepping out of her vehicle, she made a couple of lewdly suggestive changes to her wardrobe and took her special satchel out of its hiding place behind her seat. "Oh, Van – so very gullible of you. I'm just another one of your crew, so you think, and you have no idea that every time we work a primal or an event with Thurians of power or influence, you're helping me find some new pet to take care of, like this little cub." Raska always gave her regular clients instructions on how and when to bring new prospects to her attention, the requests they were to make, and how they were to act so they didn't arouse suspicion while she was "working" an event for Vanarra. She chuckled at how the high and mighty avowed were willing to efface themselves, not only to her but to potential new clients – confessing such scandalous and dishonorable behavior, all because of the rewards she tantalized them with.

Opening the door and entering the lair, she easily made her way to the exact room where her client would be waiting for her. A pet prowler padded over to her and nuzzled her leg, affectionately. "Well, he said you were a sweet heart, very easy to manage. Now, you stay down here, and I'll see you later."

After heading up a flight of stairs to the master suite, she opened the door and smiled, seeing all of the candles burning in the room, exactly per her instructions. Looking in the center of the room, she saw her client. "Oh, well now. What a good little cub you are. All ready, I see. And what's this?" she asked as she stepped forward to the small table in front of the nude, kneeling figure. "Is this my tribute?" Raska picked up the envelope waiting for her and opened it. "Very nice, little cub. I think you're a pet I'll really enjoy taking special care of."

Sahnassa returned to her lair well after high night, barely able to move, hurting all over. She had, for some reason, been tasked with every bit of loading and unloading that had been required for the event. With Flint taking a few sols off, she thought perhaps Sheffer would have done it or at least offered a paw, but Van's instructions were clear, and clearly punishment for her error earlier in the sol. "I'll … I'll ask first, next time," she groaned as she closed and locked the door.

Stepping from one empty space to another, she made it to her bedroom where some pillows and sheets adorned a spot on the floor, a few pitiful clothes hung in her closet, and her practice orlure sat collecting dust in the corner. "Maybe … tomorrow … a bed," she whimpered as she stripped off her clothes and nearly collapsed on the floor, far too tired to do anything else.

Vanarra was halfway through reviewing the feedback sheets when a heavy knock and the door opening signaled the entrance of her second in command. "Good stuff last night, Flint," she stated without looking up. "They liked us. I smell a rebook here, maybe even a spinoff or two." The quiet close of the door caught her attention. Looking up, she could see Flint was not happy, as close to angry as he ever seemed to get. "Something wrong?"

"Have you seen our Nephti this morning?" he asked almost as an admonition.

"Not really, I've been in here this morning going over this stuff," she replied, feeling instantly on the defense. "Did she not show up?"

"Oh no; she's here. Barely able to walk, barely able to sit, not really able to stay awake very well, but yes, she's here. What did you do, Van?"

"She messed up, Flint. She cut the lines to the back of the shop and didn't talk to anyone first. She cost me Raska last night, so she had to fill in."

"Yes, I heard – after I dragged that out of Sahni. I very much doubt Raska would have been tasked with all of the hauling for the evening. That would have been nearly too much work for me, Van, and you put that on Sahni? Why were you so hard on her?"

"It doesn't hurt for her to learn the value of hard work, Flint," Van replied, fixing him with a hard stare. "She also has to learn to respect the others of this office, and not take liberties with ... removing things they might need without telling them or asking them first."

"Valid points, but ... you were getting hard work from her before, Van, and if I were her and had any chance of finding work elsewhere, I would come in, tender my resignation, and leave you hanging with a rack full of expensive equipment and no way to use it." The edge of Van's irritation with her second's questioning faltered a bit, and Flint saw it. "Didn't think of that before you denied her pay for the evening, did you? And yes, I had to drag that bit out of her, as well."

"She caused Raska to lose her pay. Seemed only fair," Van replied, looking back at her work and trying to signal Flint she was done discussing the matter. Flint wasn't through.

"There hasn't been a mixed blood or a disavowed purebred we've ever treated like that," Flint reminded her sternly. "You get paid for what you work; we don't force or allow one employee to surrender their wages to another just because schedules don't work out. Raska had a choice; she could have as easily been sick or had something else to do. Now, how many in the office will try to use the same trick to blame 'the de Orturu' for screwing up their evening? Will Sahni pay for each of *those*?"

"Your point?" Vanarra sighed, looking back up at him.

"The fact that kit came back in here this morning, regular time, in the condition she was in, was more than enough of an indication she's trying, and she deserves at least the same leeway as everyone else."

"Sure she's not fooling you, Muscles?"

"I've been a masseuse for too long, Van. I know faking versus the real thing. She's one step away from needing a doctor."

Van looked up at him, exasperated. "You have got to be kidding me, Flint."

"Doesn't have a bed in her lair. Sleeps on the floor."

"I pay her well enough," Van contested, defensively. "Why the mange doesn't she have a bed?"

"House dues, student loans, and long intervals here. She finally has the money, but ... and I quote 'is finding it difficult to find time to go get one.' If you saw any of the other staff hurting like she is right now, you'd help them. Go see for yourself and tell me if she got what she deserved for accidently clipping a LineCom wire."

At that moment, there was a knock on the door. Flint stepped away from it, suggesting Vanarra allow the interruption. "Yes, come in. Oh, Raska! How did everything work out with your sick friend?"

"Oh, he's much, much better, Van," the mixed blood nearly purred from the doorway. "And he was very grateful, too. I'm sorry I'm coming in late, but he needed extra attention. I can't thank you enough."

Trying to keep her temper, Vanarra replied, "Thank you, Raska. The ... distributor has our fermentum order on the back dock. Can you see to it?"

"Looking forward to it. Thank you, again!" Van nodded, keeping her expression neutral as the door was closed.

Flint looked back at her with a bit of a smirk on his face. "I'd say you'd been had," he told her quietly.

"Yes," Van nearly growled. "Pretty damn perky and chipper for having spent all night with an invalid."

"Maybe only parts of him were sick."

"Maybe all his parts were in perfect working order, by the set of her tail. Okay, well, you're off on vacation, and I screw up. How unusual is that?" Van replied, putting her head in her paws.

"I refuse to answer that question, as it may compromise the relationship I have with my employer," he replied in good humor.

"Yeah, as if you were shy or something. So, what do I do? You are telling me I have to make this right, so what do I do?"

"Oh, I'm not telling you that, but ... you are correct. You should make it right. If you want to know my opinion, I've seen a couple of these server operations go into businesses, and Sahni is working very fast by everything I've seen. It has taken her sols to do what some outfits drag into moons."

"Yeah, Buck was pretty impressed, too," Van admitted. "Sounds like a bonus."

"Sounds like a bed to me, like you go shopping with her and spring for immediate delivery, giving her the rest of the sol off once that's done."

"You've got to be kidding," Vanarra replied, shaking her head at him.

"Imagine what you'd be willing to pay if you went into that server room and found she was gone for good."

Vanarra looked away from him and crossed her arms. "Fine. That's a ton of work I won't get done."

"If I remember correctly, your very able second in command is back from vacation this sol. He might help you out, even be willing to work pretty late ... to make sure everything *important* gets taken care of."

"Alright, alright already! I'll take the Nephti shopping and buy her a bed ... in lieu of pay for last night and a ... bonus for doing such a good job for us," Van groaned.

"Quite the noble thing for you to do, I think. Speaks well of you," he taunted.

"Alright," Van complained. "You've officially had as much fun at your boss's expense as you're allowed. You'll have to come back tomorrow for more."

"See you tomorrow, Van," he chuckled, winking. As he put his paw on the door, he added seriously, "You know, it actually does speak well of you. Just stack the feedback forms on your desk, and I'll tend to them."

"Thanks, Muscles."

He left her door slightly ajar, and taking the hint, she stood up and followed him a moment or so later, looking for the Nephti. Looking into the server room, she didn't find her, and Van's heart began to beat a little faster. Stepping up to the front, she went to the windows and looked out. "What's wrong?" Mauft asked.

"Has Sahni ... left?" she asked, worried.

Mauft stood and walked beside her boss. "No, that's her hover. She's still here somewhere."

"Don't let her out without having her talk to me, okay?" Van asked as she made for the back dock.

"She in trouble again?"

"No, I am," Van offered, stopping for a moment and whispering the answer back. Ignoring the gray one's raised eyebrow fur, Vanarra walked back to the kitchens area, and found Raska having a very happy conversation with Saiphar and Tresk, Sheffer being the only one who was actually working. "Alright, everyone! A lot to do from last night and for our event tomorrow evening; let's get moving!" A little reluctantly, the group broke up.

"Sheffer," Van asked him as he came in from the warehouse area, "have you seen Sahni?"

"The de Orturu hasn't been back here, thankfully."

"Shef," Vanarra said quietly. "That's not her name, not even her short one. It's Sahni or Sahnassa. I wouldn't permit her to call you the Anati, would I?"

"I ... I suppose not. Sorry, Van."

"Believe me, I understand. Okay ... well, now that I've probably really fouled things up, you may not have to worry about it. If you see her, please send her in my direction, okay?"

"Okay," he agreed and turned to go back into the warehouse. Van's heart was really starting to beat faster. Several thousand of her business profits had been spent on this new equipment, and without a

Sahni there to make it into something, it was just expensive techno-junk. Van walked back towards the front, nearly jogging, past Flint's open door, and finally put her nose into the server room. Looking up made her both anxious and gave her a sense of relief. An ink-dipped tail was somewhat languidly draping into the room from the ceiling.

"I never thought she'd go back up there in the state Flint said she was in." Then she heard it – a sniff. Then, there was another. "Oh, don't I feel like prowler poop about now," Van thought to herself. Stepping in, she closed the door. The Nephti working above her didn't seem to notice.

"Uh, Sahni? You ... you up there, kit?" The tail disappeared, and there was some slow shuffling above her and the sound of someone straining. The face that finally appeared made Van feel truly disgusted with herself. "I did that," she thought grimly.

"Yes ... Van. I ... nothing should be broken. Did ... did something break? I was just cleaning up."

"Why don't you come down, kit? I'm ... a little worried about you being up there right now. Come on, kit, I'm serious." Vanarra slid another of the small tables over to make the space for the ladder reasonably safe.

The face disappeared for a moment, and Van thought she was going to have to go up the ladder herself, so she stepped on the table, almost getting hit in the face with a hind paw that was unsuccessfully searching for a rung of the ladder. "Here, kit. Let me guide you a bit." Reaching out for the Nephti's hind paw, Van was able to get Sahni to the ladder safely. It took several more moments, but finally Sahnassa was standing on the table with her, stooped and hunched over.

"What were you doing up there?" Van asked.

"I ... I wanted to make sure all of the lines were secure. I didn't ... I didn't want anything else to break because of me."

"Is that something Tresk could do? Could Tresk run the new line for you?"

"I ... I think he knows how. I just didn't want to bother him and..."

"Come on off the table, kit. We need to talk a little. I ... owe you an apology." Vanarra stepped down to help Sahni onto the floor, and nearly had to support her full weight when Sahni lost her balance which pushed Van into the wall.

"Oh, I'm sorry! I'm so sorry, Van!" the Nephti effused.

"No, my fault. I should have braced better. If I hadn't been here, kit, I think you would have planted your muzzle. Let's go to my office," Van replied as she shook off the hit.

"Okay. I am still sorry about that."

Van opened the door and said, "It's alright" as she looked back and saw the Nephti was actually limping. She also had seen enough in her time to know by facial expression, ear twitch, and tail that Sahnassa wasn't faking. "It looks like … I pushed you way too hard last night, kit. I'm sorry about that."

"I … just slept wrong, I think," Sahni replied, walking past Van into her office.

"Sit on the couch, Sahni. Lay down if you have to."

"I … thanks, but I don't dare lay down," the Nephti admitted. "I … I was about to fall asleep up in the ceiling."

"Yeah, Flint told me about you not having a bed."

"Well, I had one in academy, but … it was theirs; I couldn't keep it."

"Sahni," Van stated softly as she sat down on a chair in front of the Nephti. "I … really didn't treat you right, last sol. What I did was wrong, and it won't happen again. It's not right for you to surrender your pay to Raska or anyone else. I had already talked with you; that's where it should have ended. I'm sorry. Now, I am going to permit you to give Raska your pay this one time, but I am going to give you something to make up for it. I'd like to take you shopping and get you a bed, and … if we go early enough, it could be delivered to your place and set up before tonight. Would you like to do that?"

"Oh, Van! Really? I … I'll work extra intervals to make up for it!"

"No," Van corrected. "You've already been doing that. You may have realized by now I've had someone coming in checking your work from time to time. It's Buck Harlock. He's an old friend of mine. He says you're doing a great job, and that you're way ahead of schedule. Flint's impressed, too. I … kind of have to rely on their judgment, since I don't know what's normal for this sort of thing. Just think of this as a bonus and … an apology."

"It's okay, Van, and thank you!" Sahnassa offered earnestly, seeming like she had more life in her than before. "This really means so much, and I really, really appreciate it!"

"You are welcome," Van replied, feeling more acutely shamed by Sahnassa's gratitude than she had by anything else in a very long time.

Sahnassa lay in absolute bliss, her body sinking slowly into the gel foam of the new mattress her boss had just purchased for her and had delivered. "Ohhhh," she groaned involuntarily as it adjusted to the contours of her body. She felt pretty light-headed, too, because of the medication Van had bought for her muscle aches and pains. After buying her a meal, Sahnassa had to stop Van. Something was clearly very wrong, and Van was trying to make up for it in a big way. It got worse as they shopped, as Sahni kept having to interrupt the sales staff in order to point at Van as the one with the funds. At the end of the experience, she didn't know who was more frazzled. Now, in the safety and solitude of her own lair, Sahni breathed out, "Wow, thanks … Van." Even as part of her tried to weave sensual and exotic fantasies through the wonderful feelings she was experiencing, the Nephti was already slipping into a deep and contented sleep.

Van paced back and forth in her office, feeling completely disjointed from her normal reality in a most unsettling way. She had done as Flint suggested – gone bed shopping for Sahni, but the kit could barely keep up with her, so she stopped and picked up something to help the pathetic Nephti through the next few intervals. It seemed very effective on the kit, perhaps a little too effective, because it made Sahnassa a little spacey. However, she was coherent enough that Van took her to where she had purchased her own bed, and the Nephti did fine except in one area. When Van was on her own, she was used to averting eye contact until she indicated that she had the funds to purchase; then, the purebreds would allow her to look them in the eye or near enough, without being offended. Sahnassa, being purebred and avowed, was their natural target, but she insistently refocused them on Vanarra.

It was her deference to Van that seemed to stun the sales staff and unnerve Vanarra. "This kit is going to get disavowed on the spot, if she keeps this up." However, when one of the staff was somewhat rude to Vanarra, a whole different side of Sahni showed up – one she'd never seen before. The Nephti started using some carefully chosen phrases that sounded very "familial" in nature, with just a mild salting of threat for good measure to realign the expectations of the one who had shown the disrespect. That Perratti had disappeared, and his sales manager had appeared in his place, a full-blooded Nephti from Sahnassa's own house. When Van had glanced at her, she saw her quiet little Sahni standing at her full height, eyes bright, and staring down her opponent.

As Van sat on her office couch, she decided she wasn't embarrassed by what Sahnassa had done in terms of how the sales staff might treat her in the future; she was ashamed because Sahni had stood up for her and insisted they treat her well "as she will be the one paying you for this purchase" she remembered Sahni stating quite directly.

No purebred ever stood up for Vanarra like that before, not even Sorla. Sahni was almost psychotic about it – willing to take on anyone who dared insult Van. It made Vanarra gravely regret the way she had treated the winsome, quiet technologist. "Okay, I admit it Ash, I do!" she said to herself. "I punched her in the gut, and … she stood up to defend me afterwards. I feel like burrower droppings."

A part of her argued in her defense that she was at least feeling something, but Van knew that the swirl of emotions roiling inside of her would make any real focus on work impossible. After checking in with Flint, she was out the door and headed to the gym.

That evening, just before drifting off to sleep, Vanarra was finally able to bring the events of the sol into a less chaotic focus. The heavy sparring session with her Vulpi fitness instructor, Kylie, was a good reason why; it had been a real and true fight, with Kylie only able to best Van narrowly. When Van had told Kylie a little of what was bothering her, the Vulpi suggested running on the machines for awhile.

That had proven as useful as the fight in burning off her excess nervous energy, not only because the machine allowed her to push herself as hard as she could go, but a certain nice looking Perratti had taken an interest in her as she exerted herself, and he seemed to enjoy the view. Feeling a very definite desire from him, she had somewhat coquettishly surrendered her number, and now she wondered if he would call. "Nice butt," she thought to herself, "I hope he calls."

Van knew that any liaison would be short lived, but at least she'd get to recapture a little of what she had lost when Ash passed away. Something no Perratti or Lupar would ever know when they shared her bed and company was that seldom, if ever, were her passionate feelings truly for them, but her ardor and connection was worship of a sort to that precious one she had lost – save for in the hidden recesses of her heart. She smiled a little predatorily to herself thinking about how she had surprised more than a couple of her itinerate lovers with her intensity. Thinking about the lovely body of the Perratti from the gym as she drifted off to sleep, she was amused by how a little, purebred Nephti in her office could shake up an Anati's view of the world while the same Anati happily looked forward to shaking a nice-looking male's world to its foundations.

Chapter 16: Connectivity

It does seem more alive this sol than before," Saiphar commented as he looked at the racks of humming equipment – a hum more prominent than it had been in the past.

"Oh, Saiphar!" Sahni exclaimed from the small table where she typed on her own portable computer. "Yes. The site's now active and available to the TransNet. There's not much on it yet, just a test of sorts."

"What is it you want to test?" he asked, curious.

"Oh, redundancy, security, and standards conformance," she stated plainly, and the artist looked at her, confused. Taking a moment to think about it, she explained, "I have to make sure it's reliable, that it takes the safety and privacy of Vanarra's customers seriously, and that it obeys the rules and customs required of it."

Saiphar nodded, smiling a little. "Then it should do well," he answered. "Its creator has all of those attributes."

"Thank you," Sahni replied, a little embarrassed but grateful. Saiphar was someone in the office she'd started to get genuinely close to. She appreciated his artistry, and he seemed fascinated with the technical endeavor she was engrossed in. "If I only had your talent for creating beauty, but ... Saiphar, you might be able to help. I wonder if Van would let you create some paintings exclusively for the TransNet. It would certainly be beautiful, then."

"I heard my name!" Vanarra reported, sticking her head in the door.

"We ... or I, rather—" Sahni began.

"We, Sahni. 'We' will do," the Vulpi stated calmly. Van smiled a little which made it all the more difficult for Sahnassa to continue.

"Well, uh, I ... well, we were wondering if you could allow ... might have Saiphar do some paintings for the TransNet site. His work is so amazing, and it would certainly represent your business very well."

"Filling in all of those thingies you showed me in the demo, right?" Van asked as clarification, stepping in. At Sahnassa's nod, Van answered, "I think I like that, but we'll need to map out some specifics. I pay Saiphar for each work he creates, or the client does, so I want to make sure I'm not creating art that won't be seen by anyone."

"Sahni, do you have any examples I could look at?" Saiphar queried.

"There was a really great book of that stuff in the academy library, and a few periodicals on design that talked about creating art for the TransNet. I can't borrow from there anymore, however. I'm not a student."

"Can you get it from somewhere else?" Van asked.

"Pinnacle might have them," Sahni commented. "Come to think of it, I need a place outside of the office to test the set-up here. I don't have reliable TransNet back at my place, but they've got a free wireless connection at the archive. Might work out pretty well."

Vanarra's tail swished a couple of times before she could control it. "I like that idea, Sahni," Van stated as calmly as she could. "But there's something else I want you to do if you're going there. Can you come to my office?"

"Sure, boss," Sahnassa replied, and at Van's smile and departure, she turned towards Saiphar. "You're very kind. Thank you."

"Thank you, as well, for the inspiration and ... perhaps, a few additional commissions," he smiled ironically. She patted him on the shoulder as she left, and he lingered just for a moment, enjoying the swish of her tail before returning to his own duties.

"Sahni," Van started, "I've ... heard some really interesting things about the archive. It's architecture is supposed to be very pretty inside. We kind of talked about a brochure and an index, but I wonder if you wouldn't do a little bit more for me if you're going to visit."

"What would you like?" Sahnassa asked.

"Well, here, let me make a list," Van replied as she pulled out a pen and paper and started jotting down notes. "Book on TransNet marketing, perhaps about how my sort of muzzle-to-ear advertising could make the TransNet site worth my while. I also would be interested in a book on new government taxes – I hear that's changing this season. Also, the archive index and a brochure, but also … I want pictures." Van stopped her note-writing to pull an expensive camera out of her desk. "This is the company's, and it's really pricey, so be careful, kit, okay?"

"Yes, Van. I will," Sahnassa assured her as she gently took the device from Van's paw. "What pictures do you want me to take?"

"This could cost you a little time, and you may have to be clever about how you explain it, but I want the following shots: the outside, straight on so I can see the whole thing, and then from the sides and back. The inside, from as high up in the library portion as you can get down on the stacks – I've heard that view is inspiring, and I might have an event there. I kind of want to know what I'm getting into. Also," Van continued rapidly as she penned, "I want to see any area that's themed like … like … do they have an area for kits and cubs?" she asked, although knowing the answer.

"Yes," Sahni replied. "I've been there several times, myself."

"Good, good. Don't put a kink in anyone's tail or anything, but take as many pictures as you can of even the most inconsequential stuff. If I can't visit, I might as well be able to see what it's like, right?"

"Sure, Van. I … I understand," Sahnassa replied, a touch of compassion in her voice. "I'm surprised you haven't had Saiphar or Tresk go in for you before."

"Not willing to risk it. Like it or not, Sahni, your 'de Orturu' suffix gives you a bit more flexibility should someone start poking questions at you. Disavowed Vulpi might not have any better chance there than an Anati if someone starts getting huffy, and I know you can stand up on your hind-legs if you have to." Seeing Sahni's confusion, Van explained in two words, "Bed shopping."

Sahnassa laughed. "Oh, right! Well, they were being rude! Hey, and thank you so very much again—"

"You can stop thanking me for the bed, Sahni," Van chided, but she was smiling. "Five hundred times is more than enough. Now, understand that I will pay you for the travel and for your effort. Take your time, Sahni. Do what you need to do. I'll take care of the cost."

"Thank you, Van ... for this trust," Sahnassa offered as she held the camera carefully in both paws.

"You're welcome. Oh, here's the case for it. I'll see you when you get back, okay?"

"Okay. Thank you, again, Van."

"No kit, thank you." Vanarra returned to her work as the Nephti left the office. Only a few passes later, however, Raska knocked on the frame of Van's door. "Oh, Raska. What is it?"

"Van, we need an extra paw or two with moving a few things. Have you seen the de Orturu?"

Vanarra frowned. "She's – one – on assignment for me and – two – not the 'de Orturu.' Let's stick to Sahni or Sahnassa if you can spare the energy. If Mauft's not too busy, she can help. You'll have to ask her, though."

The mixed blood female nearly winced at that suggestion. Mauft didn't respond well to requests for assistance unless the need was dire, so in effect, Raska knew that Van was saying no. "I think this Nephti has you ... deceived, Van. I don't think she's what she appears."

Van sat up and fixed her with an icy stare. "Care to state specifics?"

"Just a feeling," Raska replied with shrug.

"Hmm... Well, last name or no, she's given me no reason to distrust her motives. Minus stupid mistakes from time to time, she's as genuine as the color of my eyes. Until she gives me a reason to, say, question what she says, she gets the benefit of the doubt, just as everyone else does ... until they screw up and break my trust."

Feeling some real menace and accusation in Van's hard expression, Raska ducked in a short bow and apologized. "I'm sorry, Van. You're right, of course. I will go see if we can manage with what we have."

"Sounds like a good idea, Raska. Sounds smart," Van stated, her tone warning. Cowed and a little surprised, Raska left the room. Hearing a noise in front of her, she looked up to see Saiphar. "What's up?"

"Can I talk to you in private for a moment?"

"Sure, just close the door."

The Vulpi did and motioned to a chair. At Van's nod, he sat down. "Sahni seems like she's doing good work for you."

"Yes, Saiphar. I think so," Van answered, but then looked at the Vulpi questioningly. "Why … are you in my office talking about the Nephti?"

"You have a rule," he stated carefully. "About office … relationships."

Van put down what she was doing and sat back in her chair. "I do and for good reason. You … like her?"

"She's … interesting, shy," he offered quietly.

"Nice tail, too," Van commented, with a smirk. "Her front chassis isn't bad, either."

"There's … a lot about her that's nice," he answered with a shy smile.

"I understand," Van replied gently, "but Saiphar, my rule still stands. She's only been here a little while, and … there's a lot we don't know about her. What I do know is that you are right, she's doing a good job for this business, for all of us. If she can get the TransNet site up and running, it could allow us to pull ahead of our competitors. If she can't, we'll slip behind them, and that won't be good for any of us. Settle for friendship right now, let her … inspire you if you wish, but nothing more for now, Saiphar. Please, for all of us, and for you, too. She … she may say no. I don't want you to get hurt like that—"

"When we need to work together," he observed. "I see. She is inspiring, kind of like you are."

"Well, Saiphar!" Van chuckled. "You should never fess up to wanting to hunt the boss!"

"Not like that," he replied, embarrassed. "No, you both have survived hard things and stayed in the light. I can't tell you why I can see that in both of you, but it's true." The Vulpi stood and bowed slightly. "I will abide by your decision, Van."

Vanarra nodded. "And if things change, Saiphar, I'll tell you. I'll remember."

"Thank you."

After he was gone, she thought about what he said – how he saw the two of them in much the same light. "Maybe," she breathed, and Van smiled knowing that the normally shy Vulpi artist had gathered enough courage to come talk to her.

Sahnassa drove her hover straight to the Pinnacle center archive, a destination she knew well enough from going there so many times as a child with her parents. Thankfully, both of them were likely at work, so the chance of running into either of them was positively zero. As she headed down the fast trail to reach the archive, she started thinking about Vanarra's request for pictures. It was a little bit odd, but then again she was being paid, and the request was mostly benign, so she couldn't really find any good reason not to do as she was asked. Sahnassa was just grateful that her situation at work had smoothed out, unlike the one with her parents.

As she turned off the fast trail and made her way to the long entrance road in front of the archive, she began to feel sad and nostalgic about where she was going. In truth, the last time she had been to the archive was with her father and sisters, just before Triana went to academy. As her vehicle slipped through the small forest surrounding the Pinnacle Center, she could see its single grand spire reaching into the sky. "It is inspiring," she sighed and pulled into a parking lane alongside the hover trail.

After nearly a half interval of taking pictures from the outside, Sahnassa was in a better mood. It was a bright and sunny morning, and more than a few families and other groups had made the grounds of the archive their place to enjoy the sol, and she noticed she wasn't the only one taking pictures. "Well, enough fun out here. I'd better head inside and get to work."

She turned to walk back to her vehicle, which was now some distance away. It struck the Nephti how few times in the last five or even more seasons she had been outside on a wonderful sol such as this, and feeling a little guilty, she removed her paw-shoes and started walking through the grass to reach her hover. "Oh, this is so nice!" A whisk ball rolled in front of her, and without really thinking, she bounded forward and kicked it back in the general direction from which it had come. "You're welcome!" she called back to the group of cubs playing nearby. Laughing a little when another errant play brought the ball back in her path a few steps later, she gave it a good, sound kick which sent all of the team running to reach it. A very fast cub managed not only to catch up to the ball, but with one slicing move of his stick, managed to get the ball right into the goal. Sahni cheered and applauded for them, and several of the parents minding the children waved back, smiling.

"Oh, I need to get out more!" she said to herself. Now that she was having a decent night's sleep, Sahni was actually starting to play her practice orlure again. "It would be great to bring it out here and just play for whoever wanted to listen. Maybe, I'll ask for a rest sol or something."

Soon, she was back in her vehicle and heading towards the parking garage of the archive. Pulling into a spot after paying the fee, she clicked off a couple of pictures and then made for the lifts. Emerging in the cavernous atrium of the center, she soon found her way inside the library portion of the archive. "I've never actually had to come in for TransNet access," she thought to herself, and made her way to the information desk. There, a petite little Perratti sat with her head turned to the side, working on a computer.

"Excuse me?"

"Yes, may I help you?" the Perratti asked, and turning around, Sahnassa almost gasped at the deep scars visible on her muzzle. The Perratti smiled a rueful smile and prodded again, "May I help you?"

"Oh, sorry," Sahni apologized as she pulled out her family ID. "I … need to use the wireless to get into TransNet here, if you don't mind. Where do I go?"

"The entire archive now has wireless coverage, has had it for some time. Do you have an account with us?" she asked as she keyed Sahnassa's ID into the terminal. "Oh, well, you haven't been in here in a very long time – your account is dormant. Do you want me to reactivate it?"

"Oh, yes, please. I was away at academy."

"I understand," the Perratti archivist replied. "There, you're active and all set should you need to borrow anything. Now, there are conversation rooms on the first level, right side if you need to video conference with someone, but if your work will be relatively quiet, you can use any of the desks along the wall. They are actually quite comfortable, so I'm told."

"Thank you, very much," Sahni answered and, taking her portable computer, made her way to the rows of desks where several others were quietly working, their features mostly obscured by the partitions between them.

Sahni found the network fairly easy to connect to, and in a few moments, she had located Van's new TransNet site and started testing. "Oh, great!" she thought, nearly giggling aloud, "It's out there, just like it should be!" Although it was only a "coming soon" site, Sahnassa was able to do a fair amount of testing with it, including finding that she'd mistyped a part of the security settings, so the site was only available in non-secure mode. "That alone makes the trip worthwhile." Scribbling down some notes, she then tried a few basic volume tests with a script program, and found that the site was managing load exactly as it should be. "It'll slow down some with Saiphar's art, but it will be worth it." After trying the administrator's remote account, she was fairly certain that the site was working exactly as she wanted it to, and with a few keystrokes, she shut down her computer, folded the cover down, and stood.

Looking up, her eyes instantly locked on a pair of purple ones within a light purple and silver stripped face that seemed familiar, somehow. Cocking her head to the side a little, in curiosity, made the female she was looking at nearly shout. "Sahnassa! It is you!"

It had been so long that it took a moment for it to register who this attractive Nephti was standing in front of her. "Hylea?" she asked, furrowing her brow. "It ... it can't be!"

The Nephti clasped her paws together, eyes welling, and nodded.

"Excuse me," the Perratti archivist whispered loud enough for the two of them to hear as she walked by. "If you need to have a conversation, one of the rooms over there is open."

"Oh, sorry," Sahnassa breathed. A part of her wanted to bound across the partition and hug her sister, but she motioned to her, instead, and met her at the end of the desks. Embracing Hylea, Sahnassa whispered into her ear, "Oh, I can't believe it's you! You ... you're huge!"

"Hey, I'm not that big!" Hylea complained. "I do exercise."

"No, no, not like that," she chuckled as she released her sister and led her by the paw to the conversation room. "You ... you were like half my height almost when I left for school!"

"That ... was a long time ago," Hylea replied sadly.

"I know. Is ... anyone else here?"

"No. It's just me. I'm trying to check out schools and study up for my entrance exams, get an internship…"

"Oh, I remember that," Sahnassa replied in a normal voice as the doors to the conversation room closed behind the pair of them. "Oh, come here, kit! Let me look at you!" Hylea had a nice figure and a lovely tail that sported its own ink-dipped tip. "You … you're positively beautiful, kit!"

"You kind of look like you've lost weight," Hylea replied, sounding worried.

"Just a bit. Academy is tough; don't let anyone fool you. Do you have some time to talk?" Sahni asked.

"I … do," Hylea replied nervously as she sat.

Feeling the joyous shock of seeing her sister beginning to abate, Sahni could now sense Hylea's uncertainty with the situation. Sitting down in front of her, Sahnassa added, "If … you want to talk with me, that is."

"I do, I do, but … you have to understand, Sahnassa. It's … been hard since you left."

"It's been hard for me, too," Sahni replied, a little edge on her voice warning her sibling off if she intended to lay all of the troubles in their lair on *her* tail.

"I … can only imagine. I didn't understand a lot about what was happening at the time, and … I still don't think I have the full story from Mom. Dad doesn't want to talk about it. What happened, Sahnassa? Why did you … disgrace them like that? You basically yanked out a law meant to save the young from bad parents. Mom and Dad aren't bad parents!"

"They … they were to me, kit. I don't expect for you to understand it, but … when I told them I didn't want to be an archivist or a litigator, they just tried to crush my spirit at every turn. Dame Rothnerra, too – they nearly ruined my life, Hylea. They forced me into a school that I couldn't afford even with the matriarchal scholarship and then … then they tried to enroll me in classes so advanced that I would have failed! I … hated to do what I did, but they weren't going to be satisfied until I was crawling back to them telling them I would do everything they told me to do!"

"What's wrong with that, Sahnassa? They are both so respected in their fields and so honored! Why not follow their advice?"

Sahnassa looked her sister right in the eye. "Because it wasn't advice, Hylea, it was an order – have the life we tell you to and the career we tell you to or else you're not wanted, disposable ... disavowed for all practical purposes. I'm sorry, kit! I ... loved them; I guess I still do, but give up every dream I've ever had and everything I've ever worked for? How could they ask that of me?!"

"Is that ... really how it was?" Hylea asked, sounding doubtful.

"Yes!" Sahni exclaimed. "I felt like I was living only for the purpose of filling out the dame's roster of proud graduates – extra tail-fur and striping for her to parade in front of the other dames! That's ... not a life, Hylea. Not by any means."

Hylea looked at the floor, trying to sort out Sahnassa's revelation against what her mother had told her. "Mom ... said your grades were bad, and that proved you had chosen poorly."

"Kit, my grades suffered because I had to work to get enough money to eat and cover my school costs!"

"But they provided for you; they were forced to!" Hylea protested.

"Yeah, some of it! It wasn't enough for Harnard, and they damn well knew that when they killed off every other choice I had! Now, here! I want you to read this, kit! Here is how much they care about me!" Hylea took the note Sahnassa had in her satchel and read it.

"This isn't Mom. It's not the way she writes. It's ... it's Dame Rothnerra – that's who it reads like."

"Well, it's signed by Mom, which means she was willing to have it written and sent to me!" Sahnassa answered bitterly. "Hylea, I may carry de Orturu as my family name, but that's all I'm carrying right now! Kept by no one and yet I'm still keeper of all. I still pay my family dues! I'm ... damn near broke, Hylea, because of them! I'm in debt to my ear-tips because of them! Other kits and cubs left Harnard with their matrons lining up plush little jobs for them with nice salaries! Every technologist in my class had an offer for a job except for me! Hylea, they hurt me, and they keep on hurting me! I wish it weren't that way. If they ... if you all only knew how lonely I was – all these seasons. They ... they gave up on me. They ... don't love me anymore, and ... you and Triana gave up on me, too." Sahnassa hid her head in her paws, knowing her sister would probably walk out, but unable to keep from saying everything she had been carrying inside for so long.

"I'm … sorry, Sahnassa. Triana and I … didn't know what to do. We've talked about it so many times, but with the Compact in place, Dad made it sound like we could find ourselves in jeopardy of disavowal if we said or did anything wrong. We were afraid. I'm sorry."

"I'm sorry, too. I've … I've missed you growing up! We've … lost so many good times we might have had," Sahnassa replied, now crying.

Hylea's paw went to her sister's shoulder, and she sat beside her. "I'm sorry, Sahnassa. I didn't know. I didn't understand. Maybe there's hope things can be better between us, now?"

"I don't know, Hylea. It … would take a lot for me to get over what they've put me through."

"But it all worked out, didn't it? You've got a job now, right?"

"Just contract work," Sahnassa whispered. "It's not great, but it's something. It may lead to better things. I guess I have a place to sleep and food to eat, so … I'm not complaining."

"You know, I see how they've treated you and how harsh that must seem, but do you know, they haven't touched your room since you left? Everything is exactly as it was. Some nights, when Mom doesn't know, I … I go in and lay in your bed. It was the only way I could feel close to you, and … sometimes, I would go looking for Mom or Dad, and I'd find them in there, just staring – maybe crying. They hurt, too, Sahnassa. Maybe … maybe in time, and with a lot of … forgiveness in both directions, there won't be any need for the Compact."

"I … don't know. I hope you fare better than I, kit. I don't know if I'll ever get back their love and respect."

"What would it take for them to earn yours again?"

Hylea's question made her sit quietly for a moment and think. Finally, Sahnassa stated, "They have to put the welfare of their daughters above that of their dame or matron." She looked at her younger sister to see how that statement impacted her, and strangely enough, Hylea was nodding in agreement. "Has it been that way for you, too?"

"Some … a little … yes," came the hesitant confession, but then Hylea added, "but my problem is that I don't know what I want to be when I get out of academy. I picked archivist prep, and now they're leaving me alone, pretty much. I figured I could dual focus when I was in school and perhaps slip into something else when I went to find a job."

"You're smarter than I was," Sahnassa admitted. "Perhaps smarter than Matron Shalarra, too. She ... supported me, but I almost feel – I don't know – I almost feel like I was a ... ball in a game they were playing against one another, the dame and the matron. I suppose I'll never know."

"Sahnassa, you should know that Matron Drualla passed away two moons ago. Matron Astalla has just been announced as our new matron. She's young, well, younger than Shalarra or Drualla, and ... she's different. She can stand up to Dame Rothnerra, it seems. She's smart – knows how to walk the trail between serving her families and serving the dame."

"How can you know that?"

"The questions she asked. She pulled me into a room and questioned me pretty intensely about my choice for academy focus, and she asked ... about you."

"Me? I would have thought it was easier for her to just drop me from the list of individuals she has to worry about."

"I think you taking the Compact has never sat well with the Grand Matriarch. I've been to see her once, like you used to – she asked about you, too. They aren't asking in a bad way, Sahnassa. I think ... I think that the matriarch and this new matron feel the family has failed you. I think they want to change that. Triana and I have talked about it."

"So what does the brightest and fastest-rising new litigator in de Orturu think about that?" Sahni asked with a smirk.

"Well, at least you are reading the family news, still," Hylea chuckled.

"A little. Only when I'm ... homesick," Sahnassa admitted.

"Triana is ... angry with Mom and Dad about what happened. She's not completely happy with you, of course—"

"As if she ever was," Sahnassa interjected.

"True, but she's like me, Sahnassa. We ... lost something we'd always had – it's like you died. We've both grieved for you and seeing you now, even ... even if you can't forgive either of us for not standing up to our parents or the dame – we love you, and we've missed you. I ... listen to orlure music just to remind myself of you."

Sahni reached out and held the paw of her younger sister. "I've missed when we spent time together, when we were hurt or afraid and got close to one another."

Hylea reached back and said, "Me, too. Sahnassa, I want to do something. I want to tell our new matron that I've spoken to you. I want to tell her how you feel, your side. Now, under the Compact, she can't cause you any harm, but ... she might be willing to reach out to you. If ... if she can make some assurances to you, maybe things could change?" Seeing Sahnassa break eye contact and look away, hurt, she added, "If they only changed a little, just barely, it would be something. Any move on your part might start making things better. I ... I don't want you to be the sister I never see! I hope ... one sol, we might be together again – all of us."

"It would take a long time, Hylea. The hurt ... is deep."

"I'll tell Astalla that, too. I will make her understand exactly how you feel. You ... you may not believe this, but Dad's a little proud of you, in a way. He expected that once you'd taken the Compact, you'd never pay family dues – get yourself disavowed. Still, even though de Orturu has been horrible to you, you still honor your family. You are reaching back to them, Sahnassa. Let them reach back to you, too, okay?"

Looking at Hylea, she realized her younger sister was right. If she had wanted to, Sahnassa could have simply stopped paying anything to de Orturu, and her family would have taken that as an insult and likely disavowed her. "The ... message I got when I started paying dues. You said it was Rothnerra?"

"I'm certain of it."

"When ... when I started doing the one thing that would have shown I still honored my family—"

"She tried to drive you away with that note," Hylea completed, sadly.

"She wants to have me disavowed."

"Without a doubt. From the things she says, Sahnassa, yes. Talk to Astalla, see if she can be the bridge back for you. Don't let one horrible, sour old dame who is gray as the grave and has a backside filled with her own self importance keep you from being with us. Please?"

A tear running down her cheek fur, Sahnassa reached over and brought her sister's head close to hers and touched them together affectionately. "I ... will do as you ask, little sister. You know best."

"Oh, if only Triana would say that!" Hylea laughed, but she, too had tears running down her cheek fur.

"Don't stop breathing while you wait for that, okay?" Sahnassa shot back, laughing, and the two now embraced each other in earnest, holding each other for a long while.

"So," Hylea began as they let go of one another, "how do I contact you? You have a PawLink?"

"Can't afford one," Sahni admitted. "But I do have a TransNet mailing address now. Here, let me write it down for you."

"Just key it into mine," Hylea offered, pulling her PawLink out of her bag.

"Wow, nice!" Sahnassa breathed as she looked over the glistening device. "When did you get this?"

"You ... don't want to know," Hylea replied, shamefacedly.

"Let me guess, when you told them you wanted to be an archivist?" Sahnassa asked as she keyed with her claw-tips.

"Yeah ... that and a hover. I kind of milked that one pretty good."

"Well, good for you, honestly. You are smarter than I was. I should have just done what you suggested, but ... well, ugh, that would have taken me like seven seasons. With the technology degree, I would have never been able to pull that off."

"What is 'Sahni'?" Hylea asked, taking back the device. "And what is 'Celebrations by Vanarra'?"

"Sahni's a short name some ... friends of mine gave me. I ... I kind of like it. Celebrations by Vanarra is just who I'm contracting with, at the moment. I'm hoping that if I do well there, it could lead to some other work, maybe independent, maybe with a pack; I don't know."

"You found a job, Sahnassa – that was like shoving prowler poop in Dame Rothnerra's muzzle – just remember that."

Sahni laughed hard at her sister's coarse comment, and Hylea joined in the fun. There was a knock on the glass door, and the Perratti archivist stuck her head in. "I'm sorry, excuse me, but these are ... *conversation* rooms. Your laughter is carrying. Could you please be a little more quiet?"

"I'm sorry," Hylea offered. "We ... we're sisters, and we haven't seen each other in seasons."

"Oh! I … I understand. Sorry."

"Don't be," Sahnassa assured the archivist. "We were too loud."

"I've got to be going, anyway. Mom's going to wonder where I ran off to. I'm supposed to be lining up a shadow opportunity here at the archive."

"Oh really?" the Perratti asked, kindly. "Are you studying to be an archivist?"

"Yes, actually. I'm Hylea de Orturu. I'm Holana's daughter."

The Perratti's eyes widened considerably. "You are … *that* Holana's daughter?" Hylea nodded proudly. "I would absolutely love to sponsor you! I'm Lyssia de Oterbythe. I'll give you my card if you can come to the desk."

"Wow, that would be really, really great news! What are you going to do, Sahnassa?"

"Instructions from my boss. She wants pictures of the archive, if that's okay?"

"What does she plan to use them for?" Lyssia asked.

"Inspiration, mostly. The architecture here is legendary, and she doesn't have time to come down here or send her artist. So, I get the job."

"Well, I find it inspiring, for sure. Feel free to take all the pictures you want, just don't disturb anyone else and don't use flash lighting, okay?"

"Thank you. Okay, another hug before you go, kit?" Sahnassa asked, and she and her sister hugged tightly. "It is good to see you again, and … I do still care about you all … okay?"

"Okay," Hylea was crying as she parted from Sahnassa with one last paw-clasp, and then followed Lyssia out of the room.

For several intervals, Sahnassa went around the archive taking pictures and thinking. Going to nearly every level and trying every perspective, she examined the archive much as she was examining her own life. Hylea was right, she decided, by doing the one thing that she could to show loyalty to her house – paying dues – she had again thwarted Dame Rothnerra's revenge, and every dues payment she made did the same. "Mom's either in on it, scared, or just an idiot,"

she thought harshly. "Still, Hylea says they hurt. Maybe ... maybe I need to work with Astalla. Maybe I could take my case right to the matriarch, ask for our family to be reassigned. Wouldn't that be rich! If I could get Mom and Dad to go along with it, they've got more than enough reputation to make it stick."

As she climbed the circular steps to reach the top level, she continued trying to work things out in her head. "It would be great if they made a break, but why haven't they fought for me, for themselves?" In many ways, she thought she could guess the reason why. Rothnerra had many contacts and many different Thurians beholden to her, and those contacts had proven useful to her father, and if family news was to be judged accurate, Dame Rothnerra was close by whenever major arbitrations were signed. "Lining herself up to be the next Grand Matriarch. Ugh, then I *will* be disavowed."

Reaching the top level, she walked to the railing and looked down at the expanse of the archive library beneath her. "Wow, Van, I ... I can see what you mean," she said quietly, taking several more pictures. Putting the camera down, Sahni took a moment to enjoy the view herself. "I'm not going to be working for Van forever; she's said as much. It ... would be nice to get a little help from my family in finding something else. If I had her over to my lair ... no, that wouldn't do. I'd have to buy chairs and tables and pictures. Neutral ground, maybe here. Maybe in a conversation room. Alright, Hylea. Maybe this could work out somehow, and ... meeting here could work for a start."

After stopping to get some lunch, Sahnassa returned to the office. Quietly knocking on her boss's door, she heard Vanarra bade her enter, and she found Saiphar talking with Van – several sketches taped to the sofa. "We've been busy, Sahni!" Van replied brightly. "Saiphar's been inspired!"

"He has?" Sahnassa queried as she walked forward to look at the numerous sketches. "For ... the TransNet site?" she asked.

"Yes," he replied. "Van took what she remembered about what was needed and kind of gave me an overview. I ... had some time while you were gone—"

"To do like a masterpiece with each one?" Sahnassa asked, disbelieving.

Van smiled as she watched Saiphar's blush furs go up. She could understand why the Vulpi was finding it difficult not to fall for Sahnassa. Her praise of his work was genuine, and given who she was and what she was, Vanarra knew it was as close to official recognition as he had gotten save for those who complimented his work at events.

"This … is just a start. With more specifics, I can do better," he offered, shyly.

"Oh, then I have something for you," Sahnassa replied as she gently gave Vanarra the camera and then pulled a book out from under her arms for Saiphar. "This is a TransNet design reference guide. I put bookmarks in the pages you need to look at. It talks about the colors to use and what level of detail looks good and what just … well, gets lost."

"My gratitude towards you, Sahni. This … is a tremendous gift; thank you."

"Uh, that gift is a book that has to be returned to the archive in what, Sahni?"

"A moon."

"Yes, so … it isn't a gift, as such," Van warned.

"It wasn't the book. It was the time she took highlighting what I needed to know. Very kind, Sahni."

"Well, Saiphar, I guess you'd better get reading. You're not going to have much time before we start packing for our overnight tomorrow."

"You're right, Van. Thank you, and thank you, Sahnassa de Orturu, very kind." With that, she patted him on the back, which caused a loft in his tail that Sahni missed before he was able to pull it back down again. "I'll … I'll be going then," he said and then quietly left the room.

"He really appreciates the compliments, Sahni," Van told her quietly. "They mean a lot to him."

"I'm sincere about them. I've seen fine art growing up, but I never knew anyone who could make it. He's quite a treasure."

"Yes, yes he is. Now, take a look. Is anything here usable?"

"As sketches, probably not, but he's got the right idea. I can go through these and try to tell him what works and what doesn't."

"Sounds good. Let's take them down and stack them," Van offered, and the pair quickly had the numerous images in a pile. "Now, how did the rest of your trip go?"

"Well, the site is out there on TransNet, and it can be reached, oh, and here's your TransNet marketing book. It was highly recommended by the archivist there."

"Oh, thank you, Sahnassa. This is just wonderful," Vanarra replied as she accepted the book. "Mark any pages in here for me?"

"I started to, but then I was marking every one of them."

"So you're saying that I have to read everything in this?" Vanarra asked, flipping through.

"You're the boss, Van. You do what you think is best," Sahnassa dutifully replied.

"But I would get a lot out of this if I did read it all, wouldn't I?"

"I thought it would be very helpful," Sahni replied, again trying to avoid giving Van an instruction.

"Okay, kit. I'll have to balance that with some other entertainment that's sprung up in my evenings, but I'll fit it in. Has it got to be back next moon?"

"Yes. Unfortunately, the archive doesn't offer much leeway on that. Also, here are the brochures, the index, and the camera is positively loaded. I spent most of my time taking pictures."

"They didn't run you off?" Van asked, curious, picking up the camera and turning it on.

"No, they didn't. I spoke to the archivist; I think flattery of the archive went a long way."

"I'm … sure … it … did," Van replied, getting quieter and more introspective with each word.

After several moments of silence, Sahnassa asked, "Are they okay?"

Van seemed to snap out of her trance and sniff a bit, but then turned the camera off and laid it aside. "Very well done, kit. Very well done. Anything else?"

"Well, there was one other thing," Sahnassa confessed. "I … I ran into my sister. I … haven't seen her in five or six seasons."

Van's eyebrows furrowed. "Not in six seasons?"

"Family problems, but … maybe, just maybe, there's an opening there. Maybe … we can forgive each other, or start to."

"Sounds serious," Van observed. "Any chance she'll cause trouble for you, here?"

"No. If … if anything happens with my family, I'll make sure it stays clear of here."

"Don't want them to know who you're working for?" Van questioned.

"Don't want them taking time away from my work or getting in the way of what has to be done. She's not a client, after all, my new matron."

"New matron?"

"The old one died."

"I suppose it happens," Van observed somewhat neutrally. "So, what are your next steps getting Celebrations by Vanarra on TransNet?"

"Well, I have notes from the archive, things I need to fix, and then, I need to start working with Saiphar on art. Will he be available tomorrow evening?"

Vanarra grimaced, feeling it unfortunate that she had to broach this subject with her purebred avowed Nephti when she seemed to be in a good mood. "He … won't be. In fact, the office will be pretty much closed down tomorrow afternoon until the sol after next. We have a very big event west of Shanandrae that's going to take the whole staff."

"But … I'm not going?" Sahni asked, concerned.

"Not for this. I'm sorry, Sahnassa, but this type of event is restricted, and for the protection of my business I have to be extremely selective about who goes and who doesn't. I'm not saying that it's an impossibility, but I'll have to know you a lot longer before I trust … well, that's kind of the wrong word."

"Perhaps, it's okay, Van. I … understand. I've not been around long, and … I'm just contract help, after all. I'm not really all that good at the catering duties."

"You do a great job at the other events, kit; don't misunderstand. Look, we'll talk about it, in time. Just be patient and keep proving to me that you put this business and those who work here first. That's all."

"Okay. I will. Thank you, Van. I'll go get to work now."

"Good. Thank you, kit," Vanarra offered. "Just close the door when you leave, okay?"

Sahnassa nodded and soon was away. Van, almost fearfully reached out for the camera, but still she did and clicked it back on.

The images were transfixing her and causing emotions she hadn't felt in seasons to come rushing to the surface, and she had barely been able to restrain herself when Sahni was in the room. Now, Van surrendered to those feelings as she flipped through images of what had once been her lair.

An interval later, tears tracking well down her cheek fur, Vanarra reviewed the images on her computer's view screen. She felt so many things so vividly as she looked through the pictures, and she was grateful that Sahnassa had even accidently included the vent openings near the children's section in one of the shots. "My front door," she breathed raggedly.

A buzz from the LineCom demanded her attention, and she schooled her voice as best she could. "What is it, Mauft?"

"I have a matron up here from ... what was the house again? Oh, de Gonari—" For a moment, Vanarra didn't hear anything else, as every part of her soul was seething with anger and fire, barely within her ability to control. "Van?"

"What ... do they ... want?" she asked, trying not to growl.

"They have an event they'd like us to participate in, hire us for. Should I –"

"No, don't send them back. Have them fill out a packet and then call me after they leave."

Vanarra pressed the control to disconnect the conversation and then tried to fight her emotions down. This was the first interaction she'd ever had with anyone from de Gonari. While she was sure there were some at the events she catered, this was the first time she'd ever been approached by the matriarchy of that house, the ones who murdered her mother.

After several passes went by, Mauft called her again. "Are they gone?" Van asked.

"Pulling out now," Mauft replied.

"I'm coming up." Van slammed down the LineCom and yanked open her door. Sahnassa saw her in the hallway and took an involuntary step back, obviously fearing she'd done something wrong. She quietly followed behind Van as she went to the front.

"Let me see their packet," Vanarra ordered. Mauft gave it to her. Van, without checking through its contents, removed the contact page and dumped the rest into the trash. "Wait three sols and call them back, telling them we couldn't accommodate their request. Understood?"

"Yes, Van, I will." Sahnassa was surprised to see real fear in Mauft's eyes as she gently took the sheet offered from Vanarra's expressed claw-tip.

Then, Vanarra turned around and faced Sahnassa. When Sahni started to ask, the enraged Van growled out, "Just leave it, Sahni! Don't ask! Not ever!" Vanarra tracked back to her office and slammed the door, leaving Mauft, Sahni, and Flint standing there, stunned.

Intervals later, Sahnassa was working on perfecting the last few default features of the site. Security, financial processing, and commerce were all working exactly like she thought they should. "Perfect!" she said to herself.

"I didn't hear someone say 'perfect,' did I?" Van asked as she stuck her muzzle in. Because of the cramped space, she couldn't enter.

"Well, let's see. Let me get out of the way!" Sahni slipped out of her chair and pulled it back, and then Van entered.

"What's up, kit?"

"I think we're ready to sell something," Sahni beamed proudly. "Just a test, of course. We have to get the art up on the site and actually add real inventory and so forth, but as far as a first test, we're ready. Should I go ahead?"

"Please," Van replied, smiling. Vanarra watched as Sahnassa sat down and started keying in an order, adding her name and payment information, and then confirming all before submitting. "What did you just buy?" Van asked as she saw the order confirmation appear on the screen.

"A fribbitz," Sahnassa replied.

"A what?"

"A fribbitz, a cute little soft alien thing from one of the space fiction books I've read. I didn't have any real inventory, so … I kind of made stuff up."

"But that's a good test," Van stated. "That's … awesome, Sahni! Very good!"

"Thanks! I'm glad you like it. Now, comes the hard part. We have to tailor what I've got here to your business. Make this as effective as you are when selling to a client."

Van folded her arms. "That would be a challenge. I can be very ... persuasive," Van grinned, smiling predatorily.

"I'll bet. Perhaps I should have said ... it should be very informative."

"You're okay kit, you're okay, and ... about earlier, I'm sorry," Van offered. "I seem to spend a lot of time apologizing to you, I know, but that order ... well, I just can't talk about it." Van looked away and stared at the wall. She was struggling to keep her emotions in check, and she instantly realized she'd made a mistake; if the Nephti replied the wrong way, Van was literally, physically trapped in the room with her emotional control in tatters.

Sahnassa leaned back and sighed as she looked at the screen. "Some wounds are so deep only death can cure them," she whispered, depressed.

Vanarra was nearly in physical shock at those words; the furor that had been roiling inside of her suddenly stilled in the most amazing and unprecedented way. The phrase was so strange coming from the muzzle of the Nephti in front of her and fit Van so perfectly that the mixed blood was literally stunned. "How do you know that, kit? That's a Rahnahi quote, and ... I've said it to myself. How can you know ... I needed to hear that?"

"I've got my own wounds. That matron got to you, and ... my sister got to me. I said some really ugly things, now that I think about them. It's not that they weren't true, but ... they won't help anything. I should have said something else."

For the first time, Vanarra felt real compassion for Sahni, and a part of her own soul ached on the Nephti's behalf. "You ... get to me in the oddest ways, you know that?" Van asked quietly, putting her paw on Sahnassa's shoulder.

Sahni reached her own paw up and covered Van's. "Hurting hearts ... I suppose—"

"Hurting hearts speak the same language," Van completed, again shaken by the Nephti's compassion and understanding. "More Rahnahi. You have read her and taken her to heart." In that moment, Vanarra felt a strange pull towards Sahnassa she never had before, a kind of kinship that she had only felt with her mother and with Ash. She wondered if Sahni realized how deeply her stern and volatile boss had been touched by what she said. "You ... you are getting close to us, the Anati and the outcasts who work here, kit," Van assured her as she removed her paw. "Please, be careful with that, okay?"

"I will," Sahni promised as she turned around and looked at Van, who for the first time, looked down at her somewhat tenderly, albeit a little confused.

"I have to correct you, though. The quote is that some wounds are so deep *that it seems like* only death can cure them."

"We can hope, Van," Sahni offered. "We can hope."

"I'd ... better leave you to it, then," Vanarra stated, and Sahnassa stood up. However, instead of simply stepping out of the way, she reached out for and embraced Van. The gesture again caused the mixed blood to tense up, as she felt something inside of her start to fall apart – something she wasn't willing to let go of. "No, kit ... please don't!" she begged, backing away.

"Oh ... sorry!" Sahnassa breathed, rapidly letting Van go, her blush furs at full. "I ... apologize. That wasn't appropriate."

Van couldn't speak for a moment; she had her eyes slammed shut and was fighting a fierce battle inside of herself for control. Sahnassa's embrace made her feel like she was nearly being rape-mated – a violation of her soul. "You ... you didn't mean any harm," she told Sahnassa, although she was truly trying to tell herself that. "I ... I just can't do that – there's ... it's too much."

"I'm so sorry, boss," Sahni apologized, backing away as far as she could and lowering her head.

"My fault, my ... problem," Van confessed, taking a deep breath and letting it go. "I ... I just can't." She opened her eyes and looked at Sahni, instantly regretting everything she had just said. "I ... need to go see to some other things."

Sahnassa backed out of the way and allowed Van to open the door. Now free of the confines of the small room, Van seemed to recover much of her bearing. "I'm impressed with what you've done. It's good work. Take tomorrow as a rest sol, kit, since the office will be closed. It's going to be hard to move forward without us here, anyway."

"Thank you, Van. I'm sorry ... about hugging you."

"Doesn't happen to me a lot in the office, actually," Vanarra commented by way of reproach. "Just learn from it, okay, kit?"

"Yes, Van."

"Okay, then," Vanarra replied and walked back to her office and shut the door.

"Great, Sahni, just wonderful," Sahnassa told herself. "Way to take a good thing and just mess it up." Dejected, she went back to her terminal. Looking at it, she saw a flashing alert in an area of the site's administrative console she hadn't seen before. "TransNet mail?" With a few quick key-presses, she was looking at a message from Matron Astalla de Orturu. "Gosh, Hylea! That was quick!" she gasped. Feeling herself trembling, she started reading the message:

> To Sahnassa, daughter of our house, from Matron Astalla, entrusted with the guardianship and well-being of our family. Your sister has relayed the content of your very earnest and open discussion held at the archive earlier this sol. I deeply regret that, in your eyes, house de Orturu has failed to provide emotional and familial support to the same degree we have provided monetary support. Even in that regard, it has been made plain to us that our provisions to you were seemingly insufficient. The Grand Matriarch, upon my induction, brought your case immediately to my attention, and I have been eagerly awaiting any opportunity to speak with you.

> As an adult who is earning your own way, you are now free and entitled to make your own decisions without undue interference from your parents or the matriarchy. Your matriarch understands and deeply regrets what you felt forced to do, and in reading the notes from my predecessor, you appear to have had ample justification for your action. In the light of your faithfulness to our family, despite these challenges, and your support, I earnestly plead with you for a meeting where we may discuss bettering the relationship between us and strengthening the ties we have with one another. For the present and until you wish for it to be so, your parents will not participate in any meeting we conduct, nor will they know any details of what transpires.

> Your sister has stood in my presence as advocate for you, and in her name, I ask you to please

reply with a time and place you would feel comfortable meeting.

My thanks to you, Astalla.

Sahnassa took a few deep breaths and re-read the message carefully. Although the new matron wasn't explicitly telling Sahnassa she was right and her dame and parents were wrong, she was coming close enough that she felt a meeting could actually be productive. Given her most recent misjudgment of her boss, she thought it would be wise to cultivate a few new options. So, knowing the lack of her current employer's trust meant she had the next sol open, she replied:

From Sahnassa de Orturu to Matron Astalla de Orturu. Thank you for your kind note, and it seems like now may be a good time to try to make things better between myself and our house. As much as Hylea was an advocate for me, she was for our family. I would like to meet with you and talk. Perhaps, something good can come from it. As it happens, I have the next sol off. If we could meet at the archive, that would be better for me. I can adapt to whatever time would be suitable, since it is a rest sol. Thank you for reaching out to me, and thank Hylea for being so kind. My honor to you, to our dame, and to our matriarch, and my gratitude.

In honor, Sahnassa.

She read the message over a few times before she pressed the transmit key, but she felt pleased with it and sent it along. Sahnassa was only half way through making a back-up copy of the TransNet site when an answer flashed on the screen. Opening the message, she breathed out the request, "Tomorrow, seven intervals before high night. Meet at the information desk." Leaning back in her seat, she took a couple of deep breaths and tried to calm down, torrents of questions cascading through her mind. "What am I going to wear? Am I ready for this? Will the dame be there? What will I say? Could this be a set-up?" In only a few moments, the back-up completed, and Sahnassa realized that her mind was too distracted to do any more productive work. She logged off the system, shut down the servers, and then cut off the lights in the room as she left.

Walking past Van's door, she stopped. "Oh, I really messed up," she thought to herself. "What was I thinking?" Sighing lightly, she decided not to do anything else to make matters worse and simply walked out of the office and to her hover.

Chapter 17: Proximity

Vanarra was sitting on her office couch, holding a pillow to her chest, and trying to calm herself down. She'd barely been able to control what happened when Sahnassa hugged her, and now, as she went over it in her mind, she said to herself, "Damn, I must of sounded heartless! What … the mange happened to me? That kit … wasn't rapemating me! She … was just sorry for me? No, it wasn't that – it was something else. Damn, why can't I get this?! It's like I've lost my mind about it or … my heart…"

Van gripped the pillow almost convulsively and started to rock. "My heart…" she breathed. Vanarra realized what had happened, and the recognition was as profound as it was humiliating. This purebred, avowed Nephti had touched her heart, and Van had let that happen. "Touch my heart, open my soul," she repeated from one of Rahnahi's books. "Open my soul, change me." Sahnassa had touched Van with her recognition and acceptance of Vanarra's pain, and Van had opened up just a little. The Nephti had responded, but that had been too much for Vanarra, and the reaction inside herself was terrifying to the mixed blood. "What would have happened if I … if I let her? What … would have happened to me? How would I have changed?"

She honestly didn't know. She wondered if she would have fainted, collapsed, lashed out, gone crazy – every alternative seemed to be just as possible as her fevered mind tried to understand the growing wave that had threatened to crash into her. How she wished there was someone she could talk to about what was happening, but she couldn't trust anyone in her office – only she and Sahni were left there, it being so late at night. As always, Van realized she'd work through this on her own.

Standing and pacing back and forth, she struggled to right herself. "It's … just a weird thing. Something I'm not used to, that's all. I … I'm okay. I can be okay with it. I'm still the boss here. It's still my place, and I still make the rules. I … I can hug a Nephti and not have it mess me up. It was just … an odd moment. I wasn't ready. It's all those pictures I was looking at. Pictures that Sahni … took…" Her pacing slowed, and just then, she started to realize what truly happened. "She got to me, Ash. She gave me back some small piece of you, and I … felt for her. I'm … oh, I … that … that was heartless. After she did such a good thing for me, and if I had let her inside, I would have … might have told her about you. It's still too painful, Ash."

Vanarra held onto the door knob and realized that again, she had hurt Sahnassa. The kit had literally worked on Van's own "nostalgia" project all sol, delivered the test TransNet site, dealt with a blow to her own soul, and endured being growled at by her boss for no good reason. In gratitude for that and in response to the Nephti's compassion, Van had pushed her away. "That was a mistake," she told herself, and then Van opened the door, stepped out into the hallway, and instantly, she saw the server room was empty, the lights off, and the door locked. Her heart sank as she walked forward to the reception area. Looking out into the hover lot, Vanarra saw that the Nephti's sad little hover was gone. Van's gleaming gold hover was the only one remaining in the darkened space, alone. "I'm sorry, Sahni. I … I really am. Touch me, open my soul, and get burned," she sighed to the empty lot, putting her head against the window.

Sahnassa spent most of the next sol preparing for her meeting with the matron at the archive that evening. One of the first things to see her attention was her hover, filled to the brim with this and that; nearly three large trash containers were filled by the cast-offs and detritus which had been in her vehicle for so long. She even bought stain remover and cleaned the seats, the straps, and vacuumed nearly her body weight in fur from the vehicle's crevices. Sahni even took it in for service, and was grateful that only a few small repairs were needed, and they were thankfully within her meager budget. When she got the vehicle back, she was gratified to find the service manager had sealed and polished the outside, which, minus a little faded paint, nearly made her old wreck look new again. Getting into the vehicle, she felt a surge of pride and happiness.

That boost led her to her second area of renovation – her little lair. Borrowing a neighbor's vacuum, she cleaned the floor and the windows. Food and garbage that had been stacked here and there as she came in and out at odd intervals were finally disposed of, counters were cleaned, and long waiting laundry was finally given its due. After organizing her other possessions as best she could, she stopped and ate some lunch before turning towards her next renovation project – herself.

For the first time in what seemed like seasons, she treated herself to a long and luxurious bath, a long session with a paw-held fur dryer, and a brushing of her fur that lasted nearly a full interval. Sahnassa was beginning to realize that she had been putting in as much time at Vanarra's as when she was going to academy. While the pace of her work in school had been set by the professors, Sahni was starting to realize that in many ways, she had some control over the pace of her own work and the intervals she worked. While she was enjoying a massage-in fur treatment, she worked on her finances. A little quick math made her grimace; taking her pay and dividing it by the number of intervals she worked meant that she was actually making very little, less than a fur dresser.

"Van's really getting a bargain out of me!" she grumped. "No one else puts in the time I do except for her, and to judge by her hover, she's taken care of just fine." While she was grateful to Vanarra for her job, it was hard not to have some level of resentment about how she was being treated by the others like Raska and Sheffer. If she and her family could reconcile, then, just as Van had said, "Sahni's" contract would end, and then Matron Astalla could perhaps help "Sahnassa de Orturu" find a new contract or perhaps even a full time position at a reputable corporate pack. "Oh, that would be so nice," she breathed. In many ways, she felt she was coming to a peace with the end of her time at Celebrations by Vanarra; it was a good start, and she was grateful to Van for that, but there was obviously a limit to the attachment and friendship Van had to offer. In that way, the Anati was no different than anyone else she had ever met in her life.

Almost before she realized what was happening, it was time for her to have a light dinner, put on the dress she had purchased to work that first event for Vanarra, and take her restored hover towards the Pinnacle Center Archive. The trip there gave her more than sufficient time to think over everything that had happened to her, the times

Rothnerra had troubled her and she had endured it, when Shalarra helped her choose her calling, and then when Drualla had accepted her claim for the protections of the Compact. "I've … done things only to protect myself and preserve the honor of my house. It wouldn't have been honorable if a recipient of the matriarchal scholarship failed the first season of academy." Those thoughts emboldened her, and gave her some level of confidence.

However, there were more than a few darker thoughts to counterpoint the positive assertions she made about her own motives and choices. Taking the Compact had disgraced her parents and her dame, and cost all three of them. Her sisters, too, had felt the impact of what had happened, and the relations with those she would have hoped to hold closest were in danger of being forever distant and shaded by guilt. The matron could have been paw-picked by Dame Rothnerra, and this meeting could easily be an ambush to accuse her of misspending the house's gift, and for all her cleaning up, her last name could be forfeit at the end.

Parking in the garage, she nervously exited her hover and made for the lift. Arriving at the information desk, she saw a Nephti matron, a little taller than she with black fur, thin white stripes, and piercing silvery gray eyes sitting behind a pink nose and a kind-looking muzzle. As she drew closer, she could see the crest of her family on the matron's dark purple robes. "Greetings to you, Matron," Sahnassa stated, executing a small bow. "I am Sahnassa de Orturu."

"Indeed!" the matron replied brightly. "It is a great pleasure to meet you and to find you … so eager to talk with me! I am Astalla de Orturu, your new matron. Matrons Shalarra and Drualla thought so very highly of you. May we go and talk? I have reserved a private conference room on the fifth level for our discussion."

"Certainly, Matron. Thank you for contacting me," she stated as she walked alongside Astalla. "I'm … kind of surprised anyone from the house would want to."

"Your matriarch truly has been warmed by how you have stood steadfast in your responsibilities to this house, when it appears you have so much cause to regret doing so."

As they reached the lift, Sahnassa obeyed the offer of the matron and stepped in first. "Regardless of what happened, Matron, my house paid for my schooling and allowed me to study in the field of my choosing. That … was an enormous honor."

"An honor some in our house undertook to diminish. That was a short-sighted decision, on their part, and yes, I have the full support of my matriarch in calling out the failings of my dame. Your parents, too, by Drualla's account, have much to answer for."

"They … did support me," Sahnassa said quietly as the lift's door opened. "Although … it was clear they didn't want to. Regardless if it was a gift freely given, the house made sure they provided me with … the basics."

"Yes," Astalla replied quietly as she shut the door to the small conference room behind them, "the basics, minus love, support, and honor. Far less than the basics by the standards of this house. You have shown not only an enduring spirit but a forgiving one. Your sister felt as if you understood her situation and why she and your other sibling didn't reach out to you."

"I don't blame them. It had to be … difficult – scary. Thank you," Sahnassa stated as she accepted the matron's invitation to sit.

"Thank you, for coming to talk to me. You know, Sahnassa, that not many in our house ever feel compelled to take the protections of the Compact. Those who do are generally on their way to disavowal. You … you took the Compact and then worked as hard as you could to achieve in your circumstances. I have spoken to every one of your professors and teachers and many of your classmates. Now that you are out of school, and these individuals hold no sway over you, the Compact doesn't forbid this action."

"What … what did they say?"

"That you … valiantly, humbly, and purposefully struggled to the very end. You endured dishonor in trade for opportunity – a higher grade in an easier course sacrificed to embrace the challenge of a harder one. I know your grades, Sahnassa. They, too, know your grades, but every one of them – without exception – thought that you would do well. Does that surprise you?"

"It … does. I never even knew that they had any opinion about me, good or bad."

"They have to play the impartial instructor and pretend to be the stoic guardians of knowledge and truth, but don't ever imagine that they were blind, and that they didn't hope on your behalf. You … could have partied the matriarchal scholarship away, taken that money and bought toys and gifts for yourself, drowned yourself in fermentum with it. Did you do that? No! Every record shows you meticulously trying to stretch what you had as far as it would go. I see, for example, that your entertainment budget had to be about zero – I'm not sure there's a book in the space fiction section you didn't check out."

"Oh, sorry about that," Sahnassa apologized. "I kind of picked that habit up from a friend, but … it did make things … economical."

"I know. Your story has fascinated me, and some part of your story has been a part of each and every sol since I took this position. I have, of course, spoken to your parents." Sahnassa looked away from the matron's eyes as Astalla's tone changed. "They were disgraced when you claimed protection, but … in truth, their disgrace matched their stubborn attitudes. They, as your sister has intimated, continue to remain stubborn and refuse any talk of reconciliation, for now. I don't know, Sahnassa, if the way they are reacting is because they expect you, like so many who have taken the Compact, to willingly or unwillingly leave this house. Is that what you want?"

"No, Matron! That's not what I want. I … just want the freedom to pursue my career and bring honor to my house … in my own way," Sahnassa replied in quiet earnestness. "Not the way someone wants me to, where I can never reach my full potential, because … I can never truly love what I am doing. I am not sorry for who I am, Matron. I'm only sorry that there are those who see so little value in it."

"Your house still sees value in you, kit. Tremendous value. We offer terms to you, in the hopes that you will relinquish the rights of the Compact and allow us to care for you, not as one would a child, but as one would a family member – an adult – one we love and care about. Would you like for me to continue?"

Sahnassa nodded and answered, "Yes, please."

"First, Dame Rothnerra will not have the same sway over your family. She is being reassigned additional diplomacy duties, and those will place her off continent, on Ricia. While she will still have administrative oversight for you, unless you commit an infraction or dishonor the family, her paws may not touch you in any regard. This is a reform that has spread throughout our house, and one that has been very much needed. Second, the support of our family, my support especially, will be very freely given in the light of everything you have been denied in the past. Finally, the matriarchy will not force any reconciliation with your parents. If that happens, it will be in its own time, and it is you who will choose that timing along with Gonastir and Holana. I, myself, will celebrate that sol, but I will not force you to it.

With those protections in place, do you think that you could again accept our care for you?"

Astalla's plea was earnest, and Sahnassa could tell that the matron truly wanted this to go well. "One other condition I beg of you," she pleaded gently. "Please watch over Hylea, and do whatever you can to prevent her from coming to the same hard choice that I had to make. If you will protect her and do as you have said, then, happily, I would relinquish my rights under the Compact, and … you'd have my gratitude, Matron Astalla, as would our dear and much honored matriarch."

Astalla smiled broadly. "We agree, happily so, to that requirement. It is an honorable one, and one that shows the bonds of family still tie you to us so firmly. Well, then, would you be willing to relinquish your Compact protections tonight?"

"I would. I … I honestly have been thinking about it all sol. I … want to be closer to my family. I've been very … alone."

"And still, you support us. Amazing, kit – inspiring, even. Well, then you and I have an appointment. Would you please follow me?"

The matron was up and walking towards the door, and Sahnassa struggled to keep pace with her. "Where are we going?"

Astalla reached back and offered her paw to Sahnassa. "We are going forward, and we're not going to let the past define us anymore." Taking her matron's paw, Sahnassa followed her out of the conference room to the central atrium. Then, the pair was walking towards the doors of the lift, where two other matrons stood watch.

"My goodness," Sahnassa breathed as they entered the elevator. "We're … we're going where?"

"All the way to the top. I made some preparations in case our discussions went well, and there has been a silent observer to our discussions you were unaware of. She has missed you, possibly more than Hylea has."

"Oh, she must mean Triana," Sahnassa thought, and found herself transfixed looking at the archive falling away beneath her as the lift spun slowly on its way to the top of the spire above them.

"It's beautiful, isn't it?" Astalla asked, and in the distance, behind the archive, the sun was setting.

"Very much so, Matron. Very much so."

Soon, they entered the structure at the top of the spire, and the doors to the lift opened. "We thought a little ceremony was in order. From my review of your records, your graduation ceremony was one where we were … ill represented. My hope is that this will make it up to you," Astalla explained as she guided Sahnassa to a door where two matrons pulled it open.

Sahnassa's jaw dropped, for there was her Grand Matriarch, not dressed as Sahnassa had seen her so many times before, but dressed in the imposing and bejeweled regalia matriarchs wore when leading their house in battle. Two dames flanked her, both honored dames, also in their full battle dress. Two matrons, attired in the more practical battle armor, flanked the trio. Before she knew what she was doing, Sahnassa had dropped to her knees in respect, with her head bowed.

"State your name, you who would enter this place," one of the Honored Dames demanded.

"I … I am Sahnassa *de Orturu*, Honored Ones," Sahnassa replied, emphasizing her family name strongly. "Kept by and keeper of her family."

"Enter in, Sahnassa de Orturu," the matriarch directed. Carefully, and taking Astalla's paw as support, she obeyed her matriarch's summons. Struggling to keep her head raised against the awesome display of familial power in front of her, she felt respect and fear mingled together as she never had before. As the pair stopped in front of the matriarch, Astalla's paw lowered, and Sahnassa went back down to her knees, bowing her head and folding her paws in front of her, her tail just above the floor.

"You have truly been keeper of your family, Sahnassa. You have steadfastly pursued your schooling in the face of real and true difficulty. You have hewn a trail for yourself through a forest with no one to lead you or stand in front of you. You have not escaped unscathed, but you did emerge successfully. You surrender to this house willingly the portion it requires, neither late nor shy the smallest portion, and you do it with no urging, no reminder. Stand before me, my daughter, and look me eye to eye, in honor."

Carefully, trembling, Sahnassa accepted Astalla's help to rise to her hind legs, and forced herself to look full into the matriarch's face. Behind the headdress, she saw eyes that while serious, were happy. "You've earned that privilege. For every twenty who take the

Compact as protection, only one of those will ever return to us. You are that one, if your word to Astalla is true."

Sahnassa heard the question in the matriarch's statement and spoke as earnestly as she could, "I now, completely and without reservation, surrender the protections of the Compact. It broke my heart to take that step, and I willingly give them up."

"It has been witnessed by all here, as has been your stipulation that we shelter your younger sister so she will not feel compelled to take the same measure. She ... more than anyone else, is glad that you have thought of her."

From behind the matriarch and her group silhouetted against the sunset, a nervously overjoyed Hylea emerged, and walked around, embracing her sister. "Thank you, kit!" Sahnassa whispered in her ear, choking back a sob.

"You're my sister, and I never want to forget you!"

When the pair looked back to the matriarch, they were surprised to see that the dames to her flanks had removed her headdress, and the silver gray eyes of the matriarch were smiling down at them. "You, kit, have had a difficult trail, and I am very sorry about that. Your case, along with a few others like it, have caused us to change how dames and matrons manage the responsibility of tending families and their futures. There were some who claimed that those who could not live within the system as it was were not worthy. You are here tonight, embracing us once again, proving them wrong. Thank you for that, dear daughter."

"Thank you, Honored One. This ... means more than you'll ever know," Sahnassa breathed out. The matriarch nodded and stepped off the platform and opened her arms. Eagerly, Sahnassa walked into that embrace.

Once separated, the matriarch looked at her sadly. "It grieves me to think how we have impacted your life to this point. Things are very difficult for you, and that lovely dress cannot hide the ribs I felt. Your earnings are respectable enough for someone getting started, but your debts are crippling. As of tonight, those debts are paid," she whispered. "It is my apology to you."

"Accepted, truly ... wow, I ... thank you!" Sahnassa exclaimed and again hugged her matriarch who laughed.

Upon parting, Matriarch Selena took Sahnassa's paw in hers and said, "When you invoked the Compact, we were bound to continue the matriarchal scholarship, although there were some who argued against it. I decided that you had earned that right, and you deserved to keep it. You ... made good on my faith in you."

"My grades ... weren't the best, Honored One; I'm sorry."

"It was what you could do. Now, we will support you, and in time, those grades will not matter, not if the Thurian who stands before me is half who I believe her to be. Thank you."

"Thank you. This ... this was amazing!" Sahnassa replied.

"We were here for a photography session for the archives, and it had been scheduled for some time. When you responded to Astalla, she came to me, and ... I could think of no better way to represent to you the importance I felt over this. Astalla has been your champion and will continue to be. Your dame," and Selena cocked her head thoughtfully, "was indisposed to this meeting, as she is assigned overseas. She sends her ... regrets that she could not come." The matriarch's face was about to burst with ironic humor.

Sahnassa replied with the same irony, "Give her my best, please, Honored One. I will endeavor to prove that a technologist *can* bring honor to her family."

"I bet you will, child! I bet you surely will, and in some ways, you already have. Now, we have to leave, and I think you and Hylea should go and celebrate. You should understand that your parents believe she is attending an audience with ... who again?" Selena asked the dame to her right.

"Dame Ashina ... about ... archiving or something like that," the Honored Dame stumbled out. Hylea, to her own embarrassment, started giggling.

"Oh, something like that, okay," Matriarch Selena chuckled. "Take care of yourself, Sahnassa. Our family is here for you, now."

"Thank you so very much," Sahnassa replied happily, bowing before her matriarch.

Astalla took Sahnassa by the paw, and the three of them left the room.

A few passes later, Hylea and Sahnassa had parked in the hover lane alongside the road leading away from the archive. Walking in the cool grass with their paw-shoes off, the two sisters held each other's paws.

"We have so many good memories from being here," Sahnassa told her. "I ... I thought those sols were over for me."

"Not over. Not now," Hylea offered.

"Thank you, kit. I know you finding me last sol was kind of an accident, but … I can't thank you enough."

"You need to truly thank Astalla, too. I went to her and told her what you said, and I expected her to get mad! She didn't. She told me everything she'd been finding out about you. Drualla had two others take the Compact, all because of Dame Rothnerra, and both of them are disavowed now."

"Is it true what she said about my case changing the way dames and matrons interact with families?"

"Oh yes, Sahnassa, and here's the interesting part – Dad worked on that case."

"Really? On which side?" Sahnassa asked ruefully.

"Believe it or not, he worked on the side promoting a stronger separation of powers. I think he can see that Dame Rothnerra's interference was partially responsible for what happened with you. Now, that doesn't mean that if she hadn't been there, he wouldn't have been upset by your choice or refused to pay your school, but … he might have been more flexible. He might have made … different choices, I think."

"But he's still not ready to talk to me," Sahnassa observed. "Mother either, right?"

"Not right now, but when they hear what you've done, it may help. This was a big step, Sahnassa. How do you feel about it?"

"Wonderful and … very grateful – grateful to my bratty little sister who always wanted to play matron and forced me to play the dame—" Hylea giggled. "Oh, and who couldn't keep her mouth shut when we went for story-time with Dame Rahnahi de Dothnar!" Hylea was laughing now. "Oh, and the one who took the picture of me when I shaved off all my fur!" Hylea was now on the ground, laughing hysterically at the memory.

"Naked turf burrower! Naked turf burrower!" At that teasing, Sahnassa couldn't help herself. She dove on her sister and started furiously tickling her, which sent her squealing and trying to wriggle free. "Oh … stop! Oh stop, Sahnass … I'm … going to wet … myself!"

Sahnassa gave up and backed away and laughed hard while Hylea recovered. After a pass or two, the laughing died away, and the pair just sat smiling at one another. "I love you, sis."

"I love you, too," Hylea replied. "Thank you for coming tonight."

"Oh, kit, it was one of the most special moments I've ever had. Thank you."

"You're welcome. Come on then. Let's go get something to eat! Matron Astalla gave me a nice fat draft, and there are six items on de Kestos menu I haven't tried."

"Only six?!"

"Yeah, I really like it. Let's go!"

Vanarra watched the final morning ceremony of the primal with a limited measure of satisfaction. Her firm had performed adequately, with only a couple of small mistakes. Unfortunately, both of those mistakes had been hers. She had missed the queue during the first banquet for when the males and females were being dismissed to their camps, which meant her group had to run to stay ahead of the lines of guests and scramble with preparations once they were there. She had also misallocated her staff so that when it came time for Saiphar to leave to do his demonstrations, there was only Flint to replace him. "I'm totally off my game," she thought to herself. "Totally off."

"Hey there," Flint quietly said, coming up behind her. "Still kicking yourself in the tail?"

"Yes, dammit!" Van shot back. "I wasn't thinking straight."

"Yeah, kind of noticed."

"*What* did you notice?"

"You, staring off into space a lot. You've been preoccupied, distracted. Care to talk about what it is?"

Vanarra looked at him, embarrassed. "It's our Nephti. I … made a tail-for-brains of myself … again."

"Uh oh, how bad?" Flint asked, worried.

"I … we talked and shared some things, some … feelings and … then she hugged me, and … I … I just wasn't ready for that. I kind of pushed her away, not like physically hurt her, but…"

"You hurt her feelings, and you pushed her away, emotionally. She got to you somehow."

"Yeah, I … I don't want to talk about that part, Flint," Van warned. "I've … I've been replaying everything I felt and said and just – I don't know what to do."

"When you hurt someone's feelings, you apologize," Flint replied gently, and Van grunted. He considered her for a moment and asked, "Do you like her, Van?"

Vanarra was quiet for a moment before she answered, "I do, but I don't want to! She's going to leave at the end of her contract. There's no use in me getting attached to her as a friend or even as an employee. Her loyalty is to her house, first, and I'm just her boss. That's over when her contract runs out."

"Well, you know," Flint reasoned gently, "she could sign *another* contract. I'm sure she's got other abilities we could use in this business. She told me recently that she took some courses on videographer techniques."

"We don't record primals, Flint," Van grumped as the ceremony ended and the participants started their own conversations.

"Joinings, perhaps even some pre-joinings? I've been asked a few times," he commented thoughtfully, and Van's eyebrows furrowed. "And you know, we'll need someone to maintain the TransNet site, keep it updated after it's running, help take care of the orders and payments."

"Can't we do that?" Van asked, plaintively.

"With a lot of training and likely not as well," Flint stated firmly. "Tresk is good at turning a wrench, but computer systems? I'm not so sure."

"You want me to try to keep that purebred avowed in an Anati-run business indefinitely? Like that's going to happen!"

"Because you won't or she won't?"

"She," Van bitterly offered.

"You sure about that? You haven't even put an offer in front of her. Does she even know that you would consider such at thing?" Van was silent and wouldn't look at him. "You're afraid she'll reject you." Vanarra looked up at him angrily, but he didn't flinch. "Aren't you?"

Very quietly, her anger fading, Vanarra admitted, "Yes … a little … maybe … not a little."

"Well, she'll sure as mange reject you if you keep treating her like you're terrified of her. You're going to have to risk something, Van, if you want to keep her. You're going to have to risk being hurt."

"Ugh, I don't know if I could do that again. Flint, you're asking me to put myself out there for a purebred avowed when every time they've either left me or cost me ... dearly."

"I'm not asking you that, Van," Flint contested quietly. "You're asking yourself that, and you'd better answer soon – Vanarra Anasto is not all that patient when she wants to know something."

"Great," she sighed, watching the group beginning to disperse. "Now, I'm not meeting my own expectations. Lovely."

"Nope, lovely is what's coming up – getting paid. I see Mavia, and she's smiling big."

"Ugh, I hope she didn't see how bad things went tonight. Hopefully Saiphar's new art courses made up for it."

"Vanarra! That ... that was wonderfully done," Mavia effused.

"Are you sure? Is there anything else you need us to do, kit? I'm sure there's something we could have improved on."

"I got so many compliments on Flint at the male's camp. He did really wonderfully, and ... he's quite wise in his own way."

Van raised her eyebrow fur as she looked up at Flint, who was blushing slightly. "Really? He certainly keeps me on the trail."

"Well, he was very helpful to one of those who didn't do so well in the competition. Flint has a good perspective, I was told. And, if I could talk to you in private, I did get one other comment, as well."

"I'll go check with Saiphar and Raska, make sure clean-up and packing is getting underway," Flint stated. "Thank you very much for the feedback, Mavia. I'm humbled by it." He bowed to her very respectfully, which made her smile, and she bowed back to him. Flint smiled and stepped away.

"I like him. He's this ... huge presence, and you just expect him to be ... well, not so bright, but then he is, really."

"I'd be lost without him, Mavia," Van confessed. "He makes up for my shortcomings."

"Well, it's not your shortcomings that I'm hearing about. Honestly, you were getting some real notice this time."

"Yes, about that – I'm sorry. I've ... been a little distracted by some things back at the office, and I was a little bit more visible this time than I intended to be."

"Oh, Vanarra," Mavia chuckled, "it wasn't as visible as some of the males hoped you would be. Some of them, and please forgive me, said they found you to be ... exotic, keen, and ... quite beautiful. The males and some of the females were actually talking about asking you to compete next time. I think ... I think some of them were ... hopeful."

Van's blush furs rose a little as she replied, "Well, I've never gotten that specific feedback before. Kind of nice to hear, I suppose, but ... I really had my paws full trying to keep things running right. And you know what, everyone else can say what they want, but it's what you say that matters."

"Well, I ... I have to agree with them, Vanarra. You ... have some qualities that Primalists take notice of, and as much as I appreciate your group using the simple clothes after the shedding, there are some – myself included – who would like to see if you could possibly ... not wear them. They want to keep everything as primal as possible in the camps. So, although I can't require it of you, I ... I just wanted to state it – as a preference."

"Whew!" Vanarra breathed. "Haven't thought about having to ask my staff that, but ... you know, in reality, they've kind of already been made used to it, and as long as I keep them busy, we shouldn't have a problem. I'll talk to them. There's a possibility, a strong one, that we can ... accommodate your preference."

Mavia actually reached out for Van and hugged her, the Anati's prior experience making her a little cautious. "Oh Vanarra, you just don't know! Dealing with you is actually, in many ways, the easiest business relationship I have. Dealing with you is easier than dealing with any family house or corporate pack! When I get tired of the executive thing one sol, maybe I'll come work for you!"

"Really?!" Van asked, surprised, letting go of the Nephti and holding her back to look at her. "Why would you ever want to do that?"

"If I could figure out how to make my staff work as well as yours, I would be up for a promotion, for sure. Besides, I think of you as more than a business partner – I hope you know that."

Vanarra sighed, smiling, "I do, and you have meant so much to my business and everyone who works for me. Thank you."

"No problem at all. Here is our payment, and I think our next booking will be in ... about a moon from now. I'll contact you with the dates; I'd know now, but the resorts are in flux. The Hallows has construction that's just ruined the atmosphere of the place. It will be moons before we can use it."

"Oh, wow, Mavia! Thank you very much! My crew is going to be very pleased. I'm sure you'll find something for the next location, and if I can help, please call me, okay?"

"I will. Please thank Saiphar again. I actually had a few of the group angry at me that we didn't have him available for those paintings earlier in the event."

"Any earlier and he would have been doing it before the herding. He told me he made a very good impression this time. Hey, Saiphar and I have been talking. He wants to work some natural paw art – castings, I think – into the mix. I'll try to have some samples by the time you contact me."

"That sounds really interesting! I look forward to it. Alright, I have to talk to Apharia de Dothnar before she goes, so I'll be in touch, okay?"

"Okay, Mavia, and thank you. We do appreciate your business, so very much."

"You're welcome. Take care now," Mavia said, and soon, she was away.

Walking back into the center of the nearly empty banquet room, Vanarra thought about Mavia and all she had meant to Van and her business. "Yeah, you're sort of a ... hypocrite aren't you, Van?" she asked herself. "Mavia pays you and sends you business, stays loyal and ... gives you more than you ever had. You let *her* hug you and act all friendly – because she's paying you. You let her say how she'd like to see you running around without a stitch of clothing, and ... you're right there, agreeing to it. Willing to expose the outside, just ... never the inside. Poor Sahni. I'll ... try to do better." Seeing that the last guest had left the room, she went to gather her staff, now anxious to get back to her office and try to repair her relationship with Nephti technologist.

Sahnassa groaned as her clock on the floor sounded its morning alarm. Leaning over the bed, she looked at the time, her eyes bleary. "Not this sol," she breathed out, and keyed an extra interval of sleep into the device and rolled back into bed.   Although this was supposedly a normal work sol for everyone in Vanarra's office, Sahni had noticed that she was always the second into the office behind Van. Flint didn't arrive for nearly half an interval, and Mauft a full interval after that. She needed the additional rest time since she and Hylea had left De Kesto's shortly before it closed, just before high night. Yet, there were other reasons why Sahnassa felt comfortable rolling over and dozing for another interval.

There were technical reasons, as well, that were valid in their own way. Most of the work she had to do to prove her ability to put a TransNet site up was done, and now everything would revolve around content, and content would take time to develop. "No use in rushing when you're waiting on others," she yawned, reaching out and hugging a pillow. As she enjoyed the languid peacefulness of the morning, though, the technical reasons weren't her only justification, and she knew it.

Her reunion with her house had given her back a measure of self confidence about her future she hadn't enjoyed since before she left for academy, and the absolution of her debts went a long way in taking the edge of desperation off of her desire for a paycheck. Although it was still much needed, the threat of disavowal for failing to meet her obligations was now far less. Her own analysis of her intervals worked and her pay were also a nagging concern, and at some level, she was beginning to realize that such was within her purview to control. Van had never mentioned when she should show up and when she should leave, save for the catering events for obvious reasons. "You can't show up late if no one's told you when you should be there," she argued at a whisper, nuzzling the pillow affectionately.

It was then Sahnassa caught herself, pushed the pillow away, and stared at it a little crossly. Van's rejection of her, thrusting her away and chastising her for a show of affection, revolted the Nephti, and it felt, in some ways, like a betrayal. "Puts her paw on me and then freaks when I do the same!" she nearly growled. "I didn't do anything … weird! Merialla and I were a lot closer, and I saw hugs all over campus from time to time, even between professors and students every now and again. What's wrong with that!?"

Sahnassa sat up, the emotional pain far more effective than any stimulant in breaking her sleepiness apart and sweeping it neatly away. "I … I don't want to go in to work," she admitted, sitting up. "They … hate me there, some of them, just because I'm a purebred and avowed Nephti, a daughter of a house. What … frauds they are! They bitch and whimper about how they've been treated, but they aren't any different! Given the opportunity, they'll discriminate against someone the exact same way! They're no better."

She threw off the covers and looked at the clock, no more than a quarter interval had passed from her normal wake-up time, and she knew, now, that it would be impossible for her to go back to sleep. "Well, I will take my time getting ready, thank you very much, and I'll have something decent to eat this morning instead of trying to cram a meal into my muzzle on the way," she stated imperiously as she stamped off to the shower.

By the time Sahni had prepared herself and stopped for a quick sit-down at a local café, guilt had started to pile up against her angry rebellion. "She … she did give me a job when I really needed it, and … if I hadn't paid any dues or had to go back to my parents … that would have been really awful. And the bed. Great, now I have to apologize to Van for coming in late." Feeling a mixture of self disappointment and growing urgency, Sahnassa quickly paid her check and returned to her hover.

"Still not in," Van thought, worried, as she walked past the closed and locked server room. "For crying out to the moons, how bad did I screw this up?!" She leaned her head against the door to the server room and sighed. She was still tired from the event, even more so since she hadn't slept very well – her guilt a poor companion in bed. "What can I do to show her I'm sorry? I can't just give her things. I can't keep apologizing over and over again!"

"You're going to have to risk something," Flint had told her.

"Like what?" she asked the empty office, and the answer slipped into her thoughts, a mixture of Ash's gentle admonitions mixed with Rahnahi's teachings. "Disclosure … tell her something … something about private things, hidden. Oh I … I don't know if I can do that. Damn, that would be awkward! Hey, Sahni, come into my office so I can tell you about my rotten childhood; maybe then you'll know why I'm such a heartless bitch!"

Defeated, she turned back towards her office and sat at her desk. Looking through her TransNet mail, she saw a grateful note sent by the owners of the orphanage, telling her that her support had meant the purchase of three new beds and had let them take in as many new cubs. Pictures of the three precious little faces adorned the bottom of the message, and that instantly set her to tears. One of them looked, for all the world, like a little Ashalam.

"Van, are … are you okay?" Sahni's voice called from the doorway.

"Oh! It's you, kit! Yes, yes, I'm … I'm fine. I … just got something in TransNet mail," she replied, and Van started to close it and change subjects, but a gentle prodding inside of her told her that wasn't the thing to do. "It's special to me. Would you like to come in and take a look?"

A little nervously, Sahnassa asked, "Are … you sure you're okay with that? Really?"

"Yes, I am, Sahni. I'm sorry about earlier. Come on. I promise it's good," Van told her, motioning her over.

The Nephti stepped in, walked around the desk, and looked over her shoulder. "Oh my goodness! They are adorable! What keen little cubs!"

"Even though they're Anati?" Van asked, a little surprised, and then instantly regretted it.

"It is … possible, Van, for me to think they're adorable, even if they are *Anati*," Sahnassa retorted, sounding hurt.

"It's not possible for everyone, kit," Van admitted. "That … kind of makes you special, and a little hard to understand, at times. I have to admit, I've always seen the purebred avowed a certain way, and … you haven't been like that. I … treasure seeing little faces like this, especially when I know they've been rescued from … from … from what … I lived … through."

Sahnassa stood dead still in that moment, and so many things about her employer clicked into place. She could tell how extremely difficult those last few words were for her boss to say. "I'm surprised you could even speak to one of us," she quietly whispered.

"Some I can't," Van admitted. "There are some I can't talk to at all, and … getting close, sharing with – it's really hard for me. It doesn't mean that I don't like you. It just means…"

"That it's hard," Sahni completed for her. "I … I'm sorry, Van. I … didn't know."

"And it's my fault for not telling you more, setting you up for failure, almost. Are you doing anything tonight after work? I like to go over and see the new arrivals, meet them. If you're busy, that would be okay—"

"You'd let me come?" Sahni asked nervously.

Van looked at her, surprised. "They need every paw they can get, even if it's just someone to talk to and hold onto for a few moments."

"I'd be honored, Van," Sahnassa replied, quietly.

"See," Van told her, "that's it! You ... don't act like any purebred avowed I've ever met, Sahni. You reach out for things that no one else wants to touch, and ... it's hard to get used to that. I don't understand, sometimes, why you would bother making the effort, especially when I treat you like I do."

"We've had problems, Van, but you were so very kind to me offering me something when I really needed it, and ... I respect you for what you've built here. I hope you know that."

"Figuring it out, slowly," Van confessed. "Now, I've ... held you up long enough. What's ... what's next for the TransNet site?"

"Well, I'll need some time from you to talk about what products you want to put on the site, and how they should be organized. Also, I need to know what kind of information you want to gather. That ... packet like the one you threw in the garbage, is that something we could put on the site?"

"It ... could be," Van mused, mulling it over. "It would be nice if prospects we talk to on the LineCom could come in with the paperwork all done. Might make things go faster, and ... it would mean less time in Mauft's pleasant company."

Van's tease made Sahni chuckle. "She can be a little intimidating."

"True, but you might see a different side of her tonight. She volunteers at the orphanage, nearly every sol. She's very different in those surroundings. I – you're under no obligation to go, Sahni, but ... I would love it if you did go with us."

"I will, and you have the word of a 'purebred avowed' on that one. Shall I give you some time before I come back in and hit you with a bunch of TransNet questions?"

"Might be a good idea," Van replied. "Oh, and I almost forgot to ask you how things were on your rest sol."

"Pretty ... surprising, actually. I ... well, I saw my sister again, and ... we had a good time. First time in a long time, actually."

"Sounds nice. Alright, Sahni. I'll come get you when I'm ready. Okay?"

"Alright, Van, and thank you."

"Thank you, kit. Really," Vanarra replied, feeling a new sort of joy start to fill her. As the Nephti stepped out of sight, Van wrestled with those feelings. "I'm sharing, Flint. It's … it's working out for now, but … I hope it does work out for real."

The time passed quickly for both Sahnassa and Vanarra as they worked together for intervals gathering and organizing the things Sahnassa could add to the TransNet site. When they finally did part, both had more than enough work to consume them for the rest of the sol.

Van, seeing it was almost time to leave, quietly leaned in and looked at Sahnassa, sitting in the server room, facing the other direction. Looking at her, she noticed how delicate and well-sculpted the Nephti's ears were, the deep purple color of her fur, and the nearly black tail-tip that swung back and forth rhythmically as she listened to music, a couple of orange wires leading into her ears hinting at what was keeping her tail so well timed. "Maybe I should just go," she thought to herself. "She's … really not going to do this, is she?" Van wondered.

Just then, a square in the corner of the screen flashed, and Sahnassa sat up straight, stretched, and started stacking her papers and closing things down. Van figured she'd better say something before she was noticed. "Sahni?" she called, knocking on the door frame.

"Oh! Hi, Van. I was just cleaning up and getting ready. We still going?"

"If you want to," Vanarra replied. "It's not compulsory – strictly optional."

"I said I would go, Van, and I meant it." Sahni took the ear pieces out and quickly wound the cord around a paw-finger.

"What were you listening to, if you don't mind me asking?"

"Not at all! Rebel Monsters – it's a group from my house. They play … pretty fiercely. I kind of … well, tutored one of the members in school for awhile."

"Really?"

"Yes. They're starting to get some notice, which is good because the cub I tutored certainly wasn't going to achieve top marks academically; well, I guess I didn't either, but still, they play good stuff." Sahnassa stood up, her belongings all packed and ready to go.

"Alright then, just give me a tick, and I'll be ready."

"Okay," Sahni answered and waited while Van went back into her office.

"So, what are you going to spend your bonus on, Sheffer?" Raska asked from the end of the hallway, obviously loud enough so that Sahnassa could easily hear.

"Last night probably will get me that couch I want for my lair, maybe a few bottles of choice fermentum," the male replied easily. "What about you?"

"I have been on the hunt for some paw shoes that simply cost a fortune; last night put them in reach," Raska answered with all the enthusiasm of someone who would also receive a free sexual climax along with their purchase. "Well, I'd better go. Lots of shopping to do," she breathed easily as she walked to the front. "Oh, hello, Sahnassa … de Orturu. You have a good night."

Sahni was stewing a little at their obvious flaunting of a bonus she hadn't been allowed to earn but managed to keep her irritation from showing. "You, too, Raska. I hope you have a wonderful evening."

"Could hardly keep it from being so if I tried," the mixed blood chuckled as she swished her tail a little too close to Sahni as she turned and walked away.

"Who was that?" Van asked as she turned off the light and closed her door.

"Raska. I guess she's going … shopping," Sahni said with some small level of disappointment evident in her voice.

"Well, okay," Van replied, hearing the Nephti's tone but ignoring it, for the moment. "Sheffer?!" she called, and upon seeing his head appear in the hallway, Van asked, "Are you locking up tonight or is Flint?"

"Flint," he called back. "I'm going to spend some time at the Celestial Oasis. They've been holding back a Rician vintage for me."

"Ugh, it all makes my nose itch," Van replied dismissively. "Have a good time, Shef. Be careful."

"You, too, Van. Good night," he replied and turned away, pointedly snubbing Sahnassa.

Van could see that Sahni noticed the slight, so she whispered, "Come on, Sahni. Let's go. Just … ignore him."

As they walked past the empty receptionist area, Van commented, "Mauft is gone already. She likes getting there early when it's her evening to sit." Walking out the door into the breezy and warm evening, Sahni saw Tresk actually counting his pay just outside the door, a sizable haul from the looks of it. "Don't let that be seen in the open, Tresk," Van chided. "I don't want anyone putting a club upside your head."

"I'll be careful. You have a wonderful evening, Van … and Sahni."

"Thanks, Tresk," Sahni replied quietly. When the two of them were far enough away, Sahnassa observed, "I guess that must have been a really well paid event; everyone … looks like they're going shopping."

Van turned back to her and stated, "Honestly, I think they are enjoying rubbing it in your muzzle, kit, more than they are actually enjoying their pay – which I'll speak to them about. It's not a nice thing for them to do. You and I are spending a lot of time together putting the TransNet site up. They feel … threatened by that."

"I don't mean to threaten anyone, Van, by any means."

"But they've seen so many who did just that. I understand it, but like I said, I'll talk to them. Now, are you going to ride with me or follow?"

"Follow … if that's possible," Sahni replied, unsure.

"I'll keep the high-end maneuvers to a minimum, kit," Van chuckled.

"Alright," Sahni stated as she turned to enter her own vehicle.

Although it was a bit of a struggle to keep up with Vanarra's golden hover, Sahnassa followed reasonably well as they worked their way through Shanandrae to the interior district in the old city. Here, the buildings, while certainly of ancient architecture, bore fewer of the normal trademarks and preferences of modern Thurian architecture. The buildings here were more angular, more practical, and had fewer of those organic touches that made them seem to blend in nicely with their natural surroundings. A few of these had been converted into warehouses, one or two into "retro" museums of a sort, and some served as nominal office buildings for new or struggling businesses. The interior city did have a few open spaces and parks, usually created when old buildings collapsed or lay abandoned for a length of time. Near a section of distressingly rectangular plots of land was a light brown building that looked like several long trapezoids set one upon another in three levels.

As they pulled into the small hover lot in front of the gate, Sahni noticed that heads were popping out of the windows at nearly all levels, flashing with jubilant recognition, and disappearing inside almost as quickly. Vanarra opened her hover door and motioned for Sahni to do the same. "Prepare to get mugged," she warned. At that moment, ten or so kits and cubs of mixed ages burst from the structure's central door and into the yard, Van walking quickly to meet them.

Sahni watched, transfixed as her hard and somewhat emotionally distant employer changed right before her very eyes. Just inside the gate, she kneeled, opened her arms, and willingly allowed herself to be nearly tackled by the happy group, all calling her name over and over again. As Van tried to hug each and every one, Sahnassa was struck by the look of joy on her face – a happiness and contentment that she'd never seen before. Vanarra was nuzzling necks, licking the sides of muzzles, and ruffling between the ears every one of the happy group.

It was also then that Sahnassa spotted him, a youth of about six seasons, missing a right paw, a right ear, and hobbling on a crude prosthetic right hind-paw. As he got his time with the new arrival, Sahni caught a glance of his face – his right eye was covered by a patch, and a long scar traced the right side of his muzzle. Van took extra time with him, whispering in his ear and saying things that made the little cub hold her all the more. When he finally did go, Sahni swallowed as she saw the little mixed blood was missing half the length of his tail.

Finally realizing that Sahnassa was not alongside her and was, in fact, still standing beside the open door of her hover, Van looked back and asked, "You coming, kit? I promise, they won't bite." Just then, one of the smaller males, about five seasons, expressed his claws, bared his teeth and made a spring jump for Van, clearly in response to her statement. Van was apparently used to this cub, and slipped out of his grasp before almost tackling him on the ground and sending him into a fit of laughter with tickles up and down his sides. "Well, this one does, but I'll show … you how … to take care of … him!"

Sahni smiled a little, and closed the door of her hover, stepping forward somewhat nervously. The disfigured cub was standing at the gate, waiting for her with several others. With her heart nearly breaking looking down at him, she was shocked when a happy greeting came from his muzzle. "Welcome to Shanandrae Orphanage! It's so nice to have someone so beautiful come to visit us!"

"One of us did this to him," she thought as she reached for his extended left paw. Although she felt like her guilt and shame at being purebred avowed should keep her away from this place, the disfigured Anati cub would have none of it, catching her paw in a firm grasp and nearly pulling her inside. Quickly, he rattled off the names of every child that had gathered around to curiously gaze at the new Nephti.

"And what's your name?" he asked, politely.

"Hello, I'm … Sahni," she said quietly. "I work for Vanarra."

"Oh, you disavowed, too?" one of the few purebred kits asked, expectantly. She was a Vulpi of about eight seasons with nearly radiant green eyes and orange fur.

"Well, no … sorry," Sahni apologized, not knowing what else to do.

"She's new in my office," Vanarra explained, coming up behind the group, holding the terrifying menace from earlier still giggling in her arms. "She's been doing good work for me, and she's come to visit you. Everyone please treat her nice, okay?"

The group around Vanarra all repeated "okay" in a little chorus, and the kit who had asked her the question took Sahnassa's paw and led her forward. The disfigured male held her other paw, and between them, they pulled Sahnassa along towards the entrance behind Van.

Sahni looked around and saw that even more kits and cubs had joined the first group that had sprung out to meet them, and she was treated to an almost continual round of introductions, and did her best to say every kit's or cub's name back to them in greeting. As they approached the entrance, two somewhat elder Vulpi – a male and a female – stood at the top of the short stairs and waited, smiling, as Vanarra and her entourage approached, Sahni and hers close behind.

"It's good to see you, Vanarra Anasto," the elder male said, reaching out for Van.

"What will it take to get you to use my short name, Trif?" Van asked in mock anger as she, smiling widely, reached out for and returned his offered embrace.

"I must show some respect, for their sakes and in your honor," he explained.

"Either that, or he's flirting again," the female Vulpi said, but she, too, embraced Van warmly and gratefully. Turning to Sahnassa, she asked, "So, who did you bring for a visit, this sol?"

"This is Sahnassa de Orturu. She's working in my office right now, helping us get a TransNet site up and running. Sahni, this is Triffalion and Shenareen Batarra. They help run the orphanage and take care of this lot," Van explained, motioning to the group of children all standing with obedient patience at the bottom of the stairs.

Seeing both of the elder couple avert their eyes downward, Sahni nearly bristled. "Please don't! Right now, it's I who feel the least honored." She bowed to them, bowed in the elegant and graceful way that her mother had taught her to do upon greeting Honored Dames and Grand Matriarchs. A gasp rippled through the crowd of kids below, and when she arose, she saw that both of the Vulpi and Vanarra were staring at her, amazed and a little confused. "You are doing such a good work here. I honor you for that."

"Well ... thank you, sweet kit," Shenareen offered. "You ... you are quite kind. We do our best."

"She is a very good kit," Van asserted, smiling softly at Sahnassa. "Oh, and with the work she's doing, she'll help bring in even more business, so perhaps this can grow." Van offered Trif a draft, and upon taking it, the elder Vulpi sucked in a long breath of air.

"Well, now! Vanarra ... are you leaving yourself anything to eat on? This ... this is tremendous, dear kit!" the elder female exclaimed.

"Things have been pretty good lately, Shena, and perhaps a few more paw-shoes can come from it."

"Far more than that," Shena replied. "Children, please ... please join me in thanking Vanarra for her generous gift! What she brings us provides you with medicine, food, and the clothes you wear, not to mention it keeps your home safe and working well."

Shouts of gratitude and thanks chimed out from down below, and Van turned and went down the steps, again hugging every single child as they said thank you. Even the "terror" from earlier embraced her lovingly as he thanked her.

"She's taken such good care of us," Trif said quietly to Sahnassa as the three of them watched her. "And this is all the thanks she wants, all she ever asks."

"Are you okay, dear kit?" Shena asked.

Sahnassa looked at the pair of them and hesitated. Finally, she answered, "I … I'm not okay. They are all … beautiful, and … I've never seen anything like this."

"Those in avowed families seldom do," Trif explained gently. "Family orphanages seldom have more than a paw-ful of kits and cubs, and they get placed inside of a few moons. Here, well, it … it can take a long while, if ever. For me, it's hard to look at them, as little kits and cubs, and think of them as Anati, less than fully Thurian. They're simply children, and they don't easily comprehend what makes them different or why it even matters."

"They are bright, many of them," Shena added. "Model scholars who, if just given the chance could change our world with their contributions – contributions they'll never be allowed to make."

"Only if things never change," Sahnassa stated hopefully. "Perhaps they can. There are some out there trying – I think the Grand Matriarch Rahnahi de Dothnar, for example."

"Books on philosophy are pretty far removed from runny muzzles and torn pants, abandoned kits and cubs," Trif quietly answered. "It's a faint hope that anything will truly change."

"But it is a hope," Sahni replied. "Even if it's only a faint one. How can anyone look in their faces and not want better for them?"

Vanarra rejoined them at the top of the stairs, her eyes running with tears. "I … I just love that! Thank you both! I'd give anything for that!"

"You nearly have, Van," Trif stated. "We'll be able to repair and upgrade the bathrooms for this, with some to spare."

"More coming," Van promised, wiping her eyes. "Now, can we see our three new ones?"

"They're inside. Mauft is already tending to them upstairs. Shall we go in?"

The group of disappointed whines from the listeners below brought a chuckle to Van. "Alright, you all! I hear you! I'll be back out to play in a while, I promise." As a loud group of cheers erupted, the group dispersed, moving towards some rather nice playground equipment, Sahni noticed.

Sahnassa followed the group inside of the building, feeling a kind of sad shock she had never felt before, one that threatened to overwhelm her and drive her as far away from this building as she could get, but one she faced as bravely as she could. "So, here are our offices, up front," Trif pointed out. "The ... discipline room is right across the hall."

"Lots of sitting quietly and writing 'I will not do' something or other," Shena chuckled. "You can guess which ones out of the lot nearly call the place their own room. Here is the cubs' room, on the left, and the kits' room is on the right." Sahnassa leaned in to see long rows of small beds with chests at the foot of each one, and every bed was made neatly. Between each bed, a piece of furniture that combined a nightstand for the bed next to it gave the children their storage.

"That's clever," Sahni observed, more for the need to say something than anything else.

"Dear?" Shena asked.

"The ... wall units. "Very useful, well designed I mean."

Trif reached around Van's shoulder and gave her a brief hug. "That you can thank Vanarra for; she worked with someone to come up with the design for us. They're also built very well."

"They have to be," Shena noted, her paws on her hips, "and stop flirting with her."

"It's not my fault that our benefactor is so lovely," Trif replied in mock apology. For the first time, Sahnassa smiled, seeing that this little routine was one that had probably been practiced for a long time.

Van's embarrassment was only half-hearted as she stepped into the cubs' room and walked to one of the wardrobes. "And look at this, Sahni. Each one has a desk that pulls out from the..." Vanarra was suddenly transfixed by something hung on the inside of the door. As the others stepped around and saw what it was, all three couldn't help but stare. It was clear that one of the cubs was an aspiring artist, and the subject of his masterpiece was Vanarra – only with very revealing clothing and a tail that was far higher than it should have been, nearly draping her shoulder.

Instantly, Sahnassa was laughing, and Trif was chuckling alongside her. Shena had her paws on either side of her muzzle and exclaimed, "He didn't have that up there last sol!"

"It's ... just a tad ... well, it looks like I'm..."

"Yes, it does, Vanarra! I ... I think you have an admirer," Trif managed. "Other than myself, of course!"

Shena cursed under her breath as she stepped forward to remove the illicit artwork. "Rashall! I might have known! I'll take this down—"

"No, no, wait, Shena. Please," Van bade. "No harm done. In fact, he probably hoped that I would see it, and the chance is actually pretty slight that I would have. Let's make the cub's sol! Would you mind?" They all watched as Van drew out a marker from the desk that was a part of the wall unit and wrote on the corner of the picture in bold, black script, "To my Rashall, Love Van!"

"Oh, my!" Trif laughed. "You're hunting trouble for sure, now."

"I think it's kind of nice of her to do it," Sahnassa noted, thinking about how Van even sacrificed her own self-image for the sake of the cub's dreams.

"I ... suppose so," Shena said doubtfully. "He'll have to take it down and put it somewhere private, and I will speak to him about appropriate behavior, but ... I suppose it's okay."

"Thanks. Should we check any of the other wardrobes?"

"If you do something for one of them, you have to do it for all of them, Vanarra, you know how it is," Trif warned.

"Alright, Sahni, first task, open these up, and if there isn't a picture up there already, tack a blank piece of paper up there so I can sign it. I'll follow behind you."

"Okay, Van. Sure," Sahni replied, and happily started the work. Although there were no more racy images of Vanarra, there were more than a few pictures of beautiful scenes and even some sad and lonely ones. It was clear as Sahnassa viewed each cub's art, that they knew they were abandoned and hoped for better things, including parents to love them.

They were about halfway done when one of the kits ran to her, her golden paws covered with blood. "Shena! Shena! Come help!"

"What did you do to yourself, child?!" the elder Vulpi exclaimed as she took the kit's paws and looked at them, but the kit pulled away.

"It's not me! It's the baby kit! Outside! Someone just left it! Threw it on the ground!"

"Oh no!" Van gasped, and instantly she was out the door at a sprint, Sahnassa close behind her.

As they burst outside, it was clear where the problem was – a tight knot of children had gathered around something on the ground, and a hideous baby yowl was coming from their midst. Pushing into the circle, Van saw one of the kits holding a small baby kit, with a cub tightly grasping a stump of a tail, the rest having been sheared off. "Rashall! What happened?!"

"She was like this when we pulled her out of the box!" the cub explained, frightened. "A Faelnar just dropped the box in front of the gate and ran!"

Van looked back in the general direction of the building and then shouted in a voice which sent children diving, holding their ears. "Mauft! Mauft! Come quick!"

From the third level, the gray one's face appeared and then quickly disappeared, obviously having gotten the message.

"Now, Rashall, keep the pressure up! You did the right thing. Do you know how it happened?"

Sahnassa felt herself getting sick and had to walk away, the sound and smell and sight of what was happening just too much. Walking to the gate, feeling the contents of her stomach coming up, she looked over and saw the small tail that had been left on the ground. The box had to have been thrown, and the kit's tail was exposed through a hole.

"But where is it? How long as she been losing blood?"

"Van," Sahni gasped, but it was too quiet – forcing herself to be loud, she managed. "Van! It … was only a few moments … the … tail here … when someone threw the box. I—" She couldn't say anything more, since the Nephti hung over the gate and retched.

Not realizing Sahni's distress, Van called back, "Okay! Thanks! That's good then. She hasn't lost a lot of blood, and she won't lose anymore so long as you keep the pressure up, Rashall!"

"He's hurting her!" one of the kits shouted, worried.

"She's already been hurt. We're helping her now. We can't let her lose all her blood. Rashall's doing the right thing. Oh, Mauft, there you are! What took you so long!?"

"Went back in and grabbed the right things," Mauft explained as she took the baby kit and applied a clamp and tourniquet to the tail. "We're going to need help on this one, Van."

Looking over her shoulder, Vanarra called back to Shena, "Call the doctor, see when he can get here, okay? Tell him what it is!"

"Yes, Van! Right away!"

"Trif, get the kids away, give us a path, please!" Van ordered.

"Certainly. Children, give them room! Come over here to me, please! Right away!" Trif's stern tone wasn't disobeyed by a single one of the kits or cubs.

Van looked up and started to say, "Sahni—" but saw the Nephti collapsed over the fence, doing a good job of fertilizing the plants beneath her. "You … you stay right where you are," Van completed, disappointed. "Alright, Mauft, you've got her tail, and I'll carry her?"

"Let me, Van. Bigger paws. You're better for the delicate stuff."

"Okay, but never call me delicate!" Van teased, making Mauft actually smile a little which was difficult given the kit's pathetic howling. "Ready? Let's carry her inside – to the nursery."

"Ugh, this is going to set the rest of them off," Mauft groaned as she carefully picked up the kit, Van holding the bandage and clamp, her own paw on the kit's back to keep her from wriggling out of Mauft's grasp.

Carefully, the two took her inside and made the trek up the stairs to the nursery on the top floor.

At the front, Sahnassa was finally starting to regain her ability to breathe, keeping her eyes closed intentionally so she wouldn't look at the severed tail lying on the ground – an image she knew would haunt her forever. "It's … too much, it's too much, Van!" she cried. Without looking behind her, she slowly pushed herself to a standing position and shuffled along the fence to the gate, opened it, and made her way unsteadily to her hover.

Opening the door, she sat down, took a drink from a bottle of warm water, and wiped her muzzle with some disposable wipes, tears running down her cheek fur. "I'm … I'm not … I can't do this!" she said, and just as she was about to close the hover door, a small paw touched her leg. Looking over, Sahni saw the mixed blood, Rashall, looking at her. Looking down at his paws, she saw that they hadn't been cleaned, but looking into his eyes was the greater horror.

"Please, don't go! You aren't okay enough to drive. That's … that's how I lost my dad." His heartfelt concern made Sahni feel completely ashamed. Looking ahead of her vehicle, she saw Trif and all of the children looking at her, expectantly. Heartbroken by her own lack of strength, she buried her head in her paws and just cried.

"Well, we're having some fun now!" Van yelled over the chorus of howls and whines and cries that had erupted once they had carried the screaming kit into the nursery.

"They'll have to wait," Mauft shouted as the three of them worked to shave what was left of the kit's tail so they could apply a proper bandage.

"Where's Sahni?!"

"I saw her getting in her hover," Shena replied, sadly. "I'm ... I'm afraid it was too much for her."

"It was a mistake bringing her here in the first place!" Van growled. "Too ... purebred avowed to have ever seen anything like this!"

"This isn't normal for me!" Shena offered in Sahnassa's defense. "What beast would do such a thing!?"

"Pretty much the regular kind," Mauft observed darkly. "There, that's got it clean and shaved. When did the doctor say he would be here?"

"As soon as he could," Shena answered as she started carefully wrapping the stump of the kit's tail.

"What do we do before he gets here?"

"Keep her on her stomach, gently hold her, try to comfort her. I can't ... I can't imagine someone doing this to a kit her age!"

"Or any age, Shena. The stories I've heard ... what I've read about how this affects you for the rest of your life," Van said loudly. "I wish I could get my claws into the rape-mating bastard; there would sure as mange be two tails gone!"

"Van?" a frail voice called from the far doorway. "The ... the doctor's here."

Vanarra didn't actually hear what was said, but turned her head in the direction of the speaker and saw Sahni clutching the door frame, her nose and lips pale, as someone familiar came up behind her. "You!"

"Yes," the Nephti doctor shouted as he approached them. "And you haven't been to the clinics recently!"

"Don't need to," Van explained. "What's your name again?"

"Nadar, doctor, that is. How did this happen? Sahnassa!" he called back. "You said you saw something?"

Sahni weakly made her way and stood behind the doctor as he pulled equipment out of his bag and started getting ready to sew up the kit's tail. "I … I think she was in a box that was dropped or … thrown, and … it got pinched off."

"Nothing can be done about that now," he said. "You caught it fairly quick. For all her crying, the kit has good color. Now, I'll only need one of you to assist. Sahnassa, you up for it?"

"I'll stay," Van replied. "Sahni … Sahnassa, you can go home now!"

"I … want to help," she said as loudly as she was able. "What can I do?"

Van's temper snapped. "Try to get this lot to stop crying! Pick up a damn kit or cub and love on it until it shuts up!" Van screamed back at her. "What do you think?!"

"Easy, Van," Mauft warned.

"Okay … okay," Sahnassa replied, her ears and tail full down.

For nearly half an interval, Van paid no more attention to anyone else than the doctor and the little kit she was gently holding down. As the doctor administered medications and started stitching, Van was already regretting at how she had unleashed on Sahni.

"There, hold there," the doctor told her. "Good. You … you said you didn't need to come to the clinics anymore. You suddenly have an inexplicable case of perfect health?"

"Not really," Van replied, smiling a little. "I have a business now, and I've got a health plan for me and my staff."

"You're joking."

"No, I'm not," she replied, embarrassed. "It's hard to find doctors who want to see us, but, money can do wonderful things. A few regulars are doing very well for us right now."

"That's amazing! You've come a long way since I saw you last – that has to be seasons ago."

"I'm pleased you remember me," Van almost purred at him and winked.

"Oh now, kit, I'm too old for those types of games."

"Well, you deserve a lot of thanks for this. Hey, did anyone notice?"

"Notice what?" Mauft asked.

"It's ... quiet." The three of them looked over and saw Shena in a chair holding two of the littlest cubs, but Sahnassa had all of the rest in the play area, laying on blankets, or being cuddled, or being patted or sung quietly to. Van's quick count saw no less than eight children placed all around the Nephti who, although still weary looking, at least seemed now to have regained her color. Sahnassa, sensing the attention turning to her, looked up at them.

"Sahni, that's amazing!" Van whispered. "Thank ... you, kit."

Seeing her boss looking at her apologetically, Sahnassa was able to smile back and nod as she continued her soft little song to the infants nearby.

"Sahni?" the doctor asked as he returned to his work. "I've never heard her called that before."

"Yes. I ... came up with it. You said 'before.' Do you ... know each other?"

"Sure. I was her doctor when she was growing up," Nadar replied easily.

"Oh. It ... it was good of her to come volunteer then," Van said carefully with a warning glance at Mauft. "She ... she seems really nice."

"Been through a lot," Nadar replied very quietly as he finished wrapping a bandage around the now sleeping kit's injury. "And I don't just mean this sol. It's ... good to see her. I was worried about her."

"Why?" Mauft asked.

"Not something I can talk about," Nadar answered. "There now. All done, and thankfully, she, like everyone else up here, is quiet and asleep. That won't last, though. She's going to wake up and need to be fed in a few intervals, and she'll have lingering pain that will make her cry. Administer this for her pain, but only a drop or two on the tongue every interval, and I mean not one bit more, you understand?"

"I do," Van replied.

"You staying, Van?" Mauft asked.

"No way I'm leaving right now. When will she be in the clear, doctor?"

"She'll need to be brought to my office sol after next, but unless there's bleeding or swelling, she should be okay. Probably by tomorrow night, she'll be okay to sleep without being tended. That's … not going to be the case tonight."

"I'll arrange everything, Doctor. Thank you," Van replied and reached around the Nephti's shoulders to hug him.

"Good. I want to say goodbye to Sahnassa."

"That might be a little difficult," Mauft noted, seeing that Sahnassa had dropped off to sleep with all of the children around her.

"Oh, I'm not getting in the middle of that," Nadar stated quietly. "Alright you all, have as good a night as you can, okay?"

"Sure. Thank you."

Sahnassa awoke to movement around her and looked up. Shena, smiling, was taking one of the cubs gently off of her. Lifting her arm was difficult, since the weight of the child had put it to sleep, but she saw the time was only two intervals to high night. Feeling some bodily urgencies of her own, she was eager for the Vulpi to come and take the rest of the children from her. Finally, after a few passes, Sahnassa stood up unsteadily and slowly made her way forward. Touching the Vulpi's shoulder she asked, "Bathroom?"

"Middle level, just before the hall."

Sahni nodded and started to walk out of the room, but then she saw Vanarra sitting with the baby kit on a sofa chair, looking as happy and peaceful as she had seen her boss in a long time. "Hi, kit. You doing okay?"

"I will be," Sahni whispered, pointing to the stairs. "Be right back."

"Okay."

Van leaned back and continued to hold the warm bundle in her arms. Thankfully, they hadn't needed to give the little kit anymore medicine, as yet. Warmed milk, enriched with vitamins, had been the solace the kit needed more than anything. With infants, it was sometimes hard to see the combinations clearly, but as Van had held the little kit in the rapidly dwindling light, she thought the mix was Nephti and Perratti. "A short tail won't be so bad, then, perhaps," Van thought. She sighed, heavily, anxious about so many things – this little kit's health, the impact on the children seeing such a horror right in front of their eyes, and even how her Nephti technologist would react. What happened had clearly been a shock to the kit, one she almost hadn't recovered from. "Have to admit it was nice to see her at the top of the stairs," Van mused quietly as she stroked the little one's head.

She turned and looked and saw Sahnassa re-entering the room. "You going to go home, kit?" Van asked. Just then, the kit in Van's arms roused again, whimpering and unhappy. Even as Vanarra tried to shush her, one of the other young ones started to rouse. Rolling over, the child banged into the side of his crib and got his arm stuck between the gap in the boards.

"I'm coming! I'm coming!" Sahni whispered urgently as she made her way over and got the cub out of his predicament. Standing over his bed, she whispered to him and calmed him, and soon he was drifting back off to sleep.

Van's situation, however, wasn't improving. It was clear that between hunger and pain, their newest addition wasn't going to quiet down. "Ugh, Sahni, can ... can you help me a moment? Can you take her?"

"Sure," Sahnassa replied and sat beside Van on the couch. "Pass her over, and I'll hold her for awhile. How long since you last gave her the medicine?"

"Not since the doctor left. She's so young, she needs a feeding, as well. I'm going to go get something and come back up. Can you manage for a few passes?"

"I will," Sahnassa promised, stroking the face and little muzzle of the kit now in her arms.

"Okay. Back soon," Van promised. Within a few passes, Vanarra had used the facilities, obtained and warmed the milk, and even found a couple of juices and snack bars for herself and Sahni. When she returned to the nursery, Vanarra was surprised to find it completely quiet.

Walking over, she could see that Sahnassa was crying, long reflective paths went down the side of her cheek fur, visible even in the near darkness. Van sat alongside her and asked, "Do you want me to take her back?"

"No, Van. It's ... it's okay," Sahnassa replied uneasily.

"I can tell it isn't, kit. I'm sorry. It was a mistake to bring you out here."

"Why, Van?"

Vanarra was silent for a moment and looked away from her. "Perhaps because ... I was trying to make a point, more or less. I was trying to share something with you and maybe … prove something to you, and it was too much."

"It's not your fault this happened. What's more, she has someone to take care of her now. Can I have the bottle, please?" Van passed it to her, and with only a little coaxing, the kit began to drink. "Oh, but I can't … I can't understand why anyone would throw away a little kit like that! Toss them on the ground like trash!"

Vanarra was stunned to hear the emotion and heartbreak in the Nephti's whispered voice. "I know. This … this is what we're thought of, Sahni, by some. We're … disposable."

"But how could anyone be so cold as to do this? She's … she's ruined for life! The joy and beauty of a female … lost, and the hardships she'll go through. How could someone just throw her down and run away?"

"You throw away things in the garbage, don't you? Then, you don't have to care about them anymore. Someone has a little fling, purebred to purebred – oops, I'm pregnant! I give birth, and then walk away – problem solved."

"Murderous, evil," Sahnassa spat, horrified.

"Purebred," Vanarra whispered back, looking at Sahni.

"I would never do that, Van. I would never!"

"You wouldn't know until you're faced with that decision, when you're about to lose all that house honor and privilege for a stinking, crying, demanding Anati mongrel that's far easier to put in the garbage or drop off in a box than take care of. Only the … insane would make that choice."

"It's insane not to," Sahnassa breathed raggedly. "It's a life! She's warm, her heart beats, and she'll grow up to be someone like those kits downstairs, someone like you. Do … do you think I look at you as trash? Honestly?"

"You're working for me, so … I guess not. If you weren't, I don't know – how would you look at me?"

"You can never know what I'm saying is true, but when I've been able to, I've stood up for Anati. Please, Van, understand that as … someone in a family, we seldom see any but our own kind. My dad would take us to the archive, and … that was the only place I ever saw Faelnar or Perratti – any of them."

"The families do a good job keeping us hidden and out of sight. Big walls around their estates, rules that keep us out of places, just like the archive. I'm not surprised you grew up not seeing us. You know what bothers me the most? It's the look of shock I still get when someone sees me – it's like I'm a damned alien or something, not even a Thurian, like I'm something out of those space fiction books you read. Then ... then, some are just simply revolted or ... sometimes ... they like what they see – males, usually. They like it, for a little fun, but never for long."

"She's done," Sahni observed quietly as the sound of the sucking changed.

"You've got to burp her now," Van observed.

"I know. I had a little sister," Sahni replied as she pulled the little kit up to her shoulder.

"No, put a towel over your shoulder ... just in case."

"Good idea." There was a moment of silence while the Nephti got her charge in the right position and then started softly stroking her back. "Van, I'm ... sorry for how things are, and I can only change things so much, but ... you are fully Thurian to me. You are someone I respect, certainly more than a dame I know, trust me on that."

"How would you feel if Doctor Nadar knew you were working for me?" Van asked.

"I don't think it would matter, Van. I can work for whom I please."

"Wouldn't that ... harm your position in your family?"

"In some eyes, perhaps," Sahni answered. "However, I grew up with those who saw everything like that, and I got tired of it." A small, but noticeable belch punctuated her sentence. "Oh, wow! We have success! Sure there wasn't any fermentum in that?"

"Ha," Van replied softly, but in good humor. "Let her stay up there just for a little while longer, in case she has any more."

"I ... I couldn't take her down. She's nuzzling me, Van. Oh, you precious little kit!"

"When Nadar told me he knew who you were, I ... I was scared."

"Scared, of what?"

Vanarra sighed. "That if he found you were working for me and took that back to your family, you ... you would actually be disavowed."

"I doubt that."

"I've seen purebreds who are disavowed, Sahni. I know a lot about that. It's … a hard life, even harder, sometimes and in some ways than I think our lot is. Everything they thought about themselves disappears in an instant, and they're like this empty shell. Anati don't have a house supporting them; we never get used to it. I wouldn't wish that kind of heartbreak on anyone."

"How could I not respect you, Van, when you believe that? I enjoy doing what I'm doing for you, besides getting paid for it. Even if not everyone in the office likes me being there."

"Yeah, I've noticed that – don't think I haven't."

"Oh, she's getting squirmy again," Sahnassa yawned. "Maybe time for the medicine?"

As the kit's whimpers started to turn back into cries, Van agreed, "Yeah, let me tap my PawLink – give us a little light. Lean her back, I'll get the dose ready." After a few preparations, Van held the dropper over the kit's open muzzle, forced that way by Sahni's gentle paw fingers. "One and two. There you go, little kit. We should really give her a name."

Sahni gently cradled the little kit as her tongue lapped the medicine from the roof of her mouth. "I … I wouldn't do that. I don't think it's my right, Van. You are the one who supports this place. I almost drove out of here when this happened."

"I heard you were in your hover. What made you stay?"

"Rashall … all of them," Sahnassa sighed and sniffed back a sob. "I couldn't leave, no matter how horrible I felt."

"Here, pass her back to me," Van offered, and Sahnassa gently did so. "I didn't expect you to stay, you know. I wouldn't have held it against you."

"I would have," Sahni whispered. "You get to choose the name, Van. I don't have any right to."

"Well, I guess, but help me think one up at least."

"What can it be?"

"We're Anati, she and I. It can be anything."

Sahnassa thought for a moment and put her paw on top of the kit's head. "Hope, maybe?"

"I like that. Hope. Perhaps … Hope Rashalla – in honor of my admirer and clearly the hero of the sol."

"Oh, I like that, Van. I do!"

"There, there Hope. Go to sleep. That's it, little kit, go to sleep," Van cooed. "I think she likes it."

"Wonderful, Van. Oh, that's so amazing. I don't think I've felt more honored in a moon, and that's pretty good considering where I was last night – who I was with."

"Who's that?"

"Believe it or not, I was standing in the presence of my Grand Matriarch last night – and she was in full battle dress; that's enough to scare the tail off anyone."

"Battle dress?" Van asked, curious.

"What they wear when they lead their houses in war. It's a bit more terrifying than all the bangles and jewelry they wear normally."

Van thought about asking what she was doing there, but decided against it, not wanting to pry into the business of families – something she didn't have any practical need to know about and something Sahnassa might be unwilling to share. "And you say that little Hope Rashalla beats her? Little kit Anati with a little tail and sheltering in an orphanage?"

Sahni reached over and put her paw on Van's shoulder. "It's Hope, and it's you, Van."

Vanarra chuckled slightly, unsure if the Nephti was just being kind, trying to flatter her, or might actually be sincere. "Thanks. Now, you finally going to go home?"

"No thanks," Sahni replied. "This sofa isn't as wonderful as my bed – thank you again – but I think both of us should stay. You shouldn't have to do this alone."

"Shena would help."

"She's already asleep and has a building full of children to worry about tomorrow and this one, after we go. No, Van. I'll stay the night."

Holding the small kit in her arms, Van admitted to herself that she truly did need Sahni there in order to take care of the infant, and even though she still harbored many doubts about the Nephti beside her, she had to admit that Sahnassa was showing a good heart – at least this night. "Thank you, kit. You're kind to stay. Take tomorrow off."

"Will you?"

"Well, no."

"Well, then you'll see me there, too."

Van shook her head. "You're just plain crazy, kit."

"Not yet, but I'm learning," Sahni joked as she propped her hind legs on the low table in front of them and snuggled back into the couch, closing her eyes.

Van couldn't help but chuckle a little, and although she felt like throwing a barb back at Sahnassa for being so smug, she simply replied, "I guess. Get some sleep. I'll wake you when I need a break, okay?"

"Okay. Thanks, Van."

Sahnassa turned her head away, and Vanarra Anasto looked at her and thought, "No, thank you, kit. Really."

"You're in late this morning," Flint observed as Van came in the front door.

"Rough night at the orphanage," Van explained, suppressing a yawn.

"Yeah, Mauft called me," Flint said as he followed her into her office. "She felt bad about leaving you alone like that."

"Well, she had been up the whole night before with the other three. Besides, I wasn't alone. Sahni was with me," Van observed as she sorted through papers on her desk.

"Really? She came in this morning right on time," Flint replied, surprised.

"She what?!" Van gasped. "She's here?" Flint nodded, and Van strode out past him and went to the server room. The door was closed, but light was spilling out from underneath. Knocking on the door, she was greeted by the sounds of some shuffling and then saw Sahnassa, wearing a change of clothes and obviously somewhat more awake than she. "What are you doing here? I thought I told you to take the sol off!"

"Well, I have a lot I can get done this morning. I might ask to leave a little early, if that's okay."

"A lot early, kit," Van replied, a little grumpily. "You worked your tail off last night." Flint was looking over Van's shoulder and nodded and winked at Sahni without Van seeing.

"You worked harder, boss."

Van glanced back up at Flint, but his expression was, by then, completely neutral. "Alright, you hard-headed purebred! Have it your way, and … thanks."

"Sure. Before I leave, I should have enough put together so that you can show off the site from your office computer."

Van instantly thought of Buck, and wondered if Sahni wasn't thinking about that, as well. "That wouldn't be so bad. It's a little cramped in here, actually."

"Yes, I noticed that, too," Flint added.

"You would," Van replied back, smirking. "Alright kit, but if you start to feel too tired to drive home, come see me, okay?"

"Yes, Van, and thanks."

Flint and Van returned to her office and shut the door. "Crazy Nephti kit," Van said, once the door was closed.

"Yeah, and she's locked up in a closet – I'd go completely feral if I had to work in that space."

"My guess is that it seems a bit bigger to her," Van replied, sitting down and sighing.

"Possibly, but that room across the hall just has empty boxes in it. We could break those down, store them somewhere, perhaps … bring in a desk?"

"You want me to give her an office?"

"Well, I've nosed in a few times, and she's got things on the floor, stuck to the wall, and balanced on her knees. Most technologists I've seen or talked to had a desk of some kind, at least."

"Oh, I don't know. That's going to raise ten kinds of crap with the rest of the group."

"And how big was Sahni's primal bonus, exactly?" Flint queried carefully.

"I'm tired, I've been up way too long, and you are not playing fair," Van complained. "Yeah and they were all pretty crappy about it, except Saiphar. Okay. Go ahead! Just so long as you tell the rest of the group it's a temporary thing, while she's under contract. When she's gone, it's back to being our box closet."

"You're not thinking about what we discussed? Keeping her?"

"I … don't know," Van admitted. "I have to confess I was pretty impressed with her last night, but this is a business, Flint! We don't know if the TransNet site is going to do anything for us. For all

I know, it could be a giant pit I keep throwing money into. It's cost us a lot already, and Sahni's time isn't cheap, either."

"Granted, but you might want to ask some experts about how long it takes a TransNet site to make money and break even."

"You mean, Buck?" Van asked.

"He's the only other technologist expert I would trust with that question."

"He's my friend, Flint, but why do you trust him?"

Flint smiled as he replied, "Because you do, boss. I'm going to work on some of the feedback forms. Raska garnered a few comments at the primal."

"Really?" Van asked, concerned. "Good or bad?"

"Hard … to say. It's mixed. Some are wildly praising her, like she was some kind of matriarch or VidStar performer, but a couple were downright disgusted – mostly females. I'm trying to piece together what she was doing before I corner her on it."

"I don't like the sound of that," Van nearly growled. "She's attracting attention for herself and not for this business. Talk to me about what you find out, Flint, and then, perhaps, we should speak to her, together."

"Sounds like a good idea. Alright then, I'll talk to you later," he said and left her office.

Leaning back into her chair, she thought about his advice. Sighing and trying not to yawn, she picked up the LineCom and dialed. "Can I speak with Buck Harlock, please? It's Vanarra Anasto. Thanks."

She waited a moment, and he replied, "Buck Harlock, managing partner, can I help you?"

"Buck Harlock, you hotty!"

"Van! Hey there! I was going to call you later!"

"Really? What's up?"

"Another techno-tail fest! The group here just finished up a big piece of work, and I want to show them a good time for it. My schedule's pretty booked; I was hoping we could possibly meet tonight."

Van stifled a yawn. "I suppose so, but I was up a lot last night, so I might not be the best conversationalist."

"Well, perhaps I could cater you for once. I'll bring dinner. That seasoned creele from de Kestos still a favorite?"

"Okay, yum! Yes! If you could get the recipe off of them, I'll pay you a finder's fee!"

"Not sure that's possible. Say, would it be okay to meet at about … six intervals before high night?"

"You better bring something warm with a little stimulant in it. I just might fall asleep in your lap once you feed me."

"I can think of worse things," Buck chuckled.

"Oh, stop it!" Van laughed back at his flirt. "That Perratti I'm seeing probably wouldn't take kindly to that. You hunting any good tail right now?"

"Well, yes and no," Buck confessed. "There's a Faelnar kit at one of my client firms that seems to think I score above average. We're just kind of dancing around each other right now."

"Sounds like fun," Van mused, smiling. "I hope you get someone good, Buck. You deserve it after that whole thing a few seasons ago."

"Please, don't mention her," Buck nearly growled. "She doesn't exist for me anymore."

"Alright, alright. There's one or two that I wouldn't like brought up, either. I'll see you tonight, then. Oh, and my own techno-tail thinks she'll have something for you to look at tonight. She's been putting some forms on the site, our standard sign-up stuff."

"I look forward to it."

"Great. Thank you, Bucky."

"You too, Van. See you tonight."

Several intervals later, Van greeted Buck at the front door, unlocking it for him. "Hi there!"

"Everyone else gone?" he asked, curious, hauling in a couple of bags of food.

"Yeah," she replied, stifling a yawn. "I sent them home … a little early."

"Slow right now?" Buck asked, a little concerned.

"Not really. We've got what promises to be a wild pre-join tomorrow night, and we just finished a primal."

"Wow, another one?!" he asked, surprised.

"Here, let me get that for you," she offered as they went to the back. As he gave her one of the bags, she added, "It's like two a moon, now. Their little fringe gatherings are really starting to get bigger, and … perhaps a little worrisome."

"Really? How so?"

Van sighed, "I've started spotting a few … Foundationalists here and there. They're turning their noses up at us and trying to cause trouble between us and the organizers. So long as we stay on our game and deliver great service, I don't think they have a chance."

As Buck unpacked the bags on one of the tables, he carefully answered a tone he heard in Van's voice. "But, you weren't on your game for this last one?"

"Totally not! Blew it two times," Van admitted as she flounced into a seat opposite him. Looking at the nice spread in front of her, she smiled. "Thanks, Bucky. You're a treasure!"

"Hey, I want something, remember? And officially," he replied smugly, "this is a business expense. A meeting between business partners."

"Here's to business partners," she offered, picking up a couple of glasses she had pulled already and placed on the table. He filled their drinks with ice water, and then they both drank.

"You know, I brought something I want you to try after we're done eating. It's a wild berry fermentum – you're only supposed to drink a little of it. I thought you might like it at your next event."

"You mean your event," she replied, smiling slyly. "Alright, I'll try it, Buck, but that stuff makes my nose itch."

"Well, Maliana said hers used to itch, too, but this stuff doesn't set her off."

"Is that the Faelnar you're trying to cozy up to?" Van asked.

"Yeah. She's nice. I have no idea if it will work out. She's avowed, so I'm not getting my hopes up. She may not think I'm worth the trouble it would cause her family."

"You're worth it," Van replied as she speared a piece of creele and held it up to her eye. "I'm going to put this under a scope and analyze it," she joked after she took her first bite. "Thank you, again. It's wonderful, Buck."

"Not a problem. So tell me, what's got you making mistakes at a primal? I thought that was supposed to be everyone else's job, and you were the one clawing the fur off of the offenders?" he asked before taking a bite.

"It's the Nephti. I … continually just screw up with her – lose my temper, say the wrong thing. I don't get it! For example, just recently – I go into the server room and ask her how things are going, but it's not the real reason I'm in there. I'm actually wanting to apologize for something dumb I did, and she accepts my apology, all nice and proper, and then … she hugs me!"

He looked at her, curious. "Doesn't seem like the … worst thing I've ever heard of. Was it?"

"I … I almost lost it, Buck!" Van quietly admitted. "Something just felt so scary and so wrong about that, like … like the time I told you about when I was rapemated during an event working for Gorta. Damn, I … I didn't know what I was capable of doing to her to get her off me."

"What … did you do?" he asked, carefully.

"I backed away, kind of shoved her away, more … verbally than anything else. I made a tail for brains of myself *while I'm apologizing*! I'm not normally this big an idiot, Buck, am I? What's wrong with me?"

"She's avowed purebred, Van. You have an issue with that, right?" he asked.

"It's more than that, and it's not a Nephti thing, either. I've had a female Nephti – a customer of mine – hug me during the primal! I didn't freak out! I didn't come apart! It's killing me that I'm … really acting this … crazy around her!"

"Do you feel threatened by her, Van?" he asked. "You've told me what happened to your mother, remember? Could it be just that she's avowed? You getting a little too close to matrons, dames, and matriarchs, perhaps?"

"I don't think so. She … she kind of touched me, Buck. Touched my heart. She quotes Rahnahi at me; she seems pretty loyal. She's … even a little protective of me. Last night, we had a situation where I had taken her over to the orphanage just to kind of expose her to the kits and cubs, show her what matters to me. In the middle of it, some rape-mating bastard runs by, drops a baby kit on the pavement, sheers off the kit's tail, and runs away! Before I knew what was happening, Mauft and I were taking the kit inside, and Sahni was hung over the fence … fertilizing the flowers."

"I can understand. It sounds … hideous."

"Well, stuff like that happens to our kind," Van replied with a shrug. "I ... expected that she'd just leave – heck, that she might even quit. No, she ... almost crawls up the steps to the nursery and ends up spending the whole night with me, helping to take care of the little kit!"

"Kind of sounds like ... you might admire her, even ... like her," Buck observed. "You know, this is perhaps the toughest friendship there could be for you, save trying to make a friend of a de Gonari Faelnar."

"Ugh," Van groaned. "That's not ever going to happen! I ... I had an actual matron from that house in my lobby, wanting to hire us! I couldn't even go to the door, and then ... that's one of the things I blew up on Sahni about. She was going to ask me about it, I could tell, and I ... wasn't real diplomatic about telling her I didn't want to talk about it!"

"She's got you tripping over your tail. You know, there may just be a chance that you're a little ... afraid of committing to her as a friend."

"She's an employee, not a friend," Van corrected.

"Oh really, and what, then, are you and I? I hire you, so you're my employee in a way – at least for a short amount of time. You and I are friends, though, Van. You tell me things I don't think you tell anyone else. Why is that? What makes me so special?" he asked.

Van thought for a moment, taking some time to eat a little more while she considered. "I ... I saw you after you were clawed in the gut, and we shared that. I know you understand what it means to hurt inside. I saw you at your lowest, and ... you've seen me there a few times, too. Pulled me up a few times."

"Like after you were arrested for fighting off that rape-mating. You could have called Flint."

"Flint works for me, Buck. I couldn't let that stupid event interfere with my business, and ... you came through for me. I owe you."

"I think I owe you more," he offered.

"Well, there you have it, and one other thing: when I talk to you, I know – without any doubt – that you speak for yourself, same as I. When I talk to that little Nephti kit, she's beholden to a house. She can tell me anything she wants, and even if she believes it, her house can override it. How can you trust someone when they answer to someone else? If I take her to a primal, let's say, and I instruct her not to tell anyone about who was there and what went on; that's all great. What if her dame or matron tell her that she has to spill what she knows? Who gets listened to, them or me?"

"You do have a point, but … it's not automatic, Van," he cautioned her. "A dame or matron can ask, but if that Thurian is truly honorable, they would rather lose their last name than break a promise. The question you have to ask yourself is do you think she's that honorable?"

"Can I trust her, you mean?"

"In the end, yes," he said, quickly clearing another bite from his mouth.

"I don't know. If I want her to be that trustworthy, then isn't there a chance that I'll presume she's trustworthy when she's really not? Then, something happens, and I get burned – this whole business and … those orphans get burned. Little Nephti kit isn't worth that – not by any measure," Van said dismissively, spearing another piece of creele.

"You never know, Van – she might be worth a lot. She's here, isn't she – working for you? She's done a marvelous job getting your TransNet site up."

Van looked at the table, dejectedly. "I wish your firm could do it."

"Not our skill set," he reminded her. "Not even close. Now, if you need a factory relay or controller set up and configured, then I'm your Thurian! TransNet commerce for small to moderate businesses? Not so much." Van grunted unhappily, and he continued, "She's still doing a good job for you, right?"

"Yeah, I suppose. She gave me log-ins so you could see how things are progressing. I suppose you should meet her at some point, maybe. Would that be uncomfortable for you?"

"Not really. As long as I'm not the one having to fire her, I can manage."

Van chuckled ruefully. "Yeah, that honor would fall to me. Thanks!"

"You know, Van, I've met avowed I could trust. De Dothnar's got a lot of them. Their house holds to honor, as you well know. Any house led by Rahnahi de Dothnar is going to honor its word, no matter what. I don't know about de Orturu, but … you know, maybe you have to judge Sahni on her own merits. Anati have a bad reputation, and lots of Thurians wouldn't ever trust you like I have. So what about a house's reputation or its demands! Sahni probably deserves to be judged by what she does and who she is."

"Ouch!" Van replied darkly as she took a slice of roast grazer and put it on her fork. "I do tell you too much. You've gotten to the point where you can use my own complaints against me. I'll open up to her a little, I suppose, but I don't know. That's what Flint wanted me to do, and that's when I had the bright idea of taking her to the orphanage. That went really bad."

"The situation was bad, but did you learn anything about her? Did she prove anything to you?"

"I guess she did, and yes, I have to say I respect her a little more for sticking it out when she was so … revolted by what she saw. I just keep asking myself, Bucky, if it's worth all this trouble, all this effort I'm going through talking and thinking about this!"

"At some level, you may have already answered that question," Buck supplied. "However, getting it resolved in your head will help keep you on your best game, and keep the Foundationalists from trying to cut you out of the primals, right?"

"Damned scary bunch! Flint passed me a pamphlet he picked up from the grounds while he was cleaning up. Did you know that every purebred's problem could be traced back to an Anati? We're genetic mistakes, and we shouldn't even be allowed to 'breed' – I mean what kind of crap is that!? Don't they know we have a really hard time getting pregnant anyway? Heck, the way I've been rapemated, I should have had six kits and six cubs by now! Thankfully, when I showed that pamphlet to my customer, she said they were a fringe group, not to be worried about, but still."

"I'd pay attention to any group that thought I was a genetic mistake," Buck observed, sounding concerned. "De Caterra was never Anati-friendly, but the family I still have in there who will talk to me are telling me that the Foundationalists are starting to get a real, visible paw-hold. Watch out for yourself at these primals – they talk about sterilization and euthanasia and genetic purification; I'm not sure I would put anything past them."

"We generally keep in groups of two or more when working for various reasons," Van considered aloud. "Here's another good reason."

"Our gatherings, however, are not anywhere as problematic. We're just a happy bunch of techno-tails!" Buck offered brightly.

"Oh great, so what am I in for this time?"

"Well, we're having them bring in conveyors; I was wondering if we could use them somehow?" he asked.

Vanarra chuckled and wiped her muzzle, her meal fully eaten. "Alright, it sounds weird as usual, but of course, Buck! Tell me what I'm in for."

He smiled at her, glad that she was always willing to give ear to his crazy ideas.

Chapter 18: Interactivity

Sahnassa was frustrated. She had been having several really good sols of progress, and now a problem trying to get Saiphar's art to render correctly on the TransNet site was causing her no end of grief. She had stayed until Vanarra chased her out the previous night and had been back at it all sol and through lunch without stopping. Now, what was worse, Sahnassa felt herself getting overheated. She presumed it was just her until there was a knock on the door.

"Yes?" she asked a little frustrated, not opening the door. "Who is it?"

Vanarra opened the door and nosed in. "It's the boss, actually. Hey, it's … it's really warm in here, kit! What's going on?"

Sahnassa stood and realized that she was actually panting a bit. "Wow, I … it kind of crept up on me! Let's open the door."

When Sahni backed away and the door swung open, the change in the temperature was startling – nearly giving her a chill. "Oh my goodness!" Sahni gasped. "I … I've got to shut down. Right now!"

"Well, I'm coming in, too," Van offered, worried about her investment. Soon, both of them were in the small computer room with the door closed as Sahnassa started issuing shutdown commands. "Whoa, it's really bad in here! How long does it take to shut down?"

"It can take a few passes with some of these runners," Sahni warned, still panting.

"How did you stand it in here, kit? It's awful," Van observed, and then she crawled up onto one of the low tables nearby. Putting her paw-pad against the vent, she commented, "It's dead. Nothing coming from it. You haven't been up in the ceiling again, have you?"

"No, I haven't, Van, really," Sahnassa promised. Looking back to her displays, she breathed a sigh of relief, "All down. Cutting the power, but I'm not going to be able to get anything else done until we can manage the temperature. I mean, these boxes don't have to be treated as gently as rulla eggs, but ... they can't take being cooked, either."

"Yeah, you, too," Van observed, looking at the Nephti's pant. "Go to my office, Sahni, and wait for me. Sit on the couch, lay on it if you feel bad."

Sahnassa was going to argue, but the stern look coming from her employer forbade that possibility. Sitting in the cool of Van's office, she realized that she actually did feel kind of icky, but just a little. She heard Van's voice coming back up the hall, Tresk obviously in tow.

"Honestly, it's a cooker in there, Tresk! Nose into it yourself!" Van demanded.

"Oh mange, Van! It has to be the boards we laid up there for storage last evening. One of them must have crushed the air line."

"Meaning we have to pull up the floor we just laid so neatly, right?"

"Yeah, kind of. Maybe we can keep the damage to only a few boards, but ... I don't have spare air line. We'll have to buy some."

"How much?" Van asked, coming into her office. "You feeling okay?" Sahnassa's nod didn't convince the mixed blood, and Vanarra went to her little cooler and pulled out a bottle of water. "Drink this, slowly, until it's all gone, kit. No arguments! You're still panting a little."

Sahnassa shyly took the bottle and didn't look Tresk in the eye, his gaze at her amused. "Sounds like we almost had a case of roast Nephti."

"Roast *servers*, too!" Van shot back. "I'm not happy about this, either of you. Kit, I can't believe you didn't notice the heat! Tresk is right; that place was turning into an oven. What were you doing?"

"I've been trying to get Saiphar's artwork to line up on the site perfectly, and ... I've been having some difficulty. I don't want there to be any gaps at all, and ... I'm struggling a ... bit."

"Well, you're done in there for the rest of the sol, that's for sure," Van asserted in an irrefutable tone of voice. "I also want to ask you another question. What would have happened if those servers did overheat? Could we have lost all of the work you've done?"

"It would take a really, really bad overheat to do that," Sahnassa contested, "but ... it is a possibility. If someone hadn't been here to catch it, this ... this could have gone very bad. I was going to talk to you about the need to have off-site back-ups, but ... that would require some additional hardware. I figured you wanted to see more results before I asked for more ... equipment."

"Is it going to cost me like ... double what I've already paid?" Van asked. "Oh, and keep drinking, kit. You're still panting a bit."

Sahnassa honestly thought she didn't feel that bad, but she still took another drink before answering. "About ... ten percent or so over five seasons, but it's a good solution at a stable data center. We'd need a special piece of hardware on our end and a few new programs."

"Well, I've invested enough in this site that I don't want what I've put in to get lost. Can you buy these things locally?"

"I can."

"Well, I would like you and Tresk to go on a shopping trip. Take Saiphar, too. Perhaps you and he can talk about the art problem as you go. Take the company delivery hover. Tresk, get us some air line and whatever else you think you need to solve this problem," Van stated and then sighed. "I'll get Raska, Sheffer, and Flint to start unloading what we put up there."

"I ... wasn't even aware you had added storage up there," Sahni stated.

"We did it in the evenings after you left so it wouldn't impact your work," Van explained. "You wouldn't have been able to concentrate with everyone banging over your head. In the end, it looks like we didn't quite meet the goal. We didn't have an evening event until tonight, and Sheffer just finished loading that one out to the dock. If you three can be back in two intervals, that will give us enough time to load up."

"I'm really grateful, Van, for the ... consideration. That was very kind."

"It ... was Saiphar's idea," Tresk stated, a little reluctantly. "He wanted to make sure we were being ... considerate."

"And it was practical advice, given several of our events have been in the middle of the sol as of late," Van added. "You feeling a little cooler now, kit?"

"I am. Thank you, Van, very much. I'm sorry I didn't recognize things were as far along as they were. It ... it must have happened slowly."

"It's okay, kit. I get really involved in my work sometimes," Van offered. "Sometimes, I suppose the building could be burning down around me, and I wouldn't know it. I'll talk to you when you get back, okay?"

"Alright. Thank you, Van."

Soon, the three were riding in the delivery hover with Tresk driving, Sahni beside him, and Saiphar in the back, having deferred to the Nephti. "How are you feeling, Sahni?" Saiphar asked.

"Not too bad. I really didn't get that overheated, truly."

"Sure you weren't just chatting to some hot, avowed Nephti cub? That would do it," Tresk piped in.

"No, I wish," she confessed. "Not a lot going on there for me right now."

"You certainly are worth someone's attention, Sahni. Don't worry. In time, someone is going to appreciate you."

"Thanks, Saiphar," she said, reaching back to him with her paw for a quick clasp. "That's very kind of you to say. I guess I'm just too busy right now. Most everyone I knew found someone in academy or, maybe, they're like my sister. If any male wants to hunt her, they're going to have to run to keep up with her career."

"What does she do?" the artist asked.

"Litigator, along with Dad. She's doing pretty well, I suppose. I haven't talked to her in ... well, nearly six seasons."

"Really?" Tresk asked, interested. "You family types get into squabbles, too?"

"Yeah, big ones. My parents and I aren't really talking right now, and ... I'd ask you to keep that to yourself, please."

"You told us easy enough," Tresk contested.

"We owe her that respect, Tresk," Saiphar admonished him. "After all, it's not like we'd like our pasts talked all around the office."

Tresk glanced back at Saiphar a little angrily before returning his eyes to the trail ahead. "You just like her; that's why you're being all respectful."

Sahni was a little annoyed at Tresk's attitude, and sensing Saiphar's embarrassment, she quipped back, "Oh, and you don't like me, Tresk? Not even a little?"

"Not like on the hunt, kit – I mean, come on, really."

"Not like that. Do you like me as a friend? Or is it not possible since I have an avowed name – does that alone put me off the list?" Sahnassa asked, pointedly.

"Well … no, it doesn't," Tresk grumbled back. "It's just damned annoying how you come into the office and all of a sudden, we're rearranging everything, tearing stuff down, even that second level storage we were building was to free up room down below so you can have an office."

"What? Really?" Sahnassa asked, surprised. "Why?"

"I think Van's getting a little annoyed by the door situation in the server room, with your chair always in the way. She's spending a lot of money on you, and she wants to be able to do to you what she does to all of us – barge in whenever she pleases and have her say," Tresk stated flatly.

"You should only be so upset, Tresk. It's only going to be for a little while, anyway. I'm contract help, and … I don't think Van's going to keep me around after my contract is up. Who knows, maybe it will become your office after I'm gone."

"The mange it will!" Tresk growled.

"You should know that Tresk has an unnatural aversion to offices," Saiphar noted, a little amused.

"I'm sorry, Tresk. I didn't mean anything by that. I just mean to say that I'm sorry for the trouble my presence is causing – it's nothing I'm asking for. I … just want to get my job done, that's all."

"Well, that, I suppose, I can appreciate," the Vulpi admitted. "And the fact that you're not staying is at least some comfort."

"Tresk, that's an awful thing to say!" Saiphar nearly growled at his fellow Vulpi, an uncharacteristic menace in his voice.

"Look, Saphy, I'm just being honest here. Having an avowed around permanently makes some of us nervous, like the families are going to start moving in and taking over."

"How would they do that?!" Sahni shot back. "Van owns the business. They have no rights here!"

"With you here, they might. They might come in and try to force Van to make certain *accommodations*, fix things up for you a certain way. If that works out, avowed with better public relations might dance in alongside you and elbow us dishonorable cast outs hard in the direction of the door. Who knows, in time, maybe Flint, maybe Van would be forced out – stuff like that's happened to other businesses of cast outs and Anati. Don't try to pretend it hasn't!"

"Tresk! You … insensitive … you heartless tail for brains!" Saiphar growled, the menace in his voice becoming more than a warning.

"No, no!" Sahni bade. "I'm actually grateful to him! For the first time I finally know what's being said about me! It's been whispered as I walk by ever since I came to Van's. I'd rather know than not."

"See!" Tresk shot back in Saiphar's direction.

"It was still a horrible thing to say," Saiphar contested. "It's shameful being around you, Tresk. Just … shameful."

"Now, stop, please!" Sahni begged when Tresk banged his paw hard against the center console and looked ready to pull off the trail and have at the Vulpi artist. "I needed to hear this, really, but Tresk, please – understand something else, and … this isn't going to sound very good either, but … at least it will be honest. You and the others have nothing to fear from me or my family, largely … because well, I wouldn't do anything to harm Van's business and, really, my family wouldn't care about it. They are a family full of litigators and archivists and corporate pack directors and vice presidents and all sorts of other high-level positions." Sahni hesitated as she looked both of them in the eye before completing sadly, "They wouldn't dirty their paws with a business like ours – I mean Van's."

"I think you said what you meant the first time," Saiphar observed. "Our families – the ones we were once members of – would have. The Vulpi houses believe that having a firm grip on the doers in society is the way to stability and prestige. After all, you can always let go a few executives, but the Vulpi doing the work has to be kept so long as the business is around. If some place like Van's gets successful, they'd start sniffing around for ways to work into it. I guess … I guess that's where the fear is coming from."

"Well that, and you smell funny," Tresk replied, smirking at her.

"I'm a Nephti. I suppose we all smell funny to you. Besides, I didn't know grease was a Vulpi scent!"

"Yeah, right!" Tresk chuckled back at the jab. "Or paint!"

"I do not smell like paint," Saiphar complained.

"Well, it … it is kind of the smell I associate with you," Sahnassa admitted, "even if it's not your scent. I … like that about you, though. It reminds me of all those wonderful things you create." Saiphar's blush furs rose, and unseen to Sahnassa, his tail did, too.

"Nothing is beautiful about turning a wrench, though?" Tresk asked, sounding just a little hurt.

"You've saved me from a few big mistakes, Tresk. Believe me, I'm grateful," Sahni offered.

"You know, you're not as bad as I thought you'd be," Tresk stated, almost indifferently.

"You are horrible," Saiphar complained, pointedly staring at his fellow Vulpi. "Life would be so much easier if you just kept your muzzle nailed shut."

"No, I'm glad to actually be talking to you both. It's kind of the first time we really have since I hired on. I … like both of you. I just wish we spent more time talking to one another. I kind of get the feeling that a lot is said about me that isn't necessarily shared *with* me."

Tresk sighed. "It's a fair point, I suppose. Well, here we are. Mind if we hold off the group therapy session until this shopping trip is over?"

"Works for me, Tresk. Thank you both, though. It means a lot that you're honest with me about how you feel."

"Well, mostly," Tresk replied, smirking back at Saiphar who gave him a warning expression.

A half interval later, Sahni was getting restless. "How long is this going to take? It's not a hard thing you're asking for is it?"

"They … seem pretty distracted," Tresk observed. "Normally, there's more than just the one clerk, and he doesn't have to keep running to the back." The trio had been waiting in a fairly long line at the airflow store which seemed unusually devoid of staff.

"I've seen more than just the one," Saiphar noted. "However, there's a fairly tight bunch of them just back there ... in one of the show rooms, I think."

"Probably a visiting dignitary or some such," Tresk joked.

"Looks like the group in the back is finally breaking up," Saiphar noted.

"Well, hopefully now we can get some help and get going," Sahni replied, a little impatiently as she turned back towards the desk. The sound of the approaching group of sales staff and their customers didn't interest Sahnassa as she glanced at the computer equipment the business was using, wondering if she might be able to talk them into upgrading – with her help.

"Uh, Sahni," Saiphar quietly said to her, trying to get her attention.

"Sahni? What's that, then? That wasn't the name you were born with," an adult female voice complained, a voice that Sahnassa instantly recognized. Turning around, she saw her mother – Archivist Holana de Orturu – leading the group which had now come to a stop behind her.

"Hello, Mother," she barely managed, immediately angry and embarrassed at the same time. Looking into her mother's cold expression, Sahnassa saw no love there – only bitterness and disappointment, and her own expression, in return, took on as unpleasant a scowl.

"So, you've completely abandoned the name you were born to?" Holana repeated her complaint.

"I am loyal to our family, or perhaps you haven't noticed," Sahnassa retorted. "My friends have given me that short name. I rather like it."

"Makes you sound like an Anati," her mother grumbled and scowled, looking away.

"Then that would be an honor, indeed, given some of the Anati I've met! *They've* been very good to me and to others!" Sahni stated, emphasizing that Holana had not been. "Not everyone is a slave to how their dame sees them!"

"Impudent child!" Holana replied, looking angrily at her daughter.

"No more a child! I'm an adult, now, Mother. Thankfully, I no longer need to claim the protections of *the Compact* as I once did!"

The stunned gasps from everyone around the two of them, with the exceptions of Tresk and Saiphar, were palpable.

"That … was low. Even for you," Holana replied angrily, her blush furs at full realizing everyone around them now understood her daughter was calling her abusive to her face.

"I learned from the best," Sahni replied, disappointment heavy in her voice. "You set the tone with your greeting, Mother – so rude and so condescending! What … what could you have expected from me after all this time – gratitude?! Honor?! I wish…" Sahni was so upset that she knew she was going to cry, but she managed, "I wish you had just loved me!" Sahnassa then broke away from the group and left the building.

Saiphar and Tresk looked back at Sahni's mother who was just standing, dumbfounded and embarrassed. With no one else to turn her anger on, Holana spat out, "So who are you two, then? Useless friends?"

"Not as useless as you might think," Tresk said in an obvious snub as he turned and followed Sahnassa's path out of the building.

"Well … I … never!" the angry Nephti growled defiantly.

Saiphar, his unrequited affection for Sahni driving him to do so, stepped right up to the humiliated and upset Nephti and stared her right in the eye, less than a full track between the end of their muzzles. "No, that's not true," he contested in a tone that was as sad as it was compassionate. "You did love her once. Who could have ever stopped you from caring for your very own child?" He held her gaze level until the dark blue eyes lost most of their fury, and a different kind of shame set in, and she looked away and backed up a step. Saiphar breathed out a long, disappointed sigh, and then he, too, turned and walked away.

At the door, he stopped and looked back at the group. Sahni's mother was staring at him, but instead of an angry stare, there was an expression of loss, and those around the Nephti had walked away, a clear sign of disapproval. He turned away and shook his head sadly as he left.

Outside, Saiphar found Tresk a few steps away from the door. "Where did she go?" he asked.

"No clue, but we still need our air line."

"We can go somewhere else, Tresk," the artist complained. "Where is Sahni? We need to find her and make sure she's alright.

We certainly can't leave her here! Look for her at the hover! I'll look around the building."

"Nothing but trouble, that one," Tresk grunted, but he did start walking towards the parked delivery hover. Saiphar walked around the side of the building, the side he thought she might have gone towards. Sure enough, he found her, leaning with her head against a tree, crying.

Quietly, he walked up. "That … was very unfortunate, Sahni. I'm … sorry that happened."

"She … she cared about her dame more than she did me," Sahnassa raggedly explained, turning to face him. "Let's just go, okay?"

"Alright then." At that moment, the Vulpi wanted to comfort the Nephti, but Tresk had pulled the hover over to the edge of the lot where they were and backed it in. Sahnassa immediately saw the wisdom in what he had done. She could leave and not be seen through the windows of the store. Walking rapidly, she led Saiphar to the rear doors, popped them open, and ducked inside – Saiphar following.

"Thanks, Tresk. That was kind of you."

"I've been there. We can go somewhere else for the air line," he said, looking back at them as he pulled away.

As the delivery hover left the lot, Holana walked alone to the front, half hoping to see her daughter there, standing outside. Looking around, she saw no one. The words of the Vulpi bored through her anger and struck her at her heart – a mother's heart, and then she, too, started to cry.

"You took a good long while for that errand!" Van complained as the trio exited the hover through the back doors at the loading dock.

"Sorry, Van. My fault. We … we had a problem."

"I'll hear about it in a moment," Van replied, but then leaned back into the warehouse. "Sheffer! Flint! Raska! We need to load up, right now!" Turning back to Sahnassa and Tresk, she asked, "Did we get what we needed?"

"We did," Tresk answered. "Although the techno-tail stuff took a little while."

"That's all that matters. Was anyone hurt or did anything get broken?" Van asked.

"No, we're … alright, in that respect," Sahni managed.

"Okay. Tresk, if I leave you and Shef here tonight, do you think you can fix the air line? We need to make sure that Sahni can be productive again as soon as possible."

"We can do it, Van. I have a fair idea where things are pinched. Even if we have to cut what we've got and re-route, I can probably do it."

"I'm still a paw short, though. Sahni, could you pitch in?"

"I would be happy to, since they'll be working for my benefit, here."

Van nodded, appreciatively. "What you're wearing will be fine; I'll just use you in the back during the event, okay?"

"Thank you, Van. I'll get the 'techno-tail' purchases loaded and put away."

"I'll get started on the work upstairs," Tresk stated. "Can you please send Sheffer up when he's done, Van?"

"I've got to go up front, but tell Flint, okay?" Van directed him and then left for the front of the building. When she arrived in her office, she received a surprise. "Saiphar? Everything okay?" He was sitting on her couch, staring straight ahead, appearing unsettled.

"I need a moment with you in private, Van, if you don't mind."

Vanarra closed the door behind her and went to her desk. "I only have a moment; we have to leave soon."

"I know, but … before Tresk said something, I wanted to tell you what happened. We were waiting at the airflow store, and it was taking a very long time to get help. We found out that was because Sahni's … mother was there. She was … surrounded by the sales staff and other very well dressed Nephti. It … was a difficult meeting."

"Difficult?" Van queried. "How so?"

"Her mother was quite rude to her and to us, and it's clear that they are estranged. The exchange was brief but … quite angry. Sahni got upset and left, walked out in tears. Tresk and I followed. Whatever is between her and her mother really made it difficult for Sahni to finish what had to be done, but she did."

"That's good, I suppose. Saiphar, forgive me, but … you look like you have something more on your mind than simply telling me why you three were running a little late," Van observed.

He looked up at Van, his eyes pleading. "I need ... I ask that ... you keep Sahni and me separated, as much as possible."

"I thought you liked working with her."

"I'm ... beginning to feel more than that, and ... I know what you said, but when I saw how hurt she was by what happened..." His voice trailed off, and he looked away.

"You wanted to be there for her," Van replied, leaning back in her chair and nodding. "Make her feel better."

"I wanted to hold her in my arms and comfort her, Van. A trick of timing was all that kept me from doing so. Please, I don't want it to be obvious, but ... if I'm going to stay, and she's going to – I need for you to keep us apart."

"Even with Tresk as a chaperone, huh?" Van asked, smiling a little. "She's really gotten under your fur. You know, Saiphar, you really give me cause to stop and think sometimes. You are a wonderful painter and ... a very artful soul. You can see things in completely different ways than I ever could. You've only known her a little while, and ... she's that special? You're falling that fast?"

"I know," he replied. "I'm not proud of it. Vulpi ... I guess, have those weaknesses."

"Is it what she's doing? Is she waving tail in front of you or something?"

"No," he sighed with regret. "She's just being who she is. That ... that is enough."

"I'm glad you told me, Saiphar. I would have put you two in the back tonight, but ... I'll mix things up. I'll put her in there with Raska. There's not a lot of love there, but they don't exactly have to work close together."

"I hate to abandon her like that, but..."

"But if you don't, I'm going to have other problems, won't I?"

"Yes," he admitted. "Probably."

"It was good for you to tell me, Saiphar. I'll let Flint know, too, quietly, so we don't make things harder for you."

"Thank you, Van. I appreciate the ... understanding," he said, standing and nodding to her.

"You're welcome. Now, go help them load, and I'll be there in a few ticks, okay?"

"Okay. Thank you, again." With that, he was gone.

The next morning, Van looked up as the Nephti knocked on her door. "Good morning, Sahni. I never told you last night, but you did a really good job. Come in, please."

"Thanks," the Nephti replied, smiling. "Do you know if the new air line is in?"

"Uh, no," Van replied, a little disgusted. "Have a look at Tresk's note."

Sahnassa read over it and winced. "Sheffer broke the new air line," Sahni read aloud.

"Uh huh, and I am not happy. He's idled you for another sol."

"I could get a little work done, in short spurts – keep the door open."

Van agreed and stood up. "Let's do one better. You and I are going to take that door off of its damned hinges and set it aside. Then, we're going to have a fan blowing cool air in there. Sound okay?"

"That should work very well, Van. I might be able to work in there all sol."

"Well, yes and no. I … I want to take you to lunch. I … might need your help with something, okay?"

"Sure," Sahnassa replied. "I'd be happy to help."

"Then let's start by getting you up and running again, kit," Van replied as she strode out the door, Sahnassa following close behind.

A few intervals later, near mid-sol, Van came by and banged on the side of the door frame. "You deaf yet, kit?!"

Sahnassa took out her earphones and replied, "Not … totally, but I am kind of getting a head-ache!"

"Well, shut down! You and I are going to lunch, and Sheffer, Tresk, and Flint are going to fix things before we get back. Okay?" Sahnassa nodded and started keying commands into the computer. "Can I turn the fan off?" Van shouted. Sahni looked up at her and nodded, and Vanarra quickly turned it off. "Whew! That's enough of that. Did it work? Were you actually able to get any work done?"

"Quite a bit. I have the artwork all lining up, and I think all of the pre-sales forms are done. I've started working on how that gets presented to you, and I actually have some questions."

"Good, we can talk on the way. All shut down?"

"Yes. That's the last one," Sahnassa acknowledged as she pressed a control on the power station. "I'm ready to go."

"Then let's go," Van offered.

A few passes later, the two were riding in Van's golden hover, Sahnassa grateful that her boss was taking it slow because of her mild headache. As they travelled, the talk mostly revolved around work, specifically how Van wanted the ordering system to function as Sahni took notes. As they arrived at De Kesto's, the mixed blood breathed a sigh of relief. Given the morning she'd had, Vanarra truly appreciated the ease with which she could talk to the Nephti, and how accommodating she was to what Van desired.

As they mounted the steps, Vanarra asked a question that had been bothering her the entire time they had been speaking. "Kit, are you sure you can get all of this done in the time that's left on your contract? I mean … that's a lot of work."

"Well, you're giving me a good place to work, and there are a few tools I can use to make it easier to do. I'm not trying to mislead you, Van, in any way."

Vanarra smiled, she hoped, convincingly. "It wasn't that, kit. I just don't know if what I'm asking for is … reasonable or not. It's kind of my first time ordering up a system … with a side of files," she joked.

"Your needs and requirements are exactly that, and they need to be heard and understood," Sahnassa replied seriously, but then smiled as she added, "and the side of files then becomes my problem. I want this to work for you and not half way, either."

"I appreciate that, kit, really," Van offered.

"Can I meet you back in a moment? I need a few ticks, okay?" Sahnassa asked, with a glance in the direction of the facilities.

"Sure, kit. No problem."

As Sahni walked away, the mixed blood tried again to sort her confused feelings about the Nephti while also trying to catch the eye of the hostess. Normally, Anati wouldn't have been very welcome at such a nice restaurant, but Vanarra was a known quantity – someone nice who had money and tipped very generously. Since those tips were shared with the hostess, the effort of catching the pretty Faelnar's eye wasn't that difficult.

Sitting at the table, Vanarra noted how relaxed she was – far different than just a few intervals earlier. With Sahnassa comparatively deafened by the roaring fan, two fairly serious conversations had taken place in Van's office. First, a fairly direct confrontation with Raska about the strange assortment of comments she gathered during the primal had resulted in a frustrating series of evasions. Raska admitted that she attracted the eye of a few of the well-to-do purebreds, just like Vanarra did, and she supposed that the comments were intended to help her with her employer. Likewise, the ones who were against her she had spotted as potential rivals for those males who seemed to fancy her, and Raska supposed that most, if not all, of the negative comments were borne of simple jealousy.

Van had been unwilling to accept that simplistic view, however. Raska was clearly waving her tail or doing something that attracted attention, and Vanarra Anasto made it very, very clear that she wasn't paying for Raska to advertise herself; she meant for Raska's work to reflect well upon the business, and whatever was happening had better find a way to stop – even if that meant she changed her dress and reduced the flirtatious manner she dealt with the male guests. Although Raska was clearly offended by the insinuations, she nonetheless agreed to comply with Vanarra's wishes.

Her conversation with Sheffer was not delightful in any respect, either. Sheffer had shown an unusual amount of carelessness about the work surrounding the server room, and Van suspected there was a reason for that. Only a little prodding got Sheffer talking about everything the Nephti was doing wrong and how she was ruining Van's business – taking money that could be better spent somewhere else and just burning it up for no good reason. In the end, Sheffer didn't realize he was slamming Vanarra's judgment, and that got him a chewing out that had him backed against the wall, literally, his job hanging by a few strands of fur. After that clawing, Flint had "suggested" that Van take Sahni and make themselves scarce for a few intervals while he dealt with both Raska and Sheffer in his own way.

The Nephti, without doubt, had pushed Vanarra out of her comfort zone more than a few times and had made her as irritated and angry as anyone else in the office, but when all was sifted, Sahnassa made her mistakes out of ignorance, not out of disrespect. Saiphar's almost desperate appreciation of her was another point to consider in her favor. Regardless of how attractive Raska might be, Saiphar had never taken an interest in her – on any level. Even Tresk seemed a little soft on the Nephti, although he still complained about her. Flint clearly respected Sahni, and that – more than anything – deserved Van's attention.

"Something wrong?" Sahnassa asked, concerned.

"Oh no, kit. I ... I was just thinking," Van admitted, realizing she had been caught. The Nephti had been sitting in her seat for a few ticks without Vanarra saying a word. "Flint said it's going to be really noisy as they fix the air line, so ... since you had a head-ache and all, he thought it would be better if we took most of what's left of the sol off. You're welcome to scoot away, if you wish, but ... I have an errand I need to run – something I've had my eyes on for awhile. I was wondering if I could get your help with it. Having a couple of additional paws wouldn't hurt."

"I would be happy to. I'm actually getting a lot of good information from you, and lots of ideas," Sahnassa replied. "If you don't mind me asking questions as we go, I could still make the time worth your while."

The Nephti's work ethic pleased her. "You do good work, Sahni, and I ... I want you to know that I thought you did a great job last night, also."

"I didn't do much, really," Sahnassa replied, shyly. "Just prepped what was going out."

"But it was all correct, and it looked right, and you didn't forget anything. It surprised me that ... you didn't make any mistakes, kit. It's not that you do all the time or anything, but Saiphar told me that you had a difficult time at the air flow store. He said you were really upset – pretty hurt, actually." Sahni's shoulders sagged, and her ears drooped as she looked away. "I have to admit that I underestimated you when we first met. I guess you're made of some pretty good stuff after all when you can pick yourself up from that or ... like what you saw at the orphanage and then not run away."

Sahnassa warmed at the compliment and looked back at her boss, smiling. "Thank you, Van. That's ... very kind of you to say. I *was* distracted. I was saying everything at those plates that I didn't say to my mother and regretting everything I did say, all the same."

"Not that I'm asking about your past, mind you, but ... is there anything I can do to help?"

"Change the mind of someone who thinks more of their dame than they think of their daughter? No, I ... I don't think there's anything to be done, but thanks." Sahnassa reached across the table with her paw in gratitude, but Van looked unsure. "I'm ... sorry. I forgot. The whole touching thing." Sahnassa pulled her paw back, embarrassed.

"I'm … not made that way, I guess, by default, but … I can try," Van replied with a sigh, putting her paw on the table and reaching towards Sahni.

"Are you sure?"

"Not really," Van admitted, but Sahni slowly reached up and clasped Van's paw. "It's not you, kit, well, maybe it is. Generally, this is something I kind of reserve for the males in my life as a prelude to more *interesting* things."

Sahni pulled her paw back so quick, her blush furs shot so high, and her eyes got so wide that Vanarra had to laugh, her own paws over her muzzle. "I wasn't suggesting that with you, kit!"

"I didn't mean it that way, I promise!" Sahnassa nearly blurted. "I … I only meant to show you that … well, that was a very nice thing you said about me, and … it was kind for you to want to help me! That's all! That's all, I promise!"

"It's okay; it's okay," Van replied, settling down a bit. "That's kind of what's new for me, kit. It was only my Mom and me, growing up, and she was the only one who … well, touched me … like that – hugged me, and so forth."

"So if someone like me wants to do that, it's like I'm intruding on that memory. Oh, I'm so sorry, Van! I didn't know."

"It's okay. It's a little curious to me, that's all."

"In my first four seasons of academy, I had a roommate who was almost like a sister, very much like, in fact. We were comfortable with each other, and … our friendship was close. Grasping paws like that was one of the ways we showed the other that we cared."

Van leaned back and looked at her, nodding. "I can understand then, a little, where you're coming from, kit. So, does that good friend of yours stay in touch?"

"No," Sahni replied, her ears sagging. "I guess it was only a close friendship while we were roommates. She's joined to someone she met in school and is living off continent – who knows where, actually. I don't ever hear from her."

"That's too bad, kit. I've got a few friends, Buck Harlock, for one – he's the one that's been checking out your work, by the way. He's been very complimentary."

"And all those children at the orphanage. What a treasure," Sahni replied. "They love you."

"And I love them," Van said wistfully, but then she looked down at the table, and her voice became sad. "I have also ... lost friends, very close friends, and my mother, but ... they didn't leave because they wanted to. Some ...bad things happened to them. I most certainly know what it feels like to lose someone. Maybe it's better – in a way – when those we cared about are lost through death. At least, then, we know they didn't choose to leave us. Seeing them die is ... horrible, but watching them walk away, I imagine, has to be tough."

"It is," Sahni replied softly, regret in her voice.

"Hopefully," Van offered, looking up. "There are better things ahead, for both of us." Just then, the waitress appeared, and the two put in their orders. When she was gone, Van asked, "So, about better things, do you have any idea what you'd like to be doing once your contract is over?"

Sahnassa sighed a bit and explained, "Well, if ... I guess ... maybe that when everything is ... set ... for you, then I would reach out to my matron and see if she had anything. She's looking around a little bit, now, but I wouldn't take anything before your business was taken care of."

"I thought you said that you and your family were a bit at odds – that no matron or dame would show up in my waiting room." It was said a little more forcefully than she meant to, but Van's concerns about the Nephti's loyalty were stirred.

"When I hired on with you, that was certainly true, and I don't think you have to worry – even now – about any of my family leadership showing up and bothering anyone. Remember how I told you I took the Compact, claimed its protections against my family?"

"Yes, I think so," Van recalled.

"Well, then I told you that I met with the matriarch when she was in battle dress, right?"

"I remember that, too," Van replied as the server placed the plates before them.

"When I went to the archive for you, I ran into my younger sister. It was the first time we'd talked in seasons. She said the new matron for our family had been asking about me, and she wanted to reach out to me. I communicated with her, and then, I agreed to renounce the protections of the Compact. Those protections – they were just hurting me now because I couldn't get any support from my family. Well, the matriarch was ... pretty happy about that and when I showed up to actually renounce the Compact – they kind of had a ceremony for me. Very nice, actually." Sahnassa looked back at Vanarra and found her boss was not much enthralled with the story, and in point of fact, looked a little annoyed. "Well, so, to answer your question – my family will help me now, when I ask. However, again, they should never bother you. Sorry."

"I don't know what you're apologizing for, kit," Van replied as she cut hard into her meal. "That's what purebred avowed truly want, isn't it? A family that will cover for you? Someone to pull your tail out of a pinch?"

Sahnassa groaned inwardly as she realized what she had done and then truly thought about what Van had said. Thinking back to all of her relationships, her connection to Merialla had been the closest, even between those of her sisters and parents. The odd Nephti she had helped transform into a new and vibrant presence meant more to her than almost anyone in her life. Without really meaning to say it aloud, she admitted, "I'd give it all up for just one good friend." Sahni looked up, and Van was staring at her. Nervous, the Nephti looked away and started cutting on her grazer strips.

Van just looked at her for a moment and then, sensing the Nephti's discomfiture at such an honest and direct admission, went back to her meal. "Van? Do … do you suppose that friends you make in one place can ever … stay your friend when you leave that place?"

"I … think that's a choice, kit," Vanarra replied softly. "I've made a lot of friends over the seasons. Some of them are clients; some of them aren't. I guess part of what keeps friends together is … that they still want to share with one another, care about what's going on, and would still be willing to help if help was needed – would offer it, even if not asked. A friend isn't a friend if they're not loyal."

"That's certainly true," Sahnassa agreed, sadly. The Nephti wouldn't look at Van, wouldn't meet her gaze, and poked numbly at the food on her plate.

Instantly, Vanarra wanted to ask about Sahni's past. She was curious to discover who had hurt her so badly that had caused such a question to be uttered by the Nephti, seemingly beyond her ability to withhold. She wondered at what kind of losses could have broken the Nephti's spirit, leaving her as fragile and vulnerable as she appeared in that moment. A part of her instantly understood Saiphar's compulsion to help, but then Vanarra leaned back. Raska's protestations of innocence appeared initially as genuine as Sahni's loneliness and uncertainty, but at some level, Vanarra knew Raska was lying. She asked herself the same question here, looking at the Nephti who managed to get a bite of food into her mouth. "Is it that she's just real good at acting all pitiful? Ashamed? Is this ... all an act?" Her gut instincts swore that it wasn't a performance – the Nephti in front of her was genuine, and her hurt was genuine, but Vanarra's experience demanded caution.

Still, Van was compelled to offer some small amount of solace to the Nephti. "It takes time, kit. Trust takes time and a lot of patience."

Sahnassa, for a few moments, didn't answer, and as Van watched, she could almost tell what was happening. Sahni was lost in her own memories, but not just reliving them – the Nephti was trying hard to analyze them. Her eyebrow fur was scrunched together, and she took another bite of her food, deliberately – as if the process of eating was immediately feeding the processes in her mind. It was after a few moments of this that Sahni's expression changed, and the hurt shown through again.

"Can I help, kit?" Van asked.

Without changing expression or looking at her, Sahni started talking. "In academy, when I first got there, my roommate was ... odd. She was a little detached from reality, but her intelligence was – and I suppose is – very high. She could say the most ... insulting and ugly things, but she didn't mean them that way. She was just ... honest – she didn't have the ability to put any kind of a pretense or glossy covering on it. What she said was raw, but I learned a lot about myself pretty quickly. We got close. We got very close, and she started to change."

"She got worse?" Van queried, surprised.

"No, that's just it. She got better. She learned how to not hurt someone's feelings and how to ... feel the pain someone else was feeling and their joy. Merialla turned into someone so ... connected to me that I felt I loved her more than my family. Then, she graduated, joined, and moved away. Our friendship just ... ended, and I don't know why. I don't know what I did. I guess ... I guess I wasn't good enough for her anymore."

"Did you become friends very quickly after you met?" Vanarra asked.

"Yeah, I ... guess so," Sahnassa stated, looking up at Van.

"Friendship that builds fast doesn't last. Friendship that builds slow has an endless glow – Rahnahi. Did your … Merialla have a lot of friends when you knew her at first?"

"No. I think I was the only friend she ever had."

"Perhaps she didn't know what being a friend meant, and … the fault is hers for not knowing that or realizing how it hurt you. Maybe she was afraid to … carry the burden friendship requires," Vanarra offered. "I made a good friend of a Nephti transport driver. I was … pretty low when she found me. Sorla was great, took me in, helped me find a job. I thought we were the best of friends. When her family called, she … just left. I had to find a new place to live and that was that. She doesn't call. She never comes to visit. She's a de Dothnar, and I haven't even gotten any autographed copies of Rahnahi's books, either," Vanarra added with a smirk. "I thought the reason was because I was an Anati, but … hearing you talk – I'm not sure. Maybe it was something else," Van mused, her eyes now losing focus. "I suppose we'll never know, either of us."

"Thank you," Sahnassa offered after a moment of silence. Vanarra looked back at her, and it appeared as if some of the burden had been removed from her soul.

"For what?"

"For telling me. You never ask about my past, and you … keep pretty quiet about your own. You actually shared yours, and … it helped me to hear it. I'm honored that you would."

"There's not much honor in an Anati caterer, kit," Van disagreed, shrugging off a compliment that she felt was largely undeserved. "I doubt there ever was."

"There is. I see it," Sahnassa replied quietly.

It was an odd feeling for Van to receive the praise of an avowed purebred where the subject of honor was concerned. Family honor was just one of those creations fabricated to make the "grand and noble houses" feel superior, better than everyone else who couldn't claim such a title. This strange little Nephti kit was now applying the accolade to her.

"How do you mean, kit? No house claims me. I'm not part of any grandness or majesty."

"Family honor … it's more for show or maybe teaching or inspiring," Sahni explained. "You are kind to those who are weak, protect them, and you care about those who need you. You just drop everything when the smallest little kit – who can do nothing to repay you – is hurt. You take pity on those … well, who you might not even want to, really. There's family honor, and then there's what I see you doing. Yes, Van. I see it in you."

"I'm just doing what I think is right, kit," Van explained, arguing against the Nephti's logic. "If everyone does what they think is right, can that be called honor?"

"Only if it shows that you're willing to put others first and care about what they care about. Then, that would be honor."

Vanarra shook her head. "First time I've heard it said about me. Well, if you would do me the 'honor' of flagging down our waitress, we can get the bill, and I can pay. I'll be back in a few moments, okay, kit?"

"Yes, Van."

Vanarra went to the facilities, leaving Sahnassa finishing up her meal. Looking in the mirror as she cleaned her paws, she asked herself, "Does this crazy Nephti kit actually think I have honor? Do … I have honor?"

Walking back towards the front of the restaurant, she found Sahni standing by the door. "Ready?"

"As soon as I pay the check, kit," Van replied, confused.

Sahni presented Vanarra with her bag and stated, "I paid. You paid last time."

"I'm the boss. I pay every time," Van contested, but took the bag. "Oh, alright then. Have it your way. Thank you, kit. Let's go." As Van headed out the door of the restaurant, she smiled a little to herself. "That was a nice surprise, actually," she thought.

Back in the hover, the two of them discussed more possible changes for the site, which allowed Van to guide Sahni into some areas of interest – VidStar recordings, event images, and how the site would be supported after Sahnassa's contract expired. Van noted the temperament of the Nephti changed whenever the end of her contract was discussed. She seemed a little saddened, and while the subject was discussed, doing so was clearly an effort for the winsome technologist. As Van half listened to the discussion of support manuals and training sessions, she thought to herself, "Well, no one wants to be out of a job, granted, but … it's something else. It … feels like something else, or am I just imagining?"

"Van?"

"Oh, I'm sorry. Wandered off there for a moment. What were you saying?"

"Did you want to have the training printed out or would you like it on-line?"

"Hmm … let me think that one over for a bit. Let me ask you, Sahni, if … if something happened, and we couldn't get the site back up, could we call you for help? You'd be paid for your work, of course."

"Certainly, Van, but I'll do whatever I can to keep the site from having any big problems like that. I would come in and help you, well – if I was still living in Shanandrae."

"You're thinking of moving away?" Vanarra asked.

"I'm not sure. I suppose if I get an offer from a pack in another city or off continent, I … I would probably not stay. I could still be available by LineCom or TransNet remote, I suppose. I'm … I'm not sure what my intervals of work would be in either case," Sahni admitted, but then added, "I would make every effort, Van, to get things going again quickly. I'm never going to forget the experience at the orphanage."

"Never forget it, but would you repeat it? It's not like that every sol," Van told her. "I kind of feel bad that your first visit was so … rough. Sometimes, I just go out back and play whisk with the kits and cubs. It's a lot of fun!"

"Sounds like it," Sahnassa smiled. "I would go again, sure. I am worried, though. I could see getting really attached to them, and … that would make leaving … hard, on me and maybe on them."

"I understand. I'm pretty attached to those kits and cubs, and … they are to me, honestly."

"Rashall, especially," Sahni teased, tentatively.

Vanarra laughed heartily. "Now, didn't I just look so keen?! Oh, I'll have to do that pose for my Perratti cub! I'm sure it'll get the hunt revved right up!"

Sahni's blush furs raised. "I … I suppose."

Van looked over at her, and realizing Sahni's embarrassment, asked, "Oh, come on, kit! Ever done a little hunting of your own?" She nearly retracted the question, realizing she'd just asked about the Nephti's past, but Sahnassa's answer was too quick.

"The one time I started to, it was kind of accidental, and … it didn't go well. I … couldn't get anyone's attention in academy – not for any amount of time, that is."

Van was a little stunned. "I'm … kind of surprised by this, Sahni. I guess I'm not any part Nephti, but by most measures, you're a very pretty kit."

"Up until the point they find out something about me, and … I guess I don't flirt very well. I've been told I do things that turn males away."

"Hmm … flirting lessons. I can do that!" Van chuckled. "Just watch me, if there's anyone in this little shop worth flirting at, that is. If it's all grandfas or kits, I'm not going to, okay?"

"Well, okay, I guess," Sahnassa replied, still unsure.

Vanarra landed her hover in front of the relatively nice consignment building. "First rule of flirting, if you've got a choice, make a nice entrance. We're parked in front of the window, so the shop owner can see my little golden kit landing all nice and proper." Vanarra then opened a few buttons on her blouse, exposing the top of her chest and the accompanying cleavage.

"What are you doing?" Sahni asked, curious.

"Well, someone once called these my attention getters, and … it's true. The point of flirting is to get someone's attention and give them a good reason to keep talking to you and looking at you. Now, second, the show is always on. So the moment you step out of this hover, you're either on the flirt or not. Come out looking all shy and unsure, you won't win. Come out looking all ticked off, and they'll think you're coming after them – upset. Now, make sure you keep your tail pretty high – not over your shoulder mind you, but … just a little higher than normal."

"Should I…" Sahni asked, pointing at her own blouse.

"Hmm… not this time. Just let me have a run at it. Watch me – don't crowd me, though. Go look around at other things, just keep checking back every now and again."

"Alright," Sahnassa agreed, her blush furs a little high.

Vanarra opened the door, and Sahni was amazed that her boss had completely transformed. As she stepped out of her hover, Van's movements were graceful, slinky even. "Come come, now kit," Van bade smoothly. Sahnassa got out of the hover and almost choked at seeing how high Van's tail was. Walking behind the mixed blood into the store was another experience, as well. Van's steps were as easy as they were precise, and the sway of her hips rocked into a gentle motion that echoed all the way up to the tip of her tail.

As they entered the store, Sahnassa could see that Van's antics were already attracting attention. A male Vulpi clerk at the central desk was just staring at her, his mouth slightly agape. "Hi, sweetie," Van nearly purred out as she approached.

"Uh, hi .. hi there. Can … can I help you?" he stuttered.

"Why yes, dear cub," Van replied as if he was granting her the most wonderful favor in all the world. "There's a little item I had put back special for me. I wonder if you could help me find it."

"Do … you have a claim number?" the Vulpi asked.

Sahnassa remembered Van's requirement for not being crowded, so she walked down another aisle of the store, full of the strangest collection of knickknacks, furniture, equipment, and clothing she'd ever seen. Glancing around, Sahni saw a few items she actually might be interested in, but Van's voice pulled her back to the "show."

Van was bending over, searching her bag for the number, but the Vulpi male was transfixed, his eyes peering down along Van's chest. "How can he even see down in there with her muzzle?" she wondered, and curious, Sahnassa stepped quickly down the aisle towards the back of the store and came up behind the Vulpi, trying to get a look at what he was seeing.

"Oh, now I get it," Sahnassa breathed. Van had perfected a stance and was holding it, presumably for her benefit, but the male had an easy view of her boss's "attention getters."

Finally "finding the claim ticket," she didn't just give it to the clerk, she presented it to him, taking just a little too much glee in his nervously offered thanks for her trouble. Sahni continued to move around the store, looking for another angle on the flirt in progress. The Vulpi male was now trying to make conversation, and Van seemed to find everything he was talking about absolutely fascinating. Reaching for a rack to lean on and adjusting her bag, Sahnassa kept her eyes fixed on the Vulpi's tail, and it was rising higher and higher.

"Don't think I don't know what you two are doing," a rough female voice said quietly from beside her. Startled, Sahni turned around and was face to face with a very unhappy female Pantera. This one was a little shorter than normal, but she was still more muscular than the Nephti. "I suggest you leave before I call enforcement."

"Why?" Sahni asked, confused. "What ... what was I doing wrong?"

"Your friend is a first class distraction, I'll admit, and she covers you very nicely."

"Covers me? I'm ... sorry, I ... still don't get it," Sahnassa confessed, taking a step back.

"We've had things stolen here time and again, although this is the first time I've ever seen an Anati and a Nephti working together."

Sahnassa was simply aghast. "What?! No! I'm not ... we're not!"

"You've been watching Fushtal the entire time, making sure your friend had him good and distracted, and look where your paw was." The Pantera pointed at several clumps of equipment and old used PawLinks that were arrayed on a shelf. "Unless you can find me a better explanation of what you were doing, I think you were getting ready to shove that stuff into your bag."

"I was not!" Sahni demanded. "Look!" She opened her bag and offered it to the Pantera who took it, albeit warily.

"Nothing here, yet. So, what other cause would you have to act like you were?"

Sahnassa was then humiliated, realizing what she'd have to confess to. "I ... I was watching ... her flirt with him."

"I gathered that much."

"No, you don't understand," Sahni sighed. "I ... I am trying to learn how."

"To rip off a business?"

"No!" Sahnassa whispered harshly. "To flirt!"

"What do you mean learn how to flirt? You don't know how to flirt?" the Pantera asked, amused and surprised.

"Look, I ... I just was never – I never did. I'm ... a technologist. We don't get out much, really."

"Well, your friend is pretty good. She's about got his tail tickling over his ear, and that's saying something for a Vulpi."

Looking over, they saw that the clerk was still chatting very pleasantly with Vanarra, and she was leaning on her paws giving him exactly the view he wanted. "I'm not saying I don't believe you, but I would feel a lot better if you would return to the desk, and you and your friend had what you came for and went on your way, okay?"

"Okay. I think I've seen enough."

"Enough so that you could do that?"

"No," Sahni said quietly. "Enough to know that I couldn't."

"Who knows? You might in time. Come on, now."

As they walked up, they heard the discussion. "And I think it's the eyes that are the most attractive, and you have very nice ones, I must say. Oh, hello, Sahni. Everything okay?"

"Did you find what you were looking for?" Sahnassa asked, cutting her eyes to the side, indicating the Pantera walking next to her.

"We got a bit ... distracted," the Vulpi attendant replied, his tail dropping quickly upon the reappearance of his fellow employee. "I'll just go get it," the Vulpi replied and then was away.

The Pantera peeled off to walk around the counter, and Van asked quickly, "Well, did you learn anything?"

"Yes, I learned that she thought you and I were trying to steal from her – you chatting up the only employee in sight while I walk around and look for stuff to shove in my bag," Sahnassa complained quietly.

"Oh," Van replied. "Well, I suppose that is done sometimes."

"So," the Pantera replied. "What exactly was she doing, watching you?"

"The kit ... was trying to learn, well, how ... how to talk to a male, actually," Vanarra replied. "I offered to show her. He certainly didn't seem to mind," Van commented with a smirk.

"Well, no. He wouldn't," the Pantera chuckled. "What are you here for?"

"A dressing mannequin of a female Faelnar. One I've had them looking for."

The Pantera's features changed to shocked recognition. "Oh! Are you Vanarra Anasto?"

"That's right," Van returned pleasantly.

"It's ... that's a really expensive piece! Are you paying for it in full, now?"

"Once I see it," Van warned. Sahnassa heard the hum of a hover-pad and looked over to see a beautiful Faelnar shape covered in white fabric being pushed in by the Vulpi. "Let's have a look. Well, that is nice."

Vanarra spent several passes fully inspecting her new purchase before finally confessing, "It's exactly what I was hoping for. Here, let me write you a draft."

In a few passes, the mannequin was disassembled and placed in the rear storage of Van's hover. Once back in the privacy of that conveyance, Sahnassa finally relaxed. "I … can't believe she accused me of stealing!"

"It happens, and I have to admit I probably should have given that a little more thought," Van confessed. "Sorry about that. Next time I give you flirt lessons, you'll have to make sure you're not standing by any expensive merchandise, okay?"

"I … I don't think I could do what you did, Van. That was quite an act!"

"It's giving them what they want – making them feel attractive and appreciated. It's not all that hard."

Sahnassa sat quietly and tried to think about why she was finding it so difficult to consider following Van's example. Vanarra obviously had enormous reserves of confidence and technique when it came to the skill of appearing seductive, and her innate attributes – her "attention getters" – certainly didn't hurt, either. Part of it, she realized, was that the flirt was a lie. Van had no real intention of pairing up with that Vulpi, at least as far as she knew, and Vanarra had used him – just to teach Sahni a lesson. That, she decided, was what made flirting for the sake of it something she had a hard time justifying. "Still," she thought, "if I did find someone I liked, maybe those things would work."

"I'll have to think about it, maybe … practice in front of a mirror or something," Sahni finally replied.

"Eyes, chest, tail, and hind-side all visible if you can manage it – everything you've got in the game, telling the male you're looking at that he's your world, and you just adore him. Works more times than it doesn't, that's for sure."

"So where are we going now?" Sahni asked, wanting to change the subject.

"My place, if you don't mind. I want to get this dropped off so I can set it up tonight."

"I didn't know you designed clothes, too," Sahni commented.

"I … don't, actually," Van confessed.

"I don't understand.   Then what do you need a dressing mannequin for?"

The real reason for Van's purchase was far too sensitive and painful for Vanarra to confess. Ever since she had lost her mother, she wanted to have something to remember her by. With the loss of her home in the archive, there was nothing left to her until she had spotted a very specific dress in a different consignment store two moons ago. She was nearly trembling as she purchased it, and taking it home, it exceeded every hope she could have had. It was the dress her mother had worn on the sol they went to the de Gonari estate – at least the same design. Having it in a closet, though, wouldn't do. She wanted that dress on display near where she slept – giving a tangible physicality to a presence that only lingered in her memory.

"It's just … like, boutique art – a … conversation piece. Fits in with my décor," Van explained. "That's all."

Sahnassa could sense Van's tension about the question, and decided it was best to drop the subject. "Okay. It's … I'm sure it will look nice."

"I think so, too," Van replied. "Thanks for giving me a paw with it, kit. You're being very good about this. Sorry for the confusion in the shop."

"It's alright," Sahni offered. "And … you're welcome. I'm enjoying this, actually."

Van cut her eyes at the Nephti and smiled. "You know, I am, too, kit. I am, too."

Chapter 19: Singularity

It had been nearly a moon since Sahnassa had gotten her own office, and her run-in with her mother just prior to that event had receded into another regret, dangling at the edge of her memory. She had been too busy to dwell on that for any length of time, for the tasks she had set herself, based on the general direction of her boss, were indeed nearly too ambitious for her to accomplish. She felt desperately pressed to pursue them for as many intervals as required for two simple reasons.

First, she did not want to disappoint Vanarra. Every sol brought new revelations from the mixed blood and how she thought, what she believed, and every so often, Van would confess something – a little history, a mistake she had made, or something she cherished. However, the second reason was a date that was starting to approach far faster than she would have preferred – the end of her contract. While Van had generally been kind and done a reasonable job ensuring that those in the office didn't treat her as less than an equal, her employer had never once brought up extending Sahnassa's stay. "It'll be a great place to work and a great boss to work for, until it's not," she sighed to herself, resigned.

Seeing the end coming in less than fifteen sols, however, Sahni had finally reached out to Astalla, her matron, for help. When the subject of providing a list of her recent accomplishments came up, Sahnassa was finally forced to confess where she was contracting. That engendered a very interesting conversation where Sahni described a few of the details of how she was hired, and the time and other circumstances under which it had occurred.   Sahnassa was grateful, however, that Matron Astalla chose to put the best possible spin on it. "You have endured so much, dear kit, so many humiliations because of what's happened.   We will certainly work to find you a much better contract, in a far more honorable setting – one that will give you the rewards you deserve for such grace and persistence."

She was reading that phrase in her TransNet mail when Vanarra knocked on the door frame. "Is it ready, kit?" Van asked, her face a barely managed mask of excitement.

Sahnassa quickly closed her mail and replied, "Yes, nearly there. Just a pass or two. I want to make sure my tests pan out, and the load test is still finishing up."

"Load test?" Van asked, curious.

"To make sure the site can manage if the demand is high. It's all well and good having a pretty TransNet site, but if it falls over and puts its paws in the air if you're have a really busy sol, then it's not worth much."

Vanarra stepped in and looked over the Nephti's shoulder. The screen was covered with moving lines and graphs, showing test after test running and completing successfully.   "So, can our little pet prowler run?"

"He's running very nicely, actually. Everything's pretty well tuned, and I just finished making my last tweak. When this ends, it would be a good time to do a test. Do you have anyone in mind who might help?"

"Buck told me he'd be willing to order a few pictures and set up a request for a new event. All we have to do is call."

"Very good.   Oh look, all done!   Everything ... yes ... everything looks ... good!"

"Alright! Hooray, Sahni!" Van cheered.

"Did I hear 'Hooray, Sahni'?" Flint asked.

"I ... well, the load test is done. It's ready for you and a few ... pilot customers to try it," Sahnassa explained, a little shyly.

"Okay. Flint, order some pictures. I'll go book a few events based on paperwork I've already got, and I'll call Buck so he can do his worst – sound like a plan?" Van excitedly asked.

"Sounds good. Please, just let me know if you see anything you don't like," Sahnassa offered.

"Since when has she been shy?" Flint asked, looking down at Van and smirking.

"Ha, ha, Muscles. Ha, ha," Van returned, dryly. "I'll be testing in my office if you need me."

"Good job, Sahni," Flint said kindly, patting her on the shoulder. "You really did a very good job."

"I hope so." Flint nodded and walked out. Taking a deep breath, Sahnassa tried to relax. She knew if they found anything, Vanarra especially, it would be a long sol, fixing what was wrong until it was right. Just then, a couple of soft pings announced the arrival of a new piece of TransNet mail. "What's this?" she asked. Opening the program, she looked, and there, on her viewer was a letter from her mother:

To Sahnassa, my daughter,

You can't imagine how you've hurt me by what you've done and said. I have never been more humiliated or ashamed as I was when you took the Compact or when you recently rubbed my muzzle in it. I have also come to realize – by way of our matron – that we, your father and I, have also been at fault. I know this, Sahnassa, I do. I have been thinking about what your Vulpi friend said to me. You may not even know he did this, but he asked me why I would have stopped loving you. That question has clawed at me over and over again since he asked it. My reasons, as I catalogue them, are admittedly lacking. You have been such a failure in my eyes for so long that I refused to see my own shortcomings.

I don't know what future we can have with one another; the hurt between us is so very deep. By taking the Compact, you shunned and dishonored me as your mother, but I have come to realize, that by taking the Compact, you walked a path that was difficult, but you have ended your journey honorably in the eyes of our matriarch. I don't know if we will ever fully reconcile with you, but you should know that we at least recognize that much.

Hoping for better things, Holana de Orturu

Instantly, Sahnassa was starting to cry and felt sick to her stomach. She quickly dismissed the message from her viewer and walked out of her office towards the back dock. Shoving the door open, she walked past Saiphar and headed towards the small table under a tree where Vanarra sometimes conducted outside meetings. Sitting down, she put her head in her paws and cried, facing away from the building. A slight breeze blew across her, relieving the nausea and cooling her fur where the tears fell. "It's all about *her* hurt, how she's suffered!" she screamed in her mind. The few faint references to Sahni's "difficult journey" and her mother's mistakes were outweighed by words the burned in her mind – "You have been a failure in my eyes for so long."

"Sahni?" a nervous voice asked quietly from behind her. "What's wrong?"

Turning around, she saw Saiphar. She was a little surprised as it seemed he had been somewhat distant since his artistic contributions to the TransNet site were complete. "I'm … I'm sorry. A … note from my mother," she explained, shrugging.

He nodded and looked away. "I'm sorry. I guess it was … difficult, as before."

"Yes. She … she said one of you asked her why she doesn't love me anymore. Was that you?"

Saiphar's blush furs were in full evidence as he confessed. "Yes. Tresk walked away, and … I'm sorry. I couldn't help myself. She treated you … disgracefully."

"You … were … very kind … to say anything. Thank you."

Unsure, he stepped closer to her but then stopped. "You are welcome. Is … is there anything I can get you?"

Sahnassa would have happily accepted his shoulder to cry on, but as it appeared he was purposefully keeping his distance from her, she responded, "I just need a moment. Thank you, Saiphar."

"Okay," he replied, and then quickly, he turned and walked away, leaving her to grieve and try to pull herself together, alone.

Inside, Vanarra strode back to Sahni's office, a large smile on her muzzle. "Hey, kit! It looks just … fabulous –" She stopped when she realized the chair was vacant. "Wonder where she—" Her eyes fixed on a message that was on the screen, sent to Sahnassa de Orturu from a Matron Astalla de Orturu. Without truly meaning to, she started reading.

To Sahnassa de Orturu,
Kept by and Keeper of Her House,

Greetings and good chance to you. With the approaching end of your contract, I have been investigating possible opportunities as you requested. You have endured so much, dear kit, so many humiliations because of what's happened. We will certainly work to find you a much better contract, in a far more honorable setting – one that will give you the rewards you deserve for such grace and persistence.

I am pleased to say that several interested parties have expressed appreciation for your work they now see on TransNet. Your expertise and talents appear to have taken a spoiled rulla egg and turned it into the finest gourmet delicacy, as regards your current contract. One of the other catering concerns, aligned to our house and far more worthy of your efforts, has a very active interest in acquiring the very same type of TransNet presence that you are currently working on. Furthermore, they have a desire to retain your services on an on-going basis, offering a support contract and office space that would allow you to continue accumulating experience and truly establish your career.

As you consider these new opportunities and follow the trail to a brighter future, remember the disgraces and pains of the present sol will fade in time, and it is my hope that in a few seasons, those who stood against you will finally be behind you. We are all members of our house and from such we derive our honor. We are not cast out or adrift; we can be of one heart if we choose to.

My respects and good wishes,
Matron Astalla de Orturu

Vanarra was unable to keep her teeth from baring or her claws from expressing as she read. "Why that ... little two tailed ... avowed

… *purebred*…" Without her being able to fully control it, she pulled her paw back and prepared to claw right through the viewer itself.

"Van?" Saiphar asked. "You … okay?"

The soft-spoken question from the artist distracted her long enough for Van to regain some semblance of emotional control – stuff down the fire that had been about to consume her. "Yes. Just a little … ticked off, Saiphar. Excuse me," she growled, turning on him as he stood in the doorway. Instantly taking the hint, he quickly backed out as his tail-lashing boss exited and went into her own office, slamming the door.

"Horrible," Sahnassa said to herself as she finally got up and walked back towards the building. "She's … just being horrible about this – write your own daughter off as disavowed, ignore her for seasons, and then act all hurt when everything starts going good for me." Walking up the steps, she felt angry at her mother claiming to be the injured party. "Oh, I wish you knew what you made me feel like. I … I deserve better than that."

Walking up the hallway, she saw Flint heading the other way. "Sahni, the TransNet site looks wonderful! It's an excellent job all around."

Sahnassa sighed and smiled, "Really? I'm so glad you like it. It's nice to hear."

"Well, you put a lot of work into it. You deserve to hear that."

"I hope Van likes it, too," Sahni replied.

"I'm sure she will. I think she's in her office if you want to go ask."

"Okay. I will. Thanks, Flint."

Sahni breathed a sigh of relief. During many of the reviews, Flint had been doing most of the critiquing, and if he liked it, she truly hoped Van would. Passing by her own office without stopping, she walked to Van's and knocked on the door. "Come in!" Van shouted. When Sahnassa opened the door, she could feel the icy stare of her boss boring through her. "What do you want?"

The question, given at a full growl, took the Nephti by surprise. "Uh … just wanted to know if you liked the TransNet site, that's all."

"I suppose it will do. I suppose it's what I paid for," Vanarra replied, coolly. The golden eyes of the mixed blood held her in complete contempt. "And I suppose what I paid for will end up as someone else's possession in, oh, how long? A moon? Maybe two, tops?"

"I ... I don't know what you're talking about. The site is just for you, for your business, Van," the Nephti offered, uncertain of what was going on.

"Not if you and your matron have your way. I saw the note from her on your TransNet mail! Dammit! Rapemate the stupid Anati bitch – is that the game that all the avowed little purebreds like to play?!" Van's growls had turned to shouts.

"What?! You ... you read my TransNet mail?!" Sahni replied, stunned.

"I'll read whatever I want to – it's my business and my equipment! I paid for every damn bit of it!" Van shot back, coming to her hind paws and leaning over the desk. "Mange, and to think I trusted you! I should have never done that! Only Anati or cast outs are worth being trusted because they answer only to themselves – not some back-clawing, thieving house that claims honor on the one paw while rape-mating everyone else with the other!"

"I ... I don't even know what you're talking about, Van! I didn't read any message from my matron that said anything like that!" Sahni was starting to feel afraid of her boss; she could see the mixed-blood's claw tips expressing into the desk.

"Oh, please, please, don't take me for a fool!" Van growled. "That's the last thing you ever want to do! Her message said you asked about finding places where you could take what I've *paid* for and just drop it into someone else's lap!"

Sahnassa was backing towards the door, afraid that if she didn't leave, something bad was going to happen. Still, already angry and hurt from her mother's note, the Nephti's ability to hold back was quickly disappearing. "I did not!" she protested, putting her paw on the door frame. "I only asked her to find something for me because you don't want to keep me!"

"You're right about that, sweetie kit! What kind of damned idiot I was to let one of the avowed ever step their paws into this place!? You and your kind have taken away everything good I've ever had! You always have! I will not let you steal anything from me ever again!"

"I am not a thief!" Sahnassa had stepped forward, her fragile honor under assault. "I ... I have dealt with you honestly, and I've ... I've done everything I can – everything you asked me to! Everything!

Why … why wasn't that good enough?! You … you're a hypocrite, Vanarra! You want to be treated like an equal, but you've treated me like garbage! I wouldn't stay now if you wanted me to, and you know what the crazy thing is? I'm still not going to steal from you! Call me stupid, but I'll finish what I promised to do, document everything so then you can run it and do whatever you like! I don't care if you even pay me! I'm going to be true to my word, even if you won't be true to yours!"

"I'll keep up my end, thank you very much!" Vanarra replied, disgusted. "Anati have honor, even when the avowed don't. We are loyal, even when you refuse to be."

Sahnassa just shook her head, too appalled in that moment to even cry. "I'm sorry that you can't see past my family status or my parentage to know how truly loyal I would have been to you." With that, the Nephti turned and left, running towards the front of the building.

"Sahni?" Flint asked coming back inside through the front door with Tresk. "What's wrong?"

"I … I can't stay, Flint! She's … she's … just awful! I'm sorry!"

She pushed past him and ran for her hover, and something about how she was moving told Flint he shouldn't follow. Instead, he told Tresk, "I … I gotta go see what just happened."

"Better you than me," Tresk replied, turning back to walk around the building.

"What did you hear?" he asked Mauft as he entered.

"It's not good. Van went boom on the Nephti," the gray one replied.

"What the mange?" he asked aloud and then strode to Van's office. Walking in, he saw Vanarra standing, her claws dug into the desk and her head down. Closing the door, he asked, "What the mange just happened, Van? What … what did she do?"

"Betrayed us, sold us out!" Van answered as she tugged on her claws, trying to get them out of the desk.

"What?! What are you talking about?"

"Go look at her viewer, Flint, and then you tell me!" Van demanded. Flint took a step forward, which had Van glowering at him, adding, "And no, I don't need help getting my claws out!" Flint left, and was gone for almost a full pass before returning. By then, Vanarra had finally worked her claws free. "Well?"

"I don't see what you're talking about," he replied, flatly, if not a little angrily.

"The note from her matron?!" Van asked, dumbfounded that he didn't get it.

"I read the note from her matron, but given the kit has been offered zero when it comes to a livelihood after her contract, I can't blame her for trying to find something. She's got to eat, Van."

"Oh, she'll eat well enough! Taking what we've paid for and just giving it to our competition! We pay all the costs, and pretty little Sahni just flits out of here and passes it off to her avowed little buddies!"

"I don't think she'd do that, Van. She's an honest kit! She's been that the whole time we've known her!"

"Please, Flint, don't tell me she's got you fooled!" Van shot back, exasperated. "Come on! I thought you had some brains in there along with that muscle!"

She was stalking closer to him, and he pulled himself up to his full height, his paws on his hips. "That's enough, Van! You're not treating her fairly."

"What the mange! Do you honestly think I should feel obligated to treat an avowed, purebred ... fairly!? They've never been fair to us, Flint! Never!"

"She was! Van, how in the mange can we ever expect anyone to treat us fairly if we won't treat them the same way! You're spitting on everything you claim to hold dear, and Rahnahi de Dothnar would find you as disgusting as those who discriminate against our kind!"

"How dare you say that to me?!" Van shouted angrily, looking for all the world like she was about to pounce. For the first time since she had known him, Flint's claws expressed, and he snarled at her in warning.

"You don't want to go there," he warned, grimly. "I've only fought once, and they wiped the guy of the floor with a rag. Dammit, Van, I thought I was working for someone who had a chance of being better than everyone else I'd ever met, and damn if you're not proving me wrong! You asked her to come here! You've treated her like crap, and she's still done right by you! She's given you the very best she can, and you look at her private mail and make all these damned jumps about what she will or won't do? You haven't given her any reason to believe you cared! If you treated me that way, Van, I wouldn't stay either!"

That thought, along with Flint's impressive stature, created a shadow of doubt in Van's fury. "You can't honestly believe she would stay."

"Before? Yeah. Now? Mange, no! Would you? If your boss treated you the way you just treated her, would you stay if you had any possibility of finding work elsewhere? She's … she's the best thing to happen to this place in a long, long time, and it's a damned shame that you can't see that! What she's made for us is going to … double or triple our business, but if someone isn't around to take care of it, it'll become a pathetic joke and make your company look like a failure." As Vanarra backed away, Flint settled himself and retracted his claws. "I … I can't believe you did this, Van! What did you say to her? Did you say all that stuff you just said to me?"

Van wouldn't answer him. "You did, dammit, didn't you? You … crap, Van, by the time this is over, every bit you spent on her and her salary will have gone to waste just so you could rake her gut with your claws. We'll lose ground to our competitors who will hire her, and all because stupid us didn't keep her on contract here so she doesn't get picked up by them! What … what were you thinking, Van?"

"They've always made my life hard. I've never been able to trust them."

"All of our lives have been hard, Van, really! You … you just made them harder! Sahni … she didn't do anything wrong. I'm … I'm really disappointed in you, Van. I just don't know what we're supposed to do now." With that, he turned and left her office.

For almost a pass, Vanarra didn't know what to do or what to feel. It was like she was empty, all of the fire and anger running out of her leaving her with nothing. Slowly, she walked to Sahni's office and closed the door. Sitting down at the desk, she read the note over again. Much to her own disgrace, she realized the truth of what Flint had said. Worse, Sahni said she'd never seen the note. Flipping through the other TransNet mail, she found the reason why – the note from Sahnassa's mother. "Oh, crap," she said to herself with an exhale. Turning off the computer, she put her head in her paws.

"The kit got that kind of a claw to her heart and then … oh great, Van! Just great," she said to herself, trying to push off the feelings of guilt pressing in on her. "At least my mom loved me, looked out for me for as long as she could." Leaning back in the chair, she thought back to the moment before she had seen the note from the matron. "I was ... happy with what she did. I ... I was going to ask her ... about staying on, doing more, maybe. Maybe I would have. She's ... got every right to call me a hypocrite." She thought back to the archive and her time there. "At least if I went crazy there, no one ... got hurt. Oh, damn."

An interval later, Flint heard a soft tap on his door. "Come in," he said. Vanarra opened the door, walked in, and sat down, closing the door with an out-stretched paw. She looked at the ground, and her ears and tail were directed there, as well.

"One – I'm sorry, Flint," she said. "I deserve everything you said to me. Two – you're right. I wasn't fair to her."

"But why, Van?" he asked her. "You've got to figure that out. Why did you immediately assume she was going to hurt you? What are you afraid of?" When she didn't answer, he suggested, "She's ... she's a very likable kit, pretty special, actually."

Van leaned back and looked at him. "Maybe that's it. Maybe I'm afraid of liking her."

"Nope. I think you're afraid to trust her. You're afraid that if you commit yourself as a friend, she won't be loyal to you."

"She's had friends abandon her, she told me. I want to like her, but you're right. I'm afraid. She could cost me everything."

Flint shook his head. "That's not true! One little avowed Nephti isn't going to do us in. There have been Anati and cast-out alike that have screwed up and talked, done something that risked our reputation, but our clients always, always come back because they've learned to trust you. They know you'll do what's right. Can you be the only one? You trust me, right?"

"I do."

"What if I was only a Pantera or a Lupar, not a mix? What if I had a family but still treated you like I have every sol of the season? Couldn't you still trust me, Van, after all that time?"

"I ... I suppose I could," she offered, nodding. "I ... can't blindly trust, Flint."

"You aren't blind. Sahni's been in front of you for moons, stood by you, stood up for you. How much would she have had to do for you to trust her? How many more orphanages and kits would it have taken for you to realize that … she likes you, and I can tell you that it's broken her heart not to have you return that."

"What do I do, Flint? I've screwed up so badly there's no way out."

"There's no way out only if you won't try," he contested softly. "If she comes back, the first move is yours, and I hope you're a bigger Thurian then than you were this sol."

"I don't know. I'm going home, Flint. I … I need to think."

"Okay," he replied softly as she stood. "I'll close up."

"Thanks."

Sahnassa didn't go to her lair, at first. So upset she was shaking, she knew she had to go somewhere else. "Home," she breathed, raggedly. "I'm going home. I'm welcome there, now."

Turning her hover around, Sahnassa de Orturu headed towards a destination she hadn't visited in five seasons, her own home estate. It took her quite some time to reach it, as it was fairly far away from her lair and Van's office, but the drive allowed her to sort some things out. "I … I am not staying there. Not after that. I may be … willing to put up with a lot of things, but … not that." She had been called many things before, but being called a thief was more than she could tolerate. Sahnassa swore angrily, "Never that."

Reaching down, she turned on her music and played it as loud as she could stand, allowing it to drown out the turmoil inside of her.

Arriving at the gates of the estate, memories of distant and wonderful times came back to her. Presenting her credentials, she was easily let inside and drove towards the center of the estate slowly, just taking in the sights, the small changes and alterations that had been made in her absence. She had no illusions about returning to her parent's lair. After all, she clearly wasn't welcome there, but this place was hers, and those once familiar surroundings soothed her. She took her hover down the trails leading to her primary school, where she actually got out and watched the children playing in the athletic field. All around her, only Nephti met her eyes. They smiled and greeted her as they passed – a male or two actually bowing to her, making her blush furs rise.

Looking at the Nephti kits and cubs playing whisk on the field, a young couple sitting on a blanket under the trees, and another very keen looking male taking notice of her made Sahnassa shake her head at how strange and distorted her life had been, especially since she started working for the volatile Anati. "This ... this is where I belong," she said. "This is my home; this is my house."

The memory of Van's accusation came back to her. "What nerve, telling me I don't have honor, and she does?" Sahnassa growled. "I ... I have honor. I have this house's honor!" Instantly, she knew exactly where she wanted to go next.

Several passes later, she was driving into the visitors' section of the matriarch's keep and carefully landing her hover. She had been there so many times before – with her father and mother, on school trips, or as a part of visiting the matriarch, but now, she was of age and going there herself. Following the signs and checking in with the matron standing watch, Sahnassa soon entered the Legends Archive and the Halls of Honor – the historical repositories and museums that contained monument after monument, display after display detailing all of the times that de Orturu had accomplished noble and honorable feats. Walking through and reading the displays, smiling and nodding at the Nephti who, like her, seemed to be finding solace in the accomplishments of their family, gave her a sense of peace she realized had been lacking from her life for a very long time, long before she left her parents' lair.

"This ... this is who I am. I'll do what I said," she decided. "I'll fulfill my contract, but then I'm moving on, and I'm *never* looking back." Leaving the Halls of Honor, she felt absolutely certain of that and even through most of her drive off of the estate, but as she started to get back to the area surrounding her current life, regrets started assailing her. "Flint's been good to me. I'd hate to leave him with all that."

Walking up the steps to her small lair, she shook her head in frustration. "That's right! Even if I do like ... document everything, they ... they won't be able to take care of the site! They've got to know that – even Van has to know that! Why treat me like that?! Why shove me away?"

As she fixed herself a small dinner in her lair and watched VidStar, she tried to forget everything that had happened. Finally, she stifled a yawn and decided it was time for bed. Walking into her bedroom, she turned on the light, and there it was – the bed Vanarra had bought for her. All of those feelings of resolute strength and direction now faltered. "She ... she isn't ... bad – she's not ... evil. She just doesn't trust me." Sahnassa sat on a small chair facing the bed, one she used for getting dressed. Looking around the room, the possessions she had, as small and pathetic as they might be, were thanks, in large part, to Van having taken her onboard.

Leaning forward, she put her head in her paws, again at war with herself. She owed Van a debt of gratitude, so writing her off and walking away – heedless of the circumstances – just wasn't something she felt capable of doing. "But why? What did she see in that TransNet mail that blew her up so?"

Needing an answer to that question, Sahni got back up and turned on her portable computer. Searching, she found a wireless TransNet connection – a weak signal coming from a nearby business – and hopped onto it. Pulling back her mail, she scanned through it, surprised to re-read the note from her mother. "I'd nearly forgotten about it," she marveled. For a few moments, she just stared ahead, trying to determine which betrayal felt worse, her mother's or Van's. They both hurt, but Van's strikes on her were so unexpected, so harsh; her mother just didn't love her, simply put. "I thought Van, at least, liked me."

Flipping to the next message, she saw the note from Matron Astalla. Reading over it, initially, she saw nothing wrong with it – nothing that should have caused Vanarra to completely dismiss her as a worthwhile employee and someone she could trust. "It's all perfectly normal, Van!" she complained. Then, just as she was about to flip away, she glanced at a small portion of it.

"One of the other catering concerns, aligned to our house and far more worthy of your efforts, has a very active interest in acquiring the same type of TransNet presence you are currently working on," Astalla had said.

Sahnassa then tried an experiment. Trying to pretend she was Van, an Anati who had been orphaned, who had lived a life where – true or not – she thought she was betrayed by purebreds, she tried rereading the message. In growing understanding, as she read it – sentence by sentence, phrase by phrase – she started to slowly understand how Vanarra could have seen what was written there as yet another purebred avowed taking advantage of her. "She's never going to trust me. Not after this. Not after what I said, either."

As she stood and paced around her lair, her heart still aching inside of her as nearly every word of their argument played before her mind, leaving Van's employ started to seem less and less like something Sahni wanted to do to punish the mixed blood for treating her so poorly and more like a tragic inevitability. "If we could only trust one another. If I could find ... some way, but ... I don't see how," she breathed.

Catching herself yawning again, Sahnassa walked towards the bed. Looking at it, she didn't have the heart to lie upon it, regardless of how tired she was. The bed was a symbol, and she saw images of Vanarra in her mind – taking her in, apologizing, and trusting her with little bits of her past. Sitting in the chair once again, Sahni leaned against the wall, tired, her heart still in pain, but her body and spirit demanding relief and respite from the stresses of the sol. Resigned, she stood, pulled the covers and pillows off the bed, took them into her small den, and laid them out. Preparing for sleep, she left her bathroom and walked back into her den, sank to her knees, and then laid down upon her blankets on the floor. Part of her told her what she was doing was silly – that she should sleep in the bed. Still, she knew, at least tonight, she couldn't. Closing her eyes, she wondered, "Who could sleep in a bed given by a friend who won't trust you anymore?"

Vanarra had left work early, feeling numb and hopeless. She thought about going home, but she felt simply awful about how she had treated Sahni, and she knew she had to work some part of this through in her head. Without really realizing where she was driving, Vanarra made her way to the Pinnacle Center archive. Pulling her hover into a space along the trail leading up to it, she just sat and looked at it, the tall spire striking in its contrast against a dark and angry sky. Opening the doors, she stepped out and walked into the large grass field in front of it. With a storm rolling in, most if not all of the Thurians walking the grounds were retreating, leaving it deserted, leaving her alone.

Walking to the center of the field, she sat, placing her paws on her knees and for the first time in so many seasons, stared at the place which had once been her home. "I wish I'd never left," she thought. During that time of her life, things had been relatively simple. She had been lonely, until Ash came. "Oh, Ashalam, my love, my true, true lost love. I should have never let you take us away from here. We could have stayed together, loved one another, and ... it's all I would have ever needed." Pulling her knees up to her chest, she put her head upon them, hugging herself. "It's all I ever wanted, Ash, not all this."

Closing her eyes, she tried to imagine him beside her, sitting in the grass. "What about the others?" his voice seemed to ask her, and her mind turned to images of the orphans. The storm-rushed breeze blew around her, and small drops of rain started to light upon her fur.

"I know, but..." she tried to contest, but that line of thought was unassailable. The little faces who looked up to her, needed her, and loved her were too precious to wish away what Van could do for them.

"Taking care of others shows your worth," she remembered him reading, one of the sols where they had secreted books down into her lair. Instantly, Sahni's face appeared – not as it was now, but as she had appeared the moment Vanarra found her. The Nephti's heart was broken, and now, as heavier drops started to pelt against her, she realized the look Sahnassa had when she left this sol was the same as that time. Buck's words floated into her mind, words reminding her that even if a purebred was avowed, the honorable ones would rather give up their family name than betray a friend.

"She's been honorable," Van was forced to admit. "She's right – I've been the hypocrite."

The storm now drenching her to her skin, she stood and slowly made her way back to her vehicle – defeated and grieving.

Returning to her lair, she left the wing doors open in the garage so the seat and floorboards could dry. Soon, she was in her shower, letting the hot water penetrate her fur, chasing away the cold. "But what do I do now?" she asked herself. "I can't just keep perpetually apologizing; she wouldn't believe it if I did. I've ... I've done that too many times already. Maybe if I told her why I feel this way, why I'm always waiting for the avowed to come take what I have. Doesn't she know that already?"

In her mind, Ashalam's face again appeared in her thoughts. "You haven't told her about me," the thought came, not fully in his voice, but more as a mixture between herself and her former love.

"I haven't told very many at all about you. Sorla knew, but she's gone. Flint, I ... I don't remember if I have or haven't, honestly. What good would it do?" she asked aloud, softly.

"Don't I matter? Don't I explain one reason you hurt so?" the mingled voice came once again.

"You ... did, or you do, but ... I'll ... I'll fall apart in front of her. I can't get through that story without ... bawling like a..."

"Is Sahni worth it – a true friend for a little humiliation?" Van was unsure about this. So many times, she was looking down in respect, averting her eyes for the purebred avowed, making them feel like they were superior, regardless of how well or how poorly she thought of them. Seeing Sahnassa walk into the office still caused her to occasionally twinge, catch herself in the act of showing deference to an avowed.

"I've been humiliated all my life by her type," Van contested.

"Her type?" a distant voice asked quizzically in her head. "And here the Ugly Seed refuses to acknowledge the other flowers of the garden? Who's truly ugly, now?"

"Dammit!" she growled and switched off the water, infuriated. "I deserve to be respected, not to keep having to dip my muzzle and stoop over for every shiftless purebred who prances in front of me!" Muriella, the Faelnar who looked like her mother, came to mind.

"But she's not like that, is she?" Flint's voice seemed to ask.

"Shut up, Flint!" she demanded and stamped over to the fur dryer. Turning it on full, she let its roar deafen her mind to the contesting voices in her head.

She succeeded up until she started making herself tea, and a neglected thought seeped back into her mind. "I wish Sahni was here," she thought. Letting go of the cup and stirrer, she put her paws on the countertop and looked into her den. She could almost see the Nephti walking around, amazed by what she was seeing when the two of them had dropped the dressing mannequin off at her lair. Sahnassa had been genuinely interested in what Van had, admiring even. That gave Van a sense of pride and, at that moment, she felt some real affection for the little purebred. Now, that moment of closeness was a poignant opposite to the regret she was feeling now. "Why did I screw this up? Why couldn't I just have told her I saw the mail by accident, apologize, and ask what it meant? Why didn't I just … offer to renew her contract a moon ago so she wouldn't be in this fix? What's wrong with me?"

Like the striking of the first notes of music, those thoughts began a long and wandering symphony of soul-searching that would keep Vanarra awake throughout the night until morning.

"You're in early," Vanarra commented to Flint as she wandered into the office, feeling tired and depressed.

"I … thought it might be wise. The two of you usually get here first, and I thought it was a good idea for me to be … available."

"To pull us off of one another if it came to claw-strikes? It's not going to be like that, Flint. I don't want it to be like that. Mange, like she'll even show up! She'd be well within her rights to write us off, well, to write me off, that is," Van observed sadly as she walked into her office. "Do you think she'll show up?"

"I don't know, Van, honestly," he answered, "but if she does, then that should tell you something."

Van flounced into her chair and looked up at him, her features both tired and scowling. "*You've* been telling me things all night, thank you very much. I'd pay real money right now to get you out of my head."

Flint chuckled. It wasn't the first time he'd heard that comment. He and Van only fought occasionally, and very rarely was it as bad as it had been the previous sol. "I've … I've been going over what you said, too. I'm sorry."

"No, Flint, you're right, and I'm sorry – a sorry excuse for a boss, a sorry excuse for a Thurian," Van sighed, putting her head in her paws.

"Looks like you had a rough night." Van nodded. "Want to talk about it?"

Van, her head still in her paws, shook her head. "I'm done talking for awhile unless Sahni shows up. The voices in my skull have argued with me all night. You were just one of them."

"Come to any conclusions?" he asked carefully. "Any decisions?"

"It's all up to Sahni," Van sighed. "I … I can only talk to her, try to explain why I'm like I am."

"I'd sure like to sit in for that explanation," he grunted, but he walked towards the door.

"You and me both, Flint. You and me, both," she sighed as she sat up and started looking at her desk.

Sahnassa de Orturu looked at the entrance to Celebrations by Vanarra with an air of foreboding and skepticism. She wondered if this sol would be like all of the others when she came in, smarting from something horrible Van had done or said. Van would apologize and almost as quickly take offense, and everything that should get better, in the end, wouldn't. The slights from nearly everyone in the office would continue, the feeling of being less than everyone else. The upside down world that existed behind those doors scared her, now. She had seen how close Van had been to truly losing her temper; Sahnassa, too, had lost her emotional control, but then again, Sahni knew she wouldn't be a match for a trail-hardened Anati. "I'm tired of being the plaything of others," she thought to herself. "Vanarra is no different than Dame Rothnerra. Neither one of them trust or respect me."

Nevertheless, she still took slow steps towards the entrance. All through the night, the litigators in her mind had argued the case for and against, pro and con. Vanarra was someone who had a tough life, but Van made Sahni's life difficult, too. Vanarra was someone Sahni wished she could trust and even admire, but that trust and respect didn't flow the other direction. Vanarra was generous to her with pay and with gifts, but those gifts had a sure and certain end, an end the mixed blood didn't seem likely to want to extend. Round and round the arguments went, but the only thing truly keeping her hind paws moving towards the door was that she would need to have finished the project for Vanarra to claim it as an accomplishment. Once that task was done, Sahni knew she couldn't stay.

Walking quietly in, she felt an immense and oppressive silence. She had seen both Van's and Flint's hovers in the parking area, so both were present. Quietly, hoping not to disturb them, she made for her office.

"Sahni?" Flint called to her, softly, as she started to pass by. He motioned her in and indicated she should close the door. "Thank you for coming back this morning. Even showing up here ... it's an act of courage, and I respect that, after what happened last sol."

"Thank you, Flint. Of anyone here, you are the one I don't want to disappoint. You've ... been kind."

"Would you mind if I asked you what you were planning on doing?" he queried, gently.

"I will finish the site, and I will document it, and then ... my contract is over," she stated quietly, not looking at him.

"Thank you," he offered sincerely. "Well done. I ... I really expected for you to leave us this morning, if you came back at all. I couldn't blame you if you did."

She looked up at him and smiled, tentatively. "I've ... had to keep doing things that were unpleasant just to get by, before," she told him. "It's something I had to learn."

"It's something you and Vanarra share, but her hurt is deeper, and ... it's scarred her, Sahni. It's not made her evil or thoughtless or pitiless. It's ... it's made her afraid."

"I can see that," Sahnassa replied. "I don't know ... what to do about that, though. Everything that happened to her – I can't make that right. Her mother, the ... cruel things that happen to Anati, Flint, I never did those things, and I don't want them to happen – to her, to you, to anyone!"

"I know, and I trust you. For Van, it's harder. You know, she wants to speak with you this morning."

Sahnassa took a deep breath and let it out. "I guessed as much. Another ... apology."

"Maybe. Just try to hear what she's saying, but also try to hear what she's not saying, okay? There are places in your soul that are ten times more mature than hers will ever be. Give her open ears. That's all I ask."

Sahnassa stood and nodded. "I don't know that it can change anything, Flint, but ... okay." Turning towards the door, she stopped and looked back at him. "Flint, of everyone here, you've tried to make me feel as if I was an equal. Thank you for that. Why ... did you do it?"

"Because I never let myself forget what it feels like when someone doesn't treat you that way, and no one is going to take that away from me."

"Thank you for that," she offered and quietly left his office.

Vanarra had heard the kit come in and realized that Flint had probably called her in first. "Thank you, Muscles," she whispered. Hopefully, he was going to help, but Vanarra was still at a loss – unsure of what to say, how to undo what happened, what she, in fact, caused to happen. Before she realized it, the Nephti was standing at her door, quietly waiting.

"Sahni," she said, almost choking as she stood. "Please, kit. Come in."

Sahnassa did, closing the door behind her, but when she looked back, she found that Vanarra had left her desk and was sitting on the couch. A little unsure and unable to judge Van's intent, Sahnassa carefully sat down on the other end of the sofa. Van didn't look at her, just leaned forward and put her elbows on her knees and rested the bottom of her muzzle on her paws. "I've been awake ... all night, regretting what I said to you. I almost as quickly realized that I've probably apologized ... too many times. I've messed up ... too many times. It's not your fault. It's mine," she said sadly.

Sahnassa glanced at her, but Van still didn't look back. In fact, the mixed blood seemed locked in some internal war that made her barely able to control herself. There was a long silence, but it was Van who broke it. "I don't know what to say," she admitted. "Honestly. I don't. I can only tell you why what I saw bothered me so. I ... I have a confession to make to you. After I lost my mother, I ... I actually found a way inside of the archive, the Pinnacle Center. I had lived and scraped by for so long, stealing a book or two from a family school in a neighborhood, getting into lairs and stealing food, sleeping ... wherever I could. During that time, I saw purebred avowed, and their lives were so ... wonderful, so peaceful and nice. They ... they didn't live life afraid to close their eyes – terrified of who might be there or what they would do to you when you woke up."

Vanarra sat up and looked towards the window. "Once I found a way inside of the Pinnacle Center, I had a home – a lair of sorts. I had access to all of the books. There was food there. There ... was a little money, from time to time. It ... it was a good life for me. I stayed out of sight during the sol, when the avowed purebreds walked about. I ... came out at night and ... hid in the darkness doing what I needed to do. It was safe, and I was happy, but ... I got lonely. I snuck out, and then, I met someone. He was a mix like me, and he needed a place. I took him in. I took care of him. I ... I fell for him."

Sahnassa was confused by Van's story; it was totally unexpected, and even seemed a little fantastic. She wondered if it was a lie or if Van was simply mentally unstable. The story continued as Van stood and walked towards the window. "I loved him. It was my first time, really, and there's never been anyone like him. His name was ... Ashalam. I've ... never told anyone here about him ... until just now."

For the first time during the conversation, Van looked at Sahni, and saw the Nephti's questioning stare. Returning to the couch, she sat and seemed to struggle, trying to collect herself. "Well, uh, I ... lost him. Some Vulpi purebred ... did ... something – punched him ... punched him in the gut – messed him up somehow. He started having pains, and ... I took him to a hospital and they ... they wouldn't see us

– made us wait for intervals and intervals while he … while he was dying and while … they did … nothing! Finally, when they did come for him – too late; it was too late. I … I never saw him again. They shoved me out the door, and that was it. My love … was dead, and I … never saw him again," she repeated, almost growling out the words in a tortured whisper.

Sahnassa stood still, starting to feel afraid. If this story was true, Sahni had no idea why Van had even hired her, and fear creeped in as she wondered where all of this was going. After struggling to control herself for almost a pass, Van stated quietly, "I … I can't apologize for what I am. I can't … change the past. I can only try to change the future, Sahni. I will … try to do that. I won't ask you to stay. I … I'll just go with whatever … whatever you think is best."

The story and the offer had Sahnassa's mind reeling. "Can I honestly stay if she's been through this? Can I … really expect her to ever trust me?" Sahnassa's heart questioned it deeply, but her mind had long since been made up, and this story did nothing to change it. "I think … that I should complete the work on the site … get it turned over to you, and then … then I should go."

Van bowed her head, unable to do more than whisper. "If … if that's your decision, I'll … abide by it."

Vanarra was silent, and obviously very emotional. Fearing where that emotion could lead, Sahni stood up and made her way out of Van's office, closing the door behind her. Instead of walking back to her own office, she went to see Flint.

"What happened?" he asked, as she closed the door behind her.

"I … it was weird. She started talking about her growing up and something about hiding in the archive and this … love of hers named Ashalam. Has she told you that story? Do you know if it's true?" Sahnassa asked, confused.

Flint leaned across his desk and said quietly, "Sahni, she's never told me anything like that before. I don't think she's told anyone about that before. She's entrusted you with something … I don't think she's ever given to anyone."

"But … but why tell me?" Sahni asked, confused. "It just makes it all the more clear why she'll never be able to trust me!"

Flint shook his head. "She just trusted you, more than anyone here – including me! I usually just wonder about her past; I have for seasons. I pick up really small things, but if she told you a whole …

story about this guy and where she used to hide out, that's … that's incredibly major."

"But you can't honestly think she wants me to stay? She hasn't said anything about … extending my contract or keeping me on or anything!" Sahni contested. "What does all this matter if I'm not going to be around?"

Flint looked at her with a questioning look, and slowly, it started to make sense to Sahnassa. "If … if she's trusting me with this then, she wants me to stay?"

"She wants more than just having you work another contract," Flint offered. "Unless I'm far off the mark here, I think she desperately wants you to be her friend."

"Why … why doesn't she just tell me?"

"Afraid of pressuring you, maybe. She's heartbroken, Sahnassa. She thinks less of herself now than at any time I've ever known her. If you want, you can finish your contract and leave, but … that's not what she wants. It may be a … difficult friendship, but if you would embrace her as a friend, I don't think there's anything she wouldn't do for you."

For a long time, Sahni sat and considered what she should do, Flint quietly waiting for her to decide.

Vanarra sat in her office chair, facing away from the door, the desk, and the world. She had opened herself up like never before trying to apologize to Sahni, and it hadn't worked. Giving her history hadn't been enough, Van realized. It was no good "explaining" why she did what she did. "Oh, damn! I … I should have gotten on my knees and begged her! I should have begged! I … hurt her too much," she breathed out raggedly. "I hurt her too much. Oh damn, Ash … I … I punched her in the gut. I broke something in her. What the mange does that make me!?" Both her paws were on her head, and her chest hurt like it was about to come apart. Van heard Sahni's words from the prior night in her mind once again. "I'm sorry that you can't see past my family status or my parentage to know how truly loyal I would have been to you."

Every instance Vanarra had been discriminated against came back to her; those times she had to bribe transport drivers to allow her on board, when the hospital let Ash die, the pain that she and her mother lived through – all of it came back, not as justification for her actions, but as condemnation of them. Of anyone, Vanarra knew she should have been the one to know better, to have been better.

"No, dammit, no! Tell me I didn't do that to her – tell me I didn't make her feel like they made me feel. After ... all this time thinking I shouldn't have been treated that way, what did I do? I hurt her like they hurt me! Why? Why couldn't I – I could have done better! She had to have thought everything I just told her was a cheap fraud! She thought I made it up or just was using it to get her to stay! I ... oh, why didn't I just let her in? Couldn't I have trusted her? I'm just ... without any kind of honor at all. I'm without..."

She had been quietly talking to herself, shaking in her grief and self directed rage, but she heard the door open and Flint's grunt as he entered the room. The door closed, and she didn't even turn back to look at him; she couldn't face anyone right now. "I messed up so bad, Flint. I ... I ripped her heart out last sol, and now I can't put it back. I can't fix it. I made her feel like she wasn't worthy, like they made me feel, like she was disposable. Damn me for that, Flint! I ... I'll never be right about this one. I'll never be right..."

A presence came up beside her, and a scent that wasn't Flint's made her turn around in fear.   Standing in front of her was Sahnassa. No one else was in the room. "Sahni ... dammit, from my heart, from my soul – I'm so sorry! Everything I said was – I understand now why you won't forgive me, why you won't stay. How could you ever risk being around me, the way I hurt you?"

Sahnassa looked into the face of her boss, and somehow, she could sense the earnest desperation burning behind those golden eyes, like someone awaiting a sentence that would determine if they lived or died. Sahnassa knew that she had to make a decision, and as difficult as it had been for Vanarra to open up to her, Sahni knew that her own heart was at risk. The bitterness and hurt she had been suffering with all night was still there, but the aching grief she was almost able to feel along with Vanarra overshadowed it, and in that instant, Sahnassa could see the tender, vulnerable child hiding in the hardened shell of the mixed blood.

The fear of being abandoned by someone you cared about, separated by neglectful choice or unfortunate circumstance, was so evident to her in her boss's features that she was stunned she had never seen it before. Sahni knew that feeling – her matron who died, her parents who disowned her, her sisters who had forsaken her, the dame who had detested her, and finally, her dearest friend in academy who had abandoned her – that horrible depreciation of self that comes when someone else chooses against you or is torn away. Feeling compassion and sympathy break open her own closed heart, the Nephti reached out and took Van's paw, gently and compassionately, her decision made – a decision which she knew would be forever irreversible.

"I ... can forgive you, Van. I ... can understand; I think I know what you're feeling, why you said what you did, why you kept pushing me away. It really hurts when someone leaves you, someone you've come to trust. It doesn't matter why they leave you; it's just that they do. I've been hurt that way, too."

Van reached back and held Sahnassa's paw in both of hers, her mouth open in grateful wonder at Sahni's understanding. The Nephti added her other paw, tears beginning to fall down her cheek fur matching those streaming from Van's. "You know, I may only be an avowed purebred kit, but I'm willing to risk being your friend. If I'm your friend, and you are ... close to my soul, I won't leave you. I will be there for you, and I know you would be there for me. I can understand why you wouldn't want to risk letting someone like me get so close to you, but I would be so honored if you would take that risk ... for me."

"I ... I don't deserve you, as a friend, Sahni. I ... didn't treat you like you mattered!"

"You're treating me that way now," the Nephti told her kindly. "You ... are making me feel like I truly matter to someone, and–" Sahnassa had to stop a moment to hold back a sob. "And that's ... something I haven't felt in a ... very long time!"

Sahnassa broke down, and instantly Vanarra was on her hind-legs embracing the Nephti as lovingly and compassionately as she could. "Oh, you do matter, kit! You so do to me! I finally realized I've been treating you like I've been treated, like I swore to myself I never would. You do matter, kit! You do! You're ... my friend!"

Van wept as she held the Nephti, finally letting go of such intense pain that the mixed blood could barely even breathe from the relief she felt flooding her being. Something happened to Sahni as she was being held by this mixed blood, and it was difficult for her to even articulate it in her own thoughts. It was as if some part of her own soul had reached out of her body and touched a part of Vanarra's in a way only she could, through a portal of trust that the mixed blood had never opened before except to her. In that moment, Sahni knew that Vanarra was her family, and Vanarra knew the same.

That instant of trust speared Van through her very soul, and she clung to the Nephti, her muscles tightening nearly in spasms, and aching cries came from her muzzle she just couldn't control. For a moment, Sahnassa was startled and even frightened by the intensity, but the link which had just attenuated between them allowed her to sense the deep gashes and horrible wounds in the soul of her boss, now her dear friend. There was someone being mourned here, mourned as passionately as if they had just died, someone important in Vanarra's life. That onslaught of grief touched her, as well, and all the bitterness and frustrations over her own family came to the surface, causing Sahni's own wounds to draw into focus. Cries, nearly echoing Van's but entwined with a different kind of agony, ripped out of the Nephti's soul and poured forth. In that one moment, the pain held so deeply within both of them drained out – stories that might only be shared many seasons in the future, but whose essence was completely understood in that one instant.

Neither of them noticed the door quietly open, nor Flint's gentle smile as he closed the door, seeing what had happened.

After a few passes, both seemed to find a new emotional grounding, and breathing started to become easier. "Oh ... by the moons, Sahni," Van breathed out raggedly. "What did we almost ... miss? I've ... never—"

"Yeah, yeah," Sahnassa replied, not moving from her friend's embrace. "It would have been ... horrible ... if I had left. I think it would have cost me my soul."

"I still have to be ... your boss, you know?" Van queried, nervously.

"That's how it's supposed to be. I don't want anything special, Van. I ... I just want your trust."

"That's pretty special, kit," Van admitted, finally releasing and looking into the tear blinded eyes of the Nephti. "You have it."

"And I'll never betray it."

"What if your family finds out you work here, for an Anati, and ... this isn't a contract that's going to end. What if your family tells you to leave?" Van asked.

"I'll find some way to say no. Some way," Sahni promised, "even if it costs me everything. They haven't been as much of a family to me as you have."

"Oh, damned if you aren't the sweetest kit I've ever met, you little purebred!"

"And you ... an Anati with ... honor," Sahni replied at a whisper, smiling.

"Well, isn't that something!" Van chuckled, hugging the Nephti again.

Letting go, Sahnassa agreed, "It is. Well, I ... I guess I should go and work ... on TransNet orders or something and not worry about those silly turnover documents. They ... would just be a waste of time now."

"I'm ... glad to hear that. You ... you're a part of this place now, and ... it couldn't be the same without you."

"You are this place, Van, in so many ways. I'm happy to be here."

"Thank you for forgiving me, Sahni," Van said quietly as the Nephti reached the door.

"Thank you for trusting me," the Nephti replied, smiling. Then, she quietly left. Looking up into the knowing face of the big mixed blood leaning against the wall, she breathed, "Thanks, Flint. I ... I can't tell you how grateful I am for ... setting me straight."

"Part of the job," he replied quietly. "Now, let me know if you need anything, okay?"

"Okay, and thanks," Sahni replied, giving him a brief hug before she returned to the server room.

Vanarra watched Sahni leave the room and felt so strange about what had just transpired between them. So many times in her life, losses had utterly devastated her. With the exception of landing the first primal, very little in her life compared to the feelings coursing through her. She left her desk and walked to her couch and sat down. These weren't the kinds of thoughts to be interpreted by "the owner of Celebrations by Vanarra" but rather by Van, the Anati, the Thurian.

Staring into space, she realized the kind of link that had been forged between the two of them now had almost a physical presence in her mind. It was a "thing" that had weight, had an energy, had a warmth to it, and a strange echoing sense that kept her staring straight ahead, fighting to figure out what it was.

"Van? You okay?" Flint's voice asked her quietly from nearby.

Not wanting to lose this amazing attenuation she felt, Van glanced up and saw he had entered her office, closing the door behind him. "Yeah ... I'm ... I..."

Flint sat quietly on a chair in front of her and just waited. "I can like ... feel her ... or I imagine I can or ... I don't know," she tried to explain.

"You two came to some kind of understanding?" he asked.

"Deep ... so deep," Van replied, still staring straight ahead. "I was a fool not to trust her. Blinded. She ... truly does want to be here, and wants to be here with me as her boss. I have this connection with her, or at least ... I imagine that I do. Have you ever had anything like this happen before?"

"No, I can't say that I have, but I've read that it's possible."

"She's in the server room, right now, isn't she? Working on ... the runners?"

"I think so."

"I can tell that she's ... grateful and ... pleased and ... happy, or is that just me thinking she is? Is that me wanting her to be?"

"She was in very good spirits leaving, and happier than I've ever seen her since she started. You are still going to need to be careful with her, you know? If the two of you have come to an understanding, that's great, but the others in the office might not take kindly to an above normal level of familiarity."

Van closed her eyes and tried to shake off the spell, and to a degree, it worked. "I know, but I think she just wanted to be treated normally, nothing special. She wants to be one of us. I ... want that, too. It's going to be hard, Flint, but as much as we've tried to be vigilant telling her to be sensitive about appearing to look down on Anati, we can't let our kind in this office do that to her. We treat everyone here equally."

"Could you fire her if she spoke about a primal?" Flint asked carefully.

"No. I ... I would delegate that. It would hurt ... way too much," Van confessed. Revulsion flooded back across the link, raising it to prominence once again. "I ... think she'd sooner die, Flint, before she did something like that." With Van's trusting assertion, the sense faded, until it attenuated back to a quiet presence.

"That's how I feel about it," he added.

"I know you do, Muscles. I know. Just … take the rest of the staff aside if you need to, and let them know that if we see or hear any slights to her because she's a purebred avowed, we'll come after them as hard as we would her if she had shown disrespect to one of our kind. Make sure it's clear, Flint – very, very clear. I would do it myself, but—"

"Perhaps I could say it with a little more … detachment," Flint supplied.

"Yeah," Van acknowledged, her blush furs rising a little.

"What does this mean for you two, though?"

"That she's my friend, and as she said … close to my soul. That meant something to her … pretty … powerful. I will trust her more, and I'll lean on her more for making decisions. She's been very good about coming to me and not sounding like she was telling me what to do." Van caught Flint's smirk. "You did that?"

"Yeah, after you blew up on her when she first started. Figured it was only fair to let her know what would set you off."

"Thank you, from both of us, I think," Van offered, smiling and putting her paw on his knee. "You do such good things for me. I can't ever tell you how much I appreciate that."

"There are those incremental raises, from time to time," he chuckled, and she slapped him on the very same knee, which drew out a laugh from him, which she, happily, joined.

Sometime later, Van emerged from her office, feeling as if she should check up on Sahni. Pushing open the door to the server room, she found it empty. "Over here, Van!"

"Oh! Sorry, kit. I … I was just coming to look in on you," Vanarra said, but her paw was outstretched. Smiling hugely, Sahnassa clasped it and stood, again drawing her mixed blood friend into an embrace.

"Thank you, and I'm really feeling … happy right now," Sahnassa offered before letting go. "I … I hope you were okay with that."

In answer to Sahni's nervous expression, Van chuckled, "Probably something we shouldn't do all the time, but … yes, kit. Yes, I am, finally. I just came to tell you what I was going to tell you last sol when I lost … my mind, really. The site is wonderful, kit. It's very good, and I'm going to be so proud to show it off. What … were you doing?" she asked, curious, glancing at the viewer.

"Answering my matron's note – the one that … well, started it all."

"What are you going to tell her?   She's … going to be expecting you to jump to that purebred catering firm, right?   The one from your very own house – how … how do you turn that down?"

Sahnassa giggled. "Like this. Just read!"

Vanarra looked over the Nephti's shoulder and read the response Sahni had composed:

To Matron Astalla de Orturu,
my Honored and Appreciated Guide,

> I cannot tell you how grateful I am for your efforts on my behalf. It's truly wonderful to have a family that is looking out for me and trying to help. I have recently become aware of two items that will keep me, unfortunately, from accepting any position with another caterer. First, I reviewed my contract with my present employer and found that it has a clearly enforceable non-competitive clause which forbids me from working for another caterer for at least five seasons. I had forgotten this, but as the subject came up, I wanted to make sure I was legally clear, and it appears I am, instead, obligated to politely turn aside the offer from our own house. Regardless of the technical legality of such a clause, I gave my solemn word, and regardless of who it is given to or their available legal resources, I am bound to keep it.

> Second, my current employer has come to truly value my place here and desires to extend my contract. I believe the ambitious plans being put before me now represent more than an adequate level of challenge and present me with ample opportunities to both further my own development and bring value to my employer and to my house. I do wish to pursue smaller, tactical assignments for other, non-related businesses, and there I may be able to aid my house directly, but for the present, I am happy to remain where I am.

> No one has fought for me like you have, Matron, and I am so grateful.   I believe the

opportunities you presented gave me a real chance to reflect on where I am and what I hope to achieve. Although it pains me to have to respond in the negative, I hope you will understand, and I hope I may continue to avail myself of your expertise, wisdom, and guidance.

My sincere appreciation and in honor,
Sahnassa de Orturu

"Wow, kit, that's ... that's amazing! How did you ever learn how to write something like that?" Van asked, amazed.

"My father is a litigator, and my mother is an archivist – I guess I just picked it up," Sahni replied, shrugging with a smile.

"You," Van accused. "Just one thing though – I don't remember you signing a ... non-competitive clause as a part of your contract."

"Uh, yeah. If you wouldn't mind," Sahni directed, flipping over papers on her desk. "Please sign here, and sign here."

Taking the offered pen, Van asked, "Okay, what am I signing?"

"My original contract. Please make sure you back-date it. I'd hate for there to be any confusion," Sahni directed, mischievously.

"You're serious? Isn't ... isn't that illegal or something?"

"No, it's not. The only thing we're changing is that clause, and ... to tell you the truth, Van, I ... I could have never taken what I made for you and given it to someone else," Sahnassa offered. "That would be putting you and everyone else here at risk. It would be putting those orphans at risk. How could I do that?"

"How can you not, Sahni? That's ... that's what has me stumped about you, but ... I'm there, finally. Wait, this ... this has the original end date," Van asked her, looking worried. "You don't want to stay?"

"No! I want to stay, Van, but..." Sahnassa hesitated and then shrugged. "Someone once told me that you are the boss. You are, and I'm not going to set dates or direct work or anything else that is yours to do. That ... that would be wrong. I owe you that respect. We should draw up a new contract, I think."

Sighing, Van signed the altered contract. "And to think I didn't trust you. That's what kills me about this, Sahni. I completely judged you by every other purebred I've met, well … most of the ones I've met – the avowed ones, anyway."

"I suppose I'm not all that typical," Sahnassa agreed, appreciating Van's statement. "My past is a little … fractured here and there."

"Fine with me. Mine's messed up all over the place. So, why don't you come to my office and let's talk about what that new contract would look like."

"Just as soon as I send this," Sahni stated firmly, hitting the transmit button, sending her response to Matron Astalla on its way.

Chapter 20: Familiarity

Sahni called as she walked by Van's office door, "Good morning, Van!"

"Kit, good morning! Can you come back in here?" Van shouted back.

Putting her things down quickly, Sahnassa turned around and started to leave, but she felt a hard yank on her tail, holding her in place. "Ah!" she shouted in surprise.

Van came running, "What?!" Looking around Sahni's shoulder, she started to chuckle. "And that, my dear kit, is why we close our desk drawers all the way." Stepping around the embarrassed Nephti, Van gently opened the drawer which had snagged the Nephti's tail. "Don't pull now! You're actually caught in a couple of places. Just a moment."

"Oh, this is so ... so embarrassing, Van," Sahni breathed, putting her paws over her eyes. "Good morning, Van! Oh, can you get my stupid tail out of a crack?"

"It's a very nice tail, kit, actually," Van replied as she used her expressed claws to pull the long trailing strands of Sahnassa's ink-dipped tail out of the drawer's mechanism. "I ... saw one like it once, I think, in the archive. It was a kit who was very nice to me."

"Really? Ouch! Hey!" Sahni complained.

"Easy now, you moved! Back up a bit. I need a little slack to work with," Van directed her. Carefully, Sahni took a step back, causing her tail to sag between herself and the drawer. "Better. I think

I can get this out of here without costing you more than a strand or two."

Looking over her shoulder, Sahnassa offered, "Thanks. I'm sorry. So, you said there was a kit who was nice to you when you lived in–" Van's stern expression made Sahni drop to her softest whisper. "Sorry! When you lived in the archive?"

"Yes," Van replied, as quietly. "I was hiding out in the vent. I had gotten pretty lonely by that point and started making my way up the vent just to hear other Thurians talking, for company if nothing else. Thankfully, the children's section was pretty ... lively. One time ... one time there was a book reading – one by Rahnahi de Dothnar, Dame at the time, I think. I listened to it, and ... she was wonderful. That's how I got turned onto her, you see." Van didn't see Sahni's wide-eyed amazement as she continued to gently shift the drawer up and down, working fur out of it.

"So, I was hanging out in the vent after the reading, and some cubs, I think, started saying really bad stuff about her and ... well, Anati. There was this little kit who went back at them. It felt nice ... to hear someone, anyone standing up for you, right, even if they don't know they're doing it." Van gently guided Sahni's tail, completely freed, from the drawer and closed it carefully. "I think she had a tail like yours. Well, it wasn't stuck in anything," Van snickered. At that moment, Van finally looked at Sahni's astonished expression. "What?"

"Van, I'm ... I'm not sure. I was only a kit, and ... that was a long time ago, but ... I think that was me!"

"Really?" Van asked, curious. "Why would you say that?"

Sahnassa furrowed her brow with the effort of trying to remember. "My dad used to take us to the archive. We heard ... I think ... her read one of her books. It was a child's book – something about a seed or flowers or something. There were a couple of Faelnar there, and they were saying things that just ... rubbed my fur the wrong way. Oh, it's ... it's so long ago, but ... I think ... I think I remember saying something to them!"

Van looked back at her. "*The Tale of The Ugly Seed*. It's ... it was my favorite of hers," Vanarra replied at a whisper. "Go ... kit, walk back towards the warehouse and stop and face away from me!"

"What?"

"Just do it!" Van underscored her request with an expressed claw tip pointed in the right direction.

"Okay! Okay!" Sahni responded as Van nearly bodily shoved her towards the back.

"Stop! No, don't look back at me, kit, look forward. Oh, and raise your tail a bit. A little more. A little more."

Sahni whipped her head around, embarrassed. "I'm about to look indecent, Van!"

"Kit's and cub's tails go up high when they're happy or excited, and anyone meeting Rahnahi would be. Just do it, and turn around!"

"Ugh," Sahni groaned. "You've got to be kidding me!" With great effort, Sahnassa managed to raise her tail just about even with her shoulders, its last couple of tracks draping down behind her.

"It's ... you! It is you!" Van gasped in realization – her memory of that moment so long ago clear as it could be.

"Are you sure? She may have done several readings," Sahni called back, her head cocked in surprise.

"She didn't. Remember, I would know!" Van replied, as she approached, turning Sahni around. "I ... lived there," she whispered. "Kit, that ... moment, meant a lot to me. I can't believe you're actually that one!" Vanarra reached for Sahni and hugged her, tightly and warmly. "You stood up for me! That meant a lot to me."

"I'm glad, Van," Sahni offered, finally accepting the possibility of truth in the mixed blood's statement. "I don't remember what I said, exactly, but I'm glad it helped."

"Amazing," Vanarra breathed as she let go of her friend. "I can't believe it, but ... it's got to be true. To think, you ... you were here all along! You ... you are such a good kit, even when you are getting your tail stuck in places."

"Ugh, don't remind me! I haven't gotten it stuck like that in ages – since I was a little kit! Thank you for freeing me."

"No, thank you, kit, for giving me just a taste of what it felt like to be respected. Now, let's go up front. I have some interesting things to go over with you, okay?"

"Okay," Sahni smiled, walking towards the front with her boss and friend.

"Come on in, have a seat on the couch," Van offered, pulling a couple of juice bottles out of her cooler and giving one to Sahni.

"Thank you. Do I need to take notes? Should I go get something?" she asked.

"No, no, kit. Just you and me talking for a moment." Sahnassa sat, and they both took a sip before Van continued. "I wanted to talk to you about the TransNet site. It's been doing fine, and the registrations section is doing quite nicely, but … other than taking deposits and selling a few pictures here and there, it's not quite where I want it to be."

"Oh, I'm … I'm sorry," Sahnassa apologized. The site had been up for nearly a moon, and Sahni had tracked rising traffic and had been improving its look and feel all the while. "What's wrong?"

"It's not what's wrong. What you have there looks great, but I want to improve the product we're selling. I want you to take this sol and research buying a very, very good VidStar camera. I want one that can do still shots and also shoot video. It needs to do very well in low light."

"How much do I have to spend?" Sahnassa asked.

"I'm willing to go up to ten thousand on it. It's my last few primal bonuses. I've been holding them back for this."

"Oh, okay," Sahnassa noted. "Then, you want some software to edit the video together, make it look good, and … we sell that on the site?"

"Yes, absolutely," Van acknowledged, glad the Nephti was on the trail with her. "Every one of our competitors have been outsourcing to private video firms, and they only take a cut – a small one from what I've heard. Now, none of the avowed purebred firms will work with us, but if we can do it, then that's all profit and earnings coming into this business. Do you think you can find us something?"

"I'm pretty sure I can. I studied that in academy, so I already know how to take VidStar and edit it."

"That's very, very good, kit! Oh, and … one other thing. I know it's been painful for the others to wave their primal bonuses in front of you, and … I have come to trust you, kit. I hope I've demonstrated that since … since our fight," Van offered, a little hesitant to bring up how ruthlessly she had sliced into Sahni for her supposed infidelity to her business. "You know that, right?"

"I do, Van. I do," Sahnassa reassured her, smiling softly.

"Well, there's a primal coming up sol after next. I want you there," Van offered.

"Want … me … there?" Sahnassa asked nervous.

"Well, unless you don't *want* a primal bonus?" Van asked, smirking a little, having seen Sahni's blush furs rise immediately at the suggestion.

"I ... I ... do I have to get ... naked?" Sahni asked at a whisper.

"Not for this one, which is why I chose it. I figured that those particular ones – which are pretty rare by the way – would be a little bit more than you could manage. I mean, I like to treat everyone equally, and if you really want to go in just the fur I'm sure I could accommodate you—"

"I'll ... I'd prefer to keep my clothes ... or some clothes on, actually," Sahni stuttered, completely unsettled.

"Well, you are going to have to get some clothes made, and I'll pay for it, but don't mistake, kit. They are going to be ... a bit rustic and ... minimalist. Essentially, they'll mimic your fur coloration without allowing anyone to actually see ... anything. They will also have no stitching, so it will be just a single piece of fabric held in place by a belt. It's not the sort of thing you could walk around wearing in public, but still, at a primal, it will seem like you just happened to pick rather ... primitive clothing. It goes with the theme of the event. You think you might be up for it?" Sahnassa was thinking furiously, her blush furs still raised.

Van decided to add an additional enticement. "It can be a very ... instructive and educational event, as well. The attendees actually don't mind you having nice, long looks – but you'll need to make sure you're not so distracted that you can't get your work done. No trying to start-up a hunt with anyone, no intimate relations, and no giving of any contact information whatsoever. That's a big no-no. If anyone is doing that, I want to know it, and they'll probably be let go."

"I ... I wouldn't do that!" Sahni promised. "I'd ... I'd be afraid to."

"Well, we have one or two that have gotten a little too comfortable, from time to time, and started turning a few heads and tails in their direction. This event is about the Primalists and their organization, not about showcasing the pretty purebreds or Anati, for that matter, who happen to be catering it. I think ... honestly, kit, as a friend, this would open your eyes a little. Believe it or not, the Primalists are about more than just getting naked in the woods. They have a philosophy and a culture, almost, and some very firmly held beliefs. It's actually very interesting to talk to them."

"Okay. I'll ... try it."

Vanarra smiled, appreciating that the Nephti was tackling something far outside of her comfort zone. "That's the kit! Make sure you get plenty of good sleep tonight and tomorrow night. Go to bed early and sleep in. We'll be up most of the night we're working, okay?"

"Yes, Van. I will."

"Great. Now, I'll give you an address, and I want you to go there this morning and get fitted. It won't take long," Van chuckled, "after all, there's not much to it!"

"Nice camera," Tresk noted as they rode in the back of the delivery hover up to the primal. "A little boxy, though. Most of the stuff I've seen has been a little smaller."

"Well, it couldn't do what this does," Sahni told him. "It's got image stabilization and photo ability, but most of it is just power and memory. It's pretty well balanced though, want to try?"

"Sure," Tresk agreed and gently took the camera from her. Turning it on, he panned around looking at the others – Flint, Sheffer, Raska, Saiphar, and Mauft. Angling the camera back, he turned it on Raska. "Well, well, looky looky who's all brushed up and shiny."

"Not for you, Tresk. I'm doing it for ... our clients," she offered.

"You said it takes stills?" he asked.

"Sure," she answered and pointed at the control.

"Oh." A tick later, a flash lit up the back of the vehicle, and Raska was blinking her eyes.

"Tresk! You ignorant..."

Flint looked back from the driver's seat. "I think that's enough picture taking. Let's put the camera away for now."

"Why bring a camera to a primal anyway?!" Raska protested hotly. "No one is supposed to know what goes on, correct?"

Taking the camera back from Tresk and putting it in the case, Sahnassa answered, "Vanarra wants a record of our set-ups. She's trying to create an album to show prospective clients when they come in. She also wanted me to try the time lapse feature so we could set the camera up and let it take pictures as we get the room ready."

"I don't want my picture taken by ... that," Raska contested, seeming to catch herself at the last before saying something else.

"Even if it does take a picture of you, you'll just be a flash on the viewer when it's converted to video," Sahni offered, and unconvinced, Raska turned away from her, her back fur up.

"Saiphar, what's all that stuff you've brought?" Sahni asked, trying to change the subject.

"I do demonstrations, Sahni, of painting with natural inks and paper. I show them how to make keepsakes or pots or simple tools, even. It's been pretty popular," he noted.

"Very popular," Flint put in from the front. "He's pretty much a fixture at these things, and he has quite an audience."

"That's what shaves the fur off me," Tresk stated. "Most of these could buy expensive paper or data pads, the finest cookware and hired chefs, and get furniture that was already made. Why they want to watch you squish insects to make blue dye I just don't get!"

"Self reliance," Flint replied. "They want to be able to live without any aid of technology – if they can't make it themselves, they don't want it."

"Great," Sheffer put in. "If they don't want what their money can buy, they can just pass it to me. They can make all the mud lairs they want to, and I'll take their lovely hovers off their paws, no problem!"

The others laughed, but Sahnassa replied, "I ... I think that's great, Saiphar. I've watched that Lupar on VidStar who teaches survival lessons. He's good. He demonstrates things like you do."

Sheffer chuckled, "Yeah, I've seen that show, but he talks about practical things. Saphy here's teaching rich and well-moneyed Thurians what to do if they should find themselves in a survival situation and suddenly have an urgent need to paint!"

Sahnassa felt compelled to defend the artist, who was shrinking back somewhat at the criticism. "He's teaching them to think without relying on technology, and it could be applied to art or survival—"

"You defend him so valiantly, Sahnassa," Raska countered, "perhaps you should take him aside and command him to demonstrate something primitive on you, right?"

"Easy," Flint growled from the front.

"That's ... very unkind," Sahni shot back at Raska, her lips curled upward, after glancing at an ashamed Saiphar. "And insulting!"

"Insulting because he's a cast out and you're not?" Sheffer asked sourly. Flint's lower growl, more pronounced, forced Sheffer to reply, "What?! I'm just trying to clarify."

"It's insulting because you suggest that we both take those kinds of relations lightly," Sahnassa answered flat and even. "I respect Saiphar and truly appreciate his work. What you said made it sound like he wasn't even a Thurian, just a ... toy ... or a pet to be ordered around."

"All males are pets," Raska breathed out airily, seemingly unperturbed by the exchange. "The sooner you learn that, the sooner you can get whatever you want out of them."

"I'll remember that at your next performance review," Flint replied with a smirk. "Or your next bonus, or maybe both."

"Present company the exception that proves the rule, I'm sure," Raska sighed, sounding as if she was completely unconvinced.

Sahnassa was about to counter, but Saiphar raised his paw. "It's okay, Sahni. Perhaps the only thing worse than being thought of as a ... pet is being someone so ignorant to believe such a thing was true."

Raska shot Saiphar an angry glance, but Tresk just sat back and chuckled.

"Alright," Flint broke in. "Since polite conversation seems a bit of a stretch, let's go over what everyone's assignments are tonight, just to make sure we have it down."

As Flint started going over the various duties and schedules, Raska stared angrily at Sahnassa, but unlike all of those other times when Sahnassa had ignored it, she fixed the mixed blood with the same stare and wouldn't break it. Flint's directions to Raska were the only distraction which after acknowledging, she dismissed the Nephti with a grunt and closed her eyes, pretending to rest.

Sahni relaxed her stare and simply looked at Raska. She was inarguably beautiful, like a walking piece of exotic art, endowed with both artistic symmetry and the ample provisions of nature. "Why does she have to be so bitter and ugly?" Sahnassa wondered. "Is she ... like Van was? Is Van just further along? Could she find a way to like me – for us to like each other? Maybe, I should try to reach out to her, apologize. Maybe I should—"

At that moment, she looked up and saw Saiphar, his eyes beholding her with understanding and even a degree of tenderness. Slowly, he shook his head. "No. Stay away," he mouthed in warning.

Sahnassa was stunned that he had read her expression that clearly. A slight turn of his head with his eyes still on her emphasized the concern and begged that she acknowledge and agree. She mouthed "okay" back at him. Seeming relieved, he smiled gently before he, too, closed his eyes and relaxed. After repeating her part to Flint, she decided that rest was the best alternative, so she, too, tried to relax and catch a few moments sleep while they were in route.

Sahnassa had been getting along fairly well at the primal so far, Van using her mostly in the set-up phases at the pavilions around the ancient Nephti ruins, at first. The archaic stone structures within the overgrown forest had played very well into Van's theme for the event, and Sahni was again amazed at how well planned and executed everything was. Within a matter of intervals, an enclosed glass pavilion that at first seemed sterile soon took on the same elegant mystique of the stone spires and vegetation covered tri-ax, the ancient ceremonial forum of the Nephti tribes. Sahnassa was impressed by how accurately Vanarra had recaptured the ceremony and traditions of the aboriginal inhabitants of the Thuratan continent – even by the food that was being prepared and placed in refrigerated cabinets.

Her time lapse camera had been operating the whole time, as well, and she hoped that it would do a good job capturing the amazing work everyone was doing. While she was pulling apart horva roots with her claw tips, a preparation Van specifically instructed her on, she felt a presence come up beside her. "Sahni," Saiphar whispered, "stay away from Raska. She's got some serious ugliness inside, despite how pretty she might appear on the outside. She doesn't only think that males are pets; she thinks that about everyone."

"I wondered if she might be a little like Van, but just someone who hasn't figured out how to … like someone like me."

"She's nothing like Van," Saiphar contested. "The kindness and charity that is in Van can't be found in Raska, and she has a contempt for everyone that is toxic. She has something … strange that she does at primals – disappears and no one can find her. Don't trust her."

Sahnassa sighed. "Alright. Thank you, Saiphar. I … appreciate your perspective, as always."

"Attention everyone!" Van called. "It's now time for the grounds walk, which will take about half an interval. It's going to be dark by the time we get finished with the banquet and move to the competition fields. To make sure you know where you're going when it gets dark, everyone wash up and meet with me in the dining room."

Half an interval later, Sahni had a good idea where the male and female camps were and how to reach them. She also knew where the Commons area was and what it was to be used for. Primalist members had also started showing up and making their own preparations – setting up wooden arches, wrestling spaces, and the other competition grounds. While they were on the tour, Sahni laid back a bit, being the tail of the group. When they approached the Commons area, Sahnassa noticed Raska taking an active interest in a secluded trail that had been marked as out of bounds for the event – supposedly the burial place of an ancient Nephti healer. Sahnassa managed to appear disinterested in Raska's actions, but still subtly observed her checking a map showing the paths that connected the two camps and the Commons with the grave site.

When they returned to the main dining room, Vanarra instantly recognized a Nephti who was stooped over the camera, looking at it. "Alright everyone, back to your tasks. Sahni, come with me," Van bade and then went to the Nephti who had turned and looked at her, smiling hugely.

"Vanarra!"

"Mavia," Van replied, "it's so great to see you! Everything looking good so far?"

"Wonderful, but … what's this for?" the older Nephti asked, curious.

"Oh, let me introduce you to Sahnassa de Orturu – she's one of our team and manages the technology we use in our business. Sahni, this is Mavia, our client and good friend."

"Hello there," Sahni offered, bowing respectfully to Mavia. "A pleasure to meet you. I just wanted to try to do a little time-lapse of everyone doing set-up. That's what the camera's for. It's not going to be used for the event; it's going to be back in its case in the delivery hover."

"That's good of you. For obvious reasons, as I'm sure Van's explained, we don't permit any type of recording at these events," Mavia offered good-naturedly, but Sahnassa could tell she was quite serious.

"Do you think you've captured enough, Sahni?" Van asked, clearly indicating that she should reply in the affirmative and put away the device that was worrying their client.

"Oh, absolutely, but ... I was wondering if it would be okay if I take about ten passes or so and get some shots from the outside before I put it away for good?"

"Ten passes, but no more," Van warned. "And be very careful that no one is recognizable in what you take. Mavia's group is already out and about doing set-up, as we saw."

"I'll take care of that," Sahni promised as she removed the device from its tripod. "I just want to get the building and ruins for a collage at the end of the time-lapse. If that's alright?" Sahnassa asked looking at both Mavia and Van.

"As long as you're careful," Mavia agreed. "That has to be put away right after you do."

"Absolutely. So nice to meet you," Sahni offered as she quickly folded the tripod and excused herself.

"She seems like a very nice kit," Mavia commented, as Sahnassa departed the building.

"She is, and ... she's become a good friend to me. Her profession is a bit of an odd match for this event, though – she's a technologist."

"Ugh," Mavia feigned disgust, "bringers of the end times! You know, the funny part, Van, is that a lot of our group come from professions exactly like that. This ... is an escape for them. They can feel even more trapped by technology than any of us and have a passionate need to return to primitive simplicities."

"I suppose you have a point there," Van agreed, but quickly changed the subject. "Speaking of primitive simplicities, I wanted to show you the mix we are using for the drink – the fruit combination is exactly the same as the one used by the Nephti in ceremonial rights thousands of seasons ago."

"Really!? Van, you never fail to impress!" Mavia replied happily as she followed Vanarra towards the kitchen. "How you come up with something unique at each and every one of these is a true marvel!"

"It's my pleasure to do it, and your loyal partnership means more than you'll ever know," Van stated earnestly as the two entered the kitchen.

Outside of the building, Sahnassa was carrying around the camera in its case and the tripod, but she had no intent, whatsoever, of taking any additional footage. As she had stepped out of the building, she had reviewed what had been recorded and groaned in frustration. The camera made a small beep before it took an image, and that beep occurred every set number of ticks. In more than a few of the images, Raska's tail and hindquarters were on prominent display – an obviously purposeful foiling of Sahni's plans. That made her a little vindictively curious about the subject of Raska's attention - the closed-off paths.

Quickly, she made her way to the entrance, stepped around the rope barrier, and walked down the tree-covered path. After only a couple of passes of walking, she reached a raised mound capped by a rough-cut stone monument. "Why does she care about this?" Sahni wondered. She went over and read the inscription on the plaque sitting atop a pole a few tracks off to the side of the grave, just on the other side of a low railing. "The Nephti buried here was an ancient predecessor of the de Dothnar, a healer who had managed to halt a war between the clan of the river delta and the clan of the forest – present era de Dothnar and de Fantar, respectively. The site is rumored to have mystical powers even to this sol," she read, "and some claim seeing visions of the healer, learning a deep truth about themselves, or even being healed just by touching the stone."

Looking up at the mound and the small spires around it, it was clear that the individual was highly honored by those of her time. Closing her eyes, she quietly uttered a blessing for the dead, "May you rest well, in honor, and may you live forever in the memories of your family."

Walking around the monument, she noticed paths leading off in two directions, in addition to the way she came. Remembering the map, she also realized that the two paths came from the areas for the male and female camps. "What are you up to, Raska?" Sahni wondered, but then looking at her timepiece, she realized she should probably head back towards the hover to drop off the camera before she was missed.

Sahnassa was trying hard not to actually look at anyone as she served drinks and snacks at the female camp – she had never imagined being in a place where all manner of Thurians would be parading around without even a single bit of clothing on. Several had actually made complimentary comments to her and done things that forced her to look at them, but Sahnassa was only able to look at their faces. Raska, on the other paw, who was paired with her, was more than content to serve and exchange pleasantries with the various guests. However, Sahni noted, that not all the guests were happy to be talking with her. More than a few times, Sahnassa had heard terms like "Anati" and "mongrel" and "muddle breed" said in passing, usually by Faelnar, and despite Saiphar's warning, the Nephti did feel bad at how the exotic mixed breed was being treated. Raska, however, seemed not to even notice the discrimination and continued as happy as could be with her duties.

"Sahni, dear," Raska said to her. "I believe we're in danger of running low on … fruit juices. I will go back and get some for us. Can you manage here?"

"Sure, Raska. No problem," she answered, but something instantly told her that Raska was lying. At that moment, several other contestants came up who had just finished a match and were looking for drinks, so Sahni served them as her fellow employee stepped away.

While taking care of the needs of her customers, Sahnassa kept quickly glancing at Raska as she departed. Sure enough, the Vulpi-Nephti mix did not go down the primary trail back to the Commons; she diverted down the path to the healer's grave when she thought no one was looking. Passing out the last drink, Sahnassa grumbled, "I wish Van were here right now." Then, she quickly decided to check their stocks in the coolers hidden below the rough-cut tables. "We have way more than enough!" she grumped. Looking back to the path, she asked accusingly, "What are you up to, Raska?"

She thought about passing it off as nothing, but some instinct told her it was extremely important that she find Raska and figure out what she was doing. Looking at the table in front of her, Sahnassa decided to pre-set a number of drinks and snacks and then slip away. "Van will kill me, but I've got to know what's going on with her!"

In a few passes, Sahnassa had the table covered with drinks and snacks, and with apologies to a few who had just walked up, she slipped away. Coming to the entrance of the path, she realized that the rope barring it had been intentionally cut and tossed aside. Trying not to attract attention, she slipped down the path as quietly and quickly as she could.

Although the faint moon's light gave her more than ample ability to see the path, she couldn't truly see anything else. However, by the way the ground was sloping, she knew that she should soon come to the grave and monument. Coming up a small hill and turning beside a tree, Sahnassa stopped cold – stunned by what she saw.

The grave site had been lit by a number of shielded candles placed around it, giving it a mystical and almost reverent atmosphere. Standing on the grave, naked, was Raska along with two other male Thurians – very male by the looks of them, their tails as high as they could possibly get. They appeared to be Vulpi, and based upon their evident signs of arousal, they were ready to mate. Then, something happened that just caused Sahnassa's jaw to drop open. One of the males guided his partner forward and pushed him down into a kneeling position in front of Raska. Raska said something to him, her tone harsh and commanding – albeit still quiet enough that Sahni couldn't make out what was being said over the rustling leaves around her. The male leaned forward and planted his muzzle squarely between Raska's legs. Sahnassa covered her mouth in shock as the Vulpi-Nephti threw her head back, clearly enjoying the attention she was getting. "You've got to be kidding me!" she thought.

Just then, she heard something snap behind her, a fair distance away, but still on her path. "No one can see this! They'll blame Van for it! It's … it's horrible!" Turning around, she quietly made her way back down the path towards the female camp.

"Excuse me? Who's there?" a voice softly called out.

"It's … it's me, Sahnassa," she called back, hoping that cupping her paws around her muzzle wouldn't allow Raska and her friends to hear. "Who is it?"

The female Nephti stepped closer to her and answered, "It's Mavia. We aren't supposed to have anyone down here during the event. There is a very sacred grave down this path, and we've been told we can't disturb it. What are you doing down here?"

Sahnassa knew, at this moment, that the truth could easily create a horrible problem for Van. So, although it wasn't the most prominent truth, she decided to opt for another, highly valid one. "I … I am so sorry. I've just never been to one of these events before, and I … I am just not used to seeing…"

Mavia stepped up to her and sighed, "I understand, kit. It can be quite a shock to attend one of these for the first time, but you have to realize that this is who we are, as Thurians. Take away all of the technology we hold dear and place us back where we were meant to be, and now … most of us wouldn't know how to live, and worse, most of us couldn't find the joy in living as we used to, even for a few intervals. Come with me," Mavia offered, pulling her down the path towards the grave.

"Oh, please, let's go back up this way. I can't leave the drink table for long; Van will fire me!" she nervously protested.

"Alright," Mavia agreed, "but it won't be as private. Just so you know."

"Oh, okay." Sahnassa replied, following Mavia back towards the female camp. As they approached the entrance to the trail, more light slipped in from the raging bonfire allowing Sahni a full view of the lovely Nephti Primalist. Instantly, she averted her eyes to the ground at one side of her and away from the Nephti, standing naked in front of her.

"Now, this is what I want you to do, and I'm giving you my full and complete permission to do so, okay?"

"Oh … okay," Sahni agreed, just relieved that she was able to get Mavia away from Raska's shameful display.

Putting her paw beneath Sahnassa's muzzle, Mavia slowly brought Sahni's eyes up to meet her own. "Now, you've looked at yourself in the mirror, kit, surely, without anything on?"

"I … I have," Sahni stuttered nervously.

"I'm just another mirror, a different body but a kindred soul. I am proud of what my heritage has gifted me with, and to have another appreciate it as well – not for the sake of mating or other prurient desires – just acknowledging the truth of who we are without all we surround ourselves with; that is a compliment to me, indeed. Now, kit, I want you to look at me, from the top of my ears to my tail-tip to my hind paw toes. I want you to do it while you count to fifty slowly in your head, and I do mean slowly. I'll turn around, and you look at me. Okay?"

Swallowing, Sahni nodded and complied. Mavia stepped away and posed, but only slightly, and then slowly turned around so that Sahnassa could see every part of her. Then, she faced away and bent over, exposing her backside to the wide-eyed Sahnassa whose blush furs were so high, they were literally hurting. Mavia turned around, placed her paws behind her back and stretched forward, putting her chest on ample display. Relaxing after a few ticks, Mavia counted out "forty-eight, forty-nine, fifty. There, kit, that wasn't so bad, was it?"

"You … you're very … lovely, beautiful, keen, I mean," she offered, nearly physically shaking.

"And so are you. When you get to your lair, in private, where you feel safe and secure, I want you to think about looking at yourself in the mirror the same way; try to get in touch with that part of yourself that instinctively remembers what it meant for us to live here, as we were meant to, without any pretenses of position or technology or complex society. You may find, kit, that … this world can hold as much attraction for you as the one in which you live. That choice is up to you, okay?"

"Thank you, yes, I'll … I'll try it. Thank you very much. I'd better get back now," Sahnassa breathed, offering the path ahead of her to Mavia.

"Alright, kit. Thank you. You … were very brave just now. I'll check with you later."

As they passed the downed rope, Sahnassa appeared to notice it and said in surprise, "Oh, shouldn't this be up barring the way?"

"Well, yes! I put that there myself," Mavia commented, confused.

"I'll just retie it. Looks like someone just … made a mistake," Sahni offered, hoping to misdirect the Primalist organizer.

"I understand. That's a valuable part of Thurian life, as well. Take care now, and thank you, Sahnassa."

Mavia stepped away, and in no more than three ticks, Van was on top of her. "Sahni! Where have you been?! The drink table is almost empty, and there is no one else around! I saw you talking to Mavia for a long time! What's going on?"

Sahnassa clutched Van's arms in desperation. "Van!" she whispered leaning in. "Something's going on I need to tell you about! Raska is down that path with two other males, and … they're like … on top of a grave … having sex!"

"What?!" Van shot back, harshly. "Are you sure?"

"Raska's been acting weird all evening, and I noticed her checking out that path earlier. When I went to put the camera back up, I checked out the path myself and found the grave. Raska was going to go get some more juices, but she went down that path instead! I filled up the table and then followed her. I found her with two males – one that had his muzzle buried between her legs!"

"You are … kidding me! Okay, okay! You get back to the drink table and hold things down; I'm going to slip down that path myself for a look."

"Don't let Mavia see you," Sahni said. "She came after me when I went down there, and she almost saw everything!"

"Oh, damn, you are kidding me! That … that could have done us in right there! You did exactly what you were supposed to, kit, good job telling me. Let me go see what's going on for myself, and I'll come back up to help you. Okay?"

"Yes, Van … thank you!"

After Vanarra left, Sahni refilled the drinks and made sure she kept all of the female competitors happy. She had even consoled a Pantera who came to the table and broke down in tears, having lost the competition for grace and beauty. As the final competitions began, Sahnassa actually found herself watching them, curious. The wrestling was actually intriguing to her, seeing those females who had just triumphed for grace and beauty succumbing to the powerful upper body of the very Pantera she had comforted. Cheering the winner, Sahnassa didn't notice Raska's return.

"Well, I see you did get a little loosened up, after all," she nearly purred.

The Nephti felt a little sick to her stomach and turned around. "Oh, well, yes. She … she deserved to win. They … weren't very kind to her. How are you doing?"

"Very good, indeed, little kit. Very good, indeed," she chuckled. "Do we need anything?"

"No, we seem to be doing alright."

Just then, Vanarra walked up. "Well, you two, how's it going?"

"We're … doing okay," Sahni offered, confused by Van's lack of reaction to Raska.

"Well, there's a little help needed down in the Commons area. Sahni, I'm sorry, but I'm going to have to burden you with finishing out here and doing all the clean-up, okay?"

"Whatever you say, Van," Sahnassa replied, a little confused and disappointed. Raska's smirk confused her, as well.

"Alright, Raska, let's go. Saiphar's students are going to die of thirst and hunger if we don't get there soon." They started to walk away, with Raska's tail swish-swishing nicely. When they were a few steps away, Van stopped Raska and said, "Wait a moment, I forgot to tell her something – hate for her to make a stupid mistake." Van quickly darted back to Sahni and leaned over to whisper in her ear. "Saw it all, but she was being treated by some of the wealthiest and most powerful Thurians here. I … I had to actually escape by going through the males' camp. Saw one little cub get trounced, and then he saw me – didn't like that so much. Don't say anything about this. We can't risk causing a scene here."

"Yes, Van," Sahnassa replied, feigning disappointment. Unseen to Raska, Sahni winked, and Van winked back, smiling broadly. Schooling her expression, Van trotted back to Raska, and the two were then away.

"Well, it's finally over," Raska breathed as they watched the last few attendees leave the morning banquet effectively ending the primal. "Quite a nice time."

"Speak for yourself," Tresk grunted. "I had to endure some Faelnar tail for brains yelling at me how he had been 'shamed and humiliated' by having a female Anati see his loss. He didn't stand a chance; I could have beaten him and used his own tail to do it."

"He was kind of pathetic," Flint agreed. "Saiphar, you seemed to do well, as always."

"They want to go into some new areas," he breathed, shaking his head. "I've got some research to do."

"Like what?" Sahni asked.

"Musical instruments from primitive tools," he explained. "How did you like your first primal?"

"Eye opener," Sahni answered, and Raska chuckled.

"She was so nervous she wouldn't look any of the contestants in the eye or … anywhere else, for that matter," the mixed blood scoffed.

"As long as she kept them happy, it's not required," Flint put in. "I heard you did well."

Vanarra swept into the small anti-room where they were waiting and announced, "Well, you've done it again, team! We've been paid with a bonus, and our customer is very, very happy! She's actually very happy with you, kit – she said you did very well for a first timer! She is waiting outside for a quick chat, if you don't mind."

"Uh huh," Tresk chuckled. "Mavia has a new favorite!"

"Well, she is our customer, kit, so let's not keep her waiting. Oh, and can you take your camera and get a few pictures of that healer's monument for me? I would really like to see it, but I'm not going to have the time."

"Yes, Van. I will." Sahnassa stood and left the group as Vanarra continued her comments about the event. Stepping out into the great hall, she saw a now well-dressed and smiling Mavia waiting for her. "I ... I understand you wanted to see me?"

"Well, perhaps some sol, dear kit, but the primal is over, I'm afraid," Mavia chuckled, and then laughed when Sahni's blush furs perked up. "Oh, she said you were easily embarrassed! I'm sorry, kit; I just wanted to make sure you were okay with ... with what I did. It was unusual, but ... Nephti aren't always seen as beautiful or graceful, and you are. I want you to know that, and I'm serious about you spending some time in front of the mirror figuring that out."

"I ... I would, but..."

"You have to develop some confidence, kit – some inner strength!"

"No, I meant I ... I just don't have that kind of mirror," Sahni replied. "Just a small one." Sahnassa held up her paws and made a gesture indicating her mirror barely allowed her to see all of her head.

"Oh, well, I see," Mavia replied in good humor. "Well, as a technologist, you have options, I'm sure. That ... camera of yours. Set it up, and give yourself some freedom – put yourself on display for it – and then watch. Appreciate yourself and your primal beauty, kit. Even if you never become a Primalist, I want you to know how special you are."

Although it was pretty much the strangest conversation she had ever had, Sahnassa accepted the compliment as gracefully as she knew how. "You are very kind to say so. I'll ... I'll think about it. This is a new world for me, Mavia. I ... appreciate you being so patient and ... open about it, with me."

Mavia was clearly touched by Sahni's reply and walked up and embraced her. "You are a very good kit. Van's got a real find with you, Sahnassa! I look forward to seeing you again, okay?"

"Okay," Sahni offered, a little unsure, and the two parted.

A few passes later, Sahnassa had her camera and was making her way back down the secluded trail in the bright light of morning, shafts of radiance penetrating the forest. Arriving at the healer's grave, she started looking around. Van clearly wanted her to check and make sure that no sign of misbehavior was left that could tie her business to Raska's actions. Sure enough, Sahni found several small vials and candle pieces that had been discarded, including some that spilled hot wax onto the smooth stones lining the crypt. Using her claw-tips, Sahni chipped off the wax and collected the rest of the items, putting them into her bag.

Finally, when the grave was restored to its proper state, Sahnassa stood in front of it. It angered her that Raska had so horribly desecrated the resting place of a revered Nephti healer – someone she had read about in secondary school. Bowing before the grave, Sahnassa apologized. "I am Sahnassa de Orturu, and I beg forgiveness for those who acted so shamefully and disturbed your place of rest. Those who acted so ... thoughtlessly will be punished. I know Vanarra, and I know she will do what is right; they will never be allowed to do this again. Please know that your name is honored and taught to children, and your example is always remembered. The house of your lineage is great, and it, too, is most honored. Accept my request, noble healer, and may your honorable rest be forever undisturbed."

Sahni bowed again and stepped away from the grave. As she did, a voice said, "Thank you, kit." Looking around, Sahnassa tried to see who said that, but no one was there. Her heart pounding in her chest, Sahni turned and walked quickly away from the grave as fast as she could.

The next morning, Sahnassa was walking into the office and ran into an infuriated Raska, storming out of the building. "Raska? You ... okay?" Sahni asked, wondering if she could guess the reason for the mixed blood's anger. Raska didn't say a word and stamped off in the direction of the transfer stop. Walking into the building, she was surprised to see Mauft. "You're here early!" Sahni commented.

"Just in case, actually. Flint and Van are waiting for you in her office."

"Thank you, Mauft," she replied, and the gray one grunted and went back to her work, stifling a yawn as Sahni passed by. That had Sahni yawning as she knocked on Van's door. "You ... you wanted to see me?" she asked, sounding a little sleepier than she meant to.

"Oh, no!" Van complained, covering her eyes and turning her head. "I'm not ... I'm not going to do that ... I'm not!"

"I'm sorry?" Sahni queried, confused, looking at Van huffing and grunting all of a sudden.

"Van doesn't like to yawn in front of anyone," Flint explained, chuckling.

Finally somewhat under control, Vanarra looked back at her, and replied testily, "That's because I don't yawn, I yowl like a prowler – I saw myself in the mirror do it once, and that was enough to put me off for life. It doesn't sound good, and it doesn't look good, either. Come in, kit, that's so long as you don't ... do that ... thing, again."

"I'll try my best," Sahni apologized. "What's going on?"

"I just wanted to tell you how grateful we are that you told me about what was happening with Raska," Van offered, now smiling.

"Those vials you found at the grave – illegal pharmaceuticals," Flint explained. "A much spicier version of what they give the champions to rev up their mating drive."

"From what I saw, Raska's drive didn't need much revving up," Van offered, sarcastically. "Anyway, you saved us from a major, major embarrassment, and you saved Mavia, too, even though she doesn't know it."

Flint explained in response to Sahni's curious expression. "Raska's ... clients, for lack of a better term, are very, very well off. If Mavia had stumbled across them, it's possible those donors would pull their support from the primals or threaten to. As it is, she doesn't know anything happened; Raska's clients don't know they were found out, either, but Van's got a record of every one, though."

"What good will that do?" Sahni asked.

"Well," Van explained, "as a part of giving Raska the short trail out of the office, I told her that if she did anything, anything at all to harm this business, each one of those clients would have letters posted to their mates and families telling exactly what they did and when they did it. I also told her that I would sign her name to the letters. That would be enough to kill off her customer base, or at least wound it pretty severely."

"I'd be willing to bet that she's been using us for a long time to get to the primals," Flint speculated to the two of them. "I bet that's where she picks up new clientele."

"Well, that's enough of that. The good news is, Sahni, that – as a reward – you get not only your first primal bonus, but you get Raska's, too. Thank you, kit. You protected this business and our customer. At some point, I'll make sure Mavia knows, as well."

Sahnassa walked over and accepted the draft offered by Van. Opening it up, she breathed, "Oh, wow!"

"I think she likes that, Flint. What do you think?" Vanarra chuckled.

"I know I do," he agreed, joining her amusement at Sahni's wide open expression.

"That's … that's a whole lot of–" Sahni started, but then stopped. "You know what, Van? My … my bonus is … more than enough. Take Raska's and give it to the kits and cubs, okay?"

"Wow, kit!" Van exclaimed quietly. "That's … that's incredible of you! Raska … had it been the other way, would have never considered it. I want you to be there with me when I give it to them – okay?"

"I'd be happy to, Van. I'd be happy to," Sahnassa offered, smiling. "I … better get to work. Thank you very much."

"Thank you, kit – for keeping our trust and protecting our business."

When Sahni was out of hearing range, Van whispered to Flint, "I have never been happier to have her here than right at this moment." Smiling, he nodded in agreement.

Raska was barely conscious, struggling to understand what was going on around her. The last memory she had was going to visit a new client she had picked up at the primal – then, there was nothing. Now, like words spoken by random speakers, sensations and realities seeped into her consciousness. She was naked. She was laid out flat on her back. She felt bands around her wrists, ankles, and head holding her fast. There was a cool sensation running into both of her arms. Her mouth was muzzled and gagged so she couldn't cry out. She was aroused, more than she had ever been. She felt like her mind had been invaded by a thick and dreamy fog.

Words and sentences now trickled into her mind. "So, is this the one?"

"Yes. Quite a piece of work, isn't she? She's probably compromised half of the directors and higher in each of the major corporate packs in town."

"What are you going to do with her?"

"Well, you see she's a Vulpi mix, don't you?"

"Can you actually do that? Is there enough Vulpi in her?"

"Oh, more than enough. Her brain scan and blood-work confirmed it. She's almost at the right level to begin the process, only a few more passes."

"And then she'll be yours. Every secret she knows, and I'm sure you'll keep cultivating that little batch of well-moneyed worshipers she's amassed; they'll be perfect for putting our plans in place."

"And ... for a few other things, too."

"Oh, yes. She'll be trained to treat, although you might want to keep her away from some on the team – they have a thing about Anati."

"Don't we all? At least since you can control her, you don't have to kill her just yet."

"Well, not while she's got her looks. Little Raska here's going to be a very useful piece of property for us, a pretty valuable mongrel slut, all things considered. She's shown her value already, roping in clients we'd love to get our claws into. Now, she'll bring that value to us, like the good little pet she's about to be."

"Can I have a go at her?"

"Oh sure, but only after she's been trained – otherwise, it wouldn't be worth it. To be honest, she's actually under experienced for all of her supposed wiles."

"I suppose. She's a really great find, though. I want to watch you take her down – rapemate her mind, that's such fun to watch!"

"My pleasure. Let's go hit the cooler first – you'll want to have snacks."

Amongst all of those jumbled sensations, one more feeling entered her thoughts, generated from somewhere within her mind. It was a feeling that – had it appeared sooner – might have saved her. Now, at some level, she knew it was too late. That feeling was the fear of regret.

Chapter 21: Humility

After mid-sol, Sahnassa was working on the new VidStar portion of the TransNet site when she heard Vanarra walking into her office down the hall. "Ah, good," Sahni thought. "I've got a question or two to ask her." She got up and went to knock on Van's doorframe when she saw that her boss was laid out on her couch, a throw-pillow over her head, and her tail hanging limp onto the floor. "Van?" she asked carefully, coming into the office and closing the door behind her. "Van, you okay?"

"No," came the short and disgusted answer. Sahnassa pulled a chair over beside the couch and sat down, simply waiting. Realizing what the Nephti had done, Vanarra stated, "I'm not sure I want to talk about this right now."

"Yeah, but … you're scaring me a little. You've never done this before."

"Yes I have, you just haven't seen me. It's just most times I remember to close the door," replied her boss's mumbled voice from the couch. After a moment of Sahni waiting, Van sighed and put the pillow under her head – although she still didn't look towards the Nephti. "You know, you little purebred, dealing with you makes me forget, sometimes, that there is actually a difference between us. We're not really equal," Van grumped.

"That's not true – at least not for you and me. You're my boss and … my friend, Van."

"The rest of Thuria doesn't see it that way."

Sahnassa reached out and put her paw on her boss's shoulder. "Can you please tell me what happened? I might be able to help."

Vanarra sighed and flipped so she could face Sahni, and Sahnassa could see that Van had actually been crying. "We got turned down ... for a really nice event, an awesome joining celebration all because I'm an Anati. They ... said we had no certifications, no awards, and ... that's true. We just have customers who really like us, but apparently, that doesn't matter. We haven't been patted on the head by the right sort, and because – we get to take what they won't do, and if they want something, they take it. We don't even get to compete." Van sat up and put her paws on the floor. "The truth is, kit, that's always how it's been, but what gets me is that ... it's never going to change. We'll just keep dangling down here on the bottom of the business food chain, no matter what we do."

"Your sales are up, though. Your balance sheets are really looking great, and the TransNet site is seeing a lot of activity from our clients' guests."

Vanarra leaned back. "It's all true; it's all true," she admitted, "but my business books have an interesting chapter or two on 'market saturation' and the decline of a business so long as the competitors have an unfair advantage. They do – it's called the approval of the houses."

"But ... but you've managed to build all of this without their help. Why does this bother you so?"

"I've just never had that kind of approval before, I guess," Van stated. "My mom and I were always shunned by those who were avowed. Our lives were ... so hard. You know what I wish, Sahni, and I wish this every single sol – when I go to bed and when I wake up? I wish I could take what I make now, send it back through time, and keep my poor mom from having to do what she did for me – suffer what she did for me. It's like watching someone die in front of you, only to have fifteen ambulance hovers pull up ten passes later. Their approval cost my mother her life, and ... it cost me, too."

"I'm sorry, Van," Sahnassa offered, putting her head down in shame and sadness.

"Well, don't worry about it, kit. I guess if I keep making this business run in spite of not being approved by anyone, then I didn't really need what they have to offer. It's a dream, like being an avowed purebred. It can never happen for me, but ... it doesn't mean I still don't wonder what it would be like."

"I've seen your lair, Van. Being an avowed purebred can mean a lot of good things or a lot of bad things, and … you don't always get to choose. How about this? Just give me twenty percent of your gross pay, and I'll call you de Anasto, okay?" Sahni asked, teasing a little.

"Ouch! Twenty percent!?"

"Yeah, right off the top," Sahnassa explained with conviction. "Your rate may vary, depending on your house, but … yes."

"Hmm … I'm not sure having that little bit between my first and last names is really worth all that. What about for you, kit? Has it been worth it?"

"It's been a mix. There was a long time where it wasn't worth much at all. There were times when it was worth quite a lot. It's hard to say."

"Well, okay then. It's settled. Not going to worry about getting a family name, then. Let's just forget about it and get back to work, okay?"

"Sure, Van. If you want to talk—" Sahni started to offer as she stood, but Van cut her off.

"You'll be way too patient with me, I know. It's nearly employee abuse, kit, putting up with me."

"Has its benefits, though," Sahni chuckled and then stepped towards the door.

"Hold on a … pass," Van stated having glanced at her viewer. "We … we may have that job after all – well, a part of it, anyway."

Sahni turned around, confused. "I thought you said one of the others took it."

"Well, they did, of course, but this says there is … another reception after the joining," Van marveled, trying to sort what the message was actually saying.

"I've heard of a pre-joining, but a post-joining?" Sahni queried, curious.

"Size of it and what they want are right in our sweet spot – a little big, but doable," Van stated, rubbing her chin with her paw. "Say they're even going to have some family jewels there – few matrons and even a dame, maybe. Well, doesn't look like anyone is de Gonari or anyone else off my list. They're talking about some pretty nice money. We … we could do this."

"Not to raise the question in an ugly way or anything, but why would they jump back and ask you to do it after telling you no on the joining?"

"Looking for that, and ... ah. Well, isn't that rich? Seems like that purebred avowed catering firm can't manage both, and the other firms won't take seconds off an enemy. Hmm ... for that matter, why should I?"

Sahnassa chuckled. "You could show them up! How nice would it be if the post-joining was better than the joining and by a long, long way?"

Van began to smile, an evil, feral smile. Just then, the intercom rang. "Yes, Mauft?" Van asked, picking up the receiver. Instantly, Vanarra sobered a bit. "Level one, two, or three? Two, huh? And who are they with? Okay, right. Well, escort them back, then. Yes, I am that concerned." Vanarra put the LineCom down and looked right at Sahni. "Two dames from the de Caterra family are coming into the office. My guess is they want info on the last primal we did – who was there."

"Does it happen a lot?" Sahnassa asked.

"Now and then. Just sit up, be polite, and don't get upset at how they treat me."

Before Sahni had time to think, Mauft was opening the door. "In here, Honored Ones," she rumbled.

Instantly, Van was standing with her eyes averted down. Sahni however, kept her eyes up – as was the custom. The two Faelnar swept into the room looking at Sahnassa like she was an unwashed plate. "Who are you?" the first demanded.

"I am Sahnassa ... de Orturu," Sahni returned, defensive already knowing how the pair would likely treat Van.

"Oh," the dame replied. "Very well. I am Taslanadurini de Caterra – Dame and High Examiner for our family on Thuratan." Sahni chuckled a little inwardly, thinking back to a couple of cases where her father had sliced off the de Caterra's tail in court and given it back to them. "This is Dame Salanaragatti de Caterra – Dame and Associate Examiner."

"In honor, I greet you."

"And the same. Are you in charge of this business?" Dame Taslanadurini asked.

"I work here on contract, Dame." Sahnassa gently indicated Vanarra with her paw, and the pair turned on her.

"*You* are the proprietor of this business?"

Sahni immediately disliked their tone, but kept quiet as Van answered, "And your servant, Honored Ones. What may I do for you this sol?"

"We understand you cater at all of the primals in this area, and we have questions about a specific individual who is attending and what exactly goes on there. We want to know what he's done, in detail."

"With regret, Honored Ones, I ... cannot provide that information. I have a strict confidentiality policy which prevents me from providing that to you."

"Really?" the second dame asked, with disgust. Pulling an object from her robes, she tossed it on Van's desk. "How about a health code violation or two? These should be very easy to find around here, almost as easy as it will be to shut you down."

Van picked up the item and looked at it. Pushing it back towards them, she answered, "Well, then I might just have to break my confidentiality policy – all of it," she said, looking at them, her head still lowered. Something about the way she said it sounded like a warning.

"What? What do you mean by that, mongrel?" Dame Taslanadurini asked.

"I have a record of who, exactly, I've seen at each and every primal I've ever attended, Honored Ones, and there have been quite a few. That ... information is in the paws of someone I trust, several someone's paws – actually, and if anything happens to this business or the staff who work here, that information will be made ... public."

"You dare threaten us?" Dame Salanaragatti nearly shouted.

"It's not a threat – just a matter of fact. Primals are only an alternative venue for cultural expression, after all, and members of nearly every house are seen there. It's quite strange how many of the very rich and powerful from both business and family leadership are present at events that aren't even supposed to happen. The families have nothing to fear from me – I just serve drinks and snacks – fruit juices and rough-cut roots, Honored Ones. That's all. I have no agenda, and I have nothing to gain from knowing that an ... Honored Dame of a family is in attendance – regular attendance."

"You insinuate one from our house, you wretch?" Dame Taslanadurini asked.

"It is not an insinuation, Dames; it's an offer of help. I fear for you, knowing who this is. I … I am but a lowly Anati caterer. I have no real understanding of families or politics, and I have nothing to gain or lose if these honored individuals are found out. With all deference, that's not the case with you. You have so much to lose. Is it really … worth it?"

The pair shot Sahnassa a questioning glance, and she just – wide eyed – shook her head slowly, backing up. The elder of the dames got a worried expression on her face, and her eyebrow fur sank as she concentrated on who they might be hinting at. Several highly placed names obviously came to mind, that was easy to judge by her expression. "Very … well. You will continue to … protect … the names of any and all who attend, no matter their rank?"

"I cannot survive unless I do, and … even mere Anati wish to keep breathing, Honored Ones," Van offered, lowering her gaze in humble respect. "That's all I want – all I aspire to."

"Useful and reliable ones, maybe. Ensure you prove yourself better than your breeding, mongrel," the elder dame huffed and then walked out.

The younger dame turned toward Sahnassa, and Sahni bowed as protocol demanded. The dame returned the gesture, but said, "We trust the de Orturu, as well, to be of their word. Good sol to you."

"And to you, Dame."

As soon as they were gone, Van asked Sahni, "What was all that … stuff they did with you?"

"I don't understand what you mean, Van."

"When family jewels come in here, dames especially, they curse and call names and … well, they're just awful. These … held back," Van replied, sitting on the corner of her desk, facing the Nephti.

"Well, they … they have to address me without insult – it's protocol. If they insult me or treat me badly, then I tell my matron, and my matron tells my dame, and even if our houses aren't on good terms, that could cause trouble for these two. They still called you names, though," Sahni protested.

"Not like they usually do. The de Oterbythe were in here once – ugh! I felt like I needed a bath and to have the walls scrubbed. You

didn't notice anything out of the ordinary, kit, really? All that's …
normal for you?" Vanarra asked, disbelieving.

"They were acting pretty cautious," Sahni observed. "Since
my father is a litigator, I've heard for seasons about this deal and that
deal that was ruined because some low-level dame full of herself took
a claw-strike at someone else from another house. That … that's
enough to sink a fragile business or house alliance; de Caterra has a
habit of ruining their own deals. Maybe, there's something in the
works. Maybe, this time, they're afraid of knocking it off the trail."

"It was interesting, though. Never had a … high inquisitor or
whatever she said she was."

"But," Sahni breathed, "you … you were amazing! They could
have totally gone after you, but they just … walk away?! How did you
do that? Do you have to do that a lot?"

Vanarra sat and put her hind paws up on her desk. "Only every
so often, and generally only once per house. You see, primals are an
interesting alternative venue for cultural expression, but they are also,
as we saw with Raska, a place where temptation can run a little wild.
Nearly everyone who's not supposed to go there actually does at some
point, if they can manage it, and some of them go only once. It's only
the true believers like Mavia who are there time after time. So, my
threat about there being an Honored Dame of the de Caterra who
attended a primal isn't an empty one, and they know it. That's why
the primals have survived, I suppose. Although no one wants their
purebred little kits and cubs romping around all naked, no one's quite
sure who all the Primalists are. Fear is what this is about, Sahni. Fear
that someone higher up than they will want to stop them or fear that
too many below them support it. Mavia is actually very well placed
and pretty influential in her business. If anyone below her, for
example, were to challenge primals – well, they could find Mavia to be
a little unyielding in her criticism or punishment."

"So that's why primals continue to exist – haven't been
stamped out by the matriarchy?" Sahni asked.

"It's more than that, I think," Van offered. "They really are
onto something about the way Thurians were meant to live, and it
touches a lot of us."

"You … are a Primalist?"

"Not so much," Van offered, pulling her hind-paws down. "I
can just see their point of view, and after all, I had to live without a lot
of frill and fluff for a very long time. It's a little strange … and

actually fascinating to see purebreds trying to do what I was forced to – by them, no less. Well, sorry, present company and all that, kit." Van sighed, "It's going to take me awhile to keep from claw-swiping avowed purebreds—"

"I know you only mean some of us, Van," Sahnassa replied, smiling softly. "I understand."

"Thanks, kit. That's kind of you. Alright, I'm going to figure out how to make a 'post-joining' kick the tail off the 'pre-joining' and the 'joining.' So what are you up to?"

"I've got a couple of questions about the VidStar portion of the TransNet site, but they can keep for awhile. In fact, I'll make it both ways and then you can pick, okay?"

"I like options, kit! Go right ahead and … thanks," Van replied, gratefully. Sahnassa nodded, smiling, and left her boss in a much better mood than when she had come in.

"Wow! I've never been in here before. What do you two think?" Van asked in awe as Sahni and Flint walked alongside her through the huge arched ballroom of the Estates Resort, just outside of Shanandrae.

Sahni looked up what she imagined must be thirty tracks to the ceiling and breathed, "It's … it's amazing! It's so elegant! I don't think I've seen a room this pretty, either."

"It's … a big room. Our crew's going to run ragged in here unless we can figure out some way to manage it," Flint commented.

"Oh, but the challenge – to pull off something like this … perfectly! Now, I know why my scared and shivering competitors wanted the joining. That's easy! This … this is going to be really something special!"

"Flint to Vanarra, Flint to Vanarra – this may be too much for us, boss. We're down one set of paws, remember?"

"I can find a few more – we need to do some interviewing and quick," Van replied as she continued scanning the room, leading Flint and Sahni forward through a set of doors into a maintenance way.

"So, we do the event with a bunch of new tails? That won't go over well."

"Put your new tails in the back on a 'trial basis' and on simple tasks. Have our seasoned tails, like dear Sahni here, out front, facing

the guests and providing amazing service! Recommendable service!"
Van mused, excitedly. Flint groaned as Van continued searching
around. "Don't be so sour, Flint. I think we can do this! I'll need to
bring the twins in, provided we can find a … ah ha! It's here – a full
kitchen! We need to find out what they'll let us use and what we'll
have to bring."

"When are we supposed to meet with the organizer?" Sahnassa
asked, curious.

"In about twenty-five passes or so, but I just like to have a
good look around before we start talking," Van noted, opening an oven
door and keying the control to start it. "Looks good," she noted,
feeling it start to heat up. Turning around to Flint, who was still
looking unsure, she explained, "We've got to ask for as much set-up
time as we can, I get that. There's a ton of storage space back here,
though. If we do a lot of prep, pre-stage a bunch, perhaps add in a
rental delivery hover, we can have everything right here and just
waiting for us. All we really have to do is set-up, deliver it, and then
clean up the mess!"

"And you wouldn't book any events in front of this for like …
two sols in advance, and you'd *promise* not to?" Flint asked, doubtful.

"Well maybe if it was something small, and we could spare a
few paws," Van offered. Flint's groan garnered her annoyed response,
"Oh, come on! Not everyone would have to be involved in the prep.
If we had to pull Mauft off admin and Sahni off of her work for a bit,
we could! Sahni can practically run an event on her own now!"

"What?!" Sahni replied, surprised.

"Small office social, perhaps," Van mused checking cabinets
and turning on faucets to ensure the water was running. "Like that one
we did when I first found you – we did it with only three or … four.
Everything in here checks out." Sahni looked up into Flint's eyes
confused and surprised. Flint only smiled grimly and shook his head.
"Oh, you two. Come on! Have a little confidence! We'll talk to the
organizer and just see. Let's go! I'm sure we can do this!"

"Sahni, I don't know if we can do this!" Vanarra breathed in
worry as they watched the throng of guests pile in.

"Van, the room looks amazing! We've been working for three
sols straight, even with another pre-join in the middle of it. The food

is ready and set, and everything's working exactly like it should. You've done a great job! We all have!"

"Oh, tell me that after it's done and we have our pay," Van whispered. "I have to go check on Saiphar and his crew – you have this?"

"I certainly do, Van," Sahnassa stated as she started pouring drinks.

"Well, you'd better! Here they come. Good luck, kit!" Van offered and then sped off to go check another station.

When Sahnassa looked up, she was amazed to see the mass of guests headed in her direction. "Oh my," she breathed. "I hope we can do this."

For the next interval, Sahnassa was moving at high speed, with not even a moment to worry about what was happening with the rest of the event. The group that was already quite convivial was thirstily downing the fermentum and fruit juices – sometimes mixed together, discretely – and the appearance of several "new" employees delivering containers to replace those she was rapidly emptying was the only break in the continual repetition of serving Vulpi after Vulpi, Faelnar after Faelnar, Perratti after Perratti. Most of them treated her nicely enough, and she was working so fast that the line was never more than a few deep at any time – after the initial rush.

A loud knocking over the voice amplification system got everyone's attention, including her own. The group was being called to order, and anyone else who would have been wandering up to get drinks was diverted back to their seats by the announcer. Soon, the guests were being corralled, and Sahni thanked the last guest in her line. Without really thinking about it, Sahnassa made another drink of several fruit juices mixed together and downed it quickly. Looking to her right, she saw Saiphar giving out a final plate of appetizers, but she could tell he was really starting to get tired. Scanning the room, she saw several more of the crew who – although now getting a break – were very definitely feeling the pressure.

Quickly, she mixed two more of her special concoctions and took them over to his table. As she walked, half listening to the announcements and introductions being made, Sahni realized she was actually panting. "Wow!" she whispered as she gave the drinks to a very grateful Saiphar, "I'm … I'm really … winded."

To her surprise, he downed one of the glasses without even stopping to answer, and then said, "Oh, thank you, Sahni! I think I felt my knees shaking. Art … isn't usually … so physical."

"Yeah, tell me about it. You're doing great though! Everyone coming from your direction seemed happy."

"You, too, Sahni. Very … well done. Raska would never have kept up at that pace."

"Thanks," Sahnassa replied, blushing. "I'm going back to my station and pre-set some drinks. Then, I'm going to check on Tresk and see if he needs anything."

"He had better be grateful for your consideration," the Vulpi offered a little shyly as she patted him on the shoulder. "Thank you."

She nodded and stepped away, seeing Vanarra headed at a fast walk towards her station. Sahni nearly jogged ahead so she could beat her. "Okay, Sahni, how did you do?" Van asked, a little flustered.

"As far as I can tell, pretty okay – Saiphar, too. We basically kept up pretty well."

"Thank you, thank you, thank you," Van sighed, putting her paw behind Sahni's back. "I had to pitch in on the other side with Sheffer and Mauft, when I wasn't going to the back to check on things. We were taking some pretty … ugly comments over there."

"Really?" Sahni asked, concerned.

"Yeah – just Anati stuff, everyone was happy with their drinks and food as far as I can tell," Van replied shrugging.

Just then, Tresk walked up to them. "Van, Sahni – we've got a problem."

"What is it?" Van asked.

"Look up on stage," he directed, and Sahni noticed that his eyes were actually fearful.

As they looked, a Faelnar dame was standing at the podium finishing her speech. "And it gives me great pleasure to celebrate this night of union, not only between such a wonderful couple, but between the houses of de Oterbythe, de Kestrick, and de Caterra. All three Grand Matriarchs have gathered here with us this evening to celebrate the Caterrian Accord, bringing our strong houses into an even closer alliance. Together, we will carve out a future that will set us upon the trail towards a Thuria we can be proud of, one that holds to the traditions we have learned as the basis for our society's success."

"You have got to be joking!" Van gasped. "Three matriarchs!? Here!? This ... this was only supposed to be a ... like a ... dame or two!"

"I remember you said they were a little vague on the reason for having such a celebration," Sahni commented. "At least now we know why."

"But, Sahni!" Van asked. "What do I do to take care of three Grand Matriarchs?"

"Anything they ask you to, almost. I ... I would just wait until their speeches were over and politely ask a matron or dame near them what they would want."

Van thought for a moment. "Tresk, I'm going to put Sahni over on the other side of the room closer to me and to where the matriarchs are going to be coming off stage. I may have made a mistake making one side of the room purebred and one side not-so-much. I'll send Sheffer over here to manage Sahni's drink station and have her manage his. Can you keep an eye on him to make sure he stays focused? He was chatting up the guests a little too much on the other side."

"Great – Sheffer-sitting. Okay, Van, only because you asked."

"Good. Okay, Sahni, you're with me! Let's go," she whispered as the Grand Matriarch for de Caterra stood to make her speech.

After hustling her across the room, Vanarra replaced Sheffer and told him where to go, and Sahni was able to clean and take over his station. After the matriarch's speech, Sahni saw the elegant Faelnar step backstage, followed by her retinue of dames. "There she goes, Van."

"I'll go back there, and see if there's anything she wants."

"Be careful, Van! You don't play around with Grand Matriarchs."

Vanarra smirked a little. "Hey, nobody knows that better than me. It's not like I'm going to actually talk to her. I'll do what you said, find a matron or dame, act real humble, and just make sure they don't complain to the organizers that they weren't taken care of."

Sahnassa was still worried for her friend, but agreed, "Alright." With that, Van was away. As the passes went by and the de Kestrick matriarch droned on about her affinity and fellowship with the de

Caterra and the de Oterbythe, Sahni started getting even more anxious. Finally, Flint came up beside her. "Hey, have you seen Van?"

"I did. I think she went backstage. Flint, I need for you to cover for me, please, for just a few passes. I need to make sure she's alright."

"They'd probably respond to you better than to me. Go ahead. I'll take care of this."

Sahnassa patted him on the back and slipped towards the double doors. As she approached them, she heard shouting – angry shouting. Quickly, she opened and closed the doors, trying to keep as little sound as possible from leaking out into the ballroom. Sadly, as she approached, she realized what was going on.

"And with what *audacity* would a little mongrel bitch like you even suppose to come and talk to us!? You – the accidental byproduct of a pair of feckless outcasts who couldn't listen to the call of honor over the sound of their own ruts – mating like lower animals and weaving a genetic mistake in the desecrated depths of your dam's womb! Oh, that you would have only had the grace to abort yourself in that pitiless hole in your mother's guts."

The torrent of insults from the dame, pouring over her for the last several passes had driven Vanarra to her knees. Her head down, she had quietly approached and softly asked if there was anything they required, and that simple act had started this venomous tirade that was steadily breaking down Van's ability to tolerate. It was taking every bit of concentration she could manage to keep her back furs down and her claws sheathed. Worse, still, there was no way out. The dame wouldn't even give her a word in edgewise to apologize, back away, or even stand up and run – she was right on top of her, the dame's spit lighting on the tops of her ears.

"Excuse me?!" a voice called from behind Van.

"What?!" the dame called out, annoyed that her berating of the Anati had been interrupted. "Who are you?"

"I am Sahnassa … de Orturu, Honored One. Is there a problem?" she asked, politely.

"I would like to know who it was that sent this piece of walking excrement to me posing as a server?!"

"If you would please forgive it, Honored One, that was me, and I was in error for doing so. If you would kindly allow me to dismiss her back to her duties, I will attend the needs of you and your group directly."

The dame actually backed up a couple of steps. "That was a horrible judgment call! You certainly should have known better."

Vanarra was amazed at the interchange, but still didn't move. Sahni was shifting the focus off of Van, willingly standing in front of her like a shield.

Sahnassa bowed low. "Of course, Honored One, I can truly see that now. I can only offer the excuse that it has been a very challenging event for my firm, and we are short staffed. It was an error to send this one to you, but it was certainly not meant as an insult. I am so deeply sorry for the unintentional offense, Honored One. How can I better serve you?"

"First, remove this one from our presence," she demanded.

"Very well, Honored One." Sahnassa stepped over to Van and stood between her and the dame. Leaning down, Sahni whispered, "Please, just get up and turn round at the same time. Send me Saiphar, and we'll take care of them, okay?"

Van did exactly what Sahni directed without asking, only Sahnassa knowing how hard Van was working trying to keep her temper under control. Sahni sighed inside, knowing that Van would probably fire her for taking over like that, but glad that she was able to put some of what she learned growing up to good use. Turning around smartly, when her friend was well away, Sahni bowed again and asked, "Now, what may I get that can please you, Honored One? We have so many choices tonight."

Vanarra left the double doors feeling almost completely out of control. The insults of the dame had just beat at her again and again, and if it wasn't for the mental image of the orphans, she wouldn't have held out as long as she had. Flint could easily see his boss wasn't in a good place and quietly stepped over to her, able to talk as the gentle applause signaled the end of the de Kestrick matriarch's comments. "You ... okay?"

"Damn it, no! I just got ... cursed every way I can think of by some damn de Caterra dame!"

"Where's Sahni?

"Taking her turn with the damned purebred," Van cursed quietly. "She ... she ... helped me get away with at least a shred of my self-respect. I'll watch this station here. Go get Saiphar and send him to me. Take over for him there. It looks like Sahni and Saphy are going to take care of the family jewels tonight."

"Alright. I'll do it."

Intervals later, Van's beleaguered troops finally assembled in the middle of the empty banquet hall. "Everyone," Van breathed, smiling, although clearly tired, herself. "We ... we did it!" There were cheers from everyone, including Tresk, as she held up the draft with their pay. "You ... you all deserve ... enormous praise! I've never seen a group work ... so hard. Just ... completely ... amazing! Needless to say, you all have the sol off tomorrow with pay – myself included!" Van exclaimed as she sank comically into a chair to the chuckles, applause, and laughs all around her.

"I can't believe it!" Tresk guffawed.

"Finally! She's the one who's wiped out!" Flint chuckled.

Van's continued antics feigning exhaustion drew even more applause from the tired group. Suddenly, however, Van stood and looked right at Sahni. "Oh, but everyone! Everyone! There was one ... severe breach of procedure tonight. Sahnassa de Orturu – come here!" Van demanded. Sahnassa, a little unsure, walked up and stood in front of her boss. "Everyone, Sahnassa and I have had several conversations about *not* presuming to take charge or step beyond her place in this business. Well, she certainly did tonight! Seriously, everyone – she absolutely walked up when the client and I were having a private discussion, interrupted us, and ... well... ordered me to leave!"

Try as she might, Vanarra couldn't feign the right kind of anger – everyone around her had heard some small bit of what had happened, and even Sahni, herself, knew at this point that Van wasn't really angry. "Everyone, I ... I just can't do this!" Vanarra gave up, reaching out for her friend and embracing her, causing all those around to clap. Holding her back, she said, "Look, she saved this event. I romped right up to a dame, and she ... she just went after me. She called me everything she could think of and then she said some really hurtful, ugly things to me, and honestly, I thought I was going to be carried out by enforcement for clawing the fur off a dame when Sahni came and stood up for me. She put herself between that dame and me and got me out of there. If she hadn't, I don't know what would have happened! For all of you who covered Saiphar and Sahni while they got those ... crazy family jewels everything they asked for, thank you, and thank you two, as well."

"It ... it was my honor, Van," Saiphar offered.

"And mine," Sahni affirmed.

"Thank you," Van replied. "Alright everyone, we still have to do clean-up, so we'll save any other review for later. Let's get going!" In good spirits, the group disbanded to complete their tasks.

"Goodnight, Saiphar," Van bade as she hugged the Vulpi artist. "Well done."

"You also, Van. Sahni, it was … an honor working with you," the Vulpi offered, bowing to the Nephti.

"And for me, as well," she replied, sweetly, returning the gesture.

Looking a little nervous and unsure, Saiphar stood and added, "Uh … goodnight, then."

As he turned and walked away, Sahni and Van sat out on the terrace just outside of the ballroom, feeling the cool breeze blowing through their fur and watching the commercial flyers crisscross the skies above them. Slowly pulling her hind paws onto a chair facing her, Van sighed, "Oh, I can't believe we actually did it."

"But you did, Van! We just helped. Was that the biggest event you've ever done?"

Slowly, Vanarra nodded. "Primals – they don't have those numbers or any kind of family jewels present. Do you have any idea how many went through your station tonight?"

Sahnassa shook her head. "Too busy trying to get things done, I suppose. You know, when I did the clean-up, there wasn't a single one of your cards left on any of the tables, though. I saw several taking them as they came up for drinks. I think you're going to get a lot of new business out of this – your crowning glory," Sahnassa chuckled.

"Crowning? What's that?"

"Something from the old times. One of the Nephti clans – de Fantar, I think – actually put circles of gold on their chieftain's heads, and that's what they called it – a crown. Later, when they figured out how impractical that was, they used it as a reward or a prize at a sporting event," Sahni replied, letting her head go back and taking in a large breath.

"So, you saying I won the prize tonight?" Sahni's nod and grunt of approval, with her eyes closed and her muzzle bearing a proud smile warmed Vanarra's heart. "If I won any prize tonight, it's that I ... did what you told me to do when I was about to lose it."

"You really trusted me, Van," Sahnassa replied. "That ... meant a lot."

"That allowed you to help me. I would have never accepted that from you before – oh, how foolish I was!"

"Excuse me?" a tentative male voice called from the doorway to the ballroom.

"Oh, sorry! Is it time to lock up?" Van queried, turning around expecting to see one of the resort staff, but instead, it was a Nephti, one she thought she recognized from the event. Standing carefully, Van asked, "Is there something wrong? Did you leave something behind?"

"Well, no, actually. I was just wondering if you were the one on this card?" he asked.

Instantly, Vanarra recognized one of her own business cards. "Why yes, that's me. What can I help you with?"

"Well, I know you're probably exhausted from what you did tonight – I mean, I watched you all moving around making the night just ... perfect for everyone involved, and I wanted to thank you and ... ask a favor."

"Oh, why thank you!" Van replied, smiling – a little too tired to pull out all of her charm. "Sure, what can I help you with?"

"Well, my name is Calisair de Fantar, and my eldest is getting joined in about a moon, and we ... we are new to the area – just transferred in. We're still waiting to figure out who our matron will be and all, and we're trying to put together the ceremony, the joining – all of it. We're a little worried about the timing."

"Whatever you need, Calisair, I'm sure we can be of help. Come, sit for a moment or two, and let's talk through what you need and how we can help."

Sahni smiled, not only to reassure the tentative Calisair, but also from the feelings of happiness and fulfillment she felt coming from her friend as the two began to speak.

A moon later, Sahni walked into Vanarra's office. "Good morning! How did it go last night?"

"Pretty well, I think," Van noted looking up from her pile of papers. "Just going through the feedback sheets, now. I sure could have used you, but ... I understand. What did your matron want?"

"Dinner, actually, and ... to talk. I think she's happy with me, and thankfully, the little side projects she's come up with won't take me much time."

"Not for our competitors, I trust?" Van asked, warily.

"Not hardly, unless you want to go into the legal profession," Sahni chuckled at Van's look of disgust. "They need an extra paw every now and again to help them with back-ups and a little server tuning. That's just until their normal kit gets back from having her latest cub."

"How many do they have?" Van asked, picking up on something in Sahnassa's tone.

"Seven. Seven cubs – not a single kit. The mother swears the father is to blame—"

"He certainly is," Van mused seductively, "but he's got to have some really ... interesting technique to ... plow a male into her every time!"

"Ugh! Van! Mental image!" Sahnassa complained as she closed her eyes, and Van laughed.

There was a knock on the side of the door, and to both of their surprise, the Nephti who had been the customer at the last event – Calisair de Fantar – was standing at the door. "Oh my goodness!" Van gasped. "I'm so sorry – we were just having a bit of fun! We don't normally get visitors this early in the morning."

"It's perfectly alright. I just wanted to let you know that last night was truly amazing, and ... I have another request for you, if that's alright."

"Well, certainly!" Van replied, motioning him in, Sahnassa standing along with her boss. "Although I thought, Calisair, that you said the one that got joined last night was your only one of age. Please tell me that cute little kit hasn't found her someone special!"

Calisair chuckled, "Oh at six seasons of age, little Calliana is still playing with a new favorite each moon – leaving a trail of droopy ears and tails whenever she sets them aside."

"Oh, isn't she the lucky one," Sahnassa replied, smiling. "It's so nice to see you again. Should I go, though?

"I suppose you can stay, because it's not really a joining I'm talking about having you cater. Can we sit and chat for a moment?" he asked.

"Certainly," Vanarra replied, although it was clear her curiosity was piqued.

"Thank you," he offered as he sat. "I'm a member, one of the directors actually, of a business pack – namely the Association of Service and Commerce. We're also called the ASC for short. We represent service businesses and transport companies not only on this continent, but on several others. It's always been a part of our charter to support new and upcoming business with start-up grants, talent recognition, and awards."

"Ah, so it's a rewards banquet. We've done lots of those, haven't we Sahni?" Van asked, and Sahni nodded in return.

"I'm afraid you don't understand. I would like to submit your business as a contender in one or more of our awards programs. For example, there is an award for the fastest growing or the most charitable or even the most compelling success story." Seeing Sahni and Van return blank stares, he continued to explain. "You have to understand that the joining prior to the event you catered – the one for the matriarchs – didn't go … well. Everyone was pretty grumpy and unhappy until they made it to your event. Then, everything was free and easy and simple and good and just … nice. The joining you catered for us last night – that's going to be with us our entire lives, Vanarra. Your team made that evening absolutely magical," he said sincerely.

"But … the ASC," Van stuttered, stunned by what he was proposing and nearly speechless. "I … I mean we're not exactly a purebred business here, not avowed, anyway. Would … do you think they would … like consider us? Really?"

"I believe so. There's a local business owner in your area – Buck Harlock. He's a recipient and now on our community stewardship committee. He's a member of the ASC."

"Really?" Van replied, wide-eyed. "But … I mean he's still a … purebred, right?"

"He is, but there are quite a number of us who realize that we can't ignore the contributions of business owners who … are a little different. If you run a business that is above reproach, serve a valued customer base, engage in charity for those less fortunate, and run your operation well, then that should be recognized and lauded, appropriately.   I believe your business would be an excellent candidate. It may interest you to know that I have received several inquiries about your business even last night – in my TransNet mail. Your business is attracting attention, and even if you do submit and are not favored with a win, the exposure is substantial. Businesses may not apply to compete for these awards – they must be *asked*."

"And ... Calisair de Fantar ... you ... you are asking me?" Van queried, still unsure.

"I am," he stated firmly. "I will warn you that it is not an easy submission process, and it requires garnering recommendations from clients, opening your financials to some level of scrutiny, and business-appropriate reviews – and since your business is catering, you could expect that health and safety reviews would be part of the mix. However, entrants will have their information – especially their services and charitable contributions – shared with every other business leader in the ASC – that's more than five hundred area business leaders. The winners will be honored at a special dinner and be presented with a plaque and permission to use the association's insignia in their advertising."

Vanarra was still completely stunned and nearly panting – unable to speak. "Calisair," Sahni interjected, "this sounds like an amazing opportunity! How often do they give out these awards?"

"Only once every five seasons, here on Thuratan. Where I came from, they did it every two, but ... I think five is better. So, would you be interested in submitting an application?"

"I ... would be ... honored," Van replied, and Sahni could see that Vanarra was trying very hard not to cry.

"Very good," he replied. "Here is the application." He offered a data wafer which Sahnassa gently took from his paw. "It needs to be submitted before the next moon. I have to warn you that the pace of ASC decisions is a little slow, but that's only because we are very careful to pick exactly who deserves it."

"Thank ... you very much, Calisair," Van offered, still blinking back tears. Standing, she walked towards him. "I ... I want you to know that ... even if nothing comes of this, you've ... paid me ... a truly ... wonderful compliment. It was my honor to serve you, and I would happily do it again."

"And that," the Nephti replied, smiling, "is why you make a very good candidate. Now, good chances to you. I bid you good morning." He bowed, and still smiling, left the room, closing the door behind him.

"Sahni!   Sahni!" Van whispered, and then started crying. Instantly, Sahnassa was close to her, her paw on the mixed blood's shoulder.

"That … that was really incredible, Van! Amazing! I'm so proud of you – it's very much deserved."

"I don't know what to do!" Van replied, abruptly turning away. "A part of me is … revolted by the thought of doing everything he said to … have some purebreds just laugh me off as a joke, but he made it sound like I … an Anati … could actually … win!" Turning back to Sahnassa who was standing back a little, giving Vanarra the space she needed, Van added, "I … have dreamed my whole life of what it would be like to be accepted by avowed purebreds as an equal. I … haven't even hoped to be … applauded by them! To have one come in here seeking me out for … what?! An award!? It's … it's just too fantastic to be real! They'll never accept me – they'll never—"

Van stopped talking because Sahnassa had folded her arms and started looking at her, critically. "I did," Sahni corrected. "I accepted you, and after your crowning glory, I told you that you had won an award with me. Surely I'm not the only one who can see how amazing you are, Van! You have orders pouring in like water in a thunderstorm! You … you practically keep the orphanage solvent and supplied all by yourself! I am going to go into my office, download this wafer, and start bringing things for you and Flint to look at. That sound okay?"

"Yes … yes it does. Thank you, Sahni. Thank you … very much," Vanarra offered, lowering her head. Sahnassa was about to leave, but sighed. Looking at her usually tough boss, she could see that unique and tender vulnerability exposed as Van stood looking at the floor, her mind obviously overcome with emotions. Walking forward, she added, "I … I don't quite know how you feel about hugs sometimes, but … you really need one now. As a friend, I'm telling you that."

When Van didn't move, Sahnassa sighed again and quietly started to step away. "Sahni?"

"Yes?"

"I … uh, yeah," Van offered quietly, as if barely able to move or form words. "Please?"

Stepping carefully forward, Sahnassa reached under Van's arms and pulled her close, placing her muzzle on Van's shoulder, inviting her to do the same. Sahni was amazed at how slow and hesitantly Van was moving. Closing her eyes, she tried to imagine what her friend was feeling, and the sense that came back to her was chaotic and very turbulent, very deep. Gradually, Sahnassa was compelled to tighten her embrace on Vanarra, and the tighter she held her, the more the edge of the storm started to dull. Finally, Sahni rearranged her paws and gently squeezed Van almost as hard as she could, and finally the storm inside of her friend seemed to settle and fade. Afraid she was hurting her friend, she started letting go, but then Van's arms were around her, hugging her back – not fiercely, but gratefully – if the sense Sahni had from her was correct.

They held the embrace for a few moments longer, Sahni gently releasing her friend. When she stepped back, Van looked at her, nervous and embarrassed – the rise of her blush furs a most unusual occurrence. "Yes, well … you were right. I did … need that, I mean."

"Look, just take some time and think it through. I'll pull everything off, look at it, and get it organized for you. If you don't want to do it, I'm not suggesting you should or that you have to do anything. You are the boss, after all."

Van managed a chuckle at that one. "Okay, Sahni. Thank you, kit."

"Okay," Sahnassa offered, and then left to see what was stored on the little data wafer.

In less than an interval, the contents of that humble looking data wafer were sitting as a large stack of papers in the center of Vanarra's desk.

"You have got to be kidding, kit," Van breathed as she leaned forward and stared at the mound of paper Sahnassa had printed out.

"No, and this isn't all of it," Sahni replied, clearly daunted by what she had been reviewing. "Some of those items are only forms that have to be copied and filled out by multiple clients. There are also requirements for auditors we have to hire from a certain list and inspectors who have to look at our business – it's a whole list! We'd … we'd barely have half a moon to get it all done!"

"Oh, it sounded like such a good idea at the time," Van mused. "I don't know. I … I don't think we can keep things going for our clients if we take all this on. I mean we can't shut down our business to fill out … all this!"

"Didn't Calisair mention something about … Buck Harlock? Do you think he could help figure this out?"

"Maybe. Alright, kit. I'll try to call him and figure out if this is worth doing," Van sighed, "if we even can."

"I'll go and set up folders to save all this stuff on back-up drives. If we do this," Sahni asserted, "the last thing we'll want is to have to do any of it twice. Thankfully, we can key the information into the forms so if someone's paw-writing isn't great, we can transcribe, but everything, and I mean everything has to be witnessed, and it has to be by an uninterested third party that's certified to do so."

"I … don't know. Okay, go set things up or take a shot at it. I'll try to call him."

Sahnassa left, and Van picked up her LineCom to dial. After the initial pleasantries with the receptionist were concluded, Vanarra was surprised to be patched right into his office. "Buck Harlock, managing partner, can I help you?"

"Buck Harlock, you hotty!" Van exclaimed, and instantly the line cut off. "Uh oh," she breathed and carefully put the LineCom back in its holder. "I think … I should have made sure that the receptionist told him who … it was."

Not more than a pass later, Mauft informed her that a LineCom call had come in for her. "Who is it, Mauft?"

"He's telling me that its Hotty Harlock calling. Should I dump the call?" Mauft asked.

"No, no – I deserve that. Go ahead and patch him through," Van sighed. In a moment, the call clicked in. "Vanarra Anasto, managing to put her hind paw into it, may I help you?" she asked, embarrassed.

"Yes, you were on speaker," Buck complained, "and I was doing an employee review … on appropriate office behavior."

"Oh no, Buck! I'm … I'm like really sorry—"

"No, it actually turned out okay," he chuckled. "It was a bit of an object lesson, I'm afraid. I also didn't mean to disconnect you. I was planning to hit the hold button and … well, missed - honestly. First time, too. I'm usually pretty good about that. So, I'm sorry I sliced off the call."

"You were perfectly within your rights, Buck. It's … not exactly the most respectful greeting—"

"Hey," he interrupted. "Minus the times done when others can hear it, it's a nice ego boost! So, don't worry about it. What did you want to talk about?"

"Well," Van started as she flipped through the large stack of paper on her desk, "I had someone … Calisair de Fantar, actually, in here earlier."

"I know him," Buck commented. "Pretty good guy. I've dealt with him a few times on projects for his off-continent interests. He want to book an event with you?"

"Already did, and it went well. He … he seemed impressed, which is good of course, but then he … like tells me he wants me to apply for an award with something called the ASC."

"Oh wow, Van, really? That's pretty good – you must have truly impressed him! He's the one who put me in for the awards, as well."

"So, how many hundreds of employees did you have working on the application?" Van queried.

Buck's amusement was obvious in his response. "Oh, don't tell me that a stack of paperwork that is as high as your ear-tips is daunting the famous Vanarra Anasto!"

"Yeah … a little," Van admitted. "And from what Sahni just told me, it all has to be properly witnessed and validated as being authentic. We have less than half a moon – I've got to know here, Buck. Is this worth it?"

There was a brief pause as Buck considered his words. "Van," he began carefully, "if you were a business that was avowed, had the full support of a powerful and influential family, and had no problems gaining entry into any market you choose, then no – the ASC award wouldn't mean very much, but for my business, especially given my status, to have won that award – it … it means a lot. It's not a replacement for the endorsement and commendation of a house, but it's a very close second. We put the ASC logo on the bottom of all of our sales material with our awards and dates. They are staking their honor upon the fact we are a good business, and we've proven that. I firmly believe that bit of official recognition has helped to keep our current clients with us and bring in significant business. My client portfolio jumped thirty seven percent after the awards – every one of my new clients were ASC members."

"Really?" Van asked, beginning to become a little more interested. "I have to tell you that I was really touched that he wanted to consider me for any reward. I think ... that's a first for me, Buck."

"Vanarra," he replied encouragingly, "you are one of the smartest and toughest business Thurians I know, and you are also one of the most charitable and tender hearted. We give free computing resources to some charitable organizations, but I don't know anyone in the whole ASC who can lay claim to keeping an orphanage going."

"But will they care? It's charity – I get that, but it's for Anati or cast outs," she argued.

"Charity is charity," he replied, and she could almost hear the shrug. "It doesn't matter why the needy are needy when you're evaluating the charity of the giver. I can help you, if you'd like, get a hold on this, share what we learned from our submission, help you organize it," he offered.

"Sahni thought she had some ideas about that, as well. She said she was going to set up something on the server to hold all this stuff, if we decide to go through with it. Could ... you, like, come over tonight and talk me through some of this? I ... just know that if this could help some of those clients who back off when they learn what I am – that would be huge," she told him. "I mean, that would be fewer times I'd come back to the office feeling like a nobody because we lost a new client for being just Anati and cast outs."

"Van, for you, I would be happy to. I have the evening free."

"I thought you were looking for someone to keep your evenings ... not so free," she asked, carefully.

"Didn't work out and exactly like I thought it might. Thankfully, she broke it off before it got too far – it's less time I'll spend licking my claw-marks."

"Oh, poor Bucky," she sighed. "I'm sorry. Okay, if you come over, I'll make sure you get some good food and ... passable company."

"More than passable, Van," he chided her. "Much more than that."

"Thank you, Hotty," she teased. "See you an interval after work?"

"Sure, normal time. See you soon, Van. You know, you've really got an opportunity here."

"Really?"

"Yes. I think you could show the purebred aristocracy what Anati could mean and turn a curse into an adulation. You clawed out everything all on your own, without the benefit of a house. You've got a business that should be admired by everyone, but there was no … matron hovering over you telling you to donate something to a charity so it would look more honorable. You did those things because of who you are. That deserves some real, true recognition, Van. That deserves to be applauded."

His compliment warmed her, and she sighed, "You are such a good friend, Buck. Thank you. See you after work, okay? I may have Sahni stay, too, if she's able. I think Flint has something tonight; I can catch him up."

"Sounds like a plan," he replied brightly. "I'll see you then."

"Till then, dear Buck. See you."

Vanarra leaned back and took in everything he said. Her entire adulthood had been spent trying to eke out a life beneath the level of the purebred avowed – never having any hope of penetrating their secure little society in any real way. Now, that default competitive advantage her opponents had could possibly be assailed by the ASC logo proudly adorning her TransNet site and her sales materials. She could even have Sahnassa make first contact with those clients who were a little squeamish about conducting business with Anati. "She'd need a lot of training up on sales, but … she could do it. She … probably would, if I asked her to," Van mused aloud.

The huge, nagging worry about the ultimate viability of her business now didn't seem so impossibly insurmountable. "All I have to do," she told herself as she looked down at the pile of paper, "is climb to the top of this and have us look good when it's done." Pulling the papers close to her, she started looking through them, seriously reading to determine exactly how she could assemble all the material that was needed in the little amount of time she had.

For the past five sols, the material on the small data wafer had been wreaking havoc on Vanarra's office. What started as an awe-inspiring mountain of recommendations and reports, far too daunting to attempt, had turned into a goal Vanarra and everyone else in the office were willing to fight to achieve. Van had called all of them to the back and announced what the business had been offered, and the entire group had decided to throw in their support – wholeheartedly.

That was fortunate, because between trying to keep her normal business running and garnering all of the recommendations from clients, assembling everything needed for the audits, and cleaning every corner of her building to a high shine, the intervals spent in the office by nearly everyone doubled. Only Mauft was excused to leave at her normal time to take care of the orphans. Sahnassa, however, had been working almost as much as Vanarra, barely getting five intervals of sleep each night before running back into the office to continue keying paw-written recommendations and preparing them for signatures and witnessing.

"Sahni!" Van called as she rushed into the Nephti's office. "Where is the de Bosnar recommendation!? That one's missing from the pile!"

"Oh, one tick! Let me look!" Sahni begged, scrambling around on her computer. "It … it failed to print. Let me try again."

"Please, please hurry, kit! We only have three intervals before this has to go into the paws of the courier, and Aviale de Bosnar is coming by in like three passes!"

"Okay, trying again. What?! No, you … dumb little runner! You are NOT going to update yourself now—" Sahni growled as she reached around and yanked the network connection out of her computer. "We have a deadline to meet! There. Now, it's going to print."

Van smirked as she said, "Remind me never to update my look when you have a deadline. You just yanked its tail out!"

"Only when it slows me down! If this keeps up, I swear I'm going to change runners – this is ridiculous! Okay. Here it is, Van," Sahni offered as she pulled it off the printer.

"Great," Van replied gently taking it. "Thank you!"

Vanarra strode back to her office and found Mauft waiting for her. "What's up?"

"We have to find another courier – the first one called in and said their guy was sick."

Van was stunned. "Don't they have anyone else?"

"Looks like there's a lot of business going on right now," Mauft noted.

"Oh, alright. Pull out the high-priced one, and tell them there is something really nice for them if they can pull it off."

"Okay, Van," Mauft replied and went back to her desk.

Two and a half intervals later, Vanarra put the heavy packet into the paws of a secured courier and signed the final form, releasing it into the Pantera's custody for delivery to the ASC board. "There it goes, Mauft! There it goes!" Van nearly giggled. "We did it! We did it!"

"If anything will come of it," Mauft said dubiously.

"It already has," Sahni offered, coming to stand alongside her boss. "Van, you now know how much your customers love you and appreciate your business, and how much we do, as well. Regardless of what happens with this, you have won with them."

"Oh, thank you, kit. Thank you, both. I hope this works out; I really do. Now, comes the tough part."

"What?" Mauft asked.

"Waiting," the pair of friends said in response at the same time.

"Morning, Van!" Sahnassa called as she walked past Van's door. Over the past ten sols, Van's greetings had grown more and more subdued as no word or response had been received from the ASC submission. This sol, however, there was nothing, and that worried Sahnassa. She put her things down at her desk and went back towards her boss's office. Stepping carefully in, she saw Van, nearly scowling at her viewer. "What's wrong?"

"We've sagged on profits," Van replied unhappily.

"Why?" Sahni asked.

"It's the ASC submission," Van nearly growled. "It has to be. I spent too much time focusing on that damned thing and not enough getting new business, and now we're paying for it. I think … I think it will be a very long time before I do another one of those. You run around, prettying things up and getting all these fur-stroking letters of recommendation – all the while," Van stated, turning around to Sahni and leaning back into her chair, "you short the very customers you were supposed to be serving. As far as we know, they got the whole packet, saw who it was from, and tossed it into the garbage."

"I don't think so, Van. You … you simply had too much good there," Sahni tried.

"It's about what I am, Sahni. It will always be that. Because I'm a Vulpi-painted Faelnar, I'm never going to get respect, let alone an award from anyone of the avowed purebred set," Van stated, and when Sahni looked like she was going to respond, Van closed her eyes and sighed, "I know you do, Sahni. I know you do. You're ... just the crazy one, I guess."

"Maybe, but I guess I just enjoy being crazy," she offered. "And besides, you're not just a Vulpi-painted Faelnar."

"Oh alright – I'm a Vulpi-painted Faelnar with a few special features – optional accessories," she joked. Sahni laughed, and Van smiled, but then grew a little more serious. "I'm kicking myself, though. I ... picked a really bad time to trade out my gold roller for a new Racerra 3000. It's being delivered here after mid sol."

"Well, that's nice, right?" Sahni asked, carefully.

"Not so," Van corrected. "If I had been patient, I could have made up the difference from what I spent on my down-payment. Now, I'm either going to withdraw from my savings or short the orphanage's check this go round."

"Your savings will recover, Van," Sahni quietly stated, knowing instinctively that Vanarra would never fail to provide those kits and cubs what was needed.

"Yeah," Van replied, smiling softly at the purebred Nephti's understanding of her character.

At that moment, Sahni heard a sound behind her that was out of place. "One tick, Van. I ... I think someone's out front," she said, stepping out.

"Probably just Digger again. If he keeps this up, we'll have to get him his own key," she suggested. A few passes later, Sahni returned holding an envelope. "What was it?"

"A courier, with something ... really pretty ... for you," Sahni replied, smiling hopefully.

Curious, Van reached out for and took the offered note. "Wonder what this is?"

"It has an ASC logo on the back," Sahni replied.

"Oh," Van said, sitting up a little. "Well, let's see now." Carefully, Van slipped an expressed claw-tip into the slit along the top and drew out the letter, reading it aloud. "From the Association of Service and Commerce Awards review board – Greetings. After reviewing your very well prepared submission, the ASC governing pack leaders would be honored to have you attend the awards ceremony and dinner, next moon, at the scenic and beautiful Meeting Den Resort in the Yarvea mountains. Extensive consideration of your business's history, efficiency, profitability, and charity have led to what we hope you will consider a very positive result. Accommodations will be provided by the ASC, at no expense to you. We look forward to honoring … your accomplishments."

"Oh … my … Van!" Sahni breathed as a stunned Vanarra just stared at the invitation, wondering if it was real. "I … I think you won!"

"I … uh, well … I uh…" Van stuttered. "It … it does … sound good. Do you think it's a joke? Someone trying to set me up for something?"

"I don't think so, Van, really," Sahni said excitedly. "Call your friend! Ask him!"

"Oh, not a bad idea," Vanarra noted and, paws shaking, she pressed the paw-free option on her LineCom and started dialing. "Buck … Buck Harlock, please – oh, and does he have anyone in his office right now?" The receptionist answered no and connected the call.

"Buck Harlock, managing partner, can I help you?"

"Buck Harlock, you hotty!" Van called out to him, making Sahni cover her muzzle to hide her blush furs.

"Well, thank goodness I'm not on speaker this time. So," he asked slyly, "what causes your fair and lovely voice to grace my humble LineCom this morning?"

"I … I have an envelope here, Bucky," she started.

"And," he replied, but Sahni smiled, hearing the amused catch in his voice.

"And … it says some … things," Van replied, faltering a little.

"Most envelopes do," he commented. "If they didn't, there wouldn't be much point in sending them, would there?"

"I'm beginning to suspect that you know what *this particular* envelope says inside."

"Well, if I did, that truly would be a spectacular feat, wouldn't it now?" he teased.

"Yeah, so … they want me up there … at the Meeting Den. They are saying nice things about me. Does … what does that mean?"

"What do you think?"

"Buck," she breathed, "I … I know this must be fun for you, but this sounds just way too good to be real. I'm … it's got to be a con job, really – I mean, come on."

"It's not, Van."

"You know something, Buck Harlock. What are you not telling me?" Van nearly growled.

"All three, Van. All three."

"All three what?"

"All three awards, Van. I checked with the board steward last night, just to be sure. It wasn't even close."

"Are you saying I won, Buck? Really?" Van asked, cautious hope in her voice.

"I'm not allowed to tell you – that information is strictly private. However, you should go, and you should dress very nicely. I'm sorry. That's all I can say, but I will say this – I am very, very proud of you."

"Oh, Buck," she breathed, the truth of it finally starting to sink in. "I … I can't believe it! I … they couldn't have!"

"Hey, if last time's winner was a cast out from de Caterra, why couldn't this one be someone of mixed blood? Everyone else's business has been established and … stagnant for seasons. Yours hasn't been. Good things are coming, Van – recognition and some very long overdue acceptance – things you truly deserve."

"Thank you, Bucky," Van replied sweetly. "You … you are the best, you know?"

"Not this time," he chuckled. "Take care, Van." The line went quiet, and Van just sat there, staring at it.

Sahnassa walked slowly forward and stepped behind her boss, putting her paw on the mixed-blood's shoulder.

Vanarra was transfixed in that moment, looking at the LineCom and again at the invitation. An avowed purebred's paw offering friendship and support, an invitation for her to attend an awards banquet where she wasn't catering it – she was the one winning the award, and a future where her business would grow and flourish in the radiant glow of the sunlit sky – not cowering in the shadows; all these things swirled in her mind, connected, and flew like an arrow of light into her soul – her memories.

"Vannie," her mother offered tenderly.

"Yes, Mom?" her young voice asked.

"I love you, Vannie. Remember, I don't care what the world says about you. I will always believe in you."

"Thanks, Mom," her own voice replied, and the feeling of being embraced echoed in her.

"You've done it. Lived in the world and bloomed like the flower you truly are," her lost love Ashalam's voice called into her thoughts. "Blossoming as I knew you would, my love. Be well."

Distant echoes of watery memories played in her thoughts. "She's beautiful, Shenaria. I think … she will be … amazing. Our little Vannie."

When Vanarra began to sense the world around her again, she felt Sahnassa hugging her – embracing her. She didn't even realize that she had stood up, and the enormous feeling of freedom and hope she felt was amazing. "I … I never thought it was possible, kit. Never…" she breathed.

"With you, Van," Sahni replied releasing her, "nearly everything is possible."

The End

Epilogue

Sahni gasped as they entered the lobby of the elegant and stately resort. "Wow! This ... this is beautiful!"

"Not bad! And this area would do perfect as a pre-convention banquet," Van noted, scanning around the space. "Look, you can even direct those not attending over there to the reception desk and leave this whole section here for – look, this is the perfect space for drinks and a centerpiece—"

"Van," Sahni teased. "You're here to win an award, not cater an event!"

"Who knows," Vanarra offered as she let Sahni lead her in further. "With this award, we might actually get to cater venues like this!"

"Kind of far away, isn't it?" Sahni asked as they stepped over to a table by draped with the Association of Service and Commerce banner.

"You never know! Oh, hi there," Van replied, glancing down at the banner as she continued, "I'm Vanarra Anasto. I ... was given this invitation."

A sleek and attractive young Faelnar took it from her and, with a thick de Mistral accent replied, "Oh yes. We have you on the list! Your bags are in the receiving area, yes?"

"They are," Sahni offered.

"Very well. We have some wonderful accommodations fairly close to the lobby, but not too close, you understand, in the main building here.   I think you'll be quite pleased; the view of the countryside around is truly dramatic, and it's the sunset view. I think that's the best, and the ASC has taken care of the bill for you. However, your lair is not ready just yet. While you wait, would you like to visit the Mountain River – it's the local watering hole, down the hall to the left? They have a wild spray-berry fermentum that is a local specialty – an *award winner*," the Faelnar smiled, looking up at Van with a knowing expression.

"An award winner?" Vanarra asked. "I … should get familiar with it, I suppose."

"Excellent. Now, your bags will be transported to your room, so you don't have to worry about that. If you could check back with us in an interval, we should be all set, okay? Have a good time!"

"Thank you very much," Van replied, smiling and turned towards the watering hole, Sahnassa at her side.

A few passes later, Sahnassa shyly thanked the keen server who delivered her drink.

"What did you order?" Van asked as she took a covert sniff.

"Believe it or not, it's trufa juice," Sahnassa confessed.

"That's pretty tart," Van noted, taking her berry fermentum off the table. "What's the mixer?"

"It's just … the juice," Sahni offered.

"Wanted to keep a clear head?" Van asked.

"Well, you are kind of paying me to be here, and you've spent so much on this trip – especially if you count all of the audits and running around it took to put the packet together."

"Maybe, but I'm glad I'm enjoying this with you, Sahni. Beyond being a very good videographer, you … you really are my friend, now. It's … nice to have someone close to share this with."

"I'm surprised you didn't bring Flint," Sahnassa confessed. "He's been with you the longest."

"Flint doesn't like crowds – at least when he's not working them. I think the big guy feels a little conspicuous from time to time."

"Conspicuous?" a voice nearly purred over Van's shoulder, and she smiled. "You, my lovely Van are ever so conspicuous – but in a good way."

"Buck Harlock! You hotty!" Van chuckled as she turned around, seeing Sahnassa's obvious shock at the forwardness of the dark brown Faelnar and Van's reaction. The mixed blood stood and embraced the newcomer saying fervently, "It is so good to see you!" Releasing him, she indicated Sahni with an open paw. "You remember Sahni, from my office?"

"Ah, the vaunted TransNet developer," Buck replied kindly, reaching out for and clasping Sahni's paw. "Thanks to you, we are actually considering opening a branch to do TransNet sites. I may be asking Van if I can borrow you as an instructor."

"An ... instructor?" Sahni asked, blinking.

"So long as you hold true to that non-competitive agreement," Vanarra admonished Sahnassa solemnly. "And you, too, Buck."

"Oh, don't be that way," he fussed at her officious manner. "You know that it's only our programmable logic controller users at the distribution warehouse who want something a little more intuitive when it comes to what they deal with. I will happily stay out of the catering TransNet site design space – thank you very much."

"Alright, well, then I guess it's okay," Van replied demurely, putting her elbows on the table and gently cradling the bottom of her muzzle on the tops of her paws. "You going to join us, sweet Bucky?" Van noticed with a quick side glance that Sahni was blushing again.

"Well, no – I just wanted to stop by and say hi. I have a pre-meeting I'm supposed to attend, since I'll be one of the ones giving out awards this go round, but ... I do hope to see you tonight at the ceremony," he offered, slyly.

"Well, then you'd better be off, dear cub. I'd hate for there to be any problems with the presentation tonight."

"I hope to see you later, Van," he replied, looking at her a little fondly, Sahni noticed. Then, he nodded at her and walked away.

"Ah ... so nice," Vanarra replied as she watched him leaving.

"He does seem to be a very good friend to you," Sahni commented before taking a drink.

"True, but it's his butt that really yanks my tail up!" Van commented quietly, causing Sahni to choke and spew the remaining drink she still had in her mouth. That caused Van to laugh almost uncontrollably as Sahni scrambled to clean her muzzle and the menu in front of her.

"That ... was on purpose!" Sahni accused, her blush furs at full flight.

"Uh huh!" Van laughed. "And it was too good!" At Sahnassa's humiliated expression, Vanarra offered her a napkin and started blotting some areas of the Nephti's dress. "Sorry, kit. I … I couldn't resist."

"You could have tried," Sahni replied, nearly under her breath, but looking up, she found herself being fixed by a very stern, angry pair of Faelnar eyes. Cocking her head, she realized that the eyes weren't actually looking at her, but across the table at Vanarra who was now working on putting the table back to rights. "Uh, Van? That … Faelnar over there. He's … staring at you."

"Oh really? Another love interest?" Van asked, looking up, but then her eyes met gold ones in an angry and disconcerted brown Faelnar's face.

"Who is he?" Sahni asked.

"Uh oh," Van replied, looking away. "I remember him. Remember when Raska had her own little party at the healer's grave?"

"How could I forget!" Sahni whispered back, looking at Van. "The thought of that place still creeps me out."

"Well, I had to escape down the path to the male's camp, just in time to see cutie cuddle-cub over there get his muzzle pinned to the floor and *hard* – looking right at me. I think we'll just ignore him."

Sahni looked and saw that the Faelnar had stormed out, headed back towards the lobby. "You don't have to. Thankfully, he just left."

"All the better. Come on, finish up. I want to go back to that table and check on our room. I want to start getting ready – that was a long trip."

"It was. Would you mind if I ask you two things?"

"Not at all, kit. What are they?" Van queried.

"First, I want to go get another drink. Second, can you please let me drink it without causing me to spew it all over the place?"

"Oh, you purebreds aren't any fun at all," Van complained quietly. "Alright. I'll call him back over here and get us some sweet snappers. Then, we'll go back – okay?"

"Alright Van, and thank you," Sahni offered.

A half interval later, as they approached the ASC table in the lobby, a different set of representatives called them over. The two stern looking males – Perratti – stared at them like they were unwashed and dressed in rags. "There has been … some difficulty with your accommodations. Unfortunately, you were mistakenly slated in quarters intended for someone else. Here are your room cards. You may find the location of that room on a map at the front desk. Your … things … have already been taken there."

"Alright," Van replied, a little concerned. "Everything, okay?"

"Nothing for you to be worried about," the other Perratti answered, and then the pair left the table.

"That's … a little weird," Sahni commented.

"It happens, I suppose," Vanarra observed. "Come on, let's go see where we are now."

Almost a quarter interval later, they opened the door on a room that smelled far from fresh. "Uh, really? You've got to be kidding me," Sahni commented, crinkling her nose.

The room looked like it had been used by a bunch of academy students interested in a night of hunting females and fermentum – and the smell was exactly of that stripe. "Well, they … said they hadn't gotten around to cleaning everything."

"This late in the sol?!" Sahni replied as she – claw tips expressed – started pulling fermentum bottles off of the furniture and piling them in the already overflowing trash receptacles. "Are we sure this is our room?"

"Well, our luggage is here … kind of … roughed up," Van noted, her voice losing its normal tenor of confidence. "I'll open a window." Stepping carefully around the detritus left on the carpet, she made it to the moderate sized window on the other side of the room. Opening the curtains, she groaned. "I guess I'm not opening the window. They broke it."

The window had been taped over, hiding giant cracks in the glass. A big note warned "Do not open."

"They can't be serious, Van. This … this is awful," she breathed.

"Let me call the desk and see," Van replied. Walking over to the table, she picked up the LineCom. "Great. Dead."

"What do we do? Just … hike back around?"

Pushing several unhappy fears to the back of her mind, Van closed her eyes and sighed, "No, we really don't have the time. Let's clean this place up as best we can and then start getting ourselves ready."

"I saw some garbage bins just outside the building near the dining hall. I'll start making runs," Sahni offered, carefully lifting an overfilled trash receptacle with her claw-tips.

"Fair enough. I'll try to … clean up the rest of this," Van sighed, shaking her head and looking at the bathroom. "At least they didn't use all the towels."

A few passes later, Sahni returned from her third or fourth trip to the room which was – marginally – starting to look better. "What's wrong, Sahni?"

"There are two big Pantera security guards stationed in the stairwells – one on each side. I went both ways. They … were pretty rude, actually."

"Well, some Thurians are just that way. I think we can get enough clean here to get ready. We can complain at the desk when we go back around for the banquet."

An interval later, Sahni and Van were making their way towards the front desk. "Have you noticed, kit?"

"Yeah, I did. They're following us," Sahni whispered, indignant. "We haven't done anything wrong! Why are they treating us like this?"

"I don't know. I want some answers," Van replied unhappily as they approached the desk. "Hi there."

"Yes … oh," the stiff little Perratti behind the desk asked, frowning. "What is it?"

"Our room," Van replied, not bothering to look down out of deference, as she held up her room card with the number on it. "It's … absolutely filthy."

"And," he queried, "you want us to clean up your mess?"

Sahni was getting angry. "It was like that when we showed up! It looks like a combination between a cheap watering hole and a locker room and smells about as bad! The window in the room is broken, and we had to take out six loads of trash ourselves!"

"I apologize that things were … not to your liking. I've made a note of the room number. I'll see … what can be done. We're very busy tonight," he replied testily.

Looking up and down the empty counter, Van shook her head. "Yeah, sure! I can see that! Come on, Sahni. Let's just … go."

Still angry at the Perratti, Sahni followed her boss. However, as she glanced behind her, she saw the two Pantera security guards talking with the Perratti at the desk.

Walking down the hallway, Van followed the signs and found the banquet hall. "Ah, here it is, finally. I'm going to go to the facilities. You want to go in ahead and get something to eat?"

"No, I'll go with you. I wasn't about to touch that nasty thing in our room."

A few passes later, Van and Sahni emerged to find the two Pantera security guards standing outside of the banquet hall as Thurians came and went out of the door. As they approached, the guards stepped in to block their path. "I'm sorry. This is a private function."

"To which I am an invitee! I have an invitation," Van replied slowly, her eyes snapping as she held it up.

One looked at the other and said, "That may be, but the banquet area is currently at capacity. We can't let you in because of … fire regulations."

Sahni looked over their shoulders by standing on the top of her paw-toes. "Fire … regulations?! That … that room is nowhere near full!"

"I'm sorry. We don't make the rules here. We just *enforce them*."

"That doesn't seem to be the only *rule* you're enforcing," Van accused, but the two Pantera didn't answer. "Come on, Sahni. We … have a few calls to make."

As they stepped away, Sahnassa asked, "What do we do now?"

"I'm going to try and call Buck – this is ridiculous. Why the mange invite us to come all the way up here just to treat us like this?" she growled.

"Something really awful is definitely going on," Sahni complained.

Over the next two intervals, Van tried calling Buck and then tried leading the Pantera security guards on a circuitous trip through the admin building, emerging just at the right time to slip into the banquet room. Neither tactic was successful. Mysteriously, everywhere they went, Van's PawLink couldn't get a signal and at least one of the guards tracked them. Every time they returned to the entrance of the banquet hall, they were barred for the same reason as before.

Walking away for the fourth time, Sahni said, "This … this is completely intentional! We're being totally singled out!"

"More like me, or both of us because you're with me. It's … it's like no one told the resort we were actually on the guest list! Worse, it's like we're known criminals or something! Well, at least it's time for the ceremony. Perhaps if we're clever, we can blend into the traffic moving between the rooms and—"

"Hold it there," the security guard shouted.

"What?! What have we done?" Van demanded.

"The two of you have been acting in a suspicious manner all evening. I'm afraid you're going to have to come with me."

"What?!" Sahnassa replied, angrily. "You're … totally abusing your position! I … I … will report this to my house and file suit against you on insult—"

"Wait, Sahni!" Van replied, noticing the security guard's look of surprise when her friend mentioned a family house. "Let's … just go with him. We'll at least get a chance to talk to the head prowler around here, right? Then go ahead, sport – you lead the way."

Still angry, Sahni followed her boss as the security guard led them to the stairwell.

Half an interval later, Van and Sahni finally emerged from the back offices of the resort, a security guard leading them. "I'm sorry, Van. That was my fault," Sahni breathed.

Van, her eyes snapping, held up her paw, hushing her friend until they were far enough away from the guard to speak privately. "It wasn't you, kit. It doesn't take that long to verify house membership – I know, I've done it. They're … they're all in on it – the resort staff. At least we can go to the awards ceremony without being bothered."

As they approached the door to the small auditorium where the ceremony was being held, the two of them grimaced as the other Pantera security guard met them at the door. Sahni stood up in front of him angrily, presenting her house identification card. "You will let us in," she stated as the guard tried to again stand between them and where they wanted to go. "My credentials have been verified by your manager."

"You'll have to sit in the back. That's the requirement of the organizers for anyone arriving late."

"Yeah, because of you," Van complained.

"Those are the rules. Either follow them, or you can't go in."

"Fine," Van replied. The guard opened the door, and indeed, the presentation was already in session, with some older male Faelnar talking away about the accomplishments of the ASC over the last season. Imperiously, the guard pointed a chunky paw finger in the direction of two cheap chairs against the back wall. Fuming, Sahni and Van took their seats – with some discomfort, as there were no tail holes in the back, forcing them to sit at an angle.

"Oh," Van groaned quietly as she looked at the table on the raised platform. "You have to be kidding me!"

"What?"

"That … little cub who stared at me in the watering hole. He's up there."

"Do you think he—"

"Nothing went wrong until I saw him," Van growled. "Then, it *all* went wrong."

The distinguished Faelnar on stage was finishing his comments, and they listened.   "I would like to thank the entire advisory board and the special council, who have helped us so ably in the awards selection process. Especially, with a bit of … nepotism, I must admit, I would like to thank my son, Arnat, for bringing certain items to our attention tonight. So, it is with some regret that I must inform everyone assembled here that the selected winner in three of our categories tonight had to be … disqualified." A rumble of confusion went through the room. "The runner up, therefore, is who we will be announcing as our winner – a truly deserving candidate. Yes, it seems that certain portions of the disqualified applicant's application were found to be falsified – perhaps as an Anati business, they were thinking we would not be able to find this error and discover their fraud—"

At that moment, several things happened at once. Audience members stood up and started demanding angrily that the presenter explain himself. Others were shouting, "Fraud!? Fraud from the ASC pack leadership!"

"Let's hear from the applicant! Due process! Due process!" one shouted nearby them, and Sahni thought she saw a paw-finger pointed in their direction.

Vanarra and Sahni stood, and instantly both were accosted by the Pantera security guards who now physically pulled them out of the room, dragging them out as several of the delegates stood and watched in complete shock.

"Let me go! You ... you damned—" Vanarra screamed, but Sahni was too stunned by what was happening to even speak.

"Hush now, the pair of you!" the stiff little Perratti demanded as they were pulled into the center of the lobby. "You are being ejected from the premises for disruptive behavior. This is a world class resort, and we do not tolerate such poor comportment. Your belongings are outside the front door. You will leave resort property immediately. If you come back, I will have you arrested. Now, be gone!" he demanded and turned on his heels, nearly swatting Van with his tail.

As the guards started pulling them towards the exit, Sahni caught the eye of a beautiful female Vulpi, looking at her in surprise, empathy, and – strangely enough – recognition. It was almost as if she was asking the question, "How can this be?"

Answering it the best she could, Sahnassa shrugged, shook her head, and indicated hopeless acceptance with her arms as she was literally carried out the door.

"Bigots! Prudes!" Vanarra thundered through bared teeth as she hurtled her Racerra 3000 down the twisting mountain road. "Hypocrites!" she growled, and they took another high gravity turn which almost pushed Sahnassa over the edge of nausea. The pair of them had walked for nearly half an interval outside in the drenching rain looking for Van's vehicle which the resort had parked at the back of the valet lot on the other side of the complex.

"Yes. They were awful," Sahni said, nearly groaning. "If you keep driving like that, it's going to get worse. I'm gonna be—" Sahni had to stop talking then, and Van looked at Sahnassa. She had become almost insanely mad, unable to keep her claws from expressing themselves. If it hadn't been for the big Pantera standing at the entrance, she would have gone back in there and clawed that stiff little Perratti a new fur pattern. However, seeing Sahni's paling nose and lips, her heart almost broke. "It's not her fault," Van thought to herself, "and I'm hurting her, again."

"I'm sorry," Van said, slowing their pace to something within the posted speeds. Her reddish brown ears drooped down in apology. "Are you okay?"

"Just … about," Sahni uttered weakly, shifting her long, thickly furred tail and taking a big swallow. A few deep breaths later, she nodded.

Van stated decisively, "I'm pulling over." It was the kind of statement Sahni had learned long ago wasn't arguable, and she was secretly hoping for the chance to breathe fresh air, stretch arms, tail, and legs. The little craft glided to a stop and bobbed slightly as Van placed it in hover mode. "Better?"

"Much. I was hoping I could – what's that noise?" It was a low rumble that was growing louder. Without any other warning, Van's side of the vehicle crumpled with a loud bang, the lights went out, and they were thrown through the edge railing into a violent roll down the mountainside. Glass and dirt and noise and leaves and pain and blood and flame and blackness, and then … there was nothing.

Sahni awoke to an agony so terrible and intense, she instantly threw up. Her legs felt like she had blades stuck through them; her chest was painfully crushed against the console by a huge weight on her back. Her tail had to be gone; the pain told her that. Coughing through bloody spit and foul air, she realized what had happened; they were hit by a landslide. To her horror, she realized something else – they had been buried by it. The air was dusty, stale, and laced with the smell of burning electrics and singed fur. Worse, it was pitch black. Terror and panic raged in her with what little strength she had left. "Van? Van!?" There was no response. She would have reached out for her, but she couldn't move; Sahni's arms were pinned. She struggled, weeping hysterically and cried "Oh no, no, no, no, no! Help us! Help! Help! Oh, please help—" At that moment, she felt her heart falter, and she knew she was going to die. She felt a strange buzzing sensation all about her, and then nothing.

Breathing. She was breathing. Sahnassa felt the rise and fall of her own chest before perceiving anything else.

Continued in The Rescue: The First Visitation of Thuria

Abbreviated Thurian Reference

Thuria:

Thuria is the fourth planetary body in a sun-centered system of ten planets. Two moons rotate in slightly different orbits in perfect opposition to one another. Fifty-eight percent of the surface is water, with fairly uniform land masses in the temperate zones. While the poles of the planet are covered with ice, there are no land masses there. Each continent, to varying extents, has its mountains, rivers, lakes, and deserts, but much of the land is arable. While rich in minerals, Thuria lacks fossil fuels, so industrialization and technological advancement occurred slowly, over a long period of time.

Thurians:

Thurians are anthropoid mammals standing erect on two legs covered with thick hair or fur, and the color of fur varies. Most major species of Thurian have fur-covered tails of varying lengths. Ears, muzzles, and eyes are generally somewhat larger than those found in most sentient, bipedal species. Teeth and muzzle betray an omnivorous, but predatory ancestry. Front paws are four fingered with one being an opposable thumb. Claws are imbedded within the end of most species paw fingers, and the inside of the paw maintains a relatively thick paw-pad.

Life spans are long, at approximately 250 seasons (or orbits of Thuria around its sun), and birth rates are lower in compensation. However, this elongated life span allows for families to have nine or ten generations alive at one time. Thurians are social and very familial, with allegiance and membership to a family group passing generally through the male, unless the female is titled (member of the family matriarchy). As compensation, the familial leadership is nearly always female. Thurians are fertile by age 15 and generally lose fertility at around 90 seasons. Usually, mating produces one cub (male) or kit (female). Those terms apply regardless of species. Multiple births are not easily supported by Thurian biology. Families frequently will raise one child to full adulthood before beginning again.

Thurian Species:

Anati – (*"a-not-tea"*) any mixed-blood Thurian (derogatory term).

Faelnar – (*"fell-narr"*) Purebred species, generally of sleek to average build, with long, short-furred tails. Fur colors range from brown through golden to shades of yellow. Eye colors include gold, green, hazel, and yellow. Noses are black, brown, or yellow brown.

Lupar – (*"loo-parr"*) Purebred species. A large species (second only to the Pantera in size) with gray to brownish fur, with longer than average muzzles. Eye colors are gray to blue to green. Tails are long, straight or curved, and bushy. Fur color ranges from light gray to black and brown.

Nephti – (*"neff-tea"*) Purebred species, generally of average build. Tail fur is long and thick, forming a wide, long, and bushy tail. Fur colors from light gray to black into dark purple through light purple. Eye colors include silver, gray, and shades from deep blue through indigo and violet. Noses are black, pink, or mottled. Striping is prominent, in shades of white, silver, or grey.

Pantera – (*"pan-terr-uh"*) The largest of the purebred species on Thuria. Fur colors range from light gray to black, with no patterning except on the ear ridges (generally black). Tails are short-haired and only of moderate length. Their muzzle is thicker than most other species. Eye colors are blue through hazel to dark brown and gray. While not as sleek and quick as their Faelnar counterparts, they make up for it in muscle. Noses are usually pale pink to pale grey to black.

Perratti – (*"purr-rah-tea"*) Purebred species. The smallest of all Thurian breeds, on average, but sizes can approach average and sometimes exceed it. Tails are small and covered with short hair. Muzzles are long and almost box-shaped, with fur occasionally draping off the sides down the face and muzzle like an upside down "V". Fur color ranges between black, gray, brown, and tan. Noses are uniformly black. Eyes are silver, blue, hazel, or brown.

Vulpi – (*"vull-pea"*) Purebred species. Fur colors include white, orange-red, orange, red, and gray. Patterning is mostly limited to large variations on forearms, hind legs, muzzle, or tail. Eye colors are blue, green, silver, brown, and hazel. Tail fur is thick, forming a wide, long, and bushy tail.

House Matriarchal Leadership Hierarchy

Grand Matriarch or Matriarch

Honored Dames and Dames

Matrons

All other house members

Thurians Prominent in Purebred

Disavowed (those of no family house)

Vanarra (Van) Anasto – Anati (mixed-blood) orphan, Vulpi-Faelnar mix

Buck Harlock – Faelnar friend of Van, disavowed from de Caterra

Flint Bonar – Mixed blood Lupar-Pantera, Van's second in command

Raska – Mixed blood Vulpi-Nephti who works for Van

Sheffer – Mixed blood Perratti-Faelnar who works for Van

Gorta – Female Faelnar caterer, disavowed from house de Mistral

Tresk – Disavowed Vulpi mechanic who works for Van

Saiphar – Disavowed Vulpi artist who works for Van

Of House de Orturu (species: Nephti)

Sahnassa (Sahni) – Middle daughter of Gonastir and Holana

Gonastir – Legal council for house de Orturu

Holana – Celebrated archivist for house de Orturu

Hylea – Youngest daughter of Gonastir and Holana

Triana – Eldest daughter of Gonastir and Holana

Selena – Grand Matriarch

For Deborah ...
Most Honored of all friends,
from both of us.
Your help in this endeavor has
meant more than you can ever know.

With thanks eternal to my God,
my family,
and my friends.

Other Books
by James Todd Lewis

THE THURIAN SAGA:

The Rescue: The First Visitation of Thuria

The Aftermath: Secrets of Thuria

The Ascent: Conflict on Thuria

The Summit: Rise of the Anati

Rothnerra – Dame

Shalarra – Elder Matron

Drualla – Elder Matron

Of House de Dothnar (species: Nephti)

Rahnahi – Dame and celebrated author

Sorla – Recently adopted member of house de Dothnar, transport driver

Others:

Merialla de Fantar – Sahnassa's roommate in academy

Lashahar – Merialla's romantic interest (house not specified)

About the Author

James Todd Lewis is a science fiction and fantasy author living in Orlando, Florida with his lovely wife and two children. A native of Warner Robins, Georgia, he is a graduate of the Mercer University College of Liberal Arts and the Great Books program. He's been writing novels and short stories since 1982. At first, he just enjoyed the writing process and the fun of reading his own work. It wasn't until a hard drive crash erased several months of work that his wife, who also enjoyed his stories, insisted on making a printed copy for safekeeping. Seeing his work in print for the first time was quite a moment, and it made him wonder if others would also be interested.

Now, he feels humbled and grateful that others have been entertained by these books – doubly so when someone has been kind enough to post a review!

There is more coming in the Thurian Saga!

LIKE the Thurian Saga on Facebook for updates,

discussions with the author, and more!

Follow the author on Twitter! @hmseagle

Visit the author's website for his essay blog, book descriptions, and more in depth information: www.jamestoddlewis.com

www.ingramcontent.com/pod-product-compliance
Lightning Source LLC
Chambersburg PA
CBHW051930020726
47501CB00001B/52